CW00400165

Lee Maroney is a forty-five-year-old man. Due to his wife Sarah's physical disabilities, he has been a home carer for twenty-seven years. He has a seventeen-year-old daughter named Jess who is a film production student. Lee comes from a working-class background and having this book published is the culmination of a lifelong dream, which he hopes every reader will enjoy.

To my wonderful wife and daughter, you are the meaning to my life.
To mam and my two dads, your support was never in question.
To Anth, for believing in me all the way.
And to Big Al, you are loved and missed every day. To lose 3 parents in the span of a year breaks my heart. All my life I was loved because of you. I hope this book makes you proud; you will never be forgotten.

Lee Maroney

THE EVIL INSIDE

AUSTIN MACAULEY PUBLISHERS™

LONDON * CAMBRIDGE * NEW YORK * SHARJAH

Copyright © Lee Maroney 2021

The right of Lee Maroney to be identified as author of this work has been asserted by the author in accordance with section 77 and 78 of the Copyright, Designs and Patents Act 1988.

All rights reserved. No part of this publication may be reproduced, stored in a retrieval system, or transmitted in any form or by any means, electronic, mechanical, photocopying, recording, or otherwise, without the prior permission of the publishers.

Any person who commits any unauthorised act in relation to this publication may be liable to criminal prosecution and civil claims for damages.

This is a work of fiction. Names, characters, businesses, places, events, locales, and incidents are either the products of the author's imagination or used in a fictitious manner. Any resemblance to actual persons, living or dead, or actual events is purely coincidental.

A CIP catalogue record for this title is available from the British Library.

ISBN 9781398402256 (Paperback)
ISBN 9781398402263 (ePub e-book)

www.austinmacauley.com

First Published 2021
Austin Macauley Publishers Ltd®
1 Canada Square
Canary Wharf
London
E14 5AA

Firstly, I'd like to thank Austin Macauley Publishers for giving me this chance. To my mam who helped finance this project. To my little brother, Anth, who constantly listened to my ideas; no matter how outlandish. And to Sarah, for supporting me and making me believe that this was possible.

Chapter 1

These tears were uncontrollable, the harder he tried to resist, the more fiercely they fell. His clothes drenched, clinging oppressively to his virgin skin, torrential falling rain making his faded light blue denim jeans and jacket appear almost black. They were caked with layers of thick, oozing mud caused by his desperate scramble to escape. His hands were filthy from the liquefied earth and had spread across the cheeks of his face as he tried in vain to stem the flow of his whimpering sorrow. The sludge continually washed into his eyes, making sight virtually impossible, even though he needed his vision now more than ever. He didn't want to see, couldn't bear to see but this was desperation, there was no one coming to help.

He knew he wasn't alone. Though he couldn't see his pursuer, he could feel him, sense his presence all around, like some spectral phantasm. But this was no ghost. It was human, flesh and blood, but barely human at all. It was the spook story everyone was afraid to mention. The whisper in the schoolyard, the curse of Hallowell. The children never really believed; now, the boy had no choice, he was convinced, it was here, stalking.

His lank rain-soaked hair flopped back across his forehead. He swept fingers through the grime plastering it to his scalp. He squinted, eyes burning raw, trying to focus on through the blackness of night. The dark was engulfing, enveloping everything. He tried desperately to make out just one detail, something to use as a focal point. Where was he? He couldn't remember getting here. Where was *here?*

"Let's work backwards." His skin was ice cold, wet, why? He couldn't remember being outside, but he had to have been, he was covered in mud. There'd been running, he could remember that he was still out of breath. Running, sprinting as fast as he could, through those massive doors in the distance. But that made no sense, of all the places to hide, why here? This place was scary, more than that, it was terrifying. Christ, most people wouldn't walk past it. Then there'd been the warnings.

"No matter what, stay away from that place."

The more he thought, the more it hurt. Was his head injured? He felt for cuts, holes, lumps, maybe that was why his memory was gone. Everything seemed intact, at least there was no blood.

Visibility was almost zero. The room had to be huge, he was certain he could hear his own heartbeat echoing around its vastness. Outside a storm raged, rain pellets bouncing of the exterior platform, rumbles of thunder erupting overhead. The occasional streak of lightening couldn't break the darkness, this place had one entrance and one exit. How did he know that? When the boundary wall had allowed him to run no further, he'd searched around the room's rough perimeter, desperate for windows, finding none. He was trapped.

The child fumbled, panic stricken, his hands clinging to cold crumbling plaster, footsteps placed carefully as to cause no noise. A hiding place was essential, a cupboard or container, anywhere to lose the creature that stalked him. Something inside warned against heading back to those giant double-doors, retracing his steps simply not an option, that was surely where the monster was waiting. Delving further into these macabre surroundings felt like mental torture but what choice did he have. The place had an engulfing presence of evil. Words could barely describe its dark power, a claustrophobic almost disabling tightness, crushing his soul beyond fear, beyond terror. The worst aspects of the imagination exhausting his frail tiny body. Everything giving the resident evil the advantages over its victim. The darkness was all consuming giving it the feel of a separate entity, a cold clinging substance, unblinking, unforgiving, another tool in the building's evil arsenal. So extreme, the child could barely see his hands before his face. It was the closest feeling to blindness imaginable.

With the cold concrete surface pressed hard against his back, the boy forced himself on, attracted indelibly to the infallible guide against the blackness. Slowly shuffling his way across the vast length of the room, stopping only when the adjoining wall would allow him to travel no further, the ninety-degree tightness of the room's corner screamed out like the confines of a concrete casket and for a second, he lunged forward from its encapsulating grasp, his mind envisioning two ghostly arms squeezing him to the room's boundary. Only when he became more terrified of the engulfing blackness and the loss of the stone guide did he retreat to the unflinching sanctuary. No spectre reached for him, no strangle hold from an unseen phantasm, just crumbling plaster between his moist fingers.

Slowly, he slid down the wall, crouching to the foetal position in the corner of the freezing Hell hole; arms cradling his diminutive head, knees tucked in tight to his quivering jawline, teeth chattering uncontrollably. His timidity as evident as any time in his young life. A veiled sob escaped as he tried in vain to hold back tears, apprehension of attack always alive in his fractured psyche, surreptitious movements always essential. His thin buttocks frozen by the drenched denims pressed tightly into the concrete corner, his eyes never leaving the huge metal framed doorway across the distance, knowing at any given moment, his hulking frame could block the room's only exit.

Though time and reality were now two separate entities, an age seemed to pass and still the child's worst fears hadn't come true. The room was still as the grave. Only echoes from the outside storm could be heard across the empty shell. Strong rumbles of thunder were somewhat encouraging, reminded him that there was still an outside world. The lightening had passed which was better for his position, the darkness could now be his friend. If he couldn't see, neither could the monster.

The stench from inside this place was now becoming evident, more potent. As his mind refocused, the worse it became. Earlier, his sense of smell had been the most infinitesimal, therefore least utilised, but as his mind processed the situation, the aroma was unmistakable. This was beyond the odour which emanated from disused buildings, the musty, damp pungency that comes from years of neglect and abandonment, this was much worse. It was frighteningly like the stench from Alf Wade's farm, when every year, the rotting carcasses of decaying animals, piled high before disposal, would decompose in the summer heat. The foul stench that the neighbours feared would impregnate their homes. It was the smell of death. Pulling his drenched T-shirt across his face gave no respite, the scent was unescapable. He began to wretch, vomit almost erupting at the nauseating, contaminated bouquet, only fast acting gag reflexes saved the floor from being sprayed by stomach juices.

It was incredible. Even the corrupt air of this abhorrent putridity seemed against him. A lonely tear ran down his left cheek causing a streak across his grimy skin. His mind was fracturing; he was beginning to question what was real and not. How could this be happening? He didn't deserve this. No one did.

He pleaded with his cognizance, remember something, anything. Was this a dream, just an incredibly acute nightmare? With the index finger and thumb of his right hand, we squeezed so tightly into the flesh of his left forearm, it almost bled, grimacing at the discomfort.

"You can't feel pain in dreams, can you?"

The scraping of steel against concrete, across in the distance, the huge metal door began to move. The left one first, the wide-open exit, his only means of escape, slowly slipping away. It was the heinous noise piercing the silence that revealed itself before the visual movement, eerily reverberating around the concrete prison. Rusted metal hinges fighting years of unwavering stillness, screaming out in agony as they are awakened from their immovable slumber. Enormous steel shutters, fifteen feet in height, re-animated by extreme force, slowly, oh so very slowly, starting to seal the room like a mighty coffin lid. That doorway was the only slightest break in the darkness, the only object his young eyes could focus upon without complete blindness, now, even that was deserting him. The sound of screaming metal echoed through his mind, his fingers squeezing into his temples, crushing into his skull though he cared little about the pain being caused. He was losing control, the final remnants of sanity toward the situation disappearing. The controlled sobs were becoming impossible to mask, what was the point? This situation was unwinnable. It had gone too far, there was barely anything left to cling too, hope diminishing by the second. The only escape was vanishing before his eyes.

The left door ground to a halt, completely now; then suddenly, silence. No more screaming metal and crunching concrete. No more rusted hinges yearning for movement.

The child's imagination was working overtime. "What torture was this now? Was the monstrous savage playing games, mind games?" So many questions to which there was no answers. "Dead animals? Why did an abandoned building stink of decaying animals?" Suddenly, a thought so terrifying it was barely fathomable, invaded his brain. "What if the stench of rotting flesh wasn't coming from animals?"

His lower lip began to quiver, his eyes fixed firmly upon the room's only exit. At first, it was hard to be sure. The doors were a distance away and the vague light was obscure, but slowly, it became frighteningly evident. The dark silhouette of a human loomed across the remaining open doorway. Somehow, the child immediately regained some composure, be it one final self-preservation instinct or perhaps fear had frozen him in time. Tears were still steadily flowing but the heavy convulsions that racked his body became controlled. The room was deathly silent. Was the devilish freak aware of the child's location and simply adding to the torture, increasing the levels of with terror? Heart pounding, chest heaving, body aching like a distance runner at a marathon's conclusion, could eleven-year-olds have heart failure? If it was possible, the boy was certain he was about to become the latest victim. "Please God, don't let it hurt."

Sweat dripped into his eyes, though the searing pain was now being the least of his concerns. Clasping his palms together, he prayed for home. Lying in his own bed, quilt pulled tightly over his head, listening to his parents' petty squabbles with the realisation that he wasn't alone. He'd seen nothing of life, what eleven-year-old had. Had he done anything to deserve this? Impossible. All he wanted was to wake up from this nightmare though that didn't appear to be happening any time soon.

The monster's shadow was strangely hypnotic, like witnessing a road accident, not wishing to see the devastation, though being morbidly fascinated by the scene. Seeing detail was futile, distance and light being an invincible enemy. One thing certain was the creature's size, the hulking frame, both height and girth blocking the huge doorway. Suddenly, a flash of lightening from the dying storm bared one terrifying aspect that he wished had remained unseen. It was hanging from the grip of his right hand. The shiny metal had revealed itself, if only for a second. The unmistakable silhouette of an axe, a very large axe. It was mesmerising, swaying slightly in its owner's nightmare grip. The slight glint of moonlight maintaining its visibility. The whole vision was like something from a cheap B-movie slasher film though this was no fiction. For a second, he closed his eyes, once more in silent prayer, though his upbringing had hardly been religious. Tears were forced back, sweaty palms clenched, fingers interlocked.

"If there is a God, please make this stop. Make this thing go away." He repeated it over and over like some strange chant. And when he opened his eyes, God seemed to have listened, the creature was gone.

Had the darkness been his ally? Witnessing the monster was assisted with the vagueness of outside moonlight, but the room's interior was caliginous, no, more than that, it was pitch-black. Had fortune finally played assistance? Did the ghastly entity believe no one would be insane enough to seek refuge in the huge crypt? Perhaps it had no knowledge of the boy's presence. Maybe there was still hope?

But then, of course, it was also possible that the monster was currently sharing the nightmarish space, hiding under the cover of darkness, waiting to pounce. The child's eyes were as accustomed to the blackness as they were ever going to be. He gazed across the expanse of the room, head jerking from side to side, peering into the shadows, terrified of the slightest movement, hoping, praying. It was obvious that this odious creation would be far more knowledgeable about these surroundings than he was. Christ, he only knew his location at all because there was nowhere else that could cause this level of terror. All the hiding place, hidden doors, or channels exits and entrances. His heart rate was growing once more.

He finally accepted that there was one chance and one chance only. Head for the last remaining door and don't look back, run, and run and then run some more. If that second door closes, it would be game over and he'd be the loser. If he stayed put, eventually the thing would find him. There was no choice.

At first, it seemed the youngster's legs wouldn't obey his command. His mind was willing him to start a dash for the exit and not stop till he was in the pouring rain, out of this oppressive stifling Hellhole but his muscles were so tensed they refuse to move, paralysed by terror. Eventually, his battered courage permitted him the strength to take the first baby-steps away from the wall. Simply leaving the mild sanctuary of the rough concrete corner into the vast area made him nauseous with fear. The tears, though silent now, continued to cascade down his cheeks. His thighs suddenly felt an uncomfortable warm sensation as his bladder finally gave way, urine spreading down his already drenched denims. Strangely, the boy felt no shame, barely registering the childish error. Escape was his only thought now.

His face grimaced when his dirty cheap white trainer shoes squeaked on the lightly glossed concrete floor. He had concentrated so highly on taking small quiet steps that he hadn't lifted his feet sufficiently, a mistake he hadn't envisioned. The sound seemed to echo around the open room like a prison warning alarm alerting the world to an escaping convict. It seemed everything was conspiring against him, unsure whether to retreat backwards or continue for the door, it looks so far away. Perhaps, the beast was lurking outside, and his bravery would be for nothing. Behind, he could no longer see his former sanctuary, swallowed up by the darkness, engulfing everything once more. Confusion had made the room begin to spin. He knelt, one hand touching the cold floor, vomit rising in his stomach, head swirling out of control. For a second, it seemed unconsciousness would blank out this nightmare perhaps that would be best. He let out a high-pitched uncontrollable yell, not caring about giving away his position anymore. His body was shutting down, the repugnant horror simply too much to bear. Why fight? How can one fight something that can't be seen? He wanted his parents, his bedroom, his freedom. But they were no longer his to claim. He'd lost. The self-pity, the anguish, the unpalpable Hell of the situation. It had won. He simply wouldn't go on. He'd curl up in a ball and wait for sunrise, or death, which-ever came first. It was the only control he could reclaim, that lasted less than a minute.

The noise was vague but present. It was coming from his hide-away corner. It was footsteps, growing more obvious with every passing second and they were coming his way. Now was his chance.

He reacted on instinct rather than courage, diving, almost stumbling to his feet. The footsteps were only yards behind and he with-held the luxury of looking back. His shoes once more screeched out against the glossed concrete but for now, who cares? For once he was happy with the cheap alternative trainers his mother had bought instead of the cooler named brand, their thick rubber soles grabbing for the floor and propelling faster than he ever thought possible. Was that his pursuers deep muffled breaths or was it his own? Again, who cares? He was on his way. He felt a hand grab and miss, barely touching the jacket that clung to his back. Still, he refused to look back, eyes fixed firmly on one place, the exit. His urine-soaked jeans clung tightly to the boy's crotch, tearing into his young skin but he ignored the pain. His heart pounding, throbbing more fiercely than ever, threatening to burst through his ribcage. His respiratory system trying desperately to get oxygen into the lungs. The child was sprinting for his life. Hurtling across the slippery white surface, the door drawing closer. His energy was beginning to wane, but the creature was too close to slow down now. If he was caught, he'd be dead for sure, this was no prank. He could hear guttural breathing, like his nemesis had a cover across its face, maybe a mask.

"Good God, what would this thing look like?" Did it have an accomplice waiting at the door? Did he stand any chance at all? He was still running at full speed and this thing still seemed to be gaining, then…silence.

At first, when his head hit the floor, no pain registered, only shock. The hidden obstacle had been invisible until he struck it. A small, raised metal stump embedded in the concrete floor with no right to be there, an immovable object resembling a metal fencing post crudely hacked though and left to remain. Barely four inches above the ground with a sharp curvature, the ideal enemy for a fleeing child. He'd been just fifteen feet from the exit when it propelled the youngster through the air, rendering him temporarily unconscious upon impact. Crashing to the ground, his head took the severity of the fall, forehead lashing hard against the uncompromising concrete. His brow splitting instantly, dark sticky blood spreading from a four-inch gash, mixing with the stagnate grime and perspiration to reveal a horrific crimson mask. Instinct made the boy try to crawl, but his shattered body now no longer seemed capable. In a cruel twist of fate, he had landed outside, the cold night air feeling wonderful in a weird way. Had he been capable of walking, escape may have been possible. Instead, it now seemed game over.

The semi-conscious boy rolled onto his back, the world a swirling kaleidoscope of deplorable events, pain slowly taking hold, grasping his body in a death-like grip. And now, death was what he expected. With blood stinging his eyes, he searched for the creature that would inevitably come. The rain had ceased, and the night was deathly silent. The cold platform was drenched but not unpleasant as his body had raging heat permutating from every sweat fused pore. He could feel his blood gushing from the head wound, cascading across his face and mattered hair, forming thick pools on the ground about him. He no longer cared, he just wanted this to be over.

After a while, he raised his head from the floor. The world was still spinning, and the feel of his blood made the nausea rise once more. He stared into the room, like a dark gaping tomb from which he'd just flown. Nothing. He squinted, head pounding, heart thumping, nothing. Looking around the platform's exterior (he had been correct; this was the Abandoned railway station on the outskirts of Hallowell though how he'd got here remained a mystery) there was no sign of the monster. It had been feet from him just before the fall, why walk away now? Was this more games? Mental torture taken to the extreme? He crawled to a wall and pushed his back against it trying for leverage. Rushing wasn't an option. The head wound had numbed over, and the bleeding had slowed. He'd began to shiver uncontrollably, the cold night air and the shock factor making his teeth chatter and body tremble.

There seemed no reason for any of this. Why, when in the monster's grasp had he been spared? The end game had been in sight. It would have been as easy as swatting a fly as taking his life. Was it for the evil one sick amusement to force a child into playing these macabre games? A game it could end at any moment.

He began to slowly claw his way up the jagged brick surface. The vast doorway just to his right, still half open looked like a doorway to Hell. He shuddered more, as he thought about the room he'd just flown from. The darkness seemed even worse from the outside looking in. His legs now, fully erect, felt like gelatine under his weight. His palms pressed tightly against the cold brick surface, his body held up by its support, he noticed a tear in the right knee of the denims. With the horror, all around, the pain had barely registered before. Now it did.

He pressed the injured leg hard against the floor, unsure what weight it would bear. The pain was intolerable, and blood oozed from the wound, but it held.

A heavy rustling from adjacent woodland caught the boy's attention. The leg wasn't up to running, it would barely tolerate walking. Aware of just how vulnerable he was, the heart rate increased once more. He began to ease his way along the length of the giant structure, leg dragging, eyes never leaving the destination of the disturbance.

"Let it be a rabbit. Please God, just let it be a rabbit." The movement continued. The air was as still as the grave. He squinted, trying to make out shapes through the gloom. Nothing.

A branch snapped. Coming from deeper in the trees, something was fighting through the leaves.

"That doesn't sound like a rabbit." The upper branches swayed; something was coming. The child tried to speed up. Blood continued to cascade from the knee injury and his increased heart rate wasn't helping the head wound either. Perspiration ran from everywhere, his body felt like fire, the rustling was growing and the...

The infant howled, a mixture of laughter and relief. A dark twitching nose followed by a red-brown snout and glistening eyes, ears pointing erect, trying hard to signal out danger. Its head darted back into the trees when it heard the boy's joyful squeal then seconds later re-emerging to reveal its long sleek body, hair wet, glistening in the moonlight. A beautiful bushy tail standing to attention, alert and ready. It proceeded with caution, slow deliberate steps.

The boy looked down and shook his head with disgust. "I don't believe I pissed my pants again for a fox." The animal seemed wary, looking back toward its former hiding place, taking no notice of the child. There was no sound coming from the trees, but the animal was spooked. It leaped up onto the stone platform, thirty feet from him and stood perfectly still, head tilted to the left, staring into the darkness of the woodland. By now the boy was at the corner of the building main structure. A row of outer buildings, perfectly adjacent which related to a strong solid roof forming a desolate tunnel way, standing before him and the land's exit. And down that tunnel, there were three open doors, more than enough options for the thing that stalked him to wait, and pounce.

"There's no chance I'm heading that way." Even with the pain from his badly injured leg, the effort was worth the extra safety. Before passing the corner, he allowed himself a brief look back toward the fox. It was stopped by the open doorway, licking the salty spilled blood from the ground. It had no time to react as a hand launched from the darkness. With one repulsive swing, the animal was hauled by the scruff of its neck, high in the air, and with devastating force, smashed against the station wall. Its high-pitched scream pierced the night's silence.

Panic erupted once more. The platform width seemed so long. The monster was out of his sightline again, but the boy could hear its footsteps echoing from the concrete floor. He forced his broken frame onwards, leg dragging behind, slowing his escape, neck twisting backwards, waiting for the beast to turn the corner. The front of the building was getting closer, maybe he did have a chance. All he'd need to do was climb from the platform, the exit gate was close, Frankie never left the station grounds, everyone knew that. Would the leg hold strong when the wall was no longer there to support him? One final look back, please be gone, please let me go. Hope was rising "Thank you, God, I'm going to make it home. I'm going to survive. I'm…"

It had taken the short cut. The tunnel with the open doors, the route the boy was petrified to take. He spun, glancing off the creature's body and crashing hard to the cold concrete. With the exit in sight, hope was extinguished.

Its size seemed incredible, towering above the stricken infant. He'd tried to slide away, shuffling on his backside, pushing with his one good leg. He'd have screamed had there been any point, no one would hear, no one from town would come this close to the station, in the night, in the dark. The whole image seemed a blur, like an out of body experience, watching it happen to someone else. The only detail that registered was the axe. Long, cold, hellish. With one motion, the monster raised the weapon high into the air and clasped its steel handle with both hands. The moonlight glistered from its razor's edge. The boy closed his eyes, face grimaced in anticipation, awaiting the death blow. All that was left was for the telephone to shriek out with ear piercing urgency.

Ring, ring. Ring, ring. Ring, ring. Nick Castle woke and screamed out into the darkness. He flung his arms around his head, still not aware that he was no longer part of the nightmare.

Ring, ring. Ring, ring. He fumbled for the light switch on his bedside lamp and immediately the room was bathed in light. Deep perspiration covered his entire body and then he realised that a more pungent and gravely more embarrassing liquid soaked the bed clothes around the top of his legs. Pulling back the quilt, it revealed his sodden black boxer shorts.

"Fuck. Not again."

His heart still pounding and breathing laboured, he struggled to gain some composure. The telephone still hollered out like a screaming baby waiting to be fed.

"I'm coming, I'm coming." Under a pile of dirty clothes, Castle picked up the receiver and put it to his ear.

"Yes." His tone was more of anger than curiosity.

"Nick, is that you?" The voice was that of his estranged mother.

"Yes, yes it's me." He rubbed his eyes, head still foggy, feeling wet, uncomfortable, and seriously pissed off.

"Did I wake you?" The tone was hardly apologetic. Too much had happened between them for emotion to play a part in their sporadic conversations.

"It's 3am, what did you think I'd be doing?" This was not a conversation he needed right now.

"Well, with your lifestyle, how am I supposed to know?"

He almost hung up but realised she must have some reason to be calling at this hour.

"I don't need a row, what do you want?"

"I don't want to argue either. Listen, I wasn't sure whether to let you know this, but I figured you had a right. I got a letter this morning from your dad's mother, grandma Castle. She's been trying to call you but couldn't get through, I don't think she has your new number, and she definitely doesn't have mine."

"What she says, what's wrong."

"I'm genuinely sorry to tell you this Nick, I know me, and your dad's family don't get along but, well, there's no easy way to say this but, it's Bill, your granddad, he's dead."

Chapter 2

Wednesday October 20th, 1980

It was seven am and Nick Castle had just taken his second shot of cheap Irish whisky. At least this one was a mild diluted shot, added to a pot of black coffee, helping to battle the cold in the heat free, broken down flat in which he lived. It was excused as medicinal (it's shocking how many uses can be described as medicinal when you are a functioning alcoholic). Plus, walking the streets for hours barely clothed with only tramps and the milkman for company tends to cause a chill, he deserved that second shot. He swore to himself that this was the last drink of the day, Nick Castle lied to himself a lot.

The first swallow had been directly after his mother's early morning news, 3am was bad even by his standards. For emergencies (see medicinal), he kept an old, very old silver whisky flask engraved with the words 'man's best friend' and a crude carving of a happy, round faced, inebriated fellow, inside a small drawer in the cabinet beside his bed. By coincidence, it had been a keep's sake hand-me-down passed on from his newly deceased grandfather on his 18th birthday. Years ago, William Castle (Bill for short) was his village's police constable, a well-respected man. He'd take the flask on his long shifts, pushed tightly into a side pocket of his force issued uniform, a requirement he considered as essential as the police whistle, baton or his prized possession, silver pocket watch (Bill was seriously old-school). He was the third generation to do the job and own the watch. The relationship between the policeman and his son Michael (Mick) was strained at best and therefore, Bill promised that when he passed away, the watch was his Nick's birth right. He'd never felt deserving but somehow, throughout all the bad times, Bill Castle still believed his grandson would one day be great. There were doubts.

The flask had always caught the boys' eye, perhaps a sign of things to come. The burning brown liquid was just the thing to keep out the chill of a cold winter's morning on the beat. The old man even called it his medicine bottle a term affectionately adopted by, not only his family but around the village too. Though Bill enjoyed a warming shot on occasion, he was no drunk. In truth, alcohol gave the gentleman little pleasure and on retirement, he would quit liquor altogether, he'd seen many a good man be lost to drink when their career was over.

Unfortunately, the same could not be said of his young off-spring. Now 21, Nick was close to becoming full blown alcoholic, it had been growing for some time. Whisky worked best, his favourite, always did the job fastest. Vodka was easier to drink though, no burning sensation like the brown stuff and less aftertaste too. In fact, any spirits could happily send him to La-La-Land within fifteen minutes if you drank it fast and hard. The biggest problem with spirits were the expense and his credit wasn't good. The local shopkeepers watched him too well now, his reputation proceeding him. That's where white cider came in handy. It was said that this stuff was more addictive than heroine. Its cheap price and easy access made it a viable option for hard core drinkers. It was the alcoholic's weapon of choice, more for less, similar results. He rarely drank in pubs, the prices again were massive in relation to the off-licences, plus, pubs were social places, Nick Castle didn't feel too social these days.

Alcohol was a means to an end. A way to escape the reality of this existence. Reality was too hard to bear soberly and a night without drink was a sure-fire way for the nightmares to come. Enough drink and his pickled mind could find a hide-out.

That first shot after the 3 am wakeup call was supposed to calm him, relax him, but it failed. The self-control it took to fight, simply continuing to drink himself into an oblivion was something he rarely possessed these days; granddad Bill would be proud. The fact that it was four hours before the next tipple was a victory.

He switched on a white plastic kettle seated in the corner of a long brown workbench in his kitchen. Searching the debris around the litter strewn room, he finally came across his mug. It had been a gift from his former girlfriend, Julia. God, he missed her. The memories of the conclusion to that relationship were another reason to seek refuge at the bottom of a bottle. The coffee mug was tall and thin, much larger than average. Dark blue in colour, part of the handle was broken and there were two chips out of the rim. Across the centre in bold red writing was the words, 'World's biggest screw up'. When he'd received it, for some reason he hadn't been the slightest bit offended. Probably because the statement was bang on the money. The mug had countless stains around its perimeter and there was a strange, coloured form of mould growing on the inside base. This was because the sorry container (one of only two in the flat) hadn't seen clean water or washing utensils for months. In fact, it was quite possible that it may never have been washed. Nick didn't care.

He poured coffee granules from a half full jar of Nescafe into the grime covered mug, part of which missed its desired target and spilling onto the workbench and floor. He had previously owned teaspoons but like everything else in the flat, they were long since lost. The same process was taken from a torn pack of sugar with more missing the target than landing in pot. As he waited for the kettle to boil, he made his way to a small grey fridge on the opposing side of the room. It was there for show rather than use as it hadn't worked in six months. The door didn't even close properly and the interior light bulb had blown. As the door opened fully and the search for useable milk began, the stench rose to meet him. It was so foul, Nick had to fight the urge to vomit. He wrenched his head to the left, but the stink seemed to follow. The door was quickly closed.

"Coffee's black this morning." The kettle made a sharp click, indicating it was fully boiled and he poured the steaming water over the coffee-sugar combination. The mug was three quarters full when he tilted the kettle to its upright position and the water halted its flow. After rubbing sleep matter from his eyes and a final loud yawn, he took the silver flask from his red and white striped dressing gown pocket and unscrewed the lid. While pouring a strong measure into the coffee he muttered, "Who needs milk, taste the Irish better this way." He replaced the flasks top and picked up the mug. His passage through the kitchen to the lounge wasn't easy, manoeuvring by the empty take away cartons and beer cans could be a challenge. Determined not to spill his prize, he proceeded with caution.

The lounge itself was as miserable as the rest of Nick's life. The walls on arrival were painted a depressing battleship grey but as he had as much interest in interior design as a five-year-old has in quantum physics, the colour remained. The only picture to break the drabness of the walls was a replica print of the movie, 'Casablanca', over the fire breast wall. It was framed but the wooden brown casing was faded and scratched. It had at one time been covered with a glass protective sheet, but this was long gone, obviously broken across the realms of time.

The furniture was sparse and shabby. In the corner of the room stood a small wooden occasional table, again brown, though its paint was flaking and there were several white rimmed stains, burned on through-out the years by carelessly misplaced hot teacups. It was supported by only three legs, the fourth missing and replaced by a stack of misshapen books. On top, perched dangerously was a 14-inch black and white television set. Who knew just how old this was, the company which created it had been out of business for years? The screen was thick with dust and down one side, the sticky residue of a fallen Coke can, leaving ugly brown reminders of its existence. Remote controls were for posh people with posh televisions, which this certainly was not. The set's plastic front panel had broken off and the buttons for the second and third channel didn't work leaving the only station available being BBC1. As it was on only rare occasions the box was used, this held little consequence. The curtains which covered a small lone window in the centre of the far wall were a yellow-green mix and were quite possibly the ugliest curtains ever created. They hung far longer than required, bunching as they met the floor and were constantly closed allowing little light into the room. Again, there was a thick layer of dust across the tops and may have been home to hundreds of spiders over the years as the collection of cobwebs between the material and adjoining wall was grotesquely impressive. The carpet was of matching colour (typical 1970s horrendous fashion) and equally as filthy. A few weeks prior, a neighbour, who with his own alcohol problems had been forced to go to a drying-out clinic for a fortnight, paid Nick £10 to watch his pet dog while he was away. The dog then proceeded to piss and shit where-ever it could find empty floor space. With the remainder of the carpet being filled with trash, finding bare patches was a challenge the mutt seemed to enjoy. On one occasion, the filthy creature had blasted its waste across Nick's lovely battleship grey walls, kicking its back legs with glee. Perhaps it was the fact Nick didn't care to seek out the dog's little gifts or maybe the thought of digging through the litter was just too physically demanding, but for weeks after the animal's abrupt exit, (it had made a bolt for an open door after three days without food and Nick wasn't going to chase the beast) little dark encrusted piles continued to reveal themselves around the floor. Of course, its urine had simply sunk into whatever the dog had decided to aim it at, and the smell grew gradually worse day after day. Still, Nick didn't care.

The only other items of furniture in this lived-in cesspit were a single chair and settee. The chair had a hard, high back, like the type found in an old-folks home. It was fabricated in blue leather though again, it was torn in several places and had a long trip, down the centre of its vertical back, white cotton wool stuffing hanging loosely from the hole. Most of the inside padding was gone, adding to the increased discomfort of anyone with the misfortune of using it. It was supported by four, study, carved oak legs which had previous been varnished but, the departed animal, with no toys to occupy its time, had found the wooden supports an irresistible attraction and chewed away most of the brown paint. That £10 fee for rent was looking quite stingy after the destruction the creature had caused. As for the settee, only the bravest of souls would dare to relieve their tiredness on the flee infested rubbish dump. Fashioned in the 1960s, its material was yellow and black striped coarse wool (many times, Nick had likened it to a giant bee). It was overly long and had, at one time homed three thick seated cushions, though one had vanished before he'd moved in and the remaining two were squeezed flat to compensate for their departed sister. After years of wear, the zippers used to keep the threadbare covers in place were broken and its filthy foam interior, protruded from the useless material. Springs lay in wait for unsuspecting victims behind the upright back, happily stabbing into the flesh of anyone crazy enough to sit there. The collection of stains was again, grossly fascinating as it beggared belief that so many different things could be soiled into one piece of furniture. Once more, the smell of urine was unmistakable around this vile and unusable (expect by Nick) rest area though this time the departed dog wasn't to blame. Nick had had nightmares here too.

He held the blue mug in the palm of his hand as he made his way across the lounge to the leather chair, the liquid cooling in temperature due to the generous shot of whisky. His long dark hair hanging loosely across his face, still damp after taking a swift shower, hoping the cool water would help refresh his overworked mind. The previous night had been bad. He settled as best as anyone could in the uncomfortable chair and rested his head against the torn leather. He closed his weary eyes and rubbed the lids with the free hand before taking a long swallow from the Irish coffee. He would have happily missed out the caffeine and taken the whisky straight but today he needed a clear head, as clear as Nick Castle's mind got, anyway.

Even at this early hour, a time when normal people are starting their days, Nick was exhausted. True, the early start was a contributing factor, but he could easily feel this way, night, or day, for this was Nick Castle's life. The squalor of his home, alcohol, and medication abuse, even the alienation of most of his family, it had a deep-seated reason, a core. Something he'd fought for ten years but, after his mother's devastating announcement, an opportunity arose finally to face these fears.

After the telephone call, he'd had a strong, medium to large panic attack. These were regular occurrences' and sometimes he could control them, sometimes not. The news of granddad Bill's passing had shaken him, but it was the return of the nightmares which had caused the nervous assault. It had been a month since he'd had one this bad. Yes, he'd had smaller visions, waking to wet underwear and cold sweats but on those occasions, the images were less vivid, less realistic. A shot of whisky and a Prozac would normally quell the shaking. The breathing exercises' he'd been taught by his parent's fancy doctors had had no effect whatsoever and that paper bag bullshit (God knows how many had recommended that) was a complete waste of time. Give him a stiff drink and an anti-depressant any day.

The big ones, they were different. These seemed to go on for hours and unlike normal nightmares, every detail stayed with him, imprinted in his detached mind. Fractured by the unwavering belief that these were true images of horrific happenings and not just jumbled thoughts of the unconscious psyche. Visions of memories long forgotten, victims invading his dreams desperate for their stories to be heard, deaths to be avenged, just like Billy Scholes.

At times, the dreams controlled everything. He'd stay awake for days to avoid the images. Images of that place called Hallowell and the horrors he was certain to be true. Had his parents just been honest, perhaps things would have been different. A different life where this unknown phantasm didn't stalk his dreams. A life without doctors, without lies, in a world where people didn't think he was crazy.

He truly resented his parents for what they had done. It was their fault he was such an emotional wreck. Yes, it was their job to protect their child from harm but why lie about the motives. Children need parental support. They had had countless chances to make things right, to help him understand why his life was the way it was. Under the cover of darkness, snatching him from everything he'd ever know, ever loved. And why? Just because his friends and he had gone in that place when they weren't allowed. Had they explained why they had to keep away; the boys would never have gone near the station. Yes, it had been his idea, an idea that he'd regret forever, but he was an eleven-year-old boy looking for adventure. And okay, maybe the other lads had been scared and he'd pushed them to do it, it was Halloween for Christ's sake. Everyone deserves a good scare on Halloween. Oh, of course, Billy was crying, he was a year younger than the other three, but no one held a gun to his head, well, maybe an emotional one, the promise of endless teasing if he didn't go along with the group, but he could have said no.

And had they been warned about what was inside that place, that creature named 'Frankie' with a demented looking rubber skeleton mask and horrific intentions for trespassers, then it would never have happened. Billy Scholes would never have been dragged away, screaming for his mother, screams Nick still heard every time he closed his eyes. Why had his parents acted that way?

Instead of investigation, searching with the vague hope that Billy had survived, they had accused him of lying. Of making up a Halloween story. And when his protests had not desisted, he'd been drugged, stolen away from his home. Accused of suffering some mental breakdown as opposition to a family relocation. What bullshit. Johnny Brackett and Dan Challis were there too. Had their parents done the same thing? Why deny it ever happened? Did they hold him responsible? And why, after ten years would this shit not go away?

He hated his father most of all. He'd hung around six years before abandoning him, abandoning his family. He hated that he was a coward and a loser, for showing how to hide from his problems at the bottom of a bottle. Oh, he'd send letters or a check for birthdays and Christmas, anything that didn't take a two-way conversation. Just before he left, around Nick's seventeenth birthday, he came home drunk one night and almost…almost admitted the truth. Nick had had another fruitless appointment with a psychiatrist and was in a decidedly black mood. He'd given Mick Castle both barrels, calling him anything that would hurt, and then, his father finally snapped. Pinning his son by the throat against a living room door, he began a tirade.

"You think you are the only one who's had it hard. Don't you understand, it's all your fault? Do you think I wanted to leave Hallowell? Well, I didn't? I'd lived there all my life and was FORCED to leave. Forced to leave because of you, you, ungrateful brat. If you'd only done as you were told, everything would have been different. One place, stay away from one place, that's all you had to do and because you fucking ignored me, look what happened."

"MICK, NO," Kath Castle shouted loud enough for the whole town to hear. "THAT'S ENOUGH."

"No, it's not," Nick sensed a chance. "Go on, what did happen daddy? For once in your life tell the truth, please."

Releasing the grip, he gave his wife a stare. He wanted to continue, the boy could see that, but his wife's poisonous glare made him stop. He looked to the floor and turned, heading for the front door. Nick gave chase and as the two generations considered each other's eyes, there was almost truth. A tear rolled down the older man's cheek as he walked away. He never returned.

Perhaps, had he continued that statement things would have been different. It had all happened so fast. He was ten years old and came home in hysterics. The town doctor, Harry Bracket (his friend Johnny's dad) had got there in minutes and gave him 'a little prick in the arm' just to calm him down. When he woke, everything had changed. Hallowell, his home, family, friends, his life, all gone. He woke in a new bed, in a new room, in a new town, his parent's reaction, 'Oscar worthy'.

Hoping that medical treatment may be the answer, Kath Castle had contacted many local councillors, hoping that one may have the key to rebooting her son's fractured mind. The boy discovered the notes his mother had jotted before the final draft of a letter was comprised.

"Nick has always been a wilful boy; it is something my husband and I have always encouraged and admired about him. The town of Hallowell was our home, the only roots we, as a family, have ever known, but being a time of economic change, my husband's employers needed to downsize their local operation and we had to choose between remaining in our own village without work, or take their offer of employment in another branch. Without the prospect of alternative opportunities, we reluctantly choose to relocate. From the moment Nick was told of our decision, he changed. The fun-loving carefree boy became confrontational and obnoxious, fighting us at every turn. Things became so bad, we considered reversing our decision but, as the wheels were already in motion, this was impossible. When the moving day arrived, Nick was nowhere to be seen. We searched the village, scores of people joining us, until we finally found him.

He'd taken refuge in an abandoned railway station on the outskirts of Hallowell. We aren't certain what happened next as he was alone, but there must have been an accident. We believe he'd been climbing on a dangerous steel ladder attached to the side of the building and had fell. Fortunately, there appeared little physical damage, just cuts, bruises, and abrasions. The problems were psychological, short term memory loss being a main issue. We postponed our relocation for as long as possible, right to the final day, but my husband had a start date and we needed to go.

This was the time Nick's problems magnified. Hallowell's village doctor needed to sedate him, just so we could get him into the car. Nick slept all the way to our new home of Russellville, and when he eventually woke, he was in a new bedroom, in a new house, in a new town. It seemed more than he could take.

It was now, that the memory loss became worse. Perhaps, his brain had reset to a happier time but in his mind had blocked out six weeks of events. Nick claimed that he had no recollection of my husband's employment situation, the potential move, and of course, the accident at the abandoned railway station. There were snippets of events, but nothing made sense. Suddenly, things deteriorated even worse.

Nick's mind created a happening. It involved that railway station, so we can see where it originated from, but how his imagination could morph into something so horrible is crazy. His version of events was completely different from the truth, according to him, he was with a group of friends, still in Hallowell, the previous Halloween…"

The rest of the letter was missing, either awaiting completion, or improved upon by another worthier piece of fiction. Castle had kept this jotted note safely, showing it whenever his quarrels against his parents reached their zenith. He made photocopies, and on one occasion, plastered issues across the living room with the word, FALSE, scribbled in black-marker pen, down the centre. It was used as a stick to repeatedly hit his parents with, each time, a symbol of their broken relationship.

It was easier to have a looney-toon son than admit the truth.

However implausible, Mick and Kath Castle maintained this version unquestionably. Russellville became Nick's prison, and the only escape would be to talk to these, doctors. The first shrink, sorry, child psychologist had come highly recommended. The guardians had spoken to the quack first, ensuring that

24

their story was taken as gospel, kids tell lies, parents don't. The boy had to concede defeat, if he was in the shrink's position, who would he believe? Two level-headed, worried, hardworking, parents who were trying their best by their fuck-up son? A tale of unfortunate circumstances which forced a family to leave their family home? Or a whack-job pre-teen with a conspiracy theory? A mass cover-up involving an entire village. Scenes of unimaginable horror, a masked killer, and a murdered child? Not much of a battle.

The first prescription for anti-depressants was administered at thirteen, even though legally, they weren't allowed until after the sixteenth birthday. Special dispensation was needed as Nick was a special case, it was drugs or permanent committal. There'd been numerous suicide attempts; Nick had tried hanging himself in the outside tool-shed, but the rope was rotten, and the noose snapped. An overdose of paracetamol required his stomach to be pumped and, on another occasion, the police had taken three hours to talk him down from the school-house roof. For that one, Castle had endured a six weeks' spell, housed in the child wing of Winterdon psychiatric hospital. And still, Nick's version of events remained solid.

His parent's marriage had been crumbling since they arrived in Russellville, Mick Castle become a shell of the man he used to be. In Hallowell, he was 'Jack-the-lad', the go to guy for help, could give anything a try with a smile and a pint. Now, all that remained was the pint, every night, Hallowell working men's club, a seat at the bar and beer in his glass. The more his son's problems amplified, the longer he stayed in the bar. He wasn't a happy drunk, but by this time, all the family had given up on each other. Kath tried, at least she was bothered, would ask how the appointments went but in time, she gave up too. The marriage was over bar a piece of paper, and her son would push away any attempts at affection. She needed affection.

Now at twenty-one, Nick Castle was taking two hundred Prozac a month. By keeping his psychiatrist sweet, his legal scripts kept coming but they were topped up by Janice Briggs. Janice was a thirty something receptionist at his local pharmacy who had always had a serious crush on Nick. Plump, with short brown hair and a bad complexion, she was no one's dream girl. But she had 'skills. One day, after picked up his regular medication, her index finger stroked his hand as she passed over the package. He'd smiled and left the shop but to his surprise, she'd followed.

"I see you coming in the chemist all the time Nick, my name's Jan." He smiled and tried to continue walking, this was a relationship he had no interest in. Seeing her initial connect had had zero effect, but she continued.

"I see you coming in early for your tablets sometimes, even before they been sent over. You look so desperate, I could help you, if you know what I mean." His interest peaked.

"How's that?" She was smiling. "If you were nice to me, I could get you extra. The old quack in charge never does stock checks. If you were to come to my flat tonight, I might have a little prize for you."

And that's how it began. For six months, once a week, Nick would head to Janice Briggs home and collect twenty-five extra pills. She did it this way to ensure he kept coming back. Plus, she knew, she'd have a hold on him then. It wasn't so bad. She cooked them nice meals and supplied the alcohol. The flat was warm and welcoming; the settee didn't stink of piss. All he had to do was service her needs then roll over and fall asleep. Normally he'd sleep over, and she'd always be gone early in the morning for work so there was no need for extras. It suited their needs. She'd said she loved him once, but she knew the score. It was convenient, nothing else and this way, Nick could stay numb most of the time.

That morning had been tougher than usual. The panic attack had refused to yield. The whisky had proven ineffective, and he was down to his last strip of Prozac, so they needed to be rationed. He'd tried the breathing exercises and that was pointless. In desperation, he even found a paper bag and tried that, but it had a hole in it. He knew the only remedy was escape. The flat was becoming claustrophobic, walls closing in, shadows in the dingy surroundings taking on lives of their own. He scrambled into yesterdays discarded clothing, his dirty white trainers pulled on over bare feet, heading for the door without giving a thought for a coat, even though early October mornings are hardly the warmest time of year. He reached the exit, pulling on the door, and finding total resistance. It was locked, and the keys weren't in sight. He remembered throwing them on the kitchen workbench the night before and forced himself back along his narrow passageway, re-entering the filthy kitchen and searching through the debris of discarded litter. Reaching for a light switch the bulb crackled and died. Boxes and cans were thrown to the floor in blind panic, and he cursed his slovenly ways. Out of the corner of his eye he spotted a brass key ring behind a takeaway pizza box and grabbed for his prize. Once more, feeling his way down the passageway to the exit, he heard a noise coming from the living area. He didn't wait to see what created it. Fighting with the lock, it took three attempts to get the correct key before the cell door opened and he was free. Hurtling down a flight of concrete stairs, he almost lost his footing twice, but finally he burst through the buildings only exit and he was in the street. The cold morning air washed over him as he ran from the flat. Finally, he stopped and turned around, but nothing was following. He bent crooked, hands resting on his knees, breathing erratic. The darkness like a long-lost friend, keeping all those 'normal people' tucked up in their slumber, leaving the streets for him alone.

He walked the roads for three hours until first light, the boarded-up shops a depressing sign of the times. By 6 am, market traders were arriving, and the town of Bishopsgate was waking. Enough reason for him to head home. The cool shower he'd taken when getting back to the flat (cool because the gas was cut off and there was no hot water) refreshed his body if not cleansing his mind. The temptation to turn back to alcohol was strong but his mind needed to be sober, at least for today. The taste of whisky in the coffee holding off the craving at least for now. At 7:15 the telephone rang again.

"Hello mother dearest, what can I do for you?" He laid the sarcasm on thick.

"And good morning to you Nicky." She'd been the queen of sarcastic comments and could give as good as she received. Plus, she knew he hated 'Nicky'; made him feel like a five-year-old.

"What do you want?" He was growing impatient already. She was the last person he needed today.

"Now, Nicky, that's no way to speak to your mother."

"Stop calling me Nicky and I'll change my tone."

"Fine. Unbelievably, I was worried about you. I should have waited till morning to tell you about Granddad Bill. I'm Sorry."

"I think that's the first time I've ever heard you say those words, about anything…ever."

"Well, are you okay?" She was getting impatient now.

"Not so bad. I was actually going to call in later if you not working."

"Call in, here?" She stuttered, shocked by her son's announcement. "You must be wanting something, I assume."

"See you at eleven." He hung up the telephone abruptly and she never called back. How could she think her son could have a motive to visit his mother? Of course, he did. He needed money.

Chapter 3

The ash from the tip of a filter less self-rolled cigarette hung down in an arc ready to fall into his lap, as Nick Castle stared motionlessly through the windshield of his beat-up white Ford Fiesta. He was only a mile or so from his destination, but uncertainty had forced him to bring the car to a halt. It had been eight months since he'd seen his mother and he knew had it not been for Bill Castle's untimely passing, a visit would not have happened any time soon. Family fun time was well and truly over.

He'd sensed this was coming. For months, some form of pre-cognitive cloud hung about his being, something big was approaching, but changes in Nick's life were rarely for the good. Attempts at blocking the thoughts with alcohol and pills were futile. This was different, and he couldn't escape it.

Just four nights ago, Nick had fallen to sleep in another drunken haze, but the image before him, as reality became dreams, made him wish that the unconscious state could last forever. He was a young boy again, just ten years old, walking by the stream that ran through the woodland on the border of Hallowell. And holding his hand was Bill Castle, his grandfather, his only real, male role model. Nick smiled as the breeze made the old man's hair fall across his eyes. His firm grip, hands clenched in an unbreakable bond. He'd knelt before the little boy and beamed his unmistakable grin. "I'll see you soon." Afterwards, he wrapped his arms tightly around his grandson and wept silent tears. When Nick woke, for once, he felt peace. The images stayed with him, as firm as any vision he'd ever seen, like illustrations in a book. Not questioning why, or how. Perhaps, now, he had an answer.

Castle had never had to deal with a family bereavement and this passing was going to be hard. William Arthur Castle, a man of the people, strong, firm, hard when called upon, soft by nature. Bonded by blood, a role model, a good man. Legitimately, the only person Nick could say that at he loved, the only one he respected. Trust, that was another matter, after all, he had backed up the parent's version of events, the Hallowell lies. But his granddad always had an air of guilt around the subject, like he had gone along with the deception because he was forced, rather than by choice.

It was on rare occasions that he saw his grandparents and those visits were eagerly anticipated. They were used as a threat to keep Nick in line. Get with the program or your grandparents won't come to see you. He was also certain that, this was the threat used against them too, keep your mouth shut or you're not welcome. Obviously, visiting them wasn't an option (Hallowell out of bounds) so when the tri-annual visits loomed on the horizon, Nick would be less confrontational.

Upon one of the all too infrequent visits, a heated exchange between his parents and Bill, with his grandma Alice playing referee, had chilled the boy to the bone. With his ear to the wall and voices raised, Mick had shouted his father down, insisting that if he wanted to see their son and stay at their home then it was their way, no questions asked. Nick was terrified, losing his grandparents could well have been a breaking point from which he could never return. So, from then on, he looked upon their visits for what they were, a break from the monotony that was his life. It was also the first time ever, he'd felt hatred. Hatred for his parents, that would continue to grow steadily as the years progressed.

Something had happened once. It was the boy's 15th birthday and this coincided with a family reunion. Bill and Alice had been there for three days, and Nick knew the next day they would leave. He hated them going and was always melancholy on the departure eve. He was sulking in the usual teenage fashion, curled up on his single divan bed in the darkness. As usual, Bill Castle would come to comfort him, he could feel his pain.

The white panelled door to Nick's small bedroom creaked gently on its hinges as the patriarch emerged with milk and cookies. The boy's eyes drew toward his advancing sibling. The lighting in the room was pale, only a small standing lamp containing a low-wattage bulb on the stairwell outside the room breaking the darkness. Through squinted eyes the teenager could see for the first time the effect the advancing years were having on the old man. He'd been retired for some years now and inactivity had certainly helped slow the former policeman down, but this was different. His face had lost the fullness it once had, his flushed cheeks beginning to sag around his cheekbones. His once tight skin starting to hang loose below the eyes, wrinkled and leathery. There were small sections of stubble around the chin and throat missed from his morning shave, caused by slowly failing eyesight. His hair had started greying many years earlier and now was completely white and thinning rapidly around the crown. He looked precisely what he was, a tired old man who life had caught up with.

"Do you mind if I switch the light on, son? The old blinkers aren't what they used to be." The boy rose from the bed and reached for the blue bedside lamp on his white M.F.I. dressing table. The room was bathed in light. When Bill called him 'son' Nick would smile whereas when his father did it, all he felt was disgust.

"That's better. Thought maybe the old peepers had given up altogether there." Nick smiled generously at Bill's attempt at a joke though it was more from politeness than humour. For a moment, the two males, one just on the road to manhood and the other thick with experience, just stared at one another, the need for words unnecessary, the bond between the generations still strong. Eventually, it was the young man that broke the silence.

"Why do you need to go so soon, can't you stay just a few more days." His face bathed with pleading, as if the old man was the only link to a life he used to cherish.

Bill sighed and rubbed his tired eyes with his left hand, the right gripping his grandson's knee. "You know we can't stay; your gran has the store to run and if we stay away too long that woman working for her will steal all the stock. She's a big girl and we sell cream cakes, not a good combination." This attempt at a joke was funnier but Nick refused to crack.

"You always have some excuse."

"It's not an excuse, if we stay here the woman will explode and there will be bits of guts and cream cake all over the shop. Do you know how long it will take to clean that up?"

Bill chuckled, Nick didn't.

"Anyway boy, there's another reason. You're old enough to understand now. Your mam and dad, things aren't good there, a blind man can see that. I think with us here; it's making things worse."

"Things couldn't get much worse, believe me."

"Yes, well, if they are going to make it, things need to change. I'm not blaming you, but you need to help. I heard about the pills you been given, and I wasn't happy but, who knows, maybe they will do some good. You need to accept the situation for what it is and don't put more pressure on them. I'm sure you don't want to see them divorce, do you?"

"Couldn't care less. They don't care about me so why should I care about them." The boy's spoilt facial showed his immaturity.

"I don't think you really mean that. Whatever the situation, your parents love you and would always want the best for you, no matter what. Sometimes, I'm sure you don't understand the decisions they make but you need to trust them."

Nick was getting angry but had never shouted at Bill, he had too much respect for him, but this conversation was pushing his limits.

"Trust them, are you serious? Trust people who have lied to me most of my life, trust them to make decisions when the biggest one was bringing me to this shithole town and then lie about why they did it. I'm not stupid. I'm trusting no one."

"What about me? You trust me, don't you?"

"I'm sorry granddad but no. No, I don't trust you. I love you and grandma and always will, but I trust no one."

"That hurts. It really does."

"Like I said, I'm sorry but how can I trust you. How can I trust you when you backed them up? Backed up their lies and let me rot away in doctor's offices and popping pills to keep me quiet, keep me manageable, when the truth would make all this crap go away. Like I said granddad, I not stupid, I might be crazy, crackers, off my rocker, but not stupid. I never had amnesia, or whatever crap they claim. I can remember that night like it was yesterday, and no one believes me, NO ONE. Not you, not grandma, not them downstairs and certainly not the quacks they stick in front of me."

"I know it doesn't seem fair." His tone was down to a whisper. "One day, one day when you are older, you'll understand, believe me. It's safer this way, Hell, it must be this way. I know you're not stupid. But to be honest, I back them

30

100%. True, it's been handled badly but eventually, when you're old enough too maybe accept the truth, you'll understand why it needed to be this way."

"Safer?" the old man wanted to continue, spill the whole rotten truth but it wasn't his place. It was too dangerous.

"Look, I've said too much already. If they knew we were talking like this, that would be it, no more contact, they've told me that often enough. Just remember this. When it all gets too much, and everything is weighing you down, people saying that you're crazy, just remember, one day it will make sense. I can't say anymore, I'd love too but I can't, please just trust me"

"Take me with you. I can be packed in ten minutes' flat, screw what they say, I can go home."

"NO." His face turned red, veins popping in his temples. "Hallowell is no place for a boy like you. Hell, it's no place for anyone but especially not for someone with an inquisitive mind. I found that out the hard way and the same will NOT happen to you."

"Inquisitive mind? What are you?" The old man held his hand in defiance.

"That's enough. Now listen to me. If I've ever meant anything to you, anything at all, you'll promise me. You'll promise me you'll stay away."

Nick interjected, "I can't do that."

"Well, I can't stay then. And I won't be back. This is no idle threat. It will kill me not to see you but either you promise to stay away from Hallowell, or this will be the last time we see each other. You need to understand. There is something very wrong with that place, something evil. It's destroyed too many lives and it could destroy yours too."

"It's already done it. Don't you see, my life is in tatters, it's dead."

"Boy, you don't know what death is." There was silent reflection, neither generation knowing how to continue this argument. Finally, Bill Castle spoke. "I promise, one day. One day when you are a man, when you've got past all this shit and moved on with your life, I will tell you the truth. When I think, you can handle it I will tell you every detail. But for now, you must let this go. For me, you have to let this go."

"But that's what you don't seem to understand. I can't move on with my life with this hanging over my head." Tears welled in the child's eyes, his face distorted. "It's there every time I close my eyes."

The former policeman took the boy in his arms in a heavy embrace. He wanted nothing more than to end his pain, his suffering, but terrified what the ramifications would be if he did. From outside the bedroom on the passageway, footsteps could be heard climbing the stairs. Nick quickly pulled away and rubbed the tears from his eyes as showing emotion in front of them was something he despised. Kath Castle entered the room with a concerned expression across her face.

"And what are you two talking about?"

"He's just a little upset that we're leaving tomorrow, that's all." Bill lied and hoped his daughter-in-law wouldn't notice. "I've told him, we can't move in here, Mick and I would kill each other." His statement was only a partial joke.

"No, you can't, and he knows this, we tell him every time you visit." There was not a hint of humour in her tone and the atmosphere was as frosty as the cold autumnal night. Nick glared at his mother with hate in his eyes.

"Come on you, it's time for bed."

And with that, it was over. The closest Nick Castle had ever come to answers, had left him with even more questions.

The village of Russellville loomed large in the distance. The place that had been his unmitigated prison for eight years of his childhood, still containing the residence of her, now was a mile further along the road. No words could describe how much he hated this place. The ash finally fell from his cigarette, scattering its smouldering grey debris across the young man's grey and blue stripped sweatshirt, the only top that had been remotely clean that morning. The cigarette had halved in size as he raised the white papered tobacco to his lips and inhaled a large breath of whispery smoke into his lungs, holding the taste inside his body until he was forced to breathe out. The air in the car was thick with nicotine and his vision though the windows was impaired. Slowly, he unhooked his faded black tattered seat belt and pulled the doors silver handle firmly, pushing the rusted barrier open and allowing the sweet smell of unpolluted air to rush into the vehicle.

The fresh October morning air invaded his skin, cooling his mildly sweating face, helping to keep another panic attack at bay. He'd pulled the car over as he had felt impending trouble, Russellville had that impression on him. He had memories there too that he'd prefer to forget, things he certainly wasn't proud of climbing into the Ford, stretching his arms above his head and letting go a loud smokers cough. The cigarette between his fingers little more than a stump, he threw it remains into the gutter. Reaching into the back pocket of a pair of faded black denim jeans, he produced a crumpled Benson and Hedges cigarette packet. The box was months old and used to store his own rolled smokes as they were a cheaper alternative to store-bought packs. Without a filter, they were stronger too, a quicker route to cancer. He opened the pack and found it empty.

"Perfect day to run out of fags, marvellous." He was certain he'd just rolled a new batch the night before. What he wasn't positive of was how many he'd already smoked that morning. Annoyed and slightly more edgy, he breathed in the cool morning air, stare transfixed on his destination. Nick wondered what seeing her again was going to be like. Could he keep his distain in check? Thinking about his mother always raised the rancour inside. If he had a choice, he'd have missed the visit all together, but he needed a favour, another reason to keep his acid tongue buttoned. Climbing back into the car, he slammed the door closed, taking out his aggression on the inanimate object and wiped the condensation from the windscreen. On the third attempt, the ignition fired, and the car lurched forward, heading to Russellville.

The steep bank began to level out and soon, the village's first row of dreary houses was visible. The urge to turn the car around almost irresistible but Nick fought the temptation and drove on. This was Elm Street, where Eddy Cooter lived. He was two years older than Nick and had bullied him since day one, lasting all the way until he was fourteen. That was when, after a particularly bad psychiatrist session, Nick had snapped. Taking a two-by-four from Mick's tool-shed, the troubled teen had taken a vicious vengeance on his tormenter and three of his followers, hospitalising the ringleader and assaulting the rest. He'd got a six months' sentence to a young offender's institute for that, suspended for two years should he re-offend. Even had he been forced to serve the time; it would have been worth it to see that scumbag suffer.

At the end of Elm St, the road turned sharply to the right, and there in all its grotesque glory was Russellville. The home of Kathy Castle.

Chapter 4

It didn't seem right to just walk in. Nick Castle had lived in this house for eight years until things had become untenable and he'd left for good just after his eighteenth birthday. He'd lived in his car for three weeks until his shrink had made a phone call to the authorities and got him a place in a hostel in Bishopsgate, twelve miles away. After a few weeks, Nick had been offered the 'luxury accommodation' from where he now presided, above a stinking pizza take-away joint. Still, it was better than being back here.

The front door's colour had changed. In fact, it wasn't just the colour, it was the entire door. White plastic P.V.C. The windows too. Double glazing? She couldn't afford this. "Looks like Doctor Pete was getting his feet well and truly under the table."

He pressed the doorbell, a generic melody sounding from inside the house. It took three presses before the door was answered.

"Morning mummy dearest, how lovely you look this morning." He remembered the favour he needed and wished he hadn't laid the sarcasm on quite as thick.

"Morning Nick. Wish I could say the same for you." Her acid tongue as exercised as ever. "If you're coming in, take off your shoes, we just had new carpets fitted."

"We?" Nick tried not to sound condescending, but not too hard. "Do I take it Doctor Pete is living here now?" Doctor Peter Williams had been Nick's psychiatrist for three years from fifteen to eighteen, though he always seemed to have more of an eye for Nick's mother than his patient. Mick Castle had suspected as much and accused his wife of extra marital frivolities on numerous occasions though by this time, their marriage was already in tatters.

Nick recalled a time when his father was overheard saying, "At least Nick can have a live-in nut-fucker when I'm gone, though it will take more than Doctor Pete to fix him up."

"Peter and I are getting married just as soon as the divorce are final." Kath's statement was strong and deliberate, seeming intent on taking no shit from her son today.

"Good for you. Wouldn't have thought this place was up to Doctor Pete's standards though. Thought he'd be more of a mansion man, myself."

"We just doing this place up to sell, then we are moving into a new build in Durham city. And by the way, please stop calling him Doctor Pete, you know I hate that." Nick was walking a fine line as he needed to keep Kath sweet. He pulled off his white trainers and they walked into the lounge.

"Coffee? Tea? You do drink normal liquid still, I assume. It's not all booze." Things had been more frosty than usual between the siblings over the last six months as Nick had developed a habit of late night drunken abusive telephone calls, something Kath had grown tired of in record time.

"Coffee, please." The pleasantries made him gag on his words. "I guess I owe you an apology too. I've been worse than usual lately. My girlfriend passed away and I needed someone to take it out on. It could have been anyone, you, dad, the neighbour's cat, you were just the unlucky one, I guess. I'm sorry." It was one of the least sincere apologies ever made.

"Is that the truth? About your girlfriend, I mean?"

"No, I just thought it was a kick arse story, of course it's true. Who'd make something like that up?" This was not going to plan.

"Do you want me to answer that? The lies you've told over the years; I can barely believe a word you say."

"I'm not sure you should be talking about liars really." Tempers were beginning to fray.

"Here we go again, same old story, oh for the misery of me. If I've heard this once, I've…" Nick raised a hand.

"I didn't come here to fight. I really didn't. I thought you mentioned coffee."

Kathy Castle retreated to the kitchen and placed a tin kettle on the stove. Nick sat down on the blue chesterfield and rested his head against its leathered back. The room had been redecorated since his last visit, all bright and cheerful pastels. The opposite to his childhood memories growing up in this place. As she waited for the water to boil, she returned to the lounge doorway. She looked younger than he remembered, a stress-free life obviously suited her. Her clothes weren't worn, and her hair styled, living with a rich man had its benefits. At least something came from those worthless sessions.

"So, how have you been? Are you getting any sleep? Are you still taking your medication?" She sounded concerned for once. Even after all the wars, the arguments, and fights, she was still his mother.

"Yes, yes and yes. I'm doing okay (he lied), I'm sleeping fine (more lies) and I'm still on Prozac." (Had she known how many pills; she'd have been pissed)

"And the drinking? Are you controlling it yet? Or is it controlling you? You said your girlfriend died? Oh God, it wasn't drugs, was it?" The concern was replaced with disapproval.

"The drinking is fine too and Julia," there was a sullen pause, "is a long story but it was most definitely not drugs."

From the kitchen, the kettle was whistling. Nick took a deep breath as she walked away, desperately fighting the urge to tell her to go fuck herself. He needed a drink, badly. She returned with two steaming mugs, one tea, and one coffee. Shame there was no whisky in his.

"So, do I take it you need something, or have you just missed me?" Nick chuckled but Kath remained straight faced, afraid of what the answer could be, and having a strong suspicion she already knew.

"Oh, mother, how well you know me. In fact, I do need a favour. I need to borrow some money. I won't insult you by saying you'll get it back anytime soon but just know, had there been any other way, I wouldn't have asked. And if I had anything worth selling, I would happily have done that too."

"What do you need the money for?"

"Petrol, of course."

"Petrol? Going somewhere nice?" She already knew the answer.

"I'm going to my grandfather's funeral. And yes, that means I'm going back to Hallowell. And before you try to talk me out of it, I…" His mother interrupted.

"I'm not going to talk you out of it. Why do you think I told you about your granddad in the first place? I could easily have waited until the funeral was finished. But for once, we agree on something. I've spent years trying to keep you away from that place and look where that's got you. Hiding at the bottom of a bottle with no life at all. You are old enough to make you own decisions, right or wrong. You are searching for something and you not going to find it here. If it were up to me, I'd tell you stay away from Hallowell, but it's not up to me anymore."

She handed him a white envelope. "Open it." He looked at her with suspicion then then tore open the paper. Inside was five hundred pounds in used notes. Nick was shocked.

"I don't know what to say. For once, I'm lost for words."

"Thank you might be a start." Kath raised from her seat and walked towards her son, hoping for the first hug in years. Nick fought back tears, not wanting to show emotion but feeling overwhelmed at her action, her support. It was long overdue in his opinion.

"Of course, thank you. Thank you so much. I must admit; I didn't expect this reaction. I expected an argument, war, whatever." Nick rose and hugged his mother and for the first time, maybe in years, he felt wanted, accepted. He felt like an adult.

They squeezed tight, both fighting against tears, finally grasping a parental bond rather than jailer and convict.

"I've a confession to make!" Nick grimaced, now she was going to spoil it. "I wouldn't feel this way had it not been for Peter. I know you hate him and think I cheated on your father with him but that's not true. Your dad and I were broken long before Peter came into our lives. In truth, we were on the rocks before we even left Hallowell. I know you think Pete failed you as your doctor, maybe that's true. But he's made me feel different about everything, different about you. I understand now that you need to make your own way and protecting you from that place isn't working." Nick pulled away slightly but still held Kath in an embrace, able to see the truth in her eyes. "You're not crazy." The tears finally broke through "I'm sorry you ever felt that way. Hiding behind a stupid lie. I don't suppose you'll ever be able to forgive me but please just know, we did it for your own good. We were trying to protect you; it just didn't work."

She began to sob, her head buried in her son's chest, massively overcome with emotion. Emotion that she'd spent years hiding. This hadn't been her doing, the Hallowell mafia made the rules.

"Was it your choice? Did you make everything up, all the bullshit?" Nick needed to know. It was the only way if there was going to be a chance of progression. Kath laughed.

"Me? You've got to be kidding. Standard Hallowell practice, I'm afraid. Stanton-Grove, the place where your dad worked. Did you never find it strange that there were already other people from Hallowell working there? Other families who knew too much. I grew up in St Mara, the next village over from Hallowell, I only moved there when I married your dad. Even though I was an adult, those bastards looked at me like an outsider and they knew how to keep their secrets. The first I knew about Hallowell's dirty little enigma, was one night when your dad had had too much to drink. He rabbled the whole sordid details and I laughed, didn't believe him. Oh, I started to believe fast, when our home was being packed up and you were being drugged, so…no, it wasn't my story. I just had to go along with it, like everyone else has to." The look of disgust on Kath Castle's face told a thousand tales, none good.

"I'm sorry." Sincerity wasn't Nick Castle's strong point, but his mother had seen enough lies, to recognise the truth. "I had no idea. No idea how much this has scarred you too."

"Scarred! There isn't a plastic surgeon in the world that could fix me up son. The number of times I wanted to tell you the truth, but he wouldn't let me. He'd grown up with this wall of silence and thought it was okay for everyone else. I can't tell you the number of times I cried myself to sleep after seeing you tear yourself apart and KNOWING, knowing I could take your pain away. You can never understand how that feels."

"But he left us. Why didn't you tell me then?"

"Because I was ashamed. You were a teenager and for years I'd let you believe you were mad. Hoping that you would just let it go but you never did. You get that stubborn streak from my side of the family, sorry. And the longer it went, the harder it became. Doctor after doctor, all the pills that turned into alcohol. And unbelievably, and I'm not blaming you for this, you weren't the easiest kid in the world to love. I became numb. Me and your dad hated each other by then and I blamed him for your behaviour, so basically, I was just counting the days till you moved out. That's a horrible thing for a mother to admit but we are trying to be honest, I can't be more honest than that."

"So, while we are being honest, Hallowell. What's the truth? What exactly where we are running away from?" Nick didn't expect a detailed history, but anything would be a start.

"I can't really tell you. That's not me being evasive, I just don't exactly know. That night when you came in after being in that place, I've never seen people react like that. It was fear, anger, disbelief, all rolled into one. When the doctor gave you that shot, I slapped his face, hard. When I found out it was your dad that called him, I slapped him too. That was when I was drugged. You see, I wasn't given a choice either. The last thing I remember was being held down by Mick and your granddad who had mysteriously appeared, being told that it would calm me down because I was hysterical by then. I was confused, here was all these people in my house, talking about what needed to be done about my son, and I didn't understand any of it. When I woke up, everything had been decided. We were moving, and I wasn't given a vote. I was told that if we stayed, your life was at risk because you had seen too much. You see, Hallowell has a dirty little secret that few people know. Hell, I was involved, and I still don't know much. Those people are so afraid of the Hallowell railway station, or rather, what's inside it, that they will do anything too keep things quiet. No matter whose life gets destroyed, no matter what damage it does."

"And Billy? He didn't survive that night, I'm certain of it, that bastard just dragged him away?"

"This one you won't believe, but it's true. Billy Scholes's parents, Adam, and Joyce, their son ripped from their lives, and they accepted it. No questions asked. They were locals, through and through. There was no funeral, no police investigation. What was the point, they knew what had happened to him? It was just swept under the carpet. Like natural wastage."

Nick was in shock; how could people react this way. As if the loss of a child meant nothing.

"And Dan Challis, he was there too. Did their family need move away? Has his life turned out the same way as mine?" Kath's reply was unexpected.

"No. He was told the truth straight away. I only found that out years later and I was pissed to say the least. You see, you seemed to get the blame. Dan claimed that the whole thing had been your idea; that you had talked the others into going in the station; that Billy's death had been your fault. He agreed to keep things quiet, and it had been believed that you'd never have done that."

"You're fucking right, I wouldn't. My best friend had just been slaughtered by Hallowell's version of the bogeyman. There's no way that I'd have just kept quiet and let him go without retribution."

"And that's why we were shunted out the village. I don't blame you. Hell, if it were you that had been murdered, there's no way I'd have been willing to keep my mouth shut. His body was never recovered, you know. Those heartless bastards just wrote off a child's life. If there had been a search party, perhaps he might have been saved. They just gave up. I couldn't believe it when I was told. It was your gran that told me most of this on one of their visits. I'd been ready to tell you everything. You were about thirteen and the therapy was going nowhere. She talked me out of it. How could I tell you then? After everything you'd been through, all the lies and bullshit? I didn't know where to start. I was trapped, not knowing which way to turn. I had no one. You know my history, that both my parents were killed before I was eight, that I grew up in the children's home in St Mara. I think that's why I married your dad so young, not because I loved him. Looking back, I'm not sure I ever did. Because being with him was the first normal thing I'd ever had, that's why we stayed together if we did too. I was terrified of being alone. I know I had you but between us, we'd managed to fuck

38

you up royally. I just couldn't cope. It's no excuse and you probably think I'm the weakest person you've ever met but…"

"Mum, listen. I'm not just writing off everything that's happened. I know your role and after what you've told me, well, let's just say, my opinion has changed a little. I'm not saying you, me and Peter will be having Christmas lunch and pulling crackers together but, maybe, when I get back from Hallowell, things can be different. Maybe we can start over, try to like each other again. Hell, I might even get along with 'Dr Pete'." This time, they both laughed at the boyfriend's title. "I think maybe I can stop seeing you as the enemy and see you for what you really are. A confused lady who gave up everything for the safety of her son and got everything thrown back in her face. Perhaps, it is me that should be apologising to you. Regardless, it's time to move on and it is time today, anyway. I need to get going, get things sorted before I set off." They both rose from their seats, hugs now welcomed.

"Do you even know the way there? Perhaps, a final obstacle Kath hoped would put her son off making the dangerous trip." Nick laughed.

"I planned that route a hundred times. Set off a time or two, then lost my nerve. That won't happen today. Just hope my car makes it, it really is a piece of crap." Kath smiled then turned and walked to the mantle over the fire. She reached for a key with a Ford key ring.

"Here, take this." She lightly threw the key to Nick, in surprise he fumbled and dropped it. Looking down he realised what she'd given him. "Pete bought me it three months ago, it's the Ford Escort outside. Just leave me the key to your 'piece of crap' for emergencies. At least I know you'll get there safe."

"Mum, I, I don't know what to say. This is weird cos I'm not usually lost for words, and you've nailed me loads of times today. Thank You."

This really was idiosyncratic; Nick wasn't used to being happy in his mother's presence. It wasn't the gifts or even the warmth. It was the honesty. He'd heard and told so many lies over the years, that a lot of times he didn't know what was true or wasn't. Today had been different. It was two people talking frankly, airing the grievances, and finding some resolutions. If he could do this with someone he classed as the enemy, then maybe… He picked up the keys and opened the front door. "Won't Pete be angry at you giving me the car?"

"Excuse me mister, loaning you the car. When you get back from there, the car comes home. And don't worry about Peter, I can handle him." Again, laughing after remarks…Weird. "You think you can handle her. Two litre injections do not like yours, 0 to 60 in three and a half hours. Where the hell did you get that from anyway?" Nick opened the car door and smiled.

"That's another long story. One that you seriously don't want to hear." He put the key in the ignition and the engine fired first time. He was about to close the Ford's door when Kath grabbed the handle.

"I know you need to do this, I really do understand, but please, don't dig too far. Go to Hallowell, say goodbye to your granddad, exorcise some demons, but please son, leave it at that. That place is cursed and bigger men than you failed to break it. Stay away from that tomb. You're not the only one to have nightmares about it and I've never been in the bloody place. Just come home safe. I've just got you back, I don't want to lose you again." Nick smiled.

"Don't worry, I'll be fine." Closing the door Kath made a last call.

"That's what mothers do, you daft bugger. That's what mothers do." Kath whispered, to no-one in particular.

"Drive safe and be safe."

The wheels of the car spun once on the black, tar-masked road, the engine growling like a race car, her son staring straight ahead. She admired that profile, the same as the husband's what she was in the process of divorcing. He looked so focused, so ready. For what? She grimaced. That stubborn Castle streak ran deeply in him, just how deeply, Kath wondered. Had she done the right thing, revealing what she had revealed? What was the right thing? For now, she didn't know. All she did know was her son was on the road to destruction. The drinking, the pills, God knows what else? Had he tried hard drugs? It was possible. That really would be the end. If this is what he needed to straighten out his life, it was a gamble she was willing to take.

"God speed, my son. And God bless."

The car pulled away, the road to redemption.

Chapter 5

The curtains to Tom Daley's window twitched. Those kids had been back. It was the same every October, get a few days before Halloween and it would start: the torture. It had been so different, but that was a long time ago now, a lifetime ago. Now, Tom was hated.

His life had been happy. Born in 1922, a severe childhood infection had caused him to lose his hearing in his left ear, ensuring that participation in the Second World War would be avoided. Instead, after an uninspired education, he happily followed his father's occupation. Life in Hallowell colliery had started at 14 as a haulier. The job consisted of driving a horse or tram to the wall face, while the miners extract coal. The cargo would then be taken to the mouth of the level, this would continue across the shift with monotonous repetition. The role also included responsibility of the horse, feeding it by day and taking it home at night. His occupation required great agility in the narrow and low-roofed roads, sometimes being required to stop his tram suddenly in an instant between the rail and the side of the level, normally in almost total darkness. A speeding tram had crushed his predecessor, so he knew from the beginning that life down the pit was fraught with danger.

Underground, his progress was rapid, working as a full-time collier by the age of seventeen. Herbert Daley, Tom's father, had died, not twenty feet from him, when a shaft collapsed in the mine, and he was crushed by the weight. These perils came with the job and as such, tragedies were considered par for the course, an inevitable possibility. Ingrid Daley passed from a serious bout of influenza so with both parents gone, Tom was left alone.

Being an only-child was strange in a time when large families were the norm. Complications in childbirth had ensured that his parents would not be able to increase their number, so, in the aftermath of their deaths, Tom assumed residency of the family home.

Colliery cottages were leased to miners, being benefits of the job. Two terraced rows with twenty-five properties in each, they were a mirror image of one another, front door facing front door, with a small garden below the living room window and a short, paved walkway leading to the threshold. The rears of the properties were larger, being at a time when much of the family menus would contain home grown vegetables. Two and three-bedroom accommodations, sometimes these cottages would be home to families of seven and above, making conditions cramped and uncomfortable. Still, the properties remained highly coveted, and residents were forced to vacate, should a family member no longer be in colliery employment. This was another cause of continuous generations seeking work inside the mine, avoiding homelessness for their loved ones.

For several years, Tom Daley lived a quiet, though peaceful life. A man of small ambitions, his existence was comfortable. One of the few who considered a role inside the colliery with pleasurable fulfilment, he was proud to continue his father's legacy. The urge for female companionship rarely arose and if it did, the options would have been limited. Overly thin and short with a constant gaunt expression, his unpleasant appearance was matched only by his lack of confidence. Conversing with his contemporaries was a constant strain. Even fellow miners learned to take his aloofness for what it was, a side-effect of his pitiful shyness. Still, Daley seemed content, with the lifestyle he had chosen. His home was modest but comfortable, especially for a bachelor. The property was in sight of the colliery and the rear was adjacent with the Hallowell railway station, it was everything he needed. Suddenly, in 1967, that was shattered forever, and Hallowell would never be the same again.

June 28th, Tom had just started his shift in the six bells shaft, one of three that Hallowell colliery were utilising. The lift was lowering the men to the level required when an explosion caused by firedamp propagated by coal dust, an ignition caused by friction heat from a piece of falling quarzitic rock. The blast tore through the mine and the elevator rope snapped, cascading twenty-eight feet to the colliery bottom. Forty-five men were killed that day in one of the worst mining disasters Britain had seen in years. It took three days to dig the bodies out and survivors were expected to be few. The army had been called in to add extra manpower and when the body of Tom Daley was discovered, it appeared that he was another victim to add to the body count. When a pulse was found, great roars of cheers exploded as no survivors had been brought out for eighteen hours and most hope had been extinguished. As Tom was lifted to the surface, he was barely alive and most believed he wouldn't survive the journey to hospital. He did. His injuries were extensive, and his recovery would be a long, arduous process but Tom Daley would survive the Hallowell Mining disaster of 1967.

A friend of Martin Graham investigated the cause of the disaster. There was much conjecture when the results were made public. There would be ramifications.

Unfortunately, survival came at a price. His left leg had been under massive weight for such a long period that crush injuries were inevitable. Thankfully, blood poisoning that was part of the symptoms wasn't too severe but the devastation to the limb was too great and needed amputation just above the knee. The biggest concern for doctors though was major trauma to the head causing partial brain damage. Serious memory loss and damage to the frontal cortex left him with the mental age of a ten-year-old. He had no recollection of the death of his parents and needed to grieve for them over again. He had no family to help care for him and was in a rehabilitation centre of eighteen months. He would finally return to the family home in autumn of 1968 with the residents of Hallowell forming a care team to make the transition as painless as possible. The cottage was on one floor, so access wasn't a problem. And his best friend, Ian Gaskins, was a master carpenter, adapted Tom's home to make it as accessible as possible. He also created a special surprise but one which would eventually have grave ramifications and take Daley's life in a direction, no one could have foreseen.

Even before the accident, Tom had always felt a special bond with the local children. A family friend, Edna Warren had run a day care centre for working or single parents and in his spare time from the colliery, he would enjoy lending a helping hand. He was well known and a trusted part of the community. After the disaster, which had cruelly taken a great deal of his mobility and left him mentally handicapped, Gaskins, along with a local landscaper, George Towers, had set about transforming the back garden of the Daley residence into a playground, where the local children could, and Tom could enjoy watching their fun. It contained wooden swings and climbing frames, a fort for the boys and a Wendy house for the girls. A sandpit for the youngsters and a seating area for Tom. It was idyllic, and well received by all, especially Tom himself. Having childlike innocence, it helped sooth the loss he'd suffered in recent years.

And for years it proved immensely popular. As one group outgrew the playground, another generation would find its joys. And as for Tom Daley, a grown man trapped with a ten-year olds mind, he could never outgrow its charms. So, in its own way, Tom's life was happy. In the summer of 1972, that changed forever.

They were in a heatwave, the hottest summer for years. It was a Friday evening, ending a day not unlike a hundred gone before it. Most of the children had gone home for the day but little Agnus and Neal, the children of a Scottish couple new to the village, the McKenzie's, were still playing happily in Tom's back garden. A children's paddling pool had been donated by one of the neighbours to help keep the kiddies cool in the sunshine. It was only feet from Tom Daley's wooden bench and little Neal McKenzie, being the rambunctious four-year old that he was, decided to throw a bucket of water at their dim-witted host.

"You can't do that. I told you, I can't get my new leg wet." The children's laughter stopped immediately, shocked at their hosts outburst. Being so young, both the little Scottish children had no clue of Tom's prostatic leg and the idea of a grown man with a missing limb came as quite a shock. The new aid had only been fitted that morning and Tom was feeling the strain of newness, the stump pressing against the solid surface with no give. The pain had changed his usual jovial mood and the drenching, no matter how well natured the stunt was, pushed him to the edge. Tom rose from his seat, water dripping from every inch of his body. He wanted to shout at Neil,

"Go home! I don't want you here today." He looked sternly at the confused child, but the words refused to come. How could he scold the boy, he was his friend, and he might not come back if he sees me angry. It was only water, what harm could it do? Daley stormed across the yard, heading for the back door.

43

"Perhaps, if I put my shorts on, they'll see and understand?" A shake of the head as the children resumed their game, blissfully unaware of Tom's problems.

Agnus was two years older than her brother and when Tom didn't return, she became concerned that they'd seriously upset him. Climbing from the pool, a large white bath-towel wrapped around her entire body with room to spare. Scrubbing hard to ensure dryness, the water in her hair continually flooded her body.

"You're wasting fucky time…we need to go soon, was silly twat… Come back in the pool before daddy shouts us fucky home." The little boy still struggled through sentences, learning difficulties and behavioural issues had brought in the local social services. Speech therapy, classes didn't seem to help much. The knowledge of how to tell the social workers to, "FUCK OFF," soon ended their assistance. Another child to fall through the systems cracks, but who's counting?

"You shouldn't swear like that, Tom told us, no fighting or cussing aloud. And if daddy hears you again, he'll kick fuck out of you."

"You just swore!" Neil dipped his head under water and gulped a mouthful of the treated liquid, raising up like a dolphin, and spitting the substance with a perfect strike, her nose taking the brunt of the attack, though some managed to squeeze between her lips.

"IDIOT, I want to go find Tommy. And by the way, I'm two years older than you, I'm allowed to swear." She threw down the towel in childish rage, her hair still drenched with the pool-water. Shoulders stiffened, face scrunched, and fists clenched, she turned and headed for the back door. The gravel pathway was sharp and uncomfortable, her bare feet battling the urge to retreat. A sharp pointed stone with a razor-edge sliced a tiny slit across the base of her left big toe. Instead of selling the pain, she pushed on, not wishing to continue her argument with her baby brother.

Arriving at the back door, Agnus remembered the rules, and number one was always, "DO NOT GO INSIDE THAT HOUSE." The parents trusted Tommy…so far. But he was a grown man, and he never had female companionship. There was always a concern.

"Was he one of them?" Kids coming and going, at all hours. Surely, he must get sick, sometimes. Maybe…just maybe…well, it was a cruel world we live in. Hallowell was supposed to be a safe community, and there'd never been an incident. Plus, he was cheaper than a professional child minder. When money became a factor, Tom Daley's trust from the Hallowell parents was absolute. Still there were nagging doubts, and that rule number 1, "DO NOT GO IN THAT FUCKING HOUSE." Stay with that promise and all was well.

The solid oak door stood ajar. There were two steps to the house, and she was relieved to raise her tiny feet off that burning gravel, to the cool flat concrete. The water which still ran down from her drenched hair glistened momentarily in the fading sunlight.

The wooden barrier was heavier than the girl expected and took force to open it fully. A large set of keys, still hanging from the lock, crashed into the passage wall with a bang, as the door reached its apex, revealing some of the cottage's secrets.

"Tommy. Are you there?" The child knew that entering the house was wrong and for that reason, she wanted more. Her heart was racing, she turned and noticed her brother had lost interest in her actions and was timing himself of how long he could hold his breath under water. From outside, the home looked surprisingly normal. There was a long passageway which led from front to back of the property. Several doorways lead off the corridor and across the distance, the passage had a blind turn to the right. The walls were covered in old-fashioned woodchip wallpaper, painted in light-blue though the dust and cobwebs around the skirting insinuated that the décor was past its prime. What interested Agnus more was the collection of photographs which hid the unimpressive fashion. Each with individual frames, ranging in sizes from large to small, most of the pictures were black and white and not in the best condition. Curious, she tentatively stepped forward, fascinated by the images before her. Across all the shots, there was only three people appearing. A lady with long black hair, who looked no older than twenty-five. Her features were unspectacular but with a caring air. The long past fashions said that these had been taken a long time ago. The man was tall and thick set, tubby around the mid-section with meaty forearms and wide shoulders. Much of his face was distorted as he wore a thick beard, bushy and wild, and a matching moustache. His hair was long though slicked back across the scalp. Thick rimmed eyeglasses completed the facial disguise, Angus wondered if behind the accessories, was there a handsome man hidden? It was impossible to tell. Finally, she noticed a picture she recognised. A teenage Tom Daley dressed for the first day down the colliery. It was then, the little girl realised that the other photographs were of her host's parents. In the centre of the wall was a large portrait, all three family members seated on a long settee. It was framed in dark oak and the glass coverage was freshly polished, shimmering in the fading light. Agnus smiled, they looked so happy, so close, she wished her own family could have a moment like that instead of the constant bickering and points scoring her parents partook in. All the pictures were as symmetrical as the sizes would allow. There was a cluster of smaller prints, carefully pinned to create a heart shape, this taken work.

As she'd been so transfixed on the portraits, Agnus barely realised that she had travelled deep into Tom's cottage. The course woollen carpet rubbed uncomfortably on the soles of her bare feet, and she suddenly felt unwelcome.

"Tommy are you there?" The cottage remained silent.

"Are you mad at us?" Still no answer. There was a doorway, just to her left. Quietly she pushed it open. It was the kitchen. Everything inside was old, from the worktops to the utensils, it seemed that nothing had been replaced since his parents had passed. A large dinner table with carved legs and sturdy chairs stood in the corner of the room. The one thing missing was Tommy.

The door was left open as she returned to the passage, allowing more light into the gloomy cottage. The corridor seemed darker now and she wondered whether to go back to the yard. From her position, she could still see her little brother splashing carefree in the pool. She decided to continue.

"Tommy, where are you?" The first bedroom door was open, and it was immediately obvious that it was empty. The room was bare, just a single bed and an old-fashioned wardrobe. No curtains hung in the windows and the child could feel its unwelcoming aura. This door was closed regardless of the additional light, she didn't like that bedroom.

Agnus was becoming nervous; the passageways lack of light gave the cottage a spooky feel. Had she not felt so close to her aged host, she'd have certainly retreated. Something inside her wouldn't allow her to leave.

"Please come out Tommy, you're scaring me." Her voice was beginning to break, her emotions bubbling to the surface. Two doors remained; one was open, it was a second bedroom. The bed wasn't made, the Superman designed quilt was half on the floor and the matching pillow had fallen all the way. The matching curtains were still closed and there were clothes strewn across the black cord carpet.

"Tommy, you're scruffier than me." The girl giggled and closed the door.

There was only on room left. He was either here or he'd left altogether. There was a sound from inside, perhaps running water. Whatever it was, it seemed that this was her friend's hiding place. She reached for the metal handle, it was stiff and needed force. She grimaced and pushed hard; slowly the latch began to give, and the door pushed open.

Agnus immediately began to scream.

"I can't believe this. My favourite T-shirt and my best jeans, completely drenched, I wanted to wear those tomorrow, now I can't."

Tom Daley's clothes were saturated, the pool-water had penetrated all the way through to his skin. He stared into the bathroom mirror, even his hair was wet. The face looked tired with three days' worth of stubble and dark lines under his eyes. He sighed and gently shook his head.

"If it wasn't for my little friends, I don't know what I'd do." Slowly, he raised his arms above his head and pulled stiffly on the drenched T-shirt. There were still painful reminders of the colliery disaster whenever he dressed himself, nerve damage in his spine made even the most rudimentary tasks difficult. Tom grimaced as the top slid over his head, lying it over the white basin beside the toilet. A second sigh escaped when he noticed his white vest was soaked also, angrily tearing over his head and throwing it to the floor. Lowering to the toilet seat, he pushed down his jeans. It was tough with his false leg, but Tom was used to removing damp trousers, sometimes his bladder didn't work too well. He reached down, stretching for the bottoms, laying them beside the T-shirt on the basin. Feeling around his mid-section, he released an even louder sigh, realised that even his underpants would need changing. Raising slightly from the toilet seat, his red pair of Y-fronts slid over his wrinkled bottom and down his thighs. Dropping to the floor, he kicked the underwear across with his discarded vest. Suddenly, the bathroom door swung open.

The girl screamed hysterically. Daley froze, his naked body in full view.

"Stop screaming. Please, stop screaming."

What to do, what can I do?

Angus remained hysterical; the yells seemed to increase in volume every time she took a breath. She was frozen to the stop, her eyes glaring at areas of his person that should never be seen. Tom needed to explain but how could he, what would make her listen? Throwing a hand to the bathtub, he grabbed the only towel available, a hair dryer which barely reached around his midsection, but at least his modesty was retrieved. Still the child screamed.

Daley made the only decision he could, lunging for the girl and aiming a hand around her mouth. He didn't understand her reaction. He thought all the children knew he wore a prostatic. As for the nudity, yes it was embarrassing, but he had the naivety of a child himself. Her brother had thrown the water at him, he was just changing his clothes. What was the problem?

His hand was only loose around her mouth, terrified of hurting her, she was his friend. The next scream that pierced the air was just as shocking as the first as the little girl sank her teeth deeply into Daley's hand. He immediately pulled away and, in the fracas, dropped the towel once more, making Angus scream again. Taking her chance, she darted for the exit, and running faster than she'd ever run. Her brother had barely registered a problem, his head splashing in and out of the water. The first time he heard a scream was Tom Daley's and he thought it was part of a game. When he saw Agnus running, screaming at the top of her lungs, he immediately began to cry too, even though he had no idea why. Agnus pulled her brother from the paddling pool, her distress raising the alarm to the neighbours, curtains were twitching, doors opening. When Tom Daley closely followed, naked and flustered, red of face with only a towel to hide his modesty, the gate burst open and the hulking figure of the children's father, John McKenzie, menacingly filled the space. Sweeping the child into his muscular arms, his son hugging into his left leg, he tried to make sense of his daughter's tearful sentences.

"Daddy…Daddy…Tom chased me, he tried to put his arm around me…and he had no clothes no."

The Scotsman's eyes glazed, glaring hatred stares in Daley's direction. By now, May, the children's mother had arrived, and the little girl immediately wanted her maternal comfort.

"No, no, it wasn't like that, it was Neal's fault." The little boy immediately screamed a tearful denial.

"May, take the kids home." McKenzie swept off his jacket, throwing it to the ground and began to roll up the sleeves of his sweater.

"John please, leave it to the…" His stare stopped her mid-sentence, she was still sporting the bruises from her last beating. Domestic violence was a regular occurrence, especially on a Saturday night.

"Take them home." Another neighbour must have called Bill Castle and thankfully, he must have sensed the urgency as using the police-car was rare, the siren's unmistakable tones growing louder by the second. The giant Scotsman stepped forward.

47

"Wait, wait, please, let me explain, you see, Neal threw water over me from the pool, and I went into the house to…" The first punch was all it took to knock Daley off his leg. Two kicks to the mid-section had the mentally challenged cripple in tears and had Bill Castle, with the help of two other neighbours, not pulled the bully off, it's possible that John McKenzie would have been sporting a murder charge.

The locals had taken Tom to their hearts, and it was because of this that they felt cheated. People were always more likely to believe the word of a child over a mentally challenged adult and now they were asking questions of themselves. Was he as handicapped as was first claimed? Had he been using this situation just to get close to kids? Had he done things with any of their children? The thoughts disgusted them and even the locals without children began to keep their distance. Constable William Castle had done his best to defuse the situation, but passions were raw. He'd been forced to interview some of the former visitors to the playground that were now teenagers, but none reported any inappropriate behaviour. No charges were ever filed but Tom's reputation was destroyed. The local shopkeepers didn't want to serve him. People who he once regarded as friends would cross the street to avoid him. Once more, Tom Daley's life was in tatters.

For the last eight years, things had only gotten worse. Small town folks rarely forgave and never forget. The question of innocence or guilt was never discussed. Gossip was judge, jury, and executioner. Tom Daley became a recluse. Why go outside just to be abused?

The years had passed, and it was 1980 now, though one year was much the same as another to him. He dreaded October. The dark nights would come; Tom feared the dark. And there was Halloween. The same kiddies that once played in his garden were teenagers now and were throwing eggs at his windows. Bagging dog poop and setting it on fire on his doorstep so he'd have to stamp on it and get that nasty stuff all over his slippers. Setting fireworks off through his letterbox and scaring him to death. Enough was never enough.

Tom looked every minute of his fifty-eight years and then some. He'd learned to walk with his false leg, but now it hurt, the limp was back. His hair was long and stringy at the back but bald in top, a barber's shop had never been visited since the 'unpleasantness'. Dark rings encircled his eyes, endless sleepless nights wearing him to exhaustion, especially at this time of year. His skin was mottled, red and patchy, after a deficiency of goodness from his diet, food being the last of Tom's concerns in his meagre existence.

The curtain moved a few inches, not wanting to reveal himself to anyone passing. His dad would be ashamed of this garden. Tom had let the privet grow high, so people couldn't stare through his windows. The grass was uncut and patchy, dying in places from lack of sunlight. All the flowers were long since dead, untidy brown roots in their place. Even the apple tree in front of the living room window was dead now. The Roberts's boy from number 23 had poured petrol on it and set it alight. Tom hadn't reported it; what was the point.

He was certain he'd heard someone outside, but all seemed quiet. He didn't like confrontation, all those nasty names the kids called him. The parents were worse. That McKenzie man had punched again for telling his kiddies to stay out of his garden. They shouldn't want to be on his property if he was such a bad man. His daughter, the girl who said those nasty things, had spat at him while he was cleaning the leaves from his path. Why would she do such a thing? Disgusting. But the boy, Neal, was it? He was awful. He'd broke three windows out the back and pinched Tom's spade and rake from the garden shed. He'd heard the little bastard laughing about it with the Roberts boy, it never ended.

The gate at the side of the house creaked. He'd meant to oil it and wished he had now. If it didn't creak, he wouldn't know someone was outside. Normally, not knowing was better. His steaming cup of tea was replaced on the saucer on the coffee table because his hands were shaking. Why couldn't they just go away and leave him alone. It was dark outside; they should be at home in front of the television. Tom didn't like going outside in the dark.

There were no voices.

"I bet it's the McKenzie kid again." Tom was scared but angry too. Coronation Street was coming on soon and he wouldn't be able to enjoy it if that kid was outside. He looked forward to his programs, it was all he had, it wasn't fair. He fitted his prosthetic leg back into place and reached for his cane. "That's it. I'm going to give that little bastard a piece of my mind, I don't care what his dad does to me." Tom struggled from the seat and made his way to the front door. The back door had no lights, he was still afraid of the dark, regardless how angry he was. The lock was stiff, and it strained as it turned. The handle was heavy and old fashioned and needed strength just to force it open. It was cold for October and Daley could see his breath as he exhaled into the night air. As expected, the front garden was empty, and he had the fight the urge to go back into the warmth. The passageway to the side gate between his house and number nineteen was scary, dark, and foreboding. His limp more pronounced in the cold weather, he opened the gate with trepidation. As it creaked back in place he could here running. Tom quickened his pace and to his surprise, it wasn't Neal McKenzie. It was the Roberts's youngest. Not the little fucker that had burned the apple tree, this one was only about eight and he'd been in the garden shed. They didn't need to steal from him, if asked, he'd give them what they wanted.

"Hey, you, what do you want?" The boy, Tommy was his name, was fighting with the lock on the gate. "That locks broken, let it alone." The young tearaway started to climb the fence, determined to make his escape. "That wood is rotten, it will break. Just come this way and you can go out the front." Tommy wasn't listening and had made the top when the wooden barrier came crashing down. "I told you. I told you it would break. Have you hurt yourself?" The boy was crying, more from shock but he had cut his leg on a jagged nail. As Tom approached, the boy ran. "Are you okay? Come back and I'll help you." In the confusion, the injured boy had run in the wrong direction. To the left was a dead end, trapped in by the backs of houses and the fence to the bad place. "Don't go up that way."

Tom tried to climb over the stricken fence remains and discovered the child's blood. It was spread over his left hand, and he swiftly wiped the residue onto his cream slacks.

"You're hurt. Come back and I'll help you. I'll take you to your mummy. You're going the wrong way." Tommy realised his mistake and panicked. Daley was in the lane, and he realised there was no escape. He looked for lights in the neighbouring houses but found only darkness. It was then he noticed a hole in the fenced mesh. Just big enough for a boy to climb through. He pushed his head and body across, but Tom Daley was approaching fast.

"Don't go in there. Haven't you heard the stories; the bad man lives there." Just as he reached the hole, the boy pulled clear inside the station grounds. Tom looked at the gap and knew there was no way he could fit through. And Tommy knew it too.

"Fuck off, you, dirty old bastard." Such nasty words for an eight-year-old.

"No, No, you don't understand. You mustn't go in there." His voice down to a whisper. "That's where the bad man lives." The child was now growing in confidence, knowing he was safe from Tom's grasp.

"You're the only bad man, you old pervert. You won't get me, that's for sure."

"What's going on out there?" A voice came from one of the yards, a kitchen light.

"Mr Mc, it's me, Tommy Roberts, help me, the pervert's got me."

"Oh no." Tom started to panic. "It's McKenzie. He hates me. He might punch me again." Tom began to hobble away as the Scotsman fought with the lock on his garden gate. Tommy Roberts was laughing.

"Go on pervert, run away." He didn't see the figure behind him until it was too late.

Chapter 6

"What the fuck just happened?" Nick Castle looked in the Ford Escort's rear-view mirror as Russellville was lost in the distance. A cigarette-tip burned brightly between the first and index fingers of his left hand, as grey ash sprayed lightly across the brand-new upholstery. How could a woman's whole demeanour alter so dramatically? When he'd made the journey to his former home, just forty-five minutes earlier, Nick had been filled with all-encompassing dread. Memories of a relationship broken, trust extinguished, a house filled with nothing but misery, and an element of his life which had fractured his personality forever. Were there any other option, he'd have avoided Russellville at all costs. Unfortunately, Kath Castle was his only hope, without cash, he'd never make it to Hallowell.

Of course, this was going to sting. He'd have no choice but to bite his tongue, kiss arse, and hope she didn't see through his bullshit. If she poured it on too thick, he wondered if his strength of will would be great enough to not rise to the bait. What choice did he have? There was always Janice, his groupie from the chemist-shop, but even he wasn't that much of a bastard, was he? Nick knew he probably wasn't coming back so breaking her heart and taking her money was too much. No, instead, he'd take all his mother could dish out and drive away with whatever cash she'd allow. Still, this was going to be horrible, terrible, painful, wasn't it?

Strangely, no. It had started as expected, she'd throw a snowball and he'd volley it back. Underwhelming barbs, not enough to draw blood, just a wasp-sting or two. She'd piss him off enough for retaliation but then he'd remember why he was there and hold back just in time. Tedious, very tedious.

Thankfully, it hadn't lasted long. Perhaps, they'd both grown tired of points scoring, taking shots in a match of no winners. A truce across enemy lines. When the prospect of money was mentioned, the outcome was a surprising game changer. A plain envelope, £500 in used notes. Castle was hopeful that a small loan could be squeezed. A little guilt-trip mixed gingerly with his own brand of self-pity and perhaps he'd grift enough of a tank of fuel. But £500? Astonishing.

But even more of a phenomenon had been her openness. Her willingness to reveal details from the Hallowell incident, long since buried had been a curveball, no, a thunderbolt, which left the young man in complete bewilderment. Had his mother had an epiphany, a mind-altering eureka moment? Or had the guilt of a decade of lies become too much? Perhaps, the intervention of Dr Pete finally made her realise the damage that had been done (about time one of those head-fuckers managed to come in useful). Whatever the reason, the result had left Nick in shock and quite emotional. With Russellville, a blur in the rear-view mirror, he'd needed to pull the Ford over to the kerb, his falling tears making driving a hindrance.

His worldly outlook hadn't changed completely. The dark cloud of anger wasn't ready to dissipate just yet, the bridges which were slowly forming between mother and son would need much firmer foundations before they could be built upon. That degree of caution which came from a decade of lies would take more than the loan of a car and an envelope full of cash to make him forgive, and even longer to forget. Ten long years of deception, dishonesty, and misrepresentation of events. She'd seen him suffer, day after day, year after year, and maintaining this façade was more important than soothing his pain. He wasn't sure whether that could ever be forgiven, regardless of whatever the excuse. He tried telling himself that she was in an impossible situation, yet he still questioned whether that so-called protection was worth all the turmoil it created. He was more confused now than ever.

After his early morning start, Nick Castle had three essential tasks to complete before departure for his childhood home. The first was concluded more successfully than he ever imagined possible. Leaving Russellville with optimism, not an emotion normally representative of a parental meeting, was a welcome boost.

Next on the inventory was the collection of essential supplies. Janice Briggs's flat was always warm and welcoming, and her eyes lit up whenever he was near, like a faithful Labrador. It was a relationship of convenience; they both knew it. She'd take more in a heartbeat, as much as she'd fought against it, her feelings were unquestionably deeper than she dared to admit. She'd been more than happy to break the law for him, just to maintain the pretence of a relationship. Nick was out of her league, and she'd accepted it. In another life, and a better diet, perhaps they could have been something more. If he was capable of being a co-dependant, rather than looking for the next quick fix, maybe…

It seemed she'd been saving his Prozac for a rainy day and today was torrential. Her hook-nosed, weasel-faced boss at the pharmacy had been fired when the drugs inventory had revealed a huge discrepancy, so she'd stolen as many as possible before he'd gone. Obviously, future 'Extras' would be risky, though strangely, the news wasn't met with great concern. He could feel something happening. He wasn't sure what it was, perhaps it was the excitement of exorcizing old demons, maybe just a chance to change something, anything, from the disaster that was his life. Suddenly, drugs just didn't seem as important. But withdrawal symptoms weren't something he needed at this point so the three hundred she'd stored away were certainly handy. She'd made them breakfast and they'd made love, perhaps for the final time. Janice deserved that, and she had wept as he drove away, unsure if she would ever see him again, feeling the relationship had probably reached its apex.

The final thing Nick felt obliged to do before his long journey was visit the person who, for a while had him believing that his life could, just maybe, have a happy ending.

Normally when Castle visited Julia Martin's grave, he was too broke to take flowers of his own. Sometimes he'd pick them from the flower beds in Bishopsgate Castle's Garden, but the security guards had gotten wise and watched him whenever he walked around the grounds. Other times, he'd check out other tended graves and steal the bouquets loved ones left. Today, he'd bought his own, twelve long-stemmed lilies, Julia's favourites.

Just looking at this monument hurt, and knowing that, had she never met him she'd still be alive. That dagger stuck deep.

Nick Castle hadn't meant to fall in love. It just happened so fast, there was no control. Doctor Allen Martin (even the name made him want to wretch) had taken over as his psychiatrist at seventeen. This stubborn piece of shit wasn't like most the other quacks, all of which saw his case as a lost cause. Instead, he looked at Nick as a challenge, with relentless determination, this tenacious fucker just wouldn't go away. Firstly, he'd threatened to withdraw Nick's meds if he skipped their appointments. Next, he'd threatened to section him, due to a lack of effort on the young man's part. It became obvious that desperate measures were required. When necessary, Nick Castle could play dirty.

The plan needed thought. Each appointment would drive Castle's inner-rage higher, almost to the point where lashing out in violence would be preferential to listening to this pompous Dick spout useless advice. He was capable too, Nick's strong stature and hatred for his adversary would certainly allow him the thrust to snap the son-of-a-bitch in two. The only problem would be that this would almost definitely result in incarceration, be it imprisonment or sectioning. Plus, the young man wasn't violent by nature, yes, there'd been altercations in his teens, schoolyard scuffles and backstreet brawls, but setting out to hurt another, just for the sake of it didn't come naturally. No, it was better to pit his wits against his enemy, maybe it could be fun too. Suddenly, a chance sight would allow the seed of a plan to grow.

Was it his wife? Maybe a daughter? In a heavy silver frame on the corner of the psychiatrist's desk stood a photograph, professionally shot with a white background. The image contained could only be described as stunning. Flowing blonde hair, caught with the assistance of an electric fan to give the impression of breeze, the palest of blue eyes, which seemed to radiate innocence, enough make-up to extenuate her soft features without appearing forced or pretentious and a flowing white gown, a wedding gown, classily tailored, once more to flow a radiance without screaming, "Look at me." He'd been under Dr Fuckhead for almost two years and hadn't noticed the shot before. It was an image which once seen would be hard to forget. Whatever the connection, Nick began to plot a course which, were it to work, would eliminate Dr Martin from his life, once and for all.

It was a long shot. Everything would need to fall perfectly into place for this plan to stand any chance of success. Thankfully, Castle had two traits which could sway the scales in his favour.

Genetically, Nick swam strongly in the deep end of the gene pool. Firstly, was his physical appearance, he inherited the classic Castle profile: strong jawline, high cheek bones and thick black hair. Similarly, to the vision framed on Martin's desk, his own blue eyes could melt the hardest hearts and his soft, neutral features made his, a heart-breaking vision. He stood an impressive six feet, three inches and maintained a hard, wiry physique without having to try. His everyday presentation manifested the image of a man who didn't care. His clothes were worn and rarely clean, shaving only when necessary, and a hairstyle which could be feral and neglected. Still, it didn't matter, women would be automatically attracted to him, whether he tried or not.

More importantly, his intellect was far greater than his early years insinuated. Even with all his childhood troubles, schooling had come easy. There was an opinion that his I.Q. was partially to blame for his psychological problems, a thin line between genius and madness. He'd passed his driving test after three one-hour lessons. Leaving school at fifteen, he had nine O-Levels, skipping a year without effort. Numerous placements offers and scholarships with high-level collages were attained and refused. Had his ambition matched the intellectual ability, the options would have found no limits. Over the last few years his brain had become lazy, but it was only resting.

On seeing the picture across the doctor's desk, the assumption was, that it must be his daughter. The age difference seemed to point in that direction. Plus, why would one so beautiful even look twice at that sack-of-shit. Castle was shocked when he discovered the truth.

It was late afternoon; Nick's appointment had been re-scheduled to the doctor's last session of the day. Had the young man not needed his medication, he'd have pleaded ignorance to the letter informing him of the change and simply blew off the consultation. Being beholding to this cocksucker was a serious aggravation. Inside the waiting area, Castle's chair was positioned in a blind-spot behind the main entrance. When the young woman had appeared, he ensured that his face was suddenly ensconced in a newspaper, greatly aware that had she noticed him, the plan would have ended before it had a chance to begin. And as she exited, the same disguise was used to once more camouflage his identity. When the doctor's secretary had informed him that his wife needed a moment of his time, Castle knew that his proposed strategy's chance of success had just increased dramatically.

Were Nick's charms enough to seduce the beauty, the psychiatrist would have no option than to drop him as a patient. Plus, her incredible appearance would ensure that this mission could have a serious up-side too, everyone had needs.

Patience wasn't a trait, Castle could readily rely upon, but for this task, it was certainly required. It could well have been construed as stalking as, for three weeks he followed her every movement without being seen. He had no idea where the couple lived so, firstly, Nick had followed the good doctor home after work. It was a typical doctor's residence, newly built in its own grounds, double glazing, and a satellite dish, and most importantly, two car garages. His was a land rover 4x4 and had taken some keeping up with when being tailed by Castle's Fiesta but Julia's was far more conservative. A two door Mini said a lot about her personality, functional but not flashy, economical, though she was a doctor's wife and had no such financial concerns. At least she was easier to tail.

It was only by chance; he finally discovered the young woman's name. Whilst being parked across the street from the family home, patiently awaiting the Mini's exit, an inexperienced postal worker accidentally allowed a letter to fall from his bag. When certain there was no witnesses, Nick casually crept from his Ford and skulked across the street, dipping to retrieve the envelope without breaking stride. Julia: even the name seemed to exude class, though the sir-name still left a bad taste in his mouth.

It was rare that Nick had a project to get excited about. For a scarce time, his inconsequential existence took on some meaning, even if his activities were borderline illegal. At least it forced him to maintain sobriety across his working hours. Taking notes became essential, she was a busy girl.

On a Monday, Wednesday, and Friday, she volunteered with Oxfam, the national charitable organisation, helping to serve the public in a second-hand store. This continued until midday when she'd attend a trendy health-club, working-out until late afternoon until returning home. It appeared Tuesday was for housework, meaning long fruitless hours for her stalker, his car remaining hidden on nearby wasteland with just a busted radio and a thermos of stale coffee for company. Thursday afternoon at 2 pm, she met friends for coffee at a local tea-room. With weekends came more in-house tedium and as her husband's social engagements seemed more entwined with the local golf course, it became obvious that hers must have been a lonely existence.

Nick accepted from the start that this mission could end without success. Perhaps, it was true love, a May to September courtship with a happy conclusion. Maybe, even if there were lines of erosion in the relationship, Julia may have too many morals to partake in an affair. Were they happily married or was the situation convenient? Would Nick even be her type? Still, it would be fun finding out.

When content that he knew her schedule completely, Castle had begun a plan of attack. It seemed obvious that the Thursday social in the tea rooms would be the best option, but there'd only had one shot at making that first impression. He couldn't afford gyms and didn't think buying second-hand clothing in Oxfam would send the correct message. Normally, Julia would leave at the same time as her friends but if he could just get a moment alone with her, a fleeting glance across the room, it would be a start.

With nervous apprehension, the launch finally arrived. He'd prepared well. At sixteen, a neighbour had died, and his mother had purchased a black suit for him to wear to the funeral. It still fit, and he'd made a special effort to have it cleaned even though the fee had seriously cut into that week's alcohol budget.

He'd showered, shaved, and even polished his black leather shoes. Arriving early, he ordered a large coffee though he was aghast at paying the prices asked. There was an empty table across the room from their regular spot, close enough to make eye contact but not too close to seem weird. Julia arrived at five before two, earlier than her friends and took the normal table after ordering.

She looked as radiant as ever, long blonde hair flowing down her back, tied into a ponytail with a black velvet elastic. Enough make-up to extenuate her petite features without over doing it. Tiny frame, slim curves, and conservative dress sense, she could have been a vicar's daughter. Though she was beautiful, Nick sensed she didn't know it or at least, wasn't willing to flaunt. She looked shy and innocent, lacking confidence when another with her beauty could be quite the opposite.

He was sweating scared, nervous not to look the idiot but knowing he'd never get a better chance at an introduction. Julia noticed his stare and blushed, smiling an immature grin, like a teenager in the schoolyard. He glanced out the window to the car park and saw her friend's car arriving. It was now or never. The fifteen feet to her table seemed a lifetime away.

"Excuse me. I'm so sorry to bother you but if I hadn't, I know I'd have regretted it all the way home. This is going to sound so cheesy, but I just had to speak to you. I think you're completely stunning, I couldn't believe my eyes when I saw you walk in. Are you waiting for someone, or may I join you?" Julia's blush deepened but when her friends walked through the front entrance, she regained some composure.

"Thank you, that's lovely of you to say. I'm afraid I was waiting for someone; my friends have just arrived." Nick glanced over his shoulder, cursing his apprehension.

"That's fine, I'm sorry I bothered you. Enjoy the rest of your day." Nick didn't give her the opportunity to respond, just smiled and walked back to his expensive coffee.

He passed her friends as he walked away and heard someone say in a girly tone, "Wow, who was that?" The first piece of the plan was in place.

The following week, he was back, though not buying quite as large a beverage this time. Julia arrived with her friends and immediately noticed Nick, back in the same seat as the previous week. He could see they were talking about him, that much was obvious. The nervous giggles and red complexions due to the attractive stranger in the next booth had Julia's heart racing, mind curious. In a direct invitation, the friends departed early, leaving the young beauty to finish her coffee. One had whistled at Nick as she leaved, sharing a small laugh and eye contact, though she wasn't the one Nick had set his sights on. When the coast was clear, Castle made his move.

The walk to her booth had his heart racing. If she was interested, he'd be invited to stay, if not, it was game over.

"Hi. I'm not sure if you remember me. I was here last Thursday, and we exchanged a few words." The girl blushed, reliving the complement from seven days ago. "My names Nick. I didn't want to disturb you while you were with your friends, but I wondered if I might join you?" The redness across her cheeks deepened, vastly impressed that such a handsome stranger would take an interest. Julia searched the room, evidently hoping that no-one else was watching their interaction. When she was content that the coast was clear, she smiled and invited him to take a seat. Phase 2 was set in motion.

From the first moment, in was conspicuous that the doctor's wife was painfully shy. Her timidity could have been construed as aloofness but had there been on interest, it was certain he would never have gotten this far. He smiled after noticing that her coffee had barely been touched, insinuating that maybe, she'd wanted an excuse to remain behind after her company had left. Sliding into the booth, he took a seat opposite, not wishing to appear too familiar. From outside, the shrill honk of a car horn blasted into the quiet street and as both diverted their attention to the din, her friends were leaving in a yellow Mercedes, one waving from the passenger seat, both with knowing smiles. Castle's confidence was rising.

Being the gentleman, he offered to buy her a second drink, content that it wouldn't be needed. Preparation had been key, and Castle was leaving nothing to chance. Creating an alter-ego, a role as a successful salesman who only worked this area on certain days of the week seemed to fit, though, the less than important occupation said a lot about the young man's ambition. Thankfully, a representative for a soft-drinks company wouldn't require much imagination.

As for Julia, she seemed happy to listen, content that someone new would pay her attention. Cautious and reticent, though demure with a tiny, self-effacing smile, she stared back at the enigmatic interloper, wary and excited, fearful but intrigued. She reminded him of a new-born deer, taking its first sips of water from a babbling brook, delirious with the refreshing taste but terrified of falling in.

The two made small talk, both guarded and neither wishing to reveal more than necessary. Nick could feel himself taking the lead in the conversation, desperately hoping not to bore her. Normally, he'd have a real drink in his hand rather than coffee and cursed himself that he'd not brought along a tipple of vodka to make the caffeine more appealing. The deepening spring afternoon begun to bare clouds across the fading sunlight, and it was only then did they realise the time. Aware that questions would be asked were she to arrive home after her husband, excuses were exchanged, and Castle walked the young lady to her car. A chill wind rustled through the nearby trees though neither seemed in a hurry to end their rendezvous. Self-doubt clouded Nick's judgement, what should he do next? Come on to strong and he could scare her away, act too aloofly and she may feel he wasn't interested.

"I don't wish to appear forward but, I've really enjoyed this afternoon. I was wondering, would you like to do it again sometime?" There was a pause, a drop of the head, a held breath, a…

"Definitely."

The relief was palpable, phase 2 was complete.

It was arranged. The following Monday, 1 pm, Freddy's wine bar on the corner of Elm Street, hidden away from prying eyes. A junkshop, halfway down Bishopsgate high street was always happy to give him a price when he took in items for sale. Usually, it was his misplaced Father's collection of records, anything from the Beatles to Perry Como, if it could turn a profit, they'd take it. He'd hung on to the collection of Queen albums until last, simply because he liked their music, but as his record-player had gone in the last great sale, they seemed the obvious choice to finance the day-out.

The days leading to the meet had been long and arduous, Nick wasn't one for self-deprecation in relation to the opposite sex, but this date held greater intrigue. What if she had second thoughts? Thursday to Monday was a long time for the young woman to change her mind. And even if she did turn up, who's to say she'd be willing to do the deed. The questions filled his mind across the weekend, until finally, Monday arrived.

Nick had fought the urge all morning to take a snifter, just to calm his nerves, so when lunchtime came around, he decided to arrive twenty minutes early, enough time to down a swift pint, just for Dutch courage. Instead, he was shocked to find Julia already waiting, and three-quarters of the way down a large glass of wine, she'd obviously had the same idea. Seated in a darkened booth, in the rear of the lounge, she looked even more radiant than he remembered. A loose-fitting white blouse, off the shoulder revealing enough of her diminutive frame to appear sexy without trying, her long blonde locks hanging free around the curvature of her neck, a black-lace choker-chain the only decoration. Her cheeks were slightly flushed, perhaps the beginning of a blush, maybe the after-effects of the wine, those eyes, welcoming but timid, the gateway to more. And finally, the smile, shy and excited, reserved but hopeful. For once, Castle felt his own heart flutter, conceivably, this could be dangerous.

She rose as he approached, and he returned her welcoming gaze, kissing her softly on the left cheek before returning to her seat. He passed across the quiet room to the bar and returned with a pint of dry cider and another glass of wine for the lady, grimacing at the cost. From the start, their conversation was different from their earlier rendezvous, the alcohol helping to loosen the girl's inhibitions. Finishing off the remnants of the first glass, it seemed she'd needed the alcohols calming effects, aware that their date couldn't continue without revealing her secret.

"Nick. There's something I need to tell you before we continue. Something that you are probably not going to like, though I feel it's unfair not telling you and…"

"You're married." The young woman was astounded.

"How did you know?"

"I just had a feeling. You drive a brand-new car but have no job. Last Thursday, you panicked when you noticed the time, as if you had somewhere to be." Julia took another sip of wine.

"That's what I call perceptive." Her smile was nervous, wary of how Nick was about to react.

"And finally, in the tea-room, I saw your wedding ring."

"Cheat." They both giggled like schoolchildren. "I suppose I should ask how you feel about it, if you want to leave, I'll understand." The nerves were showing once more.

"Do you want to leave? I'm single, I have nothing to lose. I guess, it's your choice. If you're uncomfortable, I can sympathize. I'll accept it, no pressure."

"No, I mean yes, I mean, oh God, I'm getting tongue tied, it's the wine. I never drink usually, I'm making a fool out of…" Nick stretched across the table and gently took her hand, caringly stroking his thumb across her fingers.

"Take a minute. You've no reason to be nervous of me, my life's an open book (he lied). Just take your time, do you want to go?" Taking in a deep breath, she replied.

"No." Castle smiled.

"That's all that matters."

The afternoon flowed like the gentlest of streams, giggling at jokes, an undercurrent of flirtatiousness without the need for directness. The careful ebb and flow, mixed with a generous measure of alcohol, conscientiously breaking down her barriers and allowing the freedom of peace to breeze between them. And with this new-found freedom, her inhibitions quickly faded too. Suddenly, a tear formed in the corner of her right eye.

"I hate him."

"What?" The statement had come from nowhere.

"I'm sorry. I shouldn't have said that. It's just being here with you; it makes me realise what kind of life I've been leading."

It was then, Julia Martin began to reveal the painful truth about her poisoned marriage. Nick Castle rested in his chair, slowly becoming aware that he'd soon have all the ammunition against the psychiatrist he'd ever need.

"It wasn't always like this. He wasn't always this…cold. He's a doctor, well a shrink. Messing with people's heads, trying to assert power over them, loves it. He's over twenty years older than me, and I know what people thought, gold digger, but Nick, you have to believe me, it wasn't, I wasn't…" Again, Castle placed his soothing hand in the trembling girl's.

"Take your time." Once more, she paused, before continuing.

"I'm sorry Nick, we were having a lovely day and I've spoiled it by…" That first kiss was electric, their lips touching, gentle but firm, eyes fading to black, the world just falling away.

"You can tell me…anything you want." Her entire body tingled with excitement; at that moment, Castle knew she was his for the taking.

"I need some air."

The two lefts by the rear exit and directed for Bishopsgate Park. For a while, there was silence, walking side by side, hand in hand, fingers entwined in a sensual grasp. The spring afternoon was covered in a guarded sunshine, the light clouds spoiling what could have been the year's first warm day. A growing breeze whispered around the girl's bare shoulders and Castle quickly shed his black leather jacket, draping it around her narrow frame. Slowing, she turned to her beau and smiled, hopeful of a second moment of passion, though Nick's curiosity about his hated doctor was too great to avoid.

"I think you should continue, if we're going to see one another, it might be important." Castle was aware that pressing the point may make Julia cautious, but this was a chance worth taking.

"Are you sure you don't mind? It is nice to have someone to talk to."

"Go ahead."

The revelations were more than he could have ever dreamed.

"I mentioned about the age gap but honestly, I didn't care. If I'd seen a shrink of my own, maybe they'd have said I was looking for a father figure, perhaps that's right, my own was no prize. Both Mom and Dad were, how can I put it nicely, troubled. Screw it, they were fuck ups." She immediately blushed; cursing didn't come naturally. "Dad was involved in an industrial accident, he worked in a factory and his left leg was crushed in a folding machine. Problem was, he couldn't get compensation because he'd been drinking on the job. Since he could no longer work, he and my mom spent all their time and all our money propping up one bar or another. My older sister wound up being more of a mother than my own ever was." Finding a park bench, they rested, Julia's head nuzzled into Nick's meaty chest.

"I was seventeen when I met Allen. He seemed so wise, so mature. People raised their eyebrows when we first got together, I know what they all thought, but I never cared about the money. I guess I just wanted someone to protect me, to want me. How wrong was I?"

"Wrong?" Nick appeared puzzled. Fighting back tears, she continued.

"I was a trophy. Someone to show off to the boys in his club. Oh, look at me, I've a wife half my age."

"Maybe he was proud?"

"Proud, don't make me laugh. He's not proud, he's gay." Julia immediately regretted the revelation. Not for the doctor's sake, not even for her own. "I'm sorry, I'm really, really sorry, I didn't mean to snap, what must you think of me?" For a moment, Castle was lost for words, a pause which heightened the girl's paranoia. "I think I better go." As Julia began to rise, Castle regained his composure.

"Don't be silly, please, stay." She gave that shy smile, relieved at the young man's reaction. "I'm sorry, I was just a little shocked. Did you say, gay?" Silently, she nodded.

Dr Allen Martin was a gay man living a lie. Terrified the boys in the cricket club would discover the truth. Hell, how many times had he shared a joke with the guys about bender Bob, the homo fast bowler who was only tolerated because he had the best figures of any cricketer in the league. Plus, he was six feet five, built like a brick shithouse and would beat the living Hell out of any of the 'Good Old Boys Network'. Imagine that being beaten up by a queer. So, martin stayed silent. Even going so far to take a wife to hide his shame. Oh, he'd acted the loving husband for a few months, until one morning, after making love to Julia, with a look of disgust exclaimed, "That's the last time I do that with you." In addition to the young woman's confusion and distress, he'd exclaimed in a matter-of-fact fashion, the whole sordid truth. How he had no attraction to her in the slightest, how things were going to change and if she had a problem with that, she could, "Fuck off back to the council estate where he'd found her."

"Breath a word, just one word, and I'll destroy you. I'll leave you destitute and back in that shit-hole council estate where I found you." In her naivete, she'd signed a pre nuptial agreement, believing that they'd spend their lives together, that the good doctor was her knight in shining armour. How wrong she'd been. Now she was trapped in a loveless marriage, kept with minimal money and little freedom, a slave to her over-bearing bastard of a husband.

Her devastated emotions flowed continually as the devastated girl poured out the details, Castle, ever the gentleman, held her close, a wet stain of tears and mascara smudging into his white shirt's cotton material. While moving away, she noticed the mess and tried to apologise, going as far as to buy him a replacement the next time they met. It was the first time a girl had ever him a present, he was nervous to accept.

As Castle arrived home (a title his shit hole flat barely deserved) the earlier spring sunlight had faded to overcast grey. The afternoon had gone better than could ever have been imagined, the revelations of Dr Martin's sexual preferences already enough to eradicate the psychiatrist from the young man's life. Blackmail was a dirty business but the easiest route to the goal.

The flat seemed emptier than usual, more, bleak, depressing. Was he missing her already? There lies the danger. This would be an impossible relationship, that much was evident. When he pulled the trigger on his plan, she'd be collateral damage that had always been certain. It was impossible to believe this plan would work so fast that she'd give up her husband's so easily. God, she was so trusting, so pure so... No. Can't think like that.

Two days to the next hospital appointment. It would be so simple, just like flicking a switch, and the bastard would be gone forever. Obviously, the good doctor had gone to extreme lengths to maintain his secret life, risking a mouthy pissed-off patient with a grudge would be insane. Insane, strange word usage when talking about a shrink.

"Hell, I could push this further. Money, drugs, influence? Perhaps that's too far, illegality is dangerous, that cocksucker could have me banged up. Think I'll stick to eviscerating the bastard instead."

Inside the bathroom, a plastic cabinet with a broken door hung high above the washbasin. Reaching inside, Castle withdrew a glass medicine container with a snapped-off lid which carried his not-so-secret weapons. The dwindling supplies of Prozac added to his surprisingly dark mood. "Five pills to last two days." Fearing night-terrors more than withdrawal, he replaced the bottle and slammed the cabinet closed, the door's cracked mirror exterior reflecting an image the pained him to see. The glass's damage ran directly down the centre of his face, and he sniggered how apt it was. It felt like he'd become two people, the one who cared for Julia, and the one willing to throw her under the bus for his own sake. Frighteningly, the snigger turned to a fast-talking rant.

"Can I really do this? Fuck Dr Martin, this isn't about him. It's Julia? Could I keep her out of the equation? Impossible, where else would I have obtained this information? Even if by some miracle I did, my duplicity would destroy any relationship before it had chance to begin. She'd spent all afternoon pouring out her heart, her feelings, the story of one man's deceptive ways told to another masquerading charlatan. Christ, she'd run for the hills. Perhaps, that would be best. Fuck, what could I offer her, answer nothing? A shitty flat above a shitty shop, in a shitty street in a shitty town. What a catch. I'm a fuck-up, plain, and simple. A borderline alcoholic, drug-crazed, looney-toon without a pot to piss in or a WINDOW TO THROW IT OUT. THIS IS STUPID THIS IS NUTS, THIS IS… Okay, two pills, leave the rest for emergencies." Self-deprecation became a side effect of withdrawal.

The residue of the afternoon remained. The earlier pints of cider lay heavy on his stomach and left him feeling bloated and queasy. Ensuring he had the funds for the date, he'd fought the urge to drink for two days, and the swift bombardment left his head feeling flustered and confused. Another, more exuberant reminder made him smile. The taste of Julia's kiss hung decadently on his lips, residual lipstick smeared lightly around his mouth, a taste so sweet, he needed more. A craving greater than booze, than drugs, perhaps even vengeance…

So, from the vague fragments of a plan designed for revenge and ultimately, the eradication of Dr Allen Martin, an unsuspecting romance began, and it blossomed. The next appointment came…and went. Nick looked across the desk, full of vengeful knowledge, keenly aware that one word and the shrink would just, go away, and said nothing. He'd smiled, been responsive in therapy. The doctor even remarked of how he was, "Proud, that they'd made real progress."

All the time, staring through disgusted eyes, Castle thought, "You dirty, lying, horrible sack of monkey-shit. You have a woman, as fine as any woman could look, as fine as any woman could act. Loving, caring, beautiful, passionate, and you treat her with distain. You despicable human being, you shit-dipping whore-loving motherfucker. I'm going to take your wife, then expose you for the monster you really are. Do one more thing to that girl and I'll tear off your ears and feed them to you. FUCK YOU, FUCK YOU, FUCK YOU."

All while smiling, without moving his lips.

Their romance progressed, quickly. They'd walk the grounds of Bishopsgate Castle and just talk. They never seemed to run out of things to say. Acknowledging that, should the relationship go any further, a degree of honesty was essential. Immediately, during their next date, Nick admitted there was no travelling salesman job. In fact, there was no job at all. All he had was a crappy, rundown flat at the top of the town. There was no money for extras, he wouldn't be able to take her to nice places or but her expensive gifts. If that was a problem, she should say now.

"If you're not working, you can see me every day." Her reply washed a wave of relief over him. He'd gone through the speech 100 times, but it never sounded right. Instead of being repulsed, Julia seemed to have a satisfied alleviation, so thankful that her boyfriend was willing to be totally honest with her. "Nick, I couldn't care less about the job, and as for money, I'm sure we can find other ways to keep ourselves occupied (she giggled at the sexual undertone). It's just lies, I really hate them. After what Allen has done to me, I find trust hard. I want to trust you. I really, really do. Please, I am begging you, make me trust you."

Her speech stung. She was so sincere, yet there was a mountain of things she still didn't know.

"I've had serious mental problems since I was ten. A decade ago, I saw my best friend massacred. Some nights, the night-terrors come, and I piss the bed." Your husband is MY FUCKING DOCTOR, TOO SOON.

It took no time for Castle to realise that this was becoming more than a fling. Whenever they weren't together, it hurt. Alcohol became far less important, the days they were united, he stayed dry…until she left. The connection with Janice, his would-be drug supplier needed to remain, though he never saw her away from her flat and only servicing her needs when he received his drugs. For the first time in his life, he felt guilt. Still, needs must.

As date progressed, there were more tears during the expletive details of her husband's secret life. Male escorts were regular visitors to their home. After screaming, ear-shattering sex sessions with these men inside the martial bed, he'd snigger, knowing she was powerless. Hearing him in the throes of passion made her want to vomit. He disgusted her and didn't care, taking pleasure in her distress. She'd threatened to reveal his sordid pass-times, if he didn't stop rubbing it in her face; that was the first time he'd struck her. Nothing that would be visible, that wouldn't do for his reputation. Kicking her in the ribs and back had done the same job and had terrified her enough to remain quiet.

The mere mention of violence made Nick's blood boil. He was seriously new school in relation to man-woman brutality, the idea of striking a female made him puke. The topic had arisen during his parent's wars, but he'd always stepped in before an attack could occur, he'd hated at the time, but the suggestion of vehement Ramage still seemed disgusting. Whenever he was near, the rows would decrease, usually because they were about him. Power was nice.

For Julia, the violence became more vicious, he'd started to enjoy it, and made her avoid home at all costs. When his friends visited, she'd leave, get in the car and drive, anywhere, nowhere, just avoid a beating which irrevocably came in the aftermath. She believed, though had no proof, that hard drugs were exchanged in these sessions. His personality fractured, and it couldn't have just been sex. He became wild, uncontrollable. It was then that the worst thing happened.

Julia had been out of the house for over two hours, only returning when her Mini became low on fuel and she remembered her purse was still at home. The male-escort had arrived in an old-style BMW and had parked at the rear of the property. She acknowledged that the visitor had left and hoped the doctor may have fallen asleep. As her key turned the lock, she held her breath, desperate to remain silent. "Just get to the bedroom." There was a bolt on the inside for just these sorts of times, she'd be safe then. The door creaked on its hinges, making the frightened girl cringe. Once inside the hall, she looked around, all stayed silent. "So far, so good." The stairwell had recently been re-carpeted with thick Axminster and the best underlay, so her light footsteps made no noise. The fourteen stairs seemed mountain like, and a layer of abashed nervous perspiration formed across her face. Julia's eyes fixed on his bedroom door, her foot tripped on the top step, and she flayed, down across the passageway floor. Her error filled her with anger.

"How could I be so stupid? I was so close?" Beginning to climb to her feet, the master bedroom door quickly burst open.

"Are you okay?" He looked sincere, what was going on?

"I'm fine. I'm just tripped." Still anxious, she climbed to her feet. Martin gently held her shoulders, the trepidation seemed to pause the earth. He was stark-naked which made her more cautious but, for a moment, those eyes were filled with tenderness, for a moment, things felt fine, for a moment...

The first shot came from nowhere, a back-handed slap across the jawline. It happened so fast, she had no time to move, though thankfully, the blow glanced off the chin, barely making contact. The second made up for it, a straight left, full fist smash, directly on her nose, which exploded on impact. The sudden pain made her react and she grabbed for the bastard's hair, one hand connecting, a fistful of greying thatch her prize. She turned and made for her bedroom, but he was fast, double-handed pushing, just below the shoulders. She crashed heavily into the thick plastic white door which thankfully swung open, glancing her into a spin, and landing back fist, onto the polished wooden floor. The blood from her nose had spread across her face, this was the first time he'd ever marked an area which could be seen. She hoped this was the end, her bedroom was off limits, a safe area. Her wishing was in vain. His frame seemed to fill the open entrance, a maniacal grin more terrifying than the blade in his right hand. Her tears had begun to fall though sympathy wasn't a trait Doctor Allen Martin knew well.

"Get...those...clothes...off." The words were more confusing than chilling.

"Allen, think about what you're doing here. You're a gay man and that's fine. You have no feelings for me anymore, I've accepted that also. Please, just calm down, go back to your room, and let me clean myself up, you've broken my nose."

"NO BITCH TELLS ME WHAT TO DO."

The fallowing thirty minutes were a living Hell. Julia refused to divulge the details, but the harrowing incident had obviously scarred the girl deeply. She never uttered the word rape, though it was painfully obvious that this is what had happened. Her tears had stopped, she looked exhausted, it had certainly been a tribulation, deciding whether to share the horrendous event with a man she barely knew, but she believed in complete honesty and still, she could feel that he, could be the one.

As Nick absorbed specifics of Julia's tale, he felt a rage burn inside, which had never exploded before. This piece of shit deserves everything he gets, and were it time, he'd have torn him limb from limb. Visualising forcing both thumbs deep into the doctor's ocular cavities and riving out his eyeballs, punching his face until it was indescribable, breaking his legs, crushing his ribs, smashing his…Nick was upset.

Had it not been for the girl's insistence, Castle would have gone for the psychiatrist, there and then, screw the plan. He took some calming down, the taste of Mrs Martin's lips begun the reposing transformation. Still, this was one more reason to hate the self righteous cunt.

"Why didn't you press charges?" Castle's tone was soothing, this was delicate, she was delicate.

"Against a doctor. Me, with the gold digger tag and a prenup. I could tell what they'd all say. Get the doc locked up, she gets all his money. No thank you." The young man paused, one wrong word and the relationship could be over before it began.

"I'm sorry. I didn't mean to sound…Christ, I don't know what I'm saying. I'm not very good at this. It's all such a shock. It doesn't affect how I feel about you. Hell, if anything it makes me love you more. I just want to protect you from this fucking…" Julia held a hand up with a growing smile across her face.

"Makes me love you more. You just said you love me." Her grin had stretched to the diameter of her face, her perfect teeth glinting in the spring sunshine.

"I'm sorry, it was just…" Nick Castle had a serious bout of tongue tying, the words refusing to come and when they did, he'd shutter and splutter, making the girl giggle more.

"I'm sorry too but you said it, you love me, that was your words, and the rules are, you can't take it back." Finally, his composure was regained, holding her hands, staring into her beautiful eyes,

"I don't want to take them back. It was a stupid way to say it, but I do love you. I know it's crazy, we've been on three dates, but they are the highlights of my week. And when I'm not with you, I want to be. You're the first thing I think of in the morning and the last thing I think of at night. Julia Martin…I love you."

The young woman was overwhelmed. She'd hoped he may be the one, and perhaps, he felt the same way too.

Leaving Julia that evening was the hardest thing, Nick Castle had ever done. Realistically, the young man knew it was way too soon for the two to become one. He had nothing to offer but his love. 'Love', was this for real. It certainly hadn't been planned. Anything but, but he had to admit, he'd fallen hard for this girl. But sooner or later, she'd make a connection, she'd see him for what he really was.

His brain was working overtime. Plausible deniability. Two wonderful words. Yes, he was a patient of her husband, but he could demand that the two were totally unconnected, a complete coincidence. Julia had never seen him in the office, why should he know that the girl he was falling for, was the wife of a man, he had a patient/doctor relationship with. Christ, the only way he could have known, was to stalk the doctor, follow him home, then stalk her, steal her mail to discover her identity, memorise her diary, then discover the best way to strike. Dress up handsome, use all his charm to sweep her off her feet, hoping she reciprocated his advances. Unbelievable, preposterous implausibly bizarre, you couldn't write this shit.

Then came the worry. Martin had beaten her before, what if today, he did it again. Not just today, but tomorrow, or the day after, or next week, Nick would be powerless to help. The first woman he'd ever loved, wanted, needed to be with, and that bastard could beat, rape, Hell, he could kill her, and Castle would never know. He began to get anxious in the hours and minutes before their dates, what if today was the day that she didn't come? What if he was waiting, and waiting, and waiting. What if the phone refused to ring (the line in the flat only received calls, didn't make them) no letters, no knocks at the door just nothing, what then?

For months, that problem didn't exist. At the start of their relationship, it was a twice weekly rendezvous, Monday, and Thursday. At the start of the week, they would meet, perhaps having a bite to eat, talk, then partake in some heavy necking in the woodland inside Bishopsgate Park, acting more like lovesick teenagers than a couple involved in an extra-marital affair. Occasionally, they'd attend the movies, in a cinema in the neighbouring town of Oakland at the top of Debra hill, which got so little business, the chances of being spotted were minimal. Usually they'd just walk, talk, enjoy anything and everything about being together.

Thursdays were special. By now, Julia had accepted Nick for what he was. The ever-increasing levels of candour and truthfulness came as a shock, not to her, but to him. Previously, Castle had never met anyone to whom, he'd felt comfortable enough, as be able to confess details of his life which may be construed as embarrassing, or disturbing but with Julia, he finally felt free. She didn't judge or fire back with perplexing retorts. After he'd confessed huge resentment towards his parents for forcing him away from his family home in Hallowell in search of his father's employment, she hadn't given a contrary argument, but just accepted the hurt the choice had created. When he'd explained how that resentment continued into adulthood, it would have been easy for her to become belligerent to his allegations and suggest a need to move on but instead she'd listened intently without giving a counter-opinion. Soon, Nick had even divulged how he'd suffered with mental health issues, though he'd insinuated that it was more in-line with depression and had never gone into detail. Her responses were always measured, without coldness or a hint of contentiousness, keenly aware by now that, Castle was in some way tortured and she should be honoured that he trusted her enough to share these inner most secrets. Mostly, he'd conceded the poor life choices made after his education ended. How believing that destroying his own undoubted, limitless potential, would be a way of getting even with his family, and by the time he'd realised the horrendous decisions he'd made, the damage had been done. For Nick Castle, this was deep stuff, trust was a guarded possession and showing a willingness to be vulnerable, was a giant leap forward. However, some things remained off limits. The whole Hallowell backstory, that railway station, Billy Scholes (he had mentioned losing a good friend at an early age though the details remained sketchy) and the monster, which still invaded his dreams; all these things, he deemed too extreme for this stage of their relationship. His history of past and current medical professionals also stayed private. But as the bond grew ever stronger, Nick became less reticent about Julia seeing his flat. That's why Thursdays became special.

"I can't bring her here." Nick had stared around the hovel, grimacing at the ever-worsening state of his accommodation. The day was Tuesday, she'd be visiting Thursday.

Forty hours of cleaning, scrubbing, waste disposal, and D.I.Y. Dusting, washing, and trips to the tip. Ironing, vacuuming, and sweeping. By the time Julia arrived, Nick Castle's Bishopsgate flat looked like a...shithole. A washed, scrubbed, dusted, vacuumed shithole, no rubbish, litter, dirty clothes, or empty beer-bottles, but still a shithole. At least he'd tried. Still, as she walked in, he still felt mortified. The old voices inside his head,

They live in a great, big house, she'll take one look at this place and run for the hills. What do you think you're doing? He has a good job, a nice home, money, cars, power, influence. And what do you have, a shit-hole flat and no prospects. Just end it and let her get on with her life, you loser.

The knock at the door, ten minutes earlier than expected, she was always early, the mad dash down the communal staircase, he'd even tidied here, the swing of the outer door, and she's there, looking incredible. She smiles, his heart melts.

Nick led Julia by the hand, apologises ready, and climbed the dark passageway to his front door. Everything inside was screaming, "NO" but he forced himself on. Reaching the final stair, he turned to his girlfriend and with a meek smile said,

"I really don't know about this; this flat is horrible. It's only temporary, honest, but it's really not nice." His look fading to the wooden stairs which they'd just climbed.

"Nick. Don't worry, I'm here to see you, not the flat. I don't care if you're a millionaire or a pauper, I still love you. Okay."

God, Castle was hooked on this lady, more than booze, more than pills, this wasn't supposed to happen, but it had, and he loved it, loved her, the chance was growing, perhaps he'd get a job, or go back to school. He had options by God to finally put that brain to work. Hearing those words, "I love you," never failed to excite him, she was that chance. Finally, finally, finally...

Reaching forward, he planted a lingering kiss across her forehead, before opening the door. His heart couldn't fail to sink, no wonder he had depression problems living in this shithole. This first door led to the lounge. Broken furniture discarded which made the room look sparse, the television in the corner had been polished but the wooden casing still shouted damage. The cushions on the settee had been fluffed to appear bigger than they really were trying to remove the appearance of the missing one. The leather hard backed chair had been disguised with a white sheet draped across and tucked into its crevice's though it still looked like shit. The curtains had been cleaned, the carpet vacuumed, this was as good as it got.

"What have you been talking about? There's nothing wrong with this. It just looks like a guy's flat, simple but clean. It could do with a woman's touch but, yeh, I could live here."

Nick heart leaped with joy; first test passed. Did she just say she could live here? Fuck me, this is really happening, fast.

The kitchen, this had been the hardest to renovate, it was in a terrible state. The burned-on grime across the rings of the cooker had taken two hours, scratching with the tip of a spoon, just to get to the correct level. Raw bleach and scoring pads, digging in deep had eventually revealed the oven's equitable surface and more cleansing had been required to make it presentable. Cleaning the inside was deemed unnecessary, 'out of sight, out of mind'. The fridge was a different matter. All the half-eaten, mould riddled, past sell-by date food when in the trash bad. The shelving was taken out and washed thoroughly, the puddle of stagnate water inside was soaked up, even the light bulb at the back was replaced. The fridge still didn't work, there was no cool air, but it looked satisfactory. The workbenches were cleared of rubbish and the washing-up done. It was the first time since he moved in that Castle could say it looked passable. A smile from Julia appeared to say that he'd passed test number two.

Three steps across were the bedroom. Neither took any notice of the cleaned quilt-cover or the washed curtains. The vacuumed carpet and prepared clothing mattered not, in seconds, their passion erupted, clothing flying buttons bursting, flesh meeting flesh, the feel of her naked body for the first time sent electric pulses into Castle and he loved it. The bedroom door kicked shut, the moans of devotion detonating and bouncing off the badly decorated walls. Their relationship consummated over and over. The afternoon fading to evening, her eyes closed, head tucked in across his chest, meaty arms holding her tightly, silently, the two both wishing it could always be this way.

They saw each other as often as possible. His diary was empty and so long as Julia played by her husband's rules, she could do as she liked. Every time Nick had to see that bastard for appointments, the urge to tear his head off was ever present. Violence from a man to a woman, especially one as fragile as Julia was disgusting, almost as disgusting as listening to his advice. The plan wasn't working, it wasn't supposed to be this way. A quick fumble and good-bye doctor shithead. They weren't supposed to fall in love. Nick was happy and terrified at the same time. If he told her the truth, she'd run for the hills, and he couldn't handle not having Julia in his life. Twice a week no longer enough, it went to three days and then four. Oxfam lost a volunteer and the gym's exercise ended; the sweat produced from her daily trysts far more enjoyable than the treadmill.

Then, the unthinkable occurred.

It was a Thursday afternoon, their six-month anniversary. A miracle had happened, Nick had cooked. Everything was set for her visit, and it was the day he would tell her everything. It was also the day he'd decided to ask her to leave her husband and come to him. He'd had enough of running around like teenagers.

He was controlling the drinking, the pills cut down to a minimum and even the nightmares were becoming very rare. It was close to being a normal life, a life he wanted to keep.

She was never late, but today was different. 1 pm came and went with no sign. On the one occasion, she'd needed to cancel, she'd telephoned an apology. He picked up the receiver and the dialling tone was working, so that couldn't be it. He waited until two then went down the stairs, across the road to a payphone and called her home number. She'd given it for emergencies, and this seemed like one. There was no answer, just the machine with his voice, that self-righteous bastard with a robot-like single tone.

Thursday went with no contact, panic was setting in. Had he found out, and hurt her? Had there been a traffic accident while she was on route? Was she sick of him? The thoughts swirled in his head, a kaleidoscope of images, none of them good. When it reached Friday afternoon, he was losing his mind with worry. Driving to the house, he'd peered through the windows but there was no sign of life. A nosey neighbour threatened to call the police and as he'd already drank four tins of strong cider that day, the law wasn't part of his plans. He tried over and over to telephone with the same outcome. The more he drank, the more frantic he became. There seemed little option. He had to call the hospital and speak to Martin in person. The line rang to his office and his secretary answered. He demanded to speak to his doctor, but her reply chilled him.

"Dr Martin has taken a few days off. He and his wife are spending some time together, it's their anniversary. He'll be back in on Tuesday or if it's an emergency, you can speak to Dr Samuels, he's taken Dr Martins workload for the weekend."

Nick couldn't believe what he was hearing. He hung up the telephone and retreated to his own private Hell. Was it possible? Had everything she'd told him been a lie? Why go away with a man who you hate and is supposed to despise you back? The more he drank, the more he heard the voices, and what they had to say wasn't good.

"She's played you for a fool."

Shut up.

"She never gave a shit about you."

Shut up.

"He's an educated man and you're a fuck-up, not much of a contest, is there, Nicky old son."

Shut up.

"How could someone like that love someone like you?"

SHUT UP. SHUT UP. JUST SHUT THE FUCK UP.

Imagining his Julia with that animal, made him physically sick. His Julia, what a joke. The temples on either side of his brow pulsed, holding him in a vice like grip. Why had he allowed himself to be played like this? He should know better than to trust people. His one lasting acceptance of humans was the only person a man could trust was himself. He should have stuck to the plan and just removed Dr Fuckhead from his life. Well, it wasn't too late to do that. If she was using him, he'd use her right back. If she thought that six months had meant nothing, and she was going to play happy families with him, then he could sink that boat. Returning to the payphone, drunk, Nick would have his vengeance.

"Dr Arsehole, Nick Castle here. I just thought you should know I've been screwing your wife for the last six months. Every chance we got, bang, bang, bang. We even did it in your bed. Oh, and by the way, I know your little secret. I know that you're a dirty bender who prefers dick to pussy, and I'm going to make sure everybody finds out. All your friends, your workmates, your patients, everyone. When I'm finished with you, you'll be ruined. Oh, and by the way, Julia, fuck you."

He returned to the flat, opened another tin of cider and cried. He picked up the receiver of the telephone and heard there were still no messages. In a fit of anger, he threw the handset across the room and smashed it into pieces. He drank himself into an oblivion and stayed that way for four days.

It was Tuesday before Nick saw the light of day. There was still no word from Julia and the flat was claustrophobic, so fresh air seemed the answer. As he walked out into the morning gloom, the general dealer, who doubled as an off licence and newsagent was lifting the board outside with the days' main headlines to advertise. When Nick saw the words, his blood ran cold.

"Local doctor in murder suicide tragedy."

Zombie-like, he staggered into the shop and picked up a copy of The Northern Echo. By the time, he'd read the first paragraph, he felt the urge to vomit.

"Local psychiatrist, Dr Allen Martin of Bishopsgate, county Durham is believed to have murdered his wife some time across the weekend. Martin, who worked at Bishopsgate General is then believed to have taken a lethal overdose of tranquilisers at their home in the town. Police are not looking for anyone else in connection with the incident as what transpired is believed to be a tragic murder suicide."

"Nick, this isn't a library, if you want that paper, you need to pay for it." Nick stared at the newsagent and throw the paper on the floor, before leaving the shop. "What's your problem man, someone die?"

He felt trans-like; how could this be? Then he remembered the drunken phone call. He ran to the bathroom and vomited violently into the bowl. Then he remembered smashing his telephone. There was a spare in the bottom of a wardrobe, so he rushed to the bedroom and began hurling the cupboards contents around the room until he found the old-fashioned piece. He ran to the living area and plugged it into the wall. The dialling tone was disturbed, a message was available. He pressed the playback button and listened with dread.

"Hi babe, I'm so sorry that I couldn't get hold of you sooner. His mother died on Wednesday night, and he dragged me down to London with him to arrange the funeral. When I got there, I realised I didn't have my bag with my telephone numbers in and couldn't for the life of me remember it. You know what a scatter brain I am. I dread to think what you've been imagining, but at least you didn't have to spend three days with him. Anyway, it's Sunday now and I'm back home so hopefully I'll see you tomorrow. I love you, see you soon. Sleep well."

That had been two years ago, and the emotions were still raw. The grey stone monument with the craving of an angel said it all. She was his angel and he'd destroyed her. Martin's gravestone was beside hers and today was one of the few times he'd been able to fight the urge to take out his penis and piss on his grave. If only he'd waited, then perhaps Dr Martin would never have known, maybe she'd have been his now and they'd be building a life together. If only, if only.

Tears ran down his face as they normally did when visiting Julia. He knelt, kissed the stone angel, and left. Heading to the car, his next destination was Hallowell.

Chapter 7

Tom Daley couldn't lie still any longer, the springs in the overly thin worn-out mattress were protruding through the foam, impacting into his aging flesh. Plus, the blankets stank from one too many locked up Saturday-night drunks, and the greyish lifeless pillow provided was damp from his own falling tears. He needed his own bed, his own home, this wasn't fair. Swinging his legs across the bed's metal frame, his stockinged feet padded silently across the cell's concrete floor. From beyond the bars, a full-length mirror shot back a frightening reflection, dishevelled hair protruding in all directions from his misshapen head, three-day stubble and mottled red cheeks, eyes encircled with dark rings, and clothing stained and creased, the prisoner barely recognised the man staring back. With a heavy sigh, he decided to try for one last attempt to make the officer see sense.

"Constable Brackett? Are you there? Please sir, may I have a word with you?" The detainee knew the policeman was in the next room, every so often, he'd hear movement, the chinking of a teacup or closing of a filing cabinet. "Constable please, it's me, Tom Daley."

Brackett couldn't help but snigger, who the Hell else was it going to be, he only had one prisoner.

Johnny Brackett wasn't a bad guy; he just had a job to do. Keeping Daley in the cells screamed injustice, even if the evidence was damning. Sitting writing this report, even he could almost be convinced that the poor old sap was guilty. Just because this was Hallowell didn't mean that every crime originated from that place. There were witnesses that testified of raised voices of both Daley and the missing boy. Tom had been seen in the back lane, fleeing the scene and he even had the boy's blood on his clothes. It should be obvious, but there was still that lingering doubt, and it was pissing the policeman off.

This wasn't what Johnny had joined the service for, piles of paperwork, lingering from one day to the next. Sitting at this desk took up more of his time than patrolling the streets. Still, it beat all the self-righteous stares from residents that should know better, glaring looks of accusation, backed by growing belief that the wrong man was in the cells. What they didn't understand was, even if the old dummy was innocent, the police-house was the safest place for him now, Hallowell vigilante justice could be swift and merciless, substantiation of facts rarely got in the way.

"Constable, please, if you could just talk to me, you'll see that it wasn't me. I couldn't do such a thing."

"Just quieten down in there Daley, I'm busy." Tom eyes grew wide, this was the first response of any kind he'd had since breakfast.

For Johnny Brackett, this was his first real test. After the retirement of his predecessor, Bill Castle, the role of Constable to Hallowell had been deemed obsolete; bar for an occasional domestic or drunken brawl, policing was minimal in the tiny hamlet. That changed in the winter of 79 when old Charlie Bowls had murdered his wife and two children at their farmhouse in the rear of the Graham compound. Some called it cabin-fever, Hallowell winters could be particularly harsh, and the surrounding roads would regularly be closed for weeks at a time, and December of that year was a record-setter. The nearest police station was in neighbouring St Mara but with Hallowell bank impassable and no other entry point available, any investigation was forced to wait until the weather cleared. It was only after this incident that the role of constable was re-introduced, and Doctor Harry Brackett had the perfect candidate. His son Johnny was already a serving officer in the nearby town of Carpenter and seemed the obvious choice, an outsider might ask too many questions, and the residents of Hallowell had a lot of secrets to hide. In his twin role as local mayor, the doctor found little objection from the population and Johnny Brackett was installed as constable. Most days, it was a role he enjoyed, today, not so much.

"Please Mr Brackett, I just need two minutes, I can't stand this anymore. It wasn't me, please listen, you have to listen." Like a caged animal, his grip on the steel bars tightened and with additional force, the cell door began to shake, clanging an echo around the holding area. Brackett's patience was growing tested, the Autumnal cold he'd been carrying for weeks gave him a constant dull headache and the din from the next room wasn't helping.

Situated in the centre of Hallowell, on the corner of colliery lane with its rear opposite to the back of the Wheatsheaf pub, the police-station was just a converted two-story cottage, with an office in front and two holding cells to the rear. After taking the role of Constable, Brackett assumed the tenancy of the one-bedroom flat above, which proved a useful decision when there was a prisoner on site. During Bill Castle's reign as village lawman, he'd been forced to bed down in the office on the rare occasion that a detainee became an overnight guest, a position, Johnny had been adamant to avoid. Since the Daley situation was moving into a fourth day, Brackett was content with his forward-thinking choice, keenly aware that as the Village's sole law enforcement, old Tom was his responsibility.

"Can't you see I'm busy? What do you want?" The officer was tired, sleep for the last three nights had been tough to come by. True, he was in his own bed but to be safe, he'd installed a baby monitor by the holding cell, just in case. As Daley had spent most of his incarceration weeping loudly, unbroken slumber was doubtful. Like a faithful puppy, the prisoner's spirits rose at the new-found attention.

"I'm sorry, I really am. But I need to talk to you."

"What could you possibly have to say that would be of interest to me? Unless you're ready to confess, are you?" It was now the cop's spirits rising, perhaps this was about to come to an end. That hope was soon extinguished.

"I can't confess, I haven't done anything wrong. I love children."

"Yes, we know you love children, and we know what you do with the children that you love." Constable Bracket had heard it for three days. Hell, he'd heard it ever since taking the job.

"No. No, you shouldn't say that. I've never hurt a kiddie in my life. What happened years ago was a misunderstanding. I was wet and that's why I took my clothes off, and Agnus shouldn't have been in my house and I'm sick of all the nasty names and…"

"And that's about enough of that talk too. You just quieten down and when you want to tell me what really happened, then we'll talk."

"I've told you what happened. It was the man from the Station. He grabbed the kiddie. I tried to save him and…"

"And I've told you, there's no bogeyman hiding in Hallowell railway station. If there was, I'd find him, I'd arrest him. Now you shut up until the duty solicitor turns up and then I'll take your statement. And if you didn't do it, you better get me at least a live suspect." Bracket was losing patience.

"I'm telling you the truth. I'm a good boy, my mum and dad always said so. It was the man from the station, the bad man. Frankie." Bracket tore the door open and grabbed Daley by the throat, perspiration forming on frustrated brow.

"Listen to me you piece of crap. If you didn't hurt him, how come his blood is on your clothes? How come your neighbour said he heard you shouting at the boy and the boy calling for help. Now if you want to be a good boy, you just sit your arse on that bed there and shut your mouth. The sooner the police from St Mara come and take you off my hands, the better. Oh, and by the way, I don't think you should be wanting to go back to your home because I'm just one policeman and the group that wants to tear you apart is too big for me to hold off." Bracket shoved the frightened man and he stumbled onto the bed. "Now I'm warning you, any more bullshit and you'll wish you hadn't."

"But the blood was from when he cut himself climbing over my fence, I didn't…"

"SHUT UP FREAK." The volume hurt Tom's ears. "I won't warn you again."

Bracket slammed to door and heard the frightened man crying. He walked to the front desk and found a familiar face waiting for him.

"Bit rough on the old boy there, weren't you?" Harry Bracket had been the town doctor for forty years and was more than happy to use his position of influence for his own gains.

"He's getting on my nerves, all that station bullshit. That's the last thing we need, someone dredging that crap up again. He had the kid's blood on his clothes and I've a witness that puts him at the scene, open and shut case, end of chat." The police officer was flustered and looked more than his twenty-one years; it had been a rough week. The weight of the case was laying heavy, and it was one of those days where his lack of experience was showing. The doctor shot back a disapproving frown, the sort which always aggravated the young man.

In the corner of the office, another doorway led to a kitchenette, and the elder made his way across. Flicking the light-switch, Brackett senior reached for a plastic electric kettle and clicked it to boil.

"And your certain he's lying? I mean, he does have some valid points." Johnny returned his father's disapproving glare, hoping that his exasperated expression may save him from a lecture he'd used countless times before.

"Don't start dad. I'm not doing this today."

"All I'm saying is denying the possibility may be naive. You always knew that you may have to face this when you took the job. It's part of life in Hallowell that much is certain." Junior was fighting with a drawer in a silver filing cabinet that stuck constantly, trying to not focus on his father's conversation. "Are you trying to ignore me boy." Johnny hated the term, boy, it made him feel ten years old again.

"Yes." He slammed the side of the cabinet with his left hand, catching the corner and causing him to call out in pain. Harry walked across and with a short, firm tug, the drawer came open.

"That's your trouble, too impatient." He walked back to the kettle and made tea.

"And your trouble is you live in the past. Don't try to make this into something it's not."

Harry Bracket sipped from his tea, his eyes never leaving the stare of his son. "I'm not saying Daley didn't kill the kid, he probably did, hell, he's weird enough. But all I'm talking about is the possibility that he's still there, that's all. You don't have to spit your dummy out the pram."

"Yes, I'll tell you what, I'll put out an all-points bulletin for a guy with a cane and dementia, how's that? Would that make you happy?" Walking over, he snatched his tea and exited the room. His dad followed.

"You know, you really can't be this dismissive." His anger beginning to show. "Frank Graham would be thirty-four years old. Now I'm not saying that you should be investigating him and let's face it, Daley is the ideal candidate for this, whether he did it or not. He's a safe cop. But Graham's body was never found, and hell, you should know more than anyone what that animal is capable of."

"Was capable of, not is. Christ, dad, just listen to yourself for once. Yes, I accept, I do know what he was capable of, but that was eleven years ago. Eleven years. What's he waiting for? For fuck's sake, what's he eating up there, the souls of the dead. Now, you can't have it both ways, if he's as crazy as you claim, where's the self-control come from, stopping him slipping out of the railway station in the dead of night, puree a few of the locals and be home before the sun comes up. Someone who's that big a psycho would have no self-control, just a total bloodlust. Do you really believe that someone could show that amount of extraordinary patience, just guarding a derelict abandoned shit-hole?"

"HE'S DONE IT BEFORE." The doctor took a deep breath and regained his composure. "Now I honestly believed that when I got you this job, you were the ideal man because you know the history. Because you've seen the bastard up close and because, you know what would happen to this town and everybody involved if the truth came out. I'm sixty-three years old and I've lived with it for seventeen years and there isn't a day goes by when I don't question what we did. But I still believe it was what was best for Hallowell at the time and keeping him at arm's length is what's best for Hallowell now. Maybe he's dead, God only knows, I hope so. But you can't shove your head in the sand and deny even the possibility that Frank Graham is still alive and is still hiding out in the railway station." The two men fell silent, paused in quiet reflection, then the son broke the silence.

"What do you mean, whether he did it or not?" Johnny looked puzzled.

"What? Oh, Daley."

"Yes, you said if he was guilty or not. What did you mean?" He thought he knew the answer already.

"The town will demand answers."

"And you think I should fit Tom Daley up, whether he did it or not?" The tone told the doctor to tread carefully.

"You said yourself, he probably did it. Logic says he did it. It wouldn't be hard to convince everyone else he did it. It's just something to think about, that's all." Johnny Bracket slammed his teacup down on the cabinet, splashing liquid everywhere.

"I think it's time you left now daddy. I don't tell you where to stick your thermometer and you don't tell me how to investigate my cases." The doctor put down his cup and smiled.

"There's that anger again, get you into trouble one day. Oh, and by the way, if the rumours are true, you may have more to worry about than a missing child. You heard Bill Castle died two days ago? That screw up grandson of his, what's his name, Nick? He's coming to the funeral. Hot head like that hanging around, you may need to keep an eye out there." He opened the exit. "Don't forget to visit your mother." The door closed slowly.

"AARRGG FUCK." This was not the way Johnny Bracket had envisioned his day going. Slumping back on a leather swivel chair and closing his eyes, he remembered. Things that he'd tried for so long to forget.

"Constable Bracket, could I have a drink of water please." Tom Daley sounded like a pleading child and his future was in Bracket's hands.

Chapter 8

Hallowell railway station was calling to Nick Castle, there was an irresistible urge to witness the scene of his nightmares. He had no choice.

The journey had been flawless, his mother's Ford Escort, a homing beacon, drawing him home. After an absence of eleven years and short trips the total of his driving experience, Castle had begun the expedition with expected nervous tension. The geographical region of the small village was not connected with main highways, but the bright autumnal sun had made signpost reading easy. Not a wrong turning, not a momentary panic, the one hundred- and ten-miles' odyssey had taken less than two hours, suddenly, he was home, and home, felt strange. A mid-afternoon departure from Bishopsgate ensured that his arrival in Hallowell was met with a darkening October sky. When the Ford stopped for the first time, on the outskirts of neighbouring St Mara, approaching the peak of Hallowell bank, the entire town was in view.

The church of St Helen built in 1382 and which the village was born around, with its gothic steeple, the highest and most impressive sight in the tiny hamlet. Unfortunately, most gravestones were so worn that the lettering was undefinable, and many were shattered, a sad indictment of neglect across the centuries. Hallowell primary school, Nick's first experience of education, was created in the late 1800's for the village's growing populous, with red-brick walls and wrought-iron gates with a separate entrance for boys and girls. Could Mr Taylor possibly still the headmaster? Melrose drive, destination of their former family home, Main Street, where the Castle general dealers remained. His gran still the proprietor, one day it would possibly be his, he was the last remaining Castle. The town's hub was built around the communal green, the Wheatsheaf public house and Vera Henderson's bed and breakfast, the Hallowell workingmen club, and the lunchbox café. Harry Bracket's doctor's surgery was off colliery lane beside evergreen rest-home and Hallowell new-cemetery. Fred Gibson's funeral directorship, adjacent to the rest home, handily placed for aged patients. Tom Wade's farmland bordered by woodland. Every vision as effervescent in his memory as the day he left.

And then, the Graham footprint. Firstly, a highway, running horizontally across the entire expanse of the rear of the village, taking its name from the patriarchal family, ending only at the gates of the palatial family home in the north-west corner of Hallowell, the Graham mansion. In its heyday, a grade 1 listed building, eight bedrooms, built on three levels with an enormous basement. A huge ballroom with craved ceilings and interior balconies, to which the crème of society would happily visit, politicians, celebrities, even royalty. During

World War II, Winston Churchill had used the property on several occasions when meeting dignitaries away from London. It was classed as Northern England's best kept secret. A sweeping, open staircase from old Hollywood, luxury from a by-gone age. Today, the once great picture of British architecture becoming a cheerless lugubrious vision of former glories. Unrecognisable after fire had ravaged its majesty and sumptuousness, unsightly wooden boarding housed inside the window frames and doorways, vast areas of missing slate from the roofing, giving home to all manner of birdlife. The gardens overrun by weeds and decaying trunks of trees, formerly cared for lovingly by aged landscaper, George Towers, but now left to rot. A depressing disintegration of a once great institute.

And finally, Hallowell railway station. Disused since 1962, feared by women and men alike. The panicle of the Graham Empire, once mighty, once respected, now despised.

Night-time was approaching fast and Nick's grandmother, Alice Castle was awaiting his arrival. She'd need patience as Castle had a far more urgent engagement. Driving down the steep decline into Hallowell village, he had every emotion imaginable bombarding his psyche. The excitement of a child at Christmas, for he was finally home. Nerves heightened, the expectation of seeing all those faces from the past. How would Johnny Bracket take Nick's return? They had been best friends once. Now, they were opposites. There was also sadness at saying goodbye to a loved one. Not just any loved one, but his grandfather. The only type of role-model there'd ever been in his whole pathetic life. And finally, there was fear. Knowing this was the only chance he'd ever get to right some wrongs, battle some demons. His mother's revelations earlier in the day had contented him some, finally certain that the monster in his nightmares had always been real. But along with that certainty came the acknowledgement that Hallowell was truly maintaining the presence of evil, bringing forth one terrifying question. Should the opportunity present itself, would he be man enough to face that evil? One thing he was certain of; to continue living life as he was currently no life at all, that much was obvious. This was Nick Castle's resurrection.

The bank levelled as the Ford reached St Helen's church, his foot sliding from the accelerator, gently covering the brake-pedal, speed slowing to 20 mph. By the roadside, a metal signpost with the words, "Welcome to Hallowell," in royal blue lettering over a white background rose from the footpath. Nick couldn't help but allow a cheeky grin to cover his lips as the realisation that he was home fired a final registration in his mind. In the rear-view mirror, the foot of Hallowell bank was lost to the darkness and a shudder ran down his spine as he remembered that this was the one and only road into and out of town.

A decade earlier, he'd been removed from this place without consultation and now he was back. But had the young man not known differently, he could have believed that he'd never left. Like a picture postcard, stuck in another era, time seemed trapped in the past, like a weird parody of itself. Everything identical to a time when the area was ruled unquestionably by the Graham family,

Castle wondered whether this was by design. Did the population dare move past its origins?

Driving past his grandmother's general dealers, he noticed the store was already closed for the day. Nick had half expected his oldest sibling to be at the door waiting. She wasn't, it seemed the fatted calf hadn't been roasted just yet. Gregory's family butchers, still in business, neighboured Alice's business along to the right with Peter Gibson's green grocery adjacent to the left. More of the same in the land that time forgot. Turning off Main Road and heading up Colliery Lane, the shabby, stand-alone property of Ian Gaskin's auto repairs. The old handyman had been a close friend to Nick's grandfather and had been responsible for the renovation of Tom Daley's cottage after the colliery disaster.

"Wonder how old Tom is doing? Must call in some time when I get the chance." Memories of Daley's back garden playground were some of Castle's most treasured childhood recollections, that situation, one of the few things to irrevocably change in the last ten years.

To the rear of Gaskins auto repairs was the farmland owned by the Wade family. Nick remembered hearing that old Tom Wade had passed some years earlier, leaving the farmland and house to his son Alf. New owner, same picture. Castle had loved climbing trees in the woodland adjacent to the farm as a kid. He sniggered as a memory of Billy Scholes, falling from a great oak, and breaking his right arm, two days into the summer holidays entered his subconscious. The poor kid cried all the way home and wound up in a cast until September. Billy always was an unlucky child.

Colliery lane had reached its half-way point, the road turning abruptly 90 degrees leading back in the direction to the village centre. Intersecting with another straight road, Station view, which ran vertical north to south on the west side of Hallowell, the four-way junction was surrounded with terraced cottages, formerly leased to colliery workers as a perk of employment. Across the main junction from the cottages was the defunct mining works, left abandoned after the Hallowell colliery disaster, and its neighbour, hidden well back from the roadside and disguised with a thick area of woodland, was the bad place, Hallowell railway station.

The dark clouds had covered a thick blanket across the autumnal sky, October showing its early onset of night-time faster with each passing day. The streetlights across Station view had always inexplicably failed, immediately after repair, so much so that the local authorities now refused to replace the damaged fittings, blaming constant vandalism over technical malfunction. Though no resident had witnessed the culprit, most had their suspicion.

Castle pulled the Ford to a shuddering halt on wasteland between the two former Graham businesses. As the engine died, the headlight power was extinguished leaving behind only unnerving blackness. Perhaps this isn't such a good idea. Nick rested his head back on the leather exterior of the car's driver's seat and took in a deep breath. His heart racing, Castle slid a hand into the inside pocket of his black leather jacket, retrieving a half empty strip of pills. Pushing with the thumb of his right hand, the clear plastic packaging gave way, and two

Prozac were quickly bundled deep into the back of his throat, swallowing without water. Breathing deeply, he waited for the psychological effect of the medication to kick in, the realisation that their effect was little more than a momentary placebo mattering little.

Climbing from the car, he stretched and exhaled a loud yawn, stiffness caused by the journey. Rubbing his neck, he scoured his surroundings, re-acquainting himself with his former playgrounds. The mass of trees didn't seem as inviting as the vision his mind had created earlier but he knew his day wouldn't be complete if he didn't at least, see that place, if only for a moment. Over the fence was the abandoned railway line and in the distance to the left was Hallowell tunnel. And to the right…

The mesh was strong and razor wire was encircling its height, Hallowell really wanted to keep people out of the station, or, perhaps, keep them in. At ten feet, Nick decided against attempting to scale it and began to walk its length, entering the woodland and away from the safety of the town. No one even knew he'd arrived.

The rhythm of his heartbeat pounded out a faster tune as the treeline in his rear blacked out the last remaining lights from the colliery cottages. Though the Autumnal season had forced the trees to shed their leaves, the high branches were enough to block out most of the moonlight. He began to hum a tune then stopped when he realised the music, he was creating was the theme to John Carpenter's movie shocker, Halloween. He chuckled to himself and then re-focused.

Keeping the fence as a directional tool, he avoided losing his way but was continually unnerved by sounds reverberating around the darkness. The rustling of the fallen leaves, the whistling of the breeze, the cracking of bracken underfoot. Over his shoulder, the scurry of an animal, perhaps a squirrel or mouse. It was a wall of darkness now, but to his left, in the distance beyond the fence, the ground was clear. Clear, bar the mass of stone and concrete looming out of the horizon. For, not half a mile distant, stood the Hallowell railway station.

Nick felt a stirring in his bladder. Though it was the destination in mind, the sight of that place, the source of his life's destruction, came as an unwelcome jolt, like a bolt of lightning striking directly into his soul. It had been years, so many years, years of Hell. He stopped in his tracks, unsure now of how to proceed. This is what he'd craved for so long, to stand face to face with the place that gave him nightmares. So why now would his body not obey his commands. All the times he'd sworn to himself that if the opportunity arose, he'd banish the demons and face his fears. Now his body was frozen. Just twenty feet from where he stood, there was a hole in the wire-mesh barrier. An entrance, an opportunity, a trap. Yes, that was it, it was a trap, set only for him, cut open by the creature with the mask, waiting to finish what he'd started all those years ago. Nick began to whimper, a ten-year-old all over again. This wasn't how it was supposed to happen, this wasn't how he was supposed to feel. He was meant to be brave, that's what he'd promised himself, that's what he told himself he was going to do. He'd come too far to fail now.

There was a trickle on the inside of crotch, a dampness.

"Please no, not again."

He was swaying, incapable of standing still but unable to move. His left leg wanting to stride confidently into battle with his right desperate to flee. He felt dizzy, nauseous, faint. The reached for the mesh, fingers grasping, clenching, knuckles livid, eyes watering, perspiration drenching his shirt. Suddenly a step forward, a stumble, and then a run, hurtling toward the hole. He had to do it, not wanting too, needing to. He slid on moist earth as he dived for the gap. His headfirst then his arms, his leather jacket snagging on a sharp edge. He turned and fought to free his coat, not wanting to create a tear. A jagged wire edge cut deep into the skin of his left hand, blood immediately bursting from the open wound.

"Bastard." Tearing the hand away from its inanimate assailant, the laceration tore further, sending a torturous shock of pain deep into his already troubled psyche. Feeling the blood flow freely down his skin, Castle instinctively brought the lesion to his lips, the dull sickly iron taste spreading across his tongue, making him fight the urge to wretch.

"Come on Castle, get a hold of yourself."

Momentarily, he paused and took three deep breaths. He felt a trickle of his blood slip seamlessly from the corner of his mouth and wondered just how much damage he'd caused to his flesh. Still, there was no turning back now. Nick allowed himself a final look in that place's direction, deeply aware that when his whole body passed through the barrier, he'd only be fifty feet away from…

Using his right hand, he unhooked the wire obstacle from his jacket as carefully as possible, this coat was the one indulgence he'd allowed himself from his mother's financial assistance. Feeling no tear, his sighed with relief, then refocused on his mission. Pushing his body clear of the fencing, leaving just his legs to hurl forward.

"One last push."

Nick's scream as a hand launched out of the darkness, grabbing at the back-pocket of his denim jeans, echoed around the emptiness. Spinning around, the young man lost his balance, crashing to the floor of the station wasteland.

"And where the Hell do you think you're going?"

Castle was about to lash out in defence when, in the final second, something stopped him.

"I said where the Hell do you think you are going?" The voice was familiar though it had been a long time since he'd heard it.

"I fucking knew you'd pull this shit."

The young man battled confusion, childlike once again. Emerging from the blackness, a face appeared at the hole, staring down, anger plastered across his expression. With a deep exhale of breath, Nick allowed one word to escape his lips.

"Dad?"

Chapter 9

"You've got to be fucking kidding." Nick's eyes widened, pupils fixed with a glare of hatred mixed with confusion, burning deep into his father's soul. Mick Castle tried to return that same fix but the expression on his son's face filled him with dread, like reading the last line of a graphic horror story. The older man's eyes dipped to the floor, before swivelling his body away from his fallen sibling, desperately hoping that Nick hadn't noticed his concession of the battle. Mick breathed in deeply, acutely aware that this meeting would be a struggle, a conflict he'd have to lose, Nick deserved that much. Still, senior wasn't about to make it easy. From behind, he could hear Nick scrambling to his feet, desperately trying to regain some composure after his embarrassing pratfall. When certain his son had retaken his footing, Mick turned once more to face his exasperated off-spring.

"Hello nick." It was all he could muster.

"Hello nick? Hello nick? Is that all you have to say? You desert mom and me when I needed you most, vanish without a trace, not a letter, phone call, carrier pigeon, nothing. Then when you decide to reappear, all you can say is, hello Nick. What an arsehole."

The two generations stood eye to eye, separated by nothing but a weakened mesh fence, the younger man momentarily forgetting that he was in the domain of the creature, instead the monster before him seemed infinitely more dangerous. Softly and without pretension, Mick broke the awkward silence.

"I suppose I deserved that." His line of sight once more falling to his worn-out work-boots, his actions screaming for sympathy, the one emotion that his son refuse to allow him. Nick started back through the fence's hole, unsure how he'd react when his dad was in striking distance. Would it be time for a hug, or a right cross to the jaw? At this moment, his anger insinuated the latter.

"Oh, you deserve a damned sight more than that, I'm just getting warmed up. And what the fuck are you doing here anyway? You were hardly popular with your parents, now, were you?" Mick smiled; the insult was just enough to spark him into life.

"Well, that's where you're wrong Nicky." Nicky, the only thing his parents had in common was their use of the name Nicky, whenever they wanted to make him feel childish. "I've been back here almost eight months. When dad was diagnosed with cancer and he started chemotherapy, I stepped up. Took some shifts at the store, drive him back and forth for hospital appointments, shit like that. Whatever was needed."

"Well, good for you." The sarcasm was laid on thick.

"You're fucking-A-right it was good for me. Perhaps, I hadn't always been the perfect son, you'd know plenty about that, but for once, I felt needed. No one looking at me like some big fucking disappointment. I'd got so used to being treated that way, by you, your mother, even my own dad, I'd forgot what it felt like to be appreciated. It felt good."

"Felt good? Your own father was dying but that's okay because you felt good." Nick knew that senior hadn't meant for the wording to sound that way, but the insult was too great to miss.

"You know that's not what I meant. I was just…"

"How would I know? I haven't seen you for three years, you're a stranger to me now. I don't even know why I'm bothering to talk to you. Like I've already said, ARSEHOLE."

Taking three steps away, for a moment it appeared that Mick was retreating. Oops, maybe that one went a little far? Who cares, fuck him. Instead, the older man showed an impressive turn of pace, swiftly turning on his heels, bounding across the open ground, right arm outstretched, aimed for his son's throat. When contact was made, the young man was too shocked to react. As the hand clenched into Nick's flesh, junior grimaced, the pain just enough to divert his attention from the argument.

"Now, listen to me. For the first time since I was a kid, dad and I talked, I mean really talked. Not just bullshit, this was special, and you won't take that away from me. Finally, I didn't feel like a disappointment. I started to try to understand him more and I think, he began to understand me. It may sound stupid but for once, I felt like his equal."

"Equal, you? Don't make me laugh. He was a man of honour, respected by his peers. You're a fuck up." Slapping away his father's hand, the two squared up, eye to eye, shoulder to shoulder, a tinder box waiting to erupt. For a moment the tension was unbearable, an old lion ready to defend his turf against a young pretender to his throne. Suddenly, the older man smiled.

"Wow, that was intense. What do we do next, take out our pricks and see who can piss the furthest?" Next it was his son's turn to lighten the atmosphere.

"You'd lose that one too." Nick turned away, suddenly aware that the station was to his rear. As always, a shudder ran down his spine as the towering outline filled the night-sky. "So, how come I wasn't told he was ill? It would have been nice to see him before he passed. Say my own goodbye." His words were spoken with a solemn undertone, as if it was the first thing in the conversation that contained meaning instead of just points scoring. Placing a hand on the young man's shoulder, Mick gave the only retort that he could.

"It was dad's wishes. Hell, he knew you hero-worshipped him. At least now, the last memory you have of him is when he was still strong. He didn't want to see that in your eyes. I had no choice."

"Me neither. I'm not that little kid anymore that needs sheltering from the world. I do know what death is, I've seen it up close and personal." Mick frowned, aware of his son's meaning though not wishing to bring up the subject yet. "It would have been nice to have the option." His father replied with slow, deliberate words.

"And that's exactly why dad didn't want you here. Remember the promise you gave him? To stay away from Hallowell. He wasn't about to give you an invitation back to this shithole. For some reason, he believed your word meant something. That didn't last long, now did it?" Nick fired back with fury.

"You think for one minute that I wouldn't be here for his funeral? I might not have been allowed to say goodbye while he was still alive but I'm damned sure I wasn't about miss the chance to pay my final respects now he's gone." Now it was Mick's turn to return fire with all the aggression he could muster.

"Bullshit. Don't kid a kidder. I know you better than you think, boy. You used this as an excuse to come back. You couldn't resist it, could you? Dad dies, and you piss on his memory, first chance you get. Christ, maybe I'd respect you more if you told the truth for once."

"The truth. That's fucking rich coming from you. You wouldn't know the truth if it crawled up and kicked you in the nuts. And by the way, I don't care if you are my dad, you ever insinuate that I disrespected granddad's memory again and I'll punch your lights out."

"Here we go again. I thought you might have grown up after living alone for a while but that's too much to expect. Tell me something, big man, if coming back here is all about Dad's funeral, how come you end up here, staring over at that bastard, before even dropping your bags off at Mum's? I'll tell you why, because you're fucking obsessed, that's why. Always have been, always will be." The argument momentarily paused, both men struggling to catch a breath, neither willing to make eye contact, the station becoming the duo's point of view. Finally, Nick answered though his tone had lost much of its earlier bluster and bravado. He couldn't be certain, but Mick sensed his son was close to tears.

"Obsession, good word. The shitty thing is, you're probably right for once. Christ, you've seen how fucked up my life has become. I have nothing, I live from drink to drink, hangover to hangover. I've had one woman in my life that's meant something, and I fucked that up too. And yes, before you say anything, I know that most of it is my fault. With all the directions I could have taken my life, I always chose the wrong ones. Mum already gave me that lecture, so I don't need it again. But don't you see? It's this place, that fucker over there (a finger is pointed in the station's direction). Until I can put all this behind me, I'll never go forward. As far as you are concerned, I'm not asking for much, just a little honesty, that's all."

Once more, silence filled the woodland, Mick Castle keenly aware of what he needed to do though the nagging doubt at the back of his mind made it hard. Finally, a decision was made.

"Okay, you win. You're like a fucking dog with a bone and you won't quit till you get your own way. Just remember this, you can't unhear what I'm about to say. You want the truth; I just hope you can handle the truth. Once I tell you, things will change, only you can decide if it's for the better or not."

Chapter 10

Mick Castle was ready. Standing stern, he led the young man to a clearing, fifty yards into the woodland, away from the sight of that place. A pile of tinder, kindling and wood lay in a plastic carrier bag, by a large oak. Scorched earth, charcoal and discarded litter lay in a safe marginal opening, perfect for a campfire, they'd need that warmth, this was going to be a long night.

"I came prepared." The older man stretched high and torn down the ingredients. Pushing the burned earth to make a circle, he rested, knees pressing into the damp ground. "This might take some starting. It rained earlier, and this stuff been here since this morning."

"This morning? How did you know I'd be here?" Mick was smiling until he saw the stern expression on his son across his son's face. I'm not there yet with him, keep working.

"I told you Nick. I know you better than you think. When you found out about dad, that was your chance. Guess what? I don't blame you anymore. If we were going to do this, we were going to do it right. Look over there, behind that big fir tree." Nick stumbled in the dark, kicking away fallen autumn bracken, eyes trying to get accustomed to the blackness.

"Didn't you bring a flashlight?"

"It was daylight when I came earlier. I didn't think it would be so dark. No one comes here at night; I think you might know why. Once I get this fire going, you'll have all the lighting you want."

Torn newspaper crumpled into balls, freshly chopped wood, smaller twigs at the bottom and a slab of oak in the centre. Then the secret weapon, a half-bottle of turpentine, poured over everything. Mick checked all pockets then panicked.

"Nick. You…got…I. Lighter?" The young man sniggered as he found his own prize. Hidden deep in the bracken, another plastic carrier bag, this time filled to the brim with beer, and a pint bottle of whisky.

"That's what I'm talking about." Lifting the bounty clear with his damaged left hand, he reached inside and tore a can free from its neighbours. The cap snapped easily, and the taste was like manor from God. Emerging back to the clearing, he saw his father, helplessly searching his clothing, cursing his forgetfulness.

"Here, uses mine." The disposable lighter flew hard through the air, striking Mick forcibly across the right cheek, then bouncing into the prepared fire ingredients.

"Thanks, I suppose." Pushing the newspaper aside, he retrieved the lighter, its flame suddenly starting an inferno, thanks to the turpentine.

85

"Jesus. Are you trying to burn the woods down?" He smiled, the sudden warmth a comfort, and with beer in his hand, maybe this wasn't going to be such a bad night after all.

When he was certain the fire was strong and there were supplies to maintain it for the length of their visit, Mick rested on a fallen oak and snapped open the whisky bottle. Lifting his choice of booze to his face, he waited a while, taking in the smell, the aroma, its perfect scent. Then, in one swift motion, he flipped the container, pouring the contents into the earth.

"What the fuck are you doing?" Nick looked legitimately aggrieved.

"I haven't had a drink since the old man took ill. That bastard whisky had been daring me every day to drink it, and I didn't. I won, FUCK THE WHISKY. The beers are for you. You might need them after what I have to say." Senior threw the bottle deep into the trees, no one heard it land.

Instead of sharing the fallen oak, Nick scrubbed a clearing on the floor, closer to the fire. His legs outstretched, ten feet from the flickering flames, one hand pressed against the ground, the other holding tightly to the can. It was almost empty, still, there was plenty more.

"You on the waggon. Whatever next?"

"Don't worry, that will be the least of your shocks by the time we're done."

What Mick Castle told his son over the next few hours could scarcely be believed. This is that story…

"Little is known about Hallowell's history prior to the late 1600s other than the church of St Helen being erected in 1382. The tomb stones that pock mark the surrounding graveyard are far too worn to make out names and most are smashed in pieces.

The village originally known as Hallows and later becoming Hallowell was owned in principle by the Graham family. The lands were bestowed upon Sir Fredrick Graham in 1690 by the powerful prince bishops, as reward for services to king and country. Its origin was taken from Sir Fredrick's late wife Katherine's maiden name, as a reminder of his devotion after she died suddenly in her early thirties from a mysterious disease, that wouldn't be diagnosed until many years later. Her condition was discovered to be a hereditary ailment named Porphyria. The illness comes in many forms and its effects include intense abdominal pain, deadly allergies, vomiting, insomnia, and blood pressure anomalies. Heart palpitations, seizures and urine discolouration are early warning signs but the main effect it had on Katherine was mental. Porphyria can cause anxiety and restlessness, something she suffered with massively. She became confused at the slightest problem and was certain those closest to her were plotting her demise, as paranoia is another symptom of the dreadful condition. She began to hallucinate horrible creatures crawling across her skin and alien beings invading her home. It became dangerous to leave her alone as she would wander and become disorientated, not recognising landmarks that were native to her. The effects became so bad that she took her own life and that of two of their five children. She'd become convinced that the unfortunate off-springs were from another planet, abandoned on earth to infiltrate our weaknesses and lead a coming invasion. Arsenic poison in massive quantities were mixed with their food and she watched with delight as the children suffered agonising deaths, certain she had saved earth from disaster. When the realisation dawned upon her that she'd murdered her two innocent eldest children, and they weren't alien invaders, the grief was too much to bear. She laced her own meal with the same poison and forced its contents down her throat. Fearing the arsenic wouldn't be sufficiently deadly to end her life, she tied a rope to the staircase railing of the Graham mansion. Tightening it around her neck, she was disturbed by her distraught husband who pleaded with her not to execute her plan. It was in vain, as in Katherine's mind, Sir Fredrick had now taken on the form of the alien king and was ready to seek vengeance on her for killing two of his subordinates. She threw herself from the landing and snapped her neck, killing her instantly. The rope momentarily snapped, and Katherine's lifeless body crashed to the floor.

Porphyria, being a hereditary illness and with no cure became a curse the Graham dynasty had to bear. It was as simple as potluck as to whether the off springs of the future would be afflicted with the terrible disease. It's more prevalent in females, though males are also on occasion struck down with the condition. The carriers could lead a normal life for many years and then suddenly feel its horrendous effects. Some may carry it and never be affected, but it seemed that each generation had some heir to spread the disease's deadly grip.

In the early 1800s, England was at the fore of the great industrial revolution. Now, more than ever, minerals from natural resources were required to maintain this progress and Hallowell was not immune. Before this time, the lands were mainly used for farming, areas would be leased to would be workers with the family taking a large share of the profits. But as coal became an essential component in industrial life, test borings were beginning, to discover what secrets were hidden beneath Hallowell. Good coal seems were found and in 1823, Hallowell colliery was formed.

With the colliery came growth. Workers from Ireland, Scotland and Wales flocked to the little village seeking security for their families that only employment in the pits could ensure. Housing was required, and shacks sprung up everywhere. Small holdings, leased from the Graham's and not fit for purpose were taken faster than they could be built. The population boomed, and the tiny hamlet came alive. Schools and shops were created, better housing for important workers began to be constructed, everything adding more money to the Graham coffers. In 1825, a man named George Stephenson had created the world's first steam powered railway engine, the Locomotion, and the Darlington and Stockton railway company was born. Created out of necessity to transport coal from northern mines to the coast, the idea was such a success that it was repeated nationwide in record time. Hallowell needed this technology too but as the village was surrounded by hills and mountains, a solution was required. Stephenson had also designed an invention named a steam incline. Simply, a series of ropes would be attached to wagons of materials on a railway line and a winding process, powered by steam would haul the bounty to the summit and lower the cargo down its opposite side thus eliminating the problem. The

Hallowell incline was completed in 1827 and productivity in the colliery tripled instantly.

The Graham family were suddenly high-end players in the mining industry and the Hallowell railway station was constructed. A massive six story structure with two smaller side buildings connected with a lower adjoining roof and standing upon a huge railway platform, it was the jewel in the Graham business empire. The offices were situated on the top floor where the rulers could look out upon their domain. It was also the only floor to house a window as only the Graham's deemed themselves important enough for such luxuries. The lowest two floors were used as a coal washing and sorting plant and the next two were a growing iron works, creating castings for gates and fencing. The fifth floor was needed only for storage. A winding elevator was central in the structure, man powered and created mainly so the rulers wouldn't need to climb six flights of stairs. A stone staircase, spiral in design was across to the far right of the building, steep and tasking and in almost total darkness, a menace to its unfortunate users. The side buildings were used only occasionally at first but in 1898, when the Hallowell tunnel was created, and the incline became redundant, passenger services from the railway station began and the building needed to become more functional. The buildings to the left were given over to the ticket office and public lavatories and washrooms. The buildings to the right were the station master's personal quarters where he and his kin would live. The conditions were cramped for a family, but the amenities were good, and the post was looked upon with a measure of respect. The occupation tended to be filled by a close Graham ally.

The platform was white concrete surrounded with a marble trim which was highly polished. The family insisted that the building was kept immaculate as it was a possession owned with tremendous pride, a measure of size and strength. Not an easy task with steam engines thundering past numerous times a day and the cargo being coal.

As the years progressed, Hallowell colliery maintained a high productivity and good profits though those finances were rarely ploughed back into the mine. Conditions were horrendous, even by the poor standards of the day. Accidents and deaths were commonplace, but the workers were trapped into accepting what they were given as there were many who would take their place, should they complain. And with no job, would come no home as the colliery cottages were perks for the workers. It was nicknamed 'Brocken backs' as most men who ventured into Hallowell colliery would invariably contract some form of disability in their tenure. Insufficient wooden shafts would cause cave ins. A lack of affordable pit lamps meant the men would be surrounded for vast lengths of time in blackness. Some workers would lose their sanity at the prospect of a life underground. And still the Graham's grew wealthier.

World War I hit the family hard. Of the four surviving Graham brothers, three were killed in the conflict. By the wars end, Martin Graham was the sole heir to the dynasty.

Born in 1900, Martin had been too young to serve in the Great War. By the time, he would have been called upon, the conflict had ended, and he found himself in a position of great power and responsibility. He was different to the generations that had passed before him and didn't see his workers as simply robots there to do his bidding. He respected human life and he acknowledged the need for change. Embarking upon a huge modernisation of the colliery, he was hailed as a hero to many locals who had previously hated the Graham regime and everything it stood for but had been powerless to fight it. Fatalities became rare rather than the norm as Martin believed a happy workforce was a productive workforce, something his late father would have scoffed at. The colliery expanded at a frightening pace, but it was done safely and securely. Britain was part of the great 1920s depression but somehow, Hallowell seemed immune. The Graham's future appeared bright.

In the year 1930, Martin Graham finally took a bride. Iris Piper was an eighteen-year-old beauty, twelve years his junior though the age gap seemed inconsequential. The pair fell swiftly for one another and after a whirlwind romance, the two were married. Martin's life seemed complete, he had a wonderful young wife, a thriving business and all the wealth and respect a man could ask for, but one thing was missing. Though they tried continuously, the pair could not conceive a baby.

As the years progressed, it began to seem that they would never be blessed with a family, an heir to the Graham bloodline. They considered adoption but neither felt the urge to rear someone else's child. Iris fell into depression, believing she had failed her husband by not giving him what he desired the most. Martin didn't blame his wife, instead wondering if the problem lay with him. All though his life he had been struck with the Graham curse, Porphyria. Now a medical explanation had been discovered for the inherent illness, he considered whether a symptom may lie in his defective gene. Depression was a large part of the disease though Martin fought valiantly against its side effect, trying hard to stay strong as Iris crumbled. Then suddenly, the miracle happened.

On October 13th, 1946, after sixteen years of marriage and agonising disappointments, Franklyn James Graham was born. When Iris had discovered the pregnancy, she'd maintained it secretly for months, desperate not to raise the hopes of Martin only to dash them should the pregnancy fail. She need not have worried as a huge twelve pound two-ounce baby boy was born healthily to the elation of the family and the town of Hallowell. Had they known then, what had just been created, the celebrations would surely have been short."

Chapter 11

"Franklyn?" Nick Castle looked puzzled.

"That's what I said." Mick was beginning to regret his openness. Every part of his being screamed *NO. DON'T BE SO FUCKING STUPID, JUST SHUT THE FUCK UP*. He'd spent years denying the existence of this backstory and now, here he was, spouting every detail to the one person he'd hidden it from. It seemed crazy and worse; he was terrified what his son would do with this information. Still, it was too late now. He couldn't quit, Nick would be ravenous for more and would do anything to get it.

"Franklyn, wait. Frank? Are you talking about Frank Graham? That mother-fucker in that building is the Graham's kid?" Mick grimaced; this wasn't going as planned.

"Yes, yes…yes. Frank Graham was a real person. The important word in that sentence is, *was,* was a real person. I don't know whether… Look, we're jumping way ahead here, if you want the whole truth, you need to be patient. I can't explain the parts you want without telling you the whole history."

"But…" Mick raised a hand.

"Listen, just say the word and we can stop. I don't give a shit, I'd rather be home, tucked up in bed, nice and warm and not having a tree branch sticking up my arse. Now, do you want to hear this, or not." Finally, Mick acted forcibly, keenly aware of what his son's answer what be. And this wasn't a bluff, if Nick surprised him and said let's go home, senior would be fine with that. He was torn already; this was Nick's call.

"Yes, of course I want to hear it. I only asked you a question, you don't need to get all pissy about it." Mick was standing, waiting to leave, though he didn't think for a second that they would be going anywhere, he just needed to appear serious, this was a long story and interruptions would make it longer. Instead, he took more branches from the readied pile and dropped them into the flames, the instant crackle was louder than he'd expected and made the fire ever fiercer, the turpentine had seen to that.

"Fine, but I'm warning you, keep butting in and I'm off. I mean it. I'm only telling you this because you're here and if I don't tell you, you'll pester some on else and get a load of bollocks. No one else would be willing to give you the time of day, at least not anyone who knows as much as I do. Maybe no one else does know as much as I do because I got the whole story from your grandfather, and he was in the thick of everything. So, if I'm doing this, I'm doing it my way, no questions asked." Mick settled back on the broken log, content that he'd managed to quell Nick's natural argumentativeness. There'd been just a nod of the head when his father had finished talking. Staring into the flames, Mick continued his story.

"The birth of a child is almost always a joyous occasion but for a family like the Grahams, and especially with the respect Martin had garnered over the years, the whole town celebrated. Iris glowed radiance that only a new mother can, Martin played the doting dad, the family seemed complete. Finally, an heir to the Graham dynasty.

From the beginning things were difficult. When pregnant with the boy, the baby was breach and all attempts to change the bodily direction failed. Two weeks prior to the due date during a routine check, no heartbeat could be heard from inside the womb and an emergency caesarean section needed performing, fast. When the child was delivered, there was no tears, no struggling, and no noise. The doctors assumed that the infant was still born but still frantically worked to rectify the situation. The airways were cleared, and heart massage performed but still, nothing. They were about to call their efforts when Frank let loose a powerful and wonderful cry. There were audible cheers from inside the maternity unit and from the group who had congregating outside its doors, the Graham family finally had the gift they desired the most.

But the emergency birth did cause significant problems. Firstly, the baby had been deprived of oxygen for a period and the medics were unsure if the incident had caused brain damage. The year was 1946 and medical advances were primitive in their development. It was a matter of crossed fingers and prayers to God. Secondly, the early days and weeks after birth are a vital time for the mother/baby relationship. The first feed, the first hug, the first smile. But Frank was detained in hospital for over a month as a precaution after the traumatic entry into the world. Vital bonding time was lost.

Through-out the development years, the boy was puny, weak, and sickly looking, like the rut of the litter. He developed a speech impediment which forced him to stutter when talking in front of strangers. The Graham's had access to the best medical treatment available, but it seemed the problem was psychological. There were fears, the Graham gene, the condition of porphyria, could be a contributing cause but there were no juvenile tests, and it wasn't thought to be part of the symptoms. He was a target for bullies in kindergarten and withdrew further into himself, speaking only when it was necessary and then, only with certain individuals. This alienation increased the attention from cruel classmates who looked at the boy as weird and detached. He refused to mix and hated school. This desolation would be a continuing factor throughout his life.

One early warning sign that Frank may have carried the defective gene was the imaginary world he created. Most children, as a way of stretching their imaginative development, play with dolls, and create characters for their playthings, but Frank needed no such materialistic props. His mind developed imaginary friends but unlike some children who answer to an invisible force, he would take on the form of these personalities, complete with differing accents and facial expressions. Never in front of anyone though, both Martin and Iris had witnessed the troubling phenomena secretly. What made it stranger was that, whilst taking on the form of another entity, the stutter would vanish. Only the natural voice which Frank used for everyday life, would continue with the exasperation problem. Martin played the situation down, claiming his son was simply doing what all children do and it was a phase that the boy would grow out of, whereas Iris saw the condition with a more sceptical view. A psychiatrist may have seen it as the start of schizophrenia, and had Martin agreed to Iris's calls to have the boy examined, the future may have turned out very differently.

The child, at early age began to develop an unhealthy obsession with his father. A seminal reason for this was the unwavering support and affection the Graham patriarch gave his son. Martin had resigned himself to never having an heir to continue the Graham bloodline so when Frank was born, all those hopes and dreams for the future suddenly become possible once more. In the child, he saw potential. How could he fail, born into wealth and privilege, with high academic achievers before him, a family name of respect and fear in equal measures and a father who dreamed of success for his off-spring and determination to help him achieve his goals. So-what that Frank was small and timid, genetics would see him grow and confidence would destroy the timidity. He was Martin Graham's son, hell, he was the last surviving Graham. Failure was not an option. And for Frank, he absorbed all the love and attention his father would drape over him. In Martin, he saw the man he wanted to be. In his mind, no one else had a right to his father's time. As the years progressed, this obsession would grow ever more lethal.

The opposite was certainly true with regards to Iris. The maternal bond between mother and son, the unbreakable, everlasting tie that binds a woman with her own child, never materialised. Perhaps, it was that missed time after the birth when the love is at its strongest and the instinct to protect envelopes the whole situation. Maybe it was that Iris was unwilling to excuse the infinitely strange behaviour of Frank whilst Martin continued to be blinkered. Someone needed to be rational and unemotional, their son was detached from reality and there had to be a reason. Had she had more authority over his upbringing, then perhaps she may have understood her son more, and been able to see into Frank's world, the way Martin seemed capable of doing. She tried, God knows she tried, but the closer she held him, the more he pulled away. He wasn't aggressive or hostile to her, not unless she demanded too much of her husband's time and attention. He was just inaccessible to her, unresponsive to her advances. Unemotional, uncompanionable, glacial, like interaction with a stranger.

As the years progressed, a divide was growing inside the Graham family. Frank's influence over the household and especially Martin Graham was evident. If Frank had been able to choose, he'd have eliminated Iris from the family altogether. She wasn't necessary. But shortly after his tenth birthday, Frank Graham would receive a present, a gift he'd grow to despise.

Jenifer Jane Graham was born on Christmas day, 1956. At thirty-eight, Iris had all but given up hope of future children and at fifty-six, Martin was feeling his age. He was still overjoyed to be a father again but with the pressures of business and a ten-year-old son, he was concerned they would struggle with the new arrival. He also feared what Frank's reaction to a new baby would be, a fear that would be more warranted than he could have ever imagined.

For Iris, Jenifer was a Christmas miracle, to Frank, she was a threat.

Over the previous decade, Frank had transformed physically if not psychologically. He'd sprouted in height and was no longer the midget in the corner. The Graham genetics had kicked in and he filled out in proportion to his height. But he'd become obsessed with size and strength. Finding some discarded dumbbells in the basement of the Graham mansion he worked out furiously and with increasing regularity. His thick set frame became muscular and wiry, he'd run for miles with immense determination, continuing to the brink of exhaustion, regularly vomiting due to the incredible exertion he applied to the effort. He'd eat vast amounts to bulk his frame and then work out more to ensure the calories weren't wasted.

And with the transformation, the bullying ended. He'd been tormented for years, children laughing at his stammer and poking fun at his appearance. Girls would pull his hair then be defended by the boys, so he couldn't retaliate. They'd make up rhymes and insulting songs, pushing him further and further into his own imaginary world. He'd be ostracised, pushed into a corner, and made to feel worthless. Sometimes the boys would follow him home, walking a few feet behind in silence just to intimidate him. Other times, it would be worse. Many was the day he'd arrive home from school with cuts and bruises after another beating. And who could he tell? Not Martin. His dad would be disappointed, Martin Graham's son, bullied by boys and worse still, girls. Off-spring of the same commoners who worked in their colliery. He'd suffered in silence. Suffered until he wouldn't have to suffer any more. For every drop of sweat he spilled, every muscle that ached after one too many lifts, every strain, pull or tear, it would be worth it to see his enemies pay; sweet, sweet, vengeance.

As for Iris, she finally had something to cherish. She'd questioned herself, repeatedly. What mistakes had she been responsible for, which made her son find her so irrelevant? Why, after so many years of trying, could she not form a bond with her first born? Was she simply not maternal? Was she so impossible to love and therefore, incapable of reciprocating the emotion? Well, with the birth of Jenifer, her beautiful, pure innocent little vessel, she finally realised that the fault had never been hers. She was suddenly fill with love, overwhelming, overpowering, unconditional love for something which could reciprocate that emotion. And with that realisation, it made her more afraid what her supercilious son was capable of.

The infant was mere days old when the troubled pre-teen held his baby sister for the first time. Inside the private hospital room, Martin looked on, with an air of pride, gazing joyfully at his complete family, once more unwilling to see beneath the surface. The only ones aware of the frightening reality, which loomed menacingly across the horizon were mother and son. A ten-year-old cradling an innocent infant, tucked in tightly to his chest, right arm supporting the head, trying hard to manufacture a smile, trying harder to overcome an omnipresent urge growing inside, a vile, malevolent, iniquitous urge to hurl the diminutive new-born down onto the highly polished tiled floor, and then bounce, up and down on its barely-formed head, until the lifeless body was vanquished from their lives. And as he battled against the villainous vision, Iris inwardly was screaming, 'Give me back my baby. You're nothing but an emotionless monster and I don't ever want you near my angel again.' Somehow, she remained silent, even smiling at the boy as he prepared to hand her back. Suddenly, Iris's blood ran cold. An ever-so-brief glance from the damaged youth's eyes toward his sister as the precious parcel was passed across the single bed's width, appearing full of contemptuous hatred, so heinously permeated, that words could scarcely describe the magnitude. A fleeting second which seemed to pause in desolate eternity. Iris Graham had never known fear this great and was abruptly aware that protecting her daughter from this monster would become her life's work.

Once the family settled into a home-life with four members, Frank's behaviour deteriorated rapidly. Beginning a reign of vengeance against those he perceived to have wronged him during his years at Hallowell primary school, violence came easy and with his new-found size and strength came confidence, and a willingness to hurt without conscience. Content to take on boys far older than himself, an advantage he soon discovered was a phenomenally high threshold for pain. Rivals would invariably back away due to Frank's maniacal fits of hysterical laughter, after receiving whatever injury he might sustain during a violent struggle. Black eyes, bloodied noses, cuts, bruises, abrasions, nothing seemed to matter to the young tough. Happy to contest against more than one opponent, the more injuries he sustained, the harder he fought. His peers now found their dislike of him replaced by a growing realm of trepidation. Soon, he'd become the most feared youth in Hallowell.

Graham could never be accused of sexism. Females who previously, had dared to torment him weren't immune to his thirst for vengeance. The first time Frank had run the risk of juvenile detention was due to an assault on one such girl.

For Gemma Scholes, this had been a horrible day. The sort of day when you wished you'd never got out of bed. In fact, that's where the problems began; the alarm on her bedside clock had failed, again, the third time this month. Anymore, and the headmaster, old Mr Stanhope would be sending a letter home to her mother. It was bad enough that she'd have a detention to look forward too at the end of the day for her tardiness, but if her mum found out about her habit for arriving to school after class had begun, she'd lose her allowance. Worse, she'd be grounded at the weekend and Saturday was the school disco; a disco which is for couples only, and if she wasn't available, her boyfriend Paul Dalton, wouldn't have a problem replacing her.

After bursting from her bed, she got a toothpaste stain down the front of her favourite sweater, and after taking a replacement from the laundry pile, the high temperature on the iron burned a scorch on the cuff. Next, there was no milk for her cornflakes, a tuff at the back of her blond hair refused to lay down and her homework was only half done, this was going to be a very bad day.

Throughout the school sessions, things hadn't improved. Mrs Terry, a dried-up old hag who pretended to be an English teacher had taken one look at the turned in homework and laughed. Gemma replied to the snigger in-type, exclaiming that she couldn't do the old woman's detention because the headmaster had already given her one. Terry seemed to take special pleasure when she explained that her punishment would be postponed until the next day, that way she'd be nailed twice, old bastard. The canteen had run out of macaroni-cheese before she got there, toad-in-the-hole, the only alternative. And finally, to cap off the perfect day, just before entering detention, she'd seen her wonderful Paul sneaking behind the bike-sheds hand in hand with the school slut, Michelle Maze, what a wanker.

Due to an oncoming storm, the November afternoon sky had turned very dark, very soon. It was almost a quarter before five when Stanhope had allowed her to leave detention, his were always fifteen minutes longer than all the others, using the title of headmaster to exercise unyielding power. His wife had died last year and since then, he'd become harder, less approached. It was time the old twat retired. Leaving the school-gates, she could feel a light mizzle of rain begin to gain strength. Suddenly it dawned on her that her overcoat was still rested across the back of her chair in Stanhope's office.

"Shit." Turning, she started back towards the main entrance, when across in the school car park, she noticed the headmaster's Triumph-stag, pull quickly onto the main road. "You have got to be kidding? Can this day get any worse?" In a final hope, she ran to the building's rear doors, sometime the caretaker, Mr Gaskins would be the last to leave, probably stealing school supplies. Seeing the doors closed, she knew it wasn't her day, but still, she pulled onto the entrance's silver bar, finding total resistance, the realisation dawning that by the time she arrived home, her clothes would be saturated. Lifting her pink canvas back-pack over the peak of her tied-up blonde hair, she shuddered a sudden chill as, to make matters worse, a stiff, front-facing wind had suddenly appeared. The only remedy for a day like today was a strong cup of tea and a warm duvet.

This was one of those times when the positioning of the Scholes family residence could cause serious aggravation. It had been almost a year since her parents had moved them into the newly built, four-bedroom council flat at the further part north of Hallowell. True, the accommodation was spacious, ultra-modern and finally delivering a bedroom, all to herself. Not that she didn't love her brothers dearly, but a teenage girl needs privacy, which wasn't forthcoming when their former residence forced her to share a bedroom with her two older siblings. Now her Beatles posters didn't have to share wall space with pictures of Bolton Wanderers football club players or snap shots of George Best. Finally, it was all hers.

The downside was the location. Hallowell didn't have a large population, but the village was spread out, and their home was at the farthest away point. There was a school bus, but with the number of after-school detentions she'd suffered, catching the damned thing was rare.

On nice summer days, the quickest route home was pleasant, especially when her best friend, Penelope Bundy was serving detention too. A nice trek through the woodland by the railway station and colliery was a good location to smoke plenty of cigarettes in secret before getting home. Unfortunately, Penny was usually a good-girl and rarely forgot her homework, so the route was usually taken alone. In the summer, that was fine, but it was autumn now, the clocks had changed two weeks prior to British wintertime, and by the time she'd started her journey home, it was already dark. Passing the last of the colliery cottages, her clothing was completely drenched, the rain gaining strength and turning to a full-blown storm. The gusting wind made the temperature feel colder than it actually was, and the backpack had now become useless as a shield, returning to her shoulder rather than covering her hair.

'After this day, nothing could be worse.' The earth had liquified underfoot, but the first of the trees gave some respite from the storm. Was that thunder in the distance? Hanging out in a small forest was not recommended. Gemma tried to quicken her pace but almost slipped, using a large oak for support. Her breathing laboured, she suddenly wished she'd made more effort in Mrs King's P.E. class instead of smoking behind the gym with Joan Gacy.

'Cigarettes. That's what I need.' She fumbled with the zipper of the wet bag but suddenly remembered that her fags were in her coat pocket and the coat pocket was attached to the coat, and the coat was in Stanhope's bloody office. 'Fuck, fuck, fuck.'

Suddenly, a flash of memory. There was a half-smoked roll-up in her jeans pocket, and she carefully slid a hand into the tightfitting clothing, meticulously retrieving her prize. The neighbouring back pocket contained a red disposable lighter, with the bare-minimal of gas inside. With the sorry looking smoke between her quivering lips, the lighter revealed its uselessness, refusing to strike, no matter how many times the exasperated girl tried. With each failure, her anger rose until she could take no more, hurling the inoperative plastic hard into the treeline. Strange, never heard it land. The cigarette was replaced into her pocket, aware that later, it may come in useful. Looking forward into the pitch-dark woodland, the urge to take the long-way home was almost irresistible, almost...

Deep into the woods now, the only visible directions were backwards and forwards, the trees forming a thick sideways barrier which appeared impenetrable, still, they were useful to feel her way along, the earth now completely turned to mud, pathway almost impassable. Once more, she considered turning around but knew that the ground behind would be just as transformed. The rain seemed harder now, avoiding the tree-line cover and smashing into its target with depressing regularity. The only shaft of light was coming from that railway station which appeared as uninviting as ever, the residue smoke from the last steam train, still heavy in the air.

'I'm certain that was thunder. This fucker is getting worse.' Stumbling forward, she was desperate to run but knew the ground was her enemy. I must be past half-way, surely? The first definite crack of thunder rumbled overhead and made her whimper. Thankfully, it seemed ahead there was light, she'd made it, not long now and she'd be warm, dry, and full of tea.

The blow to the back of the head was painful and unexpected, her body falling to a crumpled unconscious heap on the floor. Had her situation registered in her mind before the attack, she'd have known just what trouble she was in.

The second of Tom Wade's barns was barely used, the harvest crops collected, bailed, and sold. It was lonely, desolate, only used for an occasional hide-out for horny couples, and just off the woodland path. For Frank Graham, it was the perfect location. He'd dragged the unconscious girl across the liquified earth, one shoe lost to the foliage. Not that that mattered now, its partner removed, as were her jeans, her bare ankles bound with thick twine, along with the wrists. Her body stretched out across the filthy floor, discarded sheaves of hay stabbing into her bare legs. Not that this attack was sexually orientated, Graham couldn't care less about such things. This was vengeance, plain and simple. By the time Gemma regained her bearings, it was instantly obvious that she was helpless. A gag had been forced deep into her throat, making her wretch and a blindfold had been fitted, though it had slipped free. Not that it mattered; he needed her to know who was responsible, that the tables had turned, that he wouldn't be bullied anymore, that he was the one with all the power.

For Frank Graham, this had been planned perfectly. Time had been taken for the precise place to pounce, the best location for privacy, and the ideal props to cause maximum terror, this was going to be fun.

Gemma Scholes felt the cold concrete beside her face, bare legs freezing, her ankles and wrists bound in such a way that movement was impossible, the thick twine knotted over and over, making her flesh feel raw. Still, she refused to panic, this is Hallowell, nothing bad ever happens here. Maybe it's a prank gone too fat, perhaps Paul had realised that the town bike was nothing compared to her. What she couldn't understand was why he'd even look at over girls; she never said no to him, ever. A trickle of blood ran down the side of her face.

Wait, I was hit over the head, knocked out, it is fucking hurt, none of my friends would go this far. She shuffled her head across her shoulders as briskly as she could, the blindfold slid down her face, one eye peaking over the obstacle, the room looked empty. Suddenly her eyes caught a glimpse of her bare legs, the skin was barely visible, from the tops of her thighs, down to her ankles she had been smeared with something, something sticky, uncomfortable. Her line of sight was still mainly blocked but another sense kicked in. She sniffed hard, it was recognisable, *oh, if I could just, touch it,* she lifted her right leg as high as the pain would allow, sniffing once more, Jesus, I almost hard it, rubbing her legs together, the substance squelched, globules lying across the sticky mess.

'THAT'S IT, I GOT IT, ITS…JAM, STRAWBERRY JAM, WHAT THE FUCK.'

A door across the far side of the room opened, Gemma tried hard to push the blindfold completely but managed to make things worse, only her right eye could watch the action. She wanted to shout and scream, 'Let me out of this you sorry mother fucker. Let me go or my brothers will make you wish you'd never been born.' She wanted to stand and fight and tear out hair and kick some balls…but it was impossible. She couldn't scream, she couldn't fight. She was helpless, at the whim of a madman.

The footsteps came from behind, she bent her neck in a way nature hadn't intended and saw… A long boiler suit, worn and dirty, a tear in the left knee, button up high, the signs of a white t-shirt around the collar. Long straggly locks and an attempt at facial hair. It was, no it couldn't be, not him. The arches of the face seemed pure Graham, but he'd been missing for months, left school to work for his dad, the nose, the lips, the eyes…oh God, the eyes, it is him, its Frank Graham, he's done this, but why? What did I ever do to him? Maybe a little teasing, but the idiot stuttered every time he read in class. So yes, we picked on him, it was fun, he was an easy target, he never fought back, I remember when Tommy Jarvis flushed his head down the toilet and we all watched and laughed. The rumours where Tommy had taken a piss in their first and we all called him Pissy for months, that was great, but…oh fuck, I'm in trouble.

The footsteps stopped by her feet, now she knew who'd attacked her, Christ, he was standing in front of her, and she probably knew why. What was he going to do? She was helpless, if the gag was gone, she could apologise, beg for forgiveness, it would be worth it, she didn't have to mean it, but even that was impossible. He was carrying a grey canvas bag, it looked heavy. For a moment he just stared at her with an intense smirk, knowing that he had total power, it felt great. She could only stare back, praying that the punishment wouldn't be extreme. Something inside the bag moved, and the more things did, like animals fighting, a high-pitched squeal came from inside. Then she remembered her legs, was it jam? It certainly looked that way, what the fuck was his plan? More fighting from inside the bag, Graham took no notice, simply staring at the visible part of Gemma's face. It could have been so different, all she had to do was like me, maybe give me a complement, she was the ringleader, she could have made them stop. Instead, she made it worse, her and her friends had tortured him, now it was him turn.

He'd prepared well. The stray rats were a good size, three of them. He'd caught them in traps by the station, there was plenty to choose from. They'd had separate boxes, strong wooden pallet sides, there was no escape. For three days, they'd been trapped, scratching, and chewing endlessly, one had nipped Frank's right hand when he was transferring them to the bag, a trickle of blood dripping on to the canvas, the second rat immediately wanted a taste. Once inside, they were still, unsure of their neighbours, a strange stand-off. When one would move, the others would snarl, but attack was a last resort. They all had one thing in common, none had been fed for three days, and their hunger was ravenous.

Standing before her feet, he untied the rope holding the bag closed, the knot was hard and took time. By now, Gemma had figured out his plan and began to panic, thrashing with all her might, not caring that the twine was cutting into her flesh. Mumbled screams that no one could hear, tears of terror, tears of regret…

The rope pulled free, and the bag seemed to grow in size, instead of grabbing the animals one by one, risking another bite, he threw a hand to the bottom seam and spun the bag upside down with the contents falling to the floor; three giant rats.

Gemma wasn't sure where to look, Graham seemed to have only joy for his task and the rats were momentarily blocked from her sight by the blindfold. One more thrash of the head and her vision was on longer impaired. Perhaps, it would have been better if the blindfold had remained in place, now she couldn't help but watch the rats as they approached their prize. The strawberry jam was layered thickly across both legs, for the rats, it seemed like the dinner bell. Thrashing as the approached would scare them back, but not for long. Her head throbbed, that blow must have been harder than she first thought. Pushing it from her mind, she continued to fight, what fight the straps would allow. Frank had retreated, not out of fear, he just wanted to ensure that Gemma was the target.

The stand-off continued for fifteen minutes though it seemed longer. Sweat was dripping from every part of her body, when one rat would retreat, another would take its place. It was an ongoing war that she was destined to lose. The first rat that contacted her body was the smallest of the three. Her attention had been on the double tag-team whilst the other stealthily chose its spot. Creeping from behind, the taste of the sticky desert registered in its mind, and the feeling was addictive. The spot behind the knee, where the calf meets the thigh, soft supple flesh, an irresistible mission. The teeth sliced though, blood dripped, the nose buried deep into the meat, the beginning of Hell.

By the time a passing dog walker heard her blood curdling screams and ran to her assistance, more rats had joined the party. The gag had been released from her mouth as the largest rat had gnawed through the material, just inches from were face. She'd had to endure the terror of seeing the disgusting creature, its horrible twitching nose touching her skin, praying, with the hope it would indivertibly assist her escape. Except for one, the rats fled when George Towers, a spry seventy-two years old with an army background and a stern voice burst through the barns locked doors. It had taken three strong kicks before the lock gave, he'd considered finding the owner, Tom Wade, before breaking the lock, if he had it would have been too late. The rat which had refused to flee had torn a hole in Gemma's sweater, down the middle adjacent to her stomach. The skin-tight white under-vest had caused little problem, the creature's claws making short work of the obstacle. With the sight of untouched pale skin, soft and meaty, the bellybutton in view, the rat had caused the first scratch, four inches across, the flesh had broken, and blood was bubbling to the surface. Had the old man not entered at that precise moment, the girl would certainly have perished, the blood loss would have been too extreme, and the internal organs would have been ravaged. A furious swipe of his walking cane and the creature squealed, flying and landing with a bang. It had turned back, its prize too great, the meal too sweet, but after seeing George ready for another thrust, it reconsidered, the danger seemingly too much to fight for.

The straps were difficult to untie, not because of the knots, but for the hysteria of the victim. An ambulance was called, and she was taken to St Mara hospital, her parents and Bill Castle following closely by. Initially, charges were filed, and it seemed the troubled youngster would finally face punishment for the crime. Gemma's injuries were mainly superficial, flesh wounds, bites that would leave scarring, a serious gash around her left big toe where one of the vermin had chewed through to the bone. Most would heal without the need for severe medical treatment. The greatest worriment that remained was the psychological effect the girl faced. Her personality had been shattered; where once she was brave and out-going, she became introverted and reclusive. Her schooling was over, she refused to leave the house alone, and when she was forced, it was only with accompaniment. Her dreams were invaded by filthy creatures, snakes, spiders, all manner of vermin, and rats, lots of rats. She'd wake up screaming deliriously, dementedly fighting off help, unable to comprehend the difference between the real world and the fantasy of dreams. Her psyche had been pulverised, maybe for ever. The charged were eventually dropped."

"You've got to be fucking joking." It was the first time Nick Castle had interrupted in quite a while, being too engrossed in the horrific tale to speak. "He shatters a girl's life...and there's no punishment?" Mick raised a hand and immediately, the young man fell quiet.

"I've told you, leave your questions till the end. Okay?" Nick nodded dutifully.

"The charges were dropped for one reason, the power that the Graham's wielded over Hallowell. Martin Graham arrived at the hospital almost as swiftly as the girl's parents. Looking tanned and wealthy, he acted smoothly, enquiring about the girl's condition, and commiserating the situation. Initially, Rob Scholes, Gemma's father, was irate, demanding justice and Frank's incarceration. Martin listened intently, nodding at certain stages, giving no opinion until the angry parent had finished his tirade. Then, sliding an arm across Scholes's shoulder, he delivered his retort.

Without raising his voice, he made it perfectly plain that, should his son face charge, Rob's position at Hallowell colliery would be immediately terminated. Since the family had recently moved from one of the colliery cottages, the threat of homelessness was off the table, but without a salary, the large, rented property to which they'd grown accustomed to would no longer be affordable. Option two was as such, Frank's crime would go unpunished, Rob Scholes would be promoted from his role as a miner to an office official, no more coughing up black covered phlegm and destroying his lungs, no more strenuous manual labour at a time when his body was beginning to break down, and a generous pay raise to accommodate his new profession. His sons, whom were almost of working age were promised appointments directly from leaving school with the promise that promotion would be a probability in the future. Their family's livelihood would be secure with cash to spare and an easier life. Martin delivered the choices with a frighteningly docile tone, as if this was an everyday incident and something he'd been expecting. Without any real option, the charges were dropped, and Frank became one step closer to the monster he'd eventually become."

Cautiously Nick raised a hand, like a timid schoolboy needing the teacher's attention.

"I must be losing it. You've said the name over and over, but it didn't register. Scholes? Gemma... Scholes? Was she...?"

"Yes Nick, very clever. Gemma was Billy's aunt. But remember this. Hallowell is a small village; certain families have their fingerprints all over it." This was the part Mick had been dreading.

"But..."

"If you want to hear the rest of this, shut and be quiet. Now, where was I... By 1961, Frank was fifteen but appeared more like a full-grown adult. A freak of nature, six feet four inches tall and a hard-powerful physique, it wasn't only the other children that now feared him. After the Scholes incident, Frank dropped out of school. Not that he feared repercussions as most of his peers avoided him at all costs.

No, the teenager now had a new obsession, as he'd taken what he felt was a fair amount of vengeance towards those who had wronged him, the Graham business empire, and more importantly, his father, Martin Graham. Throughout the working day, he'd shadow his forebearer, without a care that the surrounding village had nothing but distain for him. The only remnant of the Scholes incident was the huge disparagement of contempt towards the Graham family. The heinous circumstance may have been perpetrated by the boy, but it was Martin that ensured that his son would not answer for the repugnant event. Feeling that that sort of abuse of power could affect any resident who crossed the young thug's path, the whole population became evasive and cold whenever there were dealings with the family. It was obvious though hidden under a blanket of need, unwilling to anger the Graham's but the friendly posterior which had survived for so long had now vanished.

In response, the change had a seriously adverse effect on the village's main employer, who became hardened toward his workforce and the extended families. Gone were the days when he'd share a beer with the workers on a Sunday afternoon in the bar of the workingmen's club. The formerly approachable and friendly patriarch of the business empire, he'd suddenly become cold and intense, only interacting with the workforce's upper echelon, and even they were wary of his mood-swings. It was apparent that Martin had become fearful of looking weak in front of his boy, preferring to now rule with force, a disturbing trait for those closest. Knowing how the villages populous saw his son and resenting them for it, he struggled to understand their concerns.

My son has his troubles what teenage boy hasn't, but to be so ostracised by the very people that our colliery supports, the people who would starve were it not for my empire. It won't do. It's unfair, worse, its treason, mutiny in the ranks. My son will show them all, one day he'll prove what only I can see; and until then, I'll keep him safe, no matter what.

It took little time for Frank's shadow to cast heavily over Hallowell colliery. His first target was a man named Wes Hooper, an energetic well mannered, fifty-year-old with thinning grey hair and a previously handsome face that had suffered from too many liquid lunches, the lines across his brow and below the eyes quickly becoming more prevalent than had he lived a clean life. Working from the colliery floor to the washing plant inside the station, he'd moved into management after being diagnosed with prostate cancer in 1960. When the disease had gone into remission, he'd offered to retake his previous position, though Martin had seen enough of his white-collar skills to know where the man's strengths lay. After managing the washing plant for eighteen months, he became assistant manager of the whole colliery, answering only to Martin. This is where the problem arose.

Their working partnership developed into something more, the two men were of similar age and though their backgrounds were greatly different, Wes was a fast learner. His increased salary and willingness to adapt saw him enjoy rounds of golf with his boss on Sunday mornings frequent the same restaurants, all while continuing to excel in his role. Perhaps, Hooper's greatest strength though, lay in being an award-winning arse-kisser. Should Martin tell a joke, his laughter would roar the loudest to the point of being obnoxious, if it was birthdays or Christmas, his gift would be the largest, the most expensive. While those around would see the creep for what he was, Martin had taken a liking to him, classed him as a friend. For Frank, Wes Hooper was a threat, a threat that must be destroyed.

The colliery offices were positioned inside the main building of the neighbouring railway station and as usual, Wes Hooper was the last remaining employee working at the end of hours, late, Friday night. A heavy pipe smoker, something he knew his employer despised, the aging man stared out from the building's only window, the glass barrier opens to its full width as to not contaminate the office with the smell of tobacco, the village in the distance, colliery to his right, increasing troubles burdening his mind.

For months, he'd known his wife was having an affair, she'd barely tried to hide it. Her lover, a butcher named Gregory, had parked the business van outside the house while they were doing the deed. For the last week, he'd walked home on his dinner break every day, only to find his rival's vehicle parked by the kerb outside their colliery-leased house on Station view. Earlier today, he'd found the courage to enter their home only to hear groans from above. Since his cancer treatment had left him 'limp as lettuce', hearing the cries of passion just made him sad. Instead of announcing his presence, fighting for his honour, and renouncing his scarlet woman, he'd quietly closed the front door behind him and returned to his office. The conformation had come as some strange relief.

To make matters worse, earlier in the week he'd been told by his specialist that the cancer had returned. It hadn't come as a surprise; Wes was a diplomatic man who rarely enjoyed the highs of life and therefore the lows were somewhat more acceptable. The treatment last time had been almost intolerable, he'd given up so many times only to reconsider after lectures from his wife. This time, it didn't seem that he even had her support. Inside, he knew that his time, the illness would win, he couldn't face another battle.

In the distance, the house lights were shining brightly, hundreds of lives with hundreds of everyday problems. Worrying about paying bills, their kids schooling, nickel and dime shit. In the glass, he saw a reflection he barely recognised. Another chin growing under his normally tight face, too many liquid lunches with Martin, all that damned whiskey. God, his boss could drink, and he needed to keep up, double for double, treble for treble, this wasn't him but what option did he have, all the work he'd done making Martin his friend as well as his superior. He couldn't fall back; he couldn't look like a pussy. But now, that bastard cancer was back, eating him away, taking his fight, taking his manhood. Christ, he couldn't even get a hard on, he couldn't fuck his own wife, she had to turn to that stinking butcher. Fuck, what he'd like to do to that twat, WHAT COULD HE DO.

He hadn't even realised that he was holding a glass of whisky, fuck, he didn't even like the taste, it was a habit he needed to break. The glass container chunked loudly as it crashed against a set of metal drawers, sliding to the edge, and almost falling to the floor. Not that he'd have cared, the realisation that this fight was unwinnable now filled him. He returned to the open window, the evening air refreshing him, the breeze sliding smoothly across his skin. A smile grew though he had no idea why. Stepping to the ledge, he wondered what it would be like to push on through, to force his cancer-riddled body through the air and suddenly feel no more pressures, no more pain, no more…

When it landed, Wes Hooper's body had disintegrated into fragments of death, pulverised by landing across the corner of the platform, the edge slicing through his spine and almost cutting his carcass in two. The back of his head had crashed into the train tracks, the steel destroying his skull in one destructive smash, jets of blood exploding and turning the area red. Both bones on his right arm had splintered, slicing through his skin, and forming a point, the right leg folding under the body and vanishing. The left side, bar for the jetted blood stains were perfect, not a break, not a scratch, normal.

It was over in seconds and Wes Hooper was gone. Perhaps the whiskey had eroded his senses, the relaxed state, gazing into the night sky, the cool night air lowering his impressionably. Maybe he'd looked at his options, and seen nowhere else to go, death being that easy way out. Unfortunately, none of that was true.

Wes Hooper had climbed dangerous out onto the ledge. He was under the influence, desperate and depressed, lonely, and alone. He had the knowledge that the killer disease had returned, and his chances of survival had diminished. But suicide, not at chance.

The air had been refreshing. Wes enjoyed staring out at the village, seeing where he'd come from, a shitty one-bedroom colliery-cottage, and where he was now, the smartest street in Hallowell, Station View. Shame that bastard undertakers place was in the middle of their row but even that seemed to blend in. Only the cream of Hallowell got a home here. His home had been lived in by the Town physician, 'Doctor Brackett' before he bought land and moved across town. His wife had been so proud the day they moved in; life had been good then.

The office space had been darkened, all the lamps at the desks had been extinguished, the outer corridor lights too, Martin was a stickler for fighting waste. The only luminous area was a florescent strip light, bathing Hoper's desk in an orange glow. The open window was across the room, fifteen feet from his desk. His presence had been so silent for so long that if anyone else had been in the room, he'd have been easy to miss. Unfortunately, one person knew he was there.

He could see his street, there was a van parked three houses up, surely that couldn't be the butcher at this time of night, they couldn't be so brazen.

The movement into the doorway was silent, there was no light to block, no shadow to cast. He stiffened and held his breath, could he really do this, could he take this final step? Cautiously, he began to stride forward, the footsteps making no noise.

It hadn't always been this way. He'd been a man, once. A man's man. A real man. If his wife got out of line, she'd get a slap, or maybe a punch. If things were bad, he would kick her. He'd done that once. £40. Fucking £40. That's what he'd paid for that shirt, mail ordered from London, Savile Row, in 1960. £40 was a lot of money. The first time he'd worn it, he felt different, powerful. Martin had commented about his appearance immediately, it was amazing, and then…the stupid cunt boil washed it. When it came out, it wouldn't have fit a five-year old, but she'd been sorry. Wes beat her every way from Sunday, punches, kicks, he even bit her on the arm. The good old days. But then the cancer came. He went from a solid thirteen stone eight pounds to ten stone two. The treatment was horrendous and when things got bad, he didn't have the energy to take it out on her. He'd tried once, she'd made a meal when she knew the chemotherapy made him sick to his stomach. The plate had flown, across the room, smashing on the kitchen wall but when he turned to her…the strength was gone, worse, she grabbed him by the throat, pinning him to the door, and threatening that if he ever raised a hand to her again, she'd stab him while he slept. The look on her gnarly face told him she meant every word. Then there was his cock. Bastard treatment, he couldn't get hard in a room full of hookers with everything on show. He'd tried, God knows he'd tried. Magazines, blue movies, even got her to 'give him a rub'. NOTHING. What was left, no sex…ever. The trips he'd taken alone to Thailand, Christ, the pussy available there was for next to nothing, better than he could get at home, that's for sure. No wonder his cock was limp, she'd frightened him away, nasty bitch. As he lowered his gaze from Station View, a tear fell for those, 'Good old days'.

He was ten yards away, surely Wes would see him coming. What excuse could he use if he turned around right now? His pace quickened, five yards now, Frank could see his reflection behind Hooper's in the glass. One glance up and he was fucked. Graham tensed his shoulder muscles, took a strong stance, if he was going to do it, the time was now.

Hooper took a deep breath, and exhaled onto the window, the glass steaming, Wes looked up, his reflection staring back, but strangely he wasn't alone. The surprise turned to shock, then fear, the look on the teenager's face was pure rage. He spun around towards Frank, but his footing was awkward, his muscles limp. As Graham's arms hit the fifty-year-old's chest, the blow was paramount to his plan. One huge shot and he'd be gone. But the back of Hooper's head bounced painfully off the sheet of glass, momentarily knocking him senseless, the room became swirl. Instantaneously came the second commanding pummel, a harsh grip across Wes's narrow shoulders that turned into vigorous exerting thrust. Sliding clumsily past the ledge, a hand grasping ineffectually for a safety net which would never come, the body stopped for a second, both legs bent tightly inside the window, an insignificant pause, a silent scream, a man unable to grasp that his life was ending. Finally, the legs slid free, a black-leather shoe falling inside the building. For a few seconds, there was silence, and then, came the thud. Frank stepped back, not daring to appear at the window in case there were witnesses. He turned and headed for the stairs; the lift wasn't for him. Before descending the first flight, he smiled, the grin of a man content, his work was done."

"Wait, wait, wait." Nick could stay silent no longer, the tale fascinatedly gruesome, but too extreme to take in. "If people knew he was a killer, why wasn't he arrested, the Graham name couldn't have been strong enough to cover that up."

"Because no one knew he'd killed Wes, his wife was screwing the local butcher, his cancer had come back, if anyone had a reason to jump, it was him. It was just rumours, chit-chat, and bullshit. No one really believed that the psycho teenager was a killer. The proof came much later."

"Jesus." Nick's face had lost all colour.

"I think I told you, Jesus hasn't got nothing to do with this place. Now please, can I continue?"

Solemnly, Nick nodded his head. His father rose and threw a thick log onto the fire, the sparks shooting into the night sky, the oils in the dried wood coming alive and crackling in the flames. Retaking his seat, the story continued.

"From nowhere, suddenly Frank Graham was assistant manager of Hallowell colliery, a position that was despised by the men who were overlooked. One of them was Rob Scholes. The management position he'd been offered for overlooking Frank's problems with his daughter was overseeing the washing plant. Yes, he was out of the mine, all the back-breaking labour, but at what cost. The girl that was Gemma Scholes was lost, maybe forever. She spent days in her bedroom, ran when the doorbell rang, Christ, she was frightened of her own shadow. It was heart-breaking to see what that animal had done to her…and now he was Rob's boss.

His hands were tied but the feeling around Hallowell's continued odious attitude toward the Graham's refused to diminish. Iris Graham felt accusing eyes on her as she shopped in the village, heard whispers as by she passed doorways. Workers tried to find alternate employment away from the colliery, not wishing to be beholding to men they no longer respected. The family began to represent solitary figures. That Sunday drink with the boys, in Hallowell workingmen's club, joining in well-meaning banter. Now, he no longer felt welcome. The one time he had tried, all conversation had stopped, and most drinkers immediately left, making their feelings plain. Martin had been so angry, he considered firing those who had shunned him, but the union threatened to strike, and the termination plans were shelved. The days of the Graham's being royalty of the village were gone.

Rob may have been powerless for retribution, but others weren't. Adam and Carl were twins, four years their sister's senior and extremely protective. Their initial response was to go after Frank immediately but were encouraged to wait. In time, the suspects for an assault on Graham junior would surely increase, the hostility in Hallowell gaining traction. After almost two years, it was decided, they'd waited long enough.

It was a cold January evening, a little past five. The final passenger train had left, and Hallowell railway station was deserted. The thin coating of snow that had covered the platform earlier had frozen due to the stark northeast wind and the bare branches on the adjacent trees shook violently. Echoes from the colliery works rang out across the desolate ground and Frank Graham was closing for the night. The ticket vendor had brought down the shutters to his office and left, the coal washing area finished at four thirty and the iron works had ceased trading the previous year. The elevator just been repaired but Frank still preferred to use the dark spiral staircase to exit the main building. Small gas-powered lights dimly illuminated the stone steps and Frank had to extinguish each as he passed them, the shadows that remained resembled ghostly apparitions which a normal person would flee from. To Frank Graham though, this was home.

Before exiting he checked that the ground floor was empty (not that there was anything worth stealing) then heaved the huge iron doors closed. Even then, it took real strength to close them with the concrete floor clinging to metal and screaming out across the empty platform. After locking, he checked the station master quarters door, which was now disused after the role was deemed unnecessary. It had been junior's idea when he reassured his father that he was more than capable to maintain the buildings upkeep and a salary would be saved. Martin had been dubious, but his son had a way of getting what he wanted and within a fortnight, the station master and his wife were on the streets. The young man planned to move his belongings to the quarters in time, an easy way to avoid his mother and sister, but for now, the building was empty.

All that was left was the washrooms on the opposite side of the main structure. He made a swift tug on the closed ticket office shutter, checking it was secure, and was about to lock the washroom door when he heard a tap running from inside. Proceeding on, he noticed the two white porcelain washbasins in the corner of the room were flooding over. Water had reached the top and was cascading over the lip, onto the floor and had obviously been that way for some time as the whole area was drenched. Frank rushed across, water splashing over his black work boots and on the hem of his blue coveralls. Quickly, he shut off

106

the taps, noticing that paper towels had been forced into the sinkholes to prevent the water escaping. Rolling up his right overall sleeve, he forced his fingers around the sodden paper to release the deluge. More liquid spilled over the lip and splashed down over his crotch, and he momentarily jumped at the cold sensation.

'F, F, F, F, FUCKING VANDALS.' His stammer got progressively worse the more tired he became. 'S, S, S, STRING THE LOT OF T's, T, T, THEM UP.' He was so preoccupied with the flooding; he never noticed the figures standing inside the toilet stalls.

Before Frank even had an inkling of an attack, he was already on the floor. Adam Scholes fired the first blow. His aim was true, as his sawn-off broom shank struck his target across the back of his knees, dropping Graham with one shot. Falling hard to the ground in the enclosed space, his forehead bounced heavily off a basin, immediately slicing a gash just above his eyes. When he gained his bearings, there was three assailants over him, raining down blows from all angles, all armed with wooden shanks. To ensure a measure of disguise, all three wore balaclavas, only their eyes visible, and wearing Hallowell colliery issued overalls. Carl Scholes slipped in the standing water and found himself lying beside their victim. Graham made a grab for the mask but the third assailant, Charlie Challis brought a strong work boot down on the stricken teenager's arm and heard an audible crunch as the bone inside snapped like a broken branch. Frank screamed out in pain and Challis seemed visibly shocked at what he'd just done. Adam pulled his younger brother to his feet (Carl had been born 28 minutes after Adam, a fact that the older sibling rarely allowed him to forget) then continued the attack. In the mayhem, Carl had released his weapon, and, in the confusion, Frank had found it. He tried to retaliate, swinging the wooden shaft aggressively towards the three but the pain from the assault was taking a toll. Challis grabbed for the weapon and as the two fought over ownership,

With all his might, Adam fired a sickening shot to the crown of Graham's skull, becoming immediately obvious that the blow had caused catastrophic impairment, his eyes rolling back in his head, and muscles going limp. With his grip weakening on the shaft, Challis tugged it from his grasp. A fierce kick from Carl to Frank's face and the oversized teenager crashed onto his back, residue water splashing on his face, blood streaming from a broken nose and the gash across his forehead. A crater-like laceration appeared over the top of Graham's skull and blood was erupting from it, like lava from a fiery volcano. His body started to convulse, shaking uncontrollably. White froth foamed from the corners of his mouth and his eyes appeared lifeless.

The three assailants looked to one another, hoping for guidance, and finding none. This wasn't how it was supposed to go down. They just wanted to teach him a lesson, give him a kicking, and put him in his place. What if he died? That would make them murderers. They couldn't call for help, if they did, they would be finished. Adam was going to university in the summer, he wanted to be a solicitor. He could forget all that with a manslaughter charge hanging over him. And Carl, he was in the army, only home on leave. The only fighting he'd look forward to if they were found out would be fending off male rape in the showers of the prison. And Charlie, he was only here because Adam was his best friend, and they weren't sure having only two would be enough to overpower Graham. He was his mother's sole support after his father had died last year. How would she ever cope if her son went down for this.

They had no choice. Adam scrambled though Graham's pockets and found the washroom keys. Frank looked in a bad way, his skin was pale and eyes, unresponsive. There was still two inches of cold water and with the winter temperature, he could easily die of hyperthermia but what option did they have. Carl and Charlie were at the exit and ushered Adam to hurry. As he rose, Frank's hand made a final grab for him in one last defiant act. Perhaps, it was a beg for mercy, but the twin remembered the condition Gemma had been in when she'd been discovered in that barn and all the sympathy left his body. Frank's hand went limp, and Adam Scholes dropped the lifeless limb into the cold water. Crouching down to Graham's ear he whispered, 'That's for my sister you son of a bitch.' With that, he climbed to his feet and headed for the door. He took one final look back before exiting. He couldn't be sure but for a moment he thought he saw Frank smile."

Chapter 12

"Charlie Challis? Charlie fucking Challis. This is unreal. Over a decade ago, I walk into the station on Halloween night with three friends. Yes, we shouldn't have been there, I know we shouldn't have been there, tough shit. Those friends are Johnny Brackett, Billy Scholes, and Dan Challis. First, Johnny Brackett, the son of the only person in this village who has enough stroke to make problems disappear. Second, Billy Scholes, his auntie is attacked, traumatised and left for dead by Frank Graham. So, billy's uncles' smash shit out of that bastard and leave him for dead. And then, finally, there's Dan Challis. And guess what, just when things couldn't get any weirder, his uncle joins in the fun and helps leave Graham for dead. You really couldn't write this shit." Nick Castle had his fingers entwined throughout his long black hair, the insanity of the situation barely comprehendible.

"And what? What's your point? I've told you that this is a small village, everyone's up in everyone else's business, there is bound to be some cross-pollination." Mick was trying to make the situation appear inconsequential, though he knew his son wasn't stupid.

"What's my point? Come on, don't take me for a fool. There's coincidence and then there's…"

"That's it. I've had enough, I'm going home." Senior felt the best way to deflect was to attack. Refusing to be denied, Nick retaliated with fury.

"The hell you are. Stop threatening me with that bullshit, you want to get this off your chest, otherwise we wouldn't be here." Mick sat back, his eyes wide, strangely impressed with the young man's effrontery. It was true, this tale had burned a hole inside him for far too long and had destroyed what was once a strong father-son relationship. Perhaps, only honesty could alleviate that shattered bond. The truth had been adjourned for as long as he could stand.

"You got me there. I do need to divulge this shit, come clean, get it off my chest, whatever way you want to put it. Maybe this is my confessional, you can play priest." Mick paused, tears beginning to well in the corner of his eyes though he refused to allow the young man the satisfaction of seeing him cry. Still, he knew that he'd lost the upper hand, there was only one direction now. "I told you I'd be honest, and I have been. There has been no bullshit from me tonight, whether you wish to believe me or not. Now, I'm not a fan of coincidences, but this time, you'll need to take my word for it. I know my word doesn't mean all that much to you but ask yourself, what reason do I have to lie? I accept it sounds unbelievable, you, Johnny, Billy, and Dan. Four best friends, all joined together forever by the most horrible of circumstances, and then, you find out that all our

109

families are interwoven by this fucking shit too. Maybe there's some cosmic force out there, bigger than all of us that makes all this fit into place and make sense. But that's probably just a bunch of bull and like the guy says, shit happens. I mean, what were the chances that you four would be friends? You could have chosen anyone, why Billy, Johnny, and Dan. And on top of that, you guys just happen to land in the one place that brings this whole shit together. All the stuff that happened to our families, happened before you lads were born. I know that you don't want to believe me, and you have every right not too but, these things that happened, just happened, just coincidence." Nick had to admit that what his father was saying made sense. There was just one thing.

"You keep saying our families, but apart from what I was responsible for on Halloween night, what else do we have to do with this?"

"Give it time."

"Iris Graham focused deeply on her reflection, reverberating from the great antique Victorian mirror hanging in the hallway of the Graham mansion. Its value would feed half of the town for months. Dated in 1869, it was a piece that serious collectors had offered vast amounts for across the years, but each generation had fought the temptation, happy in the knowledge that every year it remained, would be an extra ring's appraisal the value tree.

For once, she saw what she liked in its reflection. It had been a long time since she'd found anything to smile about but today was a good day. The heavy lines that darkened the skin under her eyes were covered with a fresh layer of foundation, eye liner and mascara extenuated the lost beauty of her baby blues. It was disturbing how much assistance was now needed to make a once radiant reflection into something that was passable. Hopefully, today was worth the effort. If not, what would be?

She was adamant her tiredness wouldn't spoil the occasion. Hell, even Frank wasn't allowed to spoil today. The cream pantsuit bought only yesterday from Hanley's in St Mara was a little old fashioned for a forty-s… Oh my God, was that all the age she was. That smile was starting to fade. No, not today, it was too important, her marriage may depend on it.

Adjacent in the hallway, Martin preened himself before his own mirror, another antique that was three generations old, part of this lived-in tomb since the dawn of mankind. He's tried to maintain that classic Graham profile but distinguished was giving way to old age at a rate of knots. At 61, middle-aged had vanished over the horizon faster than it needed too and his disguises had only made him seem even more ridiculous. The thick black hair which he'd always prided himself upon had, in truth turned grey many years earlier though colourants had maintained the façade of a younger man until it became tiresome. At 50, the moustache had been shaved as keeping it the right colour had been impossible. He'd once tried a dye on that too, but the mixture had run and turned his top lip black. For fear of ridicule, he hadn't left the house for four days until the skin had returned to its natural pigmentation.

When his hair had begun thinning, he considered a toupee, vanity, pathetic really. There was something to be said of growing old gracefully, but Martin

Graham wasn't a man who admitted defeat easily. The paunch, around his waistline, the result of too many liquid lunches with clients who now needed to be charmed to pay the prices he expected for his coal, taking a toll on a figure that was once sleek and hard. And that extra chin he tried so desperately to disguise by wearing looser fitting shirts and the absence of neckties that 25 years ago, Iris would never have noticed because she was in love and in awe of his power. Now, she needed a reason to overlook them. It can be said that older men marry women their junior to feel younger by proxy. But surely the opposite can have the same effect. Iris was fifteen years Martin's junior but recently all she felt was old.

Damn, that smile was slipping. Better to stop staring into this mirror and enjoy their day.

Martin and Iris Graham were celebrating their twenty-fifth wedding anniversary at a small restaurant in St Mara. Things had gotten so confrontational between them in recent years that spending quality time alone together wasn't normally high on the priority list. Today was an exception. Along with the new outfit, she'd been to the hairdressers, making a special effort to look nice for her husband. Martin was still a busy man, what with the colliery and the railway station to manage but today he'd cleared his schedule, an entire afternoon and evening devoted to his wife.

Frank and Jenifer weren't part of the plan, this had to be for them. Their daughter was staying with friends, and Frank was being, Frank. It wouldn't hurt if he just vanished for the day. This was a test, plain and simple, pass and they know there's something worth fighting for, fail and, she didn't want to think about failure, not tonight. This was their time.

Incredibly, the date had lived up to expectation, eclipsing any previous hopes that she'd dared to imagine. Her knight in shining armour was back and looking good.

A romantic walk by the riverside hand in hand, a slow excursion on a gondola-driven luxury vessel along the river Steen followed by the meal, nothing fancy, just a steak as big as the plate for Martin, with a side of fries and baked beans, Iris ate seafood pasta followed by a dip in the chocolate fountain. The show was disappointing, and they exited halfway through. Not that it really mattered, there was better things to do when they both had this special feeling.

On the drive home, Iris was melancholy, sad that these days were so rare. And she knew, when they woke in the morning, normality would resume. Frank's dark moods and Martin's ambivalence toward the situation. The previous night, they had skilfully dodged the elephant in the room, but it was obvious where the problem lay. The times for excuses was over, he was a teenage boy who when provoked could become seriously dangerous; the Scholes girl could vouch for that. Had Martin supported her more, gave her greater say on the youth's punishment then maybe things would be different, more tolerable at least.

Still, that was for tomorrow, tonight had been only for them. They arrived home to a darkened house. It was only ten thirty, but since Frank was accustomed to taking to his bed when he couldn't be at Martin's side, this was expected. He'd sulk about today for weeks. No one wanted to check on Frank, his mood was expected to be decidedly frosty.

The couple shared a bottle of wine before retiring to bed. Making love had seemed brand-new for it had been so long since Martin had explored his wife's body, the feeling of tenderness heightened the sensation and the ardent-pause before penetration made her crave him even more. For a man his age, his continued rhythm and stamina was unexpected, amplifying her mood. His climax had come unfortunately at a time when hers was building to a crescendo, though she knew how to fake it, practice makes perfect. Still, she couldn't complain, maybe if things stayed this way instead for a little longer, making love may become the norm, rather than the exception. She could always dream.

The next day would be memorable too.

Martin Graham had always been an early riser, but his son was normally earlier still. Like an obedient Labrador wagging its tail, awaiting its master, Frank would patiently hold until Martin was ready each morning, so they could walk to work together. This morning, it was seven thirty and there was no sign of the teenager. Martin showered and ate a breakfast of tea and toast, all the time, wondering if his son was brooding about the previous day. He despised sharing his father's attention, always expecting appraisal for his duties and personal acknowledgement when things went right. What Frank hadn't realised was he was being groomed for high management and work-force interaction relationship was key. Martin knew that his best days were over, and Frank would need to step up, sooner than expected. The lump he found on his lower back was probably nothing, pushing through around the kidney area; and his urine had begun to flow red, in all probability, just an infection. He'd have to make an appointment to see Dr Brackett, maybe, perhaps, probably not... Plus, yesterday felt wonderful. Seeing his wife smile, listening to a laugh that had been silent for so long. A neglected woman, springing back to life. All it took was food and a bad play. No, that wasn't true. Yesterday was about them, just them. They could have taken a walk through a snake-infested forest and ate unripe bananas; it wouldn't have mattered, so long as they were together.

Obviously, there was the problem that is Frank. Martin hadn't shown the strain but even he cringed when he heard about the Scholes girl. He'd ensured that the police (Bill Castle) couldn't be involved, he had no choice, Frank's future would be devastated were he serve a prison term. And that's what would have happened, he'd have gone to jail, there was no doubt, a sobbing girl on the stand, the dog-walking witness who wouldn't be bribed, screaming parents in the gallery shrieking for justice. He'd have got a minimum of five years, annihilating everything Martin was trying to create, a ladder of ascension, Frank Graham becoming the head of Graham colliery and railway limited. Hell, he could even rename the company Graham and son, and when the boy was ready, Martin would step aside knowing the family business was in safe hands. Oh, he'd be there for guidance if needed or an opinion if there was a quandary, but in Frank, Martin saw the future. A future that would vanish if he continued down this dark path. He was a teen, lashing out at those who wronged him, and senior understood that. But there was a fine line between vengeance and criminality. Anything else, as major as the incident in the barn, with the Scholes girl, and the rats, and the strawberry jam…next time, Martin may not be able to save him. They needed to talk, father to son, just like his wife had suggested. He needed to hard, firm but caring, unyielding without the need to be impervious to his thoughts. Suggestive without being demanding, an effort to alter the boy's ravenous need for retribution. Due to his privileged position, in time, those he hated would need to crawl for employment, everybody in Hallowell needed employment and they were the number one option. Without violence, he could take his reprisal by ensuring that they got the shittiest jobs imaginable.

When the time reached twenty before eight, Martin decided to wake the boy from his slumber. The heavy wooden door creaked on its hinges as it swung open.

'Frankie. It's pushing eight o'clock. Are you coming to work today?' There was no answer. The bedroom was large and though the boy's single-bed was across to the far corner, the contents looked obvious. Still Martin needed to be certain, walking to the thick velvet drapes, and hurriedly tearing them open, the grey morning light bursting through and confirming his worst fears, the bed was made and hadn't been slept in.

Martin hurried down to the kitchen where Iris was clearing the breakfast debris. His voice was panicked as he exclaimed to his wife his findings. Iris looked nonchalant at the news, aggravating Martin even more.

'You know what he's doing don't you? He's jealous that we got to spend time together yesterday and he's punishing you, not me because he knows I don't fall for his tricks.' Martin's retort was angry and to the point.

'That's just typical of you, think the worst of him all the time.' His voice was raising steadily, little Jenifer was seated at the breakfast table, just starting his cornflakes and cringed at the prospect of another parental row. 'Don't even think for one moment that something could have happened to him, that he could be in an accident, I haven't seen him since yesterday morning, I'd have checked on him last night, but you had other things on your mind.' The little girl was crying now, partially out of concern for her brother, and moderately because she'd worked out that a few tears normally end the argument. Iris winced at the last statement; the previous night's bridge-building exploded once more.

'That's a horrible thing to say. And I didn't see you complaining last night. Anyway, I've told you before, I'm not doing this in front of Jenifer, you can see how it upsets her.' Iris was cradling the head of the distressed child, the mother slyly happy that her child's tears would end this conversation, and disturbingly concerned that part of her mind really did desire for something to have happened to him. "Just go to work, I'm sure your precious son will turn up when he's out of his mood. It wouldn't bother me if he stayed away permanently." Martin shot back a stare of pure venom then headed for the front door, clashing its hinges as he left. Yesterday's events, a distant memory.

113

The January morning was icy, with a heavy winter fog blanketing the village. Martin pulled his woollen coat in close, the lapels pointed high, trying to cover his ears. He'd left the house in such a rush, that his usual outfit ensemble, which normally included a beanie hat and scarf, had both been neglected in his hastiness to charge for the door. As his feet crunched across the gravel pathway towards the ground's gate, he considered returning to the house, but his desire to find his son took precedence. His pace brisk, but not only for the temperature. Though he'd never admit it, the thought had crossed his mind that his unsympathetic wife could be correct. Frank had punished them before but that was many years ago. That feeling of helplessness when his son had been missing was the worst thing he'd ever experienced. He wouldn't do something like that again, would he?

The seven fifty-five train from Hallowell had just departed and smoke from the engine was still visible. There were people milling around the platform as if waiting for something. It was a large group, maybe twelve people and Martin could see, their faces contained worried looks. His pace quickened when he saw an ambulance and Bill Castle's car parked at in front of the platform. Members of the group noticed Martin's arrival and began whispering to one another. He started climbing the stone steps at the left side of the platform when Castle emerged from the pack and met him before he could see what had happened.

'What's going on here Billy? Is there a problem, someone been hurt?' He could tell by the policeman's manner that something was very wrong. He raised his hands to stop Graham going any further. Martin tried to push past but Castle held firm.

'Stop a moment Martin, something has happened.' Graham struggled to get free, dread beginning to grow, anxiously determined to get to his son.

'Frank! Frank!' His voice firm but he was unable to hide a sight quiver, his brain racing, theatre of the mind creating a worse-case scenario.

'Yes, Martin it's Frank. But...' Graham pushed the policeman hard, and Bill Castle momentarily lost his grip. The by-standers parted just enough to reveal the stricken teenager being lifted onto a gurney in the washroom. The officer regained his footing and from behind, threw a firm but careful arm around the hysterical man. He pulled back gently, and Martin swung around to face him.

'Is he...'

'No Martin, he's not dead but I won't lie to you, he's not good. Now just keep back and let the ambulance men do their jobs. If you get in the way, you'll only slow them down.'

'Frank! Oh, my god, Frankie, what have they done to you?' All public dignity was forgotten as the boy's father sobbed, tears of sorrow and worry, hate and animosity and a hundred other emotions bubbling to the surface. "Just let me have my boy!" Bill Castle physically lifted the uncontrollable man out of the doorway, allowing the paramedics to carry the teenager's broken body onto the platform. The ambulance doors were open, and the driver had the engine running, every second counted.

'Martin, should I come in the bus with you, or would you like me to go and fetch Iris?' Bill Castle knew his best chance for answers was Martin but didn't expect to get much sense from him at present.

'Fuck her, you do what you want, I'm going with my boy.'

St Mara hospital was only ten minutes away though it seemed to take forever. The waiting was unbearable. Martin sat in this shitty little white room; generic NHS posters emblazoned the walls. There was a kettle but no teabags, not that he could stomach anything. The clock's ticking echoed around the room and whenever he looked in its direction, the thing seemed to be going backwards. There was a little old man waiting too. His wife had cancer and was going to die, it was just a matter of when. He studied the fellow, hunched with a flat cap and three days' stubble. The diaphoretic stench from the cigarette that hung from his lips made Martin want to vomit. There were dark rings under his eyes formed by worry, pupils glassy and hidden by thin framed spectacles that had slipped to the tip of his wrinkled nose and were probably there more for show than use. When the door burst open, Martin jumped, ready for news, but it was just the nurse calling the old boy.

'Hope your boy's okay.' As he passed by, Martin could smell the stench of dried piss and tobacco, clothes that hadn't been washed since the wife had been taken to hospital, and a coat with a tear in its left arm. Those were the little things Martin noticed about people.

'You are too. Give your wife my best.' Ever the politician, Martin could raise his game in public. Inside he was screaming, 'FUCK YOUR WIFE, FUCK YOUR SHINKY ARSED CLOTHES AND FUCK YOU.'

The old man's aroma lingered in the waiting room, and he silently cursed him for it. Smoking was a big 'no, no', in Graham's presence, couldn't stand the sight smell or taste of it. He tried to open a small window high in a corner, but it was painted shut. The room was becoming claustrophobic, and his patience was certainly wearing thin. When the door swung open once more, he was fighting panic in the pit of his stomach, heart racing with hope and fear battling for supremacy. When he realised it was his wife, and Bill Castle, the spirits dropped once more.

Iris hurried across the room, her eyes glacial, more concerned for her husband, than her son's condition. Her arms finding the neck of the devastated man, her squeeze transactional with the burden of their earlier argument, which ensured that her husband's response didn't reciprocate her passion. The hug lasted mere seconds; she could almost feel the coldness emanating from her partner.

'Suppose you'll be happy now?' His eyes filled with rage, remembering the last statement that his wife had made that morning. She was taken aback, realising for sure, exactly where her husband's priorities lay, and they certainly weren't with her.

'What are you talking about? You think I wanted this? You think I wanted my son in a hospital bed, fighting for his life?' Iris was trying to hide her emotions, keenly aware that Martin always had the gift to see inside her heart, if he saw the complete truth, they'd be divorced tomorrow.

'Well, where have you been? I've been here for over two hours. Our son could have died in the time it's taken you to arrive.'

'I needed supervision for our other child. Remember, the five-year-old who sleeps in the bedroom next to ours. I only say that because you act like you don't know she exists.' Martin raised a hand, as though to strike his wife but the policeman intervened.

'Let's just all calm down, shall we.' Martin snarled, looking across at his old friend, having enough respect for him to not cause a scene. Still, he'd have preferred it had neither made an appearance, Frank was his son, and she didn't give a shit, arriving more out of obligation than concern. And the officer, he was only here to fire questions, an interrogation played in the form of caring enquiries, an inquisition to which Martin had no answers. After the initial stand-off, the three took seats, separated by the length of the room, waiting for news on Frank's condition, the room in silence, Bill Castle ready to play referee.

After what seemed like forever, a thin-framed doctor who looked straight out of medical school entered the waiting area. He was staring at a clipboard, more for a disguised unwillingness to look the parents in the eye than searching for details. The worried expression said more than any words ever could. They were told that the initial prognosis wasn't good, and they should brace themselves for the worst. He'd been diagnosed as having serious brain damage and was being kept in a medically induced coma to give the swelling an opportunity to recede. The skull was fractured and there was severe trauma to the pre-frontal cortex, the area of the brain that controls the ability to empathise with others and separate right from wrong. His chances of survival were slim and if he did, the recovery would be long and hard, painful, and stressful. The doctors were amazed that he'd lasted this long and took that as a positive. It was the only positive Martin could cling too.

To Iris, she knew that the stress of this horrific incident would add increasing strain on her fragile marriage. Twelve hours earlier, she believed that progress was being made, bridges built, they'd been so happy, so relaxed; now, well, it was one step forward, two steps back. She wondered if there was really anything worth fighting for, they'd never been equal partners, he was the one with wealth, the oversized mausoleum which was the Graham mansion, business's power, tradition. She had nothing. And when it came to parenting, Martin's opinions had always overpowered her own though neither had any experience in raising children. The huge difference in age had sometime made theirs feel more of a father-daughter relationship and another reason why he won most of their arguments. His intimidating manner and position of power had been enough for Iris to shy away and as such, her attitude towards Frank's architecture in his early years had suffered. One thing that she was certain of, the same wouldn't happen with her daughter. Because of this, Iris had considered leaving, taking a small share of the family wealth and, along with Jenifer, vanishing forever. She wondered if they would even be missed. It was obvious that the current timing would prevent that from happening, walking away when Frank's life was hanging in the balance would be too cruel. Whether he realised it or not, Martin was going to need her, the support only a wife could give was essential if he was to exist during this most anxious of times.

When they were allowed into the private side room, Martin's emotions overtook him, tears cascading down his cheeks in rivers of misery, inner screams that were released in controlled sobs. His son laying lifeless on a hospital bed, legs covered by a white cotton sheet, the tube from a ventilator forced deep into his throat, lips involuntarily contrived apart, chapped, and dry, his lower teeth resting upon the plastic cylinder in a biting motion. The paleness of Frank's skin added a ghostly image to the already frightening appearance, his chest rising and falling only with the aid of the hospital equipment. Martin slid his fingers through the teen's dishevelled hair but was asked by the baby in the medical coat, not to touch his stricken offspring just yet. Martin had shot a returning stare of venom and the doctor had backed away, certain that this was a battle he wasn't ready to take on. Once the boy's hair was styled to something more presentable, he stroked the skin across the boy's right cheek.

'My God. What have they done to you?' Frank's father was suddenly a broken man, any sense of bravado fading away, replaced by a quivering wreck. Seeing the bruising across his eyes, blacks and purples a horrendous contrast to the ghost-like complexion, his shattered nose still broken, the doctors understandably prioritising the life-threatening afflictions before the aesthetic damage. An area of hair across the crown had been shaved to allow the medics the opportunity to witness the extent of the devastation, a bandage covering where a fragment of bone had been removed to relieve the pressure of the swelling brain. A gash down the left cheek had been corrected with butterfly stitches, the thin slices of surgical tape pulling the flesh together. The boy's whole face was barely recognisable.

The following three months had been arduous and exhausting. Day after day, night after night, Martin continued his one-man vigil by his son's bed, only leaving to shower and sleep. He'd never been an overly religious man but now, he found himself relying on pray more and more. The way he saw it, if getting close with the man upstairs would help his son recover, so be it. In total, it had taken fourteen weeks for the doctors to risk slowly waking Frank from the medically induced coma. There was a serious possibility that the teen would never be capable of breathing alone again, that his injuries had been simply too catastrophic, that he was brain dead. There had been three operations in a desperate bid to release the pressure that the swelling brain had caused. More and more pieces of bone had needed to be removed until a huge section of the skull was now missing, a protective membrane covering the exposed area. Drugs pumped through a canula into his right arm were gradually withdrawn and progressively, there were signs of life. The ventilator was still in place, the medics unwilling to withdraw the assistance until they were certain of no paralysis. When the drugs were completely free from Frank's system, the young man was placed on a twenty-four-hour watch, a role Martin Graham grasped with vigour. Encouragingly, the family had been told that the brain's damage wasn't located in the area which affected the body's motor skills, so, if he regained consciousness there was no reason to believe that there should be any form of physical disability. His limbs had been consistently exercised and remained thoroughly flexible, though certain joints had inevitably stiffened, and the muscles had begun atrophy. The essential thing now was how Frank would cope when there were no more breathing aids.

Iris's attendance at the hospital had trickled to a halt, her presence not welcomed by a husband who had become embittered towards everything but his son. Using childcare for their daughter as an excuse, the reality was that she couldn't stand seeing Martin tear himself apart, questioning his every decision as a father, cursing the events that led to Frank's assault, the guilt of not being there as the boy had been beaten to a pulp. She understood her husband's need to find someone to blame and usually, she was the target of his abuse. He'd always apologise after a aiming a ferocious barrage in her direction and inside, she knew why it was done. Martin had always been a problem solver, but before him, their son was little more than a vegetable and he was powerless to help. They couldn't even find the culprits, Bill Castle had investigated incessantly but with no witness's and the victim on life support, his hands were tied.

Iris was becoming ever more aware that their marriage was also on life support. Should Frank regain consciousness, all of Martin's attention would inevitably turn to the youth, and if he died, it would be an impossible blow for her husband to recover from. He was still the love of her life and always would be, but she couldn't help but wonder if this was the final obstacle in a marriage of turbulence.

A repulsive feeling, deep in the pit of Iris's stomach ensured that her presence at the hospital remained minimal. A consciousness so scandalous, she could barely admit it to herself, though deep in her heart, she knew that it was true. It was an indescribable guilt that maybe, just maybe, the family would be better off were Frank never to wake again. It was hardly comprehendible that a mother could feel this way and forced her to wonder if the fault lay with her. How could a woman look at her own fifteen-year-old son, lying in a hospital bed, fighting for life and think it best if the battle was lost? Visions of all the evil deeds he'd perpetrated just kept invading her mind.

At just eight-years-old, he'd taken a neighbour, Mary Berry's five-year-old son and sheathed him with pliable steel wire. Using a make-shift gag and blindfold, he'd hid the terrified youngster in the same barn that he'd used to abduct Gemma Scholes. The boy had been incapacitated for two days, the whole town searching. Christ, he was searching, all the time knowing precisely where the child was, relishing the torment he'd caused the child's frantic parents. As the child hadn't witnessed his assailant, there'd been no evidence to prove Frank was responsible, but Iris had seen the look in her son's eyes when the boy was discovered. That emotionless expression had haunted her from that day, as had the memories of her own daughter's screams.

For Jenifer's fourth birthday, they had bought her a Jack Russel puppy. Naming the animal Fluffy, it was just eight weeks old, white with black patches across its back, stumpy little legs, and a frenetic tail which lashed through the air as it ran. Quickly becoming the girl's most treasured possession, it slept at the foot of her bed, and followed her every move. Three weeks after the birthday, Jenifer woke to find her pet missing. Searching the mansion and finding nothing, the worried child went to the garden, hoping that Fluffy would be at the door, expectantly awaiting her attention. Screams pierced the morning air as Jenifer found her pet, its internal organs torn from a huge gash in the stricken pup's abdomen, the remains hanging from a washing post, blood still cascading to the floor, though the dog had long since expired. Though Frank denied any knowledge, it was obvious he was lying. The gaze across the thug's face was the exact same emotionless expression in the aftermath of Mary Berry's son's discovery, and it filled Iris with dread. She'd read an article in a magazine about children that liked to torture small animals, that it was an early warning sign for…

The closest Frank had been to a custodial sentence was due to an incident at Hallowell grammar-school. After being forced to serve an after-school detention, he'd left the classroom and hurled a brick threw the teachers car windshield. Then, he found more rocks and proceeded to smash the front office windows, narrowly missing the schools' secretary. When the headmaster tried to intervene, he was punched to the ground and beaten senseless. Had Martin been willing to allow the authorities punish the dangerous youth, things may have changed for the better. Instead, like a magician with a magic wand, Abracadabra, and the problem vanishes.

One event that altered the chemistry of the Graham family forever happened when the child was only six years old, and for the principal participants, it caused a void that could never be traversed.

For Martin, it had been a bad day. The steel company, which had been tenants inside the main building of the railway station for many years had been forced into bankruptcy, earlier that morning, ensuring that they'd be vacating the property and leaving the Graham's without tenants. Plus, the realisation hit, that the family wouldn't be receiving the six-months back rent which was owed. The national economic downturn meant new business's requiring to take on the tenancy was doubtful, leaving the Graham's finances for the remainder of the year in a precarious position. After lunch, he was told that the main elevator cable inside of Hallowell colliery needed replacing, handing Martin a bill his company could scarcely afford, and on top of that, he had flu.

Frank had spent the day home from school, sharing the same illness and ensuring that his mother suffered for it. The chicken soup, she'd prepared for his lunch had been hurled from the kitchen table to the floor when he'd been unhappy with its temperature. When she'd scolded him, he purposely made himself vomit and after being sent to his bedroom, in a temper he'd smashed the window, bombarding the glass with a toy car until it broke. For Iris the only plus point came when, for once, Martin had backed his wife's punishment of the boy, adding a spanking for an exclamation point. This was the start of an incident which would change the dynamic of the household forever.

The next day had begun like any other, Martin rose early, happy that the symptoms of his flu seemed to be passing. After eating breakfast, he visited his son's bedroom, feeling justified at the previous punishment, but acutely guilty, knowing that had his day not been so disastrous, the measure of chastisement would have diminished greatly. On entering, he opened the back-out drapes, bathing the room with the morning sunshine. It was then, to his dismay, that he realised his son was gone.

A search began in earnest, firstly the mansion and then onto the grounds. When that proved futile, the pursuit was expanded, Officer Bill Castle bringing re-enforcements and a village-wide hunt began.

St Mara police soon became involved, placing roadblocks on Hallowell bank, stationed in a prominent position, ensuring that no kidnappers had an escape route. The Graham's had always been potential targets for criminal organisations, but as the days progressed without a ransom demand, that option became less likely. The outside police force believed Martin and Iris were more probable, without any real suspects, the parents quickly became people of interest. Bill Castle had tried in vain to convince his fellow officers that the chances of filicide were close to impossible, the birth of the boy had caused wild celebrations and Martin being the most devoted father the cop had ever met. But, until the case was concluded, the parents seemed the logical option.

As days turned to weeks, the strain on the couple's marriage was becoming intolerable. For Iris, she couldn't fight the doubt that Frank himself was behind the disappearance, punishing them for their own disciplinary actions. The idea that a six-year-old child could be so calculating, just for retaliation, seemed a stretch but she'd already seen the indications of her son's dark side. For Martin, the very idea that his wife could believe their son capable of such a deplorable action made him react with fury. Not only was she expunging the boy's memory with such tales, but Martin believed that she was doing so out of guilt. Had she not overreacted with her punishment, then the lasting act would not have been one of anger. He made it plain that, were the worst to be confirmed, he would hold her responsible, and it would be impossible to forgive.

For the Graham patriarch, the scars were more than just psychological. The physical effects had left his body frail and sickly. In the time Frank had been missing, he'd barely been able to digest a meal without the feeling of nausea. Sleep became an after-thought, and when he managed to close his eyes, the marital bed felt cold and unwelcoming.

After twenty-eight days, St Mara police were on the verge of charging the couple. With no new leads and the child still missing, the finger of suspicion was pointed firmly in their direction, the authorities needed answers. Both parents were re-arrested and grilled mercilessly in separate interview rooms, any change in their stories would result in incarceration. With no new information, they were reluctantly released. Returning home exhausted, both mentally and emotionally, hope was dwindling fast, with the realisation that this nightmare showed no sign of ending. The journey back to Hallowell had taken place in silence, Iris having begun contemplation of temporarily leaving the marital home and, were it not for the authorities seeing it as a sign of guilt, the act would certainly have been completed already. As their car crunched its way up the gravel driveway, Iris was first to notice a light, shining through a window of the mansion's lower floor.

Bolting from the vehicle, it took time for the father to realise what his wife already suspected. From the hallway, the television was loud enough to hear, regardless of the lounge's closed door. Tearing inside, the parents could scarcely believe their eyes; resting on the leather chesterfield settee, the boy was back.

The initial response was one of overwhelming relief. Martin held the child in what seemed a never-ending embrace, sobbing with emotion; his son was home. From the lounge doorway, Iris watched on, joining in the reunion seemed premature until she had answers. From across his father's shoulder, the six-year-old stared menacingly at his mother, a sense of victory in his eyes, victory in a battle that Iris had no chance of winning. Finally, she broke the silence.

'Where the hell have you been?' The tone was one of accusation, and something Martin wasn't willing to tolerate. Looking back toward his wife, he answered before Frank had the opportunity too.

'Who cares where he'd been? He's home now, that's all the counts, leave him alone, there'll be time enough for answers later.' The boy's expression had changed to one of smugness, a self confidence that came from knowing his father would protect him, no matter what.

'Are you serious? He's been missing a month, we've been accused of being child murderers, locked up like common criminals. The whole village has been searching and I'm wrong for wanting answers? You've got to be kidding?'

'No, I'm not kidding. I couldn't care less where he's been, and you shouldn't either. For four weeks, I thought my boy was dead. I prayed to God every night for him to be delivered back to me and now he has been. If Frank wants to tell us, that's up to him, but so long as he's okay, I couldn't give a fuck.' Not remotely satisfied, Iris started for the child, determined to have confirmation of what she already knew, that Frank had played them for fools. Cowering behind his father's legs, the boy hid, happy in the knowledge that she'd never get close enough to strike. Martin snarled as he held out an arm, a warning that he'd do whatever necessary to defend his son.

'I'm telling you woman…don't.' It was the first time in the marriage that Iris felt physically threatened by her husband. The look in his eyes was one of deadly seriousness, and she knew that if she tried to make a lunge for Frank, Martin would strike first. It was also when she realised that this was a war she had no chance of winning, without her husband's assistance, she'd never have confirmation of the child's deceit and Martin would never push him for fear of losing him all over again. It was a vicious cycle and a licence for their son to do whatever he pleased without the fear of reprisal.

The reason Frank had never been found as the village was searched was because he'd never left the mansion. Its interior was vast. Eight bedrooms, six bathrooms, a fully functioning attic space and a massive basement. The design of the heating system required large wall cavities, where the heat would rise from the boiler in the basement and flow gently to all parts of the house. The cavities were easily large enough to pass from room to room without detection. He'd spent a month, hiding in plain sight, moving along the passageways undetected, watching his parents worry frantically. Listening to the conversations, the theories to where he was, who had him. Giggling when they argued about blame. It became a game. If he was hungry, he'd just wait till bedtime. Gliding silently from his hiding place to the kitchen was easy. No one was taking notice of the dwindling food supplies. He kept some in his hiding place for lunch and always carried enough liquid for his thirst. One night, a pacing Martin had almost caught him, but the darkness had been his ally. Other than that, it had been easy. He'd demonstrated extraordinary patience with a mission to cause extreme panic. That mission had been successful. As for the residents of Hallowell, they were told the boy had amnesia, and had no recollection of the previous four weeks. Most were sceptical though few voiced their opinions.

Ten days had passed since the drugs used to keep Frank in a medically induced coma had been withdrawn and still, his eyes remained closed. Each day that passed, his chances of survival diminished, the doctors claiming that now the last obstacle had been removed, it was down solely to Graham's powers of recovery. Physiotherapists had ensured that the young man's limbs remained fully exercised, the joints being susceptible to stiffening in his bed-ridden state. Martin would watch his son's face as the muscles were stretched, the routine would inevitably be painful, and the older man needed to know. Know if this was yet another performance by his son, a punishment for giving his wife attention. God, he hoped so. Just wake up Frank, wake up and its only you and me. Frank knew just how to deal out punishment, even if his own father became the victim, regardless of who got hurt, he'd get what he wanted. His pettiness was legendary and Martin's all-day date with Iris could be construed as unfaithfulness. This was the monster created out of love. God, he wished he could take back those mistakes, now, it was too late.

The first twitch could have been interpreted as dreaming, night terrors from a four-month sleep. The second was enough to wake Martin from his own slumber, who had taken a nap while holding his son's hand. The older man rubbed the sleep from his eyes and slid a hand across his chin, five days of stubble, grey and sporadic, leaving him looking for older than his sixty-one years. Unsure whether his son had moved or if it had been a dream, Martin's days and nights had merged into one long comatose existence. Still, he trained his eyes at the unconscious young man, desperate for anything. When a third twitch turned to a muscular spasm, his entire body jerking violently, Martin leapt to his feet, and screamed for attention.

'Frank. Frank, come on son, it's me, it's your dad, I'm right here.' The movement stopped. 'No. Fuck no, not again.' Running to the private room's closed door, he tore at the handle, smashing it against the outer wall. 'Help me. Please.' The cry was for anyone, everyone, doctors, nurses, the fucking janitor, if he could help.

In the distance, Maxine Geller, a plump middle-aged ward sister was sat at her desk, busy handling a pile of paperwork by a dimly lit table lamp. Squinting at the figure whose screams had probably just woken every other patient in her ward, she pushed back her chair, and jumped into action.

Martin's patience was growing frail, his head rotating back and forth from his unconscious son to the emerging nurse.

'Jesus' woman, can't you move any faster.' The statement was fired with enough venomous volume for Maxine to hear without disturbing the other patients on the ward. The loose skin on the woman's cheeks wobbled as her feet shuffled across the tiled floor.

'Mr Graham.' There was a pause between the Mister and the Graham, insinuating her lack of patience towards the man's urgency, sounding more like a school mistress, talking to a naughty child. 'I've told you before, you mustn't overreact every time Frank twitches. He's comatose, sleeping, it's reactions to dreams, that's all. Now it's a good sign, perhaps his brain is still firing but…' Martin raised a hand and for a split second, Maxine flinched, feeling a strike was coming, a reflex action she'd used with previously distraught families. Martin realised his mistake and immediately apologised, embarrassment making him blush.

'I'm sorry, Miss Geller, but this was different, his entire torso tightened, I thought he was about to jump up. That's got to be good, surely?' Using a sympathetic tone, Maxine replied.

'Let's look at him then.' Entering the private room, Frank looked the exact same as he'd looked for the last four months. Applying a blood pressure band to his right arm, the inflation only took thirty seconds. Checking the gage, it was…normal. The temperature clip on his left index finger had slid off, the nurse looked concerned.

'How did this happen Mr Graham? Did you take it off?' Martin smiled slyly, knowing that Frank had been responsible.

'It was the spasm, that's how it happened. I tell you, his whole torso tightened, flinched, he was waking up. Honest.' The staff nurse cringed; she'd seen this before. Families seeing what they wanted to see. She felt so sorry for this poor man, his son was fading, and he was helpless. Deciding that an argument would only antagonise the situation, she smiled politely and reattached the temperature gage to Frank's index finger.

When his hand clenched the nurse's arm, she screamed, more in shock than in pain. Pulling away, the grip was strong and when she looked to Frank's face, his eyes were open, staring blindly at the intruder by his bed. Martin whooped for joy, this time not caring if the whole hospital was woken. Weeping with relief, Martin ran to his son, an embrace finally with a conscious young man.

Frank Graham was awake."

Chapter 13

"Surprise, surprise, Frank survived." Nick was wary of speaking now but felt comfortable with a joking tone that his father wouldn't take offence. Mick took a large inhalation of nicotine from his burning cigarette and blew the smoke from his nostrils.

"Boy, you have no idea."

"Frank Graham's rehabilitation was long and painful. His muscles, with four months of inactivity had atrophied badly and his joints, though fully exercised during the coma, had become stiff and inflexible. Still, he had his father by his side, every step of the way. The more Iris tried to be involved, the more she was shunned.

She needed an escape and found it at the bottom of a bottle.

Bill Castle, the only law in Hallowell, had waited patiently to interview the teenager, knowing that was his last opportunity to bring the attacker or attackers to justice. In the village, the Graham's had few allies, and no one was lining up to give evidence. As always in small towns, there were rumours. But rumours didn't help, he needed facts, not fantasy. The policeman had learned enough about Frank to know that whatever happened, he probably deserved it, there was so many residents that hated the thug, it was impossible to make a charge. Martin's money and influence had saved his son from prosecution numerous times. But this time, Frank had become the victim and regardless of Bill's negative opinion of the boy, he was responsible for the investigation.

His final hope was speaking to Graham himself. The one person who could finger the assailants, a four month wait culminating with a bedside chat. Waste of time, Frank claimed his memory was gone, he had no idea of how he ended up destroyed on the floor of the Station washrooms. Professing to have a blank of the entire day, his answers were slow and deliberate, like reading from a carefully prepared statement. For once, Bill was unnerved at the interview, he was sat on a moulded plastic chair three feet away, their eyes locked, with the young man's stare burning though lifeless, cold, and emotionless, Castle believed he'd never witnessed evil before, but the fixed focus of that kid's eyes, made a shiver run down his spine. It was obvious that he was lying, the only concern was how he'd take his vengeance personally when his body was healed. Bill pitied the fools and secretly wished they'd got the job done the first time.

The division in the family home was growing, and the atmosphere toxic. Iris feared for her daughter, precious little Jennifer. She'd just turned six and was confused by the whole situation. Even at that age, the tiny girl could tell that her big brother despised her, she just had no idea why. Why, when she spoke to him, he'd either snarl or ignore her completely. What had she done to make him hate her so? And why was daddy heading in the same direction? Why did he not give her shoulder rides and bedtime stories anymore? That special way he used to smile when she walked in the room was gone. All his time was spent at work or with Frankie now. And why did she hear her mummy crying herself to sleep at night. And finally, why was mummy drinking the awful tasting stuff all the time and taking so many pills.

Jenifer had eaten some once, thinking they were sweeties and washed them down with mummy's special drink. She had to describe to doctors at the hospital what she had taken. The tablets had tasted horrid, and the drink was worse. She couldn't remember the liquid's name, but it had started with a V and ended with an A. Iris kept it hidden in a paper bag and that's why she'd tried it. If mummy liked it, it must be nice.

The social workers wanted the girl removed. A six-year-old drinking vodka unsupervised and worse still, taking a handful of her mother's anti-anxiety tablets. Thankfully, it was another time when the Graham name still carried weight. The hospital was in St Mara, but Martin still had enough high-powered connections, helping to make the controversy go away. But this was enough to make everyone realise, something needed to change. The parents talked of divorce, where Iris would take her daughter and Frank would remain with Martin. But the patriarch rebuffed this idea. He still had feelings for his wife, even if things were bad now. If he lost Iris, there would be no other woman in his life, and he wasn't ready to draw a line under that aspect yet. And even Iris had her doubts. If the divorce got messy, she'd walk away with nothing. She'd signed a pre-nuptial agreement when they married, never believing she'd have these problems. Iris wasn't materialistic, but she did enjoy nice things, loved her home and was proud of the life she'd created for herself. After all these years of privilege, returning to nothing was terrifying.

Also, she knew if they had the freedom, like the day they spent together on their wedding anniversary before Frank's injuries, that they could still enjoyed each other's company, they were still attracted to one another. If Frank hadn't been such a destructive force, they would be a happy couple. Plus, why should Jenifer have to live a life of poverty after living in such a beautiful home with anything a child could ever want. Martin had ensured that his wife and children wanted for nothing. But perhaps, that would change if they fought a divorce through the courts. Together they decided to stick with it, Frank was sixteen and would be a man soon. Surely, he'd calm down when he was past adolescence and until then, they'd battle through.

For weeks after the incident with Jenifer's hospitalisation, Iris stopped drinking and tried to do without the anxiety medication. This wouldn't last.

Iris Graham had had brief but devastating flirtations with addiction during her teens. Growing up in St Mara children's home, certain members of her piers came from the wrong side of the tracks. Iris had been born to well respected, catholic parentage but after they had both been killed in a road traffic collision and there were no family relations to take the six-year-old in, the child discovered what the other side of life was truly about. Many of those in the orphanage were rescue children, taken from homes with abusive or unstable parents. Some would pass through in a matter of weeks; others would be housed much longer. But all seemed to share a common trait, a streetwise ability to survive. Iris had never experienced this aspect of life and had to learn fast. Bullying, both mental and physical was commonplace and though the guardians at the home tried their best, Iris soon discovered it was sink or swim.

Iris swam. Maybe it was her Irish ancestry, perhaps strong genes, or maybe she was just not willing to take shit, but the little blonde girl who'd sat in a corner and cried on arrival became a leader rather than a follower. She was no bully, but all the other girls soon discovered that she was more than happy to defend herself when called upon. And with that, others would gravitate toward her rather than away. If she took someone under her wing, you better believe the others left them alone. If a newcomer was playing up, the guardians would ask Iris to bring them in line, and without too much fuss, she would. Other children were adopted but after a while, Iris had no wish to join a family with all the risks that that could entail. There had been too many children, who had been re-homed, only to return to the centre, emotionally scarred. She had a good relationship with all the centre workers and got little trouble from any of the children, she was respected and by some, feared. She had no wish to give that up and go play happy families with some do-gooders who thought it their Christian duty to give a home to some little waif and stray. To be looked down upon and play by their rules. She played by her own rules and that was fine by her.

With longevity came a degree of freedom and that's where Iris's problems had begun. For an attractive fourteen-year-old, the dangers of the outside world are many. St Mara wasn't a big town, but it was big enough to house some shady characters. She fell in with a crowd of teenagers, some three, maybe four years older than she was, who were far worldlier and more streetwise. Alcohol and drugs were readily available, and she experimented with them all. Smoking grass and drinking cheap vodka, she became embedded deeper into their world but soon, they stopped being free, there would be a price to pay. Little did Iris know but the oldest of their group, a baby-faced pretty boy who wasn't eighteen as he had first revealed. He was twenty-seven and ran a prostitution ring in all the small towns in the area. The premise was simple, draw in young girls with acts of kindness, get them hooked on alcohol and more specifically drugs and then introduce them to his seedy world. What made this more disgusting was that his targets were children, some as young as nine, he had clients with exotic tastes.

The first-time Iris realised just how much trouble she was in, was a night she'd been plied with so much alcohol, she'd passed out. As the teenager woke, she was being undressed and a fat slobbering creature with his tiny prick in his hand readying himself for his request, an unresponsive virgin. This was in the St Mara churchyard. Her best friend, a petite brunette called Alice, who had passed herself off as being seventeen when really, she was twenty-four and in a monogamous relationship with said baby-faced pretty-boy, was carefully removing Iris's clothes, much to the delight of the fat slobbering creature with the tiny prick in his hand who was awaiting his unresponsive virgin. She swung an elbow, striking perfectly onto the bridge of her best friend's nose, exploding the appendage across her face. Grabbing her discarded clothes, she made a dash for safety, the disappointed pervert, trousers around his ankles left wondering what had gone wrong. Her relationship with the group had now ended.

Unfortunately, her relationship with alcohol had not. The centre guardians had seen a change in her personality, but Iris had been slyly hiding her activities. Now, she seemed on a downward spiral. She'd been arrested for shoplifting so many times that she was barred from entering the stores. The centre tried to prevent her from leaving the home, but she always seemed to find a way, and always returned drunk. When the girl had snatched the handbag of an elderly lady, this was the final straw. She was kept in isolation for three weeks as a form of extreme detoxification, hoping that would help her see sense. It worked for a short while, but she eventually returned to her old ways.

Then, one night, she drank so much that she passed out in the middle of a road, narrowly missing being hit by a passing car. After arrival at hospital, her stomach had to be pumped to get the poison from her system. Later, she was warned that if she continued to drink, the ramifications for her liver and future health would be greatly compromised. This wake-up call had been a strong enough message to help change her ways. There'd been occasions when she'd tumbled from the proverbial wagon and it was tough, but eventually, she managed to stop all together. Until now.

There'd been temptation over the years when Frank's wild behaviour had driven her to distraction but for Jennifer's sake, she'd resisted the urge. Always having faith that her husband, a man she respected and trusted more than anyone she'd ever met, would eventually accept what had been obvious to others for years; that their son was troubled to the realms of being dangerous and if his behaviour continued in the downward vortex, the ramifications could be catastrophic. When the horrid teen performed an act so abhorrent that it could be scarcely believed and still Martin defended him, that faith was shattered forever.

Six months after Frank had awaken from the coma, his physical rehabilitation was complete. The visible reminders were many. Across the entire length of his brow, a white line indentation buried into the flesh, lay as a memory of the blow he'd taken after shattering his forehead against the washroom basin at the beginning of the assault. The savage kick, Carl Scholes had delivered to Graham's face had left a secondary scar above the right eye, only two inches in length but deeper and more distinguishable, the stitches had failed underneath the heavy bandaging leaving behind a raw crevice. After Charlie Challis had crunched his work-boot down across the stricken teen's right arm, the bone had snapped cleanly, but a sharp fragment had pierced the skin, a conspicuous two-inch delve on his lower forearm a forever reminder. The most unmistakable disfigurement was the five-inch scar across the crown of his skull, the result of the sickening shot from Adam Scholes. As a result, pieces of bone had needed to be removed as the brain swelled. Eventually, a steel plate was fitted to strengthen the weakened skull, but the five-inch souvenir left behind could not be concealed, hair growth around the area was affected and even if strands were allowed to grow long to cover the disfigurement, the style was always impaired.

Regardless of the physical defects left behind, it was the psychological metamorphosis which affected the Graham family most. The boy had always been idiosyncratic, his behaviour erratic, bordering on dangerous. His personality uncannily peculiar, practically abhorrent, but occasionally, he could be reached, periodically he was tolerable. After the assault, that all changed. It seemed the human being inside was deceased, his interaction with anyone bars his father, suffocated. His mother, sister, any other living soul, all irrelevant. Therefore, the next event seemed…inevitable.

Iris had been shopping in St Mara; she no longer felt welcome in Hallowell's village stores, the residents saw her son as a virus and the whispers as she passed by made her feel uncomfortable. The December chill was biting hard, and snow was falling fast. Hallowell bank was the scourge of winter, its steepness ensuring that when freezing storms struck, it became impassable in record time. As the day's aim was Christmas gift shopping, Jenifer needed to stay home with Martin. Iris was nervous leaving the child in possible proximity to the dangerous teen, but her husband reassured her; this was yet another attempt at bridge-building, playing happy families even if he made it as excruciatingly wearisome as possible.

Jenifer was in the tub, happily playing with her bath toys and marvelling at the bubbles the foam bath had made. Martin vigilantly waited in the next room, smiling broadly at his daughter's giggles, happily anticipating the coming festivities, content that his son was healthy, his daughter growing into a beautiful little girl and his relationship with Iris was showing signs of improvement. The snow increased its ferocity, beating hard against the windows and Martin's smile faded. He is becoming concerned for his wife, driving in such fearsome conditions. The grin returned as he heard her car heading up the gravel driveway and he swiftly began to descend the staircase, happy to assist with the shopping, and excited to see her purchases. As the car pulled to an abrupt halt, Martin could see a look of concern on Iris's face. Quickly unhooking her seatbelt, she bolted from the door.

'What's wrong?' Martin was beginning to panic, unnerved by his wife's behaviour.

'Where's Jenny?' Her voice's tone was filled with consternation, a trepidatious dismay that confused her husband.

'She's fine, she's taking a bath.' The bemusement in his reply just added to Iris's agitation.

'And where's FRANK!' Her overwhelming, almost telepathic feeling of dread, that feeling she'd learned to trust. Like a sixth sense telling her she had to get to her daughter, NOW.

'Oh, for Christ's sake woman, what do you think he's going to do?' Iris was already up the steps to the front doorway while her husband was struggling with the shopping bags, snow driving into his face.

Wasting no time, she darted through the hallway, toward the staircase. Her wet shoes slid on the polished flooring, and she grasped the railing for support. Stopping for a split second, she heard a tiny voice squeal,

'Help me.

'NO.' Iris restarted her sprint to her daughter. 'MARTIN, WE NEED HELP.'

Her husband had just entered the house when he heard his wife screaming. He dropped a package of groceries; eggs exploding on the dark oak tiling as he began his own sprint up the staircase.

'Iris! Iris! What the Hell is happening?'

The child's soft, virgin skin was pressed hard against the white porcelain surface. Tiny air bubbles escaping from her mouth as the baby yelled screams, no one would ever hear. Her eyes tight shut, limbs flailing, thrashing bathwater onto the tiled bathroom floor. Two hands, cold as winter with a vice-like grip pinning Jenny's chest, her fight deteriorating, the inevitable nearing, the reaper ready to claim another soul.

Her legs sprinted faster than she'd ever run, bounding the stairs, and reaching the landing on the second floor in mere seconds. The hallway branched off into a left-right T-junction with all the doors to the rooms closed. Momentarily she stopped, trying desperately to hear which of the four bathrooms on that floor was being used. By now, Martin had reached the foot of the stairs, a look of confused exasperation plastered across his face. His wife screamed,

'Which fucking bathroom are they in?' By now, her husband was beginning to understand the seriousness of the situation.

'Our room's on-suite.'

With her energy replenished, she immediately shot across to the left, frantically hoping that the door wasn't locked. Twisting the handle, the barrier swung open, and she hurtled forward. The bathroom was in site, the tub in clear view, that thing bent forward, evanescent kicks of scented water spilling over the edges, her baby's tiny feet the only part of her to be seen, the fight almost over.

With one last burst of speed, she flew for the bathroom. Iris shrieked her husband's name, causing the young monster to swivel his head, finally aware of his mother's presence. His fixation on ending the child's life had been so all-encompassing that her previous cries had not penetrated his psyche but aware that the little girl's fight was almost over, he maintained his force rather than defending the coming attack. Splashed water on the bathroom tiles caused the mother to slide, though her focus remained, rescue. The effort making her howl from the pit of her stomach, and adrenaline giving her strength she wasn't aware she possessed. Finger's entwining hair, two thick handfuls were ripped from Frank's scalp, tearing at the root. The monstrous teen grimaced with pain but refused to release his hold. Panic grew as she stared at the horror of her submerged angel. The air bubbles had ceased, the child's limbs weakening, the battle almost over. In blind panic, Iris forced her thumbs into the creature's eye sockets and finally, the hold was released.

'Martin, help me please.'

Plunging to the base of the bathtub, Iris's arms hoisted with all her mite, the child's inanimate body raising with the weight of a corpse, her lips blue, skin white, eyes sunken, hair plastered back with the force of the fluid which was attempting to rob her of life. A wave washed over the side as Jenifer was elevated high into the air, hysteria not allowing her to lay the child on the cold tiles though knowing it was her baby's only chance. She wanted only to hug, to squeeze, to protect from this monster in the midst. Looking into the lifeless vessel's face, preservation instincts returned and gently, the child was lowered to the floor, all the while, her son was still just feet away. Ignoring his dangerous presence, Iris squeezed her daughters' nose, placed her lips around the girl's and began forcing breath deep into her lungs. Noisily sucking oxygen in through her nose, removing the need to shift her lips, she pushed out with everything she had. Raising upright and using the heels of her hands, Iris began heart massage, desperate to not do more damage but keenly aware of the need for force.

Gently, the teen tilted his head slightly to the left, the way an animal might, while focusing upon his mother's frenzied attempts to save his sister's life. As footsteps approached from the hallway, echoing across the wood-flooring, Frank began to rise, stealthily sliding to his feet, seemingly still entranced by the terror etched across the woman's face. From the corner of her eye, she noticed his exit and through a cascade of tears, she managed to force the words, 'Monster. You're nothing but a fucking monster.'

'I, I, I, hate you.' His response was cold, and final. As Martin hit the doorway, all he heard was,

'I hate you back, motherfucker.'

'What the hell is happening?' The patriarch finally pushed his way into the bathroom and crouched by his wife, confused by the chaos the surrounded him. Iris was incapable of answering, having returned to mouth-to-mouth resuscitation. Martin repeated the question with more vigour and urgency. "I said, what the hell is going on?" This time the inquiry was directed towards his departing son, though Frank continued his retreat across the passageway, pushing open his bedroom door and sliding it closed behind him without looking back.

Iris forced more oxygen into her daughter's lungs. Between gasps for air, she fired a scathing retort towards her husband.

'That bastard just tried to drown my daughter!' Mouthing a silent prayer, 'Come on baby, don't give up on me.' Pounding on the child's chest once more, less concerned now with breaking ribs, wanting, no, needing, those baby-blues to flutter open, desperate for a cough, a splutter, a breath. Iris had never dared listen at her baby's chest, at a heart so young, so precious. Was that vein in her neck pulsing? God please, take me instead. Or better still, take him. Take that fuck that caused this. Oh, sorry Lord, I didn't mean to curse. I'm praying, and I use the word, fuck. What kind of a person am I? The pray was jumbled, made no sense...

Water shot into the air, like a fountain in Vegas. The tooth-fairy had performed a raid day earlier, stealing Jenifer's two front teeth and from that gap, a jet erupted, followed by a cough, a splutter, a breath. Finally, tears, both the child's and Iris's.

Thank you, Lord. Thank you for giving her back to me. Now, send the other one down to Hell and I'm content.

'No, there must be some mistake, Frank wouldn't.' Even in the most impossible of circumstances, Martin refused apportion blame to his heinous son. Iris fired a malevolent stare to her husband as she held Jenifer tightly into her drenched clothing, the child's sobs painful evidence of what the monster had tried to do.

'You are trying to defend that? After what's just happened, you are trying to defend that? So, genius, how do you explain that thing, holding my daughter under the water? Refusing to relinquish his hold, even when I tore two fistfuls of hair from his head. While she kicked, and splashed, and fought for her life, he just held her there, letting water fill her lungs, drowning her, KILLING HER. Do you hear that, Martin? That bastard would have murdered my daughter. Ten seconds more and my daughter would have been dead.' A deep flush red, coloured Iris's face while she screamed, a vein in her temple pulsed so powerfully, she expected it to explode.

'Our daughter.' It was the only argument Martin thought possible.

'What?' Iris's tears had ceased, his response shocking her to the core.

'I said she's our daughter, not just yours.' The words were delivered with a softened tone, nervous that his wife could attack him physically if she was pushed too far.

'Are you serious? You are picking now as a time to get paternal?' The incredulous stare from the soaking wet woman, couldn't respond her disbelief. The child was still coughing wildly, scented water continuing to dribble from the corners of her mouth. A large white bath-towel lay, heating on a nearby radiator and Iris grabbed the fluffy material, scooping Jenifer in its warmth, a caressing embrace, a womb-like bundle of safety. The mother's lips gently kissed the five-year old's fair hair as her baby's head snuggled deeply into the curvature of Iris's neck. Martin watched on, hoping the ordeal was over, desperately yearning to join that nestling closeness but knowing that he wasn't welcome; and certain, that after doing next, what he knew was necessary, he may never have that closeness again.

'I accept Frank was partially in the wrong. Before you say anything else, just let me speak. You say he tried to drown our daughter, which I don't believe. I think that, perhaps, it was a game that got too rough.' He paused, the words were coming, hard. If I seem too defensive of the boy, she'll explode. If I apportion too much blame, then I can't take it back, she'll want too. 'He'll be disciplined, I promise you that. I was as much to blame, I asked him to stay with Jenny while I helped you with the bags.' The father hoped his wife wouldn't respond with fury; the hope was futile.

'Well, I tell you what, Martin. Let's just blame me instead. If I hadn't gone shopping, I wouldn't have needed help with the bags. Or maybe, let's blame Jesus. If he hadn't been fucking born on December 25^{th,} we wouldn't need Christmas shopping. Or Santa Clause, maybe, it's his fault. I mean, if he went on a diet, he could still fit his fat fucking arse down our chimney on Christmas Eve, then, I wouldn't have needed to shop, meaning no bags, meaning you watching our daughter while she bathed and that fucking psychopath that you call a son couldn't try to DROWN MY DAUGHTER.' The vein in her temple had returned with a vengeance, the complexion across her face a crimson mask, spittle involuntarily convulsing as the words broke free from her lips, her eyes locked on her husband with a ferociousness she'd never dared use before, her all-encompassing maternal instinct to protect her innocent daughter destroying any respect she'd ever known for her mighty husband, Martin Graham.

'I want him charged with attempted murder.' Her words had slowed to a more deliberate, demanding tone. 'I want Bill Castle here… I want him in cuffs…in the cells… IN THE FUCKING COURTS,' a pause, 'Martin, if you've never believed a word, I've said before, never listened, never given-a-fuck. You had better hear this. That boy is dangerous. No, more than that. If he's left alone, if he doesn't get some help, he will kill someone. That much is certain. But I promise you, I promise you, if he goes near Jenifer again, if he looks at her funny, I'll still a knife in his heart, I'll kill him before he can kill her. If you want to save your son, and I say your son because he's no son of mine, if you want to save your son, do the right thing. Call, Bill Castle, call St Mara police if needs be, but get him charged, and get him out of this house, because if you don't, I can't promise he'll wake up in the morning.' Her husband's reply was concise, condensed to one word.

'No.'

His face was ashen white, ghost-like with the saddest expression imaginable for he knew that, with one word, he'd just lost half of his family. Eyes welling with the heaviest tears, he turned his head away. Away from the wife he adored, the daughter he craved. Heart breaking, he'd made a choice, his son and heir, that fractured successor, the tortured persecuted inheritor whom Graham had martyrized. No matter what, the boy would be protected.

Iris knew her marriage was over. How could it not be? This wasn't just choosing the teen over the rest of his family; this was sending a message that whatever Frank wished to do, no matter how grotesque or dangerous, that there were no ramifications for his actions. No matter how depraved, how psychotic. That daddy would be there to clear up his mess. Well this time, things had gone too far, Iris wanted out.

There was just one small problem. Martin no longer looked to his wife as an equal; perhaps he never had. But he did see Iris as his possession, and no one stole from Martin Graham. True, he couldn't physically hold her against her will. But he did have one weapon left in his arsenal that would ensure Iris Graham would never divorce her husband.

He was the all-powerful Martin Graham. Seventh generation heir to a dynasty. Owner of Hallowell colliery and employer to over 150 men. Proprietor of the Graham mansion, a grade 1 listed building and dozens of other properties across the country. He was a captain of industry, respected by all, feared by many. He had all the wealth, power, and influence any man could want. And then, there was Iris.

She'd been a gutter rat; teen years spent drinking with low lives and handling more drugs than a chemist. One of life's unfortunates who was raised in a broken welfare system and would still be scratching around on Benefit Street had she not got lucky and had sympathy afforded her when she met her knight in shining armour. Mixing with drug dealers and pimps, which, if necessary, Martin's P.I. (whom he kept on retainer for just these types of unsavoury jobs), would be able to track down, should the situation arise. Dragging one of those into court as counter-character witness would be an ace in his pack, and if the real one couldn't be found, there was plenty who would lie for a nominal fee. Then there was the situation with Jennifer's overdose. It was Iris's vodka and Iris's anti-anxiety pills that the child had swallowed. Martin had hushed it up but if questions were asked, she was responsible. So, let's be serious. There wasn't a court in the land that would give her custody of their daughter. Not when comparing his record to hers. So, iris could split if that's what she wanted. But not with Jennifer. And if Jenny stayed home, who'd protect her? Martin knew Iris was trapped; and that's the way he liked it.

Had it not been for Millie Knox, Iris's sobriety would have ended years earlier. After Frank, had been born, Martin had become obsessed with getting his wife extra help around the house. His idea was for the outer flat to become servant quarters, as it had been in past generations. His intention to hire a full-time housekeeper and cook had been vetoed by Iris, as she wasn't happy with the idea of another person, holding such a prominent role in her home. Martin had also suggested a live-in nanny and with hindsight that may not have been too terrible an idea; at least Iris would have been able to claim less responsibility for the horrific personality her son now possessed. She had compromised by accepting a cleaner who would work three, two-hour shifts as an addition to the grounds man, local gardener, George Towers, and the outside catering company which dealt with dinner parties, should the invites total above eight. The cleaner they hired was Millie Knox.

They hadn't had to look far, Amelia (Millie for short) was married to former colliery worker Archie Knox, who'd been in the Graham's employ since Martin's father was in charge. A miner, man, and boy, he'd only recently switched positions to the part time role of railway station caretaker. He was months from retirement age and the hours were an ideal way of acclimatising himself from full-time employment. Had Archie been a younger man, the role would never have been offered to him, but his retirement age date coincided with Frank Graham's 16th birthday. And when the teen broke that landmark, his aim was the job of Station master, his dream job.

The role had been obsolete since the accident.

Three months earlier, June 6th, Hallowell was during an unusually long heat wave, with residents escaping whenever possible to England's coastline, desperate for some respite from the scorching summer sun. Together with the normal railway passenger expresses and the locomotives heading to and from the colliery, there was two additional private transports on the station's timetable for that Saturday.

The first was a pre-arranged outing to Morecombe, a small coastal resort, which had always been the preferred destination for the Hallowell workingmen's club annual get-away. Lots of old ladies with small grandchildren, buckets and spades and colourful inflatables to bob on the waterfront. Leaving early on the morning, they had returned later than usual, a little after seven, the old people jolly after a rum and coke, and the kids tired and grouchy. Nothing unusual.

The second private train was also hired by Hallowell workingmen's club though this one had no minors. Strictly members only, over eighteens, a direct route to Aintree races. A day of drinking too much and gambling the wife's housekeeping. A circle on the calendar for Hallowell's finest. The train was due back late, the members had arranged a bus for an evening in Liverpool's pubs and clubs. It was midnight before the whistle could be heard as the train exited Hallowell tunnel. Awaiting on the platform was Alfred Craven, station Master.

'I don't need it at this time of night. A bunch of drunken idiots pretending to be best friends, then, when tomorrow comes, they'll be back to their normal miserable selves.' A former army Sargent, Alfred was a meticulous man. He and his family had retained residency in the station master's quarters for fifteen years. His eldest boy had followed his father's example and joined the royal air force, while his second son was still in academia; the same age, same school, same class as Frank Graham. Alfred junior avoided the thug for fear it may affect his father's position. He'd watched as Graham's behaviour had grown more and more bizarre, until one day, Frank's schooling ended. The entire class breathed a collective sigh of relief.

'I hope this doesn't take long.' The balmy summer heatwave created uncomfortable, sticky sleepless nights though Craven would much rather have been sweating between his bed sheets than impatiently awaiting the lumbering train, which was emerging from the darkness. 'There's better be no beer spilled on this platform or there'll be hell to pay.'

Craven felt one of those headaches coming on. Two scotch and sodas, that was his nightly limit, why he'd poured a third, he had no idea. Plus, it had been two fingers rather than one. Bloody late-night trains, if it wasn't for these blighters, I'd have never taken that last shot. Waiting up, while the wife was tucked up in bed, Alfred had finished his latest spy novel quicker than expected and the mobile library wasn't due for another week. Television was an invention for fools, and he wouldn't allow one in his home, so the last glass of whisky had been poured to simply sooth the boredom. Still, it was about to cause him another headache and it was that blasted late train's fault. Another loud toot from its whistle didn't help either.

Alfred Craven liked to stand at the exact spot where he expected the transport to stop. Most regular train-drivers, who were familiar with the station would grimace at the sight, realising he'd deal out a piece of his mind to anyone stupid enough to overshoot the mark. Others would pass him purposely, giggling at the disapproving glare across his face. Tonight's train had been arranged with a private company, something that was new to Hallowell station, but with the onset of road travel taking precedence over railways, it was a necessary evil. The station master frowned as the steam engine began to slowly apply its brakes. At the front of the train, the driver's cabin would usually be illuminated during night-time journeys but instead, Craven could only see darkness. The approach was faster than normal too.

Silently, from the former army sergeant's rear, passing by his quarter's front door, a shadow fell across the white marble of the platform's floor. Stealthily, its creator converged upon the agitated man.

'Who's driving this bloody thing?'

It was 7:30am before Craven's body was discovered. When he'd fallen in front of the mammoth engine, the driver had been too distracted to notice. Charlie Cookson, a foreman at Hallowell colliery had started a collection for their railway chauffer and was in the process of handing the driver the proceeds as the train pulled to a stop. A loud crack had caught their attention though the drunken passenger had assured his host that obstacles were commonplace on the tracks due to spillages of coal from the loading wagons. Since the platform was dimly lit; Charlie's explanation was accepted without investigation.

The rumours spread throughout the village like wildfire, though nothing was ever proved.

Since role of stationmaster was a one that Frank had coveted from childhood, he convinced Martin that, for the time being, a replacement was unnecessary. Being only fifteen, he was aware that his father wouldn't consider him for the role yet, so he persuaded senior that all that was required was someone to maintain the building's upkeep, and if the role needed reinstating, it could be revisited at a future time. Though he had doubts, his father acknowledged his son's advice and Archie Knox was handed the role of caretaker. The little Scotsman had been happy to fill the vacancy as a pastime to retirement. The fall in salary would be a stretch but thankfully, they could still rely on his wife Millie's income from her role as cleaner at the Graham mansion.

That role had begun fifteen years earlier, immediately after the birth of the Graham's son. Iris had been uncomfortable with the idea of a cleaner but had accepted it as a compromise. With that compromise came a happy surprise as soon, Millie became an intricate part of her employer's life.

Originally, the older woman had been just as uncomfortable, unaware of how to act in Iris's presence. She would avoid working in rooms while the lady of the house was present and should their paths cross, she spoke only when spoken too. Nervous of appearing aloof, Millie finally instigated a conversation and was amazed to discover that, many of her apprehensions were shared by her employer too. Iris feared seeming too demanding as she'd never had a domestic working for her and had therefore avoided interaction with the servant. After sharing a giggle, the two women were shocked to find that they had more in common that realised. Both had suffered parental demise at an early age, and though Millie had been raised by her grandparents, that shared experience seemed to bring the two closers. Both had grown in relative poverty, neither was well travelled and their respective marriages had both begun in their teens, with their husbands being quite senior in years. It didn't take long for Millie to become far more important to Iris, than just a mere employee. She was a best friend, a confidant, even a mother figure, be it without the authority that the parental role brought. Always ready with a hearty smile to share the good times, and a shoulder to cry on when things were tough. Dependable and approachable, loyal, and trustworthy.

As the years progressed, Iris had opened her heart more and more to the aging cleaner, becoming a sounding-board and voice of reason. She'd learned the younger woman's eccentricities, how to help with her problems and when to back away. Still, this was different.

In conversation, Iris had revealed her dark past, talking frankly about her youthful battles with alcohol and how it had scarred her forever. She'd never used the word 'alcoholic' though it seemed logical. Strangely, Millie knew that her friend still drank, but she powerless to stop her. Knowing where to draw the line and aware their relationship was still, employer and employee, frowning on Iris's actions was dangerous. Taking a motherly tone, she'd asked if the booze was under control or was it beginning to control her? Whenever Frank's actions had taken a decidedly dark turn, like the attack on the Scholes girl or the assault on the schoolteacher, her units would increase dramatically. It seemed that drinking helped sooth the dramas and since her husband was increasingly defending the indefensible, Millie and a glass of wine were her only escapes from the shattered life she was living.

At first, it was an occasional glass of wine, which soon became an occasional bottle. The more time she spent alone, the stronger the urge to drink. She tried to stay sober in front of Jennifer but the time when the child was at school was torture. Eventually, the other mothers were whispering at the school gates, veiled looks behind vague glances. Oh, they were discreet, but it was obvious. In time, Iris past caring.

After the incident with Jenifer and the pills, Iris had made a conscious effort to quit, but the loneliness of her existence was hard to fight. The passionate love, she'd once appreciated for her husband was now lost, replaced with a clouded confusion. How could he believe that their son's actions were normal? Their home life was shattered, seemingly beyond repair. Seemingly, because Martin had the power to change it, make a stand, just for once. He'd created the monster. He was Dr fucking Frankenstein, he was Bram Stoker. Martin Graham, the only person who had any control over that thing, but continually refused to access that power. Without change, their marriage was doomed but more importantly, whatever that beast dose in the future, would be Martin's responsibility.

The more depressed she felt, the more she drank and the more she drank, the more depressed she'd feel, it was a vicious circle. Wine was replaced by spirits, whisky, gin, vodka, whatever she could get her hands on. By now, the home was divided in two and with the size of the Graham mansion, they could go days without seeing one another. Iris slept in a room with Jenifer and the door was always bolted. She rarely let the child out of her sight, except for her schooling and even then, the headmaster was under strict instruction to release the child to her only, and never, under any circumstances, to her older brother.

Most nights, she cried herself to sleep in a drunken stupor. Jenifer's bedtime was eight and their room contained a spacious bathroom. Here, away from her sleeping daughter, aware that she was out of harm's way, she could drink herself into oblivion.

People in Hallowell were talking, behind whispers and glances, they giggled and gossiped and made cruel assumptions and unfair connections. Frank's actions had tarred the Graham reputation forever, so why not be callous and heartless to the mother as well. They knew nothing of what happened when the front door closed, the agony she felt at all the battles lost. And how falling into oblivion was her only way of coping. So yes, they can gossip out about the night when the house was dry, and she'd driven to the store for more supplies. How she'd clipped a lamppost and crashed into a ditch. How Bill Castle had driven her home and tried to stop the gossip spreading. Well, his efforts failed. And then there was his nosy bitch wife, Alice Castle, who'd tried a concerned reach-out only to be met with a hostile retort, making it plain that her opinion was neither wanted nor needed. For once, being in control felt good. Afterwards, she'd started making her purchases from St Mara's large supermarket and the Castle general dealers lost a regular customer.

Two years had passed since that night. The night that changed their lives forever. For Iris, it was the worst two years of her life. The only plus was watching Jenifer grow. She was such a happy child, never allowing the torturous situation to cloud her innocent. Too young to understand the shame, her brother had brought upon the family name, too young to understand the danger that that creature possessed.

One image was stuck fast in her memory from that day, and it was sad. She'd forgotten or blocked out so many things, but this one thing kept coming back. She couldn't remember where they'd eaten or what show they'd seen. Their time of departure or when they'd got back home. It was staring in that mirror in the hallway of the mansion, the last time Iris had looked in the mirror and smiled. Liked the woman reflected in its surface, a time when she still looked forward instead of always looking back. She couldn't remember that day's details, all she knew was it had been wonderful. A near perfect day. The only thing that could have made it better was, when those people had assaulted her son, why couldn't they have finished the job. A knife to the heart, an extra blow to the brain. She wondered how their lives would have turned out had Frank not survived. Just how good could things have been if that bastard was dead. But they'd failed.

Those fucking idiots couldn't even do that right. Well, now it was her turn to succeed where they hadn't; it was the only way.

Was it only two years? How could things go so far to Hell in twenty-four short months. She'd witnessed the most horrible things. Her son smashed to pieces, bones broken, body bruised, blood spilled yet her only regret was it hadn't been worse. When it had recovered, it had tried to drown her daughter, sweet innocent Jenny, the only thing left on this miserable planet that she loved (bar Millie but she had her own life) But the most shocking thing she'd seen (more shocking than Frank's heinous act because incredibly, it hadn't shocked her at all, she'd known for years what he was capable of) was the deterioration of a man she'd once loved and respected. Martin Graham was now a shadow of his former self. Age had not been kind. Where previously, he'd at least taken pride in his appearance, the downward spiral had been swift. There were no more hair colourants, his black mane now a whispery grey with a growing bald patch across the crown. His skin, once firm and vibrant, flushed by the joys of heathy living was now leathery, loose, and wrinkled. Living with a constant, five o'clock shadow and heavy bags under each eye that told a tale, a thousand words couldn't describe, he looked every second of his 63 years (and then some). The slight paunch that could be described as middle-aged spread was now fat, plain, and simple. That extra chin had tripled, and loose-fitting shirts could no longer hide this new-found obesity. His vision disgusted her.

But what was worse was his mental deterioration. All his faculties were still intact, as well as could be expected under the circumstances. But that toughness she'd once admired, even been attracted too, my God, he was no longer the same man. Employees took liberties without reprimand. Talked behind his back, worse, sometimes to his face. All that fight was gone, turning full circle. When he was younger, the workers respected him because he was fair and good and rewarded hard work and loyalty but the more that bastard was in his ear, influencing his calls and punishing where there was no crime. And now, that his strength and courage were diminishing, employees who may have remembered the man he used to be, when things were good, had more recent experiences of false force and were more than happy to exploit weakness. The man Iris Graham had married would never have tolerated such insolence. At the colliery, workers had been forced to accept Frank as their superior when, they wouldn't piss on him if he were on fire. These were mistakes that had destroyed the Graham Empire.

Iris would rather just walk away, take Jennifer, and go. But he'd never let that happen. So, there was no option remaining. While that monster was alive, Jenny was in danger and Iris couldn't take that risk. Frank Graham had to die.

The only question was how? She was a tiny little woman, and he was a beast so overpowering the monster was impossible. Poisoning was considered but it rarely ate anything Iris prepared and there was the risk, Jenny may mix up meals and that thought was too awful to consider; another way was necessary. It had started driving and an accident could be hidden. The problem was that Iris knew more about the anatomy of the spectacled cobra of India than the inside of a combustion engine and had no clue how to sabotage such a thing. She wasn't even aware of how to lift the hood so; another good option was dashed. Electrocution? He rarely bathed and getting close enough to drop a working toaster in the tub would be tough and she was only going get one shot at this. Shot? Great idea. It didn't matter how big he was, he couldn't fight a six-shooter. One problem, she didn't have a gun. Fuck: this was harder than she thought. It was strange because she was enjoying thinking of ideas of how to kill it, it wasn't that she wanted to become a murderer, it was because, for the first time in months, she felt in charge. Like her life had meaning rather than just fending off punches. She knew that, in the aftermath, there would be a prison sentence, probably a long one. She would be deemed a murdering bitch in the press, destroying her own flesh and blood. But locals, those who knew the Graham's long and arduous history would understand. Hell, they'd celebrate. Frank was as popular as the Black Death. Only Martin would miss him. He'd never forgive or forget, but at least she'd be free. And Jenny would be safe and that's why she was doing this. Back to the drawing board.

It was October 13th, 1964, Frank's eighteenth birthday. It was a man now and Martin thought it his civic duty to get the teen drunk. To Iris's knowledge, her son had never tasted a drop of alcohol and a plan was forming. She had exhausted all possibilities and couldn't reckon on anything working. He was too big, too strong, and too paranoid for most plans to work. She didn't have the connections or the resources to bring in outside help and didn't have the intellect for anything elaborate. This was going to have to be close quarters, up close and personal."

Chapter 14

Nick Castle had remained silent for fifteen minutes and his father was beginning to wonder.

"You haven't fell asleep over there, have you? I heard about people sleeping with their eyes open."

"Thought you said I had to shut up. This is the most interesting thing I've heard you say, ever. Didn't want to interrupt."

"If there was ever going to be a shot, today would be it. She might not get another so this one had to work. It needed planning, careful planning; nothing left to chance. Iris Graham became a detective.

She'd overheard about it three weeks earlier. Communication between husband and wife, mother, and son, now obsolete. They lived separate lives bar their home address. Martin would be cordial to Jennifer when he saw her which was rarely. He paid the bills; Iris did the shopping, and the kitchen was shared. In a hostile environment, it worked strangely amicably. The division wasn't announced but it was public knowledge. The only real winner was Frank, he had obliterated his mother and sister from Martin's life. The only annoyance was their continued breathing. Still, there was plenty of time.

Father and son were having breakfast, it was around eight and Iris had expected them to have left for work already. When she heard voices, she'd waited in the lobby and rested at the foot of the stairs, not wishing to provoke an atmosphere that early of a morning. The kitchen door was open and hearing their conversation wasn't difficult. Martin brought up the subject of Frank's eighteenth birthday and asked how he'd like to celebrate it. Iris had had to fight the urge to laugh when he mooted the possibility of a party. Who the Hell would they invite? They were as popular as clap in a convent. She could imagine the scene, streamers and balloons decking out a huge hall, music blaring and a free bar. And the only ones there to enjoy it being the bar staff, a D.J. and father and son, sitting with paper party hats, drunk as skunks, watching the clock saying, 'They should have arrived by now.' Hilarious.

When that idea was dismissed, Martin came up with a brain wave. Over in the town of Carpenter, ten miles north of St Mara, there was a 'special bar' where you had to be 18 for entry. In there, Frank could see the other side of life and maybe get 'lucky' if any of the girls liked him. Iris took 'special' to mean the lap dancing dive she'd once heard the vicar over in St Helens church mention in one of his sermons on the sins of the flesh. And by 'lucky', it probably meant that if they were paid enough, the freak could finally get laid. In years gone by, the thought of her husband and son frequenting such a place would disgust her but now, she could give a shit. Plus, if he came home pissed, it would make what she had to do all the easier. Frank had sounded excited, and Iris began to formulate a plan.

If everything went perfect (and she was certain these things rarely went perfect) there was a chance, but it needed precise planning and a clear head. For the next three weeks, Iris Graham went cold turkey.

God must smile on the righteous. Four days before the birthday, Iris listened at Martin's study door as he 'made arrangements. That door was always closed tight, and its thickness kept anything said inside private but for once, it stood ajar. He was ordering a booth in Rumours gentlemen's club (gentlemen, what a joke. A bunch of sleazy perverts who could only get their kicks by watching some big breasted stripper flash her cleavage at their faces). From the way he spoke, he sounded friendly with the owner, calling him by his Christian name and laughing at some crude remark no doubt. Again, this would normally have repulsed her, the thought of her own husband seeking sexual gratification in such a place, but the days of jealousy were over. If things went correctly, the only time she'd see her husband again would be at her trial.

The next call was made to a young man named Miner, an apt name for a colliery worker. She'd met his father years ago, at a work function and remembered the elder remarking that his son would be starting at the pit soon. Miner (junior) had been chosen for a special task and his line manager had been informed to expect the young man's absence on the 13th. He was informed that he would be chauffeuring for the Graham's during Frank's birthday celebration. They'd be using the Daimler and departing at eleven. He was given the option of staying in Carpenter until they were through for the day or returning home, with the express instruction to not move away from the telephone as they didn't expect to be kept waiting. If he did return home he'd be expected to drive 'like a bat out of Hell' when they needed their return trip, but also taking care with Martin's favourite car. The young man decided it was safer to remain in the seedy little town, which was well known for its gang problems and high crime rate. Taking his chances with the criminals was a better option than upsetting the Grahams.

The day before, on the Thursday, Martin had taken Frank shopping in St Mara, insisting that his clothes weren't fashionable for their next day jaunt. He'd purchased a gaudy yellow shirt with no collar, boot-cut jeans, and a long black leather trench coat. It wasn't Frank's normal wear, which was an obvious improvement, but it wasn't clothes, the eighteen-year-old could feel comfortable in. Iris imagined that, should all go to plan, they would be the final clothes he'd ever wear.

Friday October 13th. Iris had barely slept for three nights, knowing the terrible but necessary task which lay ahead. She'd accumulated a shopping list and a to-do list. The groundwork was complete, it was in God's hands now.

Miner arrived at a quarter before eleven and had dressed in a worn but well-made suit. He really hoped that his superior wouldn't expect him to wear a chauffer's hat, surely the smartly dressed attire would suffice. He'd be disappointed. The Daimler had been washed, waxed, and polished, inside, and out and had been pulled around to the front of the property. Miner had never driven anything so luxurious, in fact he hadn't driven much. The young man had only passed his driving test six months previously and the most he'd operated was a ford fiesta, 1.1 litre engine. The upgrade made him excited but nervous.

Iris had waited eagerly for their departure, wanting that final resolution that today was going ahead. She had a list of purchases that would take time to accrue and the jobs that required completion before the men returned would ensure that she wouldn't have too much time on her hands to ponder the inevitable. As the Daimler left the driveway, Iris hurried to her Volvo and started the ignition. Nothing. She turned the key again and this time the engine grumbled but refused to fire into life.

'Please, not today.' A third time and still the starter motor growled then spluttered to a halt.

'COME ON, COME ON, COME ON.' She hit the steering wheel with the palm of her hand and cursed aloud. Without the supplies, today wasn't happening. A fourth and final time and the sweet sound of the engine roaring into life, filled her ears. An audible cheer escaped her lungs as the car's gearbox accepted first gear and the journey began.

It took twenty-five minutes for Miner to navigate the Daimler to Carpenter. There'd been a few hairy moments, like when they'd arrived at a junction on the outskirts of St Mara, and he hadn't noticed an on-coming delivery van and only a last-minute heavy brake had avoided a collision. Martin had given the boy a stern glare but stopped before scolding the lad. If he pissed the youngest off too much, he might not wait around to take them home. Even the threat of the sack wasn't enough to frighten some of today's youth. He'd pushed it when he forced the driver to wear that silly hat, so the heavy-handed approach wasn't in their best interests.

Martin had considered telling Miner to park in the next street to Rumours as he didn't want the whole village talking about where Martin had taken his son for his birthday. Most thought that Frank was weird already, this wasn't something that needed to be public knowledge. But instead, he used the power of the check book to maintain the silence. As they pulled up in front of the seedy looking drinkers club, the patriarch handed the youngest a £20 note and a knowing smile. That's all it took to gain his loyalty. They exited the car, two generations of Graham, both men now, and headed into the black fronted premises, the only thing that advertised its location, a pink neon sign above the doorway: blink, blink, blinkedy-blink.

Dawson's hardware, on the corner of Chestnut Street in St Mara was perfect for Iris's needs. Used by tradesmen, tools for every occasion were in store, without the need for ordering. A spotty teen with a croaked tie and a nameplate with Steve emblazoned across it, hanging from a creased shirt pocket approached as she checked out the options.

'Is there anything I can help you with mam?' His monotone voice suggested he hated his job and hated dealing with indecisive women even more. He never made eye contact, as if he was trying his best to be rude without having to call her a bitch. Iris decided not to take the bait.

'There certainly is young man. My boy has just finished school and has been accepted for an apprenticeship at a local butcher's shop. He starts Monday and has been told he needs his own boning knife and sharpening steel. Could you head me in the direction of your stock please?' Iris had painted an inane grin across her face and the assistant couldn't fathom whether she was taking the piss or just crazy.

'Yes, this way.' It was one of those times when he just wanted to deal with the sarcastic bitch and get rid. At least he hoped it was sarcasm, if not he was about to hand a potentially deadly weapon to a crazy person. 'We don't have too much stock in now. There's three to choose from or if you want to come back Tuesday, we are getting a delivery then.' If it were possible, he had decreased even more in enthusiasm.

'No, that's too late, I'm sure one of these will be fine. Thank you so much for your assistance.' She let her stair linger a little too long and he was beginning to think she may be a crazy woman. He smiled a nervous grin and made a hasty retreat.

There were two wooden handled models, and they came with a sharpening steel, but they were far less expensive than the other one, a Matlock ever-sharp with a black hard-rubber handle and a ten-year guarantee for durability. It was his money she was spending, what did Iris care how much it cost. There was a matching sharpening steel and she bought that too; just to be sure. The irritating teen was now serving at the cash register, and he placed the items in a brown paper bag without saying a word. She handed him a £20 and a £10 and the spot factory shuffled with change and placed the coins in the bag with the equipment. Iris gave him one last glare though her earlier fake manners had now gone. As she left the store, he muttered to a colleague who was stacking shelves to his right, 'There's something not right there. Say good-bye to the next Ed Gein.'

Inside the strip club, the Graham's were already on their third double whisky. Frank grimaced at the taste, but the beer chaser had helped soften the burning sensation. The lighting was dim bar for the stage where every thirty minutes, a new stripper would perform, showing just enough to get the punters interested. If they wanted to see more, they needed to pay for private dances. Men would sporadically be led by the hand to a back area where 'extras' were available for anyone with enough money. The main bar area was empty except for a loud-mouthed group of three businessmen who called the girls, cunts and belittled their dancing. They'd been warned by a surly security man who was reassured by the £20 slipped into his shirt pocket and the offer of a beer. The bartender gestured for the tough shit kicker named Doug to speak privately and was informed that they'd been in all afternoons and were spending a small fortune. It seemed that insulting the workforce was fine so long as the cash kept flowing. Doug returned to the troublesome trio and apologised, insisting the next round was on him to which there was much back slapping and another chorus of 'Yellow submarine' by the Beatles. Frank was watching and getting pissed, he didn't like loud people. The loudest, a fat slobbering fifty something who'd already had way too much to drink caught Frank's glare and gave him the finger to which his friends cheered. The teen didn't react, just waited.

Iris realised after she'd left the hardware store that she needed oil. The conclusion to her visit had been weird and she didn't fancy the idea of a return, so she called at a service station on the outskirts of St Mara where, after filling up the tank, she bought a small tin of shell motor oil before leaving. It wasn't perfect for her needs, but it would have to do.

A big breasted redhead with too much makes up and heels that made her look seven feet tall, approached Frank as Martin used the bathroom.

'Would you like a private dance cutesy?' He'd never been propositioned by a woman before and had no idea how to react.

'I, I, I, d, d, don't know really.' His nerves were evident, inexperience shining like a beacon.

'You don't have to be scared honey, let Star take care of you.' She took his hand; it was clammy and stiff. Sensing weakness, she continued. 'Come on, let me take care of you.'

'Made a friend their son?' Martin was returning, a whisky glow covering his well-oiled demeanour. Frank saw his father and in embarrassment, pulled away his hand, shocking Star. Sensing there was still a chance, she gently slipped onto Frank's lap and kissed his forehead.

'Come with me honey, you'll be glad you did.' Martin chuckled and gave his son a knowing wink as the teen cautiously climbed to his feet and was led to the back by the scantily clad girl.

Iris had one last stop to make. Her car strained as it reached the apex of Hallowell bank and she pulled over to the side on a piece of wasteland, leaving the engine running. The still handle on the Volvo needed force to open and as it did, the cool autumnal air rushed it to meet her. When she was no older than Frank, Martin and she had picnicked just north of here where, later in the evening, he'd proposed marriage. They were the good times, how she missed them. It was still one of her favourite places though, her walks with Jenny up the bank, back through the woods and down by the railway were a personal triumph for one with such small legs. A tear ran down her left cheek at the realisation that she'd never get to do that again. She'd miss so much of her daughter's life, rotting away in prison but the important thing was, Jennifer would be safe, away from that monster. That's all that mattered. Climbing back into the Volvo, she wiped her cheek and refocused, there was still much to do.

Everything had changed. This thing in front of her wasn't the shy boy from five minutes ago; no, this was something different altogether.

Star had learned to trust her instincts, had too in this line of work. A strange cross-section of society used her services, most were lonely, middle-aged men, looking for something their wives either couldn't or wouldn't perform. Living a fantasy that ended the moment they exited the club. Sometimes they were creepy but harmless, like Weird Al. He came every Friday for one dance, always with Star, always at 6 pm. He wore a brown overcoat, down to the ground and nothing else. Some of the girls would go that 'extra mile' if there was a nice bonus coming their way, but Star was strictly look but don't touch. That suited Al fine who'd give himself a quick hand job while Star danced to the Buddy Holly hit that will be the day. Always the same time, same song, same girl. Like a broken record jumping back to a certain point. Weird but harmless.

The ones who caused the most problems were the arseholes like the three businessmen at the bar who thought they owned the girls because they paid well. She would rather stub out a cigarette in one of their eyes than dance for them, but the owner could get very nasty if the girls turned down punters. There were times Star hated her job.

But the worst was Daryl Bundy. He seemed normal at first, normal. He started coming in every few days, refusing dances, just watching. Then it became daily, the girls started a competition to see which would be the first the snare him. And finally, it happened. Star had taken him to the back and started her performance. It was just a generic dance, nothing special. As she reached just her underwear, she caught a glimpse of his eyes. It was more disgust than lust. Wearing a brown leather jacket, there was a bulge in the inside pocket and his hand slowly slid toward it. In a split second, the knife was out, and he lunged forward, the tip just nicking the flesh on her abdomen. Her screams alerted Doug the security man who disarmed to lunatic and snapped his right arm in one swift movement. Not wishing for bad publicity, Bundy was thrown out onto the streets, but the police were not informed. Three days later while watching the evening news, Bundy was the main story. He'd murdered four sex workers and was holding another captive in the basement of his house.

Looking into Frank Graham's eyes, her instinct told her he was just as dangerous. They were cold, lifeless, merciless. His hands that were clammy, sweaty with nerves were now ice. He'd transformed from that shy boy to…something else. She stopped the dance immediately, collected her discarded clothing and rushed to the dressing room, not even stopping to collect her fee.

Father Henderson had been in residency at St Helens church on the edge of Hallowell for fifteen years. When he'd arrived, he was a fresh faced twenty-eight-year-old with a strong faith and wonderful ideas to integrate the church into the community. Now he was suffering the same scars that many of his congregation felt. High unemployment and a lack of governmental investment had soured many of the worshippers and when life was bad, God generally got the blame. He'd would have had no problem fighting the good fight, had his own wife and daughter not been killed by some drunk driver a year earlier, leaving him to question his own faith. Forgiveness is preached in the bible but when he'd visited the culprit in prison, all wanted to do was tear the man's head off. If he couldn't practice his bosses' word, what chance did his congregation have.

Sunday morning numbers were falling, just twenty-seven faces had stared back last week as he talked about the upcoming harvest festival. Writing a sermon for such low numbers seemed pointless. Over the last month, only four people had used confessional and one of those didn't count; old Mrs Briggs would seek forgiveness if she discovered two knives in her cutlery draw in the shape of a cross. Was it wrong to hope for something juicy? The nearest thing was Janice Hunt, who was having extra marital relations with a guy from St Mara. Her husband had come for advice with the same story he'd heard a hundred times before (though normally it was the husbands having the affairs and the women seeking solace) He had been surprised though, to hear that Mrs Hunt had taken to beating her husband after too much alcohol on a Saturday night. This was almost always the opposite. When Mr Hunt had begun openly weeping on the priest's shoulder, Father Henderson felt himself begin to lose patience with the sniffling wimp. 'My God man, no wonder your wife is screwing around on you, be a man and…' It was these reactions that made him feel that perhaps his time in Hallowell was ending.

The church was clean. Millie Knox did a wonderful job, but it wasn't hard with such a low footfall. The vicar had fought calls to lock up the church when it wasn't manned after a golden cross had been stolen from behind the pulpit. A sign of the times when even God's house wasn't immune from the social ills of society. Henderson believed that the church should be available to the community whenever it was needed. How could that happen with locked doors. Still, sitting here, all day, every day with just a statue of Christ for company wasn't going to happen. He had better things to do with his time.

He was just about to head back to the rectory when a blue Volvo pulled into the car park. He squinted in the October sun and recognised the slim figure of Iris Graham. As a family, the Graham's had been regular visitors of a Sunday morning up to when their son had been hurt a couple of years back. Since then, there'd been no sign. The rumour mill had been in full flow about marriage problems and Henderson had listened to the whispers without retort. Still. This could be interesting.

Frank Graham was finding out quickly, the effect alcohol can have on the bladder. Three-bathroom visits in an hour was becoming tedious. The first had been to vomit, his body finally caving to the sensation caused by the whiskey's assault. That hadn't prevented him drinking three more and now, the world was a swirling haze. Aiming his stream of urine when seeing double proved challenging but he finally mastered it and the relief was palpable. Before he finished, the bathroom door swung open and the loudest of the three drunken businessmen staggered into view. Singing a chorus of Elvis Pressley's suspicious minds, he tripped and nudged into the teen's back.

'Hey, watch what you are doing there, boy.' Frank ignored the jab as he finished emptying his bladder. Fighting with his flies the drunken slob muttered, 'Yeh, you better watch yourself, big dummy.' He pulled out a pathetic withered penis and urine jetted at the dirty porcelain. Frank ended his visit and turned to leave, only for the lout to swivel and spray foul smelling liquid across the young man's shoes.

He let out an immature laugh before muttering, 'I showed him.'

The businessman was flat on the floor before he realised, he'd been hit. A large gash was gushing blood after he crashed his head on a filthy washbasin on the way down, joining his shattered nose that had exploded from one swift right-hand shot. The floor's wet tiling was slippery, but Graham's inebriation seemed to have vanished, after three huge stomps across the fallen man's brow, hit with cold precision. He'd had no time to raise his arms in defence and sweet unconsciousness ended his pain, the withered penis still leaking its contents over the slob's grey trousers.

'I've no choice father, something has to change.' The vicar could scarcely believe what he'd just heard. No, surely, he must have misunderstood. No mother could mean what she'd just said.

Henderson knew the boy was troubled. There'd been something about a pet, a dog belonging to the little girl that had been slaughtered. And he was supposed to have trapped that girl in the barn, the Scholes's daughter. There'd been talk of something that had happened with rats but surely that had to have been a mistake. Chinese whispers. No one would do that. Those places were full of vermin; no one could dream up something that evil.

His mother had called upon the priest to speak to the boy which he'd been happy to do but when he'd arrived at the mansion, the boy's father had screamed in his face and used language, a man of the clergy would never repeat. Strange behaviour for a man who'd been a regular church attendee. And when the boy had been attacked, the father visited the stricken lad in hospital but again, Martin Graham had been rude. He put that down to worry and pressure, expecting an apology once his son was on the mend. It never came. That was the last association with the family until now…

'He's still a young man Mrs Graham and some boys mature later than others. Have faith that God has a plan for Frank and in time, things will improve.'

'Fuck God.' Iris's reaction horrified herself more than the priest who'd heard statements like that before. She slapped a hand across her lips and burst into tears. 'Oh father, I'm so sorry, I just mean…'

'Don't Mrs Graham. I do understand. Frustration causes anger and we all vent in different ways. When the world is wonderful, there's no time to thank God and when it's going wrong, he's an easy target.'

'I'm sorry father.' She rose from the pew. 'I should go.' She dabbed her cheek with a paper handkerchief and moved to the end of the row.

'Iris listens.' His protests were in vain as she headed toward the exit. 'Mrs Graham, have faith, things will improve. I promise.' Iris stopped and looked back toward the confused clergyman.

'Thank you, father. You're a good man.' As she walked away, he could hear her say, 'I've no choice, something has to change.'

The dirty flowing waters of Carpenter's canal needed care and attention. Discarded shopping trollies and trash mingled with raw sewage from a broken waste pipe leaving a repulsive stench that few could tolerate. The only ones who had little choice were the women of the red-light district who'd been moved on from all the other spots in town and the police was not inclined to bother them here. Plus, it seemed the only other people who'd be around this dump would be the creeps who needed their services. If they weren't bothering decent people, leave them to it.

Miner had read six chapters of his book by the time the Graham's had staggered back to the Daimler. Leaping from the driver's seat, he'd hurried around to open the back doors and expected to head straight back to Hallowell. When he was told to make a right, down by the canal, the motives became obvious.

This really was the scum of society. Many had looked decent in their youth but years of selling their bodies to pay for a drug habit that would slowly kill them had taken a vicious toll. They wore cheap clothes and too much make-up to disguise their goodness depraved skin. Many were pitifully thin and ill looking, either buzzed out of their minds or withdrawal symptoms creating a sorry existence. They were already dead, just no one had cared to tell them.

Many had worked in the strip joint where the Graham's had just left but either age had made them less desirable or the drugs had made regular work impossible and now, selling the only asset they had left was the only option.

But then, there was Candy. She didn't only look normal, she was stunning. Hair and make-up nice, clean clothes, white teeth. What was she doing with the dregs of society? Martin made Miner stop the car and he climbed out, staggering in the beauty's direction.

'Want a date honey bunch?' A black prostitute with a leopard skin coat and broken front teeth darted from the crowd when she saw the old man was ready for business. The Daimler gave away the fact that he had money.

'Get away from me, you nasty old slut.' Martin was disgusted that such a woman would even think he'd be interested in someone like her.

'That's right you old bastard, nasty old slut. That's what we all are down here. Expect blondie over there. She thinks her shit don't stink and she's better than us. Well, let me tell you, she no better than us, same holes in the same places.' The dirty laugh made Martin think she'd used that line before.

Candy looked so out of place. Martin almost wanted to take her home with him, away from this lifestyle but knew he couldn't. Still, this seemed wrong.

What Martin Graham didn't know, what no one knew, was Candy's real name was Emma and she was fourteen years old. Her real father had died when she was only three and her mother, in desperation, married the first man who showed an interest in supporting her and her daughter. Ian King was a sleazy looking slug of a man, who's appetite for alcohol and fatty food was only surpassed by his need for child sex. He'd hidden the fact that he'd served five years for abusing an eight-year-old girl with the help of the child's mother and by the time Emma's mum Sophie realised something was not right, he'd molested Emma for two years too. Incredibly, Sophie had sided with the over-grown piece of shit, knowing that a divorce would once more see her back on the poverty line. She accused her daughter of instigating the affair (never accepting it was abuse). King had apologised and insisted he'd change his ways and shockingly, Sophie accepted that Emma hadn't, and ran away, believing that a life on the streets would be better than being at the whim of a pervert.

That was three months ago, and she'd coped by begging on street corners. That was until Dwayne Austin had come into her life. He was a fast talking, street wise pimp who piled her with so many drugs that before she knew it, she was hooked. He told her he loved her, and she believed it and soon, he was pimping her services to whoever wanted them. Tonight, he hadn't gotten her booked out, so she was forced on the streets with the other tarts. They hated her because she was so much prettier than they were and took all their clients. It was a horrible existence.

Martin took the child by the hand and led her to the Daimler. Her eyes were glassy and having trouble focusing, it had only been twenty minutes since her last shot of heroine. The needle mark on her left arm was still weeping but she felt nothing. Candy (Dwayne had chosen that name) was manhandled onto the back seat between Martin and his son. There was a screen between the Graham's and Miner for privacy and the young man didn't want to know what his employers were doing anyway. His job was to drive and keep his mouth shut.

The Daimler pulled around to a piece of wasteland away from the group of enraged hookers but still by the canal. It was 6.30 pm and the night was growing dark. Martin called for Miner to stop the car away from any prying eyes though no one would have been in that area that didn't have to be. To the right, there were disused factories, their boarded windows a depressing sign of unemployment. One had had the boards ripped off a doorway and would certainly have been in regular use by the street workers. A building in the rear had been ravaged by fire and no longer housed a roof, pigeons nesting inside its rafters and calling it home. Down by the railing to the canal, a stripped car wreck, all its valuable assets taken, windows smashed, doors kicked off, roof dented in, an enjoyable day's work for kids with nothing better to do with their time.

Martin began to exit the rear door when Candy spoke for the first time.

'Not in the car. Please, I'm claustrophobic.' Her voice was sweet and tender, nothing like the harsh black tart who'd rudely offered her wears moments earlier. Her head was swaying gently from side to side, the killer drug, obviously still pulsing through her veins. It seemed that Graham junior was also still visiting that same village near la-la-land as Candy as he seemed barely conscious, the effects of his first days drinking now wearing heavily on him. If he'd had a choice, Frank would have happily gone home to sleep of its narcotic strains, but Martin was adamant. He was a man today and as he man, it was time he…did what men do.

Martin led Frank and his birthday present out of the car and across to an open doorway of one of the disused factories. It was private enough without upsetting the girl, for some reason, that was important to him. He looked back toward the Daimler to ensure that Miner wasn't spying though it was obvious what was about to happen. When he was happy the deed would be done, Graham senior left his son to become a man.

The chilly October evening had grown cold, and a light drizzle filled the air. Inside, the doorway led to a long corridor, vision was minimal. Instead of walking deeper into the property, Frank rested his back against a grimy wall, soiled with an oil/dust residue, needing to steady himself, barely registering that he had company. Echoes from the other sex workers carried along the canals

149

length and the nearby water lapped against stone walls. The girl was still new to this life and would wait for the client to give her direction, but he just stood there, statue like, staring. He'd noticed Candy now and seemed surprised by her presence. The Daimler had driven a few hundred yards away as to not add pressure to his first time. The child, knowing that if she did nothing, she wouldn't be paid and Dwayne would get angry, knelt, eye line to the giant's crotch. She raised her right hand and started to undo his belt when a huge right knee smashed directly into her nose, sending her hurtling through the air. She landed outside on the concrete courtyard and looked for the car. The old man inside had seemed so nice, was it false? Was this what she'd been brought here for? Trying to find her feet she stumbled and fell, landing once more on her back. The blow to her face had been painful, but she was in shock and the natural anaesthetic of the heroine made tolerance possible. The grey metal poles guarding the canal were just feet away and she began rolling for their assistance. Suddenly, out of the darkened doorway, the hulking figure of the thing that had just assaulted her loomed into view. She began backing away, realisation of how much trouble she was in becoming evident. He was toying with her, moving slowly, stalking, knowing he could grab her at any moment but waiting. She began to weep silent tears, knowing that whatever he decided to do, she was powerless to fight it. Her head was touching the railings now and she thought about climbing the cold steel and running but with the monster having a standing start, she had no chance of escape. It was then, she took her only option.

The water was twelve feet below from the bank and the walls were solid brick. She'd rolled directly under the steel barrier, falling through the air, and hitting the canal with force. The icy temperature of the water made her scream and she gulped in two lungsful of vile stinking liquid. Hitting the bottom, she felt twisted metal of a discarded bicycle, its handlebar stabbing sharply into her thigh. The pain was excruciating but the panic she felt when her foot became entangled in rotting roots of long dead trees brought her to her senses. She kicked aggressively and her shoe slipped from her left foot, freeing her leg. Bobbing to the surface, the coughs of horrendously tasting water burned her throat. Her eyes stung and the world seemed black. Above the lurking silhouette of Frank Graham turned and retreated to his waiting car.

The first attempts of a fledgling killer.

What a strange day it had been. Father Henderson had wished for some excitement but the old saying, 'be careful what you wish for' had never been more apt. Surely, he'd misunderstood, she couldn't have meant what he'd heard.

It had troubled him all day. He hadn't been able to concentrate on gardener's world television show, so he'd showered, cleansing his body if not his mind. The vicarage seemed so quiet tonight. Most Fridays, Harry Brackett would visit for a game of chess and a brandy, but a case of the sniffles had condemned the good doctor to his bed. Bad timing as the vicar would have appreciated someone to bounce his concerns off. Was that wrong? He'd taken an oath to maintain the secrets of his parishioners but that was in confessional. This wasn't in the box, she'd sat on the pews as she poured her heart out, did that make a difference?

Plus, she was talking about things she planned to do rather than what she'd already done. Taking her at face value, this was potentially very serious. Surely, surely, he was wrong. No mother would plan to murder her own son.

He removed his heavy inverted eyeglasses and rubbed the bridge of his nose. The telephone was sitting right there, on the same desk he'd used to write all those pointless sermons but today he had the chance to make a real difference and was torn. If he picked up that receiver, he'd be betraying a confidence but if he didn't, a teenager's life could hang in the balance. He rose from his chair and paced the floor. Logs crackled on the open fire and Henderson forced a poker underneath, allowing flames to lick up the chimney breast. The sudden heat forced the priest back and he pulled a metal fireguard across cautiously.

"That's you John, cautious Carl, steady Eddie." The vicar was angry at his own indecision, this was a dangerous game. He looked at the telephone once more then headed to his bedroom to change his clothes.

The clock was ticking, they could be home anytime, had she thought of everything? Jennifer was safe, that was priority number one. Millie and Archie Knox were only too happy to babysit when asked; would they be as happy to do the other thing Iris had requested? After picking the child up early from school under the guise of a dental appointment, she'd spent what spare time she had with her precious daughter, knowing it would be the last chance she'd have for a long time. After leaving the child with her neighbours, she'd hugged her friend tightly, too tightly, it felt like a long goodbye and it scared Millie Knox.

Getting home by three, Iris used the motor oil to lubricate the hinges on her son's door. Using a dish cloth to wipe the residue, it had served its purpose. Stealth would need to be her friend. Taking a hammer and nails from the tool shed, she'd fixed a squeaking floorboard, thinking of any eventuality, the least sound and her presence would be detected, he slept light. The biggest concern was the key in the door's lock. He used it every night, but would he be too drunk to remember. If she removed it, he may notice, and the plan would be dead. Her answer was to fill the hole with wet newspaper then put the key back in place, hoping that it wouldn't turn and in his confused state, not fight too much with the problem. She hated leaving anything to chance but this was one she'd have to leave in the lap of the Gods.

There had been a good twenty minutes spent sharpening her weapon, knowing that she'd probably only get one strike. But the last and maybe most important thing she'd done had been prepared the night before. There'd been a lot of tears shed as she composed a heart-felt letter to her only friend, Millie Knox explaining her reasoning for the coming events and a favour that would change all the lives.

Dearest Millie,

There is going to be a lot said about me in the coming days and weeks, some will believe I'm evil, some will think I'm insane. But you, my only friend must know the truth and maybe, you can explain to my wonderful daughter Jennifer when she's old enough to understand. By the time, you read this, I will most probably be in prison. This is a decision which has tormented me for weeks, but I see no other way I can keep my angel safe from that monster.

Some time ago, Frank attempted to drown Jenny. I know this sounds crazy but it's true. I'd been shopping and Martin was left in charge. In a split second, while my baby was taking a bath, that thing crept in and tried to hold her under the water. I barely saved her. As usual Martin refused my request for consequence, I wanted the police involved but as usual, I was overruled. This virtually ended our marriage; I couldn't be with a man like that any longer. I wanted to leave but he claimed he'd fight for custody of Jenny, and I couldn't risk her being in that house and me not being there to protect her. If we ran away, he'd find us, we were trapped. If it were just my life, so be it, I don't care what happens to me anymore, but my baby does not deserve this life.

Therefore, I have come to a decision that most will find insane. The only way I can keep jenny safe in this world is to ensure Frank isn't in it. I have a plan that I will have carried out on Friday night, last night. If my plan has worked, Frank will be gone, and the world will be a better place for it. He has been an evil child and will be eviller as an adult. I can't imagine a more dangerous person and by killing him, I will have saved countless others.

You may or may not agree with what I have done, that is your choice, but know, please know my friend, had there been another way, I would have taken it.

And finally, I must ask you something that I have no right asking. When this is over, I have serious concerns at how Martin will cope. Not that I have any concern for him, had he been more supportive across the years, Frank may have turned out differently. My concern is how he'll react to Jenny. He may seek retribution for Frank by hurting her. That is why I'm begging you, please give my daughter a home. She would be far happier with you and Archie, and I know you would raise her wonderfully. There is no one else on earth that I'd trust with this request.

In closing, please remember, I did this to keep Jennifer safe. If I could give my life for hers, I'd do it in a heartbeat, so my freedom is a small price to pay. Please make her understand, I love you and always will.

Yours truly, Iris.

The letter was sent by post as Iris feared, if it was hand delivered, it may be read before the dead was done. It would arrive early Saturday morning in which time, whatever happened, happened.

The Daimler entered the confines of the Graham estate at 8.30pm. Both father and son were now the worst for drink and greatly anticipated sleep. Miner pulled the car up by the front entrance and the Grahams climbed out into the night air. Martin handed the young driver a roll containing five, ten-pound notes and reminded him that today's events were no one's business but their own to which he received a nod of agreement.

'You a good lad, you'll go far.' Frank entered the mansion first, straining on the heavy door, the hall in darkness. His father staggered up the three steps soon afterwards and Miner shook his head, partially in disgust, manly in pity.

'What kind of eighteen-year-old needs his pops to pay for him to get laid on his birthday?' Leaving the keys in the Daimler's ignition, he began his journey home, happy with his day's pay.

Father Henderson had prayed for guidance and received none. He'd considered telephoning Bill Castle and asking him to call round on the Grahams but felt it was more his own duty. A telephone conversation could be misconstrued and had Martin Graham answered, there was a good chance he'd have hung up on. If he did nothing, he'd never sleep. No, the only way was to pay a visit. It wasn't too late, and he'd probably find nothing to worry about.

He rubbed the condensation from the inside windows of his Vauxhall and started the engine. The gravel driveway crunched under the car's wheels as the vicar began the short journey across town.

Iris need not have worried. The boy had walked straight through the bedroom door without considering the key in the lock. Listening from the next-door guest bedroom, the drunken teen fought to remove his clothes. He'd taken an extraordinarily long time in the bathroom, expelling the remaining alcohol from his bladder before collapsing onto his bed. He'd given up trying to remove his jeans and lay, bare chested on the duvet. Iris had panicked at first, what if he fell asleep on his front, where would she aim the knife? She didn't need to be concerned. He was flat on his back, snoring in seconds. She peered through a slight gap in the door and smiled. Ten minutes and he'd be out for the count. She could wait.

Her last check was on her husband. She knew from experience; he was a heavy sleeper. When in drink, that was magnified, fivefold. When she saw he too was sound asleep, it was time for the deed to be done. Just a snifter of Dutch courage first.

One drink had led to three and suddenly, Iris felt floaty. This wasn't part of the plan and she cursed herself for it.

The motor oil had served its purpose. Iris pushed gently on the heavy wooden bedroom door and the hinges remained silent. Earlier, she'd removed the light bulb in the hallway so when the door creeped open, there was no fluorescent difference. There was no light at all, but still, she moved stealthily over the room's threshold into total darkness and needed to remain still for a moment or so to gain her bearings.

In daylight, she'd studied the room completely as this was a part of the house she rarely entered. Remembering back, the walls were bare bar for one framed poster of the universal released, Dracula staring Bela Lugosi. She'd stared at its picture, a horrific nightmarish killer with blood around his mouth and thought how apt it was that this was the one thing it had chosen, a monster for a monster. There was a bookcase crammed with novels of true crime, serial killers, and psychopaths. Were they used for enjoyment or were they note-taking textbooks? She'd shuddered at the thought. In the central area of the main wall, there was an open fireplace, though it hadn't been lit for years. It was encased by a dark oak surround which was bare of neither ornaments or nick-knacks; in fact, there was little personal keepsakes lying around and for a moment she'd felt sad that her son hadn't made more of the life he'd been given. She'd stopped herself soon though, knowing she had to remain dispassionate, there was a job to be done. His wardrobe had been a sad reflection on his personality too. Nothing flash or colourful, just practical, mundane garments, bought for purpose. Mostly overalls and white shirts, nothing out of place, organised, boring. She hoped the large double bed wouldn't be a problem. Had he slept on the left-hand side, she'd have to climb on the bed to strike which could alert him to her presence that was one thing she'd had no power to control. The duvet which adorned the bed had no cover, and again, she'd cringed when she considered what a spray of dark red blood would do to its white exterior.

Making her way across the open floor, all she could see were dark masses around the room. The hard skin on the soles of her feet scratched across the coarse woollen carpet, every tiny noise sounding like a base drum in Iris's mind. There'd been one floorboard that refused to stay nailed down and she'd measured it, five yards from the entrance. Walking toe to heel, putting as little pressure as she could through her feet, she felt the wooden barrier give slightly and she retracted her limb quickly; a little too quickly as it resettled with a slight click. She stopped dead and held her breath, there was no movement from the bed. She breathed out silently and continued. Sweat was pouring from her in every direction, the palms of hands the worst, clammy and slippery. Feeling the hard rubber of the knife's handle, she switched hands and dried the right on her nightdress then repeating the process with the left. Still, the handle was bathed in perspiration, a thick residual layer, a mixture of the skin's natural excretion and the ingredients in the unused rubber forming an unpleasant slimy scum. Worrying about her grip, she slid the handle under the pit of her arm, tentatively clasping the highly sharpened blade with fingertip restraints, anchoring around the dull side of the steel. Suddenly, the weapon slipped, beginning an accelerated decent for the floor. Her reflexes were sharp though not as sharp as the blade. Catching the steel, sharp edge on, Iris sliced a thin wound across all the fingers of her left hand. With the salt from her sweat, the injury stung, and she almost called out in pain; almost.

She was halfway across the open floor now. Her eyes were becoming more accustomed to the dark and she could faintly see the huge hulking frame of her son lying unconscious on the mattress, quilt pulled down revealing his bare chest. The taste of the vodka was still on her lips and tongue, would there be time for one more binge before the police arrived?

She'd begun to regret sending the letter as, if things went as planned, she could maybe have pleaded not guilty by self-defence. She could have made an elaborate tale of a drunken son assaulting a defenceless little woman and her only escape had been to use a knife. But then, there'd be questions asked; the snot-nosed kid in the hardware store would be a witness against her, claimed it was pre-meditated as she'd purchased the blade in advance. Then there was Father Henderson, how much had she told him? It was all a blur now. Maybe she could get to the letter in the morning before Millie read it. And if Millie did read it first, perhaps she'd be a good enough friend to keep her mouth shut. If she'd been cleverer, she need not have been implicated at all. An intruder could have been responsible, God knows, plenty of people hated Frank. Shit, this was so confusing, why had she drunk that vodka, her mind was focused before that.

Suddenly, there was light. She swirled toward the door, but it was still in darkness; no, this was coming from outside. It was a car speeding up the driveway. Was Jenny ill and Archie had driven her home? No, they'd have telephone first. Who the Hell was coming now, at night? She needed to think fast, act fast. The car had stopped, and a door was opening.

'Please God, not now.' Losing all caution, she strode to the side of the bed, kicking a discarded shirt that Frank had vomited across earlier, a button chinked against a glass of water standing by the bed on the floor. It was now or never. Raising the weapon high in the air, she gripped its handle with both hands, ignoring the discomfort of her cut fingers.

BANG, BANG, BANG, BANG. The shriek of the doorbell followed as the impatient visitor made their presence known. It was enough to alert the sleeping teen, his eyes springing open.

'NO.' Iris closed her eyes and brought the knife down hard, the blade cutting deeply into her son's right shoulder. Realising that the weapon had missed her original target and that the blow wasn't fatal, the knife was retracted and came slashing down once more, this time with more force than the first. Aware that he was under attack, Frank had the presence of mind to raise his right hand, the blade slicing through, snapping a bone, and becoming entangled in the teen's flesh. Again, Iris tried to retrieve the weapon but now, the monster was awake.

BANG, BANG, BANG, BANG. The priest's crashes again the front door shook the whole mansion. Slipping off his leather gloves he continued the assault, hoping his bare knuckles would gain more force. Dust blew up from the gravel road and the holy man squinted his eyes, pulling his black woollen scarf tighter around his face as the biting Hallowell wind blew leaves from the ground's trees. Pulling his long black coat in tighter, his gaunt, exasperated face mirrored his mood, surely someone was home, the hour wasn't so late? Once more, the heavy oak front door blitzed by a pounding right fist, desperate for attention.

Iris's face flushed, the teeth gritted, this was killing or be killed, but she wasn't only fighting for her own salvation, it was her daughters too. Who was at that fucking door? As the bangs echoed around the vast building, Martin finally awakened, and leapt from his bed, fearing an emergency. Still in a drunken stupor, he stumbled his way across the hall to the staircase. Noticing his son's bedroom door was ajar, he realised was something happening inside.

By now, the monster had risen, blood spewing from the double entry wounds. Iris was still fighting to retrieve the knife but was caught with a hard slap across the face, sending her spinning back and crashing to the floor. Graham carefully extracted the blade from his right hand, blood jetting from the opening. Iris thought of running but what good would it do? Once more, she jumped to her feet, but the monster was in command now. With the blade grasped tightly in the uninjured hand, he begun to thrust wildly in his mother's direction, more to cause terror than a laceration. An expression of fear had replaced her determined look, an acceptance that this plan had gone horribly wrong. In her mind's eye, there was Jennifer and the knowledge that she had failed her hurt more than the coming mutilation. The monster paused and shot a wry smile, aware that this was the end. Thrusting the gleaming blade forward, the sharp steel sliced through the soft skin across Iris's throat. At first, it seemed the strike had missed its target, but gradually blood started to become visible. Her hand shot up to the wound and momentarily stopped its flow but soon, between clenched fingers, thick red blood began to ooze. Her face turned ashen white, and her eyes rolled back. Dark red lips were mouthing silent words, but blood bubbles formed around the corners of the mouth and her standing became unsteady. With one last defiant act, she made a final grab for the knife, but her strength was failing fast. Aware the battle was done, Frank grabbed his mother's propelled right wrist, then yanked away Iris's fingers from her sliced throat, blood beginning to gush, like destroying a damn and water breaking free. Spraying across the white duvet, the thick red mass looked quite black in the darkness. Her head was spinning, legs becoming faint, Iris Graham knew her life was ending. Her son lowered his head, so they were eye to eye...and his smile grew. She kissed his cheek in an acrimonious goodbye then silently mouthed the words, 'I'll see you in Hell.'

Iris Graham lay dying on the floor; Martin Graham watched on from the doorway in horror; Frank Graham was happily content. Below, Father Henderson had retreated to his car, believing that the household was asleep, blissfully unaware that his actions had changed the course of history."

Chapter 15

"You've got to be fucking kidding?" Nick Castle stared into the embers of the smouldering campfire, its thick smoke making his eyes water. His father's words had been spoken with incredulous honesty, like a tale that was so unbelievable, it had to be true. "So, he killed his own mother?" The young man had been so entranced at the story, he hadn't noticed that his father had retreated into the woodland. When there was no answer, Nick shot around panoramic head-movement, suddenly concerned for his father's whereabouts. "Dad?" Leaping upright, he turned away from the warmth of the fire, the darkness appearing more tenebrous away from the reds and yellows of the dancing flames. "DAD?" Concern was increasing; he hadn't watched Mick leave, he'd been so preoccupied with the details of the story, the rest of the world had fallen away. The silhouette of that place loomed large beyond the treeline, Nick could feel panic rising inside himself.

"Ready to continue?" Mick emerged from behind a clump of fir-trees, thick dry logs laden across his chest, both arms gripping tightly to his prize.

"Where did you vanish to?" The young man breathed a sigh of relief, strangely surprised at how much the tale was affecting him. Emerging on his father, he outstretched his arms in a willingness to help carry the fire's fuel.

"It's fine, I can manage. What's up? Didn't think the bogeyman had grabbed me, now did you?" Mick chuckled low to himself, curiously beginning to enjoy playing storyteller. His son had been right, this was like confessional, this was something he needed to relieve himself of, this was a wrong that must be righted. Dropping the pile of timber to the floor, it landed with a thud, a large solid branch falling heavily onto the instep of Mick's left boot. "Bastard." He grimaced, bending down to rub the afflicted area.

"Told you I'd help. Serves you right, Martyr." It was Nick's turn to giggle, though he made no effort to hide his satisfaction. Looking at the fallen fuel, he remarked at its size. "Are you planning on being here for a month? You could read War-and-peace before this little lot burns away?" Looking towards the older man's face, the returning expression told him that the narrative was far from over.

Bending to one knee, Mick stretched across the fire's neighbouring scorched grassland and dragged over the branch that had landed on his foot. Carefully placing the timber in the centre of the smouldering coals, flashes of reds and yellows crackled into the night sky. Nick silently watched his elder's face, the shadowy reflection lighting from below, like the creepy image of a torch light pointed from the chest-up. "You won't be making anyone else limp in a hurry."

157

Raising his eyeline, with his neck craning backwards, he looked up towards his sniggering son. "Boy, that's just the end of part one." Turning, Nick headed back towards his uncomfortable seat on the fallen tree. Intrigued, he gave a clever retort.

"Let's have the sequel then."

"Millie and Archie Knox were enjoying breakfast with their special visitor when Iris's letter landed on the front-doormat. The aging lady recognised the handwriting immediately and a queasy, nauseating sensation fell over her after remembering yesterday's long goodbye. Asking her husband to watch the child, she retreated to the bathroom, where she could read in private. The white envelope quivering between her trembling fingertips, the sealed-back allowed a welcoming pause.

It's a suicide note, I know it's a suicide note.

Sliding a fingernail behind the crease, the firm paper casing ripped, and she quickly grabbed for the letter. Devouring every word through glassy eyes, she could scarcely believe what was in front of her. For this *wasn't* a suicide note. This was a confession to murder.

The words were so incredible, she'd read the entire letter three times. Dabbing away emerging tears, Millie tried desperately to stop her body shaking. Before exiting the bathroom, she fearfully paused at the medicine cabinet, taking in her reflection on its mirrored doors. All colours had drained from her complexion and the bags below her eyes looked red and puffy.

She's going to know. Please God, let me get through this without crying.

Taking a moment to compose herself, Millie took a deep breath and headed for the exit.

'Okay, little one. Go clean your teeth before school.' The child returned a beaming smile which almost started the woman's tears once more. What is this going to do to that little mite, her world will never be the same again? Leaving the kitchen table, the girl dropped her cereal bowl into the washbasin before heading for the stairs. As Jenifer began the climb to the first-floor bathroom, the woman could no longer maintain her carefree façade. Thrusting the note in her worried husband's direction, it soon became painfully obvious that their lives were about to change in ways to which they never could have imagined.

Once Archie had taken in the tragic narration from the handwritten note, the couple decided that sending Jenifer to school would be a mistake. For now, they knew very little, and until that changed, the child had to be their main priority. Millie rang the telephone number to the Graham mansion time after time without answer, adding more layers to their growing burden, Iris had never been unreachable when her daughter was staying at the Knox household. With each passing moment, the couple's concerns grew deeper.

Fortunately, Archie was in the middle of week's paid leave from his duty at the railway station and agreed to keep the child in his care for the morning while Millie investigated if these terrible events foretold in the letter had come to fruition. Both prayed they hadn't.

The aging cleaner's heart pounded an irregular rhythm as she passed off Graham Road, beyond the moulded iron gates, turning onto the gravel pathway towards the mansion. Her brisk pace had caused a full body layer of perspiration, her silk blouse and tweed trousers clinging uncomfortably to her skin, chaffing between her ample thighs and below the armpits. Worse still was the terrible anxiety her friend's note had created, her tormented mind racing in several directions, all at once. Surely this couldn't be true? Was her employer really a murderer?

The large-rimmed bifocals that Millie required for sight, slid to the tip of her nose and only quick reflexes stopped the spectacles crashing to the ground. Pushing them back, her eyes widened, and she found herself spontaneously holding her breath, the vision ahead causing her to fear the worst. Three vehicles were parked adjacent to the front entrance, two she recognised, the other's usage obvious from its appearance. Dr Harry Brackett's royal-blue Mercedes was neighbouring Bill Castle's light-grey Range-rover, the front driver's-side door slightly ajar as though its owner had hurriedly bolted in an emergency. The third, an indisputable requirement for such a solemn need, long and sleek, panther black estate, a plain unremarkable wooden coffin, free of decorative golden handles or nameplates, used only for the initial transportation of the recently deceased. Her hand clasped quivering lips, desperately trying to stifle a cry.

'God, no.' Her pace quickened once more, the gravel crunching beneath sensible leather shoes. The grey clouds overhead threatened to erupt their contents, the Hallowell wind gusting through the nearby trees, sending a chill down her spine. Inside the outer vestibule, bright electric lights shone from the hallway, the front double doors open, the figure of a man passing by quickly. The woman stopped dead; surely, she was wrong, that looked like Frank. The figure made a return crossing and this time she was certain, it was the troubled teen. A feeling of total horror fell over her, who was in the coffin?

Charging for the open entrance, her eyes desperate to look anywhere except for the doorway. The personalised number plate from the hearse, GIB 1, the customised advertisement of Gibson's funeral services. Inside the police car, the keys still hung from the ignition. What events had caused such urgency? Passing beyond the vehicles, all the remained between Millie Knox and the mansions interior was a flight of four stone steps. Breathing laboured, the entrance was suddenly blocked by the frowning police officer.

'Bill. Bill, what's happened? Where's Iris?' The middle-aged lawman held out both arms, palms in a stop motion, determined to prevent the woman from seeing inside. Adamant not to be stopped, Millie tried to push forward, though it was evident that the scene ahead would be too much to bear.

'Millie, wait.' Determined not to use force, Bill slid an arm around the cleaner's shoulders shepherding her away from the doorway.

'I can't let you inside, let's just take a seat in my car, I'm afraid I have some bad news.'

The options were minimal, and Millie knew it. Digression was essential and though the mere thought of accepting Martin's disgraceful version of events made her sick to her stomach, Jenifer was the priority now. A trade was the only choice.

Somehow, the former cleaner had managed to remain silent as the sick twisted story, made up by the Grahams made her want to scream at the top of her voice, LIES, ITS ALL FUCKING LIES. Bill Castle retold the tale with a sarcastic, almost dumbfounded tone to his voice.

Intruders had tried to burglarise the mansion. Two unknown low-life criminals had smashed a window by the back door and reached through, turning the key in the lock. Iris hadn't been aware of their presence and had gone to the kitchen, hoping a glass of warm milk would help her sleep. She'd immediately screamed when she noticed the intruders, waking the men above. As punishment, the lady of the house had been fatally stabbed, with a large, unknown weapon, looking something like a butcher's boning knife. The interlopers realised that their plan was gone and began to retreat, back though the open doorway. But Frank, had heroically tried to defend his family and his home, fighting with one of the fleeing criminals. He too had been stabbed, twice, once deeply in the shoulder and the other, a defensive wound in the left hand. Martin had been slow, only arriving as invading thieves had run free into the night. The scene was horrific, his wife was trying to fight for her life, but she was choking on her own blood. Dr Bracket had been called immediately, as had Bill Castle. By the time the physician arrived, Iris was dead. The policeman scoured the roads of Hallowell, desperately trying to find the assailants, all the time believing that this whole story was a crock of shit. Still, he had to investigate, it was the officer's duty. Frank Graham, the big, brave, have a go hero, was stitched, and bandaged at the Mansion, ignoring the doctors' orders of hospital treatment.

That was the best they could come up with.

What was the right thing to do? Millie's gut instinct was to take her evidence, immediately to Bill Castle. Let him sort this mess, that's what he gets paid for. Iris's letter could be enough to prove that this tale was pure fantasy. But what would that achieve? Her friend would still be gone. Fighting the Grahams would be costly. Antagonise the family, you become the enemy. Firstly, Archie's post at station would be terminated immediately. Her own role at the mansion had been mutually ended and without any income, times would be tough. Plus, there was one other factor that ensured that the note remained unseen. Jenifer. The letter could be a bargaining tool. Iris's last wish was that her daughter be protected at all costs. If the child remained in that house, with those people, she would almost certainly share her mother's fate. That monster had disposed of Iris, Millie had no concrete proof, but she knew. Everyone knew. This was the only way to ensure the child's survival.

Incredibly, Martin Graham gave up his daughter without a fight. On the contrary, he brought up the option to the Knox family, offering financial support and termination of the agreement should Jenifer become home sick. Truthfully, he knew that firstly, he no longer had the strength, will, or ability to raise a small

160

child alone. His wife had seen to the girls needs and without her guidance, he feared that her progression would be harmed by his half-arsed parenting. Secondly, and most importantly, he now knew that his son was very dangerous and protecting his daughter would be impossible. For many years, Iris had been Martin's world, before the children were born and it was just the two of them, they were so happy. Had his yearning for an heir to the Graham name not been so strong, perhaps they would have still been blissfully happy. His wife had been beautiful once, radiant, and so full of life, energetic and content. Now, she was in a wooden box and her own son had been responsible. Well, to be certain that Jenifer didn't suffer the same fate, the Knox family would be his saviours. Perhaps he'd need to sacrifice his future with the girl, but at least, she'd have a future.

As expected, the funeral was a solemn, depressing, and embarrassing occasion. Solemn and depressing because someone so young had been eviscerated from this world, living on only in the hearts and minds of those her loved her. Embarrassing because of the number of mourners. Archie and Millie Knox took the front pews to the left of the isle inside St Helen's church while Martin and Frank Graham took the pews to the right. It was decided that Jenifer was too young to understand the proceedings and stayed with friends of her foster parents. A gaggle of six Graham employees who were worried for their jobs should they not attend, took seats in the central rows and a representative from the children's home where Iris had spent her adolescent years took a seat near the back. Alice and Bill Castle felt the need to attend, Bill out of duty while Alice wanted gossip for her minions who used her newsagents. A few residents mingled outside the grounds, more out of morbid curiosity then paying of respects.

Father Henderson stood by the pulpit and tried to be professional as he read excerpts from the bible and sang 'morning has broken' in his loud operatic singing-voice, only vaguely aware his were the only lips moving. His eyes continually wandered to the eighteen-year-old in the front row, a blank expressionless mask for a face, showing no emotion, just a restlessness in his fidgeting body, as though he was uncomfortable and had been forced to attend. The priest couldn't help but remember back to that fateful conversation inside his church, less than a week earlier. He must have been mistaken. The words had run though his mind, over and over; clearly, she hadn't said what he thought she said; by God, the woman had talked of murdering her own son. And now, she was the one who was dead. Two supposed criminals raiding the Graham mansion, a likely story. The clergyman had thought of informing Bill Castle to the details of conversation, unsure if that would that prevent others with serious problems from taking his council, trust was a hard thing to earn and an easy thing to lose. His Sunday congregation had dropped by half in the last seven years and if they thought that their proclamations would be heard by more than just himself and the lord, then the confessional box would be completely redundant. And of course, the poor woman was still gone, what good would dredging things up now do? From what he'd heard, the investigation was almost over, certain Hallowell characters had been questioned though none seriously. Bill had his own suspicions, but the Grahams had been clever. The officer had inspected the rest of the house in detail, no blood was found. The only strange occurrence was a damp area on the carpet in the son's room, it stretched to quite an area and smelled of cleaning detergent. Martin explained that being Frank's eighteenth birthday, he'd taken his son out drinking and the alcohol had caused the naïve youngster to vomit violently before taking to his bed. The excuse seemed plausible but…

In the aftermath, the town gossips had a feeding-frenzy. Eventually, the coroner ruled the death by unlawful killing, something most residents agreed with. It was the cover story that the citizens found hard to swallow.

Hallowell had formed their own jury. Over the last few years, with the Graham family had given the gossips hours of chit-chat, be it that crazy son with his lunatic actions, or the drunken mother who'd left drugs unguarded where her daughter could find them. The poor little might had needed her stomach pumped, could have died. Little happened that didn't become public knowledge, one way or another.

The consensus believed Frank was responsible. Everyone knew that mother and son hated one another and with all the incidents he'd had been involved with, most believed it was just a matter of time before he committed murder. He was a bad seed, an evil child that would grow to be an evil man. It was hardly surprising that his first victim would be his mother.

A minority pointed their guarded fingers in Martin's direction. Over recent years, his personality had worsened dramatically. At one time, he'd been a much respected and even loved member of the community, a caring and generous employer with his worker's best interests at heart. As the son had gained more influence, this changed tellingly. His employees became a means to an end, nothing more. Absence and lateness were no longer tolerated and were dealt with in a swift and harsh manner. He was no longer approachable and would explode without warning, his patience was taught and his manner abrupt. Some wondered if this transformation wasn't only in the workplace. The wife had taken to drink in a big way, many wondered if this was due to marital problem. Rumours who rife of domestic violence, was that why she no longer shopped in Hallowell, unwilling to show the bruises? Hearsay suggested, the couple were living separate lives, a divide down the centre of mansion, males to one side, females the other. There was even intelligence suggesting an affair, or maybe two affairs, one each. The fabricated tale of Martin being gay, using Iris as a trophy wife, never caught on. That wasn't a rumour, just a twisted hoax, a disgruntled former employee had had tried to spread. The biggest theory was a lack of a pre-nuptial agreement, and some believed that he'd murdered Iris to avoid an expensive divorce. Most knew, much of this was bullshit but…people will talk.

Some accepted the given story, though not many…

Slowly, things began to settle. Jenifer missed her mother terribly and cried herself to sleep for weeks. But gradually, with the incredible support and all-encompassing love that the Knox family showered on the little girl, her tears began to dry, and progressively her sweet smile returned. She quickly became the daughter; Millie had always longed for. Ensuring that Jenifer didn't believe that she was trying to take the place of her mother, something that was impossible to do, the child became more and more comfortable in her new surroundings. If she wanted stories of Iris, the couple would enthusiastically tell her tales that would sometimes bring a tear, and sometimes bring a smile. As time progressed, the upset lessened, the grief was passing. Occasionally, she'd ask about her father, and on the rare times that he'd visit, there'd be hugs and gifts. Soon, these stopovers changed to telephone calls, then eventually, they dwindled to a stop. Jenifer didn't seem to mind. Strangely, the child never enquired about her big brother.

For the monster, this was finally the life, he'd always longed for. The mother, who'd he'd hated and resented so ferociously was gone, as was that brat of hers. He'd have been happier, had the little shit been in that box with the other bitch but, at least she was out of the picture. Finally, nothing stood between him and his father. Time would no longer need to be shared, there was no more family, just Graham and son, together forever. At work, at home, no divisions, no distractions, the way it was meant to be. Unfortunately, for the eighteen-year-old, a series of events would begin to destroy that utopian existence and start a downward vortex that would ultimately obliterate the Graham family.

Martin Graham, the architect of a dynasty was slowly losing his mind.

His son's version of events was just realistic enough for his belief, and he really wanted to believe. Like the best lies, much of his story was based on truth. The youth had stumbled to his bed, fought desperately to shed his clothing, before falling straight to sleep, alcohol creating an adequate sedation. A tremendous crashing at the outside door had woken him with a start, his eyes sprung open, but his body was momentarily frozen by fear. Beside his bed stood Iris, a crazed expression across her face, holding a large butcher's, knife, high in the air. Screaming a demented shriek, the deranged woman, her eyes wide and full of hate, with a huge, clown-like grin across her mouth, began slashing at him, the entry wounds to his hand and shoulder supporting the claim. While attempting to defend himself, he'd kicked out at the delirious maniac, fighting his way to the foot of the bed to flee the danger. She'd swiftly followed, the knife slashing through the air with frightening accuracy. After accepting that his unhinged mother wouldn't stop until he was dead, he'd been forced to retaliate. After finding his feet, she'd fired the knife with intense force toward his heart, the blade instead became lodged in her son's left hand. All the time, he had pleaded for her to stop, but to no avail. Back thrusting the blade from Frank's devastated hand, she stepped back, suddenly aware that against her conscious son, the attack would be futile. Still, he continued to try to reason with her, but words would have no use now. Instead, she moved to the centre of the room and started to laugh uncontrollably. That maniacal glare remained as the screeches of laughter paused. Lifting the blade to her throat, she fired her final sentence.

'They'll all think this was you, one way or another, you leave this house tonight.' With a final shriek, she plunged the blade deep into the flesh of her exposed throat. Frank had made a lunge to grab the knife, but he was too late, the damage was done.

Initially, Martin had screamed at the young man, the devastating scene pointing towards his son's guilt. Even after listening to the distorted version of events, the old man still believed firmly that Frank was responsible. Frank had pleaded his innocence and begged the old man to back him against the tidal of accusations which would certainly come his way. Martin sat on the side of his son's bed, blood still pulsing from his wife's exposed wound, not ten feet away. He'd checked for a pulse and found none. He'd even considered C.P.R. though the time for rescue had passed. Frank swiftly retreated to his bathroom, bringing three towels, two large bath ones and a smaller hair towel. Forcing the lesser one around the woman's throat, the leakage was stemmed. Turning the body onto the left side, he slid both larger towels under the lifeless corpse, then when the body was once flatter, he wrapped his mother completely. Martin watched on, lost for words at his son's efficiency.

'We need a plan.'

The tale came from Frank, like reading words from a children's book. Martin wasn't sure what scared him more? The act itself, or his effectual ability to recover a camouflaging story to cover his tracks. Throughout, the patriarch watched on, numb to the horrors before him. His wife was dead, slaughtered seemingly by their son. Whether he accepted Frank's version or not, that hideously abhorrent fact was the one gruesome constant. It was now his decision; back his boy, or throw him to the wolves?

Watching Frank place the body in the kitchen, spreading his mother's blood from the gore-filled towels, pushing on the sides of the neck to squeeze whatever remained as another prop in this twisted scene, Martin rushed to the kitchen sink, the remnants of the previous day's drinking making a swift return visit. He was about to run water from the taps when a hand clasped his shoulder.

'Leave it. It will make our scene more believable.'

Finally, Martin snapped, spinning to face his son, his hands clasped firmly on his throat. 'Your mother is dead. Do you understand that? The woman that gave your life is lying on the floor, in what's left of her blood, and you're acting like this is some fucking game. Your mother, my wife, is dead, DEAD, FUCKING DEAD. IS THAT REGESTERING WITH YOU?' Spittle splashed across Frank's face, for the first time, the monster was showing fear.

'I do understand that dad. Really, I do. I don't know if you believe anything I've told you but remember, please remember, I could never lie to you.' His words were soft, almost pleading, all his strength and bravado gone. 'I don't care about anyone else. I know this is a terrible thing to say under the circumstances but, I don't care that she's dead. If I could lie to you, I wouldn't have said that but, it's the truth. She's always treated me differently, sometimes I wondered why. Eventually, I stopped caring. If you think I did this purposely, call Bill Castle. I won't argue. But if there's any part of you that believes me, then let's get through this, we can grieve later.'

Across the next forty-five minutes, the two men cleaned furiously. The devastation of the bedroom was tempered slightly by a woollen rug in the centre of the room which had caught much of the blood-splatter. It was immediately removed but still, considerable residue had seeped through to the carpet below. Frank scrubbed with all his might, the scented detergent helping to cleanse the spoliation and remove all signs. The bed-clothing was replaced, as was the quilt, all soiled material going directly into the furnace below in the basement. In the kitchen, a window was broken from the outside in, the key hanging lifelessly in its lock. Debris was thrown from cupboards and drawers, signs of intruders searching for loot. Martin squirmed as the final piece of the horrific jigsaw was put into place. Gently, the handle of the boning knife was wiped of all fingerprints. It was taken to an area of the grounds which had a partially broken borderline fence, the teen dropping it in long grass, just visible enough to be found without seeming obvious. Frank even made two separate sets of tracks through the overgrown greenery, insinuating the presence of two different criminals. They left nothing to chance, the eyes of Hallowell would be watching.

As time progressed, the investigation found no evidence of the Graham's involvement. It should have come as a relief but inside, the damage was done, something had fractured in Martin Graham's mind. The downward descent had begun, and soon, other events would ensure he'd never recover.

Since 1963, Martin began a three-year battle which would ultimately end in defeat. Rail travel in Great Britain had been on the decline with the increased availability of the national road network. Motorways were becoming common; Busses were now a popular method of public transportation and heavy goods vehicles could be used more cheaply and quickly as a way of moving merchandise. The once essential rail network was antiquated, and changes needed to be made. The ruling government commissioned Dr Richard Beeching to make a nationwide study of how the railways could be streamlined to suit a modern Britain. His report would be the death-knell for most small railway lines and Hallowell was no exception.

With falling usage numbers for its passenger service and a more accessible road, in and out of the village, the Hallowell route was deemed unsustainable. The Graham's had built and maintained the railway station for generations and though it was a non-profitable venture, it was still a part of their property portfolio. After losing the iron works tenants and with the coal washing facility was no longer housed on site, the entire main building was empty except for their offices on the top floor. The side buildings were empty, the ticket office had closed in 65 and the station-masters quarters were now unused. When St Mara's station was scheduled for closure and there were no objections, Martin accepted defeat. November 1st, 1966, was to be the last scheduled passenger services to leave Hallowell railway station. Unfortunately, there was time for one more tragedy.

Twenty-four hours and Archie Knox would be retired. The little Scotsman was ready if truth be known. His heart had been down the colliery; the comradery of the miners, the improved conditions, it was all he'd ever known. It had been hard walking away, but the time was right; if he couldn't do the job properly, he wouldn't fake it. His fellow workers didn't deserve that. Martin Graham had been good to him. Most had turned their backs on his old boss, claimed that his attitude had changed, but Archie said it how he saw it.

The job here at the railway station helped his mind adjust to not working full time anymore, but now, even this was becoming a struggle. It wasn't the work so much, sweeping and polishing mostly. It was the hours; 5am till 8am then back at 6 pm till 7:30pm. Early mornings at this time of year were hard, and with little Jenifer now their responsibility, he liked to be home, even in tragedy, they'd received a silver lining. The girl and Millie had helped each other get past the bereavement and though the couple were both in their sixties, having little miss perfect there, had breathed new life into old bones. Suddenly, pension age didn't feel like they were sitting in God's waiting room. With Jennifer there, anything was possible.

Tomorrow would be a sad day; that much was certain. Seeing the last passenger train leave the old station would be emotional. His first trip to Blackpool had been on a train from this very station when he was five-years old. Bloody Hell, that seemed a long time ago; and Millie and he, had gone on Honeymoon after their quiet little wedding from here, changing trains at Manchester station and heading to Brighton for the week. Would probably need five changes to get to Brighton now-a-days with all the closures. 'Bloody Dr Beeching, bet he didn't travel by train much. Probably a chauffeur driven Rolls Royce for him, nosey so-and-so.'

'One last late shift then I'm a man of leisure.' Archie rubbed his hands together, cursing that he'd forgotten is gloves. His parker coat was zipped up high, the night was cold, and the positioning of the railway station offered no protection from the biting winds, the adjacent wasteland opposite seemed to help the gusts gain strength. The coats hood refused to above his head and he is getting sick of trying. 'Half seven can't come soon enough tonight, I'm bloody freezing.'

Smoke from the evening's last passenger train was still in the air. The three Hutchinson brothers, Terry, Jake, and Steve had rolled merrily onto the platform, drunk as skunks after a day's boozing in Carpenter. Terry was landlord of the Wheatsheaf public house in the centre of Hallowell and had spent his day off, propping up someone else's bar with his two brothers. They'd shared a joke with the little caretaker before stumbling away into the night, Archie smiled, it was good to see people happy. They'd been the only passengers, a sad sign of the times and a reason the line was closing.

A small electric light above a series of timetables bathed the platform in an eerie glow. A wooden bench ran parallel, and Archie rested for a moment, reaching into his overalls breast pocket, producing a pack of filter-less hand rolled cigarettes and a silver lighter. He opened the pack and pushed one of the smokes between his thin lips. The lighter fired on the third time of asking and he breathed in a lungful of nicotine before releasing it in wispy circles. He rested the back of his head against the plastic covered timetables and closed his eyes. So much had happened recently. Was he too old to be playing daddy to an eight-year-old? They'd always wanted children, but God had never blessed them. They'd never seen the point for medical tests, what did it matter if it was Millie who couldn't bare kids or whether he was firing blanks. The point was they couldn't have them, but now this. Millie had suffered a cancer scare five years ago, a lump in her right breast. It was caught in time but, God forbid, what would they do if it happened again, and it wasn't caught in time. Playing daddy is okay when there's someone else to make the decisions. A cold shiver ran down his spine.

He took two more puffs on the smoke then threw the remainder onto the tracks, a trail of orange embers scattering into the night air. Resting on his broom-handle, he pushed himself upright and prepared for his final duties. Looking across to the colliery and hearing nothing but silence, he frowned that the workforce had been trimmed so dramatically, only a dayshift remaining with the productivity of the mine was down by two thirds. There'd been a time when nine out of ten men from Hallowell worked the pit. How times had changed. He began his final sweep of his penultimate shift when a noise echoed around the platform, emanating from the old station master's quarters.

'Hello? Anyone there?' Archie paced slowly by the lip of the platform, not quite managing to see down the tunnel yet. Raising the broom in both hands like a weapon, he repeated his call. 'Hello. If there's anyone there, I'm not playing games. Come out now or I ring Bill Castle!' He cautiously approached the turning, broom outstretched, heart beating quickly. The tunnel was dark, the enclosed doorways giving no shimmer of light. He squinted, seeing nothing. As a younger man, he'd have bolted in head-first but now, he was older, wiser, more cautious, more scared. A rustling sound, surely that must be an echo, still, he couldn't move his glare from the tunnel, his instinct told him something was down there. His already rapid heartbeat pounded out a faster rhythm. 'Come on, I want no nonsense, anybody playing silly buggars will be sorry.'

Suddenly, from across the tracks in the hedge-growth, a deer darted between the branches. The little man spun on his heels, the broom shank cutting through the cold night air like a Knight's sword.

'I swear, I'm going senile.' The retiring caretaker chuckled, relieved at the resulting find. Studying into the gloomy distance, his concentrated eyes searched for the skittish animal. He smiled; a stiff pair of antlers emerged from behind the hedgerow. Waiting for the head to appear, all his attention was fixed across at the rarely seen wildlife. From the rear, the station-master's door opened silently, approaching, the looming figure's movements were ghost-like, stealthily, with vile intentions. A darkened shadow fell across the platform, but Archie Knox's realisation came a second too late.

Local dignitaries descended upon Hallowell railway station the following day, awaiting the sad, and somewhat poignant moment when the final passenger engine would depart their platform. Mayor for the Hallowell/St Mara area, Brian Marsh, and his wife Katherine were scheduled, as was a titled employee from National rail. As expected, town doctor Harry Brackett had accepted his invitation to be amongst the departing congregation, along with his wife

(Brackett was always available whenever his face could be spotted by a newspaper photographer, he was a whore to publicity) plus, a cast member from Radio show, The Archers was the token celebrity. Bill Castle had refused his invitation, scoffing at such self-important arses, and being unwilling to join the charade. An emotional, if failing, Martin Graham would be present along with forty locals who had bought raffle tickets and had been chosen at random.

It was early that morning that rumours began to spread. Millie Knox had waited until after nine to inform Bill Castle of her husband being missing. Thirty minutes earlier, along with Jenifer, she'd made the short walk to the railway station, concern enforcing her need in investigate. True, the little man was less than an hour late, but he was a considerate, predicable husband who would never deviate from the norm without an explanation. The earlier cool Autumnal evening air had dropped dramatically in temperature, and she dressed the child appropriately, bundled up with gloves, hat, and a scarf along with a newly bought Winter-coat. For Millie, no such defence was needed, the worry making her heartbeat faster, her face flush and her body permeated with internal heat.

Surveying his workplace proved fruitless. Archie was responsible for extinguishing all lights around the platform, a duty which had been performed. The darkness made scrutinising the area fully impossible, the wasteland opposite gave no assistance and the woman cursed her lack of foresight when thinking of a flashlight. Regardless of her warm clothing, Jenifer had begun to shiver uncontrollably, her disconcerted feelings about the building more responsible than the harsh inclement weather. Leaving, the tracks had not been inspected.

Once back to their home and, after seeing that Archie had still returned, Millie had called Bill Castle. Was it a normal set of circumstances, his enquiries would have waited slightly longer, but as his employers were the Grahams and his last known whereabouts was on Graham property, Bill's search began in earnest? The grisly discovery didn't take long.

The police officer's torch floated around the Station's outer building, all the doorways were firmly locked and there was no noise emanating from the colliery's direction. The local pubs in the village were to be his next port of call, Archie didn't usually frequent any of them socially, but Bill wondered if maybe he'd agreed to a drink to celebrate his retirement. As he was about to climb down from the rear of the station's platform, he noticed there was still a faint smell of smoke from a train's chimney, drifting lightly in the air. Pausing, he wondered, and grimaced, desperate to be wrong but something told him his instinct could be correct.

At first the tracks appeared clear. Castle's high-powered flashlight illuminated the iron rails sufficiently, meaning that there seemed little cause for alarm. The enlarged gravel flooring, both between and adjacent to the tracks appeared unblocked and the officer breathed an audible sigh of relief. Then, something caught his eye. It was a discarded man's work-boot, protruding from the darkened connection between the building brick foundation and floor. Bill stretched his neck, his feet balancing precariously on the platform's edge, desperate to see beneath the concrete lip. There was something attached to the boot, God please don't let it be…

Though there'd been the cancelation of passenger trains involving Hallowell station, the line was remained active to coal wagons, to and from the colliery. Remembering that the mine now ran only a dayshift, Bill rested his left hand on the cold concrete platform and carefully jumped to the ground below, content of his own safety, shining the torch's beam to the worrying blockage, the full horror soon became apparent. Due to the incredible damage to the little Scotsman's remains, Castle seemed no reason to even try a pulse.

Knox had hit the tracks, seconds before the train had arrived. The brakes had yet to be applied as the colliery was still a distance away and the driver had seen nothing, feeling a fierce rumble as his cab had crunched over the obstacle, though not worrying, as these types of hindering obstructions were commonplace at smaller stations, dangerous games but kids will be kids.

The remnants of what had once been a human being was barely recognisable. The lumbering giant had crushed Archie completely. Landing fully on his front, facing towards the train, he'd tried to spring forward, only making it to his knees before being struck. The former caretaker had been folded, snapping brutally at the base of his spine, the back of his skull neighbouring the heel of a dirty work-boot, a grotesquely fascinating mutation to the human form. The skin across his face was gone, as was the nose, leaving only bare bone, covered in a deep-red mucus/blood combination. The jaw was dislocated in a gross anomaly which only added to the repulsive transformation. One leg had been severed completely, the only thing that had altered the cop to his location and even in torchlight, Castle could see that the pooling of blood was tremendously catastrophic.

Telling Millie, of her husband's demise was one of the worst times, Bill Castle had ever endured. She'd somehow remained stone-faced though a torrent of emotion lay dormant inside. Her new foster daughter, Jenifer Graham lay sleeping in the bedroom above and the woman knew that the child had already experienced enough loss to fill two lifetimes. The questions in her mind ran rampant, exploding these new thoughts and theories. How the Hell had he managed to fall from the tracks? Why had the train-driver not reacted? Was it really a fall…? Or was he pushed? Castle tried to investigate but, there was nowhere to start. Interviewing the coal train-driver had proved fruitless, he'd admitted a disruption on the tracks, but he thought it was just kids playing 'silly-buggars', it had happened before.

'Laying logs across the iron trails, once they'd made a Guy Fawles and Mannequin, from 200 feet away and the engine going at full speed, it looked like a man. I slammed on the brakes only to find a stupid dummy with a drawn-on face. It pissed me off. After that time, I just steam on through, anyone stupid enough to hang out at the tracks deserves to die.'

With no witness's and no signs of foul play prior to the incident, the case was closed. Some people had their suspicions, and there was only one name upon their lips. Too many, this was the final straw; the coincidence was just too great. Another person had lost their lives in suspicious circumstances with a strong connection to the Grahams, namely Frank Graham.

Bill Castle became a figure of mistrust or at least, incompetence; two suspicious deaths and no conclusive evidence to apportion blame. It was the first and only time, the policeman had ever been questioned about his professionalism and he took the blow to his pride hard. He thought of retiring from the post early, but his wife had reassured him that he was still needed, that his finest hour was still to come. The worst part was that he too believed that the deaths were connected and far from accidental. After the death Iris Graham, believing that the crime scene may have been staged, he had bowed to the coroner's greater knowledge. Castle had little practical experience of such crime scenes and though there seemed a minimal amount of spilled blood for such a gruesome death, the coroner had reassured him that there was enough at the scene for it to be viable, therefore there was enough evidence to accept the Graham's version of events. Had Millie handed the officer the last note of her friend, the scattered words of a woman on the edge, things may have seemed different.

But the death of Archie Knox was more troubling. The caretaker wasn't a drinker and the post-mortem found no mentally altering substances in his blood. The scene had no obvious obstacles to cause a fall, no obstacles at all in fact. It was dark, and he was carrying a broom which, theoretically could have caught under his feet but it was doubtful. The fact that the Knox family were the current guardians of the Graham girl tied them further to the cursed family. But what reason could the teenager have for killing the little Scotsman.

And it was only the boy that Bill believed could be tied to the deaths, Martin wasn't the type. If the rumours were true (and invariably, in a village like Hallowell, they usually were) junior hated his sister, or at least had a deep-seated jealousy of her. Surely, he'd prefer her with the Knox's rather than at home with Martin. With Archie gone, obviously, there'd be more chance of the sister returning home; Millie wasn't young and without her husband, raising a child would be far harder. It made no sense. Unless, with the child being away from the Graham mansion, she'd be out of his reach. It would be impossible to stage another accident. That was a stretch, but with these people, anything was possible. But with the lack of critical evidence, he was powerless to act on his suspicions. Being a policeman wasn't always easy.

For Millie Knox, the devastating passing of her beloved husband made her make a decision that would, at least for Jennifer, keep the child out of the clutches of her wicked brother. She wasn't Hallowell born and bred. She had only moved to the village after meeting and marrying Archie. Both had ties in Scotland, Archie leaving at the age of three for a life in Hallowell after his father took employment in the colliery and Millie remaining in Glasgow until her marriage. Her three brothers and two sisters still lived in the Scottish city and the pull to return to their supportive arms was strong. She only settled on the move when, it became obvious, Martin Graham had no wish to fight against his daughter leaving and starting a new life two-hundred miles away. The aging lady had been shocked when he had agreed, expecting a battle, maybe even through the courts. If he'd objected and she'd been blocked legally, then the move would have been cancelled, as her love for the child was so strong, as was her determination to remain loyal to her friends dying request. When the two had departed, there was no tearful goodbye. Martin promised to continue to aid Millie financially for his daughter's upkeep but on the final day before the move, he hadn't even arrived to wish them farewell. For Martin, his mental state was deteriorating, for Frank, it was good riddance.

Martin Graham was becoming a very sick man. His mental health was failing but the Graham curse was attacking at the worst time possible. Porphyria, the hereditary condition that had plagued the family for generations could re-occur without warning, but stress was always a contributing factor that could multiply its ferocity leading to symptoms invading in terrible ways. Daytime was bad, night-time was worse.

His eyes would open, and all the horrors of his existence would fade with the departing nightmare. Iris always slept on the right side of the bed, facing away, but the vision of her dark brown locks, cascading across her slender shoulders always made him smile. She purred like a kitten as she slept, tiny, measured breaths, the picture of serenity. He'd slip a finger under her hair, to the top of her neck and slide the nail gently down her spine; it always turned his wife on. Soothingly, he'd kiss the exposed flesh of her shoulders, slowly teasing up around to her bare breasts, her erect nipples revealing her willingness, their undeniable attraction for one another, still strong. Eventually she'd roll gently onto her back, and he'd kiss his way up her body. When her face became visible, he'd scream, always scream.

Deep inside her eye sockets were writhing maggots, eagerly devouring what remained of its departed inhabitants. One would fall free, sliding against the decaying substance that once was known as skin and disappearing into a crevice by the protruding right cheek bone. The entire nose had long been eaten away, just the tip of a bone and a dark pit in its place. The flesh across the brow seemed shredded but that was because part of the skull was missing, and the brain was visible, pulsing as heinous thoughts exploded in her mind. The lips were intact, untouched, made more radiant by the horrendous devastation to what had been, a picture-perfect face. There was still trace lipstick though a woman of her beauty rarely needed such improvements. But as the mouth opened, it showed more gruesome revelations. Some teeth were missing, others just broken stumps clinging on stubbornly. The gums that held the shattered remains in place were dripping yellow puss, whatever blood that that had been spilled was now dried black. One thing still containing living blood was the tongue which had been bitten through but improperly healed. It hung by strings, barely attached, spewing a vile odour as the jaw mouthed words. And those words were always the same.

'Why did you let him kill me?'

'Why did you let him kill me?'

'WHY DID YOU LET HIM KILL ME?'

His screams would grow more manic, more hysterical, then he'd wake. His body smothered in perspiration; satin sheets drenched. He'd look to the right and Iris would still be there. He'd reach for her shoulder and turn her body and the hideous vision would be the same, as would his terrifying screams. He'd run for the bedroom door, but the handle wouldn't turn. The grotesque caricature that had once been his wife would slowly levitate high above the sheets. Pulling hard on the door, his sweat covered hands would get no purchase and instead he'd bray against the wooden barrier, desperate for escape. When he turned back, Iris would be standing, slowly moving away from the bed they'd shared, an evil grin emblazoned across her perfect lips. That perfection would be obliterated when the words once more escaped,

'WHY DID YOU LET HIM KILL ME?'

Deciding the door was an impregnable fortress, Martin would dash for the on-suite bathroom, slamming its entrance behind him and fumbling with its bolt for added security. As silence fell, he'd slowly back away from the door, hoping beyond hope that the barrier would hold. His knees would give way, as would his bladder, after backing into his wife's frame, who had inexplicably appeared inside the room he used for refuge. He'd fall to his knees and beg, desperate for deliverance from this horror. Curled in the foetal position, the only sound would be laughter, evil cackles as this thing loomed closer. Closing his eyes, he'd scream until his throat was raw.

Frank would need to shake him violently to break him from his terrifying slumber and the old man would cry, tears of relief that the night's nightmare was over, knowing that the next time he closed his eyes, the visions would return.

He was slipping further into his own world with the son needing to assume more control. On the rare occasions, Martin would leave the house, he'd refuse to make eye-contact with anyone from the outside world. People who had had association for years with the Graham patriarch would be looked upon with suspicion, most were now strangers. He never left home alone, and Frank would fend off the few people who were still willing to show concern for the once great man.

His appearance gave the impression of fragility, way beyond his years, and the crouched way he walked, head down, withered, unsure, projected a completely changed personality. His business dealings were ended and as such, the colliery suffered; Frank Graham was no heir apparent.

Martin trusted no one that included his son; the grotesque thing from his dreams began to make sense. Had he brought on the family's downfall by enabling the boy? Could the faceless majority be right? Was his son the true monster? Sometimes Martin Graham didn't even need to be sleeping for his mind create this altered state. The thing that had once been his wife visited whenever it felt like it. Its disintegration continued to worsen. The night-dress it had worn when the dreams started were now tattered rags and the visible flesh around the body had wilted to bone. The once beautiful hair was gone and the skin across the crown was bloodied and splitting, with more maggots gorging themselves on the deceased remains. The face was just a skull now, but its colour had changed, taking on a repulsive green tone. The lips had vanished, but the decaying tongue still hung loosely from the mouth, aiding the words,

'WHY DID YOU LET HIM KILL ME?'

Martin no longer screamed at the vision. In fact, he barely spoke at all anymore. Most of his time was spent in the study of the Graham mansion, resting in a hard-back chair beside an open fire, mouthing silently the words,

'Why did I let him kill her?'

As for the empire, the colliery, was now almost the only source of income the Graham's now had.

All the land and properties around England that the Graham's had previously owned had now been sold in a desperate attempt for the family's finances to remain liquid. In Norfolk, a 16th century townhouse with six bedrooms and four acres of land had been auctioned and had brought in much needed funds, though the proceeds hadn't lasted long. The rows of colliery cottages in Hallowell that the family still owned had now been sold to a private landlord, happily charging whatever rents they deemed adequate.

There had been investment in other mining operations throughout parts of England, but most had now closed or were in desperate need for modernisation, a process the family no longer had the finance to partake in. Mining had once been a no risk investment, once operational, the money just came to the surface. Not any longer, other forms of fuel were now readily available, and their products could now be brought cheaper from other countries. Europe no longer needed their imports, and a surplus soon grew. Labour unions ensured that the miners were now better paid than ever before, and soon, almost all collieries were running at a loss.

Due to high powered connections, Hallowell colliery still had a chance to run in profit though the main problem now, was attracting a workforce. Those who had been in residency in the colliery cottages, now had a landlord demanding rent. The homes had once been a perk of the job, now, they were an additional expense from their wages. The horrendous reputation of the family had spread, far and wide and attracting new employees was extremely tough, only the desperate and the useless applied.

A core section of miners remained, men who were hardened to the conditions and aware of the owner's incompatibility to their mentality. The boss, the hero who had started their employment, a man who had once carried their unconditional admiration and loyalty, who had helped with their problems, and assisted when they had money troubles, Martin Graham, was now just a shadow of the force he used to be. Where once stood power, now emanated only weakness. A frail, frightened decrepit memory of the architect he once was replaced by that thing.

Frank Graham carried no respect, and he knew it. The workers recognized that nepotism was his only trait to power. They stared at him through hatred eyes, hissing in his presence, content in the knowledge that they were irreplaceable, who else would be willing to work for such a person.

In return, Frank hated them too. Back in the day, they all would be gone, replaced by lunchtime with young eager workers willing to do a hard day's graft for an earned days' pay. Now, he was trapped, employing people who he'd rather see dead than give them a wage packet. This whole place, it was like one giant tomb, unescapable, unavoidable, the fated inheritance which spelled a life sentence. A foreboding future, a funeral, morose, merciless destiny for which he saw no liberation.

Staring from his office window, watching the men change into their work clothes, his inner rage boiled in the pit of his stomach. One man scowled, mouthing silent obscenities directed at him, Frank imagined the entire population of that room, choking on their own blood, some lifeless, others fighting the inevitable. Allowing a smile to creep gently across his face, the worker moved away, unnerved by his boss's reaction.

Then, the unthinkable happened."

Chapter 16

"Unthinkable?" Nick Castle felt the need to interject something, his father's flow was becoming concerning. "Worse than what you've already told me?" His father smiled.

"I've told you boy; we are just getting started."

"June 28th, 1967, Hallowell colliery. Legendary hard-man Charlie Cookson was in a bad mood. His wife was battling cancer and seeing the woman he loved fighting through round after round of painful treatments had eroded his patience to the outside world. Taking solace in alcohol, today he was struggling with a particularly vicious hangover, meaning he'd overslept and missed breakfast.

Formerly a loyalist to Martin Graham, seeing his fuck-up son resting in the once great leader's office made the huge Yorkshireman's blood boil. Staring through blood-shot eyes, he was ready for a confrontation. The other workers were arriving, and the atmosphere was understandably grim. Inside the grimy cloak room, the men were throwing lunchboxes into metal lockers and discarding dirty overcoats. Some were changing footwear in safety work-boots when a young employee, Curtis Russel, broke the uncomfortable silence.

'So, is there any news Charlie? Tommy Jarvis got a start over in St Mara, that new Recycling plant that's opening next week. He's put a good word in for me, reckons the job's mine if I want it. It doesn't pay as much as here but it's better than nothing. Plus, in the winter, it's not four-months of darkness to look forward to.' The agitated foreman remained silent, though his expression said more than words ever could, a cold, stern, scowl sweeping across his face as he continued working on an irritating knot in his left bootlace.

'Come on then Charlie, what's the word.' The youngster was pushing his luck and the senior miners knew it. Donald Davis, a miner bordering on retirement and exhausted by life's rigors gave Russel a cautionary stare, coupled with a knowing shake of the head, a warning the up-start did not heed. 'Charlie, we've a right to know. If I'm going to out of a job in three months and I've got chance of another, it would be nice to have a heads-up. Plus, Anne and I am looking for a flat, how're we supposed to afford that with no work?' Curtis's trivial concerns pushed the grizzled veteran too far. Throwing his steel-capped boots against the locker-doors, he flew at the frightened kid, who backed away and cowered as Cookson appeared to double in size. Grabbing Russel by the scruff of the neck, he screamed his angry retort, aware that his new boss would easily hear the blast.

'Firstly, you disrespectful little twat, it's Mr Cookson to you. Secondly, if you don't like it down the mine, fuck off somewhere else cos your work is shit anyway, and thirdly, if you want answers, see that prick in the office and not me, okay.'

'I didn't mean any disrespect Mr C, honest. It's just we look at you as our boss, not him. We respect your judgement and know you watch our backs.' The foreman automatically regretted verbalising the kid, knowing it was the situation and not the lad's manner that made him react, but when the office door opened, he immediately saw a chance for retribution.

'P, P, P, Problem here.' Frank preferred to avoid work confrontations knowing the men had no respect for his authority but after hearing the commotion, he felt the need to face his detractors. Charlie pushed his way through the workforce and went nose-to-nose with the boss's son.

'Yes, I have a P, P, P, problem.' The sarcastic stutter made the men snigger quietly. 'This place is in the shitter, and you are ready to flush. Five years ago, there was two-hundred men working in this pit and now there's less than fifty. We lost a lot of good men, family men, guys who you aren't good enough to lace their boots. Most had to leave Hallowell because there was no work and that's you and your bastard father's fault.' Frank stepped forward, anger plastered across his face; not because of the accusations of mismanagement, because Cookson had the cheek to insult his dad.

'Y, Y, Y, You, watch your mouth, D, D, Dickhead.' There was an audible hush.

'D, D, D, Dickhead. That's almost funny; take a long hard look in the mirror, mother fucker. What your prick's have done to this place is criminal. You should be ashamed. Still, you know all about killing things off, don't you?'

'I suggest Y, Y, you get back to W, W, Work while you still have a job.' Unwilling to strike first, the younger man turned and started back toward the office, holding his breath, awaiting an inevitable blow. Instead, the big Yorkshireman clasped a meaty hand onto his rival's right shoulder and spun Graham back around, the two once more locking eyes, reminiscent of an old lion, staring down a young contender to his throne. Cookson was one of the few men who could match up physically, their height and weight almost identical, an unstoppable force meeting the immovable object. With anger in his eyes and hatred in his heart, Graham lunged at the grizzled veteran, firing a push with both hands into Cookson's chest; the foreman didn't move an inch. The cloakroom was deathly silent, none of the workforce daring to make a sound, both out of fear for their jobs and in respect toward their colleague. Charlie was a legendary bar-room fighter but smashing the boss's son was dangerous ground. Still, backing down wasn't an option, the men were watching.

'Okay then, psycho. Perhaps, we should take this outside, or maybe you're only a tough-guy when you're standing in front of a woman.' There was an audible gasp, the workforce knew exactly what their foreman was alluding to and though he had their unreserved support, to a man, they were sure that this was taking things a step too far. Graham's eyes scoured the room, his hatred now multiplying to the bystanders too, ready to fire anyone stupid enough to snigger in his direction. Donald Davis, the man who'd tried unsuccessfully to warn off you the youngster, Curtis Russel, just moments ago, realised that, if he didn't intervene immediately, things would get seriously nasty. Best case scenario, Charlie would only be sacked. Worst case and…

'Right, that's about enough of that shit, we all got work to do.' Sliding between the warring duo, he gently but firmly, steered his friend out of harm's way. 'Come on bud, it's not worth it, think of your pension.'

For a second, the stand-off continued, neither man willing to look away first, believing it to be a sign of weakness. Finally, the foreman smiled a victorious grin after raising a hand to his mattered, grey, beard and watching as his combatant flinch. Davis pulled a little more forcibly at his friend's arm and at last, there was distance between the two alpha-males. Cookson crossed the room and retrieved his discarded work-boots, anonymous mutterings from his colleagues giving their leader some quasi-victory, though most felt the score was even.

After pausing long enough to save face, Graham retreated to the office but watched through its window as the workforce sniggered and joked at his expense. One by one, they finally all filed out of the cloakroom, heading towards the mine-shaft's elevator. The last to exit was Charlie Cookson, still sporting that self-righteous grin, waving a two-fingered salute in his boss's direction before vanishing from sight.

They are singing.

The elevator door had slammed shut, but the voices still carried throughout the floor. The tune was, 'London Bridge is falling down,' but the words had changed. Their voices were in unison, singing as one, fuck, it sounded practiced, staged, solely for his humiliation.

'Frankie Graham's falling down

Falling

Falling

Frankie Graham's falling

What a wanker.'

This was too much. The lift-carriage was lowering and still, it continued, chorus after chorus, most singing, others laughing. Inside his mind, the words reverberating. Cruel, sadistic, relentless. Suddenly, he was a child once more, back inside the school classroom. The bullies, with their tyrannical laughter, their depraved, sinful, malevolent tormenting. Taunting his looks. Mimicking his speech impediment.

He slammed the office door but still the taunts echoed from the elevator shaft.

Stop it, p, p, p, please, stop it.

Falling to his knees, he clung to the office wall for guidance, crawling along the tiled floor, seeking solace in the corner. Buttocks pressed in tightly, his body curled into a ball, hands clasped tightly over his ears though still, the taunts barbarously rebounded in his mind, shutting down rational thought. Eyes closed feverously as he knew that the bullies stood before him. Perhaps, it was that Scholes girl, her vicious tongue whipping the rest of his school-class into a frenzy. Or maybe, it was her brothers, ready to smash him back into a coma. Perhaps it was Charlie Cookson and the rest of that rabid scoundrels.

His arms pulled his head down further, pressing uncomfortably into his thighs. Perspiration dripped down into his already blood-shot eyes, causing them to sting further. Calloused palms rubbed furiously, giving the impression of tears. Or maybe it was tears, by now, he barely knew. There'd been no crying since childhood but, as he was now a child once more, a weeping sniffling little wimp, frightened of bullies, of girls, maybe he should cry. Perhaps, he should bawl and scream and show the whole world exactly what a pussy he really is.

The skin across his cheeks was reddening by the second, his hands sliding from his sweat soaked face to his crown, fingers entwining into his thick bushy hair, the urge to tear it from its roots almost irresistible. His eyes still closed tightly, terrified of what awaited him in the room's artificial light though the tempered darkness give no respite to his torment.

His breathing now, uncontrollable, coming in short, repetitive bursts, causing his barrel chest to ache like a long-distance runner, exhausting him from the inside, out. His navy-blue coveralls now dampened with the same perspiration which had invaded his face without warning, now assaulting the rest of his body. His internal temperature reaching critical breaking point. Still, those same excruciating rhyme lyrics bombarding his mind.

'Frankie Graham's falling down

Falling

Falling

Frankie Graham's falling

What a wanker.'

Suddenly, he could take no more. His laboured breathing had stopped altogether, he was choking, all the air had left his lungs, those reddened cheeks turning a hideous shade of blue. Fingernails clawed at the walls, the blue-painted brickwork giving no traction, the tips of his fingers slipping on the shiny surface. Without warning, his thick calf muscles tensed into action, emerging with a forceful leap and swiftly, he was upright, stumbling forward towards the closed window across the room. With his eyes squinting, (still terrified of the bullies all around him), his speedy excursion instantly crashed to a destructive halt, his foot catching the leg of a sturdy oak desk, sending him hurtling back down to the tiled floor, his head colliding violently into the dull vertical edge of the room's only iron radiator. Strangely, the sudden pain seemed to re-boot his breathing, the sudden intake of oxygen making his head feel giddy.

Opening his eyes, he scanned the room. It was empty. The bullies from school…they were all gone. Remembering back, he'd taken swift revenge on all those who'd wronged him. The Scholes girl, she'd been the ringleader, oh how he'd avenged all her crimes. The rats had been a particularly nice touch. And her brothers? That was coming.

His hand lifted to the wound on his forehead. An adequate reminder, two, maybe three inches, the blood was pouring smoothly; his fingers touched carefully as to not disturb the flow. The head gently tilted backwards and slightly to the left so the river could ebb, breezing a continual progression between his eyes and down both sides of the nose equally. It felt warm and sticky, his face a crimson mask. The pain was an afterthought, a worthwhile sacrifice to feel this…normal. Pain was good, pain was the answer.

Maureen Sanders, a twenty years old, naïve, unsophisticated secretary, passed by the office window and peered inside. Had there been anyone else working on that floor, they'd would certainly have run to her aid as the scream she called out at seeing her employer's face covered in blood was as loud and terror filled as one could achieve. Graham watched in joy as the young woman fainted, crashing to the same tiled floor to which he'd recently frequented. Resting in a moulded plastic chair, he rubbed his hands heavily across his drenched cheeks, marvelling at the amount blood-loss, one wound could achieve. His tongue lapped across his lips; the acidic, almost metallic taste not unpleasant. He thought about the young woman, lying unconscious in the corridor outside his office. How easy it would be for her to just…disappear. But what would that achieve?

Then he recalled that vision. All the workers, choking on their own blood. Their bones broken, skulls crushed, laying in their own desecration. Suddenly, a plan began to form.

He'd seen blood, felt blood, tasted blood…Blood was the answer. The only answer. The only escape from the drudgery, which was his life, it would be liberating himself from the invisible ties, finding his freedom. This was the way, an escape, an abdication; but it would mean the total eradication Hallowell colliery, the end of an era…and so much more.

Frank left the office, a strange aura about him, like a great weight had been lifted. The blood was drying now, and the volcanic wound had ceased to spew its lava. He wore the contents like a badge of honour, and why not? The secretary was having a nice nap and no one else worked in this part of the building, not until the miners returned from their shift. Wearily farmed into the elevator, patently waiting as the decrepit lift climbed the 180 feet to the summit. Martin had planned to replace the cables long ago, they had been deemed unsafe on inspection numerous times, yet still they were used, day after day, month after month, a constant grind carrying far more weight than the safety limit. He'd passed poor Maureen, such a silly girl, she had so much growing up to do, maybe? She'd fallen in a strange manner, the wall had taken much of the force, there didn't seem much damage (if she'd hit her head, it would be lucky, her brain didn't work anyway). Had she woken whilst he was passing, she would have probably fainted again, luckily, she continued her slumber.

Immediately to Graham's right were the elevator doors. For the last seven years, they had never closed properly, and with a little effort, they could be pulled fully open. Staring down the dark shaft, imagining what damage his sick plan could do, he began to laugh, his cackling humour echoing all the way down to the mine below.

The official story was that an explosion occurred, caused by firedamp propagated by coal dust, an ignition caused by friction heat from a piece of falling quarzitic rock. The blast tore through the mine and the elevator rope snapped, cascading 165 feet to the colliery bottom. That's what the investigator's report said.

That investigator was a man named Michael Knight. A well-respected person who would leave no stone unturned to discover the truth when dispatched to the scene of a disaster. That was, every disaster, bar Hallowell colliery. If his history had been looked at thoroughly, he'd have never been allowed the task of deciphering the nature of the catastrophe.

Knight was a Graham disciple, ten years Martin's junior who owed his entire professional life to his mentor. As a boy, he'd been apprentice in the Graham colliery but had been fast tracked from the coalface to the offices when his intellect proved greater than his brawn. Martin used Knight as his pet project and his ascension through the ranks was swift. After ten years, the young man had made assistant manager but after marriage, his wife had itchy feet and wanted a change of scenery. Not content with small village life, she longed to return to her roots in London and Knight reluctantly conceded defeat. Martin tried everything to keep his bright employee but when the fight seemed futile, he used some of his considerable connections to ensure that Michael's career would continue to flourish. There'd even been rumours of a gay sexual connection between the men though nothing was ever proved. When a post became available in the colliery inspector's office, Graham ensured his friend was offered the post without even an interview. The head offices were in London, so the Knights were overjoyed. Martin did have an ulterior motive though, connections in that department meant that there was less chance of surprise inspections on his property, something that could come in useful in the future.

Michael Knight never forgot this kindness and their friendship remained throughout the years. His intelligence had propelled him through the ranks and now, he was head of the disaster investigation team. When he was told of the tragedy in Hallowell, he appointed himself to the case though it was not his working area. Time to repay that debt. He found his friend a broken man and his son, Frank, almost in total charge. After seeing many incident sights, Knight immediately recognised this was no accident. It took a matter of hours for him to come to his conclusions and a little while longer to find a cover story. Had the truth come out, it wouldn't only have been Frank who was blamed. There would be questions asked and fingers pointed, there'd be a trial and scandal. The Graham family would be ruined, Michael Knight wasn't about to let that happen. Martin couldn't survive prison.

When Knight revealed his findings to his mentor, he wasn't certain the details had truly been understood. He was talking about murder, plain and simple. Forty plus men dead, Martin just stared into space. He looked like a dementia patient, recent incidents destroying what normality remained. It was for him, that his true findings were buried.

After the men, had lowered to the colliery floor, the rage inside of Frank Graham had been too much to bear. He'd been insulted for the final time, now they would pay. The acting manager had devised a plan so repugnant, even he wondered if he really had the hatred needed to carry it out.

Martin Graham had never liked the idea of using heavy explosives underground. Many collieries did but he was old-fashioned, and perhaps a little stubborn. He believed that it would risk the lives of his workforce, he'd seen explosions before and the atrocious results it could cause. As a young apprentice, there'd been a natural eruption due to escaping methane gas and, when the six workers in the blast zone were found, there wasn't much left to send home to their families. That memory had lived with him, his entire life and he had no wish to increase the likelihood of seeing it again.

He'd finally bowed to peer pressure in 1963 when for the first time, Hallowell colliery used dynamite in its extraction. The price of coal was dropping and the need for more product with a lessening workforce, necessitated it. He still hadn't been sure and had insisted on being present during the first blast, being unwilling to ask his employees to do something which he wasn't willing to do himself. A series of holes were drilled along the coal bed and dynamite was inserted. When the explosion occurred, the coal wall would crack into pieces making extraction faster. Unfortunately, one of the borings chosen was an extremely weak area and the controlled blast created a cave-in. Two workers were hurt and though the injuries weren't life threatening, it was all the evidence Martin needed, arguing that it was far too great a risk. The dynamite was locked away in the stores and forgotten about by everyone. That was everyone, bar Frank Graham. A couple of years previous, he'd considered stealing the explosive to blow up his mother's car while she was in it. Obviously, he never took it past the fantasy stage, but this plan was many times deadlier.

The explosives hadn't been difficult to find. Packaged deeply inside wooden crates, Martin had wanted them away from the colliery altogether, his fear of an accidental eruption growing to almost phobia-like proportions. Instead, storing them on the top floor of the railway station-main building, in spare space beside the Graham offices, had seemed the safest option, content in the knowledge that only Frank and himself were aware of their location.

Retrieving the crate required, had taken an aggravating amount of time. Heavy wooden boxes containing miner's helmets and lamps, coveralls, and boilersuits, filed timesheets, both used and plain. Hoarded documents which now served no purpose and were growing thick with dust, tied up in coarse-feeling material sacks. A hugely heavy metal cage containing empty fire extinguishers had been the penultimate obstacle and had taken all his force to manoeuvre it aside before finally, the prize loomed into view. Frank's torch-beam cut through dark, musty air, dust mites causing the young man to cough, his throaty splutter reverberating against the tight, bare-brick walls. Squinting against the obscure murkiness, he could see a wooden crate, a red plastic sign, the word explosives written in white lettering attached to its vertical length. The monster smiled, his doubts of whether the dynamite had been removed without his knowledge, extinguished. Kicking away the concluding obstruction, a heap of folded cloth sheeting, he knelt and excitedly reached for his requirement. The lid was firmly attached but Graham had come prepared, a strong crowbar had been slid through a loop at the waste of his customary overalls, along with a small tap-hammer, and in no time, the inside was visible, the creature had his weapon.

Inside a plastic box, Frank Graham carefully placed four cylinders of dynamite, eight inches in length, 1.5 inches in diameter and weighing less than a pound each. Made up mainly of nitro-glycerine, along with certain stabilizers for transportation safety reasons, the highly volatile explosive required very careful handling, something the monster was keenly aware of. Whilst in storage, the cylinders had sweated, forming a pool in the base of the crate which had crystallised on the outer of the sticks, making them even more shock sensitive. His new method of transporting the explosives, a small, foot-long plastic container was filled with cotton balls, to which the capricious, hazardous ingredients were packed tightly. When content he'd taken the necessary safety requirements, Frank put back together, the jigsaw puzzle, that was the railway-station storage room, determined to not draw unnecessary attention to his movements. After locking the storage room's mess-fenced door, he turned to his lethal weapons, knowing that his plan would alter the history of Hallowell forever. The devilish smile immoveable from his lips showed a monster without remorse or feeling. Without compassion, compunction, or guilt. It was a knowing smile, an evil smile. It was the smile of a psychopath.

That fact the incomparable nauseating event had fallen upon a Friday was significant for two reasons.

Firstly, with the weekend looming, he'd have needed to wait three days to carry out the heinous task, and had that delay taken place, had there been a whole weekend to mull over the ramifications of his actions, it was possible that the loathsome episode may never have happened. Though Frank had no compassion for his would-be victims, the expected punishment for the crime may have been enough to make him reconsider. Friday ensured that there was no time for doubt. It was act now, worry later.

Secondly, and most importantly, all other non-mining employees would have vacated the premises by the time the colliers shift had ended. Due to Martin's continuing mental deterioration and Frank's lack of both experience and leadership capabilities, seventy-six years-old Jack Price had been chosen to help steady the ship. Six years after retirement, the slight, diminutive Hallowell resident with thinning white hair, heavily wrinkled face and crooked drooping nose had been a strange choice for under-manager and the old man had taken some persuasion. A Graham proponent and an especially close ally to Martin for many years, he'd felt a certain sense of obligation to help the family in their time of need. Price had only agreed to return due to the realisation that, perhaps, his own brand of gentle leadership qualities would assist his friend's son, while the family strived for greatness once more. Jack had lost his wife to cancer, eighteen months earlier and expected his own tedious tango with the grim reaper until they were reunited in heaven, so to become useful once more, no matter for how short a time, had come as a pleasant surprise. Unfortunately, the assistant manger's Friday shift ended an hour before the miners were due to resurface, along with his secretary's. As for Frank's unfortunate subordinate. Maureen Saunders, the calamitous worker who had fainted earlier in the day at the sight of her employer's blood, she'd felt unable to continue with her working day after enduring such a shock, leaving the colliers fate resting alone in the hands of a maniac.

Ten minutes before five, Frank rested in his office chair, the clear plastic box placed carefully on the desk before him, the deadly ingredients inside wrapped tightly in cotton wool for safety. Lid adjacent, the crazed young man slid a finger across the soft white material, its pleasant texture disguising what horrors lay inside its catacomb. A large black and white clock hung above the office door, its incessant ticking the only noise to break the silence. Frank's gaze was one of a cat's, prowling, ready to assert its power over a defenceless mouse. Would the blast kill him too? The fireball would almost certainly have no other means of escape, the elevator shaft could cause a returning jet of fire, capable of exploding from the weakened doors, engulfing the entire colliery. Not that his own death gave him any measure of concern, ending Charlie Cookson and his band of bastards would be a fair trade.

Five minutes before five, they would be hovering around the timeclock now. The union had tried to get the workers an early finish on a Friday afternoon…no chance. Finish early, take less wages home that was the option. Greedy fuckers, always wanting something for nothing. Gone were the days of workers mining until they were told differently. That was the trouble with the labour of England today, bastard unions becoming more powerful than the owners. Frank continued the day's evil series of grins, let's see what the union thinks of this. He couldn't remember when he'd last been in a mood this good.

Two minutes before five, Frank was at the top of the elevator shaft, the doors fully open. He knew the lift hadn't begun its climb; the echoing grind would be heard throughout the entire property. Still, the crash of iron doors opening, muffled voices toned with joy that only the end of a working week could bring, plodding footsteps as the men squeezed into the less-than-comfortable space, no-one wishing to miss the first car as the wait for the next turn would mean an inpatient interim, knowing that their compatriots would be three-quarters of the way down their first pint while they were still heading for the pub. Frank was growing just as impatient, in his hands were tubes of death, more lethal than a rattlesnake, more frightening than an unexploded bomb. For once, Graham was sweating scared, not for his own demise, but to ensure that his noxious plan came to fruition. Finally, the booming voice of the foreman, Charlie Cookson drifted up the concrete tube.

'All aboard?' Someone had the sound of a tooting steam-train whistle while others laughed, the jovial nature of the men continuing to grow. The doors squeezed shut, and after a brief pause, the groan of the mechanism, the carriage began to climb.

Graham took a long, lingering stare at the weapons in his hands. Do this and there was no turning back. All his previous crimes were forgivable, even the killing of Iris could be construed as self-defence. But this? It was pre-meditated.

A thought out, hand crafted, unmistakable mass-murder. The village would want vengeance, it was their loved ones who would be slaughtered. Survive their wrath and it would be life imprisonment without parole. The death penalty had recently been abolished but even Frank baulked at the prospect of going down forever. Was it worth it? His mind was changing. Cookson could be dealt with quietly, and the others weren't important enough to give up his liberty. The grin had diminished, this was something that had excited him, the anticipation of destroying all that scum, the contemplation of ridding himself of the millstone that was Hallowell colliery. The carriage was now midway through its journey to the surface, their conversation was now somewhat clearer. But that wasn't talking, it was singing.

'Frankie Graham's falling down

Falling

Falling

Frankie Graham's falling

What a wanker.'

Suddenly, the anger had returned. The considerable ramifications were now inconsequential, the disrespect they'd shown was now more important than even his own freedom. Some were singing, verse after verse, others were laughing, the growing noise ate away at his soul. Tears welled once more in the corners of his eyes, not of sorrow, but of frustration. Having been on the verge of recoiling his deadly plan, the apparent weakness made him feel physically sick. Had it been weakness, or was it apathy? Whichever made little difference, those feelings were now gone. There was just one thing left to do."

Chapter 17

Nick Castle sat wide-eyed, staring into the flames. It was barely comprehensible and yet the young man accepted every word. So many things were now making sense; answers to questions long since buried. He had no wish to interrupt, fearing against breaking Mick's momentum. The interjection he used was kept short.

"This is incredible."

The older man simply nodded, feeling almost overwhelmed with emotion, for now, his own involvement was looming. An admission was worrying, but he'd come too far to stop now.

"Hallowell had once loved Martin Graham, hero worshipped him. He was the modern father of the town. Now, all that had changed. He was as responsible, if not more, for the tragedy. He'd spent a lifetime excusing that monster, aiding him, growing him, enabling him. Everyone else could see how that creature would turn out, even its own mother. But Martin was untouchable which meant Frank was by proxy. Now, things had gone too far. If the authorities wouldn't help them, they'd have to do it themselves, old style.

The news broke suddenly and out of the blue. The investigator, Michael Knight, the man responsible for brokering the lies of the colliery disaster was dead. Killed in a motorway crash while heading back to London, rumours of intoxication behind the wheel were expected but not confirmed. His Ford Anglia had veered violently into the on-coming traffic and been crushed by a heavy-goods eighteen-wheeler. No one else had been injured. The rumour mill had been in full swing, some said it was suicide, not being capable of living with the horrible thing that he'd done. Others claimed that the alcohol had been to block out the terrible truth. Whatever the reason, Knight was dead and so was the resident's hopes for justice.

The accident investigation authorities had accepted Knight's version without question. Why wouldn't they? His record of employment was impeccable, his understanding of the situation, flawless. Hell, the man had even worked in the damned place, who else could have done the job any better? What had happened was a tragedy but, mining was a dangerous job, unfortunately, sometimes workers die, if a man like Michael Knight said the explosion had been of natural origin, there would be no questioning his findings. Still the residents smelled a cover-up, and were determined to expose the truth, whatever it took.

Charlie Cookson's widow, Karen, had ensured that the controversy had remained the focal point, beginning a petition which had been signed by over 300 people, desperate for answers, even more desperate that those silent voices be avenged. A small consortium of grief-stricken families made a pilgrimage to the London offices, a venturesome frenzied group, determined to ensure that a second investigation be made. The petition was the only reason the faction got inside the building and when an officer finally agreed to take a meeting with the audacious assemblage, they were told with extreme certainty that the matter was closed. The signature sheet meant nothing, their conspiracy theories meant nothing, their best man had worked the case and found no negligence on the part of the owners. So far as the accident investigation authorities were concerned, game over. Without the option of a legal recourse now dashed, the only choice seemed private justice, vengeance, whatever it took.

Bill Castle's position was precarious, for the last few years he'd played the role of mediator between the Grahams and the rest of Hallowell. His close ties to Martin ensuring that his feelings of loyalty had persisted, making on-lookers perplexed. Now, this had over-stepped the mark and even the most optimistic of people would struggle to see a happy outcome. The Graham's had lost all leverage, the railway station, gone, business interests, gone, even the chances of the colliery re-opening seemed unlikely. They weren't seen as Hallowell royalty anymore, they weren't employers, they were just avenging, a role they had no idea how to play, and an accumulation of residents were determined that they pay for their crimes, one way or another.

Word spread quickly about a town meeting, which had been scheduled for the day after the failed London siege. Local landlord, Terry Hutchinson had been asked to host the congregation in the Wheat-sheaf public house but quickly realised that his establishment wasn't big enough to accommodate the numbers involved. It wasn't by invitation, all were welcome. Hallowell was a colliery village, and the tragedy had struck almost every family. Some lost a father, or a son, brother or uncle, others had lost friends, loved ones who had been slaughtered at the whim of a madman. Everyone was affected, everyone's wrath demanded retribution.

The venue was changed to the large concert hall inside the workingmen's club, which could comfortably seat 250 people. As the association began to assemble, even that number appeared small, this was going to be crowded.

An unseasonal heatwave had made the Autumnal evening, stickily uncomfortable. Alfie Harris had been the chairman of the workingmen's club for many years and frowned as none-members were allowed to enter his hallowed building. With a flat cap and a woodbine smouldering from the corner of his mouth, he watched women entering the men only area and frowned even more, he was a stickler for rules.

Several colliery workers who hadn't been on shift during the disaster weren't only fighting the horror of losing colleagues, but now they had to face the prospect of unemployment. Simon Grayson, whose brother had been tragically taken, had sat at the bar since midday, conversing with whoever appeared, sporadically shedding tears and drinking, heavily. Charlie Cookson's son, Harry had spent much of the afternoon in the same way and by now, it seemed a race to see who would pass out first. Their mood had changed, from shared grief, becoming increasingly confrontational as time progressed. The undercurrent of aggression which had bubbled under the surface, their increasing discontent at the seeming lack of advancement toward justice, causing the men to gradually turn on one another, raised voices and macho posturing causing bystanders to intervene numerous times until eventually, the congregation, tired of their histrionics, decided to let them go at it. With the audience losing interest, their jets began to cool, pickling themselves with booze taking precedence once more.

It was early evening before the multitude of residents had assembled into the concert-room and had taken their seats. Once some form of order had been given, Bill Castle, flanked closely by Harry Brackett, who by their statures of authority and seniority had been elected as co-chairmen, took their position. The doctor appeared to be enjoying his role of power whereas the policeman would have been happier being seated with the mob. And that's exactly what this had the potential to become, a mob, or more importantly, mob rules.

A make-shift pulpit had been erected on the stage for the chairmen to stand behind, a high table with covered vertical lift which was useful as Castle's knees were shaking uncontrollably, public speaking was not in his comfort-zone. He called the meeting to order, and silence was given, a sign of respect the rank and file had for the officer affording him their attention. Bill tried to hide his nervousness though his reddened cheeks and stuttered start gave his secret away.

'Okay, ladies and gentlemen, I think we should begin. This is a very strange, almost surreal situation, one would none of us have ever been in before. I've spoken to many of you individually over the last few weeks but let me start by giving each one of you who have been directly affected by this tragedy, mine, and my wife's deepest sympathy at this most upsetting of times.'

'We don't want your sympathy, we want JUSTICE.' The voice hailed from the back of the room, still chugging on a bottle of beer, Simon Grayson's words were readily acknowledged by the crowd, even if some seemed angry at the disturbance. Harry Brackett pushed forward, eager to justify his position of co-chairman.

'Yes folks, we all agree what is needed but calling out without having the floor is not the way forward.' The doctor's authority notably lesser to the policeman used his raised articulation to appear more important. A throng of voices from all corners had begun their own conversations, Castle's frustration at the interruptions began to overtake his nervousness.

'Right, knock this shit off. If someone else wants to chair his thing, feel free to do so, otherwise shut the fuck up until it's your turn to speak.' He suddenly became aware of his language and regressed, not wishing to start off the session confrontationally. 'Pardon my language but, if we carry on this way, we'll get nothing done.' Turning to his co-host his next retort was aimed in his direction.

'And Harry, nothing has been decided yet, that's why we are here, so we can all have a voice and then, decide what's to be done.'

It was now, the physician's turn to feel embarrassment, taking a step back to the left. 'Fine, if we're all in agreement, let's continue…'

187

'Tom's going to be okay.' Kenneth Dooley, a young miner who wasn't on shift that day, burst through the doors at the back of the room, an excited grin plastered across his face. A huge ripple of joy spread across the room, tears falling, men hugging men, the sudden burst of exhilaration fracturing the tortured souls. Tom Daley had been the final man pulled from the disaster site, most believed him dead, but a pulse had been found. 'It's still touch and go, but the docs say he should make it.' Finally, a reason to smile. It didn't last.

The gathering lasted over two hours. Anyone wishing to speak was granted impeccable silence. There were tears, from both women and men. The only child allowed in the assembly hall was a boy named Dean Cundy. He'd lost his father and grandfather to the colliery disaster but managed to maintain an air of eloquence and dignity that most adults appreciated. A single tear had rolled down his pale, freckled cheek as he told of his mother who had been under sedation for much of the interim after losing both her husband and father. It wasn't until his time was growing to an end when the youth's face had contorted into anger, mercilessly exclaiming that the monster behind the tragedy deserved to die for his actions. A cheer had erupted in agreement and the child was afforded a standing ovation and wild applause. Bill Castle shook his head, knowing that the mass conflux of irate residents would accept nothing more than blood, an eye for an eye, a life for a life.

Though most knew already, Adam Scholes, a successful solicitor and regular passivist, put aside his non-violent stance, as he reminded the audience of Michael Knight's close ties to the Grahams and his historical connection to Hallowell colliery. Local schoolteacher, Daniel Murphy had been dog-walking on the morning of the catastrophe and had seen Frank Graham leaving the stores of the railway station, looking timorous and carrying a package which the monster appeared to try to hide. Jack Hunt, a former ticket vendor and station employee added that explosives were in those same stores and colliery worker. Sasha Wolf remembered that there had been explosive remaining after Martin had ended their use inside the mine.

The courtroom had spoken and the jury of two hundred plus and emerged with a verdict. Frank Graham was guilty of mass murder, sentence…death."

Chapter 18

"Wait, wait, wait." That last statement set off an alarm in Nick's young mind, this whole tale seemed to be coming to an abhorrent conclusion. "This was England in the 1960s, not the medieval days. This shit sounds like a 'GET YOUR TORCH AND PITCH FORKS' moment. You trying to tell me that," His dad interrupted.

"I'm telling you, what you wanted to know. If you can't comprehend it, tough, this is what we've lived with for a lot of years, and now you get to share, lucky you. Now shut up and let me finish."

"But this is unreal."

"Oh, it's real. For once, know when to shut the fuck up and listen. You said you needed to know; I'm telling you. So be quiet and all will become clear."

"It was October 13th, 1967. Some claim it was the day Hallowell's innocence died. The village was never the same. It also happened to be Frank Graham's birthday. They'd waited all this time for the official report on the catastrophe, praying that taking matters into their own hands wouldn't be necessary. Their fears were now realised, it was private justice or no justice.

When the plan was finalised, there was no turning back. Rumours had spread that Martin Graham was now barely coherent and rarely left his home. If it were possible, the plan was to avoid a confrontation with the patriarch, believing that the knowledge his son was dead, was punishment enough. He hadn't perpetrated the crimes, only enabled them. Frank shouldn't have been too hard to find. The colliery was now derelict, the railway station closed, and he rarely ever ventured out of town. The mansion was the obvious location. If Martin stood in their way, he'd be moved, one way or another.

They'd met by the railway station as to not draw attention to themselves; the last thing anyone wanted was crowds of people cheering as they descended upon their target. What was going to happen, it was barbaric, uncivilized, some may say inhuman, but so was their target. He'd destroyed without remorse, robbed children of fathers, stolen sons from mothers, the law was an ass, it was unavoidable.

There seemed little sign of movement in the old building which stood out scarily in the late afternoon mist; a vision of a by-gone era. During the march to the mansion, most were silent. Few wanted to land the final, lethal blow and wondered if they'd be man enough, should the task fall to them. It was around 4 pm when they entered the mansion grounds and most wished they'd scheduled the assault earlier in the day; the light was already fading and maintaining their courage wasn't easy. The gravel crunched underfoot in the driveway, breaking the eerie silence.

Dean Cundy, the young man who'd impressed the congregation by speaking so eloquently about his lost family members had insisted he be present. There were objections immediately, most of the men who'd been chosen for the heinous task looked at the youngster as a child, someone who would need protection rather than be an asset to the group. It was Bill Castle who stood for him, argued for him, took responsibility for him. Cundy had been closing to tears as the policeman had exclaimed,

'This kid has more guts had half the men in this village. To stand before a crowd, to speak like he did, he's the sort of MAN, I want by my side.' A few grumbles from inconsequential people were all the argument heard. Dean was on the team.

Bill kept the youngster close.

'I was with dad, every step of the way.' Mick Castle's face seemed to beam with pride, he and his father were partners.

'So you were there?' Nick had been expecting it, but somehow it still came as a surprise.

'Oh, I was there, I was part of the whole damn thing.' It was a group of thirty men. Urban legend claimed the number almost double; those were mainly men who had later claimed participation for fear of accusation of cowardice. Bill and Harry Brackett lead the team, though after the town meeting, the doctor's position of power had seemed to diminish quickly. Mick Castle shadowed his father, mainly to give and receive protection. Bill's friend, the off-licence owner Tony Jayne walked step for step with the lead group though remained in silent thought. His boy, Archie, who had just turned sixteen and had only begun work at the colliery three weeks before the tragedy, now lost forever. The boy had been vibrant and enthusiastic, optimistic with a good education and an exciting future, the monster had stolen him. Inside, a part of Tony died that day too and if anyone from the group would have the guts to land a killer blow on that creature, it was him.

Young Dean Cundy seemed dangerously excited, as though the magnitude of the situation hadn't quite taken hold. Bill watched as the youngsters' feet shuffled, rather than stepped. His legs moved as though dancing to silent music, the officer knew it was the kid's way of pretending that he wasn't quite so scared shitless as he really was. Bill smiled and then noticed the lad was holding something in his right hand. It was hard to make out, so he asked, 'What's that you got there?' The lad now smiled though his face had flushed slightly with embarrassment. Moving in close, he used both hands to flatten the item out.

'This was the last present my dad ever bought me.' Stretching out his arms, he revealed the most revolting Halloween mask, the policeman had ever seen. The face was sculpted into the shape of skull though some of the skin had yet to decompose. Created in thick latex, the eyeholes were larger than usual with smaller holes at the tip of the nose and mouth. Considering the mouth, it had two rows of discoloured rotting teeth (some were missing) with a square jawline and prominent cheekbones to add to the repulsive visage. The rubber flesh was coloured in a dark green shade, but more protrusive was the black scraggly mass of fake hair which started at the brow, covered across the crown, and hung shabbily down to the neck. There were no holes for hearing which would make conversation difficult. As the youngster stretched his prize out fully, beaming with pride at the would-be disguise, Castle could only grimace, feeling strange that the final present given to a boy from a father should be something so repulsive. 'What do you think?'

'Well…yes…it's very…I don't want to say nice but,' Dean giggled, reminding the officer, just how young his charge was. 'Do you like it?'

'Of course.'

'Well, I suppose, that's all that matters. Plus, I kind-of like scary things so, I like it to.'

The leading group were only 100 yards from the front door when a voice from behind called out excitedly, claiming a sign of life at the attic window. The curtain fluttered; a figure had passed it by. The question remained, was it their target?

'I'm sure. I'm sure I seen someone up at that window.' The agitated man was butcher, Malcom Gregory, who had been happily lagging with the second group. A small, meek looking chap with pure-white hair, (short back and sides) easily distinguishable from the rest of the men as he'd arrived still wearing his white butchers coat with red and white striped apron. He burst forward, desperate for Bill Castle's attention. 'Honest, up in that top window, I really seen someone.' The cop smiled, he'd known Malcolm since they were children, and this was the most enthusiasm, the butcher had shown, about anything, ever.

'Don't worry mate, just take a breath. Of course, I believe you. Hell, that's you're here.' Sneaking a look at the little man's attire, he sniggered. 'Didn't you have time to get changed, Malcolm?'

'What's the point? If any blood gets on these, who gives a fuck?'

'Good point.'

Fifty yards from the main front entrance, the group seemed to stop in unison, this had suddenly become very real. Partial conversations from men taking up the rear also came to an abrupt halt and momentarily there was silence. Gregory squinted back towards the attic window, had he really seen someone, or was it an optical illusion? Maybe it was nerves, who knew?

The front entranceway seemed less impressive than most remembered, flaking varnish on the solid oak door and its frame gave the impression of age, and the glass vestibule which surrounded it, was begrimed and scummy, a pane to the left housing a large crack down its centre. The three steps which lead up to the porch were tired grey concrete, covered with autumnal leaves and blown in litter, the whole thing seemed a sad indictment of the once great mansion.

From the pack, the portly figure of Fred Gibson, an unlikable slug of a man who most found highly disagreeable, pushed his way forward and rushed the doorway, twisting the handle, only to find it locked. The sealed entrance surprised few, what bewildered most was that Gibson had volunteered to take the risk in the first place. The proprietor of Hallowell's only funeral directorship, most looked upon the overweight slob as a coward, and his actions were completely against type. Bill Castle felt the need to check before taking the undertaker's word, believing that this was a way to avoid entering the dangerous situation. When the handle refused to give, Gibson gave the officer an exasperated stare but said nothing, his true spineless personality returning to the surface.

'Looks like we'll have to try the back-door before smashing our way in, best not adding break and entering to our list of crimes.' Castle still wasn't completely sold on their plan but knew it was happening, regardless of his participation. At least this way, he could try to ensure Martin's safety, even if the patriarch's will to live would greatly diminish once Frank had expired.

Terry Hutchinson and his brothers Jake and Steve enlisted their services, along with another family of siblings, the Simpson brothers, Aaron Oliver, and Barry. The latter had a reputation for criminality, theft being a key component, and Castle warned them, stealing was strictly off limits. Harry Brackett decided to lead the mission, promising to keep a watchful eye, with Barry returning a sarcastic smile.

The rear of the property gave more evidence of the Victorian architecture that had made the building, grade 1 listed. Gothic carvings above the doorways and stained-glass mouldings embedded in the split windows, it looked more like a church than a stately home. There were several outhouses around a large courtyard, which would all require searching, should the monster not be discovered in the expected locations. Some generations previously, Lord Walter Graham had been a keen horse enthusiast, owning several champions. Once beyond their racing days, the horses would return from the trainer's yard and go to stud here. The former stables were still on site and reasonably well maintained, even though it had been years since they were used professionally. Aaron Simpson peered an inquisitive head through the stable door and found it empty; shame, that would have been an easier target than the main house. The brothers had been on this land once, pouching pheasant, but Martin had chased the off, firing a loaded shotgun in the air. A three-door garage built far later than the other structures was off to the right with a slip road circling to the front of the mansion. The doors were bolted tight, but most people knew what was inside. The Daimler, long, sleek, and black was fit for royalty, while the Ferrari 250 GTO, which was regarded as the best model the industry giant ever created, was enough to make young men would drool. A three litre V12 engine, five speed manual gear box, rear wheel drive and a top speed of 175 mph, it was a collector's dream. There had only been 39 ever made, ensuring that Martin would only use it sporadically. Neighbouring those, Iris's Volvo looked a poor relation. Oliver Simpson tried to squint through frosted glass to catch a glimpse of the collection, but the windows were at too high an angle. Cursing, he re-joined the group.

Next was the tool shed, though the terminology gave no relation to its size. Stretching across a vast square footage, the group noticed its doors slightly ajar, allowing the men to explore its wares. They were cautious, fearing their target to be lurking inside; he wasn't. Once more, the Simpson boy's collective eyes lit up at the well-stocked storage house. Everything from manual to power tools, gardening equipment, both hand-operated and electrical. A ride-along lawn mower looked especially tempting to a career thief but, unfortunately Harry Brackett was watching, spoil sport. Once certain the building wasn't occupied, they tentatively moved on.

A large terracotta plant-pot, standing beside the back entrance had fallen, smashing into hundreds of tiny shards. Manoeuvring the debris with a tatty work-boot, Oliver Simpson called out in excitement as a long metal key revealed itself. The doctor, wallowing in the role of un-official leader of the sub-team was presented with the treasure. With a strong sense of trepidation, he forced it into the door's lock. Gripping hard, the latch refused to turn. Applying force, he tried thudding the solid oak with his shoulder though it was obvious that the key didn't fit the lock. Trying to hide his sense of relief at not being the first to enter the mansion, he extracted the metal object and placed it into his pocket.

'Here, let me try.' Barry Simpson nudged the physician aside, grabbing the key as swiftly as an expert pickpocket.

'You're wasting your time, lad. It's bolted on the inside,' Brackett was becoming agitated at the young up-starts arguing. 'You'll snap the key in a minute, just give it here, and we'll get in round the front.' Simpson still ignored the old man.

'It's coming, it's coming.' The resulting 'Snap' was audible around the courtyard. The handle of the key remained in Barry's hand, and his face turned a deep shade of red.

'Told you, idiot.' Nothing else was said, the sub-team started the short journey back to the main body of men, partially relieved that they weren't the ones needed to face Frank alone.

'No luck lads. Plan B then.' Ian Gaskins, the mechanic from town had started working on a small window by the front door.

Three days earlier, young Dean Cundy had started a personal assault on the mansion, his private torment gaining the upper hand against common sense. Bricks had been hurled, and glass had been broken, the window of the vestibule by the front door taking the brunt. He'd retreated before being noticed and though a replacement had been fitted, the putty was still pliable.

'It's nearly out, Bill.' Tommy Wright, owner of the Lunchbox café was standing rigid, ready to catch the glass when it fell; he failed. The heavy pane slipped from his grasp and shattered on the floor into a million pieces.

'Sorry Bill, thought I had it.' The chef blushed as the others watched in despair, knowing the sound of breaking glass would be a loud alarm bell.

'Don't worry Tom, few minutes and they'll know we're here regardless.'

The policeman absorbed the scene with dread, the missing windowpane was too small for everyone to fit through; everyone, but Dean.

He stepped back, desperate for another way, there had to be another way. All the large windows were led-lined meaning the glass would break but the barrier

193

would remain. The front door was solid oak, and the back was bolted twice. Scanning the group, all he saw were middle aged men with beer-battered-bellies, the soul willing but the flesh weak. And then, there was this fifteen-year-old boy, with pimples and greasy red hair, carrying a fucking Halloween mask, and *he* was their only option.

The boy was waiting eagerly though the officer needed an offer, he couldn't ask the kid to do this, it had to come from him. Finally, Cundy plucked up the courage.

'I can fit through sir (the kid was always respectful), straight in and out, no problem. Just give me a boost and I'll be in, unlock the door, game over.' Waiting like an impatient Labrador with a hankering for a bone, with a voracious appetite to assist the invasion, his eyes pleaded for a chance. Bill sighed, *what other choice do we have?*

'You are sure you're up to this? With his slender frame, the kid was the best suited to climbing through the open entrance. Dean nodded, though now slightly apprehensive, in his heart he didn't expect to get the job. Still, he stood strong, trying hard to stay brave in front of Hallowell's finest. 'Okay, listen. Like you said, we'll give you a boost and hopefully, there'll be a key on the other side of the door. If there is, unlock it and we'll be in, quick as you like. If there isn't, or if there's any sign of him, don't be a hero. Get the Hell back out sharpish and we'll break the door down if we have too.' The youngster, wearing jeans and a black hoodie, felt special, knowing that not only was he part of the group but, his mission was one of the most important aspects. That front door was almost impenetrable, and it would take a battering ram to knock it down. It was this way or no way. The boy took a deep breath and, with a boost from Gaskins and, Malcolm Gregory, he was hoisted up to the sill. Slipping his head through, he timidly scanned the hallway.

'Do you see anything lad?' Bill Castle didn't like this, sending a boy to do a man's job.

'No sign sir, coast is clear. I'm going in.' the adrenaline was pulsing through his veins as his thin torso squeezed through the tiny gap. Holding on to a metal curtain rail, he pulled his legs through and jumped to the ground. The air was cold and still, like the inside of a museum. Artwork in carved frames adorned the walls, a vase standing on a smoked glass unit was probably more valuable than it looked, and it was so tempting to give it a little push. The carpet was thick and heavily patterned, and his footsteps made no noise as he slowly moved along it. The front entrance was housed inside a glass vestibule, but the youth could see immediately that there was no key in the front door's lock. Passing the glass patrician, he gently squeezed the front door handle, already aware of the answer to the question posed.

'Shit.' He forced open the letterbox and Charles Malone, the town pharmacist was peering through the other side, making the lad jump in surprise. 'Sorry, there's no key. What should I do?' Castle had rushed across and answered for the chemist.

194

'Come back out. We'll find another way in.' The boy was about to obey the order when suddenly, he remembered the report from the recognisance team who'd investigated the mansion's rear.

'I could nip through into the kitchen. The other men said there was a key in the back door, all I'd have to do is turn it and we'd be in. Honestly sir, I know I can do it, trust me please.' When Bill heard the word 'sir', it made him remember just how young the kid was.

'I told you, don't be a hero.' This was a dangerous game, should the monster be lurking, the boy wouldn't stand a chance.

'I'm not doing that sir but it's the only way. That door is too big to break down and you guys can't fit through that little window. You could meet me at the back door and if I see Frank, I'll be back here in a shot. It really is the only way.' Without waiting for a reply, Cundy was back out into the hallway. Bill wanted to call him back, but volume would be foolish under the circumstances.

'Bloody daft kid. Castle emerged quickly from his crouch and started mobilising the troops. 'Right, Simpsons, Hutchinson's, Randal (schoolteacher) Tommy (Lunchbox owner) Paul (Jayne, off licence owner). You men stay here, the rest come with me, the kids heading for the back door.' A group of twenty-four men ran at differing speeds at Bill Castle's demand. The others stood guard, waiting, and wondering if the front door would spring open any time soon. When he knew, he couldn't be called back, Dean's pace slowed. Never having seen the inside of the house, he was directionally blind. There were doors all along the hallway, any of which could have headed to the kitchen. But, also, any could be housing the monster. His bravery was waning, regretting volunteering for the selfless act. He'd never even been in a fistfight before but at least he could rely on speed, and if he saw Frank, he'd certainly use it.

Before him to the right, was an impressively sized entrance, bigger than the others, with two white panelled doors closing to meet one another in the centre. Was it the kitchens? Perhaps a dining room? His imagination began into over-drive, envisioning catering staff hauling silver trays of food for society dinner-parties. Carefully prying one of the doors open, he soon realised that it was neither, though something forced him to continue his investigation. Listening carefully, there were sounds he recognised emanating from the far wall and, pushing the barrier open a little further, he soon discovered that inside, was an impressive personal library, the length of the room becoming a wall of books twenty feet high, assisted by a portable wheeled ladder. There was an air of comfort to the surroundings, aided by three red leather chesterfields, positioned around a fine walnut coloured coffee table, and a magnificent central window with heavy velvet burgundy drapes. The sound that he'd recognised was the crackling of wood on an open fire, blazing high up the chimney with a gold-coloured fireguard. More shocking was the figure of Martin Graham, resting in a soft leather recliner, feet from the raging inferno.

Dean backed away, suddenly afraid to take one more step forward. The old man remained still, had he not witnessed the boy's entry? Did he care? Wearing a blue housecoat and pyjamas, the skin across his tired, old face was pallid and loose, every line magnified by the reflected flames and pale, shade-covered lamplight. The shadow cast upon the far wall was that of a diminutive old man, not the once majestic figure Martin had once portrayed. The eyes were closed, and Cundy could scarcely tell whether his host was still living, only the chest surging to intake breath, giving the secret away.

Even from a distance, the youth could feel the ferocity of the open fire, suddenly aware that a layer of perspiration had formed across his entire body. He couldn't tell whether it was the heat or just nervous tension causing the dampness, all he was certain of was it wasn't pleasant. Studying the old man, Dean was locked inside his own stillness; it was only when he heard footsteps from above that the trans was broken. It was unmistakable, heavy footfall was passing across the higher floorboards. The monster was here. Springing to action, he darted from the library, allowing himself just the briefest final glances towards Graham senior, shocked at the sickening parody of himself that the patriarch had become. Heading back into the hallway, he peered up the staircase, desperate to not see his nemesis descending floors. For now, the coast was clear, though he knew that couldn't be relied upon for long. It was essential he found the kitchen; he couldn't do this alone.

Reinforcements were just a door's width away but, what if there was no key to unlock the barrier. Brackett had claimed there were moveable bolts but that couldn't be certain. Starting to run, he opened doors with careless abandonment. The creature had to know the men had the mansion surrounded, the shattering glass had echoed around the entire grounds. Riving at door after door without finding his desired destination, he cursed, panic becoming all-encompassing. An entrance towards a study, with an oak desk and chair, another was for a lounge area with a luxurious sofa and tasteful décor. When he found the dining room, massive, polished wood table surrounded by twelve chairs, his heart lifted, perhaps he was getting close. Instead of leaving, he noticed another doorway at the back of the room, and he sprinted for it. Those footsteps were on the stairway now so heading back to the hall was no longer an option. The wooden door swung on its hinges and Cundy yelled with relief, suddenly bursting into the kitchen. There were voices from outside, silhouettes shadowing a large led-lined window, but the terrifying footsteps growing in volume. Scanning the room, a passageway turned off at an obscure angle, this was his only chance. Sprinting across the expanse of the kitchen, Dean caught the corner of a steel, preparation table, a large, empty cooking-pot crashing to the tiled floor, echoing loudly across the mansion's lower floor. Holding his breath, he listened intently, the sound of footsteps had desisted, where was the monster?

Turning the hidden corner, Cundy's eyes lit up with glee at the sight of the mansion's back door. The doctor had been correct, there were two bolts, one at floor level, the other a stretch for the diminutive teen. The lower latch slid across easily but the higher one was stiff, the boy having to press all his weight against the barrier to assist his fight. Eyes continually turning to his rear, Graham was nowhere to be seen. Allowing himself a self-satisfied smile, the handle turned and...nothing. The door refused to give. Bill Castle's booming voice could be heard from outside, how the boy wished he was beside the policeman now. Pulling with all his might, finally the seemed movement.

'Move away Dean, we'll do the rest.' The teen willingly obliged as he listened to heavy thuds emanating from the courtyard. Five stern kicks and still the lock held. Cundy fought back tears, Graham had to be aware now, the sounds were unmistakable. The solid barrier appeared impenetrable, no matter how much force was registered, the latch held. A sound from the kitchen panicked the teen even more, his young heart fit to burst. Peering into the room, the coast remained clear, the noise obviously an echo from the team's effort. Finally, the wood began to splinter with the increased pressure. The joy was palpable when the barrier smashed clear from its holding, the vigilante mob were inside.

The policeman grabbed the boy, dealing out a relief-filled hug.

'Well done son, have you seen anything?' The flustered lad regained his composure and responded.

'The old men in the library in front of the fireplace but, well, he looked strange. Like he saw me, but not really. I don't know how to explain it. And I heard footsteps from above and I'm certain they were coming down the stairs. I didn't hang around to see who was making them though.'

'Good lad, you did great. Right everyone, listen up. He's here, somewhere. The lad heard footsteps behind him, and he'd have no way of escape. We'll split into groups. One searches downstairs, the other up. Between us, there's nowhere for the bastard to hide. Harry, you stay by the front door and scream bloody murder if you see him, Tommy, you are too. Dean, you run as fast as your legs will carry you, back around to the front of the house and get the others round here. Tell them to pick a couple of guys to stay there though, just as lookouts. Adam (Scholes, the solicitor) and Walter (Williams, the estate agent), we need to find that front door key. I'm thinking drawers, cupboards, maybe a key-rack. Okay, the rest of you, form two groups, I'll take the downstairs team, Dean said he thought he heard the steps coming down here. Let's get to work.'"

"Christ, Granddad knew how to organise people." Nick was totally engrossed in the terrifying tale now but hadn't spoken for a while and felt the need for an obligatory remark.

"Tell me about it. I was there." Mick regretted that quip as he'd tried keep personal ties down to a minimum.

"I'd never thought about you being part of the community. How old was I then?"

"It was 1967, you were…" Mick was struggling.

"Eight dads. I was eight. You can remember all this shit but have bother with your own son's birthday." Now it was the lad who regretted his smart mouth. What if his father got pissed and refused to continue? Thankfully, Mick ignored the barbed shot and progressed with the history lesson.

Bill Castle's group contained his son Mick, Gavin Holt (postman), Ian Gaskins, Robert Henderson (bed and breakfast proprietor) Jimmy Glass (former pro footballer) Charles Malone, Charlie Manson (pharmacist and apprentice pharmacist) Ed Kemper (greengrocer) Malcolm Gregory (butcher) and Daniel Murphy (schoolteacher).

Harry Brackett took charge of the team number two. Head of Hallowell primary school, Manuel Drake, a lanky, stick-thin forty-something, believed he should have led given his standing in the community. That was rejected because most people thought he was a pompous twat. Sasha Winter, the school caretaker had taken special delight in watching his boss brought down to size, not so fucking special now, boss man. Next were Neil Myers and Duncan Holms, two rough, tough farm labourers who unbeknownst to the village were in a same-sex relationship together, though no one would have guessed and even if there had been suspicion, few would dare mention it. Jack Hunt, James Collins and Winston Reid had all been laid-off in colliery cut-backs, probably making them the luckiest of all, as they would, likely have been killed in the tragedy too. The last man of team two was Daren Peacock worked as mortician Fred Gibson's chief pallbearer. As he scoured the men, he wondered if any of these folks would need his services by nightfall.

Spreading out, William Castle led his team towards the library. Being familiar with the mansion's interior, he'd felt the urge to see if Martin really did seem as incoherent as Dean claimed, the cop had to know. A wave of nausea swept over him as he witnessed first-hand, the extent of his former friend's deterioration. Once a super-power in relation to Hallowell, now, a life-beaten shell of his past self. Staring into the flame's abyss, this wasn't a man, the policeman recognised. Bill didn't know who this was.

Iris Graham was there too, though only visible to Martin. Stooped on one of the leather chesterfields, her own deterioration was complete. The head was now just a skull, all skin, scar tissue, blood, becoming a distant memory. The bone had maintained a strange green colouring (like the appearance of Dean Cundy's Halloween mask) but other than that, it looked nothing more than a medical school prop. The hair did remain. As thick, black, and full bodied as the day she passed. Unfortunately, now, it appeared more like a mannequin wig. Her clothes had been replaced with a white death-shawl; the one Fred Gibson had dressed her in while preparing her body for the funeral. Her hands and feet were skeletal, the index finger on the left, pointed in accusation towards her husband. The skull's bottom jaw was mouthing silent words which still rung loudly in Martin Graham's ears. Pure terror blanketed his expression, causing Bill to place a soothing hand on his bony shoulder. Watching as the former businessman's lips quivered, Bill crouched, desperate to hear the words emanating from the petrified man's mouth. Calling out to the chattering mob for silence, Castle brought in an ear closer. It was hard to be certain, such were the whispered tones, but he thought he heard the words, 'Why did I let him kill you?'

After searching the library's few available hiding places, the group headed for the exit, in preparation to continue the lower floor search. Bill paused, for some reason feeling that this would be the final time he saw Graham alive. They had been closing once, and even though he agreed with the consensus that Martin had been partially responsible for the horrendous happenings, there too was a

198

feeling a tad of sympathy for the stricken old man. The officer wondered how he'd have acted in the same situation, defending his son against the indefensible. A tear welled in the corner Castle's eye. How did things get this fucked up? Kneeling before the leather recliner, he took Martin's gaunt hand in his own and said, 'Goodbye old boy.' As Bill rose, Dean Cundy returned, hurriedly rushing to discover his mentor's whereabouts. With his youthful zeal, the boy had slipped his Halloween mask back across his face, a feeling of safety after his earlier scare permeating his emotions. Suddenly, after appearing almost comatose just seconds earlier, Martin's paralysing catalepsy was swiftly broken as the horrific rubber disguise, complete with a head of thick black hair loomed into view. The Graham patriarch began a series of hysterical screams which echoed throughout the stately home and as the team completely exited the library, the old man began his final journey into total insanity.

The rest of the floor was searched with the same meticulous fashion, though still without success. Inside the kitchen, cupboards, pantries, even drawers, nothing instigated a clue. The main living area was sparse of hide-outs though everything was still checked, nothing was left to chance. The hardest parts were large storage cupboards in the area under the staircase, filled with years of clutter and generations of crap. Huge boxes, covered in grey shadowy dust which made the men choke when disturbed, heavy sacks hanging from hooks big enough to hide a man, all of which were poked in the hope of a squeal. The requested silence when a chance noise was heard only to see a mouse dash from its darkened bolthole. Everything checked, double checked then checked again, still nothing. The same went for the upper floor, as Harry Brackett, directed his troops to every possible hideout, only to be disappointed. The door to the loft needed forcing and, as it was locked, it appeared the most likely spot for Frank Graham to lurk. All the upper floor searchers had bound into the attic, all ready to have their shot at the target. The air was thick, musty, and damp, the relics stored here obviously hadn't been witnessed for some time. The door hadn't been locked, it had just been so many years since it had been opened, that the hinges had grown rusty and stiff with inactivity. It soon became apparent that Frank couldn't be hiding here; not unless he could fly. The men made footprints in the carpet of dust but theirs were the first that had touched the floorboards in years, and the teen would certainly have made tracks, were he lurking in the shadows.

Winston Reid thought he saw someone fleeing down the gravel driveway as he looked from the loft window, but the afternoon was becoming evening and the light was fading fast. He couldn't be certain who or what he'd seen. Adam Scholes had found the front entrance key and the whole group congregated together in the downstairs hallway.

'Fuck it, let's torch the fucking place.' Aaron Simpson was losing patience with the search and had a date for later that evening.

'Don't be so stupid.' Farm worker, Duncan Holms, who'd had a running feud with the Simpson family wanted to beat the snot out of the troublemaker. 'You really are a piece of shit, you and your whole fucking family.' Oliver Simpson had a dive in Holm's direction, but Neil Myers stepped across in his friend's (boyfriend) defence. There was pushing and shoving, name calling and abuse until Archie Cookson, the one man no-one messed with, shouted above the din the loudest.

'Knock this shit off, now.' His face was red and a vein in his right temple looked fit to burst. 'There'll be no firebombs, no vandalism and by the way, you (pointing a finger at Aaron Simpson) take that snow-globe out of your fucking pocket now and put it back where you got it.' The young tear-away looked sheepishly away and did as he was told. 'Now I don't know about your arseholes, but I came here to find the mother fucker who murdered my boy. Not to have some jolly-up, not to go thieving and not to beat up anyone else, though if you carry on, I might change my mind. Right, now we've checked upstairs, and the loft space and you lot have checked down here. Has anyone thought about the basement?' There were embarrassed expressions as it was the one area, no-one had considered. 'No, okay fine, may I suggest we do that before we move on.' It was said as a demand rather than an option.

Archie was a grizzled veteran of countless barroom brawls and even at seventy-eight, few would bet against him in a straight up fight. Losing his wife of forty-six years to cancer had been hard. Losing his family in the mining tragedy had been worse. He was a man with nothing to lose, making for a dangerous opponent. Cookson shook his head, his wrinkled, leathery face and tightly shaved grey hair making the look of a tired old man, which is exactly what Archie wasn't. He still walked five miles a day, still worked rounds on the heavy bag in the same boxing gym he'd used for the last sixty-five years, back when he'd been an exceptional amateur fighter but never had the chance to turn pro. He could still do more push-ups than most men forty years his junior and had enough hate in his heart to take on Frank singlehandedly if the needs be.

It didn't take long to find the entranceway. Two heavy wooden doors with large rusty hinges underneath the main staircase. It was reasonably well hidden to the untrained eye, but Bill Castle's determination to see this through had sharpened his senses. There was a strong padlock thrown on the ground nearby, insinuating that the basement had been opened recently. Ian Gaskins and Tony Jayne pulled open a door each and a dense, engulfing stench rose to greet them. The policeman took charge and lead the way. Spider webs stretched across the stone stairwell, but most were broken, as though someone else had recently used the same path. Tony Jayne had been the only man sensible enough to think a flashlight may be handy and happily passed it forward, content with the chorus of congratulation on his quick thinking. Castle flicked the switch and a beam of light tore through the gloom. Slowly, descending the stairs, the sheer size of the basement became apparent. It seemed to stretch beyond the width of the mansion and when the men saw the number of cupboards and doorways that would need checking, there was a collective shudder. The vast number of searchers made it more manageable but the restriction of one torch made had the men uneasy. Some used cigarette lighters to break the darkness, others waited until their eyes had become accustomed to the surroundings. There were no outer windows and it seemed there was only one entrance/exit. Though they searched no one could find a light-switch and the investigation became slow and pondering. Rows of desks and folded chairs, anywhere a person could hide needed to be checked. Any dark corner or hidden bolthole, all were searched but it continued to be fruitless. If Frank had been here earlier, he was not here now. Frustration was increasing, and the Simpson boys were once more hindering rather than helping.

'This whole thing, a fucking waste of time.' Aaron was annoying people more than the inability to find their target. Young Dean Cundy was as surprised as anyone with the failure to find Frank's whereabouts.

'This makes no sense, no sense at all. I heard him walking down the stairs inside the house, I know I did. I can't understand where he could be. There were guys outside all the time, and we checked everywhere in doors. It just makes no sense.' Simpson tutted loudly and shook his head.

'Listen kid. You were shitting yourself in there and y ears played tricks on you. I knew we should have picked someone else to go in first. Send a boy to do a man's job. Fucking pussy.'

'No, it wasn't like that.' The kid was becoming emotional, vexed.

'Yes, yes, y...' the punch old Archie landed on Aaron Simpson's jaw dropped him to the floor. His brothers ran to his aid but said nothing, knowing that the old man was ready to dish out the same to them if he needed too. There was audible laughter from all bars the troublemakers, but Bill Castle had seen enough.

'Okay, I've had it with this shit. We supposed to be united trying to get this son-of-a-bitch and you three arseholes are making it harder. Now, when we get out of here, we heading to the railway station next. You three choose now, either shut the fuck up or fuck off home.' Tony Jayne interjected.

'Bill, I think you need to look at this.' Across in the far corner there was one last doorway but instead of being vertical, this one headed down. Everyone rushed across to the shopkeeper's find and tried to peer over each-other's shoulders to look. 'There's another layer here, going further underground.'

'Well spotted, mate.' The policeman fought through and, with the torchlight, stared down at the new discovery. 'I don't believe it. This isn't a room, it's a tunnel though where it goes, fucked if I know.'

'I do.' It was the first time that day that Archie Cookson's facial expression showed concern. 'I remember a rumour, back, when I was a kid. Martin's father, just before World War I, they said he had breakdown. Two of his kids were killed in action and he figured the Germans had it in for his family. It was back when kids were being shipped out of the cities because of the bombings, there were a bunch sent here. Graham started thinking that one of the children was a German spy, crazy shit, unbelievable. Anyway, he figured that they'd been sent to burn the mansion down and they'd all fry while they slept, so he wanted an escape route. Started sleeping down here and the first sniff of smoke and he'd be away. We all thought it was just some bullshit rumour, but the story goes, he paid to have a tunnel dug between here and the railway station. There's supposed to be another doorway up to the house too, don't know if that's right. Anyway, no one believed it, looks like we were wrong.'

'It backs up the kid's story.' Bill looked to Cundy and smiled who in turn looked at the Simpsons and gave an 'I told you so' face.

The whole congregation climbed back out into the open air, a welcome departure from the stifling atmosphere of the basement. The evening was changing into night and the long shadows of the Graham mansion helping the darkness assume control. Everyone looked to Bill now for guidance but, even he was unsure of how to progress.

'Okay, there's enough evidence to accept, Graham used this tunnel today. Dean says he heard him in the house, I believe he heard him in the house. One thing for certain, he's not there now, no-ones that good at hide and seek. So, the obvious thing to do is head to the railway station. The only problem is, he could come back along that tunnel, and we miss him. So, I think, half of us head over there above ground and the rest go along the tunnel. That way, we got two shots at nailing him. He could have done a runner altogether and there's not much we can do about that but at least, we can carry out the plan we had at the beginning and give it our best shot. Now, is there anyone who can't do the tunnel for any reason?' Barry Simpson raised a hand.

'I'm claustrophobic.' There were titters of giggles and someone fake coughed the word, 'pussy'.

'Fine, I take it you lot are staying with the topside group?' There were dull nods of agreement. 'Fine, you three stays up here and the rest of you guys, get into two groups. I'll stay with the tunnel team, Harry, you lead the above group.'

'I have extra batteries in case you need them.' Tony Jayne was feeling like the wisest man on the planet.

His smile desisted when Bill said, 'Great, you're on my team then.' No one would admit to it but, to a man, they all wanted to be with the open-air group. The idea of heading along a passageway and not knowing where it would exit made even the most confident of men shudder.

'Did you head down the tunnel with granddad?' Nick Castle was beginning to forget his own past problems and becoming more aware with every passing minute, the magnitude of what had happened in Hallowell's past. He also began to find sympathy for his generational off-spring. Mick nodded slowly and thoughtfully.

'Dad wasn't letting me out of his sight.'

The torchlight was beginning to dim as they passed the halfway point of the journey. It was like a long concrete tomb that felt like it had no beginning or end. The group stopped and as the batteries were changed, the darkness was all encompassing. When Bill flicked the torch ignition, the bulb refused to fire.

'What's happening? What's wrong?' Jayne's heart rate was of similar increased speed to the rest of the team though he was the first to allow his panic to show.

'Chill out. I think I might have put the damn things in the wrong way.' The policeman fumbled with the thick batteries, and one slipped from his grasp, falling on the ground with a clunk. 'Fuck. A pint to the first man who finds it.'

Dean Cundy was already on the floor feeling for the lost item when a foot accidentally trod on his fingers.

'Ouch. Whoever stepped on my, oh wait, here it is.'

The boy jumped up, clutching his prize. 'There you go Bill; you owe me a pint.' Bill took the battery and smiled, fixing it properly in place and bathing the tunnel into light once more.

'And you shall have one my lad, soon as you reach eighteen.'

'Spoilsport.' There was a round of laughter, which soon faded as the journey continued. The ever-present echo of rats in the below sewer system made some uneasy but others relished the fact that there was still life in the outside world, no matter how foul it may be. Adam Scholes was at the tail end of the group and found himself constantly glancing over his shoulder, the thick wall of blackness, an indefinable foe. He wondered just how close someone could get before he'd be seen, ten feet, maybe twenty? He certainly did not want to find out. As his glances became more frequent, he began to see something, but were his eyes playing tricks? It wasn't a man, not even a figure; it just seemed that the air had taken on a slightly different colour. At first, all the lawyer could see was black, but this was different. He knew the eyes saw more acutely, the longer they were in a certain environment, even pitch darkness, but this was strange. There were wisps of grey, fog-like. By the time, he stopped the team to announce his suspicions, the terrifying truth exploded in his mind like a thunderbolt.

Martin Graham still hadn't stopped screaming, even after the group had discovered the basement, his guttural, throaty cries, reverberating around the deserted rooms of old building. The vision of Dean Cundy, wearing that grotesque rubber mask, which so resembled his decaying wife, had driven him over the final hurdle to total insanity. His hands, bony and discoloured, months of malnutrition robbing a once full physique into the frail dishevelled shadow that remained today, clingingly tightly to the chair's wooden arms, knuckles livid, veins pushing behind loose fitting skin. His face, a combination of terror mixed with an ungodly grin, skin hanging loose under the eyes and around the cheek bones with pigmentation of red blotches under a pale, almost white complexion. Five days' stubble, grey and wispy, covered the chin and under the nose though not down the sides of the face, as though a shave had been started but not completed. His hair, mattered and greasy, flattened to his head without the aid of a brush. But his eyes, the windows to his madness. Red and bloodshot, they were now no more than slits as the face's constant grimace, pain of the soul showing in this sub-human image.

Suddenly, the hands released their grip on the chairs wooden frame and the bony fingers began tearing at his head. The screams intensified as he began tearing huge clumps, handfuls of slippery, unwashed locks, straight from the root. Riving, with his hands clasped tightly around huge fistfuls, the screams were more of frustration than pain when his fingers would slide from the greasy target without success. The inhuman cries turned to odious, devilish laughs, when he'd been capable to rip enough mattered hair from his head, so he could see the contents before his own eyes. Throwing his prize into the hair, he'd blow as the despatched locks floated gently through the air, delighting in watching them change direction, just with the help of his breath. Then it was back to the self-mutilation, until he could tear enough to start the process over again. When there wasn't enough hair left to yank and blood was gliding gently from the tears in his withered skin in the aftermath of his unconventional haircut, his urge for destruction intensified.

Everywhere he looked was Iris.

'Why did you let him kill me?'

'Why did you let him kill me?'

'WHY DID YOU LET HIM KILL ME?'

The voices, oh my God, the voices. His hands clasped his ears, but it didn't help. The same line, repeatedly. He rose from the chair and stumbled, legs weak from malnutrition, he grasped for the chairs aid but then releasing its stability to cover his ears once more. My God will this ever end. He opened his eyes and the decayed figure of Iris still lay on the chesterfield, mouthing the ungodly line, time and time again, refusing to stop, mockingly competent, the skulls jawbone rising and falling as the line starts again. Making a dive for the spectral aberration, he fell onto the couch, only to find it missing. He opened his eyes, and she was standing by the chair, which he'd just vacated. He rolled onto his knees, head tucked down, there was no laughter anymore, just those guttural cries which had unnerved Bill Castle so. Pushing against the leather surface, the slippery material gave no purchase but instead, he forced his weak legs into action and returned upright. There were still voices from the hall. Christ, there were still voices in here. Couldn't this bitch just go to her grave and leave him alone.

'Why did you let him kill me?'

'I wish you were here now, you fucked up, decaying twat, it wouldn't be Frank that killed you. IT WOULD BE ME.'

He rubbed his hands across his face and head in despair and finally acknowledged the pain caused by his D.I.Y. haircut. Listening, the voices out in the hall were diminishing. Were they leaving? Who cares? There's only one way to shut this bitch up permanently.

On the far wall of the library was a secret passageway. Like something from a murder mystery film, a case of books slid forward, and the pathway was open. Martin stumbled forward, his slippers with their rubber's soles sliding under his feet until his legs regained some measure of strength, and he was upright, running, head-long down the passageway and away from the vision of Iris.

The mansion contained a maze of secret walkways, the same hideouts which Frank had used as a child to torment his parents after their temerity to punish him. Just wide enough for a grown man to walk crab-like, the first exit came into Martin's personal workshop. As a young man, he'd spent hours here, it became a getaway from the pressures of business. Its large double doors, which neighboured the garages in the courtyard, big enough to drive cars into. Oh, not the classics, like the Daimler or his Ferrari, no, here, he'd tinker with beat-up motors, bought for a pittance. Like the mini he'd bought for three pounds from a lad who could no longer afford to run it. He'd tuned up the engine, fixed the bodywork, replaced broken windows. All self-taught, he was quite proud of the work he'd achieved. But that was years ago, before business had become his God. Before earning money became more important than having a life. It was a better time, a more innocent time. But 'Why did you let him kill me?'

Oh fuck, leave me alone.

Where is it?

That group, who'd entered his home uninvited, had found the entry-point to the basement. It wouldn't be long before they found the tunnel to the station. God, he hoped Frank was safely away.

Smashing open doors, desperately searching. There were tools for weapons but what would be the point? He was outnumbered, thirty to one. And his strength had deserted him when he needed it the most. No fucking uses. Plus, that bitch was here, asking the same fucking question all the time. The words pounding through his head. No wonder Frank killed the fucker, I'd like to kill the fucker. She might have lost the battle, but she was winning the war now. Thieving his sanity was the last 'fuck you' to her loving husband. This insurmountable unstoppable uncontainable haunting, continuous images, unquenchable thirst for vengeance. There was only one way to stop this nightmare.

Riving at the doors, their contents thrown to the ground, tins of paint, half full, flammable rid of this woman, once and for all. Turpentine, that's better, not enough though. Need more, the whole thing must but not fast enough, I must get burn. A cupboard at his feet, why won't it open? A padlock well fucks you. That drawer over there had tools, a crowbar, that will do. Its heavy, need to pry this lock off. Its stiff, God its strong. Must force it, please make it snap. EUREKA get it. That's what I need, PETROL!

Two large cans, one half full, the other never opened. Should be enough. He lifted with all his strength, grimacing at the full can's weight. Coming back out of the workshop, he used the secret passageway to return to the library. That bitch was following, asking the same fucking questions. Well soon, that zombie-looking mother fucker will be saying, 'Why are you burning me?'

That's where he started the annihilation. Using his mould-covered teeth, he broke the seal across the cap of the full tin. It was stiff and a molar on his lower left-side jaw cracked painfully, but when he managed to release the stopper, the curtains, chesterfields, and chair were doused in the accelerant. He spilled a trail to the door then realised he needed matches. Peering out into the hallway, the invading voices were coming from the basement now; all except HER'S. There were always matches in the kitchen, that became his desired destination. Instead of wasting a journey, he heaved the half-full contained across the floor, a thick pungent trail leading back to the library. She was behind him now, her words turning to mocking laughter, the skin-free jaw clattering as the teeth clashed together. He refused to see, maintaining his focus upon the kitchen. Entering his destination, he allowed himself the briefest of glimpse to is rear, the thing was gone. Undeterred, he spun on his heels, heading directly to the drawer by the stove. Before him, in his path, the hideous apparition appeared, the repulsive sight so ungodly, he wished his eyes away. Nerves fractured, body trembling, psyche destroyed, he barged forward, passing through the spectral phantasm without touch. Thrusting the drawer from its hinges, he searched, throwing debris and clutter to the floor. Finally, in the furthest, corner a full box, swan vestas. He was almost giddy now, throwing accelerant across the cabinets and over the dinner table, drenching the blinds hanging in the window. Conclusively aware of what his actions would bring, the moment came, the sweetest moment, when a flame would shine, and fire would quench all ills.

The first match snapped, force and excitement making Martin a tad too eager. He took the second from the pack. Breathing under control, he took a last look at the life he was giving away. The tip scratched against the bevelled card, and it ignited, perfect fire. With his vigour, he almost missed the target, the dark oak kitchen dinner table and its six chairs, but the match caught the edge of its wooden frame and the petrol burst into life. Its force shocked Martin, intense heat exploding around the room. It spread with incredible speed, the doors of the cabinets, melting and splintering under intense pressure, the blinds swaying into the glass, the clear barrier fighting hard to stay strong but wilting quickly as the flames get closer.

Martin's demonic giggle returned, his plan taking shape. The library was the main target.

'LET'S BURN THE BITCH, LETS BURN THE BITCH.'

His earlier frailty had now diminished, he was a man possessed, crazed with the power at his hands. The thick velvet curtains were doused, expecting the need for accelerant to be great. It was then he remembered, it had already been prepared. Time for the matches. Oh sweet god of the flame, how I love thee. The match struck on the first time. He was standing by the chesterfield, right where the bitch had mocked him from earlier, with that fucked up face and that black hair; just like that kid who'd been here earlier. I wonder if I could burn that bastard too? The wooden strip was dropped just before it burned his fingers, and the chesterfield was alight. He smiled a huge, face stretching grin as he imagined the figure of his wife, frying, fizzling, VANISHING.

One thing, Martin Graham had forgot, the trail he'd left to the door. The flames ran like Olympic sprinters, the thick Axminister carpet, which had been doused minutes earlier was the perfect partner to form a formidable streak, five feet high. The doorframe immediately burst into life, its layers of lead paint bubbling and crackling, passing its deadly contents over to the door itself. The flames heat was unbelievable and by the time Martin discovered he was trapped; it was too late. The books were ablaze as the doorway to the secret passage. The couches and rugs were roaring with yellow and red licks, licks which turned to nibbles, then bites, until the fire was eating everything. And the more it ate, the bigger it got. Martin Graham accepted his fate with the grace and dignity of his former years, his better years. The hard-backed chair, his hard-backed chair, the one he'd spent a pretty penny buying, was free of fire. He stumbled across, flames nipping at his pyjama bottoms and took his seat. The smoke was getting bad now and his giggle was replaced by a cough. Hard, choking, carbon dioxide searing his lungs, the flames getting closer. Inside the chaos, the decomposed figure of Iris Graham walked through the room, unaffected by the flames. Martin wasn't screaming, giggling, even coughing anymore. As she stood before him, her image began to reverse. Blood began to re-emerge, skin grew rapidly over her skeletal features, her face was beautiful once more. Her re-animation complete.

'It's time to come with me now, Martin.' Her voice was sweet, no longer filled with accusation or rage. She took his hand and smiled. The flames didn't seem to matter, he could no longer feel their intolerable heat. His chocking had stopped too. What was happening?

'But I've done so much wrong. I'm responsible for him. Don't you understand, I don't deserve to come with you.' A single tear rolled down Martins face but when he raised a hand to wipe it, the hand was young. The flesh was tight, as was the opposite one. He raised them to his face in amazement. 'What's going on, I don't understand.' Iris slid her fingers through his and pulled him to his feet.

'You will.' Together, the spirits of Martin and Iris Graham vanished. He vacated body of Martin Graham burned, like everything else.

The group outside, using the fields as their route to the station, saw the flames first.

'Oh Jesus, what's that now.' Archie Cookson, who was now starting to tire, his 78 years beginning to show, noticed a red glow as he glanced back toward the mansion. 'Simpson, did you.'

'It wasn't me Mr Cookson, honest.' Aaron Simpson, with a new-found fear for the old man knew he'd have the finger pointed firmly in his direction after his earlier idea to burn the place down.

'Well, whoever is responsible, it doesn't really matter. The bastard is burning.' The group stopped and huddled together, trying to get a good look at the flaming landmark.

'What should we do?' Oliver Simpson was always first to ask a question but never quick with an answer. With a sigh that came from the pit of his stomach, Archie Cookson said,

'Like you said earlier Simpson, let it burn.'

With that, the group turned in unison and headed for the station. Most of the men were quiet, an occasional rude remark from a Simpson which was continuously followed by a knowing and dauntingly fearful stare by the aged leader; most were in silent contemplation. Martin Graham, a man who had given employment to many of this vigilante group was almost certainly dead and that was a shame. He was only responsible for enabling the monster, he hadn't been responsible directly for anyone's passing. When Barry Simpson began the chorus of, 'Graham, roasting on an open fire', to the tune of the Christmas song Chestnuts roasting on an open fire, by Nat King Cole, it wasn't well received openly by anyone though a few secretly giggled inwardly at the loud-mouths clever word replacement. Cookson was becoming more agitated by the moment and was on the verge of sending all three homes, though something inside told him they may be needed. He was not only having second thoughts about this plan, but he was also having third, fourth and fifth thoughts too. Had he been in charge from the out-set, it would never have gone down this way. His plan was to send out two reconnaissance teams out, first thing in the morning. It would only take four guys, two teams of two, one stationed outside the mansion and the other at the railway station. Four young, fit, quick lads who could watch and wait, then, at the first sign of life, one could follow wherever Frank headed and the other could haul arse back to headquarters for re-enforcements (Charlie had served in WW II with distinction and the old army phrases had stuck in his brain). That way they were certain of hitting their target without raising the alarm that they were coming. It had been deemed too risky for the lads chosen, should their cover be blown. Archie had argued hard that, if they were careful, there was no chance of that happening, but he was overruled. It was Bill Castle's show, and the old man quietly resented the policeman for it. He was inwardly satisfied that this effort was slowly turning to shit. The bastard could well know that the group were baying for blood and vanish into the night. And that was another thing, it was fucking night now, the sky was turning black, and they had ONE torch between them. Inside that station building, there were loads of little rooms, off-shots and hiding places and HE knew all of them, a damn site better than any of them did. It could easily become a one-man ambush. Why they hadn't started earlier, Archie couldn't understand. It was obvious that this could take time and a late afternoon start was asking for trouble. Still, it wasn't his responsibility. It reminded him of the Nazi soldier's excuse, 'I was just following orders.' Most of these arseholes around him were sheep, blindly doing what they were told. It made Cookson sick.

Robert Henderson, the co-owner of a bed and breakfast in the village ran forward to Cookson with a worried look on his face. He was only young, about 37 and he'd inherited the business after his parents had been killed in a car accident. His wife Kelly had assumed the day-to-day running of the guest house, Robert was mildly retarded and needed help with his daily life. He was fortunate that he'd also inherited his father's movie star looks, most of the town's women secretly lusted after him though few would have been happy being tied to someone so mentally challenged.

'Mr Cookson, I just had a thought.' Archie didn't expect much but humoured the lad, ready to let him down gently. The chances of Robert finding something of note before anyone else were Jack and shit, and Jack just left town.

'What's up kid?' Cookson wasn't the most patient of men, but he had been friends with both the lad's father and grandfather, so he was more willing to listen than he'd normally be.

'The fire. The fire up at the mansion.' Henderson's face was red and flustered, as if he'd given this a lot of thought before he had the nerve to bring it to Archie's attention.

'I know son. It's not nice. But even if we headed back there now, there's no chance that we'd be able to save the old man. Maybe he got out before it started eh.'

'No, no, no, I didn't mean that.' Rob was shouting, and the old miner was quickly losing patience, he was tired, grumpy, and unnerved.

'Okay, what's wrong then?' His tone was sharp, and Henderson knew he needed to get his point across quickly.

'It's the men in the tunnel. If the house is on fire, smoke will waft along the tunnel too. What if they can't get out at the other end, if the doors are locked or something, they'd be trapped.' Cookson couldn't believe that no one else had thought of it and cursed himself for doubting the young man.

'Fuck, you're right.' The old man stopped dead in his tracks and called the group to order. 'Right, listen up, Rob's just thought of something, none of you brain-boxes did. The guys in the tunnel. Smoke will be drifting along and if they can't get out the other end, they're fucked. There's nothing to say that Graham didn't lock the tunnel doors at the station end when he got out, so we need to haul arse and find them doors, now.' To a man everyone's pace quickened vastly; the fittest were running, the older or fatter of the species broke into a fast walk. One thing was for sure, if Robert Henderson was right, their friends might not have much time.

Adam Scholes was certain now. He bolted through the team, many giving a disparaging stare at his abruptness. He was determined not to start a panic, the close quarters of their surroundings didn't lend themselves to desperate people, but he was greatly aware that the position could become dire in a hurry. Bill Castle had led them to this position, he could damn well lead them out.

'Excuse me William, might I have a word in private.' The policeman knew there was a problem whenever someone called him William, only his wife called him that, and only when she was pissed about something.

'You're welcome to lad; this place isn't arranged for privacy.' The schoolteacher, Randal Meeks overheard the beginning of this conversation and though he made every effort to seem unaware, his inquisitive instincts (nosey) had him determined not to miss any details. Brackett's low tone made eavesdropping tough, but the tutor was professional busy-body and world class gossip, Meeks gently creeped in closer and moved his head to a ninety-degree angle so the sound waves would carry better.

'Listen Bill, I don't want to cause alarm, but we may have a problem. I think, maybe, the mansion is on fire. There was a grey mist drifting our way, from behind, a few moments ago; I was concerned but as there was no odour, I thought it was perhaps just an optical illusion. Then, I smelled it, the stench of smoke, it was unmistakable. Now, if this walkway isn't much further, it shouldn't pose too much of a problem. But if it continues for any length of time, then we may be in trouble. Smoke travels fast, especially in enclosed spaces.'

The policeman couldn't believe what he was hearing. Today had been one long cluster-fuck from the start but if Brackett was right, things may have just got a damned sight worse. 'Are you sure about this Adam? I haven't caught any smell up here. Could it possibly be just your imagination, we're all on edge?' Scholes was becoming agitated; Castle was insulting his intelligence now.

'You don't imagine smoke, William. You might be happy to stick your head in the sand and ignore it, but I have no wish to become a new flavour of barbecue.'

'Don't throw your toys out the pram, it was a perfectly normal question. Now provided it is what you say it is, what kind of bother are we in?' The lawyer sighed as the answer seemed perfectly obvious to him.

'Well, if this God-forsaken tube ends soon and there is a means of escape, then nothing, but…'

'What do you mean IF we can escape?' The answer was dawning on Bill without the need for answer, though Scholes was still happy to reveal one.

'Well, we could reach the exit, only to find it locked None of us have any knowledge of what we're dealing with down here but, if Graham has any intelligence at all, surely it makes sense that he'd have locked the exit-way after using it, especially if he knew he was being pursued. I know I would.' Castle was more than a little agitated himself now.

'So, if that's what you'd do, didn't it occur to you to mention that before we started trailing along this fucking thing. Your incredible insight may have had some use then.' Bill Castle rarely lost his temper but, had there been fewer witnesses, he could happily have punched the self-righteous twat on the nose.

'Now just wait a minute Castle, don't dare try to blame me for this bullshit, this was your idea in the first place. Oh, you're so very good at barking out orders but as soon as something goes awry, you start looking for someone else to blame, well it won't be me friend, that's for certain'.

'Keep your voice down Adam, we don't need a battle between us, now do we.' Mick Castle spoke for the first time, ready to defend his father at all costs.

'Panic? Why would we panic?' Dean Cundy's look of concern spread to the entire group.

'Gone wrong? What's gone wrong?' Walter Williams of Williams's estate agents had overheard the argument, the secret was out.

'The mansions on fire.' Randal Meeks answered for Bill who in turn fired a death stare in the schoolteacher's direction.

'We don't know that for certain.' The policeman was in danger of losing control of the situation and this was a bad position for panic. 'Adam said he could smell smoke but it's coming from behind us. If we keep going the way we're heading, we're bound to find the exit soon.' Manuel Drake, head of Hallowell primary and the man pissed for being overlooked as sub-team leader earlier added proverbial fuel to the fire.

'I can smell it too. What if we can't find the exit, we'll be trapped. I propose we head back the way we came while we have a chance. Perhaps, the fire isn't too out of control yet and we can still escape. We need to get out, I need to get out, I can't stand this, oh my God, I have to get out.' The frightened man began walking back toward the smoke.

'Don't be an idiot, that would-be suicide.' Scholes finally said something, Castle could agree with. 'If there's smoke this far along, then the exit is the only way to go. We need to have faith that we're close, what choice do we have.' Drake was almost hysterical now and it was obvious to everyone why he'd been overlooked for a position of leadership.

'And if it's locked?'

'Then we have faith that our colleagues will find us and unlock it for us. We have to keep moving.' Thanks to his support, Castle's urge to punch the solicitor had waned. They moved off quickly, hoping they were right.

The railway station building was now a sad sight. Had it only been a year since this place was bustling with life, scores of men using it daily for employment or transportation? Now, life had moved on and the concrete giant, which had once stood proud in a position of strength, overlooking the township of Hallowell, was a forgotten relic, a memory of a time more innocent. And like the station, the Graham family was just as desolate. A few short months ago, it had four members of varying popularity, living, working, and schooling in the village. Now, two were dead, one had been evacuated and by the close of today, with God's help, the last of this cursed clan would be eviscerated from Hallowell's population.

One by one, the team, led by Archie Cookson and Harry Brackett climbed the wooden sty in Tom Wade's farm field, onto the gravel pathway leading to their target. The evening had a chill, but the air was still and quiet, clouds covering the half-moon, adding a darker feel than the time suggested. Simon Grayson, the man who'd spent much of the town meeting drunk, walked, balancing along the disused iron of the railway tracks, the rubber sole of his white trainers squeaking against the metal surface. Conversation was minimal, the smoke from the burning building still filling their nostrils. The fittest of the group were a distance ahead, the Simpson's for once willing to lend a hand without the promise of something in return. Jimmy Glass had been a professional footballer for Blackburn rovers in another life before a cruciate ligament injury had robbed him of his dream occupation. He'd tried comebacks, but his weakened limb always broke down in the end. He planned to stay in the game, management or coaching was always an option. It had been an option for four years but the depression of not being able to do the thing he loved had driven him to drink. His career shouldn't be over at twenty-eight. Still, he could run when he needed to, Frank Graham would be the perfect foil to take out his built-up rage. He'd been the first to arrive at the railway station, followed by the Simpson brothers and Ian Gaskins, the mechanic/handyman. The darkness made finding the entrance tough and though all the men were enthusiastic about ensuring the monster got his comeuppance, none fancied the idea of heading into the darkened building alone. As more of the group arrived, the volume of the voices increased but when the town butcher, Malcolm Gregory heard faint banging and even fainter yells for help, the din of the searchers ceased immediately.

It had only taken a matter of minutes for the team, down in the tunnel, to reach a dead-end, though it felt far longer. The odour of smoke had increased, or at least it seemed to, now the burning was public knowledge. Those at the rear had begun to cough constantly and Bill Castle couldn't help but feel it was the idea of fumes causing this reaction, rather than the smoke itself. He couldn't blame them, though he felt Manuel Drake was playing for sympathy, if he was the great leader to claimed to be, shouldn't he be trying to maintain an air of calm rather than help increase the panic. The policeman was certain that the teacher's reputation would be shot if they finally made it out of the concrete hellhole. And if it wasn't, it should be.

To a man, they all feared the worst and when the torch beam began to dim, Castle began to feel that the Gods were conspiring against them. He asked for all men with cigarette lighters to move to the front of the team, as they may be needed. This had added another layer of doubt amongst the group but when the light revealed a solid wall, bouncing back its fading stream, the spirits were lifted. There was an initial rush along the stone walkway and the chemist, Charles Malone, slipped and was almost trampled by those in his rear. Hands grabbed the stricken pharmacist, and he was unceremoniously yanked to his feet.

Two heavy wooden doors stood between the men and freedom but to their horror, they were locked, bolted from the outside. Most took a shot at forcing the barrier, some, two or three at a time, but the wood was too thick and the lock too powerful. Drake once more led the cries of panic and it was down to his fellow teacher, Danny Murphy, to manhandle his boss into submission. He was warned that he'd be sorry for his reaction when they were back at school Monday, Murphy replying that if Drake didn't chill out, he wouldn't see Monday. There was talk of heading back to the mansion, but the consensus was, that the time for retreat had passed. If the fire wasn't too great to pass already, it would be by the time they walked back. Their only hope now, was their companions on the outside.

The banging was faint but certainly audible. The Hutchinson Brothers stood inside the huge entranceway of the main building, but the noise was no greater; it was decided that the doorway had to be located somewhere outside. The side buildings were searched but most were too small to contain a secret walkway. The old station-master quarters were locked but the door was easily forced, though again, with no luck. The echoes were increasing in volume and the team cringed at the conditions their friends were dealing with. The red glow of the Graham mansion, flames jetting high into the dark night sky was still visible. The situation was becoming critical, and then…

'Here, Archie.' The excited cry of Malcolm Gregory startled the team, who in unison, ran towards his voice. Inside the ticket office, there were loose floorboards below a movable desk. The more the butcher jumped on the thin wooden barrier, the more the trapped men banged back. The Hutchinson's were the first on the scene and the desk was thrown to one side with surprising ease. A woollen rug covered the wooden barrier and when the ply-wood seal was removed, two large wooden doors became visible. There were two long bolts which were stiff but pliable, but the strong, heavy padlock was more of an obstacle. Terry Hutchinson called for tools, something like a crowbar which could be used to force the padlock. The men inside had grown quiet when they heard their rescuers attempting to save them but the longer it took, the more concern re-grew. It took an age but eventually a steel bar was brought from the old iron works. Sliding it through the rounded metal, it refused to budge. More force was depressed and Terry's brother, Jake took hold of the opposite end and began twisting. Both brothers were sweating with the exertion and calls of encouragement were yelled from all sides. Just when Terry was about to hand the bar across to a fresh pair of hands, the lock snapped and came away. There were audible cheers as the broken residue was thrown aside and the heavy doors were hauled open. A puff of trapped smoke rose from the hole and the team scrambled from their prison, fresh air never tasting so good.

When the exhilaration of freedom wore off, the whole group emerged from the ticket office and joined forces on the empty platform, there was still a job to do.

The hunt was back on.

Evening had turned to night and as such, the unlit area was completely dark. Bill Castle had questioned his leadership abilities inside the tunnel, but he was still most qualified to head the assault.

'Okay, we need a plan. My suggestion is we form smaller groups of five. There are six floors so if each group takes a floor and searches, and the rest stay here in case he makes a run for it, then we covered all ends up. Now if anyone spots him, don't be a hero. Shout and scream until your blue in the face and don't tackle him till all your groups there. He's a big nasty son of a bitch and if he knows we here, he could be armed. Whatever floor he's hiding on, if he's spotted, he'll have thirty odds on him soon as you like so don't take unnecessary risks.' Dean Cundy, with his youthful bluster interrupted.

'If I see him, he's fucked.' The group laughed but Bill interjected.

'Listen here. skull boy, (the mask was still in place) if you see him, let the others know and stay away from him or you'll have me to answer too. In fact, I think you can be in my group, so I can keep an eye on you.' Once more the group laughed though the magnitude of what they were about to embark upon was slowly sinking in.

'But Bill, what do we do when we find him?' The lawyer in Adam Scholes made the question seem more pertinent.

'When we find him, we drag his arse back out here where we can all see what's what, then we get ourselves some private justice, Hallowell style.'

'How do we know he's still here?' Randal Meeks, a schoolteacher in neighbouring St Mara had a fair point. 'He could have run for it when he heard us coming?' Disgruntled whispers agreed it was a possibility.

'If he's bolted, there's not much we can do about that. We've given it our best shot.'

'He hasn't bolted, be certain of that.' Daren Peacock, the grave digger, had been quiet most of the mission so when he spoke with such confidence, people listened.

'How do you know that, Daren?' Castle was curious.

'Because I know him. I done work for the family, odd jobs, shit like that.' Small but thick set, the gravedigger looked like a human battering ram. He took a heavy drag on a self-rolled cigarette and released the smoke through his nostrils. 'We became, friendly. Not friends, I don't think he ever had a friend, but we passed the time of day. If I was ever out front, having a ciggy, he'd come over and have a few words. Some of the shit he'd say, when his guard was down, freak anyone out, me included.'

'What like?' Bill didn't want to push; Peacock was well known for being a loner who didn't suffer fools gladly.

'Too much to go into now. But this place, he was obsessed. Called it his birth-right. There's no way he'd let anyone run him off, that's for sure. No, he's here, you mark my words.' Peacock had an air of assurance that few others.

'Well that's enough for me.' Bill was looking confident. 'The only way he gets away is through us. Now we have no torchlight left, the batteries on this thing almost died in the tunnel so...' Jack Hunt raised his hand in excitement, like a child in the classroom.

'In that old storage cupboard, next to Graham's office, there's some old colliery supplies. I'm sure there's some miner's lanterns, not sure if they still work but it's worth a shot. Only thing is the door is locked up.' Neil Myers, six feet four, twenty stone monster whose claim to fame was appearing on world of sport in his job as a professional wrestler, stepped forward and kicked the door, smashing it off its hinges with one blow. Jack Hunt smiled. 'Guess it's open now.' There was a collective laugh.

Inside they discovered nine lanterns. Two were broken and two had no fuel but five were in working order. Bill Castle began to organise the men. 'Okay, six groups of five we need to start sorting yourselves and whoever is left, stands guard here. My group will take the top floor because there is a window, so we'll have a little light, the rest of you can share the lanterns out. Mick, I want you with my group.'

'Someone's coming.' Tony Jayne's eyesight seemed better than most, and in the distance, coming from the direction of the roadside, a figure began to form. The entire team prepared for battle, their search would be unnecessary, who else would be foolish enough to roam these streets alone? The silhouette was large, and suddenly a second form emerged two. As they approached, it became obvious that it wasn't their target.

'Whose there?' The policeman pushed through the group, determined to face whoever materialised. There was something called back though the words were inaudible. 'What? Who is there? Identify yourself.' The duo were opposites, one seemed tall, lanky, and slim, the other short, pear-like overweight blob. Immediately, the cop knew who they were dealing with. 'Gibson? Is that you?' This time the reply was heard.

'Yes, it's me, I'm here to stop this. I have Father Henderson with me.' There was consensus grumbling, the priest had purposely been omitted from the town meeting, knowing a man of the cloth would never accept the brutal plan in place. Castle's anger turned towards the undertaker, realising that he must be responsible for reporting the plan to the father.

'This has to stop now.' The dulcet tones of the priest spread throughout the group, arguing with God wasn't part of the deposition. As the two emerged from the shadows, it was obvious Gibson was exhausted, his face flushed red, breathing laboured, whatever exertion he'd taken part in had certainly enervated his energy.

'Where did you go?' Archie Cookson's question was on everyone's mind, the mortician had earlier been part of the investigation team.

'I couldn't take it anymore. You people were acting like rabid dogs, we are taking about a human-being here, whatever you think he's done, this punishment to too much.' Tony Jayne could take no more.

'Listen here, your fat mother-fucker. That thing stopped being a human-being, the moment he destroyed the lives of all those men. You saw that devastation. Remember how they looked, how my boy looked? His neck broken, ribs crushed, face smashed to Hell, remember that? And you're defending him? How dare you?'

'It's not defence. I just don't believe that murder is the right option, ignore him, banish him from the community, refuse him services and purchases, there are other ways to deal with the situation. This is one step away from being a vigilante group. We are supposed to be a civilised people; what's next? Burn his body at the stake? How about placing his head on a spike for the whole village to see? That would be a good image for your kids to think about just before they go to sleep.' The undertaker's rant had once more stolen his breath, the vicar placing a hand on the fat man's shoulder in a calming way. That peace didn't last.

'An image for the kids to see before they go to bed. Well, Mr Gibson, my eighteen-year-old boy won't be dreaming of Graham's head on a spike. Unfortunately, he won't be dreaming at all, because he's dead, murdered by that cunt inside that building. Now I swear, you say one more word, and we'll need a new undertaker, and his first job will be preparing you for burial, understand?' Jayne's were slow and deliberate, spouted with venom and menace and the mortician knew that the man before him could break him in half and no-one would intervene.

'But...' The vicar's words were cut short before he could start. Tony Jayne was on a roll.

'Before you say anything John, read your little book there. What does it say? An eye for an eye, life for a life. That overgrown piece of shit can't give us all those lives that he annihilated, he has only one to give, his own. And I want it. We all want it, a life for a life father, you can't argue with the man upstairs.'

'But where does it end?' Gibson's words were spoken with trepidation, cowering in the priest's shadow.

'It ends with him, six feet under. If that means I'm going to Hell, well, fuck it, that's a price I'm willing to pay.' There were calls of encouragement, Aaron Simpson called 'bravo' which broke the tension. Immediately, the focus shifted back towards Bill Castle, the objection was noted, and ignored."

"Christ dad, you were part of everything." Nick Castle was shocked, having always taken his father for something of a coward. "Where was I while all this was happening?"

"At home with your mother, where do you think? You'd just turned seven years old. I only went for your sake, if we didn't have you, I'd have said fuck it, none of my business. When you have a kid, you'll do anything to protect them and if that means going up against the bogeyman, so be it." Nick opened his mouth and swallowed a large slice of humble pie. How could he have been so wrong? If only they'd have explained early, life for all of them could have been so different. "Didn't you ever wonder how I knew so much about this shit?"

"I just figured granddad told you. I had no idea you were directly involved." Nick's respect for his father was growing by the minute.

"He was my dad, I didn't know that half the town would turn out, I thought he'd be on his own, doing his policeman hero shit. If I'd known that all those guys were going to be there I would…no, that's not true. Dad looked at me differently that day. I'd finally done something that made him proud rather than just being a fuck up. I wouldn't have swapped that for the world." At that moment, Nick knew exactly what his father meant.

Chapter 19

"So, wait. I don't get this. Thirty of you guys find Frank, kick the living shit out of him, how come he's still around?" Nick was at the height of his inquisitiveness, the drama told by his father all consuming, altering his mind-set, answering questions. The tales were horrific but in a fascinating way, he knew the conclusion was soon, but his excitement was making his entire body tingle.

"Just hold your horse's mister, there's plenty to go yet." Mick was beginning to show signs of weariness, to his rear the sun was beginning to rise, they had pulled an all-nighter.

"Well, get on with it, this is great." Mick's no expression changed to a look of confusion.

"This isn't great. It's a long way from great. Use that term again and I'm off, my bed's waiting for me." Nick immediately cursed his choice of words, the night's bridge-building could easily begin to shatter their foundations if his terminology remained the same. An apology was necessary.

"Sorry, I didn't mean it that way. Can you continue, please?"

"'So, you in?' That deliberate menacing tone to Bill Castle's voice had returned, this had been a long night. All eyes were on the invading duo, few wanting their participation. The vicar could be forgiven, but the undertaker…

'I won't be a part of this. This isn't justice.' Henderson stood firm. His own faith had been tried recently, and if this was a test from God, the priest was determined not to fail. 'And I'll say one more thing before I leave, if Frank is found and damaged in any way, you all will be reported to the proper authorities, we live in a civilised society; this is not civilised.' Henderson looked to the mortician, everyone looked to the mortician, his future in Hallowell hung in the balance.

'I'm sorry, but I agree with John.' His retort was short, meek, and embarrassing, just like his personality. Castle smiled.

'Good, we didn't need you here in the first place, but know this, should any resident ask about your participation, they will be told that you were asked and refused. A conscientious objector, perhaps? More like a fucking coward.' There were sniggers of laughter from the group. 'Now, fuck off and leave this to the real men, blood will be spilled tonight.'

The last of the evening clouds had dissipated, replaced with the blackness of night. In the distance, the sound of Fred Gibson's car engine, could be heard firing into life and moving off from the railway station car park; few would miss him. Some members of the squad had been concerned about the priest's threat and Castle informed them that anyone wishing to leave would be shown no prejudice in the future, no one accepted the offer.

The crisp fresh night-time air felt refreshing to those who had been trapped inside the underground tunnel and few relished the prospect of once more, being entombed in another pitch-black Graham strong hold, though that was now the prospect.

There were mutterings as the men self-formed into small groups. Peter Russel, Steve Hutchinson, and Oliver Simpson had all been employees of the iron works, formerly housed inside the main building so they were told to ensure, none of them were in the same group as each other, they could serve as partial guilds. Bill Castle too had a certain amount of knowledge after his frequent visits to Martin so again, he wasn't paired with any of the other three. Other than those parameters, the groups formed quickly, family members or close friends bonding to form trusted cliques, teams of five ready to fight to the death for one another…and the loved ones they had lost.

Group One

William Castle, town constable.
Mick Castle, seventeen-year-old kid who had no business being there.
Gavin Holt, second-generation post-office manager.
Ian Gaskins, thirty something loner, auto mechanic.
Harry Brackett, town doctor.

Group Two

Charles Malone, a fourth-generation family member and town pharmacist.
Tony Jayne, off licence owner, father to a colliery disaster victim.
Peter Russel, a family man with a wife, three children and a fruit and veg store.
Malcolm Gregory, another fourth-generation family member and owner of Gregory's butcher's shop, along with his son Steven, who was asked to partake in the vigilante group and refused.
Dean Cundy.

Group Three

Archie Cookson, seventy-eight and still hard as nails.
Walter Williams, co-owner of Williams reality with his wife Cathy.
Tommy Wright, co-owner of the lunchbox café with his wife, Louise.
Adam Scholes, successful solicitor.
Robert Henderson, proprietor of a small bed and breakfast with his wife Vera.

Group Four

Terry Hutchinson, landlord of the wheatsheaf public house.

Jake Hutchinson, former colliery worker who wasn't on shift the day of the tragedy.

Steve Hutchinson.

Charlie Manson, young apprentice in Charles Malone's chemist.

Danny Murphy, Irish immigrant who moved to Hallowell with his wife Jennifer and young son Jamie, working at St Mara high school as deputy head teacher.

Group Five

Randal Meeks, schoolteacher in St Mara high.

Jimmy glass, ex-pro footballer.

The Simpson brothers, Barry, Oliver, and Aaron. The village bad seeds with convictions for breaking and entering, violence, and drunk and disorderly. They were only aloud in the group as there is safety in numbers.

Group Six

Jack Hunt, former ticket vendor.

Neil Myers, professional wrestler and one tough son of a bitch.

Winston Reid, the only black man in Hallowell, his wife Gemma was the only black lady.

Simon Grayson, former colliery employee.

James Collins, his was a different story to the rest. He was working the day of the tragedy but wasn't inside the lift as the explosion occurred. He'd had left his shift thirty minutes earlier for a routine dental check-up, otherwise he would have been a victim too.

The remaining people stood guard. Dennis Hill was the strong silent type, Tommy and Lee Wallace were more former colliery workers, Fred Challis, a healthcare worker whose wife owned a flower shop, Fred and Andrew Lambert who were brothers in their seventies who had come, more for support than use. Not a rustle of breeze could be felt as the final preparations were made. A thin layer of mist had formed, swirling about their feet, rising from the ground up, adding another eerier aspect to the already terrifying setting. Bill called the team to order, it was time.

Moments earlier, the side buildings were searched thoroughly, without success. The station master's quarters had proven tough, though the Simpson boys had been keen to lead the way, everyone knew they were just doing recognisance work for a later theft run. At this point no one cared. The bedrooms had been the worst, large cupboards, bed spaces, wardrobes, all places the target could hide. The kitchen was easier, with the exception of the walk-in larder, every checkpoint was too small to fit a man. The scullery was the same and soon, it became obvious that Frank wasn't here. The ticket offices and public toilets were checked, though few felt it would be a suitable hiding place for the monster. When all the checks had been carried out, the entire squad converged to the main building.

The groups entered, slowly. To a man, everyone was filled with apprehension. It was true what had been said earlier, Frank Graham knew this place way better than any of them. He'd been brought up here and had always had a strange affinity with the building. Perhaps it was the ugliness of its appearance. Or its daunting presence on the skyline. Whatever the reason, he would know every inch of it, its hiding places, dark corners from which to strike. The workings of the elevator which had been installed beside the staircase when the upper floors had been leased to the iron works company. Key operated, something only a Graham would have. Everything inside was a potential weapon, another advantage to the dark, evil creature the men pursued.

The whole group scoured the ground floor hoping to get lucky. The conveyer belts used in the coal washing plant were still in place and all needed checking as the base of the machinery was hollow and big enough for a man to hide inside. Every time one of the searchers poked in a speculative head, they could have been face to face with the thing they hunted. Across in the north-west corner of the floor, there was prefabricated office space with desks and cupboards, all potential strike-out spots. Thankfully, for now, they had use of all the working lanterns but that wouldn't last as the teams ascended the staircase. After fifteen minutes of searching, it was accepted that Graham wasn't present. Group six remained on this floor, just in case, waiting at the base of the stair well, ready to ascend should they hear a signal. The lanterns departed with them; the floor was now in total darkness. None of group six were upset that their floor wasn't Frank's hideout, their job was done.

The staircase was pitch black, only illuminated by the low light of the lanterns. Solid concrete formed each step, built to last. To arrive at each floor, there was four turns, a squared off spiral its formation and around every corner, the lead man would peer his head before continuing, anyone could be lurking there.

Floor two was mainly office space, more prefabricated walls and old wooden desks, metal filing cabinets and notice boards. Everyone needed checking. The troublesome Simpson brothers knew this was their floor and barged to the front in the lead role. They felt, as they would be stationed here when the rest left, it gave them some authority and began barking out orders to anyone who would listen. Bill Castle quickly brought them back down to earth, letting them know directly that they were a small cog in a large machine and to do their job, quietly. If Graham was hiding, it would be nice to still have some form of element of surprise. With the brothers shouting the odds, that would be lost. The policeman had had enough run ins with the Simpsons over the years to know how to handle them.

The main office space maintained for the plant manager was much larger than the rest with a small area for a secretary neighbouring for easy access. It was the only one with artwork on its walls and spacings between its flimsy barriers so that the boss could watch out at his workforce and ensure no one was slacking. The desk housed an old, red telephone with cylindrical numbering and a flip top registry beside it. Barry Simpson picked up the telephone and to his surprise, there was still a dialling tone. Someone must have forgot to inform British Telecom that the coal plant had moved. His brother Oliver smiled.

'When this is over, there's some good gear here we could nick.' He kept his voice low as to not alert Castle. 'Yes, some of this stuff is worth good money over in the junk shops in St Mara. We could clean-up.' He was beginning to get excited, almost giddy.

Aaron Simpson joined them with a similar glint in his eye.

'Hey lads, the scrap in this place is worth a fortune.' His volume was not low at all and seemed to echo around the room, his brothers looked at him with distain. Bill Castle tapped him on the shoulder.

'This gear, boys, is still property of Graham coal limited and should any of it vanish, then it's still considered theft, so stay the fuck out.' The three skulked away and Oliver punched his younger brother in the arm for his tactlessness. However, it was still a plan.

When the floor was deemed clear, twenty sets of footsteps climbed the concrete with Bill Castle giving the Simpsons one final glare. Floor three had never been overused and therefore seemed quite sparse. It was shared between the two companies and contained a working shower system used not only by the buildings workers but that of the colliery too. Martin had always been a considerate employer and had installed the bathing area to help the men recharge their batteries after a long day's work and so their wives wouldn't constantly be nagging the husbands about bringing their mess home with them. There was a changing area and lockers that the miners could keep their belongings safe in and though it wasn't supposed it be for the Iron works above, when their workers used the facilities, no one complained. Hiding places were very rare and it took a matter of minutes for the search to be concluded. Group four, led by landlord, Terry Hutchinson, as the others had done remained on the floor, but they were left with a working lantern. Something the former groups no longer had the luxury of having.

If floor three had seemed sparse, Floor four was positively empty. This had been Nicholson Iron's storeroom and there were no longer products to store. Even the men's breathing seemed to echo. It was a decidedly creepy environment. On the far wall, there was an outer doorway of sorts, but this was bolted shut. Previously a small crane was positioned on the outside to transport the merchandise to awaiting carriages on the railway line. When the crane was removed, the door was sealed. Pub landlord Terry Hutchinson was elected a reluctant leader of his sub team by seniority. When the last ten men climbed to floor five, the Hutchinson's along with pharmacist Charles Malone, and Irishman Danny Murphy watched their colleagues exit with an uneasy feeling of dread, the hiding places were becoming rare, if he was here, he was upstairs.

There were now three possibilities. Either Graham had managed to flee before the crowd had descended upon the station, he'd been missed in their searches and was in a good hiding place below them or, and this was the most terrifying option, he was awaiting their entry from above. As each floor was searched, the numbers dwindled. When the men looked at one another, it was obvious that their fears were growing. Like players in a game of Russian roulette, only swapping the relief of the empty gun chamber with the knowledge that Frank Graham was not on their floor. Talk between the men had ceased, only passing comment on whatever was necessary.

Floor five, like floor one and needed extra attention. The main work area for Nicholson Iron, the hideout possibilities were endless. Long workstations, once more with hallow bases, enclosed weld compartments with metal walls and a couple of small offices. Everything was searched two by two and as such, the time it took increased greatly. When Bill Castle was satisfied that the area was clear, he reluctantly acknowledged that his floor was the final hiding place for the monster. As was now usual, the five assigned to the floor remained at the base of the staircase, and Bill couldn't help but look at young Dean Cundy and wish he'd never let the teenager come. The boy was trying to act tough, but it was obvious the nerves were taking hold of him. He glanced for a final time and winked, and the teen gave a half-hearted smile in return. The lad pulled his green skeleton mask, down over his face, hiding the rouge tear that descended his right cheek.

The twenty-four steps it took to reach floor six seemed to take a lifetime. Each turn taken with trepidation, Bill Castle always leading the way, his son close behind. The policeman had known Frank Graham since birth and watched his development carefully. Ever the politician, he had tried to circle away from charging the boy when his crimes weren't too serious as Martin held a lot of power in Hallowell and could influence people in high places. Also, the businessman was someone Castle had called a friend. Now that friendship was over, it looked for all probability that Martin had perished in the fire storm, and the lawman wished he'd been harder on the boy when he had the chance, time in a young-offenders institute may have been enough to straighten the kid out. It was too late for reproach now, he had a job to do, and he intended to do it, one way or another.

This floor came as something of a surprise as there was clutter everywhere. The room was cordoned off into two sections. One, back in the day would have been quite luxurious. It was the office space for Nicholson Iron and contained a small conference room. A large oak table surrounded by sixteen carved, high-backed chairs and tasteful art on the walls, it was the only area of the building that contained an outside window. Used to impress potential clients, the office space too was quite impressive with leather chesterfield couches and a modern, contemporary feel. With the money spent on this area, it wasn't difficult to see why the company had quickly run into financial trouble. Hiding places were sparse but the second area was anything but. A former canteen for the workforce, with a fully equipped kitchen and serving area, numerous wooden tables with plastic moulded chairs and a large bathroom area, everything needing careful inspection. What made this part different though was that all the equipment seemed to have been vandalised. The tables were overturned, and many were broken. The chairs seemed to have been hurled across the room with one hanging perilously from a ceiling light fitting. Glass in the serving area was smashed and

222

the kitchen utensils strewn in all directions. In the bathroom, two of the lavatories had been pulled from the wall and a sink was broken in two. There had certainly been flood damage as the smell of stale water was unpleasant and the carpeting still squelched underfoot. Wires hung from the ceiling and the light fitting was broken, it seemed like a hurricane had blown through the place and made searching difficult. But still, they continued.

On the other floors, the men passed the time as best as they could. The Simpsons regretted not being on the ground floor, so they could have moved some merchandise to a location easier for future theft. Randal Meeks tried to keep his distance from them, they scared him. Jimmy Glass tried to keep his boys quiet in case anyone should call out. Some groups stayed rigid in the stairwell base; others re-searched places that had already been covered. And on floor five, Charles Malone listened intently for his colleagues above, ready to spring into action if needed. Due to the emptiness of floor four, he'd volunteered to continue the climb, desperate to be part of the capture. Malone, the town pharmacist was an ex-professional boxer until injury cut short what was once a promising career. Still a fitness fanatic, he looked forward to a possible faceoff with the young psychopath, confident he'd have little trouble putting the kid away. The other four from his group had fanned out across the room, checking and rechecking, leaving no stone unturned. Malone had kept the lantern and peered out across the vast expanse of the room awaiting their return. He saw what he believed was Dean Cundy, heading back in his direction. The only way he could tell was the fifteen-year-olds rubber mask, too sizes too big and making his head appear huge.

'Kid, would you take that thing off, it's giving me the fucking creeps.' The chemist chuckled but the figure stopped ten yards away, just outside of the lanterns range. 'Dean? You, okay?' Still no movement. He raised the lantern and stepped toward what he believed was the boy. 'Dean, what the fuck are you doing, stop screwing around, this is no time for jokes.' The mask was now strongly visible, its evil features seeming more ominous with the lamplight shadows. 'Dean? Are you…'? His sentenced halted as the intense pain of a large butcher knife piercing his abdomen took the breath from his body. He tried to call out, but the words wouldn't come. With a swift twist, the blade ripped through his stomach and blood spilled from his mouth. When the knife was retracted, the chemist fell to the floor, with two twitches he was gone. Graham returned to the shadows.

On floor six, the investigation was almost complete with still no sign of the monster. In a corner to the far right beside the bathroom door, there was a set of steel steps and a doorway out to the roof. Castle climbed the steps and tried the door but found it locked. He gestured his son and the two, shoulder barged the exit. After three tries, the barrier gave, and cool evening air cascaded in. light rain had started and the freshness on their skin felt re-invigorating and pleasant. A small brick structure on the roof housed the exit and the highest point of the elevator. Metal doors blocked the lifts access and Castle was a little relieved that it did.

'Looks like we wasted our time boy, the bastard gave us the slip. Let's get down and get the other boys and get the Hell out of here. And let's hope, the Simpsons haven't started tearing the copper wiring out the walls.' Bill patted his son on the back, making Mick feel important and the two chuckled together. They returned to Gavin Holt, Dr Brackett and Ian Gaskins and made their way back to the stairwell, unaware of the horrors that lay before them.

'Jesus.' Nick Castle could scarcely believe the words coming from his father's mouth, this was too much. 'You guys do this invasion, and you wind-up losing a guy?'

'I wish that was all we lost.' His sombre tone told a story of its own.

'HELP, HERE, HERE.' The tone of the policeman's voice struck terror into everyone, the man who feared nothing, sounded petrified and that cascaded down to the group. After leading his team back to floor five, he'd found no-one waiting. With his senses heightened, he held up a hand and kept his boys back, if there was anything to face, he'd face it first. The men were silent and held their collective breaths. Holding the lamp high in the air, he hadn't noticed the pool of blood that had accumulated on the floor. His boots slipped on the surface, and he lost his balance. Mick stretched to keep his dad from falling and began to slip too. The officer placed a hand on the floor and felt its wet sticky substance between his fingers. With career experience, he immediately knew what he was feeling. Lowering it to ground level, it revealed the ashen-toned lifeless face of Charles Malone.

After raising the alarm, the other groups came running. To a man, the sound of heavy footsteps fighting their way up the stairwell echoed around the whole building. Archie Cookson was first on the scene, he'd bounded the stairs like an athlete, but his arrival wound be too late. Charles Malone, a man he'd been friends with for thirty years was lying on the floor looking like something in a butcher's shop, his insides on the outside, blood spreading like oil on a lake, glistening with the lamplight. As more people arrived, some were mesmerised, unable to take in what was happening. This wasn't how it was supposed to go, they were the good guys, fighting evil and tyranny, standing up for the people of Hallowell and the victims of the colliery tragedy. It never happened like this in the movies, good always triumphed over bad that was the rule. Some turned away and fought the urge to vomit, Aaron Simpson failed that fight and erupted all over his brothers. But the true horror of the situation didn't reveal itself until all the lanterns were present and the room was bathed in light.

Peter Russel had lost two sons in the colliery disaster. The forty-five-years-old greengrocer, a man with a wife and five children was rested on a metal chair. At first, from behind there appeared no abnormalities. His head was crouched a little forward, but he could simply have been relaxing. When Bill Castle put a hand on his shoulder and the head tilted back, it was obvious that nothing in Hallowell would ever be normal again. A length of thin steel flex had been tied around his chubby thick neck and pulled with ungodly strength. He'd managed to get a hand up, but the force of the garrotte had sliced through the fingers and into his throat. The steel cable was tied so tightly, it had cut all the way to bones in his neck. As the head came back, it tore what was left of the flesh and the head fell to meet his back. Aaron Simpson vomited again; others wanted to do the same.

His father-in-law was Malcolm Gregory. The butcher was only six years Russel's senior, but the grocer had married his youngest daughter after her first marriage failed. He hadn't approved of the mob mentality but had agreed to take part in hope of restoring some order to the proceedings. A god fearing catholic, he believed in forgiveness and hoped that, should Graham be caught, he could persuade the vigilantes to take the boy in and use the ways of the law. Though he'd lost two grandsons at the monster's hands, he felt that it was God's will, and his divine light would rectify all wrongs. The hammer blow that caved in the base of his skull may well have given him a different view.

Tony Jayne had witnessed what Frank Graham was capable of after his son's confrontation with the beast. A playground argument had turned to a vicious battering by young lunatic. He'd always been such a confident boy but after the beating he'd received at Graham's hands, his personality changed completely. He went into his shell, no longer vibrant and bubbly. He suffered with night terrors and stopped wanting to leave the house alone. Later, he began stealing alcohol from his dad's off-licence, needing increasingly more just to get through his days. When the drink turned to drugs, Tony had taken him to a doctor outside of town but that created more problems than it solved. Eventually the teenager overdosed and was admitted to hospital. Over the next six months it happened three more times. When Tony's wife, Anne, found the boy hanging with a rope around his neck in the garden shed, the emergency services were unable to save him. Tony believed that his son had been another victim of Frank Graham, even if he hadn't struck the killer blow. Today, he really wanted to be the one to take the bastard down. With the tragic connections to the disaster too, Jayne had been seriously determined to take his vengeance…if only…

No one would ever know if the shopkeeper had seen Graham and decided to do it alone? There were signs of a struggle, but Jayne didn't really know what he was fighting. His throat had been crushed; the marks were still visible. Graham's fingers had penetrated the skin and ripped out the innards, he'd been forced back into a corner of one of the office spaces and the monster had taken his time, enjoying his work.

The final member of the floor five team was Dean Cundy. All the remaining twenty-five members searched frantically, forming a line across the length of the room, no more than a few feet apart from the next man, and forensically inspecting every inch, desperate for a clue to the boys thereabouts. They found nothing. To a man, there was tears, not just for the dead, not just for Cundy, it was the frustration at their collective failure to apprehend their target. This day had been a monumental cluster-fuck though most managed to maintain an air of dignified regret, all except for the policeman, Bill Castle."

"Granddad?" Nick's eyes widened at the realisation that the policeman had been willing to show such unequivocal emotion before his peers.

"I know." Mick had tears welling, the memory of his devastated father's face, too much to bear. "You know dad. In all the time while I was growing up, I think I saw him lose his temper two, maybe three times, it just wasn't in his nature. I got suspended from school once, just a couple of days, nothing major. A teacher caught me smoking behind the gymnasium. He wasn't fussed about the suspension, but smoking, that was a different matter. Another time, I smashed a window. A mate and me were playing rock fights, just kids' stuff. An old woman's window got broke. He wasn't pissed about the glass, or even about having to pay for the damage, it was the fact that I lied about doing it, he hated lies. That's about it, I can't remember any more, anyway."

"Except that day?" Nick kept his tone soft, without a hint of accusation.

"Yes, except for that day. You see, I watched him change that night, crumble. He went from being the man everyone could depend on, everyone could follow, to being normal, just another card from the pack. I don't mean in my eyes; he was my hero before this happened and he'd be my hero afterwards. I don't even mean towards the other residents of Hallowell, inside they all knew this was an impossible situation and he'd always do what was best for the village, no matter what. No, it was in his eyes, in his heart. The plan hadn't been his, but he'd gone along with it, he didn't want to Kill Graham, but he'd agreed to it. And he knew that Dean Cundy had no right to be there that night, and he let him come anyway."

"Wait. What does Cundy have to do with this? He didn't turn on you guys, did he? Run off, or let slip the group was coming?"

"Christ don't be so fucking stupid. Were you listening to anything I've just been saying? That kid had lost everything, home, security, family. That's the dumbest question I've ever heard." Tiredness was beginning to grind, and Mick's patience was becoming tested. Immediately, Nick attempted to back-track.

"Sorry, I didn't mean to sound insulting, it's just…"

"It's just, nothing. No, he didn't turn on us. He stood shoulder to shoulder, at fifteen, showing more balls than most will in a lifetime." Mick's taught temper was still frayed though he didn't want a blow-up at this late stage, so instead of raising his voice, he delivered his words slowly and coolly. Seeing his father calming, Nick pressed on.

"So what then?"

"He'd vanished. We found four bodies. What that monster had done to those men, the mutilation, this wasn't just murder, it was overkill. We searched every inch of that place. Every floor, every cupboard, every hideout, there was nothing. Oh, there was enough blood to know Dean had to be dead, but his body, there was no trace." Nick wasn't certain whether to press his point but something inside made him ask.

"Don't take offence here but, is there no chance at all that he ran. I mean, who could blame him, he sees grown men destroyed, he'd have been terrified."

"Of course, he'd be terrified, we all were, but Dean would never have done that to us."

"Fear makes people do crazy things?"

226

"It was nothing to do with fear. That kid wouldn't have run. And even if he wanted to, there was no escape. There were guys at the foot of every flight of stairs."

"So, what happened?" Nick was keenly aware that his questioning was taking a toll but had no wish to miss out on the final chapter. His voice took on a sympathetic tone, it was the only weapon in his arsenal.

"I don't know, none of us did, it made no sense. It hit dad hardest. He could cope with explaining what happened to the families of the fallen, they were grown men, they knew it was dangerous and they accepted it. Even Dean went into this thing with his eyes open, Hell, he'd have turned up whatever dad said. It wasn't so much, the kids passing had hit dad so much. Obviously, he was upset, we all were, but it was the not knowing that drove him crazy. It sounds nuts but, if there'd been a body, if we could have had a funeral, maybe it would have given dad some piece of mind. I think that's what made what happened next so hard to take."

Nick was apprehensive but had to ask. "What did happen next?"

Mick's tale was ending, there was just one final chapter.

"The time had come to make a choice. No one could have imagined the horrors, the tiny hamlet would have to endure, and now, more than ever, Hallowell felt like an island. The village was in mourning, it had begun with the colliery tragedy and then, five more souls had been lost, compounding our misery. The one constant agreement was the killing had to stop.

Therefore, a second town meeting was called, this wasn't a decision which could be made unilaterally. Once more, the location was inside Hallowell workingmen's club, the concert room on the second floor, though this time all tables were removed to allow all attendees entry. Every family was represented, such was the importance. Again, Bill Castle and Doctor Harry Brackett were co-chairmen, though this time, they were joined on stage by Archie Cookson, Wheatsheaf landlord, Terry Hutchinson, and Father John Henderson, who, after his objections to the previous assault, was adamant that changes needed to be made.

6 pm, Monday 27th October. It was decided that the bars inside the local pub and the club would remain closed until the meeting adjourned, and anyone deemed to be under the influence of alcohol would not be granted entry, it was important that the discussion be allowed to flow without the interruptions of hecklers, emotions were raw, tension at breaking point. Over 400 residents packed the hall, eagerly waiting for the proceedings to begin. A strange hush had covered the congregation, the atmosphere differing from the previous occasion, everyone knowing that by the night's end, a choice that would affect, each one of them had to be made. Unfortunately, few had the solutions and those who did have a strong opinion were afraid to share their feelings, no one wishing to be blamed should their idea fail, Hallowell was being torn apart, no one wanted to be responsible for making that first rip. Each resident was handed a blank sheet of paper.

Brackett took the lead, rising from his seat and moving to centre stage. For once, the power-hungry doctor did so under duress; Castle had threatened to vacate his role as co-chairman if forced to become the meeting's figurehead. The officer was content to be involved but, after the disaster of the previous plan, he had no desire to be blamed again. Not that the residents had blamed the policeman, instead, it was Bill himself that had shouldered the responsibility, as lawman, the buck stopped with him.

Brackett sheepishly asked the floor for suggestions. When all that returned were blank, silent responses, he asked again, though this time with additional force. Again, all that was reflected were frightened, non-comital stares, this was going to be a long night. Seeing that leadership was required, Bill sighed and stepped forward, placing a thoughtful hand on the doctor's shoulder. Harry released a breath which was pure relief, raising a half-smile toward his friend before returning to his seat.

'Okay, ladies and gentlemen, here we are again. I must make one thing clear from the start. I'm willing to be a part of whatever is decided tonight, and as a police officer, I'm content to play a pivotal role, but this is going to be a group decision, and as such, I expect contributions from all corners, I won't be solely responsible. So, I'm going to open the floor, but if no one is going to commit to a suggestion, we may as well all go home, the choice is yours.'

'We need to head back over there, find that mother fucker, and put an end to this, once and for all.' Aaron Simpson had smuggled in a pint bottle of Gin and had drunk over half already, the strength giving him unlikely confidence. A chorus of objections from all corners put the troublemaker back firmly into his shell.

'And what good would that do?' Mechanic, Ian Gaskins' question had weight.

'It worked out great last time.' Aaron's brother, Oliver was the one to deliver a retort.

'This time, we plan it better. Go earlier, take flashlights, weapons, more guys?'

'Yeh, and what good would that do?' Gaskin's passion was impressive, Bill Castle could only hope that others would follow his lead. 'You were their last time; you saw what he did. He carved through those boys like a hot knife through butter. He knows every inch of that place, we don't, all the hideouts, tunnels, we wouldn't stand a chance.' This was becoming an argument between the Simpsons and everyone else, with Gaskins playing the role of spokesman. Aaron Simpson was adamant not to be shot down, believing a raised voice would win the day.

'How can you say we'd have no chance? You might be a pussy but don't include us in that.' The mechanic rose, ready for action.

'Call me a pussy again, I dare you. And you'll wish Graham got to you first.' There were outbursts of laughter, mixed with faces that thought the retort was in bad taste. Aarons face flushed red with embarrassment, the booze was giving him a headache.

'RIGHT. NO MORE.' Bill Castle was ready to walk. 'This is not a pissing contest. Now, Mr Simpson put forth an option. I know a lot of you here tonight think the brothers are a trio of pricks but, at least he had the balls to speak up. So let's discuss it, does anyone agree?' The three brothers looked at one another, unsure whether they had just been insulted. Karen Cookson, Charlie's widow climbed to her feet. The heavy rings under her eyes, dark and raw, insinuated that sleep had been an option lost. The drawn skin across the cheeks, loose and wrinkled told a tale also, the sudden weight-loss she'd endured in recent days implied that holding down food had been an impossible task. The woman looked tired, weary, as though a stiff breeze could blow her from her feet. But still, she found the strength to participate in the discussion.

'One thing we must ensure, there can be no more killing.' Grunts of agreement came from around the room, even though her tone was too quiet for many to here. Clearing her throat, she continued. 'As many of you know, my family has been decimated by that animal, and if there was a chance, I'd kill him myself. But we need to be pragmatic about the situation, he holds all the advantages. As Mr Gaskins has just stated, last time, he sliced his way through our men without a scratch and when I got my Charlie's body home, it was more than I could bare. I would spare any of you that same fate.' She paused, the memory of her beloved's shattered remains, still tearing at her heart. 'We need to be sensible, sending more men into that place is suicide…that's what I think, anyway.' Her words had been spoken with such poise and dedication; it would be difficult to argue. Instead, Bill reopened the floor for an alternative. Adan Scholes took up the challenge.

'What about fire.' All faces looked at one another with confused expressions. 'We could head over there, on mass, take cans of petrol and burn the place down.' Realised words in private conversations muttered throughout though no one felt the courage to argue. Finally, the priest, Father Henderson responded.

'That was something I'd considered over the last few days but there are three problems. One, the structure is pure concrete, meaning that without material, it would be very difficult to burn sufficiently. We have no access to explosives and even if we did, none of us is qualified to carry out the task.'

'What's the third?' Scholes, who wasn't aggressive by nature was annoyed at the vicar's interruption.

'The third, what if we miss?' Again, there were mutters of discontent, though many silently agreed. 'What if we did manage to burn it down, but he wasn't there. There are no guarantees, with that blasted tunnel to the old house, it's not certain. What if we destroy that place, and he's not home? Now, there seems to be an unholy truce, he's inside there, we're out here.'

'What are you saying?' Bill's response was more questioned than accusation, wondering if the holy-man's continuation would be what, he himself had in mind.

'What I'm saying Bill,' looking towards the policeman was easier than staring out into the crowd, 'while he's in there, and we're out here, everyone is safe (more mutters or agreement). Let's look carefully at these choices put forward. The first, to send more men to slay the beast (after last time and his objections, his participation was more about getting his congregation back on side than finding a solution, it just seemed this was the best way) would be suicide, just as Mrs Cookson has said. Frank would hold all the advantages. Oh, and by the way, steeping out from my role of priest for a moment, and I truly hope the holy father forgives me for saying this, but if I had the chance, I'd kill the bastard myself,' this time the laughter was audible, it seemed funny to hear a clergyman swear, 'I just don't see what good sending more men in there would do. The second choice put forward by Mr Scholes, was destroying Graham's building in the hope he'd be destroyed too. Now again, and once more, holy father forgives me, if there was any guarantee that creature would be slayed, then I'd say do it, stack wood high, block all the exits, and watch it burn. But there can be no guarantee. And should his home be destroyed, and he's still roaming free, then none of us would sleep safely in our beds.' A ripple of fear vibrated through the crowd, this was a situation few had considered and now… 'I do have a third option, though as clergyman, I fear many of you will believe that I say this from a pacifist stand-point rather than a citizen of this wonderful village, and truly, that is not the case. What I suggest, is,' taking a deep breath, he paused, knowing that these words could come back to haunt him in the future, 'we lock him in.'

'What do you mean father?' Bill's question was on everyone's lips.

'What I mean constable, is we take a large team of men to the railway station, no one is left alone for a moment. Where there is fence, we secure it tightly. Where there isn't fence, we create one. All around the perimeter of the land. Not directly on the building, that would be too dangerous, but all around the wasteland that surrounds it.'

'What good would that do?' Aaron Simpson hadn't spoken in some time, but the Gin had taken a serious hold now, his words slurred, translucent saliva dribbling from his mouth.

'What that would do, Mr Simpson, is not only prevent him leaving the station, but it would also stop anyone else from entering it.' Realisation was beginning to spread, though many were sceptical. 'I'm no expert on the Graham family, for many years, they have stopped participating in Sunday mass, and most of them have never asked for my council.' Again, there was a pause, remembering the conversation with Iris Graham, the day before her death.

'Father?' Bill's simple word brought the vicar back to the point in hand.

'Yes, I'm sorry. As I was saying, I only really know about the Graham's, what I've been told. I must admit, most of what I've heard has been terrible, but this is no time to go over their rap sheet, did I say that correctly officer?' Bill smiled and gave a nod, the vicar's words had a soothing tone which didn't seem right for such an occasion, though it seemed to have taken much of the angst out of the proceedings. 'Thank you, Mr Castle (he returned Bill's grin), What I have discovered is, the boy, Frank, has always had a strange affinity with the horrible railway building. I've been told many times how, even as a child, he'd spend his days, roaming the floors, climbing to its roof.'

'Shame he didn't fall off.' That was the first thing Aaron Simpson had said all night that the room could agree with.

'Well, perhaps you do have a point there.' The priest continued, 'But he didn't, so let's get back to the point in hand, shall we?'

'What is your point father?' Harry Brackett was beginning to become impatient and…it had been a while since he'd spoken.

'Yes, I'm sorry doctor, I do have a habit of rambling. My point is this. With him inside there, and us out here, we are safe. If all he wants is that infernal building and to be left alone, I say, let him have it, it's his birth right. It's October now, if he stays in there through the winter, without heating, he'll freeze to death, Mother Nature will do the job for us. Don't think for one moment, this is a head in the sand solution, this is a pragmatic one. We secure the lands, Hell, we make it illegal to step foot there, anyone stupid enough to do it gets a week in the cells, what do you think, Mr Castle?' Bill smiled though gave no response. 'Should he exit the station, then, how do the bookies say, all bets are off. If he exits it, then he loses all advantages and then, we get him. And if he stays there, we are all safe.' Many in the room agreed, though, as at the beginning of the meeting, most didn't want to be blamed, should things turn bad. As the rumblings of private conversations died down, the vicar retook his seat and Bill returned to centre stage.

'Okay. Does anyone else have a differing suggestion?' He paused, though no one took up the challenge. 'Right, now the way I see it, we are down to three options, the three choices put forth by the floor, and as a community, the fairest way to decide our future actions is, one resident one vote.

Choice 1, Mr Simpson's suggestion,

Choice 2, Mr Scholes suggestion,

Choice 3, Father Henderson, and Mrs Cookson's suggestion. Does everyone agree?' There were no objections.

'Fine, behind this curtain, (Bill pointed to his rear, half-way across the stage, a thick velvet shield, used countless times by hopeless singers and rubbish groups, desperate to entertain a drunken audience) there are three boxes, labelled A, B, C. As you entered, everyone should have been given a blank sheet of paper, for anyone who hasn't, there are spares available. We will leave the boxes at the rear, so the voting stays private, the area is well lit so there's no problem. Once everyone has cast their votes, we will publicly count them. What we must accept is, the majority rules. Plus, anyone voting for option 1, it would be appreciated if you add your name to the sheet, should you wish to volunteer, there are pens by the boxes. Anyone tampering with someone else's cast votes will be dealt with severely. Once a vote has been cast, it is there permanently. Does anyone have a problem with anything I've just said, any objections at all, now is the time to say?'

The blank staring replies, and mutterings of agreement, told Bill, it was time to proceed.

The voting began with the policeman. William Castle, the law in Hallowell, the proud defender of all that was right, clenched his white sheet, fingers trembling. Walking to the boxes, this was against everything he stood for. There was a tear forming in the corner of his left eye, he knew this was admitting defeat, but what option was there? He couldn't stand to see anyone sacrificed in the hunt for this enemy. Was it just him against Frank Graham, he'd have taken that challenge, even if the years were growing long, wrinkles forming in the delves of his face, reflexes slowing? With a heavy heart, the paper was slid into Box C, sacrifice justice to maintain peace.

Dr Harry Brackett was next. He didn't hesitate, Box C once more was his only option. There was no way he'd be laying his life on the line again, just to save face. If there was a way to get Hallowell back to some form of normality, he'd take it, and this was as close as they were going to get.

In the hall, an orderly line was forming, little conversation was being passed and the ones that were speaking kept the noise down to a minimal. It seemed like a wake, everyone was sober, deep in reflective thought, weighing up the options before them, this was a choice that change people's lives.

The voting seemed to take an age. The bar at the back of the hall had now opened, there was a free drink to anyone who had voted, those still queuing looked on enviously. Couples were allowed in together; they would obviously know how each other was polling.

Karen Cookson left the stage in tears, balloting her single sheet when in her heart, she felt she deserved two more, one for her wonderful husband, and another for her eldest son, both lost to that psychotic piece of shit. Even though she'd suggested one of these options, her fighting spirit almost made her alter her mind-set. Her paper hovered over the box for choice A, proposed by that horrible Simpson man. Was he correct, should they go back in? Everyone wanted vengeance, everyone wanted justice. Tears began to roll, her heart breaking for the loss of her family. And that's why she balloted choice C, so no-one else would be cursed with her constant grieving.

One hour, forty-five minutes, a man with the unfortunate sir-name of Graham (no relation) posted through his choice. It had gone relatively smoothly, though when the Simpson family were in the make-shift booth, Bill Castle had sensibly spied through a gap in the curtain. His concern wasn't justified, the three brothers, flanked by their equally troublesome alcoholic parents, were in and out in seconds, obviously voting for their own suggestion. Bill couldn't help but remember the nuisance they had been during the first raid, and he was determined that should the ballot go in their favour, the brothers would be forced to take the greatest risks. Bill had done his bit.

Volunteers to bring the boxes back into the main hall were many, the anticipation of the result was palpable across the congregation, though most already knew what the outcome would be.

'Choices, what choices?'
'It's hardly a contest, now, is it?'
'Do you think it's fair asking us to make this decision?'
'Is it weak?'

'Are we weak?'

'What happens next?'

Small private conversations, only audible to the next person, spoken in whispers behind hand-shields. Blame was already being apportioned, though everyone was 'too nice', to point fingers, Bill Castle could tell what they were saying, knew what they were thinking.

'WHAT THE FUCK DO ELSE CAN I DO? SHOULD I MARTARISE MYSELF, HEAD TO CERTAIN DEATH ALONE IN THE RAILWAY STATION JUST TO SAVE FACE? WELL, FUCK YOU.' The officer kept his thoughts to himself; this was no time for internal war.

Carl Jones and his partner carried a box each. A gay couple who lived on the edge of Hallowell, and had refused to participate in the earlier hostilities, fear had brought them to the workingmen's club tonight, as it had with others. Some feared the Grahams, others feared for the lives, some just feared being left out of the loop. But still, fear was the common denominator. Many were still angry, grieving for loved ones lost, but that unquenchable terror of what's next had forced them to bow to the consensus. Harry Brackett carried box three, his strain insinuating that his was the heaviest. All three were placed on a central table on the stage, without asking for order, the crowd began to silence.

On the stage, Bill Castle pulled back; Doctor Brackett had wanted to lead, this was his chance. Shooting the officer an uncertain glance, he began to speak.

'Ladies and gentlemen, let me begin by complimenting all of you on how professional you have acted tonight.' There was nothing like blowing smoke up a crowd's arses to get them on side. 'As co-chairman, let me just say that the decision we make here tonight will mould the future of our great village, and whatever happens, just remember as physician for Hallowell, you can always...' Bill had heard enough already.

'Okay Harry, you're not running for president.' Those who could muster a smile, did. 'Let's just get on with this.' The policeman grabbed the nearest box, labelled with the number 2. Adam Scholes idea had been to destroy the railway station, either use explosives, or to simply burn the building, forcing Graham out in the open, and then a vigilante team could extract Hallowell's vengeance. It was obvious from the weight of the box that few residents had agreed with his vision. The lid was opened, and the votes totalled, four. Since Adam had been accompanied by his wife and both parents, the paltry total made the solicitor blush. Castle quickly moved on.

Harry Brackett opened the lid to box one. Immediately, it became obvious that this one would be competitive. Aaron Simpson was universally hated by the residents of Hallowell, along with his entire trouble-making family, but his idea for a second assault of the station had support. Placing the open cardboard box on the central table upon the stage, inside there seemed an awful lot of votes. As the audience waited, Bill Castle and Harry Brackett began to count. It soon became self-evident that their original perception of numbers had been over-exaggerated, the precise number coming in at 97, still strong as many had claimed not to be voting for any idea put forth. As the officer counted, he smiled at all the papers without the names, volunteers which he'd asked for, many wanted blood, but most weren't willing to chase it. Some had volunteered, surprisingly, most were women, Hallowell's girls were tough. Paying special attention, he saw that none of the Simpson brothers had put their name forward. The final vote paper lifted from the box was counted by the doctor and had been labelled, the signature…Bill Castle, his bravery and sense of duty not allowing to chase the easy option.

Just lifting the lid of box three gave away a spoiler of the result, sheets were bulging over the top. Father Henderson's influence as a clergyman may have dwindled in the passing years but his idea made sense, sometimes, that was all that was needed. Still, the formalities were needed, the nay-sayers needed proof.

Most had lost interest in watching when the numbers passed 100. The battle was won. Still, the policeman and the doctor continued, 150…200…250…300. The final count was 308, almost everyone in the room had voted, even those who claimed they would abstain. The consensus had spoken, almost three to one had voted in favour of the vicar's plan.

Adam Scholes Station destruction 4 votes.

Aaron Simpson Second invasion 97 votes.

Father Henderson Station lock down 308 votes.

Hallowell had spoken. Some were happy, content, relieved. Others were agitated but remained dignified; all except for the usual suspects. Aaron Simpson began a drunken tirade, screaming that most had voted against his idea because they were too afraid, too terrified, that they weren't men. A wave of anger was rising, and the tsunami was about to crash over him, even his brothers were growing tired of his histrionics. Inexplicably, his denunciative lecture was turned toward the police-officer, Bill Castle, bad idea.

'You. You call yourself the law, you're a fucking disgrace.' The volume of his voice ensured the entire hall could hear; Bill had no choice but to retaliate.

'Are you talking to me?' Castle waited for a reply. Keenly aware that he was wading into deep waters, Simpson's brothers tried harder to drag their drunken sibling to the exit. They failed.

'Yes, I'm talking to you. A lawman, what a fucking joke. It's your job to protect people from things like this, I bet you voted for a fence off. Let's make it nice and easy, so I don't need to get off my arse and deal with it. What's the point in having a policeman if…' Castle had heard enough, his face contorted with rage, a vein throbbed at his temple, complexion beet-red.

'Right, you little cocksucker, listen to me. First, I agree that, as a policeman, I should have dealt with Frank when I had the chance, but he was protected by his father and no-one was willing to testify against him, for fear of their jobs, my hands were tied. But I still agree that I should have done more. For that, to everyone here, I apologise. And second, let me say this. Yes, it was a blind election, people were free to vote whichever way they liked. But I asked that, if you voted for a second station entry, I'd need volunteers. Now, you can ask Harry there, I voted for your option, the only time in history I've agreed with the

Simpsons. But when I say, ask Harry, that's because he saw, I'd signed my name, I was volunteer number 1. You three, (pointing in Aaron Simpson's direction) I don't know how you voted, what I do know was you didn't volunteer. Oh you have plenty mouth, but when it comes to it, you're just a fucking coward. Now, as policeman for Hallowell, I can't walk over there and punch your face in. I'd be dismissed immediately. But should you throw the first punch, I'm legally allowed to defend myself. So I'm asking, no, begging you, come and have a go. The first shot is free, there's my chin, if you are lucky, that first punch might knock me out. But I'm warning you, it better. Because if it doesn't, as God is my witness, I'll end you. This has been horrible for everyone, the whole village has been to Hell and back, but we've all dealt with it with quiet dignity. Everyone except you three, you lot are the fucking disgrace.' There were faceless calls of hear-hear, from the crowd, and Bill's son Mick moved forward to stand shoulder to shoulder with his father, just in case the Simpsons were man enough to take on the officer. His attention wasn't needed, Bill's words were enough for them to skulk off quietly into the night.

"Wow." Nick Castle had never been prouder of his family history, even if the resulting decision left a lot to be desired. "So, did it work?"

"For a long time, yes. As we said, the station was fenced off, thick mess with razor wire across the top. Of course, it was just for show. It he wanted to get out, he could simply cut through the wire. But it made the residents feel safer."

"And did it stop all the trouble." Nick believed he knew the answer but was surprised by his father's reply.

"Mostly. For years, there were only three more victims."

"Three more? Who were they?"

"The Simpsons, of course. Those idiots couldn't resist the chance to make easy money. They cut through the fence, off to raid the station master's quarters. We got their bodies back three days later. There wasn't much left. Other than that, things were quiet. Christ, there were times we forgot he was even there. He became some fucked up legend. A lot of people thought he was dead, there was never any sightings. It worked fine, until…"

"Until?"

"What do you think? Until you guys decided to go trick or treating." Nick's head lowered.

Chapter 20

The comfort of Mick Castle's car passenger seat felt good, Nick's weary body as exhausted as his battered mind. An entire night of revelations had answered so many questions, the shattered carcass that had been his adolescence, which had been swallowed by one horrific event, now made some semblance of sense.

So many had been affected by their actions that fateful night, some more than others. True, his own life had veered in a nightmarish tangent, the future he'd expected, with his hugely high intellect and academic ability, destroyed. His stubborn streak ensuring that schooling would fall to the lowest of priorities. Broken relationships, a fractured parental marriage, alcohol abuse, drug abuse, all created by Nick himself. The wallowing in self-pity, now made him feel very childish. For the greatest loss was reserved for Billy Scholes and his grieving family. Billy Scholes, small, feeble, easily led and gone. Murdered by that monster, he'd paid the ultimate price, as had his parents. His father, Adam, whose name had been mentioned time and again whilst Mick recited the historical nightmare of the Graham legacy, each time Nick had heard the word Scholes, he'd felt sick with guilt.

The ties in the small, frightened village, with its cast of scarred characters, ran deep. And now, those characters were plus one, for he was now part of it, he was back. The saying, 'Be careful what you wish for', constantly reverberated through his mind. He'd wanted this with every fibre of his being and now, his wish had come true. It had taken his grandfather's passing to facilitate it but, however sad the situation, he was back. It was his time; it was his chance. Chance for what? He had no idea, after last night, the sensible sounded preposterous and the insane sounds judicious, what was next? God, he was tired.

Mick climbed into the driver's seat and pushed the key into the ignition. The men avoided eye-contact, both had regrets, and both understood, one another's failings. The night had been so important, the young man was now privy to a huge secret, but Mick still had concerns as to what Nick would do with his new-found information. Still, the older man had few regrets about sharing the tale, his son had a right to know, continued lies were no longer an option. Slowly, the car pulled out of the clearing and onto the main road.

Mick could now allow himself a few seconds for his own memories. Days after the second town meeting, scores of men volunteered for the fencing project. Three teams, hammering, digging, carrying materials, always with at least two lookouts watching the station for signs of movement. A massive square, hundreds of metres in length, close enough to box the monster inside, distant enough to ensure the workers safety. Was the plan perfect, no. Did anyone believe it would work, probably not. But what other option was there? At least they were being pro-active. Mick had played his part, working hard for over two weeks, standing side by side once more with his father. Once the barrier was complete, he suspected that their relationship would most probably return to the way it had always been, loving but distant, but for now, they were partners, and that felt good.

As for now, Mick's role had come full circle, he was now the father, looking out for his own son. He'd made mistakes, but finally there was a chance to rectify the situation. Bill Castle had been a great man but as a father, his emotions were always deeply hidden, showing affection was always difficult. Promising himself not to replicate the policeman's fatherhood choices, he'd only realised he'd done exactly that when it was too late. Nick hadn't been an easy child to love, especially when the boy had reached his teens, but that was no excuse. And watching how Bill had mellowed, comfortably sharing warm and devotion with his grandson when the patriarch had been emotionally anorexic toward him during his adolescence, had caused jealousy to emerge, and he'd felt resentment towards both his male family members. That had desisted in the closing months of the old man's life, they had finally shared a closeness which had been missing for so many previous years. With one bridge built before it was too late, Mick was determined not to squander another day in his relationship with Nick, time was too precious a commodity to waste. Last night had been a start, where it would end, neither man knew.

"The more things change, the more they stay the same." Driving into the village at 7 am, the tiny hamlet just waking from its slumber, looking the same as any other working-class town. A long-haired teenage boy, acne marked face and B.M.X. bike, delivering newspapers to its rising residents. The milkman, heading home after yet another early morning shift with a tired expression on a weathered face. Men in coveralls waiting on the early bus to go wherever they worked. Normal, average…boring.

An aging Jack-Russel struggled to keep pace with its master. The gentleman appeared around fifty, with a well-to-do manner and stylish, though slightly dated clothing. His eyes were somewhat hidden by a pair of expensive looking spectacles, though his expression insinuated that he'd recognised the young stranger, even if Nick had no such recollection. That expression was troubling though not threatening. Perhaps it was because he was seated beside his father, a resident far more familiar to Hallowell's populous but the man's reaction lingered concerningly in Nick's mind.

"Who's that guy?" The young man had catching up to do. "The pompous looking bloke with the pooch and walking stick?" Mick frowned, knowing immediately who his son was referring too and what being seen by him meant.

"Don't you remember him? That's Dr Harry Brackett. Since your granddad's passing, he's finally risen to become Hallowell's higher power. The old bastard has been vying for the role for years, but he's never commanded the respect that dad had. He seems to think that being a G.P gave him instant credibility. I was hoping he wouldn't see you yet, that will feed the gossips for the next few days."

Mick's disapproving glare toward the man made the doctor look away. "I can't stand the old bastard."

"Brackett? That must be Johnny's dad, right?"

"Yes. And you know what job, the good doctor managed to fix up for his boy don't you? He's Hallowell's new constable. The Brackett's are now the law too, how perfect is that?" Mick rubbed a hand across his cheeks and chin and found two day's stubble. The all-nighter had taken its toll and he was ready for his bed but knew his mother would want an explanation before sleep was considered. "I don't know what reception we'll get when we get home. Your gran was against this. Carrying out your granddad's wishes I suppose. When she heard, you were coming, I was told in no un-certain terms that details of the past were strictly out of bounds. When she knows, I told you everything, I may be looking for alternate accommodation."

"Don't worry, I can wrap gran around my little finger." Nick smiled.

"Don't bet on it. Your granddad was the push-over. Always was, mum is harder than she seems. Small town life will do that to a person."

The car took the final corner into Melrose drive and pulled up three houses from the end of the terrace. The Castle family home: still with the same white, picket fence, wild rose bushes under the lounge window, neatly trimmed lawn containing border plants which had lost their colour in the autumnal temperature, new double glazing had replaced the shabby old window frames but other than that, everything was exactly the same. It felt welcoming, homely, and Nick frowned at the wasted time. Living on a diet of shit, booze, and pills. Bouncing from one failed relationship to another, and never caring. Hurting those who dared get close. The effigy of Julia Martin suddenly flashed across his mind's eye. In another life, they could have made a home here, they could have been happy, settled. Recently, he'd learned to block-out the image for self-preservation, when he thought of her, he hurt, the events were still too raw.

The white net-curtain twitched as the engine died and the tiny figure of Alice Castle rushed to the door. She met her grandson at the doorstep, greeting him with a welcoming smile and a huge embrace. Even while standing on the threshold, the old lady only came up to her grandson's chest. She smelled of pagan perfume and her clothes carried the odour of fabric softener. Her silvery hair immaculate and thin-framed glasses covering the tiredness in her eyes, hiding the fact that she'd been waiting all night for their arrival, never finding the comfort of her bed for fear of missing Nick's return.

"My goodness, let me look at you." Holding onto the young man's broad shoulders, she pulled back, staring into his deep blue eyes. "My god Nick, will you ever stop growing?" Heading inside, young man realised that it wasn't just the exterior of the house that hadn't changed. Neutral beige still covered the walls of the hallway and the expensive thick carpet with deep underlay still had a long runner mat all the way to the base of the stairs. Four pairs of shoes stood on a rack by the front-door and Nick remembered to the no footwear indoor rules, his grandparents had upheld over the years, and he instinctively kicked off his black trainers before entering the lounge. As he led the way, Alice gave her son a questioning glare and Mick looked to the floor, certain he'd be blistered as soon as they were alone.

The lounge had changed some, the sofa and two chairs which couldn't have been more than a year old seemed a size too big for the small room and had obviously been bought for its astatic purpose rather than comfort, its rigid wooden frame and hard cushions hardly pleasing on the arse. A large colour television and video recorder were housed in a stone alcove which adjoined with the fireplace and huge open fire, crackling as it burned its way through a sturdy log. There were pictures in large frames adorning the walls, mostly of him in various stages of his childhood. And there was a silver picture frame containing a shot of his grandparents on their wedding day, Bill Castle standing proud in a blue pin-stripe suit with his young bride by his side. They looked the picture of happiness and Nick was jealous, would he ever feel that way?

Alice made tea and placed the pot on a tray with three cups. She poured two streaming measures for herself and Nick but left out her son. Mick reached across and poured his own, knowing that mother was angry.

"So, I take it he, has been telling tales," The welcoming face of the Castle Matriarch had changed, Mick had told his son that Alice was no push-over, years of living with a policeman toughened you up. "I can tell from your face that he's been talking; how much do you know?"

"He knows enough." Mick continued to stare at the floor, trying desperately not to make eye contact.

"Was anyone talking to you?" To the world, it was obvious, Alice was pissed.

"I had no choice. I found him heading over there. Would you rather me just let him nose around himself. Or worse, go in, you know what he's like."

"Excuse me, I am here you know. The days of talking at me are over. I'm a grown man and deserved to know the truth." Nick had gained a new-found confidence, knowledge is power.

"Okay, I'm sorry Nicky, I know you've been through a lot, but I'm just trying to defend your granddads wishes. He didn't want you mixed in this stuff and neither do I." She rested back in an armchair and sipped her tea. "Damn, I forgot the sugar." The old lady retreated to the kitchen and Mick thought this was his chance to leave.

"I'll leave you to catch up, I'm going to bed for a few hours, hopefully she's calmed down by then." Mick was whispering the words as he as he is heading for the lounge exit.

"Running away as usual, that's your way, isn't it?" Alice knew the words that stung the most.

"Not running away mother, going to bed. I've been awake all-night I'm tired."

"I think we're all tired gran. Obviously, we all need to talk, but now's isn't the time. And I could do with something stronger than tea."

"Well, that won't be happening either. I've heard that you have something of a drink problem. If you're planning to stay here, that stops now. This house is a dry house and that goes for you too Houdini, slopping off for a sleep. No booze for either of you, okay?" Nick solemnly nodded, knowing that he had little option, the money his mother gave him would dwindle fast if he had to pay for board and lodgings. "Go on then, I've made up the spare room for you and the water is hot if you want a shower first." Nick smiled; it felt like home.

Looking into the silver framed mirror beside his bed, Nick barely recognised the person staring back. His usual square-jawed, dark skinned, handsome vision, now looking ten years older, those eyes of the deepest blue were blood-shot, watery exhausted, early aging lines embedded in the skin below which would hopefully vanish after a good sleep. His complexion had borne the brunt of a miserable diet, ready meals and fish-shop grease causing a layer of impurity, which again, would hopefully dissipate after round of his grandmother's cooking, real food, real meals, his stomach feared the change. Finally, his wonderful thick black locks, shoulder length, was now mattered, reaching for the sky, his fingers had unconsciously clawed, tugged, pulled, while listening to his father's all-night tale of terror, a habit which added to his dishevelled appearance.

He remembered the mirror. In-fact, he remembered everything, the whole room, nothing had changed. A decade had passed and all that was different was the duvet cover. Everything just looked…old. The carpet pile was flattened, a pathway from the door to the bed which shaded the material from cream to an off-white grey. The wardrobes and draw unit were no longer pristine, the wooden surface had faded for its former brilliance to a dull indifference, merging into an ordinary background. This room was just like Hallowell, trapped in time, incapable of moving forward.

Castle stripped to his boxer shorts, desperate for sleep. For once, his discarded clothes were folded neatly, his respect for his grandmother's home enough to alter his bad habits. Heavy velvet curtains blocked out most of the daylight and the thick feather-filled duvet wrapped tightly like a safety blanket, that's exactly how it felt, safe. For the first time in years, his comfort wasn't medically induced. The drugs would still be a problem, withdrawal could be rough, but for now, he'd need a clear head, there was things to do, people to see. Controlling the booze would be harder, the pills had been for depression and being home could eradicate that. Alcohol was more readily available, and he knew there was a need, controlling the desire for one more, then one more, then one more… Still, that was for later, for now, it was time to sleep. Resting his weary head onto a flattened pillow, his eyes drooped, flickering into lifeless matter. Sleep was easy but, his final thought before drifting into sweet unconsciousness, please God, just for once, keep the nightmares away.

Sleep came and went all too quickly; perhaps the room was too nice, too comfortable, the thick quilt didn't stink of piss (yet). Whatever the problem, sleep didn't seem to be the solution. He spent twenty minutes in the shower, the water cleansing his tired muscles, southing the horror of the Hallowell story. His mind was the enemy for now, the details revealed by his father, too fresh to allow a peaceful rest.

He dressed in new denim jeans, bought with some of his mother's money and a white shirt that wasn't too faded. Once more staring into the mirror, the shower seemed to have helped, his hair now brushed into a central parting and a shave removing the dishevelled look. His skin still looked pale and sickly but that was due to the start of withdrawals. Deciding to go cold turkey with the drugs, if things got too bad, there was a supply for emergencies, but for now, that wouldn't be necessary. As expected, the craving for booze was more severe and he had no intention to combat the urge completely. The battle was to ensure he didn't get shit-faced, but if the worst happened, he could always sleep in the back of Kath's car.

In the neighbouring bedroom Mick's vehement snoring reverberated off the walls, the contented feeling of sharing the truth with his son helping to aid a sound slumber. Passing the bedroom door, Nick smiled, it was hard to fathom how one could miss something so unpleasant. Descending the stairs to an empty house, a terrible thought entered his head, "What if this is a dream?" Pinching the flesh on his left thigh, the registering pain felt good. This is all he'd ever wanted, now he had it. Where his future would lead had yet to be revealed, the only thing that was certain, he was home, and he was never leaving again. He was sick of existing instead of living, the subsequent road ahead was scary, and exciting, and for the first time in years, he felt alive. That was something it was impossible to put a price-tag on.

For Johnny Brackett, this had been a long day. Being constable to Hallowell was hardly a tasking job, some might say, boring. But he got paid to keep it that way, the way the residents liked it, the way his dad liked it. Being *stationed* in his home village hadn't been an ambition, the role had just fallen into his lap, once more, his father's influence being a key factor rather than his own will. All he'd ever wanted was to get as far away from Hallowell as possible, London? Maybe Scotland? Somewhere he could make a difference. Locking up a drunken yob who'd started shit in the working men's club on a Saturday night wasn't going to make that difference but, as with most thing in his life, control was only something he could dream of. Following Bill Castle was hardly a task he treasured either, the man had been lofted into legendary status, appreciated more after leaving the role, Hallowell's residents were so fucking blind. If they'd only stopped to think, they'd realise that all the troubles revolving around the station happened on Bill's watch, allowed to spiral out of control across his time in duty, blind, so fucking blind.

The station, and namely, Frank Graham, was the only challenge, the constable could imagine being remotely interesting. For years, things had been deathly quiet, so much so that some had begun to believe the bastard had croaked. The last episode had been ten years ago, when he and his so-called friends had stumbled across the monster on Halloween night, the night Billy Scholes had been slaughtered. Oh, Brackett had shed few tears over the runt's passing, the idiot should never have been there in the first place. But it was the aftermath that had affected Johnny. Losing his best friend, Nick Castle, whose parents had shifted the bed and whisked him away to some far-flung corner of God-knows-were, instead of facing the consequences like a man. Brackett's father, the good doctor, had managed to shield his young son from much of the flack, most people didn't even know he'd been in there. Nick deserved the blame, why not, he was no longer here to face the snide remarks and uncomfortable stares. And if there was any more blame to be apportioned, Danny Challis could eat it, he's future was always going to be pig-shit, what difference would a little more misery make. But now, there was this Daley thing. Tom Daley, the big dummy, wrong place at the wrong time. Many had managed to convince themselves of his guilt, it was easier than facing the truth. Still, Johnny knew better, he just wasn't the type, odd yes, dodgy, perhaps, but murderer? Not a chance. Thankfully, most of the evidence did point in his direction, a jury would easily be able to swallow it, alleged kiddie-fiddler, child's blood on his clothes, raised voices heard, both his and the child's, it would be a doddle to get the numpty banged up for a long time. Of course, that would never be allowed to happen, the powers that be (namely his father) would never take that sort of risk. If Daley got cute and started spouting off about railway station killers and cover-ups, questions would be asked. Even if the authorities saw it for what it was, a desperate man doing desperate shit, there was still a chance that curiosity may be peaked. No, it was too iffy, eventually this would fade away, the investigation would be quietly wound down, witnesses' memories getting hazy, evidence lost, it happened more than one would think.

Still, it was a pain to have to run after the big dummy, feeding him three times a day, he was a policeman, not a chef. And listening to his incessant whingeing, day after day, night after night, it was more trouble than it was worth.

And then there was problem number two.

Nick Castle, the prodigal son, returning to cause more trouble. This was aggravation Johnny didn't need. Oh, they'd been friends, best buddies, but that ended the day he left town. Turning up at a time like this could never be good, what with Daley in custody and a missing kid, emotions in the village were raw. Him, stirring up a hornet's nest would only make things worse.

"Well, if he's coming back to start shit, I'll be ready. Maybe I didn't want it, but this is my town now, I'm the fucking law. He's not the leader anymore, he has no authority." Johnny had said those words, over and over in his head since the news broke of his former friend's impeding return. All he needed now, was to force himself to believe it. Because Castle was the one person who'd always managed to intimidate him, even without trying. It had been over a decade, so much had changed.

"Have I?"

Whatever the truth, Hallowell was about to lose that boring tag. Brackett shuddered at the thought.

Chapter 21

They had no choice; if Sarah didn't get shelter from this storm, she'd die. She'd got continuously worse, and the doctors wanted her in hospital, but she refused, there was no way she was leaving Pete out in the cold, she loved him too much and her feelings were reciprocated tenfold. There was only one place with a roof, maybe start a little fire, keep her warm. Screw the stories, bollocks to the bogeyman, they had no choice.

They were two tragic souls bound together by the horrendous events that scarred their existence. And that's all this was, existing. Begging on street corners, getting moved on by the hero policeman, living on scraps that people throw away. Saturday and Sunday mornings were best, there'd be half eaten pizzas, chucked by people running taxis. Donner kababs with bite marks round the meat but most of the salad left in bins, necessary for a balanced diet, provided you don't mind searching through the other crap people throw away. Occasionally, begging on those nights could be profitable, sometimes a drunken twat would stagger over, trying to impress some bit of skirt, and show how generous he is by giving them a fiver. One ruffled his hair and told him to get a bath and a haircut; he'd have chinned the cheeky bastard, but he pushed two ten-pound notes in his shirt pocket. Twenty quid, the best grift he'd ever done, they ate well the night. But then there was always the violent drunk, some piece of shit that lost a game of pool or got blown out by a girl and decided to take it out on the beggar in the street; three times that happened, he got a good kicking once. That scared them off for a few weeks but last night they grifted a little further out from the town centre, there was less people around and the only got two pounds and twenty-seven pence (some dick threw the seven pence in the hat, I wouldn't have bothered) but Sarah was ill, and they cut the night short to get out of the rain. Her clothes were still drenched, and the flu was really taking hold. Tonight, they needed shelter.

It hadn't always been this way. He'd had a life, once.

His dad was Danny Murphy, another illustrious member of the failed railway station invasion, though he'd never mentioned a word to his only son. For Danny, Hallowell had been an escape route, from his Irish ancestry and a tyrannical father, whose prejudices against Catholics, would make a lasting relation with the girl he loved impossible. And that was all that mattered. After meeting Ellie Pender, he felt feelings, only written about in romance novels. Cupid's arrow, love at first sight, all that bullshit that he hadn't believed in until it happened to him. Perhaps it was forbidden love. He'd first seen her in a wedding procession leaving a catholic church, wearing a pink bridesmaid dress with carnations weaved into her hair, outshining the bride without trying.

Even on pushbike, he managed to follow the wedding cars to the hotel of the reception. When he was certain of the location, he'd hurtled home, showered shaved and changed in record time, then caught the bus to the far side of Belfast in the hope she'd still be there. He worked his way into the hotel bar, trying desperately to look inconspicuous, and lingered around the hotel lobby, desperate to have that second shot at a first impression. As he peered tentatively into the reception hall, he noticed a long wedding table, decked with a silver cloth, the bride and groom sitting centrally. At first, he thought he'd missed his chance, as, whilst he scanned the room, there was no sign of the beauty. Moving further into the hall, with a kaleidoscope of movement, a group of smartly dressed gentlemen huddled around an older chap who seemed to be the bride's father, cigar smoke and exaggerated laughter, back-slapping, and congratulations. Children played tag, running under tables, and hiding behind heavy open curtains. One boy, around six or seven was showing off, sliding on his knees across the dance floor and then bursting into tears when he was scolded by a plump, round-faced killjoy of a woman for getting dirt stains of his trousers. The deejay played 70s soul and a couple of middle-aged women, dressed in Marks and Spencer's finest and hats, danced to the beat, aware that a similarly aged lothario with greased back hair and a thin panatela smouldering between his lips was watching their every movement.

And then finally, she was there. Swaying gently to Lionel Richie and the Commodores with her fellow bridesmaids. His heart was literally pounding, palms sweaty, she was even more beautiful than he remembered. Hair red as fire, wild and alive. The flowery decoration that had adorned her hair in the wedding celebration was gone and her locks now flowed freely, cascading across her perfectly rounded face and over her shapely shoulders. Leaving the dance floor and retreating to the wedding table, she sipped champagne, the bubbles tickling her nose and making her giggle. If extra-sensory perception exists, perhaps this was evidence, as his willing of her to see him, if only for a moment paid dividends. A brief, fleeting connection, eyes meeting eyes. A shy look and smile, then turning away, if only briefly, and then another glimpse to ensure she hadn't been mistaken. It had to be her, there was no-one else he could be staring at. Lynn, the matron of honour, the girl most boys swooned over, was still on the dance floor, waiting for everyone to notice her. Agnus, the bride's sister was the next chair over but, she wasn't what most would describe as attractive (a nice way of saying she was a pig, with piggy features, piggy hairstyle and farmyard body odour, Christ, it was a wedding, couldn't she at least of taken a bath). No, it was obvious, and he was making it obvious too. Glancing from the corner of her eye as to not make it too plain she was interested, she could see he was tall with broad shoulders, blonde hair, shoulder length, with a lovely smile. It was normally her friends that got the lookers but… She excused herself from the table and glided across in the direction of the doorway but stopped just before, so he'd have to make the first move, which of course, he did. The first meeting of an eternal partnership. She was catholic, he could give a shit. His father, that was different.

Ian Murphy, the millionaire owner of Murphy haulage, of protestant parentage, had maintained their beliefs and prejudices. So much so, he became a unionist/loyalist supporter and anonymous benefactor to the loyalist organisation, the Ulster Defence Association (UDA) and the Ulster volunteer force (UVF) which had resolved to use violence to resist the republican paramilitaries and to oppose Irish unification.

He was adamant that his wealth and standing would be eradicated should the nationalists gain too much power and increase their position in government. The provisional Irish republican army, the main republican paramilitary organisation in Northern Ireland was uninterested in any solution to their country's problems, short of British withdrawal and Irish unification. The Provisionals had split from the official IRA in the late 1960s and become subsequently known as the IRA. To Murphy, all Catholics were IRA scum and his prejudice led to hatred. His beliefs were hard to believe considering the wife he chose came from Catholic parentage. Their marriage was short and violent.

Danny was all that came from the traumatic relationship and his earliest memory was one that shaped his future life and beliefs. The child was only three, cowering and crying in his bedroom as his parents screamed and fought outside his door. When he heard a terrifying crash, he squeezed open the exit and peeped through a crack. His stricken mother, Lyndsey Murphy, was laying at the foot of the stairs, her body broken and lifeless, while his father was telephoning for help which he knew was hopeless, but necessary for an alibi. It shaped a continual division between father and son, a harsh and domineering father who employed fear as a way of achieving respect. Lyndsey's death was ruled a tragic accident and as many of Ian's contemporaries held office in the police force, the matter never investigated further. Only Danny knew the truth.

Lyndsey was a non-practicing Catholic who believed in God as a central religious figure but with humanist values, believing that God was not responsible for man's actions. Though in time, the memories of his departed mother faded, her beliefs stayed with Danny, who was a loving and non-violence presence, who hated the death and destruction, which invaded all aspects of life in Northern Ireland at that time. Realisation at an early age, that his father had connections to leading figures in the groups responsible for much of this violence, it only added to his already growing detest for the patriarch of the Murphy family. This man, already responsible for the death of his mother, a wonderful caring free spirit of a lady, who was content to be financially supporting what was essentially an organisation, happy to kill for their cause.

He was shipped off to boarding school at twelve, which made Danny happy, as it meant spending less time with his father. The rift between the siblings was wider than ever; Ian could already see that his son had taken more traits of his late mother than he ever would from his own image and the boy became tiresome. Soft, with no killer instinct, how did he ever hope to be a master of industry with such weak outlooks. From boarding school, it was directly to college, and with that, more disappointment for Ian Murphy. The boy had some stupid idea of wanting to be a teacher. Playing nursemaid to a bunch of snivelling brats, what was he thinking? It was obvious that Danny would never be up to running the family business, but this was going too far. Was the kid queer or something? Such a let-down.

Had he known of the secret love, blossoming between Danny and Ellie, his son and a…catholic, then he'd have no doubt taken drastic action, this was taking it too far. If the people he dealt with daily, discovered the horrendous truth, his family fraternising with the enemy, things could get very dangerous indeed.

The couple instead, met away from the city or in places where they weren't known. Ellie had little family to speak of her mother had died in childbirth and her father had left before she was born. She'd been delivered in a hostel for un-wed women, and after her mother's passing and no claims made from grandparents, she'd been passed to the Carlisle family, who readily accepted children, simply to claim state hand-outs. During a routine inspection of the family home, all the children in their care were found in disgraceful conditions. The five children they were fostering, ages ranging for seven years to six months, were all found to be victims of serious malnutritional, living on scraps while their *carers* gorged on whatever they pleased. The meagre clothing the children possessed was worn and unfit for purpose, unwashed and filthy. Their hair were lice infested and the beds riddled with bedbugs and other parasites, the bedding filthy and soiled. The children's skin had angry sores, infected and painful, due to lack of proper washing and the baby's nappies were rarely changed leading to infected rashes. What was worse, the kiddies were regularly beaten and verbally abused, none were registered for school, so no hard questions could be asked, and the eldest, a seven-year-old girl named Elisa, had accused the male carer of sexual abuse, though it was never investigated seriously therefore never proved. Eventually, the foster parents were charged with severe neglect and were given custodial sentences and the children were once more passed into the care system.

That was the way Ellie's life continued, she'd stay with a family for a few months, get settled then be moved on as those caring for her wanted only to be foster parents and not adoptive ones. It wasn't until she was ten when she found a real home with the Pender family, so much so, she took their name. They were a wonderful, caring loving couple who accepted Ellie as their own from day one. Even with her traumatic up-bringing, the girl had always maintained a friendly outlook on life, if maybe a little guarded about getting close to others, the fear of losing those important, ever-present. It had taken a while for her to accept that the Pender family was a permanent home rather than a temporary one but when the realisation hit, that this home was for keeps, her true personality bloomed. She excelled in school, made friends quickly and became integrated into family life. Plus, there was one huge bonus, religion, or therefore a lack of it. In her time, she'd stayed with staunch Catholic families who had tried to force their beliefs upon the child. Then she'd be moved to a protestant family who would do the same. With the religious confusion in a child's mind, she felt enveloped in neither form of worship nor therefore homing her with a family would be difficult. The Pender's were different; oh, they had their own views, but they believed that religion was a private and personal choice, that a person should be free to choose their own path without force or recrimination. This came as a welcome relief in such stifling times, that Ellie went neither one way nor the other. She worshipped God but agreed with the humanist beliefs that no one controls a person's actions or thoughts but themselves. The exact same belief system the Lyndsey Murphy lived by and what Danny had maintained throughout his life. It seemed that, in a country obsessed with religion, to find another with the same differing belief system must be fate, they were two kindred spirits coming together as one.

One person who would have never accepted the union though was Ian Murphy. The fact that the girl had served as bridesmaid in a Catholic wedding would be enough to rule her out as a potential daughter-in-law. Danny also feared that his father's darker contacts would be more than happy to make such a problem vanish, permanently. Remembering how his own his mother had lost her life at the hands of her obsessed husband, still made the young man shudder, and he had no doubt that Ian wouldn't think twice about having Ellie suffer the same fate, should he discover the girls lack affiliation to his staunch Protestant beliefs. Danny had seen dangerous looking individuals meeting with his father, men he recognised from their pictures in the newspapers who'd done *favours* for him against business rivals. People who used the backdoor and left with paper bags stuffed with cash. Those were the people Danny feared. He realised that if he wanted to make his secret relationship with Ellie permanent, they'd need to leave Ireland for good.

Danny knew it wouldn't be easy, Ian wouldn't let him go without a fight. It was the bigot's stubbornness that stood between himself and freedom. He'd accepted his son would always be a disappointment, never becoming what was expected. With his insipid ideas of education as a career, he hadn't even managed to beat it out of the boy, lord knows, he'd tried. There were times he wanted to bang his head against a wall and bray some honour into him; in fact, he had, several times, well, it was necessary, sometimes children needed tough love, spare the trod and spoil the child, that's what he was, spoilt, had everything too easy. Never knew what it was like to go hungry, to take a risk, put it all on the line for a shot at greatness, so what if a few people got hurt along the way, the greater good, that's all that mattered.

A speech Danny Murphy had heard so many times, he could recite it perfectly. No, if they stood a chance at a future, it was total deletion of the life he knew. And when Ellie announced that she'd fallen pregnant, the decision was final.

It was like running from the mafia, going into witness protection. Her adoptive parents would need to be left behind, there was no other way. When they were settled and safe, she could inform them of their whereabouts, provided they kept it secret. It was for their own safety, when Ian discovered his son had fled, he'd no doubt use any means necessary to find out his location and when he became aware that his son's partner was with child, he'd make it his mission to force them home. If Danny was a disappointment, perhaps his offspring may not be. The couple decided that, if they truly wanted to be free, leaving Ireland was the safest option. Not only from a tyrannical father, but the troubles that plagued Belfast. They needed a small town where it was easy to blend in, to settle and make a foundation of a new life. They chose Hallowell.

The little village was a dream come true. Danny quickly got a job teaching in the primary school and the savings that they'd accumulated were enough for a deposit on a home. After a few months, their son, Peter was born, and the couple married in a quiet service with the few friends they'd made. Ellie was upset that her adoptive father hadn't been able to give her away, but they were still too afraid to reveal their location. All the parents knew, was she was safe, happy, and settled, for now, that was enough.

The Murphy's were content, and they became prominent members of the Hallowell community. Eventually, they moved to a larger house, Danny was promoted to deputy head of the little school and Ellie began a child-minding service. They were part of neighbourhood watch and Danny registered as a volunteer fireman, they were as integrated into village life as was possible. Therefore, when many of the male population agreed that justice was needed for the slain colliery workers, Danny Murphy reluctantly agreed. After a lifetime of pacifism and a deep-seated hatred for violence of any kind, it was a decision he'd laboured on. But when the truth was known, this was violence to stop violence. Without putting an end to this monster, no resident would be safe. After surviving the disastrous invasion, Danny would have nightmares until his dying day; unfortunately, that day would come sooner than anyone could have predicted.

Years had passed; it was 1979 and Peter was fourteen. A straight A student in St Mara grammar-school with ambitions to follow his father into teaching, the teen was a happy, popular, well-adjusted boy from a close-knit family. Danny was now head of Hallowell primary and Ellie maintained her business from home, a child-care service for working parents. The one disappointment in an otherwise idyllic existence was that the couple hadn't been able to have more children. Danny had previously been diagnosed with testicular cancer and after having one testicle removed, he'd no longer been fertile, stopping the growth of their family. But rather than dwelling on the negative, they put all the energies into Peter, giving the boy all the love one child could wish for. Unfortunately, on Christmas Eve, 1979, their wonderful lives turned to tragedy.

The tree was set in the same position every year, standing tall and proud in the bay window of their living room. Each passing Christmas new decorations were added, dating all the way back to the bauble with baby's first Xmas, red plastic with white lettering and scattered snowflakes. Tinsel, all colours, and lengths wrapped around imitation green branches. For years, a real tree was purchased but after the annual tradition of picking pine needles out of the carpet until February became tiresome, a nice artificial decoration was seen as the way to go. The fairy on the top had remained the same, retiring such an iconic figure seemed somehow wrong, but other than her watchful eye, the progression to find decorative perfection continued. This year's addition was an expensive new set of fairy-lights; crystal ballerina's, on a thin green wire, each with a tasteful white bulb housed inside the dancer's glass slippers. They'd been ordered from China and had, just barely arrived in time for tree decoration. Ellie always prided herself on her artistic flare, but this year seemed to have surpassed all previous efforts. Peter was way beyond believing in Santa Clause, but his parents still insisted on his retirement to his bedroom before presents were scattered under the tree, some yearly traditions deserved respect. Danny and Ellie hugged one last Christmas embrace as they gazed with pride at the selections, they'd chosen for their son's Christmas treats before too, retiring to the beds, excited as children, for the coming morning.

As for Peter, his times of a sleepless night, fearing St Nicholas would by-pass their home, were now in the dim and distant past. Like most teenagers, sleep was far higher on the importance scale than a new pair of trainers of designer jeans. The snow-ball battle with friends across the afternoon had zapped his energy and the chill he'd caught from not using adequate clothing had made sleep, even more important. Ellie had given her son a mild sedative and some cold medication helping the Sandman deal him an upper-cut and knock-out blow; he was unconscious in seconds.

The chaos the teen woke too was nothing short of terrifying. His bedroom was filled with thick, choking, death-inducing smoke, which stung his eyes the moment he opened them and caused temporary blindness. He pried the lids open once more when the toxic fumes threatened to kill him where he lay. Around the bedroom door was an orange glow, while the wood crackled and strained against the intolerable heat. Increasing black smoke squeezed under the embattled barrier, rising in gusts, pluming along the bedroom ceiling, joining the thinner wisps, escaping from the floorboards. Heavy padded curtains blocked the windows but still, the boy could see flashing lights of the emergency services. They were his only hope, as the inferno outside, on the house's passageway, beyond his bedroom door was an impossible route. He feared for his parents, across the hall, two doors away. Had they discovered the fire and escaped, perhaps raised the alarm. Doubtful, as his dad would stop at nothing, even laying down his own life to rescue his son. Maybe they too were trapped and needed help. The thought drove him on, rolling from his bed, down low on the floor, desperate to avoid the thickest of the smoke. His incessant coughing was searing his throat, soot scratching his windpipe and entering his lungs. Flattened against the carpet, the incredible heat from below permeated the floorboards, Peter couldn't imagine the nightmarish scene in the lower floor, their home roasted, destroyed. Clawing his way across the floor, his head dizzy, unconsciousness a heartbeat away, he fought onwards, his only wish to reach his stricken parents. His fingers became entangled with a discarded vest, and he grabbed the cloth, tying it around his face, trying to cover his nose and mouth.

In what seemed to take an age, he finally reached the bedroom door, aware it was almost certainly suicide but unwilling to release the hope of reaching his parents. Waves of heat penetrated the wooden barrier, scorching his already raw skin. He'd have yelled out in pain, were he not already barking out desperate attempts to breathe. Using the wall for leverage and stretching for the doorhandle, he finally allowed his scream to take precedence over his continual coughing, as the unquenchable agony of the burning metal melted the skin on the palm of his right hand. Tears formed tiny rivers down his grime covered cheeks, though the liquid was dried before it reached the jawline. He sunk, once more to the floorboards, fully aware that his battle was over, there'd be no Christmas miracle. Just desperate that his parents could re-build their shattered lives if they'd somehow managed to escape the inferno. Lessening coughs still burst forward from his smoke-filled lungs though out of reflex rather than effort. His eyes slid closed, head flopping forward until his body crashed to the floorboards with a sickening thud.

Peter Murphy woke in the burn's unit of St Mara general hospital, the medically induced coma administered by the doctors, gradually removed. His face was still lightly bandaged though it was hoped that in the future, the scarring would be minimal. His right hand had been seriously damaged, and the doctors were still concerned about its long-term usage. His lungs were seriously affected too, though it was too soon to say what lasting problems could occur. The inhalation of deadly fumes was thought to have caused the teen's death but when fire-fighters broke their way into the flaming house, a pulse was discovered, and the crew had managed to save him. The biggest concern though was psychological, Danny and Ellie Murphy had both perished in the firestorm, not even escaping from their bed, toxic fumes killing them while they slept. Neither had taken life insurance and their savings were ploughed back into paying off their home. That had obviously now been destroyed, the teen was left with no family and no security.

Investigators discovered faulty wiring in a set of Christmas tree lights was to blame for the blaze.

The blistering wind howled around the railway station grounds, rain pellets stinging their skin, drenching further the meagre clothing the couple wore. Peter's intuition told him the decision to seek shelter inside the abandoned building was wrong, so very wrong: but for his partner, it was a risk he was willing to take, she was all he had left in the world now. Clutching her freezing right hand, he offered a weak smile, a desperate attempt to give reassurance, before asserting slightly more pressure and leading the young woman towards the foreboding building, their accommodation for the night.

For Sarah Pullman, this was the first and only time, anyone had ever made a sacrifice for her, the sole time she'd been afforded any sort of affection. In Peter, she saw a lifeline, if only they could change the nightmare of their existence. Her life was pre-ordained for struggle, even before birth. Conception had been the result of rape, her mother Janet, had an addictive personality, be it sex, alcohol, or more dangerously, hard drugs. A habitual smoker of cannabis since the age of eleven, the first time she'd been paid for sexual favours was at thirteen, selling blowjobs behind the bike-sheds to horny teenagers on the rare occasions that she bothered to frequent school. Playing the role of a whore never troubled Janet, her reputation was soiled before even reaching secondary school due to her family name, a notorious clan of former travellers who had settled in Hallowell after years of pounding the roads.

The cannabis was soon mixed with booze, though the search for new and more exciting highs inevitably lead to experimentation with harder drugs. Mixing with older teens, the first line of cocaine, which had vanished up her nostrils, consumed days after her fourteenth birthday, left a lasting smile across her face. When she'd begun to spike the veins of her arms with hypodermics of heroine, that exceptional high for which she'd always dreamed had now been discovered. In the aftermath, nothing else would do and a life of serious addiction ensued. Selling herself to fund the habit hadn't been a big deal, Janet enjoyed sexual activity and, were she not desperate for money, she'd have no doubt given it away for free. The alleged rape, which had resulted in the pregnancy with her daughter, was only such, because the client had been unwilling to pay for the services in the aftermath of the tryst. Janet filed no charges with the authorities, partially because everyone knew her chosen occupation and would doubt the validity of her claims, and secondly, she was so chemically obliterated at the time, she had no idea who the alleged rapist was.

The screams of a child, born with an addiction to heroine are an incredibly heart-rendering sound. Unfortunately, as the authorities had no knowledge of Janet's pregnancy, and with the delivery occurring in a filthy, vermin-riddled, boarded up squat, rescue was without chance. Post-birth, the baby was suffered withdrawal symptoms and her cries were more than hunger, more than fear, it came from an unnaturally brutal pain that pulsed through her veins, the body's need for sustenance, only heroine could provide. As for her mother, her daughter's screams would simply fade into nothingness, the moment that needle would spike her scarred-up forearm. Her fall to oblivion, the vortex between the real world and the fantasy land that the drugs provided. With only other drugged-up low-lives sharing the squat, it's a miracle the child survived at all.

She'd attempted to sell her daughter on more than one occasion, but no one wanted to buy a drug addicted kid. And the bitch was so stubborn, she refused to give up the child for free, nine months of pregnancy had to be worth something. Suddenly though, Janet Pullman had an idea. The circle of scum that the whore associated with sometimes had tastes which ran to the exotic. From four years-old, Janet Pullman began pimping out her own daughter.

For the next nine years, Janet didn't discriminate. Fat, thin, black, white, a group of Asians, mainly from the same family, were regulars, good customers. There was a teacher from Carpenter, Janet had enjoyed blackmailing him for three months until his suicide; a doctor too, though when she tried the same trick with him, he had three guys hospitalise her with the promise of more to come should she ever come back. It hadn't been worth the risk, Janet wasn't intelligent enough to be a master criminal, there was money to be earned without the risk of violence. Most punters were just seedy old men with a history of paedophilia. There'd been a woman too though she'd lost a child and just wanted to hug, freak. Pullman didn't care, just so long as they paid. The strangest was an anaesthesiologist who didn't want sexual favours. He enjoyed violence, five minutes in the room just to spank the child, over and over. Janet refused at first, but when he offered triple, her going rate, the prostitute agreed, so long as he didn't mark her daughter's face. Hand marks on the arse might turn some of the weirdos on. Sarah would scream when he entered the room, it seemed to excite him more.

As for Sarah, she was kept in line with regular beatings and was rarely allowed out of their grungy bedsit, which at least was an improvement on the squat. Given only basic food rations so she didn't get fat and put off the clients, the offer of drugs was readily available, if she was addicted, she'd be easier to control. Usually, the teen could resist, knowing even at that early age that escaping her mother's clutches would be virtually impossible with a dependency to hard drugs. Sometimes though, the urge to block out the agony of her life was just too strong. Her vein would be spiked, and oblivion would be the release.

And then finally, it ended. The woman who'd supposedly needed her services to sooth the horror of losing her child was an undercover policewoman investigating a paedophile ring. Originally, her visit was just to gain information on the Asian family but when she discovered that Janet Pullman was prosecuting her own daughter, the team moved swiftly. There was enough evidence to convict but a liberal, bleeding-heart lawyer managed to compose enough of a sob-story to give Janet a back-door escape. When the judge heard about her life of abuse from violent parents, (lies) her being forced into prostitution in her teens by a vile sadistic pimp (more lies) and a drug dependency forced upon her by the same sadistic pimp (yet more lies, she never even had a pimp) she was given a choice. Complete a six-month drug rehabilitation program at a housed centre in Manchester or be given a six-month custodial jail sentence. Rehab was her preferred decision. As for her daughter, St Mara children's institute would be her new home, the chance of a new life, a new start.

Peter Murphy and Sarah Pullman arrived at the centre only hours apart and therefore formed a connection immediately. The girl had been under medical supervision for two weeks prior to the move as medics needed to evaluate whether the sporadic drug use across her childhood had stunted her development. They were pleasantly surprised at how well adjusted she seemed, slightly inverted and wary of strangers, especially men and their motives. The appearance of a male doctor who had been a regular client when she was only seven years old made the girl cringe, though she decided to keep her knowledge secret. The middle-aged pervert, who wore with a misshapen toupee and stank of a revolting tobacco breath, recognised the teen, and avoided her stringently. On the only occasion, he'd been forced to interact with Sarah, he'd backed into the room, desperately trying to hide his face, reading her chart, and signing for medication before exiting rapidly. The girl sniggered, if her mother knew, he'd know doubt become a victim of her blackmailing scam. As for Sarah, just knowing of his whereabouts gave her power, for now, that was enough.

As for Peter, most of the outward scars had healed sufficiently. Like Sarah, he projected his feelings inwardly and buried them well. Self-harming was his and his alone. The sudden rush as his hidden blade sliced cleanly into the flesh of his thigh was a punishment for surviving the fire, living on as his parents perished. He always ensured that the wounds weren't too deep, always down his inner thigh, a rag would hide the blood-flow, ensuring that his secret stayed hidden, continuing his own private Hell.

Every time he closed his eyes, the dreams would come. Flames chasing him down a darkened pathway and no matter how hard he ran, the fire streaked faster. Then the earth would fall away beneath his feet, and he'd descend into an inferno vortex, demonic eyes all around as he grabbed thin air. And above, the giant faces of his parents, a giddy snigger erupting into roars of laughter as he screamed for assistance that would never come. But again, this was his own private Hell, the doctor's reports said he was doing fine.

Their first interaction was an act of bravery. Three boys, all of which were sixteen and on the verge of being moved on to a more adult placement had heard of Sarah's former life. They cornered the girl inside of her bedroom and closed the door. The ringleader, an acne covered slug named Harris sleazily asked how much she charged? When she tried to flee, Lewis, Harris's dogsbody and general slave was forced to push the frightened teen on the bed and hold her down. While Harris undid his belt-buckle, Peter burst through the bedroom door, brandishing a kitchen knife. The last of the three, a weedy, slickly looking boy named Domain who had been guarding the entrance, ran terrified from the room and staff members came running. The police were called, and the sixteen-year-olds were immediately moved on, and a bond between Peter Murphy and Sarah Pullman began to grow.

Their connection was immediate and absolute. In Sarah, Peter saw a tortured soul, an innocent who had been hardened by a childhood no one should ever have to endure. A mind numbed by the one person who should have been a protector and trust eroded infinitely of humanity. Her body language shunned others but her eyes showed a need for human interaction. She'd built walls the authorities found impregnable, but Peter was just as damaged. In truth, probably more so; he'd had a wonderful family life with parents who idolised him, he'd had that protection, shielded from the dark side of nature and now, he was alone. Sarah was streetwise, aware that the world could be cruel, and he desperately needed that. She believed in him, could be herself with him, and knew he'd always be there, no matter what. Peter was the thing that had always been missing throughout Sarah's childhood, a solid, reliable, and trustworthy soul. They fit perfectly.

The idea of being separated was unthinkable but that's exactly what they faced. Believing it was in the boy's best interests, Ian Murphy was traced. It took time and clever investigatory techniques as Peter, when questioned had denied any knowledge of living family members, knowing what the outcome would be if he revealed the truth. Danny Murphy had never hidden the painful disdain he felt for his father and had been completely honest with his son about his past, desperate to ensure that the boy would never have to endure an adolescence like the one he'd faced. It was the thing that Peter now feared most so when the lines of communications were opened with his grandparent, he faced drastic action to avoid being shunted to Ireland, and away from Sarah. Ian Murphy had showed no emotion at his son's passing but *was* interested greatly at the chance to finally have an heir he could mould in his own image. It would also be a lingering fuck you to his defiant son.

In addition to Peter's worries, Sarah heard the news that her mother, Janet Pullman had successfully completed her six-months rehabilitation program was soon to be released, her daughter was horrified, knowing that she'd be expected to return to her mother's care. Janet was a good actress and could manipulate situations to her own needs, but Sarah knew that if she was passed back to her custody, the nightmare of her previous existence would return, sooner rather than later. With both the teen's situations at critical breaking points, running away was their only option. London was the preferred destination though Manchester and Birmingham were considered too. Anywhere that no one would recognise them, where they could start a new life; maybe find jobs, a nice flat, a car? But that would take time and more importantly, money. For now, what they had was what they had. Sleeping in shop doorways or under cardboard boxes. There was a burned-out shop just off Musgrave Street in St Mara, but the stench of charred wood brought back unwelcome memories for Peter, ensuring that it wasn't an option. There was another store, out of business and boarded up but the back door had been kicked in and it was a dry, out of the way haven. That soon lost its appeal though when, one night, the young couple entered, only to find two men, in their late twenties, one unconscious, a hypodermic needled spiked into a vein on his left arm, a small trickle of blood coming from the wound and a trail of drool, spilling from the right corner of his mouth, while the other was pouring whisky down his throat and staring at Sarah with lust in his eyes. They retreated swiftly, never to return.

Now the weather had worsened and with Sarah's severe case of flu, there was only one option left. An option neither wanted.

The once mighty fence that had guarded the station boundaries for eleven years was dying a slow, painful death. Where once volunteers of Hallowell had expertly maintained it, the need for protection against Frank Graham seemed to have diminished. Sightings had once been commonplace, now, the residents were contemplating whether he still existed at all. The oak posts were now weathered, brittle and worn and one had collapsed completely after woodworm had vanquished all its strength. The steel staples which held the wire mesh in place were still strong though and the weight of the fallen shaft had considerably weakened its two nearest neighbours. Some months earlier, a group of teens from St Mara had visited the site with dirt-bikes using the location of the stricken fence post as a means of entry. Now there was a clear pathway for anyone foolish enough to use it.

The lights from the nearby terraced houses illuminated the land slightly but the sight of the station, dark and foreboding, was enough to give anyone second thoughts. As the couple scrambled across the fallen wire mesh, Peter took one final look bad towards town. He was seriously apprehensive now, but Sarah needed shelter and the village held no other options. The girl slipped on the liquefied grassland and Peter lunged to save her from falling. Her cough was incessant, and her pale skin only added to her sickly appearance. The flesh on her hands was bitterly cold, as was his own, this was no time of year to be homeless.

They'd waited if possible and Peter now regretted that; if they'd descended on the old building sooner, they could have made plans, found wood for a fire or maybe material for bedding. Now it would be pitch black, God knows what could be lurking in those shadows. The no trespassing signs had made them wary of arrest, but few people ever ventured around this part of town. It was 8.30pm now and the streets leading to the station were empty.

The rain had fallen steadily all day but now the wind was rising, making the frigid water feel more like sleet. Inside their clothes was rolled up balls of newspaper, used as insulation against the cold, living rough meant you needed to be a fast learner. Both had made make-shift ponchos from black bin liners, holes cut for their heads and arms, but Peter's central hair-parting had now formed a natural ravine for the rainwater to run, flowing over his brow and off the tip of his nose in a constant stream. Sarah had had the sense to use a white supermarket carrier bag as a hat but with the increased velocity of the rain, the plastic barrier was becoming less effective. Her teeth chattered, skin pale and colourless, eyes sunken and dark, tiredness an indefensible foe. Peter wished he'd forced her to remain in hospital, she was too ill for this. Placing an arm around her shoulders, he pulled Sarah in tight. She tilted her head toward him, and he tenderly kissed her brow.

"Nearly there. Then we can get warm." Sarah raised the left corner of her mouth in an attempted smile, the best she could muster right now. Bodies pulled in close, they continued to trudge across the open wasteland, the station yards away.

Gravel crunched beneath their sodden shoes as they approached the platform. The two tunnels either side of the main building stared out like all-seeing eyes and the massive doorway in the centre, a gateway to Hell.

"I can't go in there Pete, please don't make me." She pointed her left index finger at the gaping doorway.

"Don't worry. That's not where we are heading. One of the other boys from the home told me about a family quarter in that side building, that's where we are going." Sarah forced a smile as she placed her hands on the cold concrete, ready to roll onto the high platform. "Here, let me help you." Peter slipped his hands under her armpits and with a swift hoist, she flew into the air, the buttocks of her wet denims squelching onto the drenched concrete surface. He noticed she seemed lighter than usual, four square meals of zero a day, an effective weight loss diet.

With a quick hop, Peter was on the platform, but he noticed Sarah was struggling to even climb to her feet. Once more he slid his arms under hers to help but his own strength was waning.

"Last push babe, nearly there." Continuing to cough violently, she rolled to her knees and pushed her way up, using the young man's body for leverage, their clothes now completely saturated. They walked past the open doorway to the main building though neither allowed themselves to peer inside. Once beyond, Peter darted a swift glance, ensuring no one was about to lurch forward. The coast was clear. Perhaps it was his imagination, but he could have sworn a shadow fell across that doorway.

"What's wrong?" Sarah saw the startled look in Peter's eyes and in turn, became more nervous too.

"Nothing, just a case of the willies, that all. Let's keep going." The crescent moon was hidden behind a dark, raincloud and whatever light that had been visible from the terraced street of houses was now out of range. The rain was firing like bullets, exploding off the hard-concrete platform and the wind was blowing hard in the direction they were walking. In the distance, Peter thought he'd heard a low rumble of thunder and preyed he was wrong; Sarah was terrified of thunder and lightning. He needed to get her inside and settled, perhaps she'd be sleeping before the storm arrived.

Reaching the corner of the main structure, a gust of wind roared through the tunnel which sent Sarah stumbling backwards. Peter gently grasped her arm and began leading her toward their destination. The walkway was black, jet black, and at the far side there was no break in that darkness. Momentarily they paused, beyond the stage of second thoughts. The make-shift plastic hat that adorned Sarah's head blew off, soaring high into the night sky. Again, the girl looked to her boyfriend for guidance, unsure why he'd delayed. His face felt flush, heart racing, he wanted to be anywhere but here now, but he knew Sarah could never take another journey and even if she could muster the will, there was nowhere for them to go.

"Are you okay? We can go someplace else if you're unsure, I don't mind." A big part of her wanted Peter to agree but realistically, she knew what his answer would be.

"No, honestly, it's fine. We've done the hard part and it won't seem so dark when we get used to things." He held her hand and cautiously strode forward, apprehensively Sarah followed.

The first door they came too was locked, or maybe it was just massively stiff. Either way, it seemed sensible to move on. Thankfully, the next entrance was clear, and it was the section they were searching for. The stationmaster's quarters were the obvious shelter, it had two doors, the open one before them, the second was the one they'd just passed; maybe it wasn't locked, it was an escape route should they need one. Inside, there was a sparse selection of furniture though all felt damp and weathered. Peter poked his head around the door and scanned the first room. It was the main living area and the coast seemed clear.

"You wait here, just for a moment. I'm going to check inside and if it's okay, I'll come and get you." The young man tried to enforce a stern tone, so Sarah wouldn't argue but it was futile.

"No chance, you're not leaving me alone here." Sarah's face had changed, the exhaustion and illness replaced with by a concerned glare.

"Sarah, this is a deal breaker." Peter could be just as serious and the fear he was feeling was comparable of a man on death row after getting his date for the chair. "I'm responsible for us being here, it was my idea, therefore my responsibility. If there's anything in there, I'm faster than a hiccup and we could be gone before you can say 'psycho-killer', but if I need to get you out too, we'll be chopped in sushi." Peter's tone was humorous, but Sarah knew that his words were based in truth. He'd happily offer his life to defend hers and that's what scared the girl most, loneliness would be the ultimate Hell. "Two minutes and we'll both be inside relaxing. Either that, or we leave now?" The firmness in his voice told her that he wasn't going to relent. Without another word, he was inside the stationmaster's quarters and Sarah was alone, in the dark.

Peter reached into his wet denim jeans pocket, remembering a cigarette lighter he'd found in the gutter the previous night. A white disposable, the silver mechanism that caused the flint to strike was rusted and stiff. He'd been surprised to find it worked first time and with alteration, the flame grew to an impressive height. He'd never smoked a cigarette in his life but, living on the streets gave you a healthy respect for items others threw away. Now, it could be useful. Unlike the previous night, it didn't strike on the first try, but when it did fire, the flame caught his thumb and he cursed at the sharp pain. When the flame erupted for a second time, he ensured his digits were clear.

Holding the lighter high, the room was still barely illuminated. He could make out shapes, a chair, wooden and uncomfortable looking in the right corner. A settee, centrally, though he couldn't decide whether it was useable. The floor was carpeted but it squelched under-foot, proving that there was a break in the roof above. Looking up, the all-encompassing darkness hid the damage. There were two other doors, bar the one he'd used to enter, and he knew he'd need to check every room before they could settle. Once he was satisfied the quarters were empty, the entrance could be barricaded, then they'd be safe. Tentatively, he headed through the first.

Outside, the tunnel seemed so much darker when she was alone. Sarah's head darted in all directions, her fear never allowing her the luxury of a breath. Looking forward, towards the uncomfortable unknown, where once crowds had gathered, the hustle and bustle of business life, passengers leaving this shit-awful village to somewhere better, fuck, anywhere was better than this. Now, there was just an unwelcoming wall of darkness. Staring to the rear, the direction to which they'd just came, she remembered that Pete had appeared nervous, had he seen something? Was there something sinister lurking and her boyfriend was to brave to share it. Finally, there was the room before her, the place that her brave lover was now investigating. Her mind raced, panic grew, what would she do if he never returned?

Outside, the wind's force seemed to grow with every passing moment, the rain lashing to the floor with frightening power, the sound bouncing off the walls, magnified by her surroundings. To the rear, Sarah saw the briefest flash of lightning across the distant treeline, her bladder stirring, and a whimper escaped from her throat. When a crash of thunder burst above the howling wind, the whimper turned to a cry. She didn't want to scream, she just wanted Peter back.

The room had formerly been a kitchen though everything seemed derelict now. A cooker powered by gas stood at the back of the room. The grill pan was missing and the glass door on the oven was smashed, three knobs on the front panel were gone too and the metal grid above the rings was in pieces. Pete turned the remaining knob and was amazed to hear the escaping of gas. Holding his lighter above, it burst into life and the room immediately didn't seem so black. If there was still some form of gas supply, would there be electricity too? Even if there was, lights would draw too much attention, so he resisted the urge to try. An old refrigerator was by the cooker, the door closed, a wooden shaft holding it in place. Forcing the heavy obstacle, he yanked had on the door and it opened without a fight. The stench from inside was repugnant, two dead rats its only occupants. Though there was no light inside, the cold air told Peter that the fridge was still powered, meaning there must be an electricity supply somehow.

One rat was rancid, maggots devouring the innards, the eyes already long gone and its curved teeth in a permanent snarl from its open mouth. The other was fresh, barely cold, whoever had placed it there had done it recently. He could hear a faint mewing and bent closer to inspect. The second rat was still breathing though the young man could see from its position that the back was broken. Unable to take the sight anymore, he slammed the door, immediately aware of how much noise it had made. Without the wooden shaft, the metal barrier swung open once more, the rat's feeble cries tugging on the young man's heart strings. Its eyes glinted in the darkness; Peter couldn't resist its desperate squeals any longer. Slowly stepping forward, the shattered vermin was feet away. The mere idea of touching the prone creature made his face grimace, his stomach churned, bowels clenched. Tugging on the white metal grill on which the animal lay, time had rusted the shelf to the sides. Even with more force, the grill refused to budge. Seeing the plan thwarted, he searched for something to slide under the creature, its mewing growing louder as though it knew its time was short. A rag by the sink seemed perfect. Wrapping the material around its body, he gripped tightly, the feel of its tiny bones beneath its damaged flesh caused nausea to rise once more. It attempted one last fight for life, the tiny right front leg firing a feeble slash of its withered claws. Peter ignored its effort, now gripping tightly with both hands. The fingers of his left hand around its pathetic little head, one fast tug, the neck was broken. The mewing fell silent, he could feel the life drain from the little vermin. His feeling of revulsion was echoed by another thought.

"That's the only thing I've ever killed."

Sliding the rat back from where it came, it rolled off the material back to the metal grill, ensuring that, whoever had placed the vermin inside the fridge had no idea it had been touched. Once more he shuddered.

"Fuck. That looked like someone's lunch."

Pushing the refrigerator door closed, this time he remembered to force the wooden shaft back in place.

As for the rest of the kitchen, there was little of any repute. An old wooden table, fashioned from scrap wood, fixed together cleverly with rounded screws, took up residence to the room's centre, four equally abstract stools stationed between each table-leg neighboured their larger host. A stone alcove in the far-right corner, which would probably have been used as a food pantry, unnerved the young man, it was just large enough to hide a lurking figure. Tentatively, he paced lightly to the hide-out, his already overworked heart jumping summersaults in his chest. Deciding to tear the band-aid off quickly, he shot a head inside, finding nothing but a decade worth of cobwebs, the unpleasant strings making him frantically wipe his face for solace. He soon became aware that the only window from the room lead out onto the platform tunnel, another reason why the darkness was all-consuming. His thoughts drifted back to the rat from inside the refrigerator. Who would have placed it there? What sadistic beast would leave the defenceless animal half alive, half dead? The torturous act had no meaning, even if it was a potential food source, why on put the stricken creature out of its misery. Also, Peter couldn't help but wonder why he was so bothered? It was only vermin, diseases riddled vermin, why should he care? But he did.

Confused, the room began to take on a claustrophobic feel. This was where they were supposed to spend the night? Backing all the way to the kitchen door, a scream tore through the quarters. Sliding on the saturated carpet, the young man sped across the expanse of the kitchen, his knee clashing painfully against the leg of the roughly constructed table. Still, he ignored the stinging affliction, all too aware of the recipient of the scream.

Unable to cope any longer in the terrifying tunnel way, Sarah had entered, desperate for the company of her partner. Passing into the lounge, she'd manoeuvred around the uninviting settee. Suddenly, a noise from her rear forced her to spin on her heels. Passing the doorway, an external shadow fell across what little light was available. Backing away, her entire body began to tremble. Eyes fixed on the open entrance, the urge was to run and smash the door closed, to pile every stick of furniture as a barricade and pray. Then suddenly, it was too late.

Meow. The brown tabby-cat which stepped into view made Sarah squeal with relief. Just then, Peter emerged from the kitchen, placing a hand on the girl's shoulder, forcing her to scream out in fright once more.

"Are you okay?" Peter's question was delivered, partially with concern, partially with fear.

"Yes. That bloody cat in the doorway, its shadow scared the hell out of me." She'd begun a nervous laugh but when Peter's expression didn't match her own, she immediately knew there was a problem.

"Babe, what's wrong?" Sarah needed an answer, though really didn't want one.

"Which cat?" Peter's eyes studied the entrance, the vague light revealing little.

"The one in the doorway, silly." She now returned her stare to the entranceway, soon realising that the animal was gone. Returning the sightline to her partner, the concerned expression across his face spoke volumes.

"I think we need to go, now." Fear returned, jabbing at her psyche, aware that Peter wouldn't react this way unless…

"Why? What did you find?" her involuntary shiver had returned, a mixture of cold and adrenaline. The chattering of her teeth was audible and echoed around the stillness of the room. A crash of thunder, the loudest yet seemed to rock the building causing the frightened girl to jump into Peter's arms, clinging on tight.

"We need to leave, NOW." His stern tone scared her more.

Outside, a shriek of anxiety, a wail of consternation, followed by a high piercing yelp of agony. Finally, a sickening thud, as the cat's skull exploded against an outer wall. And then, silence. Earth shattering, ear-piercing silence, broken only as the pet's lifeless carcass hit the floor. A huge flash of lightning momentarily lit up the room and for a split-second, it was bright as daybreak. Sarah's scream shattered the air, as the doorway suddenly became blocked. The silhouette of a mammoth, hulking creature, its features hidden by the darkness, standing between the terrified couple and freedom. Only one detail could be seen, the monster carried something in its right hand. Something long, and heavy.

Chapter 22

Hallowell workingmen's club survived on its regulars. Every other Saturday night, a music group or comedian would be booked to appear, and the concert hall would be packed, even if to just see how bad the act would be that week. Friday and Sunday evenings were bingo nights, and all the old girls would flock to see if this was their week to win their fortune. But Monday through Thursday, only hardened drinkers kept the club afloat. It was restricted to members only though virtually all residents over the age of eighteen had joined. It was a rite of passage, a coming of age, now they were old enough to sit in one of the town's biggest shitholes whenever they felt the urge.

Nick Castle took a deep breath as he approached the outer doors. He'd only ever been in here once; a family friend had booked the concert hall for a wedding reception and the Castle clan were on the invite list. He was six years old.

The main entranceway led into a narrow passageway and then, after more double doors, the final hurdle before the bar. Sitting at a plain wooden desk, reading the Racing post, smoking a Woodbine, and wearing a chequered flat cap, Alfie Harris, the club secretary, held the protective barrier between Hallowell workingmen's club and non-members. The door creaked on its hinges and Nick tentatively walked through. Harris didn't register his presence, just turning the page of the newspaper to the previous night's football results. Pausing, the young man began through the hall towards the open doors of the bar. The secretary's eyes never left his reading as he called out in a low gruff voice.

"And where do you think you're going?" His throat was gravely after forty smokes a day and made a guttural rasp at the end of the sentence.

"Just heading into the bar, swift pint, that okay?" Nick knew the answer but tried to remain courteous. The guy looked about a hundred and mean as a Rottweiler, his wrinkled flesh and watery eyes making his, an unpleasant visage.

"You a member?" Now it was Harris's turn to ask a question, he already knew the answer to. No one became a member until Alfie stamped your card.

"No. I just got into town last night for my granddad's funeral. I'm…" The old man raised a hand and Nick stopped immediately.

"I know who you are. You're Bill Castle's grandson, aren't you?" It was said as a statement rather than a question.

"Yes. Yes, that's right. Bill was my granddad. Like I said, I just got in last…" the old man interrupted once more.

"Well, I don't care who you are, or who your family is. You could be Prince Charles for all I care, we have rules. No one gets in here without being a member." The gruff old bastard had still never made eye contact with the young man and went back to reading his newspaper, taking a long shallow from a pint of mild without taking the cigarette from the corner of his mouth, a strangely impressive sight.

"But I…"

"No exceptions." He finally raised his head in a final warning of confrontation, no one messed with Alfie. Nick would have argued longer but knew it was futile.

Walking back through the doors he whispered to no one in particular, "Small town hospitality." He almost reached the buildings exit when he remembered something which may yet gain him access. Opening his wallet and searching a hidden compartment, he pulled a piece of card from the leather bind which made him smile.

"Will this, do you?" Handing Harris, the crumpled paper, the old man snatched it, irritated that Castle refused to go away. After his eighteenth birthday, Nick had been made a member of Bishopsgate workingmen's club, knowing that the prices in these establishments were far lower than regular public houses. As a bonus for membership, he'd been given an affiliation card, meaning that he was automatically given access to all sister clubs in the country. Alfie squinted at the card; Nick's name printed across its centre.

"You got other ID?" Nick couldn't believe it, he was trying to buy a pint of lager, not run for office. "Something else with your name on?" Harris was just trying to be awkward. Nick searched his wallet and to his amazement, found an old library card. It was ten years old, but it did have his name on. He handed it to the argumentative old git and after more squinting, he growled,

"You'll have to sign the visitor's book. And if you're coming in often, get someone to nominate you for membership. You can only sign in three times with this, I don't care what the bloody thing says. It's what I say that counts here." Nick said nothing else, knowing that antagonising the stubborn man would only make matters worse. He printed his name on the ledger and signed in the neighbouring box. As Castle headed toward the welcoming arms of the bar, he was amazed at Harris's closing statement.

"Hope you enjoy your visit." Not a trace of sarcasm in his tone, the young man smiled and shook his head.

As he entered the lounge, all heads turned, bar one. He could feel the stares burning holes through him and his pace quickened, hoping to find sanctuary at the old-fashioned bar.

"What can I get you lovey?" The smiling face and pleasant tone were such a welcome distraction. The woman was in her fifties, few wrinkles adorned her face as her plump stature kept them at bay. Her hair made her look older than she really was, a salon ready blue rinse, tight curls and short at the back and around the ears, the image of an eighty-year-old granny style. Her thick framed glasses hid much of her face, but her friendly eyes were welcoming and happy.

"Can I have a pint of Carling-black-label please?" The tension he felt was beginning to ease, this was going to be the first drink of the day, despite the evening hour rolling through to night-time. This cold turkey thing was going to be tough, the pills were easier, for now, but an occasional tipple might keep the shakes at bay.

"Coming right up, straight glass, okay?" He'd never been asked that before; this woman was eager to please.

"Fine, whatever is easiest." As the pump flowed the light brown liquid, he noticed the lady was wearing a wedding ring, though her plump fingers made it look tight and uncomfortable.

"I was sorry to hear about your granddad. Good man, William. Served this community well." The statement shocked Nick. Smiling, he asked,

"Thank you but how did you know who I was? I just arrived last night." The lady looked up as the glass was filled and passed the drink across the bar.

"Small village life, Nick. Everyone knows everything in Hallowell. Before your car stopped last night, word spread you were here." Her tone dipped to a whisper. "Made a few people nervous too. Anyway, how's your grandma coping? Must be tough for her?" Again, Castle paused, momentarily lost for words, and then gained his traction once more.

"She's okay, what did you mean, nervous? Why would anyone be nervous of me coming?"

"Pint here when you're ready Betty." Fred Gibson, the town funeral director called from the far side of the bar. A portly, rotund man with a bald head and dark circles under his eyes, he seemed concerned at how the private conversation was going.

"Right with you Freddy." Betty rolled her eyes as she smiled at the young man. Nick offered a five-pound note as payment for his drink. "On the house lovey, welcome home." As the friendly lady moved across to serve the impatient customer, he turned away from the inquisitive stare of the undertaker and faced the remainder of the lounge. While taking a long swallow of the lager, he noticed other eyes rapidly removing their gazes, returning to whatever conversation had been present before his arrival. He wondered how many of those conversations had been about his arrival. He used to call this town home, now he was a stranger in a strange land.

Just along from his position were a series of high bar stools and he took one, seeing that the mirror around the optics would give him a great vantage-point of the entire room. It was closer to Fred Gibson, who was having heated words with the barmaid and hardly being discreet about the fact that he was the topic of their argument. His face had reddened and after throwing a pound note on the bar, he stormed away from Betty mid-sentence.

"You're Mick Castle's boy." Again, it wasn't a question, and his tone were impatient and demanding.

"It would appear so." Nick swivelled in his seat and faced Gibson, man to younger man, his own patience and temper beginning to stretch. "And what can I do for you?" His smile sarcastic and took the fat-man by surprise. "Oh, I get it, you're the welcoming committee." Betty sniggered from behind the bar but stopped when Gibson flashed her an angry glare.

263

"That's not far from being true." A sweaty, podgy hand was offered, a gold sovereign cutting into the index finger which looked like it would need surgery to have it removed, fat almost covering the thin circle on the opposing side to the knuckle. Nick studied warily, unsure if his unpleasant encounter with Alfie Harris was clouding his judgement of Hallowell people. Cautiously, he offered his own hand and the undertaker grasped it firmly. "I'm Fred Gibson, funeral director for the village." His grip didn't lessen, and the young man was unsure if this was a test.

"Yes, I remember you. I'm Nick, you're right, Mick is my father, Bill was my granddad." The handshake was becoming damp and unpleasant, Castle tried to withdraw but Gibson maintained the hold. "Sorry but I'm going to need that hand back." Nick smiled as though his statement was a joke, but the joviality of the director's demeanour was diminishing fast.

"In time." His expression was now down-right aggressive. "I just thought I should ask what your plans are now you're in town. Wouldn't suppose you'll be hanging around long after the funeral." These people seemed to have a talent of making a question appear like an order. His words were spoken slowly and deliberately as to cause no misunderstanding in their nature. The force of the grip was becoming painful, and Nick decided to reverse the pressure. A loud crack came from Gibson's bones, and he finally released his hold. Nick wiped the fat-man's perspiration from his fingers and rose from his seat.

"Right, now we've got past the, who's dicks bigger contest, why don't you tell me what you want. Either that or go away and leave me to my drink." Nick climbed back onto his chair and finished the remainder of his lager. The barmaid, who was waiting across the way, trying desperately to make her eavesdropping seem less obvious called across.

"Another one Nick?" Fred Gibson was becoming increasingly irritated at being unable to control conversation.

"I don't think our young friend will be staying." Directed at Betty whilst staring at Castle, Nick had had enough.

"I don't mind if I do love. Might take a whisky chaser too. I'm celebrating being home." The stare down could easily have turned violent, were the funeral director anything other than a self-important coward.

"I'm watching you boy. Not only me, but lots of others are also. You're not wanted here, the sooner you realise that the better."

Turning on his heels, Gibson waddled to the door, having a last look back in Nick's direction before leaving permanently. Betty refilled the glass, but Castle withdrew the order for the spirit, not certain whether his willpower would give him the ability to stop at one.

"What a nice chap." The barmaid handed him the lager, taking payment this time as it was obvious, they were still being watched.

"Don't worry about that old wind-bag, full of piss and vinegar that one. No one takes any notice of him. That's why he sits on his arse in here most days, trying to get some attention." Nick smiled, the lager relieving most of his stress. Using the mirror as a guild, he realised many of the patrons who were there when he arrived had left and of the others, most had lost interest in him anyway. "Just like chip shop wrapping."

"Pardon? You need to run that one past me again."

"Well lovey, today's newspaper headlines are tomorrow's fish shop wrappings. Same with your arrival. All of them that's rabbiting about you today, will have forgot you here by tomorrow. You mark my words." Nick laughed and sipped his drink, wondering if that was true…but doubting it.

"So why are you being so friendly? I'm not complaining, it's just, I thought it would be one for all, and all for one?" The young man maintained a smile on his face as to not appear audacious.

The barmaid returned a pleasant smile, the removal of the spectre of the undertaker now freeing her to speak more naturally. "I take people as I find them. Anyone decent with me, I'll be decent with them. Oh, I can give as good as I get but, life's too short. Self-righteous windbags like Fred Gibson like the sound of their own voice, makes them feel important. Happens a lot in small villages. I suppose, everyone likes attention."

"Not me. Now, it would be better if I was invisible." Nick chuckled though the barmaid appeared more serious with her response.

"Invisible? In Hallowell lovely, there's no such thing." A random voice called from the neighbouring lounge, desperate for refreshment. "On my way Johnny." Delivering a final smile, the lady left the scene.

Most of the remaining faces rolled into one. Groups of three or four, some louder than others, all in varying degrees of inebriation. But across in the corner…that guy was different, familiar. Nick maintained his stare in the mirror, studying the face. He was younger than the rest and on his own, pretending to read a newspaper but his tell-tale glimpses over the top blew the disguise. He was so familiar, just couldn't place him. Looked older than Nick, so a classmate was doubtful. Was it age, or was it that he seemed, troubled? He was obviously drunk, but his gaunt appearance and pale skin made Nick assume it was a regular occurrence. So, damned familiar, so damned…

It struck Nick like a thunderbolt. Was it true? They'd been great friends, classmates, now he looked ten years older than himself. Nick rose slowly and turned. The man seemed to know Castle's thoughts and got up to leave but Nick was too quick, cutting him off at the door. He threw a hand on the man's shoulder, but he didn't react immediately, just stopped walking.

"Hello nick." He turned and was face to face though the man refused eye contact. Standing in front of Nick Castle, was Dan Challis.

The pint of bitter tasted foul. He barely touched alcohol and only frequented the Club when there was a Saturday night fight. His eye-line was perfect, an adjacent mirror gave a full view of the bar from his stool inside the lounge, a spying grand-slam. Hearing the raised voice conversation between the mortician and the newcomer, it was obvious that he was still as quick witted and confident as ever, few people got the upper hand on Fred Gibson. That was fine as he'd be a challenging adversary, watching Castle scour the room without being seen was fun. When his former friend had risen to leave, he'd been disappointed. But seeing Nick pause before exiting made him curious, who was he talking too? As the newspaper had lowered and the booze-riddled face of Dan Challis appeared, he'd cringed, this was too soon. Constable Johnny Brackett waited until both men left before following closely behind.

Chapter 23

The room was still as the grave, the monster's work done, his home protected once more. Killing no longer exuded the same emotions, the excitement of the chase, anticipation of the strike, exhilaration of victory. His youthful bloodlust replaced with an older man's poise, murder had consequence, brought unnecessary attention to his solitary existence. Perhaps they were loners, unaware of his legendary curse. If not, they'd be missed, men would return, his tranquillity destroyed.

The storm was passing, thunder rumbled to the west, towards the coast but the wind had lost its bluster, the rain dying to an intermittent patter. Dust mites filled the air, disturbed by the struggle, the queasy stench of disuse floating past the rubber disguise into his wide nostrils. He would remove the mask only when certain his work was done. The girl was dead, of that there was no doubt, but the boy, his body was still twitching. Was it the throws of passing from one world to the next, or was there still life in his broken carcass? Graham raised a heavy work boot, and with almighty force, crashed it down, upon Murphy's exposed skull, A sickening crack told the monster the boy's death was now absolute. This gave him no pleasure, just a job of protecting what was his.

Frank Graham scoured the room, a final check that only two souls had been stupid enough to enter his domain. The wooden frame of a double bed situated in the far-right corner, with a large oak wardrobe standing as a divider, to a child's single divan were all that was housed in the former station master's bedroom. The killer had hauled both mattresses to the main building's upper floors, needing more protection when at rest, then the ground floor accommodation provided. Inside, he had the advantage, all the hideaways, escape routes and darkened corners from where to strike. Should he be outnumbered, the odds would still be in his favour, whereas inside the residential unit, he'd be trapped.

Whenever they came, it was always inside here. Too afraid to enter the main building, the station master quarters were like honey to a bee. Desperate loners, passing strangers, suicidal idiots, always the same. That's the reason Frank left the entrance open, they entered but never left. Always falling into his trap, believing there were two entrances, two means of escape. The second door was nailed shut and as for the bedroom window, whenever they tried that method to flee, they were as good as dead.

That's what the girl had done. The same as so many before her, his masterpiece of manipulation. Graham had forced a steel spike into the window's wooden frame, leaving just an eight-inch gap. Victims would either battle to force a larger exit or try in vain to squeeze through the meagre hole. Either way would cost them precious time and invariably end in failure. Sarah had come closest of all those who had attempted to climb through the miniscule space, her head and shoulders managing to circumvent the obstacle before her. The tiny breasts, inherited from her junkie mother, finally proved advantageous as her torso pushed past the coarse wooden frame, freedom was in sight.

Had Graham been seconds later, Sarah Pullman may have been the first to successfully flee. The boy had tried in vain to gain his beloved girlfriend more time, showing incredible heart and courage, having already lost his right leg below the knee. Bravely, the fifteen-year-old had swung a kick towards Frank's abdomen, only for the monster to grab the flailing limb; a swift gruesome shot from the steel-bladed weapon, slicing cleanly through, just below the kneecap, the severed leg thrown aside like trash in the gutter. Peter crashed to the floor, screaming agonising, blood-curdling cries, hands desperately trying to stem the hot jet of spraying blood. Sarah had cried out in terror, aware that her partner was all but dead, knowing the odds were, the same fate awaited her. Trapped in the bedroom, the window was her last lifeline. She shot a glance at the glass barrier, noticing its partially open offer. Looking back to Peter, knowing that she couldn't attempt to leave without his approval, he yelled with his wavering voice, "GO."

His scream brought her to life, and she darted for the exit. Though the monster was only yards away, self-preservation demanded she try. Peter made one final effort to assist, knowing his own situation was terminal, the blood loss too catastrophic for him to be saved. He used both arms, grabbing tightly around Frank's left leg and hung on, trying to slow the killer's progress. The masked face looked down, strangely impressed at his victim's tenacity but unwilling to be thwarted in his pursuit of the girl. Rather than fight, Graham dragged the teenager as he stepped, Murphy's own blood causing a slippery aid on the filthy floor. Aware that his efforts were having little impact, the boy opened his mouth wide and sank his teeth deep into Frank's left calf. The monster groaned with the sudden sharp pain and returned his attention to the gutsy teen. Stretching down, he grabbed a huge handful of Murphy's hairs and wrenched his head away from the leg, his own flesh tearing as the boy's jaws locked in position fought to maintain their grip. A trickle of blood ran down Frank Graham's calf as he raised his weapon high, crashing down on Peter's skull with the dull edge, for fear of missing his target and impaling his own flesh. A sickening gash appeared across Murphy's brow and his grip began to weaken around the killer's leg. Peter's blood-covered fingers were flexing and relaxing in an involuntary motion, his entire body shuddering as his essential organs began their final duties. A last grasp at the hem of Frank's coverall trousers had no effect, and the monster strode away, in Sarah Pullman's direction.

Whilst Peter had fought valiantly to gain the girl time, Sarah pushed the window with all her might, quickly becoming conscious that the small gap was as good as it got. Refusing to waste time, she began her fight to escape. Forcing her head through the window frame, the cold air shocked her heated skin. A wooden sliver had become embedded into right cheek, tearing a severe gash below the eye, but the pain barely had time to register. Her shoulders and arms passed the exit with ease, as did her upper torso. With a strong push, her stomach was through. There was a real chance now. As she prepared to pull her legs into the darkened tunnel and run for help, the wooden fragment that had torn the flesh on her cheek impregnated the dirty pink coat she was wearing and refused to release its hold.

"Please, not now." She tugged at the woollen material, but the wood was dug in deep. Panic was returning, and the shadow of the killer loomed large. When the material refused to tear, she began trying to remove the coat, but the fastened buttons were obscured by the window frame. Wriggling her arms and shoulders free, she crawled forward but the bunched material made the tiny gap smaller. With one last defiant tug, the coat ripped, the material gave, and one final opportunity presented. If she escaped, perhaps it wasn't too late to save her beloved Peter, perhaps she could get help in time, perhaps…

The first strike was delivered with such momentum that the blade severed the spinal column and almost cut the tiny teen in two. The twelve-inch blade struggled to retract, such was the depth of the injury, but when the axe was forced free, the second sickening slash was thrown with equal intensity. The monster grunted with hatred, not for the victim but for the whole of humanity. The horrific weapon crashed down, again and again, and by the sixth strike, Sarah Pullman's lower half slid to the bedroom floor while her upper torso fell with a heavy thud into the outside tunnel, finally free of the bedroom's confines. The blood-loss was massive, smearing a gruesome trail below the bedroom window. Part of the teen's intestine was still intact, the only lingering connection of the upper and lower sections of Sarah Pullman.

Graham exited the bedroom, morbid curiosity piquing his interest of the girl's splattered upper remains. An immense pool of coagulated blood surrounded the half-body, eyes fixed in unrepentant terror, fingernails broken as an involuntary grasp had scratched claw marks into the cold concrete floor. Raising his weapon once more, he slid the razor-sharp edge across the window frame, the lasting entrails severing, the evisceration of the girl complete.

The door to the old public washroom was hanging on one hinge and scraped across the concrete when it moved. There was so much blood, more blood than usual, and the girl's screams, so loud, maybe the storm would have stopped them carrying.

The axe felt heavy. He tightened his grip and raised it over the sink, the steady flow of water turning pink as the blood was washed clean from the blade. Dropping the cumbersome metal into the basin, the stained grey porcelain, objecting to the blow, calling out with an echoing thud. The surface was smashed beyond recognition from its former glories, back when the building was seen with pride and county wide envy, water cascading through a large crack, formed pools on the uneven floor. Running the cold liquid through his fingers and around his hands, even more thick red residue disappeared down the wastepipe, sins washed away in an instant. The jet of blood that erupted from the girl as the weapon had sliced threw her spine had covered his dirty overalls, adding to stains from crimes long since forgotten. By tomorrow, it would be dried, and they'd be forgotten too…hopefully.

A long wooden bench stretched the length of the room and Frank collapsed to a sitting position, his legs weak, spirit worn. His head drooped to below his shoulders, eyes closed, everything hurt. It was always like this now, every time he had to kill. The bloodlust of his youth had passed, all he wanted was to be left alone. But that would never happen, not really. What right did they have to come to his home? He was just protecting what was his, a birth-right, a legacy. He'd even considered leaving. Questioning whether, after all these years of solitude, could he live back in a society that had shunned him. Not here, that much was certain. His face was imprinted on the memories of everyone, old enough to remember what they claim to be his crimes. Burned into their nightmares. Were they really crimes at all though? Yes, he'd killed, but in self-defence and retaliation, and later, protecting what was his. Was that really crime? And where would he go? The family fortune was gone, all that remained was this building and the burned-out shell that had once been the Graham mansion. No, this was safer. Society wouldn't accept him anyway, not the way he looked.

Raising his head, a broken mirror, covered with twelve years of dust and grime, sat staring back in his direction. The mask was almost ever-present now, after the fire. It was so stupid, weeks after what they call, the invasion, when the men had finished building that damned fence on his property, Frank was waiting to die. He didn't fear it, in truth, he welcomed it. A reunion with Martin, away from the pain of living.

It was deep winter; January snow had blanketed the land and made hunting pointless. He'd lived on rabbits, caught in simply snares, whatever vermin he could catch, rats were better than mice, more meat. When it was dark, he could venture to the woodland across from the main building and forage for berries and black currents. But with the harsh temperatures, came hibernation and hunger. It had been weeks since his last meal, thankfully, water wasn't a problem. If the idiots from town had a clue, they'd have cut off all the services, forced him out. They didn't. Even the electricity supply still ran though he used it sparingly as to not draw attention. He was losing weight rapidly, the body eating itself to maintain the essential workings. It wasn't going to be fast. And just when it seemed death would come, a sweet release from this existence, he'd came.

Appearing as a mentor, a master, Frank had been intrigued. The instinct to kill quelled, if only momentarily. A cowardly psychopath who'd dreamed of being the next great serial killer, but his timidity refused to allow the urge to grow to fruition. Still, his compulsion to deal with the dead, to do things with their unresponsive corpses had been enough to satisfy his deviant desires, for now. That's why he'd become the town undertaker. Touching the naked flesh, probing parts no living being would allow him to investigate. And when the time was right, when all the snivelling, whining maggots had stopping wailing by the coffins of their departed loved ones, when he was certain there'd be no last gasp efforts to hold the dead fleshy hand of a deceased wife or husband, no police needing one last look for clues or forensic swabs, he was free to have fun. The first time he'd removed a foot from an elderly granny, the night before her cremation, his excitement had been unbearable. What if they pulled back the satin sheet to discover the missing limb? What if the funereal fires went out and the body wasn't turned to ashes. He'd had to hide his elation once the curtains closed, and flames extinguished his remaining fears. That was the first.

He enjoyed taking trophies. His freezer in the basement of his home was crammed full of body-parts. A hand from a deceased schoolteacher, the kneecap from a miner killed in Hallowell colliery. He'd almost been caught when he decided to take the penis of a black man, who had legendary status for the size of his appendage (something that had been vastly over exaggerated) and his wife asked to see the naked body of the departed one final time. He implored the woman, for decency's sake, and amazingly, she agreed. He stopped for a while then, the fear too great, but it couldn't last. His crowning achievement, the removal of a busty teen's breasts, hours before the burial. He still used them a lot. Thawed them out and…you get the idea. He wasn't sure if he'd overstepped the mark when the left leg of an eight-year-old girl, killed in a road accident was taken. Plus, he had to cut it in two, so it fit in the freezer and the thigh just looked like a Sunday pork roast, wasteful really. It was then that he decided, why waste money on meat.

He'd roared privately with laughter when a visitor had been served freshly cooked rump meat from an overweight, fifty-year-old woman between two slices of crusty bread. Sautéed in a red wine sauce, the travelling salesman had raved at the wonderful taste. The heart of an old codger who died of natural causes had been tough and disappointing but normally, his varied cuisine gave him all kinds of pleasure. Maybe that's why he was so overweight. Even his pet dogs, a Jack-Russel and a Yorkshire terrier were fed from this staple diet. And it was all his secret.

And there laid the problem. He had no one to talk too, no one to tell. They wouldn't understand, all those muppets who sank pint after pint in Hallowell workingmen's club. Workingmen? Most were on benefits and hadn't worked a day in their sorry lives. How he'd like to eat them, at least they'd be useful for a change. And that fat bitch behind the bar, what was her name, Betty? She'd have enough blubber on her to feed the whole town for a month.

And then it happened. The Graham family imploded. He was one of the few people, Martin had called friend and the even fewer people that paid Frank any attention (bar anger and hatred) He could see past the youthful antics, looking to the man the boy would become, a full-blown psychopath. It was obvious, those same eyes that, as a younger man, he'd seen staring back when he looked in the mirror. The body language, the loner tendencies, if he'd had the chance, he'd have loved to mentor and guild the boy to become the killer, Fred Gibson had always dreamed of being. Steering away from the obligatory attacks on locals and spreading the net, further afield. Frank could have killed them, and Fred would fry them up for supper, and get extra business in his parlour too, everyone's a winner (except for the murdered folk but like mom used to say, "You can't make an omelette without breaking eggs.")

He'd been pissed when the chance passed him by, what good was the boy doing, hiding away in the railway station, such a waste of talent. Regardless of the boy's motives, the undertaker's urge to protect Frank continued as the invasion was planned. He'd used the local vicar, speaking the word of God, trying to change the minds of those idiots, vying for vengeance. When that failed, he'd put his own reputation on the line by refusing to be part of the manhunt. Oh how he'd laughed (privately) when news of the station massacre broke. He'd seen what the result would be, well before it happened, Frank Graham was a killing machine, they were amateurs, there was always only going to be one winner. Thankfully, his disappointment was short, the business boost he'd received with all the funerals of the fallen exploded his bank balance, and his collections took on some interesting additions.

Unfortunately, things were getting boring. No longer satisfied with his depravity, it just wasn't the same as killing. He'd set out for St Mara on Christmas eve, the previous year, adamant that another day without murder was another day not worth living. Armed with a hammer, crouched on a hidden pathway, he darted from the shadows and struck out at a woman jogging, but missed. She screamed and ran, so did he (in the opposing direction) and fled the scene in a blind panic, his one and only effort at his lifelong ambition. When the police didn't break down his door (he'd had the sense to take a disguise, crazy not stupid) he accepted that he'd never be the next great serial killer. What a blow.

So, visiting the station, some would call it lunacy, he felt it was an investment in the future. If he could get through to the young man, perhaps he could be a killer by proxy, live a moment though his eyes, walk a mile in those boots. Frank knew him, maybe trusted him, perhaps even liked him. Worth a shot.

He'd been terrified walking through those giant doors, at night-time too. The only time when no one would be watching. He was cautious, sweating scared. The flashlight was handy, but the killer could have been lurking anywhere. He decided to make noise, plenty of noise. Not wishing to startle the boy, he needed the chance to speak before being struck down. With his heart racing, so fiercely, he needed to rest and that's when the boy revealed himself. God, he was good. Appearing out of the darkness like a fucking vampire, Gibson had raved at a hundred miles an hour just, so Graham didn't kill him where he stood. But he was gaunt, sickly looking, even with the mask on. (Gibson never saw him without the disguise and wasn't willing to push his luck) His frame had shrunk, clothes hanging loose and baggy. It was obvious, Freddy was just in time. And the gifts, pre-cooked shin from a real murder victim (not exciting, the young woman had been bludgeoned by her boyfriend but at least it was a wrongful death) Frank gorged and was grateful, so much so, he allowed the undertaker to live. And to return, provided he brought back more sustenance. The funeral director maintained the killer, throughout the winter months. Inside the canteen on an upper floor, a deep freeze still worked, and Gibson continued his steady supply of meat, happy in the knowledge that nothing would go to waste. Sometimes pre-cooked, sometimes fresh. It didn't seem to matter.

Fred Gibson became Frank's link to the outside world. To say they were friends would be a stretch, the monster's voice now a distant memory, speaking would be a sign of trust and that was an impossible task. But the undertaker ensured that Frank was informed about everything he could need to know. Whatever the events in Hallowell that were connected to Graham, he'd pass on swiftly, also ensuring that the killer had all dietary needs covered. In return, Gibson could briefly live vicariously through the eyes of the creature he so vehemently wished to be. Desecrating the remains was deviant but taking a life from one world to the next, that was the ultimate thrill. If he was incapable of performing the act, collaborating with someone as merciless and savage as Frank Graham was the next best thing. And who knows, should some idiot dare to wander onto station lands while he was present, his life-long dream could still come true. One could only hope.

Frank was literally exhausted. The act of murder drained him, both physically and emotionally. Whilst performing the heinous act, every sense would be heightened, all targeting the goal, defend what was his. He had no fear of being overpowered, his massive bulk and frame more than a match for anyone foolish to enter his domain. Plus, his willingness to do what others wouldn't always gave him the edge. But still, that element of doubt, a mild lack of self-confidence kept his mind focused, no mistakes. And once the deed was done, the intruders vanquished, and all signs of the existence removed, there was the continual worry, would they be missed? Occasionally, he needed to make a judgement call. Like the time a group of pre-teens had stupidly decided to use the outer station courtyard to ride their bicycles. From a hidden vantage point on the top floor behind the only window, he'd watched. Had no-one told them of the Hallowell railway station curse? They seemed so ambivalent to their surroundings, so removed from fear. He considered showing himself upon the platform walkway, a sharp fright to remove the problem. But if he did, would it bring unnecessary attention? They weren't in the building, just doing what children do, thrashing around with juvenile abonnement; still, they were breaking the rules. When an adult called to them from the outer fence and the children scattered, Graham felt relief. An amazing about-turn from the psychopath of his teens. Murder was now a means to an end, nothing more.

His slumped figure in the station washrooms was so far removed from the person he once was, it was hardly recognisable. Killing was a chore now; he needed rest. The wetness of the blood that drenched his coveralls was unpleasant and made his skin raw. He knew that removing the half-carcass of Sarah Pullman was necessary, it was in view to the passing public, where was Gibson when he was needed? Slowly, he rose from the seated position, his bones cracking around their joints. Stretching, he breathed in deeply, the rancid stench of sweat-impregnated rubber from his hideous disguise filled his lungs. Raising his hands to the scalp, he took two fistfuls of the mask's fake hair and started to pull forward. The stinging pain immediately registered in his brain, forcing his retraction. How long had it been since his face had been free from the disguise? Weeks? Months? Perhaps it was years? The outer skin becoming one with the inner skin. For the first time, the monster felt claustrophobic. Staggering forward, he caught his image in a broken mirror. Green latex shaped crudely to form a skeleton, white misshapen teeth in a constant maniacal grin, eyeholes unnaturally large with dark lifeless pupils staring out. His muscles suddenly tensed, body rigid, breathing held. Is this what he'd become? Was this vision of horror in the cracked glass a true reflection of who he was?

Finally, his breathing softened, returning to its normal slow rhythm, the perspiration which had covered his body began to dry. The aches which had invaded his muscles suddenly eased, and the dense frown which had masked his inner skin vanished. It was now that he remembered, what he was, what he'd always been…and what he would always be. A smile, hidden by the latex, crackled out of sight, and a silent laugh tried desperately to escape. For now, the truth re-emerged. He was a killer, plain and simple, his legacy, the taker of souls, the pornographer of violence… Frank Graham was a monster…and he loved it.

Sarah Pullman's shattered body wasn't going to move itself. He turned and headed out into the cold night air, extra vigour in his steps.

Chapter 24

A decade earlier, these two young men had been close friends. Comparable age, comparable background, now, there seemed a ten-year age difference, time has been cruelling to Dan Challis. As the pair crossed the workingmen's club car park, headed towards Castle's borrowed Ford, Challis's limp grew gradually more pronounced, the cool Autumnal temperature adding stiffness to his arthritic left knee. Sliding the key into the driver's side door, the central-locking mechanism triggered, Castle shifted effortlessly into his seat. The interior light ignited and now more than earlier, Nick could see how the torturous events of the last decade had taken a devastating toll upon his former friend. Taking three painful attempts to lower himself into the passenger seat, Castle almost felt obliged to help and had been greatly relieved when Challis had finally landed in place. The exertion taking a toll, Dan's breathing was laboured, chest heaving, the mangled limb sending shooting unbearable shocks from the knee, though both the thigh and calf muscles, the pain drawing invisible tears to his eyes, had his company not been Nick Castle, the urge to fight the emotion may have been lost.

This wasn't how their lives were supposed to go.

Dan Challis had allowed himself to become one of life's losers, buried under the hypocrisy of Hallowell's lies. A fall-guy for the Billy Scholes debacle, with people more than happy to maintain the momentum and crush him under its weight. For there was no-one to protect him, to defend him. His father was a flaccid, cowardly, excuse for a parent who cared more about his rudimentary little green-grocers store than his son. A scrawny, nervous, evasive man who avoided confrontation at all costs. This was almost certainly a contributing factor in the loss of his wife to another man years earlier, which as ever, he accepted with his usual aloof manner. The only real loser in the situation was Dan, finding himself without a mother from the age of three. The father/son relationship was fractured from then on with Victor Challis there only for financial support, rather than emotional. Soon, the boy was parenting himself, aware he was free to do whatever he pleased if he stayed out of trouble.

This allowed his first forays into alcohol abuse, bypassing its odious taste for the welcoming arms of oblivion. He progressed fast, his first hangover at six, at nine, his first hospitalisation due to a drunken fall from a first-floor window and alcohol poisoning at eleven which required his stomach to be pumped. Throughout all this time, Victor Challis did nothing to intervene. The boy had always had a talent for hiding the shameful facts from his friends, coincidentally, the first time he allowed his mask of normality to slip was on the night of Billy Scholes's demise.

Was it not for his group of friends, the alcohol dependency may have progressed even faster, for they had become the only support in his life? First there was Nick, his opposite in every way, popular, handsome, with a solid family life, everything Dan wished he could be. Not that there was jealousy, he knew where he stood in life's pecking order and accepted it; he was happy to have the association, a brief glimpse of popularity, being in Castle's presence made him cool by proxy. Plus, Nick's family had taken a shine to Challis, even if it was underlined with pity. Invites for meals made him see what a real family could be like. The granddad was funny, grandmother, sweet. Castle's father was distant, but nothing compared to his own. A happy vision of what could have been, had life been different.

Then there was Johnny Brackett. Their relationship was more comparable, probably because they were both slightly in awe of their popular friend. They would sleep at one another's houses at weekends or on holidays, and both were a year ahead of Nick in school. The friendship was the longest of all the boys too, which made what eventually happened even more painful. Doctor Harry Brackett, Johnny's father held a façade that was designed to be friendly but was clearly false. A devious, over-ambitious man with illusions of grandeur, he always looked down on Dan, aware *his son* could do better. An intimidating presence who enjoyed using his wealth and position to force his will on others.

Finally, there was Billy. Though Johnny was reluctant to accept the youngster into the group, Challis had no such reservation. He admired the boy's tenacity and trusted Nick's judgement.

Had Challis been bestowed with the same genetic make-up of the Castle family, perhaps his life may have been more tolerable, the world saw beautiful people with different eyes. His childhood appearance, though hardly enviable, had deteriorated rapidly. His hair was long though not fashionably designed, thick and mattered with memories of a homemade cut gone drastically wrong, though which had probably seemed a good idea in a drunken state. The roots showed the early onset of grey, inevitable with his increased youthful stress levels. Across the scalp, the thickness gave way to a thinning patch and his hairline was receding at an alarming rate, a trait of the Challis family tree. The skin across his face was ashen white bar the cheeks which were flushed red, a sign of raised blood pressure and his lips were cracked and dry, the alcohol causing severe dehydration. Scarring from serious teenage acne had left his complexion irrevocably damaged and several broken noses from drunken fights had distorted the appendage forever. Poor genes had created a ski-jump shaped mountain in the centre of his face which commanded attention, above his other facial abnormalities. It's said that the eyes are a gateway to one's soul. If that were true, Challis's soul must be black and broken. Bloodshot and raw with deep entrenched circles below, it screamed of a man on the edge. One who would welcome the sweet release of death rather than flee, a man with nothing left.

Castle had watched as Dan struggled across the car park, his left leg dragging slightly behind, instantly realising why, a painful daily reminder of that night. He'd have commented but Nick wanted this conversation to be lighter and less accusatory, something told him Challis would be needed in the future.

Dan crouched into the Ford's passenger seat, stomach rested against his thighs, right hand propping up a laden head. His fingers in perpetual motion, rubbing back and forth across three days of stubble, his entire body in a constant agitated state. His eyes gazed out of the side window but saw nothing, the evening darkness giving the club car park an eerie feel. Surprisingly, it was he who broke the uncomfortable silence.

"You don't have a drink on you, have you, Nick?" Castle rested a hand on his old friend's shoulder, understanding very well, the hold addiction could have on a person.

"Danny, I think maybe, you've had enough mate." Challis didn't respond, the answer pretty much what he'd been expecting. "Christ, Dan, what the fuck happened to you?" Bemused, Challis finally allowed himself to make eye-contact.

"After everything that happened, you have the nerve to ask me that question." Castle felt his face flush, immediately aware that he'd said the wrong thing.

"I didn't mean it that way. It's just…you look like you're struggling." Challis laughed.

"Struggling. That's almost funny. I passed struggling years ago." Castle remembered his grandfather's silver whiskey flask was inside of the glove compartment of the car and hoped there was some residual liquid still inside. Opening the catch by Challis's knees, he reached inside and took the container, relieved when a splashing noise erupted from the interior.

"There's a little left, you're welcome to it if you like." Handing over the flask, Challis quickly pulled at the lid then gulped the remaining fluid. "Dan, keep drinking like that and you're going to die."

"Is that a promise?" Nick gently shook his head, legitimately concerned for his old friend's health. This conversation wasn't what he'd had in mind.

"How did things get so bad?" Challis reached for the doorhandle, ready to leave but Nick protested. "Wait, Danny please. I don't want to upset you; I just need to talk." Challis nostrils flared, eyes staring harshly, and with a deep intake of breath, allowed his frustrations to flow.

"You've some nerve. I've spent the last ten years cursing the day I ever met you. Johnny Brackett might have treated me like shit, but at least he was here. At least he didn't run away."

"You think that was my choice?"

"Well, wasn't it?"

Instead of disputing the point, Nick could see that his embittered neighbour needed to vent. He'd expected as much and was ready, if Dan wanted to take a shot at him, Castle had decided he'd take it without reply, feeling Challis deserved this retort.

"Let me tell you a story, Mr Fucking Perfect." Nicks continued flawless, effortless appearance added to Challis's grief. "It's Halloween night. Four friends, who obviously mustn't have had half a brain between them, decide to explore the creepiest place in town. Sorry, let me back-track, make that one silly bastard, for arguments sake we'll call him Bobby-big-balls, wants to prove that he's the bravest of them all, and three fucking sheep, who are too dumb to quarrel with Bobby-big-balls, follow along dutifully, without a bleat or a bar to be heard." Nick grimaced, keenly aware that every word so far had been true. "The fearless four enter said creepiest place in town. Sorry, again I must back-track, one fearless warrior, three scared-shitless sheep, enter the creepiest place in town. With Bobby-big-balls leading the way, at first, it's not too bad; oh, it's dark, cold, stinks of piss, but at least it's quiet. That's until HALLOWELL'S VERSION OF THE GRIM REAPER DECIDES TO MAKE AN APPEARANCE." Challis paused, aware that his raging, vociferate delivery was reaching dangerous levels of aggression, nervous that should this altercation turn physical, Castle had a reputation of being a tough son-of-a-bitch. "Now, I don't need to go into the gory details, but in the aftermath, one sheep is slaughtered, one sheep leaves almost crippled. The third, who had taken an active role in the evening's entertainment and had never challenged or complained to his fearless leader Bobby-big-balls, strangely appeared to have never actually been there. Peculiar, but the railway station had the notoriety of being haunted, maybe the image of Johnny Brackett, wandering around freely with the group all night, was a fucking ghost. And finally, we come to our intrepid, courageous leader, Bobby-big-balls. Well, he must have been a fucking magician because once it was over, the mother-fucker vanished." Once more, Nick was desperate not to interrupt, though part of Dan's tirade made no sense.

"I don't understand, what do you mean about Brackett?" Castle's confused expression told his irate neighbour that Nick was mystified about this aspect of events.

"You don't know?" A shake of the head was the only response needed. "This was the hardest part for me to take." Challis's tone now carried less accusation, quieter, more thoughtful. "I was in hospital for over three months." Dan eyes glassed over, tears quelled by shear willpower alone, the circumstance obviously still a painful memory. "The first operation I had went horribly wrong, the surgeon caught a nerve behind my kneecap, arsehole, it took three more operations just to get back to where I started, it's been fucked ever since. Anyway, I had a lot of time to think, going over and over and over, in my mind what happened that night. Then I'd fall asleep, and the nightmares would come, it was a never-ending circle of shit. I was desperate for someone to talk too.

"It's amazing just how slowly time goes when you're trapped. They took me to the children's ward, over at St Mara memorial. The only time I could leave my bed was in a wheelchair. It wasn't bad when the nurses had to help me take a piss, but other than that, it sucked. Kids would come, kids would go, I stayed. They brought a boy in, about seven years old, been hit by a car. They worked on him for four days, back on forth to theatre, operations on this and that, in the end, it made no difference, poor little fucker still died. That was about as interesting as it got. My mind was going numb, I'd counted the tiles on the ceiling, the flowers on the curtains, anything to stop me thinking about what had happened at the railway station. As time went on, I was sure that you and Johnny had suffered the same Fate as Billy. If I asked dad, he'd change the subject, if I asked for coins to use the pay phone, he'd say he never brought money. It was like I was being cut off from the outside world, it made no sense. Add together with the fact that my leg was killing me, no matter what painkiller they doped me up with. Plus, and remember I was only eleven, I was going through booze withdrawal. By then, I was used to drinking every day, suddenly I'm trapped and there's not a drink in sight, I was going through Hell." Dan took a breath, suddenly energised by the chance to vent, for someone to listen. After a steady pause, he continued.

"Finally, after more than three months, they say I can go home. I was so excited; it was like being paroled from prison. Then, the night before I'm due to be released, my father arrives unexpectedly. Suddenly, all my hysterical buoyancy…turned to shit."

"What happened?" Nick was legitimately confused, he'd listened intently to Challis's sorry tale and had begun to believe that the devastation to the knee was the reason his former friend had become so embittered; as more details emerged, his point of view was gradually changing.

"It's funny you should ask. My dad's a piece of crap and I only saw him twice a week, so when he called unannounced, I knew there was a problem. At first, I thought the doctors had changed my release, that they'd found another problem with my knee. Soon, I was wishing they had kept me in." Challis paused, composure was needed, this was the big reveal. "It seems that, the day after our Halloween adventures, my wonderful father had been visited by Harry Brackett."

"Dr Brackett? Johnny's dad? What did he want?" Castle was legitimately confused now.

"Well, I don't know if you remember, but there was a time when Brackett was buying up properties. Investments, all over Hallowell. There were three houses, couple of flats, he just let them out, usual stuff. The problem was, he bought two of the shops on Main Street, one became a hairdresser, and the other was the lease to my dad's green grocers. My father had the chance to buy the lease, but the daft bastard missed out, so for the last three years, he was dad's landlord. Now, it really hadn't made much difference, the rates were practically the same, the only change was, each tenancy was only for a six-month period, just in case someone came along and offered a fortune for the shop, Brackett would have an out. Still, dad thought nothing of it, signed the extension twice a year, no problem, sometimes it would expire, it made no difference, one of them would remember and sort it. So long as dad paid the rent, everything was fine."

Nick suddenly had a sickly feeling; this story wasn't about to have a happy ending. Silence was his friend, if he had to speak, his mind was blank, the words would have stuck in his throat. He wanted to ask, though knew he'd receive an explanation without his enquiry, that was better.

"So, it's the day after Halloween, the morning after what happened, that fucker wasn't waiting. Dad opened the shop, even though I was in hospital, having surgery, the twat was still more interested in his shop. The first person to over the threshold was the good doctor, and he meant business. It was perfect timing, the contract had just expired, and he happily brought a new one."

"Why do I feel there's a but coming," Castle hadn't spoken for a while and thought the comment may make Dan realise he had his full attention. Challis returned with an ironic grin, the but was coming.

"Oh, there's a but…" Reaching into his inside pocket, the troubled young man returned with a pack of hand rolled cigarettes. Offering Nick one gave Castle hope, it was hard to read where his former friend's story would end, and where his personal blame would lay, it was obvious their history intertwined uncomfortably. "The contract he offered was amazing. It would be open-ended in favour of Mr Challis, meaning Brackett wouldn't have the power to terminate the contract, but Victor could walk away at any time without notice. There would be no more future worries, the shop would be his for ever. Next was the rent. It was 30% less than dad had ever paid, with a promise never to be raised. Inflation didn't matter this was also a price forever. Financially, the change would be massive. There was a promise to replace the cracked windowpane in the front door and bring a locksmith to replace the slack handle on the back door. Any other repairs dad reported would be fixed immediately. It would be the perfect contract, everything he'd ever need."

"So, what's the catch?" Nick was almost certain what the answer would be but needed confirmation. Challis's tone had quietened, his earlier anger slowly turning to self-pity. If anyone had the right to wallow, it was him.

"The catch, yeh, it came with a strange request. According to the doctor, the Brackett name carried respect, self-righteous motherfucker. He only had one son and soon, it would be his burden to carry the name with pride. That would be damaged, should the residents discover that Johnny had been there, inside the railway station, the one place everyone knew was off limits, when a small boy was murdered. Everyone knew the risks, the whole village was going to be pissed, and they'd want someone to blame. The Castle family had gone, vanished, never to be seen again. Obviously, Billy was dead, so he wasn't going to have fingers pointed, that just left Johnny…and me. Brackett's offer was simple. The shop, fixed up, cheap rent, no danger of eviction, dad's for as long as he wanted it. All he had to do was…keep me quiet."

"Jesus?" Though Nick had suspected as much, the confirmation still burned.

"So, that's what dad hit me with." His gaze drifted towards the passenger window, a rouge tear welled in the corner of his left eye, he had no wish for his former friend to see him cry. It burst forward, gently drifting down his reddened cheek; he'd hoped that if he ever the chance got to talk about this nightmare, it may be therapeutic, saying the words out loud rather than echoing around his mind may release some of the pent-up frustration. That hope was mistaken, this whole thing was a mistake, he was feeling worse, his heart raced vomit threatened to erupt from the deepest realms of his stomach, a stress-based migraine clenched the temples of his forehead in an unbreakable, constrictive crush. Castle visibly noticed the change, trying not to panic but this looked serious.

"You look like shit Danny; I'm taking you to the doctors." Challis managed to laugh between the endless waves of debilitating discomfort.

"The doctor. Are you pulling the piss? The fucking doctor is the same man I'm talking about now, the piece of shit, I'd rather die than see that cunt." Castle, still trying not to panic, slowly started to panic.

"Well, we have to do something. I can't leave you like this." Nick was now unconsciously sweating too, being a doctor had never been on the wish list.

"Get me home, my medicine is there, I'll be okay when I get my medicine." Challis looked certain, even if Castle wasn't. What choice did he have? Forcing the key into the ignition, the engine fired first time.

"Hold on Danny, we'll be there soon." Pushing his foot down hard on the accelerator, the Ford lurched forward, almost stalling before Nick rescued the miscue. Its light beam shone brightly as the car moved off, Nick's eyes firmly on the road ahead; had his sight veered slightly, a stalker watching from a safe distance may have been visible.

Outside the car, across the road in the side alley beside the workingmen's club, the paltry figure of Fred Gibson looked on, cigarette smouldering in his left hand, remnants of his last whisky in the other. Tossing back the last few drops, he placed the glass quietly on the floor at his feet, eager not to be noticed. Pursing the cigarette between his lips, he breathed in a lungful of smoke before releasing it through his nose, hiding the lit tip behind his free hand. He'd watched as the pair had taken their seats but without audio, the undertaker was unable to tell the nature of the former friends meeting, leaving a troubling concern. As the pair sped away in Castle's Ford, he realised his fact-finding mission was futile and began the ponderous walk home, he had serious concerns.

Robert Henderson was on the front doorstep of the small bed and breakfast his family had owned for three generation. Holding a cup of hot chocolate to keep out the autumn chill he'd decided to finish off his cigarette and then call it a night. The earlier gentle breeze was gaining in strength, Hallowell was prone to changeable weather, and he worried about his television antennae, perched high on the chimney stack. It had been working lose for some time and it was a job he hadn't gotten around to yet.

He was more worried about the new resident that hadn't arrived. She'd been due to check in hours ago and hadn't telephoned to cancel. She was booked in for a week and it was custom he could scarcely afford to lose. In the distance, he could see the waddling figure of Fred Gibson. Regular as clockwork, staggering home from the club, half pissed. Henderson frowned, if he had half the money, Gibson spent swilling that poison down his neck every night, he wouldn't need to worry so much about lax customers.

"Hello there Mr Gibson. Had a nice evening." Robert always spoke with a pleasant respectful tone even if the person he was referring too got on his nerves, and Gibson was one of those people, creepy bastard.

"Nice enough, I suppose." His slur was slightly more pronounced than usual, a definite sign that he'd had one above his limit. "What are you doing out here this time of night? Thought that pretty little wife of yours would have you tucked up in bed by now?" Robert wasn't the only one who found Gibson creepy, his wife, Irene, avoided the fat slug whenever possible after, when at an evening function two years previously, he'd spent the entire time staring in her direction and making underhand lurid comments about her breasts. The 'pretty little wife', comment brought back the memory, but Henderson fought the urge to spit in the pervert's face. Instead, he decided knowledge was power.

"No, I'm late tonight, I've been waiting for a new resident arriving, but you'll know all about that I assume?" The smug grin across the B-B proprietor's face troubled the drunken man as he prided himself on knowing everything that happened in the village…first.

"What are you going on about, new resident? How am I supposed to know who you have staying? Normally you're empty this time of year." A large belch erupted from his stomach, momentarily seeming it may progress to more, but a flabby hand over his mouth stopped a more embarrassing episode.

"You okay there Fred, not going to be sick, are you?" Henderson was enjoying this now. Not so high and mighty now, fat fuck.

"I'm fine, I'm fine. Come on, who's your new resident then?" The more Gibson tried to stand in one position, the more he swayed. Henderson prayed he'd fall on his fat face.

"You mean you don't know? I thought it would be the talk of the village now." This was fun, the undertaker's eyes were beginning to water, Christ, it looked like he was about to cry. Finally, an idea dawned on him.

"I get it. You got that Castle boy staying here. I just seen him in the club, gave him what for, that's for sure. He knows not to mess with me. What's wrong, even his own grandmother does not want him in the house?" A self-satisfied giggle followed, proud that he'd solved the mystery without help. Without waiting for a reply, he began to stagger past only to be stopped in his tracks.

"No, not Nick. I heard he was back but he's not staying here. No, it's another returning Hallowell original that I've got booked in, if she ever arrives." Gibson twisted his neck, back to face the smiling landlord.

"She?" The mortician just wanted his bed now, but curiosity wouldn't allow him to leave without the information.

"Yes. Can you remember the young girl, Martin Graham's daughter, Jenifer? She's the one booked in. Walter Williams, the real estate agent made the booking. She's coming back to put the old Graham lands up for sale."

Gibson's bottom jaw dropped, eyes fixed, staring back in disbelief. His whole body shuddered, and he rocked, barely capable of maintaining his footing. This cannot be. Why wasn't I told. My God, this is a disaster. When he'd managed to regain his composure, he turned and began a fast walk home, an alcoholic top-up was necessary.

"Goodnight there, Mr Gibson." Henderson laughed and went back inside.

This had been a long day. Her journey, originating in her adoptive town of Paisley, just south of Glasgow, to her village of birth, Hallowell, had been due to take only a little over two hours. After departing around lunchtime, Jenifer Graham expected to arrive in the village by mid-afternoon. More than enough time to check in to the bed and breakfast, unpack her meagre luggage and re-acquaint herself before dark. That was the plan.

Only a few miles down the A74 motorway, a five-car pile-up had closed the road for more than two hours. When traffic finally began to move once more, Jenifer's Mini-metro had driven across debris from the accident which punctured her two passenger side tyres. After an hour wait for a tow-truck, and a further ninety minutes delay while the repairs were done, it was now after nine and she still hadn't arrived. Night-time clouds had vanquished the last of the autumnal sun. To Jenifer, Hallowell was a distant and painful memory, she'd never returned since her initial departure. As her confidence in map reading skills left much to be desired, finding a signpost with the words Hallowell, 8 miles, caused a wave of overwhelming relief. The concern now was, would her room still be available, or did she have a cramped night on the tiny car's back seat as a conclusion to a tremendously stressful day.

Having sworn never to see Hallowell again, this hadn't been a decision taken lightly, it was born out of necessity, her financial life depended upon it. Having graduated grammar school, Jenifer had followed up her dream of being a hairdresser by studying at a technical college in Glasgow. Once her training had finished, she'd taken a position close to home, at a small salon, leaving her perfectly happy. That contentment was tragically destroyed when the proprietor, a lady named Susan Campbell had suffered a fatal heart attack, leaving the premises in danger of closure.

The late hairdresser's family had grown fond of the young collage graduate and felt uncomfortable seeing her redundant, jobs were hard to come by in the area. It was a business Susan had started from nothing and, with its regular, loyal clientele, it was still a viable opportunity from someone with drive. Therefore, Jenifer was offered the chance to purchase the premises as a going concern, the Campbell family wanted nothing for either the name, or the trade, just a fair price for the building. It was a shop-flat combination and though the young hairdresser still lived at her adoptive parental home, the urge to spread youthful wings and taste freedom was an instinct. A decision was necessary.

Originally, it was an option Jenifer believed to be fanciful and out of reach and therefore she'd gratefully declined. Being a girl in her early twenties, the project would need serious finances and though the family were being generous with the asking price, she'd still require a mortgage and deposit, something most banks wouldn't be willing to risk with a person without collateral or credit history. The situation was exasperating, it was a chance at something great, a business of her own. There was ready-made custom, the competition was virtual non-existent, she knew in all probability that with hard work, this could be her future. Still, it was a future out of reach, without that initial capital, it was foundations built on sand. That was until a familiar hero stepped in to help.

Learning of the situation, her adoptive mother Martha decided to selflessly re-mortgage her home, keenly confident that the girl's strong work ethic and sound business acumen would be enough to grow the salon into a thriving investment. Jenifer had protested, the pressure of such a financial endowment was terrifying. The demurral only made the older woman more adamant, trusting her daughter above all others, knowing that her efforts would be multiplied ten-fold if the family home was used as collateral. The emotional young woman finally accepted the gracious vote of confidence and the sale happened, now, Jenifer Graham morphed from hairstylist to entrepreneur.

Things began well, the business was turning a decent, if not strong profit, but enough to pay the bills. The clientele was perennially older ladies and though they were loyal, it was hard to build the future around a senior generation. Still, things looked promising and if she could tempt younger patronage, the chances of increasing turn-over were viable. Jenifer's work ethic was phenomenal, her obligation to a six-day working week ensured that a lack of effort would never be an excuse for a business failure. There were no employees, bar for a teenager who only worked Saturdays as a shampoo girl, so wages weren't an issue either. In fact, any situation which could be controlled, was. Unfortunately, Jenifer Graham suddenly realised that control was only an illusion. From nowhere, two events threatened to derail her business, attacking from an angle which could scarcely be believed, and which desperate measures would be required for her future to survive.

George Mawson was a neighbour in more ways than one. His gent's barbers ran almost parallel to Jenifer's salon, a straight 'proppa' man, a former army sergeant who had brought that alignment and structure to civilian life, an old-style short back and side's man who cut one way, those who wanted fancy, went elsewhere. The old man had created a niche for himself in the village and had stood in service for over thirty years. A massive heart attack later and George was gone.

The barbershop had remained closed for three months, some of the local boys had even ventured across to Jenifer, daring for an occasional perm, perhaps highlights, Miss Graham was adding style to Paisley. She could feel a definite rise in trade, so much so, that she considered adding staff. That was until the barbershop was closed no more.

BLADES. A huge salon chain with branches in every major city in Scotland. Four full-time stylists, introductory offers, senior Tuesdays where all the old girls were half price. "Fancy your hair done at home? Our girls will be there in a flash." Paisley was plastered with posters, advertisements, special rates. Jenifer Graham was in trouble.

Her fight back, she began aiming at the male clientele, the void left behind by the great George Mawson. Cutting snot-nosed kids' hair while they twisted and squirmed, it was Jenifer's nightmare. But she was a fighter. Her adoptive mother had gambled everything to make her dreams a reality, she'd be damned if some Johnny-come-lately was going to run her out of town. Her regulars stayed loyal, they didn't fall for the Tuesday-specials, demeaning bastards, if this was a war of attrition, she was up for the battle, working fourteen-hour days, trying desperately to keep the dream alive. Terrifyingly, debts began to mount up, the younger generation to which she was aiming had taken the cool option, the expensive option, it wasn't as if the competition were particularly good stylists, some of the things leaving that salon were laughable, laughable if the situation wasn't so dire. She was losing sleep, the stress of the situation driving her crazy. Should she sell? Surely someone would have a use for the building, she'd already moved back into the family home with Martha so she could let the flat above; her little palace, her pride and joy, now habited by two drunken louts who play loud music all day and all night(shit music too, heavy, heavy metal, the meagre clients were getting pissed) the bastards were a month late on the rent, money she needed for the mortgage, Christ, she needed to toughen up, she was a Graham for fucks sake, oops, can't say that, I hate cursing. Customers were growing less and less, the situation was becoming critical, the sale board was ready to be erected, and then...

BANKRUPT. BLADES WAS BANKRUPT. The giant chain, who had run rough shot over small business's everywhere had expanded too quickly, borrowing too much, too fast, and suddenly, the banks called in their loans, only to find the company was overextended. Thirty-six shops across Scotland, scores of employees, BANKRUPT.

It was like new-year's day. All the customers who had defected returned in droves. And not only did they reappear, but the dissatisfied friends came too. Suddenly, she was booked solid, days, nights, weekends, appointments all jammed in, so-much, that she was turning away custom. The enemy was dead, but their wounded soldiers needed resurrection. Over and over, the former employees of Blades would ask for work, the brash, arrogant, presumptuousness of superiority was replaced with a sorrowful desperation. Jenifer took pity on one girl, a newly qualified stylist, straight out of school who'd only worked for the adversary at weekends. Paula Reed was a sixteen-years-old who was helpful, energetic, and most of all, respectful to her employer. Jenifer had won the war of attrition, she had her flat back from the louts, redecorated, refurnished, and returned. Oh, she loved her adoptive mother, but the freedom of her own flat was astonishing, the flexibility and liberty to live alone was intoxicating. After a hard day's work, her employee would leave, and she'd go upstairs, her plush comfortable armchair, placed perfectly before the flats main window, overlooking Paisley, a welcoming end to a wonderful day. She was living the dream; her debts which she'd accrued during the battle were repaid. The salon was flourishing, she was an employer now for f, no, no cursing. Jenifer finally felt grown up, life was good.

During the battle with Blades, one bill was neglected. So much so, that the building insurance on Jenifer's salon was cancelled. She'd seen the final notice but, at the time, she had bigger fish to fry. When the good times returned, the restoration of the building insurance was on a 'to-do' list. Surely its importance could wait, the salon's structure was sound, there was plenty of time.

Paula Reed. Paula f...king Reed. Yes, she was helpful, energetic, and respectful. Yes, she was pretty and attracted the passing teenage boy trade. And YES, she was forgetful, ditzy, and dangerous.

It had been a particularly gruelling thirteen-hour shift, Jenifer had left the premises exhausted, the strain on her lower back and thighs needed some Vodka-tension. Climbing the stairs to the flat above, her employee called her own farewell, she'd worked the entire shift too and was equally frazzled. Paula's last client of the day was Tina Harden. As she was known as the town bike (everyone's had a ride) her sir's name was regularly changed to Hard-on, as in, she like those hard-ons. It was bitchy chit-chat, mostly because Tina was glamorous enough to take anyone's boyfriend, should she set her mind to it. The young woman was anything but promiscuous, it was a rumour started back in school days. Sometimes the stories were hurtful, other times she'd just laugh it off. Tina had been with her current boyfriend for over a year, her conscientious devotion ensuring her faithfulness. Her visit to the salon *was due* to the date, their first anniversary, tonight they were celebrating, with a meal and the cinema over in St Mara. Enjoying diversity with her appearance, she asked for her thick auburn hair be straightened, a style many of the young women were partaking in recently. Content with the result, Tina left the salon, Paula was happy that her shift was over.

Jenifer had fallen asleep in her favourite chair, the single glass of vodka-tonic untouched on the occasional table by her side. Opening her eyes with a startle, voices from out on the street were screaming, the sirens of a fire engine, blaring harshly in the distance, increasing volume by the minute as it approached. Someone was kicking the locked side door, the bolt standing firm. She was suddenly aware of the smoke, just a small splutter, more out of expectation than necessity, it hadn't taken hold here yet. Bursting into action, she leapt from the armchair, running bare foot for the exit. Opening the door into the passageway, a sudden barrage of deadly fumes bombarded her senses. This time, the cough was severe, navigating a passageway into her lungs, the exhaling croup releasing less than was taken. Her eyes stung, both hands trying to cover her face. There was one exit and it appeared blocked, she slammed the door closed, desperate to keep out the killer smoke, the room was filling, not as astringent as the passageway...yet...but the relentless journey meant that the lounge would soon be as caustic too. It wasn't in her nature to panic but her home and business was burning, her life was in danger, rescue was her only chance. Returning to the main window, a crowd had gathered outside. Concerned, useless faces, watching, not helping. Fighting with the catch, finally the lock opened, the huge window swinging from the centre, wide enough to leapt clear should that become the only option. the height was scary, would any of the watching crowd catch her in mid-flight? Probably not.

The fire engine sirens were increasing in volume and suddenly the huge red appliance roared into view. Hallowell was considered too small to require a fire-station, so any emergencies came from its big-brother, St Mara. In winter, whenever Hallowell hill became blocked by the huge snow drifts that regularly attack, the message was clear, don't set your house on fire, no one's coming to help. Jenifer was now rested high on the windowsill, trying to avoid the raising smoke, gasping for fresh air whenever possible. Downstairs, the glass had yet to shatter but its hypnotic twirling dance was somewhat hidden, soot charring the clear shield, no one brave enough to get too close. The fire engine was now stopped just feet before the front door, men leapt from the growling giant, busily working their roles, the chief barking orders, they were a well drilled team. The lead man immediately noticed Jenifer, precariously perched half out from the high first floor window.

"Don't worry miss, we'll have you down in no time." His voice was tender and caring, even with the raised level of volume. Jenifer only returned a smile; he was too busy for conversation. Now that rescue seemed inevitable, her thoughts turned to the damage. Only the night before, she'd remembered about the lapsed insurance, intending to reinstate it when she'd had time to visit the bank. If only she'd done it yesterday, or at lunchtime or...

"Jimmy. We'll need to smash in the front door, bring the big red key." The big red key was a large weight of iron with handles, so the men could swing it hard, locks and hinges wouldn't stand a chance. The young hairdresser cringed, for every item damaged, would be another item that to fix. Luckily, she felt a bulge in her jeans pocket, it was the keys, would the chief be willing to use the easy option.

"Excuse me." Jenifer waved her arms furiously, she needed attention now. "Hello. Excuse me please." Someone had forgotten to switch off the appliance sirens so grabbing a fireman's attention was potluck. "HELLO." Finally, the chief noticed her cries.

"Yes miss, I haven't forgotten you, you'll be down in a jiffy." He started to turn but the young woman's shriek returned his attention.

"NO, LISTEN, I HAVE THE KEYS, YOU DON'T NEED TO SMASH IN MY DOOR." Jenifer was twirling the shiny bunch around the first finger of her left hand. The chief now seemed to have the point. Cupping his hands, she gently threw them, the fireman grimacing as the heavy set struck his palms. "It's the one with red tape around the end, you might need to shoulder bump it, it can be stiff."

The aftermath was devastating. The flames had spread from the visible salon, into the downstairs kitchen. All the walls were covered, thick black soot mixed with filthy streaks where the fireman's jets of water had mixed. All electrical equipment was destroyed, the fire-investigation team soon discovering that it was the forgotten hair-straighteners which had caused the blaze. Paula, the young apprentice, was horrified to discover her mistake. Jenifer comforted her as she wept uncontrollably, even though, deep inside, she would have rather strangled her. The furniture was destroyed, the carpets squelched underfoot, the entire place was now useless. Her dream seemed over.

Jenifer Graham suddenly had one option only.

As the sole heir to the Graham family, she was bequeathed the deeds to all property and lands inside Hallowell. As the only living descendant (bar Frank) this was her birth-right. A solicitor had contacted Martha, days after fire had destroyed the mansion. It seemed that, as per Martin's will, his children would be sole beneficiaries of all he had. The money was gone, after the colliery tragedy and the economic downturn in mining in general, Graham had been using his savings to keep the family afloat. At his death, Martin Graham was debt free, but his only remaining assets were the defunct Hallowell colliery, the charred remains of the Graham mansion, and a closed down railway station. The mansion was well beyond repair and neither business assets (station, colliery) were sellable as going concerns. But there was one beneficial credit too which she could use. Land was scarce in the area, but the fashionable trend for successful businesspeople was a second home in a quaint village, somewhere away from the hustle and bustle of the city. The land available to planners in the south-west corner of Hallowell could be a gold-mine. The current government was desperate for developers to create new homes, planning permission had never been easier. All it would take is foresight, guts, and a good demolition team.

Originally, Jenifer wouldn't hear of it. She was a mere child when leaving Hallowell but still, the memories ran deep. Her mother had been her world and the events leading to her demise had created scars. Martha had been a saviour and leaving the village had been the right thing to do, but it hadn't been able to eradicate the hurt of losing Iris and the idea of returning to Hallowell, even if it was only to sell the properties, seemed like defiling her memory. These things were her father's possessions, taken from his father's family, the Graham dynasty, which was now dead. Jenifer had never felt part of that lineage, the name the only continuation of in her mind. As for money, she'd always wanted to make her own way in the world, carve out a niche for herself without hand-outs. Even the money taken from Martha had been received under duress, the risk of her adoptive mother financing her business with the re-mortgage of their family home a frightening prospect. And had it not been for the potential of that home being repossessed, then the young woman may never have agreed. It had taken time for Martha to convince her that this was the right thing to do, and now a decision was made, Jenifer was all in, her trait of decisiveness something that had always served her well.

At night, the panoramic view from the top of Hallowell bank was quite beautiful, just a smattering of lighting illuminating prominent roads and the thoroughfare of main street. Jenifer smiled as memories returned, the brightness just enough as to make out the house Martha and Archie Knox had shared throughout their married life, mid-way along a small cull-de-sac called Melrose Drive. The property contained a small, private, back garden containing a large oak tree, in which the little Scotsman had created a basic rope swing hanging from an upper limb, just for her. She'd spend hours rocking back and forth, rope scratching between her knees, fingers grasping onto the coarse material, the old caretaker pushing her gently, giggling at her childish squeals while her mother and would be adoptive mother shared a chat and a cup of tea, seated on a home fashioned outdoor bench…bliss.

How things could have been different had her father not shown so much bias in favour of her brother. Even at that early age, Jenifer had realised where she stood in the order of things, her resentment eroding whatever love she may have previously felt for him. They'd been a home divided, female's one side of a huge chasm with the males, carrying explosives, demolishing bridges wherever possible.

She'd never seen the mansion since it had been destroyed by fire and wasn't certain what emotions it would produce. Thankfully, the darkened night sky hid any sign, now wasn't the time. Iris Graham had never truly felt the mansion was her home, more a huge museum for generations of Grahams past. Now there'd be no more generations to be burdened with the family name. When she had children, Jenifer was adamant that they would either bare her husband's tag or take the title of her adoptive family. One way or another, the Graham lineage would die.

The old railway station, the second of the two properties she hoped to sell, had never been part of her adolescence, unlike her wicked brother. She'd had no interest in the family business and Martin had never encouraged one, so Jenifer was as much a stranger to the derelict old building as anyone, it had been Frank's obsession, not hers. Now, it was just an opportunity to pay back Martha and rebuild her salon.

Originally, she'd been scheduled to meet the estate agent, Mr Williams, earlier that afternoon and now was relieved that the appointment had been delayed by 24 hours. Had it been possible to sell the god forsaken buildings without ever setting foot back in Hallowell, she'd have taken the option gladly. Instead, he'd claimed that it was essential that they meet in person before posting the listing for sale. There was something she didn't trust about Williams, though she couldn't put her finger on what it was. He'd been polite enough during their telephone conversation, even if a little rushed. It was the fact that he'd seemed, flustered, almost afraid of what she represented, a peculiar position for a man on commission. Perhaps, she was just being paranoid. Booking into the guest-house open-ended, there was hope that the business would be concluded sooner rather than later, Hallowell held no mystique for her, no longing to search for answers. Becoming rich wasn't even the aim even though the land was considerable, and the value had never been higher. No one would want either building for anything other than demolition and the cost of developing the land would be high, but not as high as the profits a good builder could expect. There was room to create many homes on the site, a good architect was worth his weight in gold. Still, as far as Jenifer was concerned, they could store nuclear waste there so long as she got as cheque and never had to visit this terrible place again. In her heart, she knew it couldn't go as smoothly as she hoped but, this was a start.

Slowly, her mini metro navigated its way down the steep slope of Hallowell bank, back to her own private Hell.

Nick Castle's borrowed Ford pulled in tightly by the kerbside. The road had three consecutive streetlights broken, one of which had a smashed out-casing, the debris scattered below on the floor beside a hand-sized rock, the obvious culprit to the damage. A grass verge, between the roadside and the parallel street was torn up, irresponsible drivers flaring up earth, just because they could. A burned-out Fiat was abandoned overly close to the houses, with charred fenceposts of the end property's back garden, the only surprise being that the entire border hadn't turned into an inferno. That same end-property's outer side wall was a victim of ugly, unnecessary graffiti, spray-paint, chalk, anything to mark-up the bricks was used, with uncomfortable profanity and racial slurs, looking like it had been scrawled by a pre-school five-year-old.

Even under the cover of darkness, it was obvious that the area was beyond deprived. Back in the day, these colliery cottages had been well kept, under Graham ownership, the homes were used as a perk to employees. As the owner's fortunes had deteriorated, the properties were sold off, one by one, usually to private developers who leased them at high rates. Now the tenants were perennially low-income families or single people living on benefits, those desperate, with nowhere else to go. Exactly Dan Challis's position.

Nick paused whilst his former friend exited the car, not wishing to hang around the area outside any longer than was necessary. A scream erupted from an open window of a central property. Castle's eyes darted in the direction, the look of concern across his face making Challis smile.

"Don't worry. Those fuckers are lunatics, they are probably pissed again. In fact, she's worse than her husband, hears voices." Castle shook his head, this place had down-hill, fast.

"Christ Dan, what the hell happened here, this used to be a nice area?" Challis returned an ironic chuckle, the reason for the place's demise connected to their own troubles.

"If Martin Graham had sold to decent people instead of the dick-brains who own them now, things would probably have stayed okay. The fuckers who bought them couldn't give a shit, so long as they get their rent." Not waiting for a response, Challis turned, heading towards his back door. When Castle saw that he was aiming for the graffiti covered scorched fence end-house, his face grimaced, wondering how bad the inside must be, and, just how far his former friend had fallen.

The garden gate was open, hanging on one hinge. As Challis fumbled with his keys, Nick took a brief inspection of the garden. There was a wooden shed in the left-hand side corner away from the house. The door was missing, the felt from the roof had been torn away by vandalising children and its small window was broken. Around the base were more scorch-marks, seeming that those same young vandals had attempted to burn the outhouse down. Concrete flagstones had been improperly fitted across the yard, weeds growing between the joints, and centrally, one had been removed, eviscerated grass beneath sporadically trying to make a comeback. By the border wall, a fallen washing line lay lifelessly in the dirt. Finally, there was a single plant-pot, full to the brim with earth, a single yellow rose flourishing inside. Castle was surprised that something so elegant could grow between all this chaos.

Once inside, the foulest of smells immediately caught Nick's attention. An amalgamation of greasy food and stale booze, unwashed clothes and body odour, a stench which obviously, Challis must now have become immune too. Taking in the scene, Nick was reminded of his own dump back in Bishopsgate, empty beer cans and fast-food takeaway boxes, sparse furniture, and outdated décor. Did his flat stink too? Julia had never complained, perhaps she was too embarrassed? Having similar battles with addiction and a wasted adolescence, Castle thanked God for his superior family genes, aware that, should he finally defeat his psychological issues, he'd still have a shot at a good life. For Challis, it seemed there'd be no happy ending looming across the horizon.

Passing through the kitchen, Dan stopped at a wall cabinet and hurriedly opened the door. To Castle, to appear obvious that this was meant for food storage, though it could hardly be called well stocked, just a few condiments and a can of tomato soup between Dan and starvation. A half-eaten ham sandwich lay on the bottom shelf, the white and green mould spores covering the exterior indicating that this was one of the ingredients adding to the vile overpowering smell. Challis's fingers fumbled across the top shelf, grabbing at thin air, desperate for the prise which had so far eluded him. As his hand touch glass, a relieved expression bathed his face. Carefully prying the bottle forward, Nick noticed a red label, vodka printed across its centre. Trying to hide his disapproving glance, Castle could see that the seal wasn't opened, the high alcohol percentage and the full pint volume ensuring that Challis would soon be delving into sweet oblivion once more.

Inside the lounge area, there was more clutter, though if Challis was embarrassed by the state, he hid it well. Kicking off his shoes, Dan flopped into a reasonably well-maintained armchair, the brown leather material free from tears and the reclining mechanism still in working order. Challis pointed toward its not-so-pleasant neighbour, Nick realising that this was his invitation to sit. Slowly, he lowered himself, careful to avoid an awkward spring which had foraged its way to the surface.

"Okay genius, what's your story?" Challis's words were deliberate and concise, the vodka had taken an immediate effect, soothing his agitated nerves, and making him more than a little curious as to how Castle's story compared to his own.

"What? What do you mean?" Nick's composure was suddenly lost, afraid to reveal his tale of woe as he knew that no matter how well it was delivered, it would fade in comparison to Dan's. Sensing the advantage, Challis began to relax.

"Listen, Nick, I may be thick, but I'm not stupid. As much as I'd like to believe in my animal magnetism, I'm certain that's not why you're here. And as impressive as my humble abode is, your gran's is nicer. Since you turned down my offer to share this fabulous vodka, there's only one option remaining, you need to vent your story. I watched you in the car, while I poured my heart out, you never flinched. And what's more, you reserved an opinion which meant one of two things, either you already knew my history, so it didn't come as a shock, or you think you had it worse. So I'll ask again. What's your story?"

Nick rose to his feet, happy to have an excuse to get out of that God-awful armchair. Challis's stare was burrowing deep, and for the first time, the alpha felt intimidated. Not wishing to make eye contact, his stare dropped to the ugly worn carpet to which his feet were sticking too. Passing across the room, he held out his right hand.

"That offer of a drink still there?" Reluctantly, Dan passed the bottle, Nick hesitating before accepting.

"You too?" Challis had a knowing expression, strangely content that knowledge was power.

"How do you mean?" Castle was beginning to see that his former friend was more perceptive than he'd originally seemed.

"The booze. You hesitated before accepting, like you wanted a shot, but didn't too. When you've been a drunk for as long as I have, you learn the signs. It's nice to know I'm not the only one." A returned half-smile was all the reply necessary. "So nick, are you going to spill the beans, or perhaps you have nothing to spill?" Castle's half-smile turned to a nervous laugh, knowing that, whether he wished to or not, the tale would now have to be told. There'd be obvious comparisons and after Dan's horror story, his own seemed less harrowing. Returning to the uncomfortable armchair, he lowered himself back into place, this was going to take a while.

"Okay listen, before I start, let me just say, what happened to you was unreal, and unfair. No, more than that, it was fucked-up. Make no mistake about it, if I could go back and change things, I'd do it in a heartbeat. But I can't, you didn't deserve it, Billy didn't deserve it, that's my cross to bear. I suppose I should start at the beginning. It's been over ten years and I can remember things as if it happened yesterday. God knows I've tried to forget but I can't, it's burning into my mind." Closing his eyes, it was obvious that Castle was already struggling. "You remember, when I got out, I ran. But please believe me, it wasn't out of cowardice, I just knew that I had to get to my granddad and bring back help, otherwise none of us was getting out alive. I knew you were hurt, and I wouldn't be able to carry you alone. In the confusion, I lost track of Johnny, so I knew I had to get reinforcements. So yes, I ran. I ran as fast as my legs would carry me, so much so that when I got to granddad, I could barely speak. When he realised what had happened, he was out like a shot."

"Yes, it was old that pulled me out." Challis had no wish to interrupt but felt he owed the old man his gratitude.

"That was granddad, if it had been his choice, I'm sure he'd have gone after that bastard again. He'd have gone back, and back, and back, until one of them was dead." Dan's expression changed, as though he knew something but wasn't saying. "When granddad came for you, I wanted to come back with him, show him where you were. I was overruled and locked in my bedroom to make sure I couldn't get out. I even tried climbing out of the window, but the fucker was locked. I tried everything, kicking the door, punching it, I screamed until I was horse, and still I was ignored. Finally, the door opened, but instead of my family, your favourite guy, Dr Harry Brackett was waiting."

"Brackett?" Challis's own memory of the crooked physician returned and there was momentary silence. Eventually, Nick continued.

"By now, I was frantic. Like I just said, I was certain Billy was dead and I knew you were hurt. But I had no idea whether granddad got to you in time, or if that monster reached you first. And I still had no clue about Johnny. For all I knew, my three best friends could all have been killed and no one was telling me anything. So I tried bursting past him, so I could get out of the house, but Dr fuck-head pinned me down on the floor. I remember my grandma trying to calm me down but by now, I'd just lost it. That's when Brackett pulled out this needle and stuck me with it. Supposedly, it was just to make me chill out, that's the last thing I remember. When I woke up, it was three days later."

"What?" Challis could barely believe his ears, though something told him Nick wasn't lying. "How many drugs did he give you?"

"Good question. Perhaps my folks were giving me boosters, I really don't know. What I do know, is when I eventually woke up, everything had changed."

"How do you mean?"

"I was 100 miles away, in a new bedroom, a new house, a new town."

For the next fifteen minutes, Castle went into as much detail as he could remember. The supposed mental breakdown, the psychiatrists, the medication, the lies. How the relocation fucked with his head, how he'd learned to trust no one, not even his grandparents. He even mentioned the tragic tale of Julia Martin, knowing that total honesty was the only way that Challis would believe him. In turn, Dan's face flushed with embarrassment, at the extent of his rage toward his former friend. In his own mind, there could have been nothing more harrowing than his own history, his physical pain and mental torture coupled with extreme loneliness and desertion by those he cared for the most. But at least, he had the comforts of home. When things got bad, he could lock the front door, leaving the troubles exiled outside. He'd had freedom to make his own choices without parental pressure and the peace of mind to know he was blameless for the situation. Nick didn't even have that. Castle had suffered just as much, maybe more, with the added token of guilt. The realisation that a friend's death had occurred mainly due to his actions. Challis wondered if it was possible to overcome something of that magnitude and was thankful it was his burden to bear.

This had been a strange night, both young men feeling very differently from when the evening begun. And strange as it sounded, their shared experiences meant that maybe, their former friendship could be rekindled, it was something both were badly in need of.

Walter Williams sat in a large, high backed leather chesterfield chair, his spacious study in darkness, illuminated only by a huge open fire which commanded attention in the centre of the room. A newly placed log crackled under the intense heat and a knot in the wood shattered, echoing out and breaking the silence. His wife had retired to her bed early, whenever her husband was in this kind of mood, giving a wide berth essential. But this had been different, he'd been in a world of his own for three days, ever since that telephone call.

The ice floating inside the scotch and water he'd been holding for the last thirty minutes moved inside the tumbler as it melted. Williams moved his fixed stare from the dancing flames and watched, as he swirled the glasses contents, before draining the fiery liquid, his throat burning in protest. The lenses on his thin rimmed spectacles had misted and he slid them off the tip of his nose, wiping the condensation on the sleeve of his stripped pyjamas. The stress related headache refused to release its grip on his senses. Ever since he'd taken that damned phone call, how could things get so messed up?

His business was nice, simple. If someone wanted a property in Hallowell, he was your man. If you were leaving town, he'd find you a buyer, trading up, trading down, didn't matter, for real estate, Walter Williams was the go-to-guy. It was easy, take some photographs, advertising, as strenuous as it got was planting a for-sale sign in someone's garden. It was safe, commission based, put his two daughters through college and paid off his own mortgage seven years early. At 57, he was considering retirement, Hell, they had savings, he and Janice had always wanted to travel, stress was the last thing a guy who'd had heart bi-pass surgery eighteen months ago needed.

When Harvey Spector, a solicitor from Glasgow had called claiming to represent a former Hallowell resident, he'd been intrigued. When he discovered that resident was Jenifer Graham, his heart had begun to race. When the details of her request were revealed, he'd felt like vomiting. And he'd maintained that feeling ever since.

If he rejected the offer to handle the auction, someone else would take it. Someone from outside the village, who'd never heard of the Grahams, or Hallowell railway station or the God forsaken invasion. And yes, he still remembered the invasion, remembered it very well as he'd been a major player in the event. Fuck, he still had nightmares now, after all these years, finding those bodies, men he classed as friends, slaughtered like something in a butcher's shop. How many times had he questioned in his mind, the sequence of events that left the Village in this limbo? How many times had he visualised finding the bloodied remains of the child, what was his name, Cundy? Dean Cundy? Fifteen years old and torn apart. What if it all started happening again? Would people think of him as responsible?

Harry Brackett had been his first telephone call. The good doctor had ascended to the pinnacle as far as decisions for the village, and with his son now town constable, he was the obvious choice for advice.

It was almost midnight but still the doctor couldn't sleep. He'd tried watching television, but his mind continually drifted to the problem, Hallowell's problem, his problem. Earlier, he'd taken a walk to clear his thoughts. He'd seen Fred Gibson, waddling his way home from the workingmen's club, worse for drink, as usual. The undertaker had almost run in the doctor's direction, irate at not being informed of the events that threatened their secret. When Brackett had argued that he had intended to inform him the following morning, Gibson scoffed, certain that his position as advisor was no longer welcome. Brackett had planned a meeting for the next night, in the back room of the community centre and had invited many of those who had been present all those years earlier when the problem originated. Brackett also claimed to have telephoned Gibson's home and received no answer, that being the reason he hadn't been informed. Still agitated, Fred had stormed off, though strangely, not in the direction of his home. Still, the doctor didn't care whether the fat slob's feelings were hurt, he had bigger fish to fry.

Before arriving back home, Brackett had witnessed a new model Ford, passing through town. In the darkness, he hadn't seen the drivers face but something told him it was the Villages other returning resident. Nick Castle's arrival had caused him almost as much concern as the Jenifer Graham problem. From all accounts, the kid was a rash hot-head and if he discovered the truth about his grandfather, there was no telling what the idiot would do. With the Roberts boy's disappearance last week and that Daley moron yet to be charged with the murder, there was too many loose ends. Johnny would have to buck his ideas up if he wanted to keep the job of lawman in his village. Just get Tom Daley charged, if he hadn't done it, who cares?

He returned to a home in darkness. Ellie, his long-suffering wife had taken to her bed and after Johnny had moved to the flat above the police station, the old house seemed lonely. He poured a generous measure of brandy in a crystal tumbler and rested on his long, leather settee. Laying on an occasional table beside the telephone, his personal number directory book was still open, the earlier calls he'd made to his fellow conspirators still fresh in the mind. Informing Adam Scholes had been tough. The former solicitor had lost more than most, his only son perishing ten years earlier and his wife's subsequent suicide leaving one of Hallowell's brightest, a shell of his former self. Terry Hutchinson, landlord of the Wheatsheaf public house had taken the news with surprising acceptance and had offered to help spread the news to others involved. Bed and breakfast proprietor Robert Henderson already knew, and Brackett was more than a little irritated when the landlord had accepted her as a guest. As for the rest, word of mouth would ensure that the meeting was well attended. Almost every resident in the village had some tie to the invasion, and the secret that the town had kept together.

Brackett rested the back of his head against the arm of the settee and wished Bill Castle was still here. As the brandy took effect, his eyes began to droop.

The time was almost 2 am and a majority of Hallowell was sleeping. As Nick Castle had driven through town, back to his grandmother's home, a young woman had been banging on the locked door of the bed and breakfast. The security light above the hallway revealed just enough. Her appearance, it was uncanny, the long blond hair, tied tightly into a ponytail at the back, small in stature, petit figure, conservative dress sense, and beautiful, so beautiful, she looked so much like…he pulled the car over to the side of the road just as the door was answered. The proprietor didn't seem amused at the late hour and Nick was certain he could see her blush. Even her mannerisms, the image of Julia

Martin, his lost love. He knew it was impossible but the urge to run from the car and, just be certain, was almost overwhelming. When the door closed behind her, the option was gone.

The drive back to his grandmother's home was a blur. He knew it couldn't be her, all common sense told him that. Julia was gone, he'd attended the funeral. How many times had he visited the graveside and still, he couldn't get that vision from his mind? When he'd arrived home, Nick was surprised to see his grandmother still up.

"You needn't have stayed up gran, I have a key, remember?" The old woman looked different to when he'd left, strangely vulnerable, something he wasn't used to seeing. "Is everything okay?" Alice Castle smiled, touched at her grandson's concern.

"Yes, I'm fine, just couldn't sleep, that's all." Inside her bony hands sat a steaming cup of tea, used more to keep out the night-time chill than for refreshment. "Just having a nightcap. Would you like one?" The old lady began to rise from her hard, wooden chair, part of a set of four around the old-fashioned dining table in the kitchen. Beneath a plastic skullcap was a set of rollers, wound tightly around her hair, held in place with clips, ready to be removed the next morning to maintain her immaculate appearance. But tonight, with her blue flannelette night-dress and red chequered house coat, she looked every day of her seventy years. The wrinkles under her eyes seemed slightly more pronounced in the dull kitchen light and a recent weight-loss had made her skin lose and slack.

"No, I'm fine, guess I'm just tired. Something strange did happen though." Nick pulled out another of the dining chairs, its feet scratched on the tiles below. Lowering onto the solid seat he continued, "Shook me up a little." Alice was immediately concerned where this conversation could go.

"Strange? What do you mean? You haven't been near that place again, have you?" The colour had drained from her face, terrified what the response would be.

"No, no, nothing like that. I've had quite a nice evening. Saw some old friends. What was strange, I was coming home when I passed the bed and breakfast opposite the communal green. There was a girl, looked about my age. She must have been late arriving because she had to wake the owner up. He didn't look to happy." Nick giggled then continued. "Anyway, a couple of years ago, I was dating a girl, Julia was her name. The funny thing was, this girl tonight, she was the spitting image of Julia, same hair, same features, same dress-sense, everything. If I hadn't known better, I'd have sworn it was her."

"Was this Henderson's?"

"Yeh, Henderson's that's it."

"Well let me put your mind at rest, it wasn't, what was her name, Julia?" Puzzled, Nick quizzed further.

"How do you know?"

"Believe me, I know." Alice stopped without revealing any more details. "Now you must be shattered. Get yourself up to bed, we'll have plenty of time to catch up in the morning." The young man knew better than to argue with his grandmother so without needing more encouragement, he agreed.

"Night gran." Castle headed to the rooms doorway but looked back at the old lady. "Feels great to be home." Without waiting for a response, Nick was gone. Alice Castle breathed out in relief and took a sip of the tea.

After hearing her grandson's bedroom door close, the old lady retreated to the comfort of the living room. In the corner stood a plush, grey, velvet covered armchair, Bill's armchair. Alice lowered her tiny frame, its thick seated cushion still holding the mould of her late husband's ample frame. Pushing herself back, she stroked her face against the luxurious material, closing her eyes tight so to not allow tears to escape. It still held his unmistakable sent, God how she missed him.

Above the mantle, over the residue of a long dead fire, his picture, looking so handsome in his policeman's uniform encased with glass and a silver frame. That smile, shining teeth under the broadest grin, wide shoulders, and taught stomach. He was so good under pressure, all those years in the force giving him healthy discipline and continuous respect. Now she had all the decisions to make, important decisions.

When Brackett had telephoned earlier, she'd been sharp in her response. His smarmy tone and condescending wording. Claiming his call was simply a one of courteously, that her appearance at the coming meeting was optional and should she decide that, with the passing of her husband, she would be too emotional to attend, he'd obviously understand. As though their family wasn't as intertwined with the troubles as anyone could be. If Bill were still here, he'd be the one making the telephone calls and not Mr High and mighty Harry Brackett, he was only a doctor when all said and done. When Alice had snapped that, of course she would be attending, he'd forcefully insisted that she should come alone as only direct opinions were deemed important, and indirect way of saying that Nick was not welcome. He'd also insinuated that, in his opinion, her grandson should not be told the truth about her husband's passing. At that, she'd hung up on him, that Castle fortitude as evident as ever.

It did raise some interesting choices though. Was it fair to continue the charade with Nick? Bill's death: if her grandson knew the truth, she didn't even want to think about what would happen if he knew the truth. Natural causes, what a joke. It was the last lie, the last thing that needed to remain secret. Was it really a lie? Well…yes. But a lie that was told for the greater good. The young man had been through enough, had to endure so many changes in the previous few days, if he discovered that that monster had been responsible for the death of his grandfather, it could push him over the edge. It was terrifying to think about how he'd react, the family had already lost so much due to this nightmare, losing Nick too was almost too horrible to imagine. But and this was a big but, what if he discovered the truth by another means. Talking to Johnny Brackett, or worse, Johnny's horrid father, it would be easy for the authentic reason to become known. There were others that knew too, it was a small village, and in small villages, gossip was rife. Should Nick become aware of yet more lies, the trust which had been gained in the last few days would be eroded, possible forever. He was a man now and deserved to be treated as one. Bill would certainly not approve but his closeness to the boy had always clouded his judgement. Her husband had been the first to see that the Castle gene ran strong in Nick, the stubborn and headstrong decisiveness, but had also been keenly aware that too much had already been lost in the Graham affair, this was a fight they couldn't win. If the old fool had heeded his own words, he'd still have been here now.

It was hard, if she continued the lie, perhaps Nick would leave post funeral. If she could choose, she'd take that. But in her heart, she could see that the boy was home. If he left, what would he have to go back to? If it took a risk for him to re-evaluate his life, was it worth it? Maybe it was time to trust him to make the right choice, or at least the best one for him. It was so confusing.

Alice Castle drained the last of her tea and headed for the stairs. Before switching off the lounge's light, she took a last look towards her husband's photograph.

"Night Billy. Sleep well my love."

For Johnny Brackett, living in the shadow of a powerful father hadn't been easy. Law enforcement hadn't been his choice, rather one chosen for him. Something that was expected rather than desired. He'd always craved something more than village life, an escape from prying eyes and small-town gossip. But it was what it was, this was his life now, for better or worse. Being constable to a town like Hallowell was a thankless task. He was following a legend; Bill Castle had been in the role longer than most residents had been alive. Even after his retirement, most would go to him when there was trouble, rather than report it to the real officer. But what made it more frustrating, the interfering old bastard would respond instead of telling the morons to get lost. If he'd just stayed retired, he'd be alive today but no, he had to be the fucking hero, the stupid old... How could Johnny ever be expected to get the respect he deserved when he was constantly being undermined. Especially when most people thought that he was only given the job because of who his daddy was. Which brought it back to living in the shadow of a powerful father.

The truth was, Johnny Brackett was good at his job. He'd done all the training, six months hard tasking at the academy. Then another six months working the beat in Carpenter. He was sound in modern techniques, firm but fair with young tearaways, did additional education in his own time and wasn't afraid to go in hard when it was needed. Knowing Hallowell perfectly, he knew what was expected and where the line was drawn, he was a damn good police officer. But as ever, there was a glass ceiling. And that barrier was Hallowell railway station. If he could bring the monster to justice, he'd have all the respect and then some. But he was one man, what option did he have but maintain the status quo.

The Tom Daley situation was bad, very bad. True, he *was* the perfect patsy, hated by most and distrusted by the rest. If any child went missing, village justice would be knocking down his door first. He had previous and had been seen chasing the boy, there was forensic and witnesses, everything pointed in his direction. But in his heart, Johnny knew it was bullshit. The guy was simple, disabled. Just another average Joe who wanted a quiet life. Maybe he could have just snapped and nailed the kid, the Roberts family were scum and he'd complained about being pestered on numerous occasions, but it just didn't fit. Looking in Daley's eyes, the guy was terrified and wasn't bright enough to make up a story like that. Especially using Graham as cover, most people wouldn't even mention his name unless it was necessary. He had no history of violence and had spent all his time in the cells, crying like a baby.

But the locals wanted blood. Someone had to pay for a missing child, even if he was innocent. As though, they would feel better, have a clearer conscious, if someone was done for the crime, even if most probably knew who was responsible. It was the feeling of helplessness that came from having a killer on your doorstep and being powerless to remove him. Graham's legend had grown immeasurably over the years, and Johnny Brackett hated it. He knew the horror stories; his father had held nothing back. Of the invasion and its bloody ramifications, the death and destruction that the monster had caused and the fear that had grown, year on year.

But he was the law, he had an obligation to protect his residents. What use was convicting a nobody like Tom Daley when the real killer roamed free? Still, he was one man.

Having been restless all evening, Johnny had patrolled the streets. He'd driven down Colliery Lane, by Daley's cottage, only to find the kitchen window smashed, mob rule. Having called upon local handyman, Ian Gaskins, to repair the damage and being satisfied the property was secure, he'd moved on. After walking the backstreets of the colliery cottages, he felt obliged to check the woodland bordering the railway station. The hole in the fence had once more been torn apart, no matter how often it was repaired, it would always be re-vandalised. After considering recalling Gaskins to make it safe, he decided that the morning would be soon enough. Leaving this entry-point agitated Brackett, but it was after midnight, surely no one else was stupid enough to walk these lands at this hour.

Earlier, he'd driven past an angry looking Fred Gibson and wondered if his father had broken the news about Jenifer Graham's imminent return. Aware of just how pivotal the event could be, he was also strangely excited by the prospect. It would take something monumental to evoke a second invasion, and this could be it. How else would he ever get the support needed?

Brackett's worst fears were confirmed when, after visiting Hallowell workingmen's club earlier in the evening, he'd noticed the returning Nick Castle. Worse still, he'd left with Dan Challis, that couldn't be good. It was obvious what their conversation would centre upon, and the officer didn't need, it is raking up the past. Alone, Challis was no threat to Johnny's position, but with Castle for company, that was different. His secret had been hidden for over a decade, Hallowell knew nothing of his cowardice, how he'd deserted his friends to save himself. The doctor had even ensured that his son's participation on that fateful night did not become public knowledge. Challis had been afraid to speak up and even if he had found the balls, who'd have believed him? But with Castle

299

back on the scene, things could get decidedly sticky. That respect he so desperately craved would be lost forever if the truth was known. This was seriously dangerous. He'd followed the Ford to Challis's shithole on colliery lane but after thirty minutes, he got sick of waiting.

Finally, the constable had driven past his father's house, the light still shining in the lounge. He'd considered calling, but decided against it, their earlier conversation still leaving a bitter taste in his mouth. It was after 2am when Brackett finally took to his bed, aware the coming day would be vital to Hallowell's future, to all their futures.

Fred Gibson arrived home, his face red and sweaty, the front of his grey slacks damp where he'd had trouble holding his bladder. A translucent trail of saliva hung from the corner of his mouth after improperly wiping the residue of vomit from his face after an eruption behind the bins of Evergreen old folk's home. A faint whimper had been emanating from deep inside after discovering the frightening truth about Jenifer Graham's return. That whimper became a moan that grew to a cry and by the time he'd burst through the doors to his spacious home, he was openly weeping, a low guttural howl like a wounded animal.

Slamming the door behind him, giving no consideration to the sleeping neighbours, he scurried through to the hallway before stumbling into the kitchen. As the refrigerator door slammed across the neighbouring workbench, the light inside momentarily made the mortician squint. Making a grab with his podgy hands, the cap was hurriedly torn from a half-full bottle of gin, and he drank as though it contained the antidote to a poison. A choking splutter escaped from his throat and for a second, it seemed that the contents of his stomach would once more be making a return appearance. When he'd regained some composure, he took another sip then slid the bottle onto the workbench, only luck keeping the clear glass container upright. Forcing open a stiff drawer, just right of the cooker, Gibson began to search frantically for a set of keys, the only set to the door on the far side of the room. Wastepaper and debris were thrown in all directions as location of the prize remained hidden. He stopped and tried to clear his mind.

"Where are they, come on Gibb, think!" Closing his eyes, he tried to remember; he'd had them before going to the club that much was certain, the compulsive side to his nature would never allow him to leave the house before ensuring all doors were locked. He could picture checking the funeral parlour, the door giving sufficient resistance to know it was locked. Trying the showroom door, which contained several coffins to which clients could choose from, was more habit than need. The only time the room was ever opened was arranging funerals or, sometimes, if the mood took him, he might sleep in one of the caskets when his insomnia occurred. It was the key to the last of the three doors he craved. He'd spent most of the afternoon down there, so he knew, he had to have had those keys.

"THINK, YOU ARE FUCKING IDIOT." Gibson could feel his blood pressure rising. He'd take a pill but finding the keys was more important. The drawer's contents were now strewn across the kitchen floor but there was still no sign. His head hurt and he could feel his temples pulsing. Resting a hand on the workbench for support, he felt as though he was about to pass out, the room was spinning and the urge to vomit once more began to grow.

"That's it!" Finally, his memory registered the information needed. Staggering back out of the kitchen, he made a grab for the grey sports-coat he'd worn to the workingmen's club. The chink of metal on metal made him let out an excited giggle. A sweaty hand fought with the lining of the pocket stitched inside and when his fingers wrapped around the cold steel, Fred Gibson let out a loud shriek of satisfaction. Throwing the coat across a nearby chair, he stumbled back into the kitchen, stopping only for a last swig of the gin. Fumbling through a set of eight keys, he found the longest and impatiently, pushed it into the hole, fighting with the mechanism until the door clicked open. A set of ten stairs lead downwards toward his destination and on several occasions, he almost lost his footing, clinging to the rail for safety. By-passing the parlour and the showroom, he hurried to the doorway at the end of a small passage. Forgetting the lock, he barged straight into the barrier, hurting his shoulder in the process.

"Come on Gibb, calm down, almost there." After trying three keys in the gloomy hallway, he finally interjected the correct one and the door swung open. Hitting the light on the wall by the entrance way, the sharp change was painful, and he closed his eyes momentarily. The room had no windows and was bare, bar for three large chest freezers on the far wall. The number one was scrawled on the first but he by-passed it, heading for a smaller version in the corner. It was new and had only been delivered two days earlier, but the driver had been given instructions to leave it outside in the hallway; bar for Gibson, no one entered this room.

The lid opened upwards, and a gust of cold air wafted in the mortician's direction. Expect for two items, the space was empty. Fred reached down far into the bottom and grasped his prize. His fingers wrapped tightly, he held it close to his face, the feeling of it being frozen taking away some of the pleasure. The plastic carrier bag that was wrapped around it was discarded quickly and a smile of relief overwhelmed his face. Opening his mouth, he began to suck furiously, the nipple from the right breast of a woman recently deceased tasting like an ice lolly for a child.

Chapter 25

"Christ, I'm confused." Nick Castle rested his head, closed his eyes, and considered the incredible kaleidoscope of emotions from the last forty-eight hours.

Firstly, the devastating loss of his grandfather. Bill had been his one constant, a sounding board, a high point in an otherwise horrendous adolescence. It had been a long time, too long since they'd seen one another but it was always an option. Now that option was no more, and it hurt.

The rendezvous with his mother had been just as shocking but for very different reasons. The frank exchange of views was nothing new but her willingness to reveal truths that had been hidden for so long came as a frustrating if not refreshing departure from the norm. Her accessible responses were a complete U-turn from the sequestered oblivion he'd encountered as a teen. It stung so much that things may have been so different had they had this conversation two years, five years, even ten years earlier but, he found himself sympathising with her, something previously, he'd have never believed possible. Beseeching the requests, no, demands, of her husband and in-laws wasn't an option, wavering to their greater judgement on a subject to which she knew little, she'd felt obliged to continue their lie, even when she could see the damage it was doing to him. Dispelling the story for the truth after all this time took guts and though she only had so many details to reveal, her voluntary beginning made it impossible for Mick to deny. He'd left his mother, for the first time, not feeling that usual acrimony and glacial animosity but, with hope that their detached relationship could still be bridged. It would take work but, it was a start. Perhaps he was finally growing up?

The loan of money gave him a feeling of independence he'd long since lost. Borrowing his mother's car too, helped him step away from his broken personality. He was returning to Hallowell, doing so in a beat-up banger and penniless would have continued his inferiority complex whereas appearing with an impressive vehicle and cash in his wallet portrayed a position of success. It was a welcome departure from reality.

Arrival in Hallowell had been disconcerting for so many reasons. This had been his dream, to return to his spiritual home, the land that had beckoned him since the day he left. The car had travelled like a homing pigeon, taking no effort at all, not a wrong turn, never needing to glance at a map, gliding through the motorways and back-roads alike. The childish excitement made his heart race, the anticipation of a triumphant return, seeing family and a few old friends. But suddenly, memories of those same friends made the ever-present horror flood his thoughts once more. The persisting instinctive terror he felt when he remembered that thing that inhabited that place. The reason that he hadn't been able to call Hallowell home for all these years. The repugnant, nauseating phantasm that destroyed his life and haunted his dreams. He was immediately forced to pull the car off to the side of the road and wretch. His body had quivered involuntary, all that impetus that he'd felt faded once more and he was back to feeling a jaded wreck. But as he lifted his head, the remnants of an earlier meal splattered on the floor before him, he became aware of his surroundings. High on top of Hallowell bank, the entire panoramic of the village before him, he regained his decorum, aware this was now or never, face his fears or run and hide. But if he chose the latter, he knew he'd be running forever.

Seeing that place again hadn't been as tough as he first thought. It was just a building, plain and simple. Had Mick Castle not appeared on the scene, perhaps he'd have even ended up inside its daunting walls. Searching for its masked occupant. But had that been so, he may have never discovered its heinous secrets.

Listening to his father revealing every detail, telling an unbelievable tale, with all its deplorable facts, trying desperately to defend the decision to create a catalogue of lies and deceit, making him believe he was ill when he wasn't to protect their secret, all in the name of his own protection made his blood boil. But the longer the story continued, the more it made sense. He knew he'd never accept that there was no other way, but it became apparent that after the events of that Halloween night, nothing would ever be the same again. Seeing the emotion displayed across Mick's face, understanding just how much all their lives had been turned upside down, did give Nick another perspective. Would he ever be able to forgive his father for the dishonesty? Who knew? All he did know was, holding on to the bitterness would accomplish nothing. Parents make mistakes and this was a whopper. But, if he was in the same position, would he have been willing to sacrifice everything for the safety of his own son?

When he'd seen Dan Challis earlier this evening, he understood more. He witnessed just what could have happened had the family stayed in Hallowell. His friend had been gradually destroyed too, but without family support, he'd had to battle those demons alone, the only solace found at the bottom of a bottle. It made his own alcohol abuse seem more manageable, barely.

The drinks he'd consumed earlier that evening in Hallowell workingmen's club were just enough to keep away withdrawals. His idea of going cold turkey with the prescription medication would be harder than expected but he decided that taking a dose, only when his day was done to aid restful sleep was the way to go. His mind and body needed to be sharp and the zombie-like state the pills created was not conductive to getting things done. There was a lot of people who'd like to see his return end in humiliation, he had no intention of fanning those flames. But still now, alone in his grandmother's spare bedroom, a room he'd slept a thousand nights in as a child, the act was over, he could relax.

As he lay naked inside the comfortable single bed, thick continental quit pulled high to keep out the coolness of the room, he felt home. The more things change, the more they stay the same, the heavy sent of lavender from the detergent his grandmother had used since the beginning of her marriage wafted from the sheets and quilt-cover. The feather filled pillows moulded gently to the contours of his head and in no time, he fell sound asleep. And then…the dreams came.

Sometimes the dream would be through his line-of-sight, reliving the details in the first person but tonight, it was like the playback of a home movie. Watching from above, with perfect cinematography, while screaming at the screen for the idiot characters to not do exactly what they were doing. For some reason, this nightmare terrified him the most…

The browns and yellows of fallen leaves grouped in piles around bare trees, gathered about every wall and building, blanketed fields, and roads; Autumn was sweeping the land, the farms harvested, children back in school, BST clocks reset to GMT, October was ending but for one last day, all Hallows eve, Halloween.

For Nick Castle, this was Christmas, birthday, and holidays all rolled into one. His favourite day and especially night of the year, when his devilishly mischievous sense of humour and fun-loving pranks were celebrated rather than frowned upon, when his eyes lit up with glee at his willingness to be just that little more adventurous than everyone else, and the one time when he was willing to use his influence over his friends to get what he wanted rather than accepting the consensus.

Because Nick was the leader of his group, unspoken of course but leader none the less. He knew it, Billy Scholes knew and welcomed it as did Dan Challis Even Johnny Bracket knew it, though not without a certain amount of resentment. And tonight, for once, he'd use that leadership, he had a plan.

Even at the age of eleven, Castle had the kind of aura that others gravitated towards. Tall and sleek with and athletic physique, a natural sportsman in both team and individual disciplines, captain of both the school football and cricket squads and a standout in track and field, all elements adding to the respect from his peers. And along with that respect came a healthy dose of fear. Not due to bullying, that wasn't in the boy's nature, but his strength and unwillingness to back away from a challenge, regardless of the opponent made him a feared adversary. It also created a situation where his need to fight was diminished as rivals would be wary before a punch was thrown. Nick's intellect and quick wit also added another layer to his popularity. A dry sense of humour coupled with strong diplomatic abilities gave an air of maturity which his peers enjoyed, and his handsome features and sense of style were an automatic attraction with the opposite sex. He truly had an all-round package.

And that created friction with Johnny Brackett. Though he was Nick's best and longest friend, his jealousy regularly bubbled over into resentment. He was a good sportsman though never exceptional, bright rather than intelligent, he was almost handsome, almost popular, and as such, it made him try way too hard. He enjoyed Nick's company but found it decidedly cool in the Castle's shadow. He refrained from challenging his friend for superiority for several reasons, unwilling to risk a long friendship, knowing that a split from Castle would destroy most of his own popularity (some only tolerated him for Nick's sake) and mostly, if things turned physical, he'd loose. Instead, he remained by his pal's side, aware it was better on the inside looking out than the outside looking in.

Dan Challis was the third member of their group. He had no leadership aspirations or illusions of grandeur, an opposite to Nick in every way. Bright ginger hair with tight curls and a less than stylish sculpture, early onset of acne and a decidedly unathletic build, narrow shoulders and puppy-fat around the midriff. An orthodontist's dream with protruding front teeth and crossed lowers, wide-rimmed, large-lensed spectacles, and a crooked, bird-like nose, he'd have been forgiven if he'd hated Nick and all those genetic advantages, but the only thing Dan hated, was God. That's because one of the almighty's messengers, a smooth talking greasy haired false profit named Thomas Scripture (Bob Done, but that never sounded as holy) had convinced Challis's mother, Elizabeth, to leave the family home and join their religious sect, The Brotherhood of Christ. Travelling from place to place, preaching the word of God, enjoying freedom and even freer love (it was the 1960s) Liz walked out on her family when Dan was just three years old, never to return. Such was the scandal, some in town thought her husband had murdered her and buried her with his vegetables in the back garden. Thankfully, witnesses had seen her leaving and the farewell note she left was soon authenticated. Challis senior, a painfully shy and some may say, boring man never remarried, but rather than comforting his deserted son, became a workaholic, spending all his waking hours, tending to his main passion, the small green grocer's shop he'd built from nothing. Some blamed this as the reason his wife had ran off, her husband having more interest in cabbages and tomatoes than her. It wasn't long before Dan realised, he was alone in the world. His father provided well, materialistically, but he was emotionally absent and the main reason the boy clung so much to his group of friends. Especially Nick.

Much to the shagreen of Johnny Brackett, Billy Scholes was the fourth and final member of their quartet. Since he was two years younger than his three compatriots, Brackett felt he was beneath their circle and ensured everyone knew it. The boy was small and skinny but what he lacked in stature, he made up for in enthusiasm, guts, and tenacity. And that's what Brackett feared the most; his potential, the potential that Nick saw right away. When Johnny looked at Scholes, he saw a yapping puppy, chasing his master, a master that wouldn't flinch at promoting from within, promotion to the best friend position, his position. Banishing Billy from the gang would protect that position but, day by day, the youngers ties grew stronger, and Brackett hated it. He couldn't use his standing to eradicate the threat, Castle would never allow that, his only option was to try and break the newcomer's spirit, both psychologically and physically. Even Nick couldn't protect the child all the time though he would intervene when things got out of hand. But Castle was determined to allow things to run their course, afraid that should he use his influence too freely, Billy may take advantage of the protection and never organically grow to being their equal on merit. Scholes had to learn to fight his corner, even if it got rough along the way. One such instance was during a bout of play fighting and Brackett saw an opportunity to deal out some punishment 'accidentally', breaking the child's nose. Billy could easily have wilted, crumbled with the pain, and regressed to junior member but instead, held his ground, willing to take more to gain the respect he so greatly craved. Nick smiled like a proud big brother and even Brackett had to begrudgingly apportion a measure of acknowledgement. The tests would continue but the small boy jumped a huge hurdle that day.

Due to Dan Challis's relaxed nature, he never had a problem with Scholes being taken under their wing and Nick was adamant that the new cohort be afforded a place at his table, Johnny Brackett knew he'd have to accept the situation for the foreseeable future.

The dream began around the residential streets of Hallowell. A relatively new holiday pastime across Halloween, known as trick or treating, going from house to house, demanding gifts for safe passing of their home from childish pranks seemed more like a protection racket and even though most adults detested the yearly hijacking, children looked forward to the haul of candy by the nights end. Though some parents felt it was little more than begging, the four friends were determined to partake in the growing tradition but when it became obvious that most adults were unwilling at answer the front door, the activity soon lost its allure. Not that Nick minded, this night was too important to waste on petty childish games, this was Halloween, the night when the worlds of the living and the dead collided, when spirits roamed free and the lines of good and evil were blurred. He wasn't about to spoil his favourite holiday being ignored by boring old farts, too greedy to hand out treats. He had bigger fish to fry.

For as long as he could remember, he'd always been captivated by the old railway station on the edge of town. And the fact that his granddad seemed so evasive whenever he'd ask him questions on the subject only made it seem more fascinating. What was it about places that were out of bounds that seemed so attractive? He could vaguely remember going inside there once, just before it had closed. Not inside the main building, instead waiting on the platform with his family and friends for the annual Hallowell workingmen's club outing to the seaside resort of Blackpool. He'd managed to peer inside the huge metal doors, just a peak, enough to spike his interest. It was so dark and lifeless and for a brief second, he could have sworn that something moved inside. It terrified him and he'd ran, clinging to his grandfather's leg. That's all it took to begin a lifetime of curiosity. Nick was incapable of backing away from the things that scared him.

The dream suddenly changed location. The safe well-lit streets of the village were now just a memory. No more gangs of adolescents on a sugar rush, armed with eggs and toilet roll, no more frustrated parents hoping their children would get tired so they could head home early. This was the dark side of town, the wrong side of the tracks. Just a wire-mesh fence, complete with a man size hole, stood between them and that place. Dan Challis took a match from a pack brought from home and scratched it against the box's rough exterior. The wooden stick ignited giving a brief respite from the darkness. The expression across the boys faces, illuminated by the flame told their own stories. Nick's excitement could barely be contained, this was the Mount Everest of Halloween locations with untapped potential. The parental warnings only added to his interest; he was too wise to believe in the bogeyman. Brackett was wary but unwilling to show weakness. Anything Castle could do, he'd prove he'd do just as well, be just as good, act just as brave. The friendly rivalry between the two alpha males always had the potential to erupt into something more serious but for now, an unspoken truce was the order of the day. Brackett had always had this undercurrent of jealousy toward his long-time friend, an unhealthy obsession with Nick's popularity and abilities. He knew that when people saw them, he'd always be Tonto to Nick's Lone Ranger, the sergeant to Castle's chief. In a town of Hallowell's size, being number two could be a lonely position. He was tired of playing second fiddle but knew that most people only associated with him out of respect for his well-liked pal. It was also reason that many saw him as a bully, frustration at being unable to express himself on an individual plain causing him to rely on fear to gain his own respect. For Johnny Brackett, tonight was a test, and he was determined not to fail.

Dan Challis was more concerned, having heard whispers about the station curse, but his fear was smaller than a desire not to look like a pussy in front of his peers. The dark vortex they were about to enter was like Danny's young life; scary, hopeless, and certain to end badly. And if something did occur inside, hey, shit happens.

And finally, there was Billy. His eyes were already filling with tears as he climbed through the wire barrier. His parents had had the sense to tell their son enough to leave him terrified of the place and that knowledge left him frozen. The more he attempted to act brave, the more the tell-tale signs would reveal themselves. His hands trembled, lower lip quivered uncontrollably, and his silence buried the fact that should he try to speak, the tears he'd tried so valiantly to quell would certainly have burst forward, kick his arse, and spray his cowardice for all to see. That wasn't an option. Truthfully, he knew he had little options, period. Be one of the boys, do this crazy dangerous shit and put everything on the line or pass; admit to being terrified, admit that any moment he could very easily piss in his cheap tracksuit bottoms, admit that if the thing in the station didn't get him, he'd most probably be a victim of juvenile heart failure. It was no contest, fear of looking like a wimp in front of the boys was a clear winner. Plus, Nick had gone to bat for him when Brackett refused to accept him into the fold. There was no chance he'd let his friend down now. With gritted teeth, he pushed on.

Underfoot, course gravel and dirt crunched beneath their feet. The hole in the mesh, which was the only access point, had been repaired many times but as ever, the gaping entry point re-emerged. Sliding through was physically easy, but psychologically, it was like climbing into Haydee's, with the next stop, Hell itself. In daylight, the station could seem like any other abandoned building, lonely, derelict, lifeless; but at night, it came alive, every shadow that danced as the wind blew, every crack that echoed with magnified veracity in its vast empty rooms, every tortured soul who cried silent screams, its memories, its victims, its resident.

An earlier downpour left the air fresh and crisp but an eastly wind had driven back the clouds. The branches of nearby trees swayed, vanquishing the remaining leaves and the tunnels by the main building above the platform caused a high-pitched howl as the rushing air fought against the concrete monster. On the sixth floor, a lone window stared out towards Hallowell and behind its broken glass, a figure moved aware of trespassers.

The massive main building loomed large before them. The shape of the two roofed walkway tunnels appeared like black unblinking eyes, staring deep into their souls, aware of their fears and eagerly awaiting their entry. A tear rolled down Billy's cheek though it was swiftly wiped away before his peers could notice. Challis's pace had slowed, delaying the inevitable and even Brackett was now desperate for an out, praying that one of the others would break first so his terror could remain hidden. Castle had needed to use all his influence over the group to ensure that his dream came true, maintaining some semblance of leadership of his small group meant leading his troupes into battle. This was the stuff legends are made of. Having the kudos to brag, Monday at school that his gang had conquered the station, explored, and lived to tell the tale, on Halloween night of all times, it was worth the risk.

The platform was long and high, the white marble now dull, and deadened, a depressing sight that had once shown strength, now shattered by dereliction. Billy Scholes struggled with the climb, his height even shorter had his shrinking courage and the earlier storm had made gaining purchase on the slippery surface a chore. Bracket sarcastically offered the boy a boost which was rebuffed with a swift, "Fuck you, Johnny." Scholes rarely used profanity and regretted the retort when he saw Brackett's steely stare.

"Okay ladies, we're all friends here." Nick was growing tired of his role of peacekeeper but also knew that without his protection, Brackett would happily kick Billy's arse and banish him from their group. Playing godfather was the only way to maintain the status quo. Silence befell them once more, the air of distention hanging thick. Castle placed his hands on the marble and with a swift spring, bounced to the platform floor, privately content that when Brackett had tried the same thing, it took two attempts to complete.

After each had climbed to the platform, Challis reached into the inside pocket of his green parka and shocked his pals by producing a pint bottle of Smirnoff Vodka.

"Jesus Dan, where you get that?" The others stood wide-eyed as Challis cracked the seal and unscrewed the cap. Raising the bottle to his lips, he gulped a long deep swallow of the bitter clear liquid, his facial expression not altering as the fiery splash cascaded down his throat, indicating that this wasn't his first foray into the world of underage alcohol abuse. After taking a second sip, he answered Nick's question.

"Swiped it from my dad's liquor cabinet."

"Fuck man, he's goanna nail your arse when he finds out." Nick was giggling as he accepted the bottle, taking a sip but grimacing at the liquid's strength.

"Dads never nailed me since mum left, eight years ago. So long as I don't get in his way or take up too much of his precious time, he could give a shit what I get up too. You guys all told your parents some story so you could stay out late tonight, mine didn't ask." Billy was offered the bottle but declined, one line he was unwilling to cross just to be part of the group. Brackett snatched the bottle away, shaking his head in disgust, calling the youngster a pussy into the bargain. He swigged hard from the vodka, but the harshness burned his throat, causing him to splutter. Nick laughed,

"Not the only pussy, eh? Fucking lightweight." Castle's insult stung and Johnny was about to retaliate when a noise echoed from the main building, stopping all four in their tracks. Billy was the first to say what Brackett and Challis were both also thinking.

"Listen lads, I don't think this is a good idea." Though Brackett had been desperate for an escape excuse, his alpha male pride once more overtook common sense.

"Told you he was a fucking pussy. Why we must put up with this snivelling little mama's boy, I'll never know. I'm sick of listening to him bitch and moan and another thing, if…" His words were cut off as something large crashed onto the roof above their heads, causing all four to dart for the platform edge.

"Sorry, call me what you like but I'm off!" Scholes was about to jump down to the ground below when Nick put a hand on his right shoulder.

"No, you're not." Castle rarely forced his opinions on others, but this was one of the exceptions. "I brought you into this group cos I like you and I thought you had balls. You spilt now and don't come back. I mean it." Pointing a finger in Brackett's direction he continued. "And you, leave him alone. He's my friend, the same as Danny is, the same as you are. If that's not good enough then you can go fuck yourself too. Now this is Halloween night and I'm going exploring. The bangs are either the wind moving shit about or another group already in here, fucking with us. If that's the case, how's it going look Monday, we get into school after running off like a bunch of pussies and we find out its Jimmy Knowles and his mates pulling the piss, we'd never live it down. Now I'm going inside, if I have to go in alone, I will but desert me tonight and that's us finished. Up to you." Dan Challis spoke first.

"Calm down Nick, we came here together, we go in together." Brackett begrudgingly nodded his agreement then all eyes went to Billy.

"Don't suppose I've much choice. Let's just get it over with." Castle grinned at his band of brothers.

"That's more like it. Smile for fucks sake, this shit is supposed to be fun." After a pause to ensure all was quiet from inside, Nick Castle led his friends into a darkened tunnel, heading for the giant steel doors at the station's rear.

His hair wet, cheeks flushed, body drenched in perspiration. Arms flinging uncontrollably in reflex, eyes opening and closing, pupils rolled back in his head looking demonic white. Why couldn't he just wake up? His whole-body twitching, not for fear of what was happening but what was *about* to happen. For this was a dream with a pre-determined ending. A replay of the same scene over and over, Nick knew what was coming.

Another new scene. They were on the top floor of the station staring from the building's only window. How they'd skirted the inner bowels of the main building, Nick had no memory, but they had, and the group were filled with triumph. This was great, the boys could dine out on this for months and they knew that the other pupils of Hallowell secondary school would hang on their every word. This was huge, conquering the station, no-one else's group would have the balls to try that, and on Halloween too.

The wooden window-frame was embedded with sharp jagged nails which had been used to keep heavy timber planks across its length. The monster had removed them to ensure he had good vision over his property and an area to see Hallowell from afar and as such, the glass panes had been smashed allowing air the cascade in freely. The cool evening air refreshed their sweaty foreheads and a gentle breeze rustled discarded papers on a lone desk by the window. Challis suddenly had a terrible thought; they knew they'd explored the station but what proof did they have. Anyone could lie and tell the same tale, what they needed was a souvenir, a keepsake to ensure no one could question their word. Danny began rummaging through the papers for something they could use as evidence.

"What you are doing, Dan?" The problem hadn't occurred to Castle as, since he carried so much respect from his peers, others questioning his integrity didn't seem possible.

"Trying to find something to prove we been in here. Something with a name or address, so those fuckers at school won't think our story is bullshit." He continued sifting through the papers, but most were just blank sheets. A match he was holding burned down to the wick quicker than expected and singed his first finger and thumb. Letting out a quick squeal, Castle laughed out loud.

"Christ, Dan, don't worry about it. People will believe us."

"You maybe? I want a prize." The desk had a small draw and cupboard to its left side and Challis began tugging to free them. Using too much force, the draw sprang from its runner and smashed to the floor, a loud crash echoing around the sparse room. He looked around at his friends with a sorry look across his face.

"Jesus Challis, can you make any more noise, I think an old biddy in St Mara might have missed that?" Johnny Brackett was beginning to bore of the surroundings and felt it was time to make their exit. "He's loud enough to wake the dead!"

"IIIII, CEERRRTTTAAIINNNLLYYY HOOOOPPPE NNNOOOTTTT." Nick's terrible impression of a ghost, complete with slow, spooky tone was enough to lighten the mood and raise a giggle from his three pals. Challis continued to wade through another stack of papers when he yelled,

"Eureka, I got it." An envelope labelled with the railway station address and written to Martin Graham was waved high in the air like an eighty-year-old with a winning bingo card.

"Very clever, now can we split?" Johnny's patience was running thin. Nick looked to his wristwatch and stared at the pointers, trying to make out the time in his gloomy surroundings.

"Guys. It's almost ten, we been in here over two hours, can you believe that? Where did that time go?"

"Bollocks, your watch must be wrong." Brackett looked at his own timepiece then raised his eyes in surprise when he realised his friend had been right. "Fuck me, I can't believe that there's no way we been in here that long, is there?" Billy Scholes immediately began to panic, being more afraid of a parental reprimand than being in the station in the first place.

"Oh shit lads, I need to go. My mum and dad will go nuts, they told me to be in by nine." Quickly, they began heading for the staircase in the room's far corner when a noise stopped them in their tracks. Billy, in his panic didn't hear what the others heard. "Come on man, hurry up. I told you I'm late."

"Bill, shut up a minute." Nick's words were whispered rather than spoken, the three eldest boys standing as still as statues, trying to focus on the noises place of origin.

"Come on, I'm in trouble, don't play tricks on me now, I got to get home." He continued to walk but the others stayed frozen. Suddenly Scholes heard it too. Heavy footsteps gaining in volume, walking toward them, climbing bare concrete of the stairway.

"Nick, what the fuck is that?" Brackett was showing signs of cracking. "I swear, if you fuckers have set me up for a prank, I'll…" His words ended in mid-sentence. The only detail they could make out from the thing blocking their exit was its size. Its massive frame filled the doorway, and he was carrying something. Something long, cumbersome, hanging down by its right leg. Only when a brief hint of moonlight caught the blades edge, did they accept just how much danger they were in.

"No, no, no, no." The bedclothes were drenched now, sweat and something far more embarrassing turning the sheeting into a waterfall. His eyes now crunched closed, grimacing as though to avoid a coming blow. A swift kick caused the quilt to fall to the floor, his naked body writhing uncontrollably, heart pounding, breath laboured. His right hand clenched into a fist; his subconscious aware that the dream had one chapter still to run.

Up on the roof of Hallowell railway station, the boys used their bodies as a human barrier, ensuring that the steel doorway they had just slammed shut behind them would not be re-opened by their pursuer. After initially feeling resistance, the monster had desisted, aware that the children were trapped. Sixty feet in the air, a fall would be just as deadly as Graham's blade. After a moment, when their racing hearts had slowed, Challis broke the silence.

"What, or who, was that?" The boys stared at one another, none wishing to answer their friend's simple question. "And where did he come from? One minute there was nothing and then…this is bad."

"It's that ghost people at school talk about, that bogeyman guy, Fred Graham. That's who it is, we just saw a ghost." Brackett looked once more at Billy Scholes in disgust, his immaturity becoming too much to bear.

"It's Frank, not Fred, and he's no fucking ghost, arsehole."

"And how do you know it's not a ghost, genius?" Billy's terror at this situation was making him braver with his real-life one.

"Two reasons. One there's no such thing as ghosts. And two, we listened to him WALKING UP THE STAIRS. I wouldn't have thought that Casper the friendly arsehole would shake the room with his footsteps. Prick!" Scholes flushed red with embarrassment but then decided he'd had enough of Johnny's taunts.

"You know what Brackett, fuck you. You think you can pick on me cos I'm younger and smaller than you. Well, I'm sick of it. I don't care what you think of me cos I think you're a prick too. And if that gets me beat up, tough shit." Nick stepped away from the door, standing between the two as to ensure things didn't turn violent. Suddenly, with his peripheral vision, something caught his eye.

"Guys, shut up a minute and look." Castle pointed across to the far edge of the roof where two metal poles protruded from the concrete, heading down over toward the lower side building's roof. "I can remember noticing before, there is a ladder attached to that wall. Let's look."

"What about the door? That motherfucker could come barging through here any moment. It'll take all of us to keep it shut." Dan Challis had a good point, but Nick's argument was strong.

"If that is a ladder, let him come. By the time he gets onto the roof, we'll be home having coco."

Silently they regarded one another, their hands still pressing weight tightly on the grey metal door. Carefully, Nick decreased his force, eventually moving slowly away. Next came Brackett, and still the barrier held firm.

"Can you feel any difference boys? Is he pushing it from his side?" Castle prayed his question wouldn't be answered with the door smashing open, and those prayers were granted. Billy and Dan simultaneously released their grip and still the doorway remained closed. "Come on boys, let's check this out, it's the only chance we have bar barricading that door until morning and hope that someone rescues us."

Stealthily, they deserted the sanctuary of the blocked door and headed for what they hoped would be salvation. The night air was cool and crisp, half-moon hiding behind darkened rainclouds, stars just dot across the blank canvas. Challis realised his hands had begun to tremble uncontrollably and quickly forced them into the pockets of his parka. The vodka lay in wait and the terrified boy quickly unscrewed the cap, gulping until his throat burned. Brackett walked step for step with Nick, determined to be just the leader his best friend was. He arrived at the ladder first and cautiously peered over the edge. His expression told its own story.

"It's short. Only goes halfway down the wall." Castle turned away and cursed while Challis fought the urge to vomit. Billy Scholes seemed the least concerned.

"Okay, we go back to the door and keep it shut. Like you said, when we are missing, folk will come looking for us." Brackett raised a hand to interrupt.

"Wait. I think this is doable." Staring down at the ladder, he began to smile. Nick looked too but wasn't sure what his friend was thinking. "Listen, we climb down when we reach the bottom rung, let your feet hang free. If we hold on tight and work our way down so we are hanging off the bottom rung, the drops not that far. Maybe fifteen feet, if we land properly, we should be okay."

"That's stupid, I'm not jumping off the side of a building, no matter how far you think it is. I'll break my bloody neck." Billy Scholes was adamant, but what he'd never revealed was he was acrophobic, heights terrified him. Even on the roof, he'd kept a low centre of gravity and refused to go near the edge. This was the boy's worst nightmare. "Please, can't we all just stay here, someone will rescue us soon and then we'll all be safe."

"He has a point Johnny, that jump could be lethal. This way we are all certain to get out of this okay." Nick was swaying but after seeing the terror on the young boy's face, he felt a sense of duty to protect him.

"Nick, surely you're not scared of a little fall." Brackett was using underhand tactics, trying to get under his skin knowing that Castle rarely ducked a challenge.

"I never said I was scared. I'm trying to keep everyone safe. Billy looks terrified to jump, if he hurt himself badly, I'd be responsible. I brought him along, not you."

"You know what Castle, you're right. He is your responsibility, I don't even like the little shit. So, if you want to stay here and guard him, be my guest. But I'm not waiting here for that thing in there to get bored and smash his way through that door. I'm giving it a go. What about you Challis?" Dan stared at the floor, unhappy at being a pawn in this power play.

"You go first. If you okay then…sorry Nick, but I'll give it a go." Scholes was backing further away, openly crying now. As Nick went to comfort the boy, Brackett was on the ladder, starting his descent.

"Nicky, when I get out, I'll send help." With that, he was gone.

The steel rungs were cold and wet from the evening's earlier shower. His feet were on the fourth rung before his head passed the roof top, but he climbed quickly. Metal studs attached the ladder into the brick surface, maintaining a sturdy grasp. Johnny's knuckles were livid, only releasing their grip when it was necessary. The descent had slowed, the rooftop looked far away. From above, a figure was watching his efforts, probably Challis, he couldn't tell. His heart was beating way too fast, that macho façade now a distant memory. Looking down, he couldn't believe what he was about to do. Castle was right, this is way too fucking high. He thought of stopping, climbing back up, but what would that prove. He was wrong, yet again. No, no please, fuck it, I'm here, my idea, I'm going for it. He reached the final rung; his feet had nowhere left to go. He closed his eyes in silent prayer. His hands were on the third rung from bottom, feet still refusing to leave their safety net. They needed to be hanging free, come on, just one kick and we can go for it. They slipped away, one at a time, now only his hands on the cold steel. They reached for the second bottom rung, the skin in the palms burning now, still the urge to retreat battling to break his will. Sliding his arm through the bottom rung, armpit taking the strain for a second, but then, he was there, time to go, too late to retreat, both hands hanging from the bottom rung, legs dangling in space, that looks a big fall, more than fifteen feet. Fuck it, no choice.

He released his left arm, so the body swung sideways, away from the wall. Looking up toward his friends, to God, he let go. Remembering something on TV about how when paratroopers land, they bend their knees and roll, let's try that…falling, hitting the lower roof, landing, rolling, ALIVE.

A deep puddle of cool rainwater seeped through the barrier of his donkey-jacket as he laid still, back pressed hard against the tarmac rooftop. His heart was still pounding hard but that was just residual shock from the fall, it had been higher than he'd originally thought. Lifting his head gently, he glanced down toward his limbs, no incredible pain, no bones piercing skin; he sat upright quickly, too quickly and the world span. His base of his skull had bumped hard on landing but that was a small price to pay. Perhaps a mild concussion and a headache, the important thing was he was free. Using the wall as leverage, he climbed to his feet, still no major injuries revealed themselves. This time he'd been right, he could be the hero, swooping in to save the day. Two heads bobbed over the rooftop edge, hugely relieved that their friend didn't seem hurt. In a low voice that seemed to carry across the entire station grounds, Nick enquired about Johnny's condition to which Brackett replied simply with thumbs up. That was enough for Challis, who was immediately over the side, starting a fast descent. Billy Scholes had dared himself to join Nick, peeping cautiously as their friend began his escape.

"Take it easy Dan, fall from here and you're dead."

Nick regretted his words when Scholes immediately backed away once more, the urge to vomit rising from the pit of his stomach, his disabling fear of heights making what was expected, an impossible task.

Challis was rushing way too much, the wet steel giving little purchase to his grip, cheap plastic soled baseball boots sliding under his feet. Still, he hurried, knowing that if he thought about, he was doing for too long, he'd back out. The wind was gaining strength, whistling through the adjacent trees, blowing his damp, lank hair down across his eyes. He was halfway down the ladder's length when he allowed himself a second to brush the obstacle from his face. At the very moment, a side-wind gusted strongly, hitting him full force, causing his cheap footwear to lose their hold.

The fall was fast and violent, just a final desperate grasp for the bottom hung stopping him from crashing thirty-five feet to certain death. Challis was crying as his body crunched into the brick wall, his face smashing into the concrete breaking his nose instantly. Brackett had seen his pal fall, but his braveness had deceased, instead of moving into position to break Dan's fall, he threw his arms over his head and ran in the opposite direction. Nick threw himself over the edge and was about to head down the ladder to aid his friend when he saw the fleeing figure of Billy Scholes.

The frightened boy had witnessed Challis's terrifying slip, ensuring that there was no way he could follow the group. He'd began to back away quickly, heading toward the rooftop doorway. Nick saw his retreat and called out after him. He was torn, try to assist the stricken Challis, knowing the chances of hauling him back onto the ladder were slim or stop the youngster darting back into the station building, knowing alone, he stood virtually no chance. As he stared down the ladder, his choice was made for him.

Dan had clung on gamely, pushing hard against the wall with his feet as he tried to take the strain off his burning hands. The wet brick surface offered no assistance and with Challis having little athletic strength, the chances of hauling himself to safety were minimal. Brackett had returned and was shouting advice and encouragement though was still unwilling to break his friend's fall. Breathing through his broken nose was laboured and as tears streamed down his cheeks, he had little option than to release his grip, his body beginning its frightening plunge to earth.

When Brackett had fallen, he'd allowed his body to swing sideways away from the wall, but Challis didn't have time. His legs were stiff as he hit the roof but as they buckled, the knees bent, smashing hard into the unforgiving concrete. Dan screamed out in agony as his kneecaps splinted, blood exploding from deep gashes, flowing down the insides of his grey tracksuit trousers. Brackett stood helpless, unsure what to do to help his stricken friend but as the looked up to Castle for direction, he was nowhere to be seen.

"Fuck Bill, don't go in there." As Nick clambered back onto the roof, his mesmerised pal was heading into the top floor of the station, the horror of seeing Dan Challis crash to the floor, more terrifying than whatever lay ahead inside the cursed building.

Castle slipped on the tarmac surface, barely maintaining his footing, such was his panic to pull Billy from the monster's lair. Running with all the speed he could muster; he was at the doorway in no time. Bursting through, the darkness rose to meet him like sudden blindness. Feet away, there was a flight of ten stairs, turning in the middle, hiding the final five. Nick took in a deep breath and began the descent, holding his arms out before him as a shield from the blackness.

"Billy. You there?" His voice was in whispers though he knew any noise would travel across the emptiness. Pausing, he waited for a response, there was nothing. Reaching the turn in the stairwell, he envisioned the monster waiting, holding Billy's hostage, but there was only darkness. At the bottom of those stairs there was a small doorway, though the door was open. He imagined Billy, running blindly, deathly afraid, too petrified to stay on the roof but equally pessimistic about what lay before him. What chance did he have alone in here? What chance did either of them have? Still, Nick knew he had to try.

The space was so vast, Nick couldn't tell where the top floor began and ended, a darkened version of an arctic white-out, where all that can be seen is one tone. His eyes fought to accustom themselves to his surroundings but the more he tried, the worse the situation became. His mind raced, every fluctuation a potential threat. Leaving the sanctuary of the outer wall was terrifying but Billy Scholes had to be here somewhere, the chances of him making the escape of six floors, implausible.

A strong dose of déjà vu swept over him, the more he thought of his frightened friend, the more his mind scrambled. Was he locked in some unescapable trap, a lidded coffin slowly depriving Scholes of air, expelling the last remnants of oxygen from the stricken child's lungs? Was he being tortured, unspeakable atrocities fracturing his physical body as well as his psyche? He could visualise the boy pleading for his life, standing no chance. Or was it already over? Had the monster snuffed out Billy's life immediately for having the temerity of entering his domain? For that much was true, this truly was his domain, and they were trespassers.

Nick began to feel stupid, stupid, and arrogant. They'd all been warned in different ways, some with gentle persuasion, others with a more direct order, but each knew the risks. But it was Castle who'd been the driving force, the insistent leader, more worried about a moronic Halloween activity than the safety of his pals. And now this was the result. One friend outside screaming in agony and another…

He needed to focus. Without him, Billy stood almost no chance. He shuddered at the question of what chance they had together, but first things first.

The stench of mould and charred timber consumed the air. Leaving the sanctuary of the room's perimeter so hard, again that feeling of being here before entered his mind. The wood from the room's entry way doorframe was splintered and a thin sliver sliced beneath Castle's fingernail; he hadn't been aware his grip on the barrier had been quite so forceful. Trying to suck out the invading wood, he bit deeply into the tip, the taste of his own blood, acidic and sickly on his tongue. Spitting the residue onto the floor before him, he noticed something, something out of place.

As he knelt, his bones cracked, echoing around the expanse of the space, appearing far louder than. The cold concrete floor penetrated the knees on his denim jeans and the dust felt course between his fingers. It would have been so easy to miss but, there it was, like it was meant to be, a prop in the sick creature's games.

Nick grabbed the plastic casing of a clear disposable lighter and shook it by his ear, hoping above hope that it still contained enough fluid to take a spark. The gentle splashing made Castle smile but when he tried to ignite the flame, the metal mechanism was rusted and stiff. Pressing hard with his right thumb, it took several efforts just to move it slightly but with patience, the wheel began to turn. His injured finger squeezed the back of the casing making it bleed more but the pain was now a secondary emotion. The light from the flame would give him hope, a chance. An equaliser against the thing that roamed these hallways.

His mind was focused totally on making the lighter work, but frustration was growing. The more urgency he performed, the less effective his efforts. As his temper grew thin and the urge to hurl the aggravating prop increased, the flint sparked, and a bright yellow light banished the darkness. He squealed an immature celebratory yell, forgetting his surroundings momentarily. Had he not been so encapsulated with the rudimentary task, perhaps he'd have seen the thing to his rear, perhaps...

Billy Scholes's face was already red and bloated, the huge forearm of Frank Graham held tightly around the child's scrawny neck like a deadly garrotte blocking the flow of air to his lungs.

He tried to call a warning to his, mentor but the words wouldn't come, moving lips mouthing silent lines. His body was shutting down rapidly, limbs that seconds earlier had flayed in retaliation now had no energy left to fight, his feet dangling eight inches from the ground. He had managed to squeeze his own arm between his throat and the monsters grip on being snatched as he'd already be dead. With one final supreme effort he managed to splutter a single word.

"Nick."

It was soft and timid, barely audible against the roar of the outside wind. Castle heard just enough to making him spin 180 degrees, standing just yards from evil itself. The initial instinct was to run but, how could he? Billy was his responsibility; how would he live with himself if he deserted him now.

Nick took a step forward, ready to try, he had to try; but the vision before him was truly grotesque. Its massive frame blocked the stairwell doorway, its clothing merely shadow. But the face, the mask, illuminated by the flickering flame, a true visage belonging to nightmares. Thick, nauseating rubber moulded into the form of a rotting skeleton, white carved teeth around a small mouth-hole, square jawline and two black shapes under which lurked its eyes. Eyes that contained no humanity, no compassion, no mercy. Long black fake hair covered the crown, continuing to the shoulders, dishevelled and wild. The shadow caused by the unnatural lighting only added more horror to the repugnant appearance.

Nick was frozen, his bladder fit to burst, all pretence of bravery long since forgotten. He considered crying for help but who'd hear? Inside the station, no one could hear you scream. It was those eyes that had Castle hypnotised, like a cobra with a snake charmer.

In the creature's free right hand, a crude, butchers boning knife, six inches in length was clasped tightly inside its fingers. The blade glistened by the dancing flame, Graham held it aloft to ensure both Nick and Billy could see exactly what was about to happen.

Slowly, the beast brought the blade toward Billy, bringing forth a final struggle, though the child was no match for Frank's massive strength. Gently rubbing the point across the tip of Scholes's nose, this was one act Graham was determined to enjoy. The apocalyptic terror he was causing, knowing without doubt that he could do anything he wished heightened every pleasure sensor.

Moving the tip of the blade below his forearm, it sliced into Billy Scholes's chest like a hot knife through butter. The ribcage across the sternum gave more resistance but Graham used greater force, taking pleasure in the challenge as the blade snapped its way though, until it reached the fleshy stomach area where the weapon once more gained speed. When the time came to retract the knife, the child was split from throat to crotch, the insides spilling wastefully onto the filthy floor. All at once, the life force drained from the boy's face, head drooping to the left, tongue lolling over the lower lip, a faint trail of blood slipping from the corner of his mouth. It was the eyes which haunted Nick Castle, his dear friend, Billy Scholes, the whites fading to black, the pupils fixed and dilated, until the lids closed, the final remnants of a life lost forever.

As for the monster, there were no eyes, just black crevice's, hiding behind the horrific latex, the vision was too abhorrent, too detestable, too ungodly. The picture of evil.

Nick began to scream, scream uncontrollably. His eyes shut tightly, refusing to see anymore. Two hands pressed hard against his shoulders and shook violently, cold water splashed against his face blocking his nose and mouth, making him splutter for air. And when he finally allowed light to shine into his eyes, both his father and grandmother were stood before his bedside, a small lamp bathing the room against the night-time darkness. His heart pounding, body covered in perspiration, and other, more embarrassing fluid lower down his body.

Chapter 26

The chink of glass bottles landing on the doorstep, delivered by his milkman, told Fred Gibson that the opportunity for sleep had passed him by. Not that he'd tried, the terrible news of Jenifer Graham's return to Hallowell and the possible ramifications that may come from it ensuring that sleep was suddenly unimportant.

He'd spent most of the night downstairs in the small hide-away, along the corridor from the funeral parlour, playing with his favourite possessions. Normally, he'd have the items back in the freezer before they began to defrost, the smell of decaying flesh was difficult to disguise, but last night, he'd allowed the breasts of Sarah Parker to become soft and pliable, the saliva from his tongue speeding up the process considerably. The soft skin on the hands of Kasey Becker felt different when frozen, but they were so beautiful, he couldn't risk decomposition, so he only used them on rare occasions. Last night had been one of those times. After removing them from her tiny teenage body, he'd wrapped the fingers around his penis and then maintained that position on freezing. Now, he had a perfect aid for masturbation, returning them to the cold storage before they had time to alter.

Each body-part was labelled, though it wasn't necessary; his power of recall sharp when searching through his collection. Some were easier than others to recognise; the second deep-freeze contained mainly feet, the simplest and safest souvenir to steal. Loved ones sometimes demanded one last hold of a deceased family members hand or a final kiss on the cheek, few ever asked to rub to soles of a foot or a last clipping of a toenail. The bodies were always hidden with a silk cover so seeing a missing appendage was doubtful.

If Fred had been born into another family, his life would almost certainly have turned out differently…but he wasn't.

The Gibson family had a lineage in Hallowell dating back to the 1850s. Michael Graham, who at the time was the eldest son of colliery owners, Alex, and Diana Graham, married a shy, blonde-haired beauty from neighbouring St Mara named Mary Gibson. Having betrothed into great wealth and power, Mary used her influence to have the Graham's finance a business venture of her brother Thomas. He'd spent five years training to be a mortician in Sheffield and was looking to open his own establishment. Alex agreed, and gave Thomas land and a stake, unsure of its viability, but reluctant to refuse his new daughter-in-law the simple request. The business struggled at first, as outsiders, the village looked upon the new family with distrust. But as the establishment had been founded with Graham money and therefore backed by Hallowell's first family, the funeral services were soon thriving. An outbreak of influenza in 1853 wiped out one quarter of the village's population and the caring and professional way Thomas dealt with the crisis helped his reputation grow. In 1878, it was passed on to his son's, Alfred, and Arthur, thus beginning a tradition that had continued across six generations. That legacy was destined to end with Fred, as he had no children, had never even married, his deviant nature wasn't conducive to a happy family environment.

Born in 1928, he'd missed conscription to the armed forces by mere months, the war against the Nazis ending before his selection. His mother, Maureen, had suffered serious complications during childbirth and though her son was born healthy, it was revealed that she would no longer be capable of maintaining a pregnancy, thus ensuring that the Gibson's would be one of the village's smaller families. Geoffrey Gibson, Fred's father was a serious, stern man who ruled his family with fear. He'd taken on the role of undertaker more out of obligation than desire. His own father had died when the Geoff was only twenty and as his siblings were all female and not expected to partake in the family business, he was the sole recipient. Even his marriage hadn't been by choice, Maureen falling pregnant outside of wedlock would have been a great scandal, so a rushed ceremony was arranged. Geoffrey soon found himself with a business, a wife, and a child on the way, all at the age of twenty-three. His dream had been to travel and continue into extended education but, suddenly he found himself trapped into a life he'd never wanted. His relationship with his wife was unconventional, they avoided one another as best they could, Geoffrey enjoying more of a relationship with a bottle of Jack Daniels. Maureen knew her role and played it perfectly. To the outside world, she appeared the doting wife, always by her husband's side at social events and family gatherings, maintaining a clean and tidy home and raising their son to the best of her ability. The fact that she had been sleeping with an old boyfriend named Ted for most of her married life was inconsequential, he was married too and had four children. Had he given Maureen any encouragement, she'd have left Geoffrey without thinking twice, but Ted was only using her for sex. She knew that and constantly felt ashamed, cheap, sordid and though she'd tried to resist his charms, Ted was her own personal addiction. At least it made the drudgery of her marriage more tolerable.

It was hardly surprising, with the air of indifference inside the family home that Fred grew up idiosyncratic. Introverted and unconfident, he was painfully shy and as his father had disciplined with force, the boy became timid and avoided confrontation at all costs. Craving parental acceptance and finding none, Fred would retreat into a make-believe world and loved reading. It wasn't until he began to share Geoffrey's working responsibilities that a fatherly bond would grow, by then, the damage was done.

The mortuary was an impressive looking structure, situated on station view, one of the better areas of Hallowell. Its architecture style was Victorian gothic, as was immediately obvious by the stone gargoyle carvings, above the curved oak front door. Three steep steps from the street led through the entrance, into a glass vestibule and then into a long wide hallway. The ceilings were high with casted plaster mouldings as coving and an impressive, patterned centrepiece around the light fitting and a low hanging glass chandelier, shaped as crystal candles (these were added in the 1920s and the building was one of the first in the village to be fitted with electricity). On the walls of the hallway were large, photographed portraits, images of the Gibson family lineage, the frames heavy and professionally hung. Completing the décor was thick, carved dado-rail running the entire length of the passageway. The floor was tiled and always kept immaculately clean, giving the impression of a museum. There were three doors, all in sequence along the right-hand wall, the first leading to an imposing office/showroom.

This had barely changed since the business's inception. Immediately parallel with the front entrance, set back in an alcove on the far wall was a large sturdy, containing an old-fashioned desk, the inkwells by its right-hand edge giving away the cumbersome piece of furniture's age. A hard, uncomfortable high-backed wooden chair accompanied it and made the newly installed grey metal filing cabinet seem evermore out of place. Adjacent was a large open fire and slate hearth, utensils polished and in place beside it, more for show than use, the fire was rarely lit. Along the length of the wall between the doorway and the desk ran two red, leather, chesterfield couches for the comfort of bereaved families whilst deciding for their dearly departed loved-ones, and a plain oblong coffee table ran horizontal, housing a good supply of tissues. To the right of the room was a huge bay-window with plush, full length black velvet curtains, which would naturally be closed when a body was being stored. Coffins took the rest of the space, in varying price ranges and standards of finish, the cheapest ones housed in the rear.

Along the corridor was the original office of Thomas Gibson which had been left as a reminder of days gone by. A small window, high on the back wall, hardly added adequate illumination and gloom always seemed to fill the air. Thomas's first desk was still in place in the room's centre, and a small, gas-lamp gave memories of simpler times. An electric heater now stood in the place of the previous open fire, the stone surround remaining, and yet more ancient family pictures adorned the walls. Though the room contained much of the Gibson family history, it was a place Fred rarely used, the door remaining locked whenever possible.

The final room on the floor was used for body preparation and again, was invariably locked. During Gibson's childhood, his parents had never hidden the truth from their son of what their family business entailed but they had waited if was possible before allowing him access to this area, concerned that as a pre-teen, grasping the details of what the occupation contained would be difficult conversation. Plus, it was hoped that one day, their son would take the helm of the business but, if he was scarred as a child, it could eradicate those plans. As the family lived in the flat above, there was a doorway at the back of the kitchen which led to a staircase and the business below. Keeping this door locked seemed the most sensible and secure solution and worked fine. Until one day, a simple mistake would alter the course of the child's life forever.

Anthony Robson was an old man whose illness had been obvious for all to see. A former miner who'd worked for fifty plus years in Hallowell colliery, his later days were spent destroying his liver and kidneys drinking cheap gin while pining for his wife who'd died suddenly of heart failure. The internal organs had begun to shut down months before his death, cirrhosis crushing the body's ability to remove impurities and combat the devastating consequences of the strong alcohol. His days were consigned to drinking and vomiting, food a long since after-thought. After death, his skin had become yellow, as had the whites of the eyes. Strangely, the cause of death was not directly alcohol related. During one of his better days, he'd decided to wash the windows of the two-story house he'd shared with his late wife. The effects of inebriation did cause him to slip from a wooden ladder, he'd perched precariously against a kerb in the street below. As he crashed to earth, his abdomen become impaled through a small picket fence around the property, the sharp upward V's penetrating the guts and causing Robson to bleed out before assistance could save him.

The task of preparing the body, so his grieving relations could say their final goodbyes, was particularly unpleasant. Geoffrey had been friends with the old man, not close, just a wave as he crossed the street or a word in the news agents shop. A friendly face, a passing smile. Anthony had been devastated at the loss of his wife and had been grateful for the caring way that Gibson had arranged her cremation. Knowing the old lady wasn't insured, Gibson had tried his best to ensure costs didn't spiral out of control and didn't exert undue pressure when Robson had struggled with the final bill. The old boy was covered with colliery life insurance so at least that wouldn't be a problem this time. Having watched the former miner fail so badly over the previous few months, it was hardly surprising when he received the call about his passing. What he hadn't expected was the brutal and messy way death would finally take him.

It was two days out from the funeral and the body had been correctly processed and prepared. The wounds had been cleaned as best they could, and embalming fluid had replaced Robson's blood. A coffin had been chosen by the old man's brother and was due for arrival the coming day. Until then, the body would unfortunately have to remain on the table inside the preparation room, a sheet covering him completely. It had taken longer than usual but Geoffrey was happy that he had served his old friend well. Having washed his hands, he pulled off his blue coveralls and folded them neatly before placing them in a draw. He was tired, always feeling slightly more drained when his work was carried out on someone he liked. Father Harris of St Helens church had asked him to call to ensure the details for the service were correct, he was an old fusspot, but his heart was in the right place and though Geoffrey just wanted to relax with a nice glass of scotch, work came first.

After the mortician had freshened up, he decided to walk the mile distance to see the vicar, the preparation room could become claustrophobic after time, and the cool autumn evening was just the job to lighten his spirits. As he was leaving the property, his son was arriving home from school. Maureen was away 'shopping', but Geoffrey trusted the boy enough to be home alone, Fred was very sensible for a six-year-old and he'd only be gone an hour. Throwing down his schoolbag and kicking off shoes, the child headed to the kitchen for a snack; it was then that his father's mistake became apparent.

Pulling open the refrigerator door, Fred reached up and grabbed a milk carton from the shelf. Taking a long gulp from the container, he returned it and pushed the barrier closed. It was then he noticed something that seemed too good to be true. After Geoffrey had finished his work and had left the mortuary, he'd made an uncharacteristic mistake.

The door at the top of the stairwell was always locked, more out of habit the necessity but as his mind had wandered, he hadn't noticed the mechanism hadn't latched and with the breeze from the opening front door, the barrier had swung wide open. The boy's curiosity was unbearable, this was his chance.

The stairway was dimly lit, and young Fred had no idea where it led. The soles of his stockinged feet glided silently across the bare floorboards, though the child listened intently for every crack.

"Daddy?" The boy knew what he was doing was wrong and that a hiding was probably headed in his direction when his parents discovered he'd passed the no-entry point, but something inside wouldn't allow him to turn back. "Daddy?" Fred wasn't sure if it was a test. Obviously, he'd seen his father leave but he wondered if the door had been left ajar on purpose and Geoffrey had rushed to the other entrance below, waiting to discover if the trust he had for his son was unwarranted. By now though, Fred was almost certain that his father was gone, but still wanted plausible deniability were he wrong. After a third call received no reply and he satisfied that no parental interference would repel his exploration, he'd reached the bottom of the stairwell and directly before him stood the outer doorway, and after a 180-degree turn, three more doors gave the youngster choices.

A golden doorknob on the first was stiff and initially, the boy thought it locked but with extra pressure, the latch clicked, and the heavy wooden barrier swung open. The hinges were old and in need of oil and the sound they made as the door creaked open made the child wince. Inside was a sturdy oak desk with a neighbouring metal filing cabinet. Plush leather sofas stood at ninety-degrees by the bordering wall, looking so comfortable, Fred couldn't resist trying it in the hope it's elasticity would make a suitably trampoline. Pouncing across the arm, he let out a childish whoop as he face-planted into the firm material, spinning and coming to a stop on his left side. The look of glee across his face soon dissipated when, across to the right-hand side of the room, four coffins stood up on their end, displayed for potential clients, what was on offer for their dearly departed. Fred's natural inquisitiveness soon replaced shock; he already knew what the family business was and now, the opportunity to see the inner workings was too bigger prize to lose. The wooden caskets were highly polished, and their brass handles glinted in the fading sunlight. Smooth silk material lined the interior, and the boy couldn't resist the urge to climb inside, the feeling upon the bare skin of his arms felt cool and luxuriant. In the room's corner, a far less elaborate and inexpensive model for those with a meagre budget stood. The wood wasn't as polished, it contained no handles and there was no material inside. Trying to make it a less attractive option meant more profit for the undertaker.

After exploring everything the showroom had to offer, Gibson returned to the hallway. Approaching the next door, he could see the barrier was closed. Once more, he called out for his father.

"Daddy?" There was still no reply. Pushing the barrier gently, he grimaced when the door held firm. Twisting the handle and nudging with his shoulder gave no help and Fred soon lost patience and interest, there was more to explore.

Approaching the final doorway, he felt a strange apprehension that he'd never experienced before. This was wrong, he knew it was wrong, but something inside willed him forward. The discernible excitement of risk, the fascination of witnessing something he had no right to see. Once more, the handle was stiff, but Fred was determined that this was one obstacle he'd overcome. The wooden surface was smooth, glossed in white paint, heavy and firm. Holding with both hands, he twisted the golden doorknob with all his might and pushed hard with his left shoulder. The barrier refused to move. His palms were sweating making purchase on the metal utensil difficult and several times, he'd stop and wipe the residue across his trouser legs. It seemed that the barrier would be impenetrable, and frustration was growing. Pulling down the sleeves of his sweater to cover his hands, the material seemed to grab better against the metal and suddenly, there was movement. Encouraged, he re-doubled his efforts, aware that his time was short. His face grimaced as he tried to force a way through, his shoulder was sore, but he'd come too far to stop now. Inch by inch, the handle twisted until...click.

The hinges were badly in need of oil and creaked loudly as the door swung open. The room was in total darkness, no windows allowing in natural light. The air smelled foul with chemicals and young Fred pulled the neck of his T-shirt across his nose and mouth, but still the stench passed through. Also, something in the air stung his eyes, a misty residue of something he'd never experienced before. The state odour of blood and decay mixed with the chemical composition of embalming fluid. Finally, the door was fully open, and he began to make out shapes. His eyes fought against the darkness and the boy began to feel across the inside of the wall for a light-switch. The property was one of the first buildings in Hallowell to be fitted with electricity and the child was unsure of its usage. His tiny frame could only reach so high, and his arms stretched to their full length. Eventually, he discovered a small round metal growth protruding from the upper wall by the doorframe. His fingertips at full stretch and standing on tiptoes, he could feel the switch in the centre of the casing. It was just out of reach. He began to jump, missing the target several times and once more his frustration was showing, childish squeals of disconsolation as each time he failed in his mission. Then, with one final leap, the switch flicked, and a long strip-light crackled twice before bathing the room light.

The smile across Fred's face at defeating the obstructions before him soon faded when he discovered the wide room's secret.

A long metal table was housed in the centre of the room and, a sheet was covering something across the top. The cover was dark grey, but housed stains in all directions, deep red splotches of all sizes, some larger than others and a huge patch which seemed to subdivide the sheet into two halves. The marks appeared mostly dry bar for one. The red was deeper and glistened in the artificial lighting, obviously fresh. Slightly to the right, a smaller table stood by it, shining metal instruments scattered on its upper surface. One looked like a knife, sharp pointed tip, and smooth handle. The blade was covered in dried blood and some of the residue had spilled across the table, a small puddle forming by the knife's tip. Across to the walls at the back of the room, glass fronted cupboards containing bottles of chemicals were placed high and out of his reach but, it was what was on the long metal table that interested him the most.

White ceramic tiles covered the floor. Slowly, his feet padded across the room, the tiles squeaking under foot. He noticed a small pool of blood had spilled onto the floor under the table. His heart was racing, partially with fear of parental discovery but mainly of what he was about to see. Across in the room's corner, a small wooden stool would give him the access he needed. It was heavier than expected, solid, homemade from waste wood, scattered blood stains embedded in the upper surface. Lifting the cumbersome object, he turned and headed to the large table, his inquisitiveness peaking, his eyes transfixed on the thing below the sheet. The stool fell hard onto the floor tiles and the loud bang echoed around the room. His fear of being caught had now faded, this was worth a beating. Scaling the stool, left leg stretching followed by the right, suddenly he was face to face…with death.

Carefully, he hauled the sheet from the body. The head appeared first, skin yellow, eyes closed, he just looked like he was sleeping. This wasn't horrible, he was just a man who had passed, not a ghost, or a zombie, or a ghoulish thing, just a man. Fred stroked the cheek, it was cold as ice and made him cringe but soon, it just felt normal. Lifting the skin on the brow, he pulled an eye-lid open. This did seem strange; they were yellow too, not like normal people. He didn't like that and quickly pushed the eyelid shut. Gently pulling the sheet away, it began to expose his upper body. Neck, shoulders, chest, normal, then suddenly…

The wounds in the abdomen were deep. Three jagged gashes, marks where the old man had been impaled on the fence. All had been stitched, in a fashion, quickly held together with black thread to stop the innards from being exposed. Fred winced at the sight, the blood, still weeping from the wounds. He considered pulling the sheet back in place and running but something wouldn't let him. He had to see more, feel more, know more.

The grey sheet slid from the table and crumpled in a heap on the floor. The body now fully exposed, thin winkled legs with oversized knees, the toenails on both feet were black and overgrown, a withered, flaccid penis squeezed between his legs. And the holes, the deep penetrative wounds, covered in lifeless blood. He couldn't remove his gaze from them, it was almost hypnotic. Fred knew he should be afraid, repulsed even, but he wasn't, this seemed strangely natural.

Perhaps he was pre-prepared due to the family history, was that even possible? Whatever the reason, he knew he couldn't leave, not without, touching.

With one finger, he stroked the thread. It was thick and tight. Each wound had three large stitches, but there was space between each one. Scratching with his fingernail, he found a gap. This was wrong, this was so wrong; so why couldn't he stop? Sliding two fingers across the skin below the first wound, there was a lip which hung slightly loose. It was almost black; the dried blood had begun to curdle into a scab before the old man had expired. The fingers probed deeper; Fred thrilled at the feeling. With a little force, his index finger found an open hole, he looked away, not bearing to see but needing to feel. The finger was deep to the second knuckle, the fatty tissue moulding around; the feeling was indescribable, his first finger had joined its neighbour, two appendages deep inside the body, stroking gently. The stitches held firm and stopped anymore access to delve deeper but the delirious, feverish, joy; exploring the insides of someone else's body. Even though he was only a child, he could feel a stirring of in an area where he never felt before. Cursing when the third digit couldn't gain entry, he pulled the fingers from the wound, blood and fatty tissue clinging to his skin. It was cold, lifting the hand before his face, he dared himself to taste his prize; tongue protruding, fingers emerging, the crash of a door closing above.

Fred began to panic. Grabbing the sheet from the floor, he wiped the residue on the rough surface and tried desperately to re-cover the body. Pulling the sheet high, he allowed himself a smile as the head went out of view, giving the cheek one more stroke. When he was satisfied the corpse was how he'd found it, he ran to the door and stretched for the light.

The boy was given precious time as Geoffrey paused inside the hallway, struggling to remove the shoes from his aching feet.

"Freddy! I'm home." The mortician frowned when there was no response. "Where's he got too now? Fred, are you there?"

The child frantically stretched for the light-switch but knew if he waited any longer, he'd be caught red-handed. Instead, he closed the door to the preparation room quietly, terrified as he heard his father's footsteps moving across the floor above.

"Oh, no." From entering the kitchen, Geoff immediately noticed the doorway to the lower floor open. "I don't believe it!" Marching directly across the room, he threw the open the barrier furiously but was forced to stop with a start. His son was sitting on the top step with an inquisitive look across his face.

"Hi dad. What's down here?"

Geoffrey soon realised that his son was more mature than most children his age and after gentle persuasion, had given the boy a guided tour of their family business, ensuring that a body wasn't in storage first. He was vaguely concerned that Fred was perhaps too interested in the workings of what their occupation entailed but was thankful too that the boy wasn't repulsed by the idea of making a living by dealing with the dead, the business was his birth-right and he was the only possible heir. By eight-years-old he was cleaning the mortuary, mopping the floors, and wiping away spilled blood, washing the utensils, marvelling at the sharpness of the scalpel. By then, his father allowed him to assist in the preparation of a deceased body. Again, it was a man, old age the cause of death. There were no outward wounds, he'd been a heavy smoker and the stench of nicotine was embedded in his skin. As he helped dress the man in his Sunday best suit, he noticed the size of his penis was tiny and couldn't help to giggle. Geoffrey frowned; certain he knew the reason for his son's laugh but unwilling to join the joke.

By the boy's teens, his duties had continued to grow, gaining increasing responsibility. He was now allowed to enter the mortuary at will. Neither of his parents were suspicious of his motives so exploring exposed bodies became easier. The feel of the cold flesh was addictive, as was the sliding his inquisitive fingers into places living people would never allow. His depravity was steadily growing.

His grotesque hobby helped ease the pressure of the other elements of life. His teenage years in school were a misery. By fifteen, he was seriously overweight, and his diet of fatty, greasy foods caused his skin to be savaged with acne. Huge boils and pimples exploded across his complexion and added to his unpopularity with his peers. Boys either shunned or bullied him and girls just thought him weird and ugly. Even in the school uniform, green and red blazer, black trousers, white shirt, he looked scruffy and out of place. School was a place he was forced to go rather than wanted too. He was known as the undertaker. Strangely he liked that. It was a nickname, the cool kids all had nicknames so, why couldn't he? That's what he was. That's what he's always going to be. It eventually got shortened to taker which was better. If people were calling him taker, they weren't calling him fat spotty bastard. An improvement.

Fred had one friend. The Gregory family had ties to Hallowell dates back generations. Of Irish ancestry, they opened the first shop ever recorded in the village in 1850. Originally a pork butcher though as years progressed, they became a more complete meat seller, generation after generation would inherit and run the store, each as successful as the last. The family had an old Victorian style gothic mansion on the outskirts of town with their own slaughterhouse, extended out of the back. They had a contract with the Wade family, another well respected clan who owned the farm adjacent to Hallowell colliery and the railway station and bought perennially sheep and pigs to which they would slaughter and sell in their main street shop.

Years may have progressed but the Gregory's seemed stuck in time. The mansion, which had previously been the most luxuriant property in the village bar for the Graham mansion became dilapidated and in desperate need of renovation. The roof would leak, shutters on the windows hung loose and the glass in those windows was mainly cracked and broken. The garden was overrun with weeds and decaying trees, the dirt-track driveway had huge potholes which made many horses trip and become lame as they were taking their meat, to and from their slaughterhouse. The stench from a leaking septic tank could waft toxic fumes across the village when the wind blew in the correct way. It was the last house to convert to electricity and even then, it was only to assist in their slaughtering of the animals. Year on year, the once mighty property became more derelict but still, the entire family would continue to live under one roof.

Even though they were one of the wealthiest families in Hallowell, the children walked the streets like urchins. Shoes with holes in the soles, trousers, either three inches to short or baggy and dragging on the ground, hand-me-downs from the previous generation. Their hair was unkempt and greasy, and all their peers would avoid them as they always seemed to stink of blood.

Malcolm and Nathan were the eldest of the latest generation of Gregory. Siblings ranging from fourteen to just four, the brood of seven were the latest in the lineage to have a dishevelled appearance and prospects, only tied to the family business. Malcolm was learning to butcher as soon as he could hold a knife. Watching the livestock brutally killed in the back yard became as natural as breathing, seeing rivers of animal blood drying in the afternoon sun, the stench of death omnipresent. The boy was small for his age with a raft of psychological problems, ranging from bed wetting to fear of the dark. Constantly struggling through school, the child longed for the day when he could leave the teachers and classrooms behind and take his rightful place as the next in line to the Gregory's butchery empire. Where the fuck was, he ever going to need to know the square route of six million, what year was the battle of Hastings, algebra, geography, learning French, what the fuck. It was a waste of time. School was the shits.

And what made it worse was the children whom he had to share those classrooms with. Thin and sickly looking, he was the typical boy in the corner. As his bed wetting had become so severe, the urine seemed to have penetrated his skin permanently. His mother rarely washed the sheets, just hung them on the line to dry, so the imprint of the stench was present, each time he took to his bed. Whether he soiled the bedclothes again or if his sweat made the embedded pee became revigorated, the child would constantly stink of the embarrassing episode. Ridiculed and bullied, Malcolm began to live inside himself. Fantasise about taking those who tormented him to the slaughterhouse and…

Perhaps things may have been easier had he the support of his twin in school. Unfortunately, Nathan was slow witted, originally believed to have down syndrome but eventually, the doctors changed their diagnosis to the boy having autism. His parents were good people who tried their hardest to push their son on, but his limitations were great. Thankfully the child had been blessed with a handsome face and strong physique. The brothers were not identical twins, far from it. To see them together, most wouldn't even have believed them siblings. But as Nathan grew, his mind regressed and his condition deteriorated, leaving the house alone was impossible and even the most menial of tasks were beyond the boy. He was gentle of nature but occasionally, his frustration at his limitations would see him explode into fits of rage. These would usually dissipate quickly, and he'd return to his position of gentle giant.

As Malcolm couldn't rely on his twin for assistance, he was delirious when he became close friends with Fred Gibson. They seemed kindred spirits, bought together out of need and a hatred for the tormenters of a school that refused to see past their deficiencies and eccentricities, to see the people inside. True, Fred was odd, he lived in a funeral parlour and had a morbid fascination with death, and Malcolm stank of urine, mixed with blood, wore holy, unfashionable clothing, and came from a family of animal murderers. They were outcasts who had no friends, were of limited intelligence and little in the way of athletic ability, they were easy targets for bullies and stood no chance with girls. But finally, at least they had each other.

Malcolm was a year younger and therefore a class below at school which meant that they still had to endure the classroom alone but at break and lunch time, they were no longer forced to hide away, desperate to avoid another beating. There was strength in numbers and though they were only two, fellow pupils tended to let them alone. Fred would try hard to ignore his friend's foul smell, carefully trying to broach the subject occasionally in the hope that some new soap or scent could mask the odour. And Malcolm would listen intently to Fred's tales of the macabre, from inside the funeral parlour, though the mortician's son kept his own private activities secret, unsure how his only friend would react. Trust was a major issue for Fred Gibson and, even though he felt a growing bond between Malcolm and himself, risk and reward were considered. He wanted a partner, someone to share his obsession with but that was dangerous.

His depravity had grown steadily as his confidence to not be caught increased. The taking of souvenirs had begun early. A lock of hair, a nail clipping, anything small that wouldn't be noticed. After saving his money for what seemed forever, he'd purchased a second-hand polaroid camera from a pawn shop in St Mara. This was the key to taking his hobby to a new level, snapping photographs of each body the business processed. Some were given extra attention than others. Had the death been particularly grotesque, the wounds would be shot in intricate detail, close-up and personal. He'd once used a whole reel of film on Tommy Jarvis, a young man in his late teens that had been crossing the railway line after seeing his girlfriend, just as the last coal train had passed by. The injuries had been catastrophic, and Gibson had been almost orgasmic as he took shots of bones protruding through skin, phenomenal blood-loss and half a crushed skull. Then of course, there were the ladies. Most were hags, old, cancer-riddled, repulsive. But occasionally, he'd get lucky. Like when Alice Vasey passed.

Alice had mental problems throughout her life. After losing her mother to a drug overdose at just six-years-old, she spent her early years back and forth between St Mara children's home and foster parents that always seemed to tire of her highly-strung ways. As a teen, she took the same path as her late mother, alcohol leading to drugs leading to prostitution. Few seemed to care when she was discovered in a back alleyway behind the shops in Hallowell Main Street, a hypodermic needle hanging loosely from a vein in her left arm. Even less were surprised when she was pronounced dead at the scene. It was two days before her twenty-first birthday.

Though the hard living was already taking a toll, Alice left a beautiful corpse. Long black hair, shoulder length with a natural curl, dark gothic eyes, and full red lips. Her body was overly thin, but her firm youthful C-cup breasts re-invigorated her curves, and her petite stature gave her that child-like quality.

It had been early evening when the body had been discovered and after the formalities, the corpse didn't arrive until almost midnight. Geoffrey Gibson had already drunk four large measures of whisky before even receiving the telephone call with the news of the girl's passing, so he allowed his son to greet the coroner and the policeman when taking delivery of Alice's remains. Arriving in a black, zipped-up body-bag, the young woman was placed on the slab of the mortuary and suddenly, Fred was alone with the girl of his dreams.

He watched her many times from his bedroom window, late at night, drunk out of her mind or high on drugs. Sitting on one of the children's swings inside the nearby park, swigging from whatever bottle she could get hold of. She fascinated him, her ways; she seemed so free, little did he know the torment inside her mind. He'd tried to approach her once; he was barely thirteen, and desperate to get her attention. By then, everyone knew she was selling herself to pay for her habit. He walked over and handed her a £1 note but couldn't get the words from his lips. She'd looked at him and laughed heartily.

"What do you think you're buying with that? Bet your little pecker can't even get hard yet." With that, she scrunched the note between her fingers into a ball and threw it at him, all the time laughing that filthy cackle. Fred's facial features crunched, and he almost burst into tears, embarrassment mixed with disappointment, he began to run, the money blowing away with the wind. As the teenager fled into his home, he ran to the bedroom but continued to watch. He smiled as he noticed the girl searching the undergrowth by the swings after realising the money would be useful. Recovering the paper ball, she uncurled it and pushed it into her denim jeans pocket. Enough for another hit. Once the body was in place, Fred had to fight his natural urge. Though his father was overly intoxicated, he may have still been awake when the policeman had left. Perhaps he'd come downstairs and check everything was correct. No, it was better to lock up, switch off the light and make sure, he made plenty of noise before going to his bed, so his parents knew he was upstairs and going to sleep. Then, if he was patient, he'd have time to sneak back down later and see his prize. By 2 am, the house was silent.

Creeping from his bedroom and avoiding a creaky floorboard on the outer landing, he carefully placed his feet with as little weight as possible on each stair until he reached the bottom. Pausing for a moment to ensure his parents weren't stirring, he made his way through the lounge and into the kitchen. The locked doorway to the mortuary was always stiff and still in need of oil on the rusty hinges so the teen moved the barrier tentatively, cringing with each movement as the arthritic door seemed to echo around the house. With the entrance open, he moved a kitchen chair, forcing it under the handle to hold it in place as to not cause any more unnecessary noise. Carefully, he descended the last staircase, and switched on the mortuary light.

Pausing for a moment to ensure his parents hadn't heard his descent, the house was still silent. His patience had prevailed, before him, the girl of his dreams.

The clasp on the zipper of the body-bag was stiff with a sharp point which penetrated Gibson's thumb. The pain barely registered such was his excitement. Holding tightly to the material with his left hand, his right hand yanked firmly on the zipper, and it began to open. With each click, more of her became visible, that beautiful long wavy black hair, hanging loosely across her face, her pale skin, cold as ice, lips the shade of cherries, she looked just like she was sleeping. Pulling further, her slender, swan-like neck, those narrow shoulders, and then, finally he could see, perfection.

Fred hadn't expected the body to be nude. Sometimes, after the coroner had pronounced the cause of death, the corpse would still be in the clothes they had died in. But today, Alice Vasey had been stripped naked. Perhaps they had needed to inspect the body for any other possible causes of death. She *had* died in a filthy backstreet. They had to check if she was carrying any other injuries or if there had been sexual interference. Then Fred began to get angry. What if she had been stripped to satisfy some perverts sick fantasy. What if someone had defiled the body before bringing there? Who would do such a thing?

"No. No, I can't think like that. Who cares what happened before?"

The zipper reached its apex and Gibson reached inside, carefully lifting the legs, one at a time, until she was fully uncovered from the black leather body-bag. Rigor had already begun to take hold, the limbs stiff and losing their flexibility but with force, the teen managed to lay his prize out perfectly flat on the cold marble slab. He'd carried with him, a small brown-paper bag and inside was his polaroid camera. After marvelling at the girl's beauty, he began lining up shots. Her head and shoulders, her breasts, below the public line, each taken with care and precision as to not waste the negative. Climbing onto the slab, he stood above Alice, trying desperately to obtain a shot of her in its entirety but always, either the feet or the top of the head was missing. He tried resting the corpse on its side and moving to the far reaches of the room, but the head lolled lifelessly onto the shoulder and the left arm kept flopping over the areas which he prized the most. His frustration was growing when he decided to prop the head up on pillows and lie the intruding arm behind the girls back. It looked wonderful, as if she were sleeping. Staring through the viewfinder, he began to smile, knowing that this shot would be one of his most treasured possessions. Pressing the button across the top of the camera, nothing happened. He did it again with the same response.

"What the fuck?" Turning the polaroid, he opened the flap which house the photographic paper; it was empty. "No, no, no, this can't be, I had fifteen, I've only took fourteen." Sifting through the shots he began to count. "Twelve, thirteen, four…NO." Two sheets had fused together and as he carefully tried to pry them apart, they began to tear. "FUCK, FUCK, FUCK." He looked at the body, Alice Vasey's face, it seemed to be smiling. No, surely, it was a trick of the light, he moved closer, the corners of the mouth did seem raised. "You knew this would happen, didn't you?" Jabbing a finger in the dead girl's face, he became angrier at the lack of a response. "You knew those sheets were stuck together and it would spoil my fun." Pushing the body at the shoulder, it slowly rolled away, onto its back. The push, though not forceful, excited him. He could do anything he wanted, and no one would know. The first slaps were gentle, across the thighs and wrists, the abuse arousing him like never. "You need to be punished. I was having fun and you spoiled it." A back-hand slap across the left breast made a mark and he immediately regretted it. He rubbed the area profusely, but it just made things worse. Fred began to whimper. "I'm sorry, I'm so very sorry, I didn't mean to…" the mouth still appeared to be smiling in a mocking retort. "Stop that, whore. That's right, you're nothing but a stupid, street walking whore. Well, there's only one thing that whores are good for." Gibson threw down the camera and quickly began to fumble with the belt of his trousers. "I'll show you, whore. No slut will mock me." His slacks fell to the floor, and he kicked off his slippers. With a knowing smile, Fred Gibson began to climb onto the marble slab.

Alice Vasey was the start of a greater depravity. The living held little interest in Gibson's mind. What was the point? He had everything he needed without the fear of rejection. He soon realised that it was not sex which excited him, it was the power he held over another. He didn't class himself gerontophilic or paedophilic, he wasn't gay, straight, or bi-sexual. He had no prejudice, for him, everyone was fair game. It was barely even about sex at all. It was the desecration of another person's remains. Perhaps the soul had passed but the remains were his to do with as he pleased. Fuck the living. Even if he discovered a girl who could see past his less than attractive appearance and questionable personality, it was doubtful that she would allow him the freedom to partake in the sick activities that the dead afforded him.

Soon realising that it wasn't only the female form that aroused his loins, he began to defile the bodies of males also. The first had been the corpse of Timothy Jenkins. A tall strong blond-haired boy who was in a year ahead of Gibson in school and a specimen the girls swooned over, had been struck by a car halfway up Hallowell bank and killed instantly. Jenkins had been a ringleader of a group who had seemed to live to make he and Malcolm Gregory miserable. His handsome looks and athletic ability made him the perfect candidate for popularity and with that came the freedom to either help or destroy another's existence. As far as the outcasts were concerned, he chose the latter. Neither Gregory nor Gibson would use the lavatories in school in case any of their enemies were lurking. Malcolm had once made the mistake of leaving for school without using their home facilities and by lunchtime, was desperate to empty his bladder. Jenkins and another boy, Tommy Doyle, had witnessed the frightened teen enter the restroom and quickly formulated their plan. Eight boys either urinated or defecated into one of the toilet bowls but instead of forcing Malcolm's head into the sewage, he was made to do it himself, adding to the youngster's humiliation.

When Fred had seen the body of the boy who had made his life a misery for the past five years laid lifeless on the mortuary table, he squealed with delight. Across the three days the corpse was in storage, Gibson took the chance to exact a vengeance on the bully, hoping above hope that his spirit was somewhere watching on in disgust. Slicing open the boy's scrotum with surgeon-like procession, his removed one of Jenkins's testicles, but instead of keeping it as a souvenir, he boiled it on the stove until cooked through and then baked it to add a crunchy exterior, giggling as he sat in the school lunchroom not twenty feet from the ringleader's group as he munched it between a slice of wholemeal bread.

Next, using a needle, he forced the sharp implement under the nails of his fingers and toes, wondering if Timothy's spirit was screaming in agony at his actions. A sick satisfied grimace covered his face as he imagined the pain his actions would be causing were his nemesis still alive. The guttural choking cries that would be emanating from his foul acidic mouth. Yes, that was fun. But the final humiliation would be the closing victory.

On the eve of the cremation, deep in the early hours of the morning, Fred Gibson once more descended the staircase to the mortuary slab. His father had been visiting with Jack Daniels and was snoring uncontrollably and his mother was under her usual Valium sedation so he could be certain not to be disturbed. Still, he was careful not to make any unnecessary noise as the act he had in mind would take privacy.

Earlier, he'd assisted his father in placing Timothy's body into its final resting place, a highly varnished gold-handled Smith and Stimson coffin. Fred could never understand why people would go to such expense for something which in several hours would be burned to ashes, he could only guess at keeping up appearances. The casket had been moved to the front room of the property though the curtains had been closed as a mark of respect. Fred flicked on the electric light-switch and the sharp glare made him squint. Several coffins were standing on their ends across the far wall, but the Jenkins casket had been placed on a study pine table in the centre of the room. The lid was closed, and a golden plaque was fastened tightly into the polished wood.

Timothy Jenkins
Born January 28th, 1927
Died October 13th ,1943
Sleep well our special boy.

"Special boy." What a crock of shit. Was he special when he was beating the crap out of anyone, he felt the urge too? How about when he was humiliating Malcolm, terrifying him enough to flush his own head in raw sewage just to avoid another beating. The mother fucker got what he deserved. And now…the final vengeance.

Gibson lifted the caskets lid, it was stiff and had been forced into place earlier, damp weather always made the wood swell. Carefully placing it across the doorway, he spent a few seconds gazing at his enemy. The body was covered in white silk, only the head was visible, his blond hair neat, parted down the left side. Removing the material, Timothy's parents had bought him a football strip, Preston north end, and had requested he be dressed in it for the ceremony. Again, such a waste, there'd be nothing left after it went in the flames. Fred pushed an arm under Jenkins's shoulders and with one hoist, lifted the corpse to a seated position. Sliding his right arm behind the bend of the knees, he heaved with all his might, taking the lifeless body up and over his shoulder. The coffin slid and for a moment, Fred feared it would crash to the floor. He quickly deposited the body across onto a long leather chesterfield and rushed back before it could fall to the floor. His breathing was laboured with the exertion but also from the excitement of what he was about to do.

Timothy had fallen into a seated position, the head and left arm slumped slightly across the chesterfield's wooden barrier. Fred gazed once more at the body but had a sudden moment of doubt. True, the antagonist had been a vicious bastard who destroyed countless days of schooling for the frightened boys, but he was dead now, was this going too far? A strange feeling of compassion that the teen had never felt before was growing and Gibson had a sudden need for affection, gently sitting beside the body, placing his left arm around its shoulders, and pulling it to him. Holding the corpse in a tight embrace, he kissed its brow and stroked the blonde hair back in place. He was having second thoughts, was this one depravity too far? Yes, he'd been with deceased females and had touched private areas of male anatomy but that was mostly out of curiosity and never with one he felt an emotional attachment to. This was something he could never take back.

Fred pushed the body away and leaped to his feet, pacing the room in startled confusion. He hated Timothy Jenkins; of that he was certain. He was glad he was dead, and he was certain of that too. So why was he hesitating? This wasn't a sexual need, this was just violation, a final act of vengeance to a sworn enemy. It wouldn't mean anything in the long term. It was just a deed that needed to be done.

It was decided. He slowly let his dressing gown fall to the floor and shifted Timothy's corpse into a more suitable position. A single tear rolled down his cheek as the desecration begun.

This became Fred Gibson's life. In 1948, when he was just twenty, his parents were killed in a fire. They had been staying at a small guest house in the coastal resort of Blackpool when the property had been engulfed in flames while they slept. He became the sole proprietor of the family home and the funeral business, it served him well and afforded him a comfortable living. He remained friends with Malcolm Gregory who by now had become owner of the butchery on Main Street and the two continued as drinking friends. Women became more of a mystery to Gibson, the burning need for a mate quelled by his continued violation of the deceased. His manners toward the fairer sex ensured that, should any female see past his unattractive façade; his personality would chase them away too. Fuck them.

But still, there was one need, a burning ambition that he never managed to fulfil. With that, he'd need help.

It was the summer of 1960. The long August days were during a heat wave that had gone on for weeks. Tempers were frayed and alcohol consumption had increased dramatically. The temperatures inside Hallowell colliery had reached unsafe levels, miners were suffering heat stroke, the situation was reaching breaking point.

Alvin Wilson was a married man with two children, in his early forties, he'd worked the mine all his employed life. He was a mild-mannered family orientated fellow who supported his mother, liked a drink at the weekend and smoked roll-up cigarettes. He didn't cheat, barely gambled, and gave his wife most of his wages for the house keeping. That's what made what happened more bizarre. It was a Tuesday evening, he'd finished his shift, washed, and read his newspaper and sat down to dinner with his family. Midway through the meal he got up and excused himself from the table. As his daughters ate and the wife cleared the dishes, he went out to the garage and got himself a hammer. On re-entering the home, he proceeded to bludgeon his entire family with the weapon, smashing in all three of the skulls before tying a rope to a beam in the attic and hanging himself. Some said it was a mental breakdown, others claimed his wife was seeing another man, there was only one thing certain. The bodies weren't discovered for two days. Two long hot days in the blistering summer heat. By the time Fred Gibson was called and the police released the corpses, the decomposition had already taken hold.

The undertaker prepared the remains as best he could, Wilson's brother lived in St Mara and assumed responsibility for the costs. But there was something different about this situation that Fred couldn't understand. These were the first murder victims he'd ever had in his care, and his emotion troubled him. It took time to pinpoint the reason…he was jealous.

The wife was a plain woman, average height, slightly plump around the midriff, loose skin hanging below the arms where there'd been some weight loss, but the flesh had lost its elasticity. He could tell her bleached blonde hair wasn't natural, it didn't match with patches on other areas of her anatomy. From the crime scene, it appeared that she had been the last to die, standing at the sink, only alerted to her husband's presence by the sickening thud of the hammer crashing through their eldest daughter's skull and the terrified screams of the two-year-old who watched on. She had defensive wounds on her hands, but Alvin was a powerful man and had easily overwhelmed her and had given his wife an extra two blows into the back of the skull for the temerity of fighting back.

The eight-year-old had one clear indentation, at the base of the skull with the rounded edge of the 10lb weapon and a long slice across the brow where her head had struck the edge of the dinner table while falling to the floor. The younger child was less straightforward. After the heavy steel hammer had crashed through her crown, it became embedded beneath the bone and as he tore the weapon free, part the child's brain had followed.

As for Wilson, his face had turned purple, and the nylon rope had cut into his flesh. With the decomposition of the skin, the head and body were only attached because of the spine. It appeared that his neck hadn't broken as he'd intended and he'd been strangled to death by the cord, it would have taken some time and been deservedly painful. He was the only member of the family that Gibson had taken a trophy from, removing his penis and testicles, and storing them in the deep-freeze. The girls were left intact, even Fred had principals.

It was days later, well after the funeral services, that the troubling emotion revealed itself. He wasn't sad for the victims, in the funeral business, empathy was a luxury one could seldom afford. It wasn't even disgust for the act itself, quite the opposite. He was sad because he wished he had the guts to perform murder himself. All these years, countless bodies, clearing up the mess others had left behind. He just wished he could be responsible for once. He'd tried, God knows he'd tried. But when the time came to strike that killer blow, to take that final step and become a murderer, his courage alluded him.

The first time was with a prostitute in Carpenter. She'd taken him to a deserted shop for privacy, the back entrance was broken, and she assured him they wouldn't be disturbed. As the woman performed oral sex upon him, he reached into his jacket pocket and produced a folding hunting knife. Snapping the blade into place, he was about to plunge the cold steel into the young woman's neck when one of her fellow sex workers burst in to use the property too. An argument erupted and Gibson fled, disappointment embedded across his face. The next time was once more in the neighbouring town of Carpenter, inside a wooded area used by joggers. He had hidden in overgrown brushes, ready to pounce when an unsuspecting runner would pass by. Brandishing a large butcher-knife, he saw a girl in her late teens approaching fast. His heart was racing as the sound of trainer-shoes crunching on the gravel track got louder and louder. It was dusk and the visibility was poor, but Gibson had decided it was too late to back down now. As the final seconds passed, he moved into place. The wooden handle felt loose between his sweaty fingers, only the width of a tree between himself and his lifelong ambition. But just as he was about to pounce, the sound of voices froze him solid. The sound of two police officers chatting as they approached from the other direction made him dive back for cover. The jogger heard the disturbed branches and stopped to investigate. Fred held his breath and closed his eyes tightly in silent prayer.

"Please God, let me get away and I'll never do this again." He heard the officers call to the girl to ask if she needed assistance. If they investigated, he was done for sure, a middle-aged man lurking in woodland brandishing a butcher-knife. He thought of throwing the weapon but that would only bring more attention. Finally, the teen told the police that she was fine, just a little spooked by her surroundings. They laughed and went their separate ways and Fred Gibson cried with relief. It was then, he was certain that the horrific ambition would of his would have to stay unfulfilled.

That was until 1967.

The year Hallowell went to Hell. The colliery disaster, the destruction of the Graham's, murder, mayhem, and devastation. And the undertaker was perfectly placed to watch the entire unfold.

Fred had always known when to keep his mouth shut and who not to upset. Links between his and the Graham family were long and impressive, dating all the way back to the village's birth. William Graham, Frank's great, great, grandfather, had given the Gibson's land in Hallowell to form the funeral business in the 1850's as payment for a lavish ceremony after the death of his mother, Maude. William's grandson Michael had married Mary Gibson, Fred's grandmother causing a blood-line link and even recently, Fred and Martin were relatively close friends and Gibson was made godfather to Frank and Jenifer. The undertaker knew how to make friends with the right people. When the Graham business empire had begun to crumble, Gibson acted as a confidant, and when his wife died, he performed the ceremony, free of charge. Fred's only payment was the amputation of both of Iris's feet, tagged and placed in the Gibson deep freeze, they were very shapely.

Fred hadn't participated in the town's invasion of the railway station, instead, gaining the support of the local priest to bring a halt to the proceedings. He'd done so in a way to save face, aware that to disagree with the consensus could be detrimental to his standing in Hallowell. Trying to appear concerned for the men's safety, he secretly feared for the future of his godson, afraid that the sheer numbers may be too much for even Frank to overcome. After the failure of the debacle, inside, he was giddy with relief, caring little about the residents who had perished at the hands of the psychopath. It was also then; his sick brain formed a devilish plan. If he couldn't perform a murderous blow to cause death, his godson could, and he could watch.

First, Fred needed that initial contact with the young monster and hope that his roots with the family could be enough to form trust. If not, he would probably become the next victim.

He waited two weeks after the invasion to allow time for the dust to settle. Plus, those idiot Simpson brothers had defied the borderline agreement and entered the station to see what they could steel. The only thing they found was death, which for Hallowell, was deemed as a good deed, they were nothing but trouble, good riddance to bad rubbish. Still, the funerals were a nice little earner and Fred had taken all their penises for his collection in the deepfreeze. It pushed back Gibson's plan slightly, but it gave him more time for his plan of action.

It was a little before five on a cool November morning. The village was covered in a thick blanket of fog which helped Fred's mission. It was barely light and when the day broke, the mist stopped the sun's rays penetrating the gloomy air. The mortician needed to be careful, the eyes of an early morning dog-walker noticing his decent into the station would spread through Hallowell like wildfire. So, entering the grounds directly was too dangerous, there were colliery cottages nearby and even if it seemed the coast was clear, it was impossible to be certain. This had to be private. Thankfully, Fred knew an alternative.

When those morons from the village had discovered the tunnel from the Graham mansion to the railway station, they'd forgot to block that access when the fence was erected. It was an ideal escape route for Frank and an easy access to anyone crazy enough to enter the station. Plus, in their haste, no one had noticed a hidden doorway, halfway along the tunnel, containing enough to satisfy the monster for a long time.

Martin Graham had become extremely paranoid after World War II and the atomic bombs dropped in Japan. He was certain that other countries would soon have access to such weapons and, in his mind, he previewed what the devastation would be like in Hallowell. Towns, villages, capitals, destroyed be the press of a button. Well, if that was coming, he'd be ready. The tunnel had been erected years earlier but at the halfway point, a room was created. It was full of canned food, dried food, hundreds of bottles filled with fresh water as obviously, after the nuclear attack, our natural water supply would be contaminated. There was an air conditioning unit to help with the natural airflow, there was an electricity supply and a back-up generator in case the blast kills the power, a television, radio, changes of clothing and a small bed. Martin hadn't constructed it for himself, where it was his time, he'd accept it. It was created for Frank, desperate that his son would survive and continue the Graham legacy. Had he known what it would eventually be used for, he probably wouldn't have bothered.

Passing by the woodland around the Graham mansion, he searched for a fallen fence to make his entry. A well-worn path had torn into the grass, where local kids with no respect to the Graham name had skidded around on bicycles, but it helped Fred discover an area where the green-mash fence had been torn down by vandals and thieves. Gibson lumbered clumsily over the obstacle, stumbling, and almost losing his balance. When he finally passed the test, Fred cursed and kicked the awkward mesh, happy that the incident was over.

He could still smell the foul stench of charred wood and smouldering rubble. Weeks earlier, he'd watched the flames destroy that once beautiful fortress with no alarm to a fire service, this was town business, questions would be asked if the firefighters from St Mara were called. Yet more Hallowell secrets, hidden in time. It was ten days before the fire was fully extinguished and even then, sporadic blazes would erupt. He'd been worried the main building had been destroyed so badly that, it would collapse upon itself, and his easiest access point to the tunnel would be blocked. Treading carefully as he approached the front door, seeing the devastation would never get easier. Fallen masonry and broken glass crunched underfoot, it was beginning to look obvious that this access point would be impossible. Both doors had turned to ash but inside, the hallway ceiling had collapsed, blocking the entire area. Looking to the windows, they appeared more of the same and even those that may be passable contained huge razor-like shards of glass embedded in the frames.

"Fuck." Frustration was growing, if the outside was like this, what would the interior be like. Stepping back, he dug the heels of his brown, Dr Marten boots into the earth and exhaled a large sigh. Each of the blackened window-frames stared out like lifeless eyes and the heavy mist shrouded the devastated roof from sight. Was it worth it? This risk he was taking could go very badly, very quickly. If by some chance he managed to navigate a path through these derelict remains and find the tunnel way to the station, there was always the chance that Frank's madness maybe too great for Fred's reasoning to combat. It had been some time since he'd part of the young man's life and the way he'd dispatched the station intruders had been clinical and merciless, perhaps his friend's son would be just too far gone. The temptation had been great to just turn on those worn-down heels and be home in time for breakfast. There was just something inside that wouldn't allow it.

His journey to the rear of the property was swift, just because the hour was early didn't mean that the whole of Hallowell would be sleeping. The mechanic, Ian Gaskins was a keen hunter and would regularly stalk the village's woodland in search of rabbits with his air-riffle. Fred had seen him slip onto the Graham estate on a few occasions even though he'd tried to warn him off. Another with no respect. He had a big mouth too, especially after a few beers, trouble making Mother Fu... "Focus Freddy, focus, don't get side-tracked."

His sigh of relief was audible when the rear doors appeared unblocked. Buildings like these were built to last and though the damage was still extensive, the walls had held firm and most of the roof was still intact. The back door was locked but with little force from his meaty right shoulder, it gave way easily. A remaining glass pain fell from the casing and shattered on the floor, making Gibson cringe as the noise echoed around the courtyard. Stepping into the kitchen, the stench of charred material made him cough and he raised a hand to his mouth. The shiver that ran down him spine had little to do with the cool morning temperature, this still felt wrong to be inside a friend's home, even if that friend had passed. He still felt that closeness to Martin and the grieving process was still underway, Fred had so little in the way of friendships that losing one hurt deeply.

Exiting the kitchen into the hallway, the site of the magnificent staircase, reduced to ashes made tears well in his eyes. More than the Graham's wealth and possessions, this had always impressed Gibson the most. A vision of a bi-gone age, strength and beauty, plush carpeting, tasteful décor, and fine artwork hanging from the walls; all reduced to a blackened waste. Quickly, he turned away, no longer wishing to see the awful sight and headed toward the basement.

The door was blocked with fallen timber, which was tough to remove, a French dresser that had been positioned in the passage had wilted under the intense blaze, but its steel frame had prevented its total annihilation. Gibson took a strong footing and began to lift, only for a floorboard to give way under his weight. Stumbling forward, his shin cracked against the splintering wood, cutting a hole in his trouser-leg, and slicing a gash into his flesh. The pain registered immediately, and he yelled out, as much to the shock as the injury. Carefully, he pulled the stricken limb free and kicked out in anger at the fallen piece of furniture. The unit shifted and collapsed into pieces, causing a cloud of dust to erupt. When the debris settled, the pathway was clear.

Gibson made steady progress down the stone steps, finally confident enough to use the flashlight he'd brought from home. The small door to the basement was wide open and the undertaker was surprised that there appeared to be little damage inside, just the usual stench of burned remains. He wondered how much time had passed, wanting to reach the station grounds before the rest of Hallowell woke so he quickened his pace. There was a discarded hammer inside the basement workshop, and he considered taking it as a means of protection, deciding against it when he remembered he needed Frank to see him as a friend and not a threat. "Threat." That would be funny if he weren't so terrified.

Once inside the tunnel walkway, he was glad he'd remembered the torch as visibility without it was zero. The tight wooden boards that made up the walls floor and ceiling were reminiscent of the tunnels inside of Hallowell colliery. The height was barely above six feet and Gibson continually found himself crouching, claustrophobia was never something that had troubled him but inside of here, the tight space made him seriously uneasy. His breathing had become laboured, and he could feel panic raising inside him, the sooner he reached the halfway point and the secret bunker, the better.

The door was easy to miss, no handle, just a small gap, enough space for four fingers. The only other clue to its location was the directional lines of the wooden slats, the walls ran vertical whereas the doorway material was horizontal. Bar for that, the entranceway was completely hidden. Gibson slid his podgy digits through the space and tugged firmly. He needn't have used such force as the door sprang open with ease, indicating it had been used recently. The hinges still whined as only rusted metal could and the shrill call made Fred grimace once more. A heavy smell of spoiled food rose to greet his nostrils and he spun his head away sharply, the unpleasant odour making him wretch. Regaining composure, Gibson breathe in deeply from the tunnel air and continued, unaware he was holding his breath. A translucent layer of perspiration covered his wide body and though the early morning air carried a chill, the anticipation caused his skin to radiate heat, his dark blue polo shirt clinging to the base of his back and appearing black in colour. The lack of oxygen soon caused him to feel dizzy and with his free hand, he clung to the doorframe for balance.

As the torch light flashed across the bunker, he was surprised that it was far larger than his memories recalled. Fumbling in the darkness, he rubbed the interior walls desperately trying to find a light switch. The smooth surface indicated that it had been professionally plastered and as Martin Graham had been a furiously private man, Gibson guessed that the work would have been contracted to a company far away from Hallowell. Finally, his fingers ran across a plastic casing with a metal switch in its centre. Firm and stiff, the button fought against being moved from its off position but eventually the mortician snapped the lever, and the room was bathed in light. Again, he couldn't help but be impressed with the magnitude of the bunker and its many contents. The fact that it was connected to an electricity supply was great feat of engineering and the sink and lavatory confirmed that a good water supply was available. The smell of spoiled food was soon overpowered by the heavy smell of paraffin and in the far-right corner stood an emergency generator for all eventualities. The furniture was sparse, just an unmade single bed and two hard backed chairs, ensuring that the designer didn't have comfort in mind. A 19-inch portable black and white television set with a metal Ariel rested on a brown coffee table, neighbouring a silver transistor radio with tape player and a white kettle, all necessities rather than luxuries. The floor was bare stone, broken only by a rough wicker mat below the sink. To the left was a separate doorway leading to another room. On inspection, it became obvious that this was the larder, five shelves covering the entire wall, containing any number of dried and canned foods. Nothing fancy, enough to maintain life, just add water and gag it down before the stomach has chance to rebel. Cornflakes had been spilled across the floor and crunched under the undertaker feet. The rancid smell was from a large tin of canned peaches, half eaten and then left to rot, the orange fruit now growing green storks with white fur. Knowing that Martin Graham was such a fanatical neat freak and would never leave the room in such a state, it was obvious that Frank must be using this lifeline to maintain his diet. The thought of meeting the killer in such a confined space made Fred shiver, it was time to move on.

Turning off the light in the bunker was hard, leaving this semi-normality to venture further into the railway station was a formidable task, one Gibson wasn't certain he could do. Standing by the door, there was a choice to make. He'd come this far but the uncertainty of what he was about to do made him feel nauseous. Slowly, he pulled the barrier closed, light still seeping around its edges. Turn left and head home, shower breakfast, just another normal day; turn right, God only knows.

The door clicked shut, shining the torch in the station direction, "Oh, fuck it, let's go." Then a sound pierced the air and stopped in dead.

He was certain it was coming from the direction he needed to travel. Just faint, he held his breath, the rhythm of his heartbeat for company. Were his ears playing tricks, his imagination running wild? No, there it was again. A vague scratching then, eek, eek, eek. The worst memory he ever had was flashing repulsively in his mind.

It was three years ago; he'd been requested to remove a body. An old hoarder named Royston Sterling hadn't been seen for two weeks. When a neighbour had broken into his bungalow, the hot summer weather had speeded up decomposition. Gibson had been warned to expect the worst. Bill Castle was retired but agreed go along and assist if needed. The old man's home was a maze of shit, years of hoarding everything from old newspapers to plastic bottles containing his own urine. The stench was overwhelming, and it was a fight to climb through the clutter to find the victim. Sterling had been felled by a stroke but that hadn't been the cause of death. As the old man lay helpless, unable to move or cry for help, the vermin he shared his home with, saw a breathing feast.

When Gibson first saw the body, it appeared he was still breathing, the chest cavity still raising up and down. The undertaker shrieked in horror when the twitching nose of a giant black rat gnawed its way through a hole in Royston's bloated stomach. The nervous monster could barely move as it had gorged so greedily on the deceased man's innards, but then without warning, it shot from the carcass into a hole between the walls of clutter, leaving only a trail of gluttonous remains in its wake.

After that incident, Fred had a growing phobia of rats and the anticipation of passing a lair along this tunnel just added to the nightmare.

He continued, almost in a trance, the situation was barely tolerable. He could hardly remember why he was doing this now. He could still hear the rats, imagining their unearthly faces. Still, he walked on. Wooden planks on all sides, tilting his neck forward to avoid the roof. Thousands of tons of earth above his head with just wooden slats protecting him, he was sure this was getting lower. The torch light revealed nothing; the air willed with dust mites. His pace quickened, "Just get there. Just fucking get there." Trotting gingerly, counting the steps in his mind, anything to pass the time, step, by step, by…

CRACK. Gibson stopped dead. Where had it come from? It sounded like it came from behind. Should I run? Which way should I run? CRACK. His torch beam scanned the area, seeing nothing. Fred began to whimper; this was a big mistake. His pace turned into a jog, his heart rate bouncing, he was still heading in the station direction. Or was he? Who knew now, all he wanted was to be somewhere, anywhere but here. CRACK.

"FRANKY? IS THAT YOU? ITS ME, UNCLE FRED." He added the honorary title of uncle in the hope it resonated and gave him more chance of survival. There was no answer. Fred was openly weeping now, any feeling of machismo long since gone. He stumbled forward, his grip on the torch loose, sweat flooding from every pour. The scurry of rats now gone, what had chased them away? Bending forwards, almost on all fours, scrambling like an animal.

FOOTSTEPS. Christ, was it footsteps? He couldn't tell anything anymore. It could be just his mind fucking with him. The torch spun 180 degrees, "That came from behind, FRANKIE." The light shook violently, his legs still heading away. A broken wooden beam across the floor had him crashing in a heap. Gibson scrambled back to all fours, crawling, scratching, scurrying like the rats he so despised. The footsteps seemed to be getting louder but there was still no one in sight. Suddenly the tunnel's end was coming. He could see the doorway in the distance.

"Twenty feet, come on, I can make it." He stopped momentarily, there were no footsteps, behind was just darkness, silent as the grave. Fred breathed in deeply, he'd made it across the tunnel. Now, the final step.

The door was sold wood and filthy with years of dust. A sliver handle shone as the torch beam struck it.

"Please don't be locked." The torch swapped hands and he wiped the sweaty residue on the trouser leg. He breathed in, fully focused, the world fell away, all that was left was the door. An outstretched arm, five powerful fingers, an awesome grip, Fred screeched in pain, his shoulder crunched inwards, his head spun around and before him, a giant skull shaped mask, a 12-inch knife…

Fred collapsed in the corner and threw his arms around his head, an explosion emanating from his bladder and flooding into his black jogging bottoms and swiftly forming a pool at his feet. The undertaker tried to speak but his vocal cords were paralysed. The monster's shadow engulfing the man's quivering frame, his feet fighting for purchase on the dusty floor, but the cold brick corner prevented any retreat. Frank Graham's thick right arm took aim, lifting his deadly weapon head high, ready to bring down Hell upon his terrified victim. The razor-sharp edge of the blade caught a reflection from Gibson's torch and from his lower vantage point, the evil horrific mask looked even more ghastly. Finally, the petrified man forced his voice to speak.

"Frankie. Frankie, you remember me. Its uncle Fred. Your dad's best friend. Please, I'm begging you, don't do anything silly. I'm here to help you."

Slowly the creature lowered the weapon and tilted his head slightly to the left; animal-like curiosity struggling to understand the bravery of this inconsequential little man who had invaded his domain. Weeks had passed since Graham had had any human contact and even then, it ended with a bloodbath. Its mind had fractured completely, and the outside world was now the enemy. Slowly raising the blade once more, it seemed Gibson's pleas would be in vain.

"Frank, listen. Just listen for one moment and if you don't believe what I'm saying, you can do as you please." Once more the stalking deceased. "I'm here to help you. I don't know if you saw me when those idiots from the village tried to invade this place. I came to stop them..." Frank stepped forward, "I did everything I could to stop them, but they wouldn't listen. Thankfully, you didn't need my help, they got what the deserved. Those stupid mother-fuckers had no right to come into your home, this place is yours, it's your birth-right. I was overjoyed when you dispatched so many of them." Gibson's words were hurried, afraid that should he slow down, Frank would dispose of him as swiftly as he had the others. "But what you don't know, there was a town meeting afterwards, they wanted to blow this place up. There were explosives left inside the colliery works and they wanted to use them to blow this place all to Hell. I stopped them. I came up with a plan where they would just build a fence around the station and leave you in peace. If it weren't for me, this place would be flattened now with you inside the rubble." The mortician's lies gave him a stay of execution, but it was still unclear whether it was a temporary reprieve.

"That was just one thing, but Frank, I can help you with so much more if you just trust me. The reason I'm here, is a promise I made to your father before he passed. He asked me to watch out for you, his precious boy, if anything ever happened to him. He was worried that the world wouldn't understand you the way he, and I of course, do. And he was proved right. Look at what those savages tried to do, when all you wanted was to be left alone. Now, I loved your dad so much that I was willing to put my own life at risk, coming here today, just so I could fulfil that promise I made. I knew you may not believe me, and I knew that you had the power to kill me where I stood, but I wasn't willing to break that promise, no matter what it took." The lies the mortician was spewing were seeming to be breaking through the monster's guard. Martin Graham was the only thing in the world that Frank cared for and though his psyche had been shattered, deep inside, that pain of losing his father still ached.

"I know you think you don't need anyone but how long do you think you can survive on the rations in that bunker. When winter comes, you'll starve. There'll be no rabbits to catch, you won't last long living on a diet of rats and mice. I can help. I can bring you food, bring you drink, anything you need. Any supplies you wish for, I can provide. And then there's information. Whatever happens in that shit-hole village that you need to know, I'll make sure you find out first. God forbid, those morons decide to come back, wouldn't it be good to know in advance? I can do that. And make no mistake about it, you could kill me now, of that there is no doubt. But if you do, it would be for nothing, I am no threat. Those people fear you and because of that, they hate you. They would love nothing more than to see you dead. I am your only friend. Kill me and there is no one else." Frank seemed to be listening, but the mask hid all expression. It was impossible for Fred to know if he was making a dent.

"So, I'm asking you, trust me for now, and if what I'm saying isn't true, kill me later. If I'm lying to you, I deserve to die. I'm not asking you to do anything other than let me help you." Gibson was still a blubbering mess and all his words had been spoken between sobs, but his confidence was growing. Slowly, he pushed through his knees and straightened his legs, though he was still unwilling to step away from the cold brick corner. Standing upright, Frank didn't strike out. Lowering the knife, the monster reached for the tunnel door and the passed through, into the station. Tentatively, Gibson followed.

Keeping a safe distance, Fred walked, step for step in the giant's shadow. He occasionally spoke, asking for permission to follow and he took the silence as an okay. The sun was slowly rising outside but the light had yet to filter through the vast brick walls. Gibson's eyes were fixed firmly on his ghastly host, still unsure if he was being led to his doom. He'd visited the station on several occasions before, usually as Martin's guest and once in his professional capacity. Charles Cyphers, a man nearing retirement age who was trying to squeeze one last year in employment before living on the state pension had suffered a fatal heart attack whilst working at the coal washing plant on the ground floor. Falling forward, he fell into one of the giant presses and his skull was crushed; certainly, one of the more gruesome jobs Fred Gibson had been called upon for.

The darkness of the interior meant that the undertaker was reliant completely on Graham for direction. He was still carrying the torch but felt it would antagonise the young psychopath were he to shine it forward, so he continued venturing into the blackness, hoping that he wasn't being fooled into a false sense of security. As they reached the stone spiral staircase, Fred stayed three steps behind always, not wanting to follow too closely but ensuring he didn't fall too far behind. The climb seemed to continue for ever and Gibson was soon breathing heavily, his weight issues proving a problem. Floor after floor, the struggle continued, not wanting to protest but fighting to catch a breath. Finally, the top floor was reached.

It was the only part of the building with a window and the sudden flooding of light was a welcome distraction. Long and across the room's centre, Gibson noticed a pane of the glass was broken but soon understood why. An area on the concrete floor was scorched and a makeshift wall, three layers high had been built from discarded house bricks where Frank had been creating small fires. Around the scene, large chipboard barriers, taken from the office space had sectioned off an area of the vast room which the killer was using as a sleeping area. A single mattress had been dragged from the station master's former living quarters and a filthy quilt was crumpled in a corner. A wooden stool was the only other item enclosed and this was positioned by the window, ensuring he could see anyone entering his domain. Embers were still smouldering as Frank pushed the makeshift chair with his right foot, indicating for Gibson to sit. Slowly Fred lowered his frame and stared up towards his host.

The mortician had bi-passed the first obstacle, the visit concluding as well as could be expected. He'd continued to talk at 100 miles an hour, not wanting to leave the monster with any time for doubt. Stories of Martin were a safe subject, the more a connection Gibson claimed to have had with the Graham patriarch, the more trust he hoped to create with the son. Not wanting to outstay his welcome, he'd left after fifteen minutes; Frank not objecting when he rose to leave. Gibson had wanted to ask the young man to remove the mask, its image detestable, but fear had prevented it. Asking questions was pointless as it soon became obvious there would be no response. As he headed in the direction of the staircase, his footsteps were taken backwards, not daring to remove his eyes from the hulking figure and when he finally began his descent, the steps were quickly, still unsure if Frank would have a rethink about allowing him to leave alive.

Fred had promised to return, Tuesday mornings offered as the designated time, though Gibson had no idea whether anything he'd said had been understood, the horrific mask a barrier between revealing his expressions. It was months before Gibson began to feel confident of his safety and even then, he still couldn't be certain. The monster continued to wear the disguise whenever the mortician was present and refused to utter a word. When Fred plucked up the courage to enquire why he refused to speak, there was no response. Not wishing to push the subject, the topic was never raised again.

In time, the mortician became accustomed to his strange friend's silence, happy to do all the talking. He'd pass on information from Hallowell, whether it was relevant to Graham or not. If there had been a particularly gruesome call in his role of undertaker, he'd share all the gory details and if it had been a quiet week, he'd lie, the made-up tales more enjoyable than the real thing. Ensuring that there was a regular supply of stories involving Martin continued that connection and reminded Frank why he allowed Gibson to come and go freely.

And so, an uneasy truce was formed. Graham tolerated this strange, unsure creature who talked too much but usefully brought food to help sustain him through the cold winter months. Somewhere in his fractured mind, there were memories of this person and more importantly, links to his father. His former life was but a distant vision, locked away as he existed inside this concrete prison, happy recollections were a luxury his poisoned psyche would not allow. But his father was one aspect of that life he was reluctant to forget, and Fred Gibson could ensure that those memories could live on.

As for Gibson the adrenaline rush, he'd feel stepping into the daunting structure with an untamed, uncontrollable monster, unsure whether the next time could be the last time, his heart rate quickened, pulse raced, and he loved it. Plus, it gave him someone to try out his cannibalistic dishes out on. Graham would never eat while the mortician was present, his unwillingness to remove his disguise making it impossible, but Gibson was confident, the food he delivered would not go to waste. Soon, the ingredients of the tasty treats changed. Instead of pork chops, lamb shoulder, or topside of beef, the meals began to consist of human heart, roasted kidneys, or slices of pre-cooked human thigh. Diced human shin marinated in a red wine sauce was a particular favourite of the deranged chief as was female cubed liver (liver from a man always seemed tough and chewy) cooked with sliced onions and thick gravy. When he eventually confessed that the meat was taken from the dead, he was surprised that this revelation didn't seem to faze the monster. It also made Fred curious as to whether his protégé had already partaken in anthropophagy as a way of supplementing his meagre diet, it was possible that other victims may have fallen foul to the killer's strike.

A favourite pass-time of the mortician was sharing details about his deviant behaviour with his psychotic partner, safe in the knowledge that the tales could go no further. For years, he'd longed for someone he could trust enough to share his dark actions with; as a young man he'd considered Malcolm Gregory, but the risk was too great. Though they had remained friends for most of their lives, the chance of the butcher being repulsed and informing the police was too much to bear. Now Fred had the partner he'd always dreamed of, and he relished the chance to finally share every sordid detail. It felt like confessional with a dark priest though there would obviously be no absolution gained.

Months turned to years and the relationship gained strength. They both brought something that was irrevocably theirs; Gibson provided a link to the outside world and in return, Graham allowed the undertaker to continue living. It was a bond of convenience which strangely seemed to work...

And that bitch sister was trying to wreck everything. Fred needed to inform Frank before it was too late, she had to be stopped, one way or another.

Chapter 27

It was barely light, ten before six, a cool autumnal breeze was swaying the branches of the trees, speeding up the leaf's demise and leaving behind a rustic carpet of browns and yellows. Through the fallen bracken, a lone grey squirrel feverously searched for supplies as hibernation would soon be upon it, nervously twitching its nose, eyes darting from side to side, trying desperately to avoid predators and make it back to its newly fashioned lair with its prize. The cracking of twigs under Nick Castle's boots made the little vermin spring into action and hurtle through the foliage into a hole in the trunk of a large oak tree. Nick smiled, wishing his life could be so simple.

The nightmare had been expected, though its ferocity had caught Nick by surprise. It was the one he feared the most though was powerless to prevent and returning to his slumber had been an impossible task. To make matters worse, the dramatic reduction in the medication he'd been taking had caused restless legs syndrome but remedying the problem with more pills would have been admitting defeat, Castle didn't like to lose. He'd listened intently, ensuring his father and grandmother had returned to their own beds before quickly dressing and silently leaving the house. When anxious, he preferred to be alone and out in the open air, a barrage of questions from concerned siblings was least in his list of priorities. The cool breeze re-energised his senses and calmed his twitching limbs and for the first time, he begun to believe that vanquishing the sedatives from his system altogether was a genuine possibility. He'd been warned that any reduction would need to be gradual as in some extreme cases, seizures and other serious side effects were possible but at least this was a start.

From his family home, midway along Melrose drive, he made his way towards the church of Saint Helen, turning right at the bottom of church lane, and headed up Main Street. He'd passed the main thoroughfare yesterday but only by car, not having chance to take in its timeless quality. Gregory's butchers' shop, a large double-fronted premises which had served the needs of Hallowell since 1850 was the first store in the street, neighbouring his grandmother's newsagents. Her assistant, Michelle Myers, a kindly woman around the same age as Alice, who had taken the reigns for the last few days after Bill's passing was waiting at the door for the newspaper delivery. Squinting through large, lensed spectacles, she peered across the street as Nick passed by. Recognising him from a framed photograph her boss hung on the back-room wall, she waved a hand and Nick smiled in return.

"My daily star here yet, Shelley?" The voice from Nick's rear startled him, not noticing the approaching figure, a wild-bearded portly chap with a large bunch of keys in hand. He stopped at the door to the butchers and Nick assumed it was Malcolm, the latest generation to run the family business.

"Must be running late today hon, hope they hurry up, the paper boy will be here soon." Once more Nick smiled, remembering that he'd carried out that role as a child. Continuing his progress, he noticed the two were now in whispered conversation and was certain he was the topic of their gossip. "Small town life."

To the left-hand side of Alice's store, a florist had taken the place of Loomis hardware. Nick remembered Sam, the old man who owned it, had no family to inherit the business, a rarity for small village life. No such concerns for the final of the four shops, the Jayne family had a four-generation lineage for their off-licence, and the latest owner, Tony, their tradition would be upheld for the foreseeable future. Directly opposite was the Wheatsheaf public house. The landlord, Terry Hutchinson and his two brothers, Jake and Steve were well known for being proficient with their fists and therefore, anyone who wanted to cause trouble after one drink too many would be well advised to take their nonsense elsewhere. Terry was a former bare-knuckle champion who fought gypsies for money and though he was now in his fifties, it was a brave man who'd take him on.

Castle was amazed just how familiar everything was, even after being away for so long. Beyond the street of shops and the Wheatsheaf the road split in two and surrounded the communal green. This pleasant, football-pitch sized piece of land was the centre of Hallowell and where the annual carnival was held. The grass's perimeter was guarded by a low, white picket fence with wooden park benches, each containing a gold or silver plague, engraved with the names of former residents as a mark of respect for those passed away. Nick frowned as he imagined his grandfather's name would soon adorn one of the seats.

To the right side of the green stood the lunchbox café, already the succulent smell of fried bacon wafting from its open front door, ready to service those who started their working day early. Adjoined was Hallowell workingmen's club. His experience the previous night with the unpleasant Fred Gibson made Nick curious as to whether the fat slug had an ulterior motive for wanting him out of town soon or was, he just a self-important prick. Time would tell. On a more pleasant recollection, he looked left to Henderson's bed and breakfast and wondered which room, that beautiful girl he'd seen, was sleeping in. It had been a mere glimpse but enough to peak the young man's interest. She'd been the last thing he'd thought about before falling asleep, shame he hadn't dreamt of her instead of his nightmarish vision.

His pace quickened once beyond the communal green, except for Gavin Holt's post office, most of the rest of the properties on Main Street were private houses. Reaching the roads apex, he continued to the left along Graham Road. This was aptly named as it led to the burned out remains of the Graham mansion. There'd been the option of using a secondary road, colliery lane, but the only sights to see were a newly built retirement home named Evergreen and Gibson's funeral parlour. Either road would have taken him to his eventual destination, but he decided on the scenic route.

It was almost 7a m as he reached the driveway to the Graham estate, his leisurely pace turning to a crawl as Nick enjoyed the cool morning air. As a child, five, perhaps six years old, he'd gone with his grandfather to see Martin on irrelevant village business. It was the first time Castle could remember seeing the building in all its former glory; the pristine gardens, the huge out-buildings, beautiful sports car parked by the front door. After being invited inside, the boy marvelled at its splendour, museum like architecture with high ceilings and immaculately kept furniture. With total recall, Nick could remember thinking it was a home for royalty, now it was fit only to be demolished. Walking up the driveway, weeds had invaded the gravel road, blown litter, and fallen leaves adding to the depressing deterioration. Grass from the lawns was knee high, flopping wearily against gravity and a small birch tree had succumbed to a storm, uprooted, and dying across the gateway. The house itself was derelict in every way, walls falling, windows shattered, the roof a distant memory. Nick had planned to explore the interior but thought better of it when he discovered its precarious state. From the corner of his eye, he was certain he'd seen someone skulking around the back of the property but felt it wasn't his place to care. Perhaps his imagination was working overtime, but he thought he recognised the intruder, Fred Gibson. Nick soon dismissed the notion, what would a man like him be doing climbing through a demolition site at this early hour. Instead of retracing his steps, Castle headed to through the gardens, to the woodland in the rear of the mansion. If his memory served, there was a pathway which led to the railway track and colliery.

Once more, there was evidence of thick overgrowth, but Nick soon found his bearings and passed the Graham property border, out onto the disused railway line. The great wheel from the former mine was still intact but there was evidence of vandalism everywhere. Like the Graham mansion, the site had fallen into dereliction, and it was hardly believable that just fourteen years prior, this was the source of a majority of employment for Hallowell. Nick grimaced when he considered the deaths of all the stricken miners and remembered that this was the first stage of failure for the Graham family. One act of terror and so many lives destroyed, his own included. Not wishing to remain longer than necessary, he quickened his pace, the railway station now in sight.

Castle couldn't understand why he continued to torture himself this way, was it penance for the death of Billy Scholes? There were no answers to be found, not from the outside, that was for certain. He'd purposely taken this route to ensure he could see the back of the building, the main doorway. Positioned on the outside of a constant, high, chain-mail fence, there was a vague safety-net between himself and entry. Not that he feared entering anymore, no, he feared not being able to stop himself entering. For he knew that it was his destiny, combating those demons the only way he thought possible. It was obvious that Bill had been correct, his only reason for returning to Hallowell was to face those fears, and there was a chance that doing that would be disastrous.

A trickle of blood ran down the palm of his hand, he'd been so transfixed at the sight, that he hadn't noticed a barb on the wire mesh fence. With fingers curled through the holes, knuckles white and livid, the sharp tip had impregnated the skin, sticky red residue squelched between his digits. Pulling the hand away, Nick noticed the cut was deeper than first appeared and he reached into his jacket pocket, relieved to find a clean handkerchief to stem the flow.

"Fuck." Castle was more aggravated at the inconvenience than registering the pain, his adrenaline overtaking the sting. Suddenly, something caught his eye. Through the tunnel between the main structure and the right outer building, a car was visible. Small and white, a Mini Metro if he was not mistaken.

"I've seen that before, I know I have, but where?" In the distance, the car door opened, and the question was answered for him. The petit figure of the girl he'd seen just six hours earlier, rapping at the door of Henderson's bed and breakfast. But what the hell was she doing here? Quietly closing the barrier behind her, she stretched, her head tilted backwards, hair flowing in the breeze. Her resemblance to Julia was uncanny and for a few seconds he was tempted to call out his lost love's name, before sense returned to his thinking.

"What is she doing?" The girl was leaving the sanctuary of the small carpark and heading in the direction of the demonic structure. "Christ, she can't go in there, I got to stop her." Nick started to climb, aware that the injury to his hand was throbbing but having no time to care. His feet fought for purchase against the tight mesh, but arm strength helped propel him higher. The footing of his left trainer-shoe slipped against the fence, but he was already almost at the summit. Pulling with all his might, his right leg clung to the top, the barrier bending with the weight. Pushing on, the crotch of his jeans snagged against another barb, and he heard a rip as he fell to the inner floor, a four-inch rent forming in the most embarrassing of locations. Still, there was no time to worry, the young woman was inside the grounds now and Nick was in a race to stop her entering. Swiftly, he hurtled around the outer perimeter, not wishing to climb onto the platform unless it was completely essential. Arriving at the front of the building, he was relieved to see she'd stopped midway across the courtyard. Hearing Nick's running footsteps, Jenifer looked startled, unsure of the intruder's intentions.

"Don't be afraid Miss," Nick's words were laboured, the exertion of climbing and running showing his current lack of fitness. "I, I saw you from behind the building and, well, I wanted to warn you. It's very dangerous." The alarm on the girl's face was still evident though her initial fear had subsided.

"Dangerous? How do you mean, dangerous?" God, she even sounded like Julia, not her accent, a trace of Scottish intermingled with a local dialect; but the way her diction delivered the line, soft without a hint of menace. As Nick approached, he expected her to back away, but she seemed to have trust in his sincerity.

"I just mean, inside, it's derelict. A lot of people have been hurt over the years inside there, it's not safe." Castle's variation of the truth seemed wise; he had no wish to appear a crazy person, spouting tales of vengeful killers and urban legends. "I'm sorry if I scared you Miss, my names Nick. Nick Castle." He offered a hand and with a sense of trepidation, she took it, softly shaking in a friendly gesture.

"I see. Thanks for the warning, my name is Jennifer." She neglected to reveal her sir's name, unsure whether the sins of her family would make her an unwelcome visitor. "It's nice to meet you." Nick held on a little longer than necessary, lost in the uncanny resemblance. "Do you think I could have my hand back?" She giggled shyly and embarrassed, Nick replied in kind.

"Of course, I'm sorry. You just remind me of someone I used to know. It's nice to meet you." As his grip released, the girl smiled, the feeling of relief growing, no longer concerned that this attractive stranger had appeared out of nowhere. His looks were unconditionally striking, in another day, in another time…

"Well, thanks again." Jenifer slowly began to turn, wondering if he would make a move and unsure what her response would be if he did. "Bye." A step toward the car, slowly, then another, he mustn't be interested. Castle was unsure how to proceed, the attraction was mutual but asking someone on a date after meeting in such auspicious circumstances seemed forward. Still, he knew he couldn't let this opportunity go to waste.

"Wait." Jenifer allowed herself a wry smile though she was facing away from her beau. Gently, her body swayed, he looked helpless, surely with looks like his, he couldn't help but have confidence with women. "This is going to sound crazy but…well…would you like to have a cup of coffee with me. There's a café not far from here in the middle of the village?" Jenifer considered her watch tentatively. "I'm sorry Miss, you must be busy, sorry for bothering you. You have a nice day."

"Stop apologising." Said with another giggle, she felt like a schoolgirl all over again. She was curious as to whether he'd seen her blush. He had.

"Sorry." The two laughed now, his nerves proving that Nick wasn't a regular lothario, regardless of the way he looked.

"I have an appointment at 10 am but I could be a little late." Nick couldn't hide the grin though he tried to conceal his excitement, this was the first good thing that had happened in a long while. "Would you like a lift, or do you have a car here?"

"I was taking a walk, my cars at home…well, my grandmother's home."

"Great, let's go."

The lunchbox café was empty bar for one man. He was dressed in a yellow, safety jacket, with dishevelled hair and three days stubble. From his vast waistline, the three bacon and egg sandwiches he was ordering would be just a starter in his daily unhealthy consumption. Nick pulled out a chair and the girl smiled, strangely impressed that her companion still had time for chivalry. The room was plain but clean, random pictures on white walls and carpet tiles for flooring. Each table had red and white chequered tablecloths, but the plastic fabric made them seem cheap and tacky.

"What can I get you hon?" The waitress that appeared by their station was late twenties with a tight curly perm and no make-up. With a fake smile, she seemed inconvenienced by their presence and appeared relieved when they only ordered drinks.

"Tea on a morning? I'm barely alive without my caffeine jolt." Nick's attempt at humour was a simple icebreaker, restarting the conversation before a chance of a dreaded awkward silence.

"My Godmother would never let me drink coffee as a kid and by the time I could decide for myself, I couldn't take the taste. Always said she was overprotective." Nick used the statement to Segway into a prying mission, desperate to discover this young woman's story.

"Godmother? What about your real parents? Was it your Godmother who raised you?"

Jenifer paused, apprehensive to reveal too many details but aware that saying nothing would come across as cold.

"Yeh, she's a wonderful woman. Actually…she's all the family I have left. My mum died when I was little, and my dad and brother were killed in a fire."

"Fire? That's terrible. I'm so sorry, I didn't mean to pry." The girl took a breath, aware that she was about to pass on details that would reveal her real identity.

"I suppose you've heard all the stories?"

"Sorry, but no. I've been away from Hallowell for ten years too. Only came back two days ago." Jenifer seemed more susceptible, happy that this young man could be something of a kindred spirit. Small village people had equally small minds and gossip seen as fact. After the controversy of the family history, it was refreshing to speak to someone who appeared to have similar roots to herself. He had a caring face and as a tear welled in the corner of her left eye, he reached out a hand, running a finger down her cheek. "Listen, and I make no apologies for saying sorry again, but I really didn't mean to push. If you don't want to talk to me about this, forget it, it's fine. I know more than most what it feels like for people to stick their noses where it's not wanted." It was her turn to be curious but felt if she turned the tables, it would seem evasive.

"It's fine, honestly, it's just…well, it's a long story." Nick smiled.

"I've no plans."

"Unfortunately, I'm afraid I have. You see, my father was Martin Graham, I here to finally get rid of the family assets, as such they are. I'm supposed to meet the real estate agent, Mr Williams I think he's called," looking at her watch, "five minutes ago, shit." She raised a hand to her mouth at the curse like a schoolgirl in class. Nick was so shocked at her revelation; his voice momentarily froze. Jenifer saw the colour drain from the young man's face and immediately wished she'd held her tongue. "I'm sorry Nick, I have to go. It's been lovely meeting you." She offered a hand and the sudden end to their rendezvous brought Castle back to his senses.

"Of course, you're busy." He took her hand and gently squeezed it. As she began away from the table, Nick made a final desperate plea. "Are you leaving straight afterwards?" Relieved, the girl paused and smiled.

"No. This is the first time I've met this man and, well, I'm hoping for a quick sale so I'm staying in the village for a few days."

"Great." Castle tried the cool approach, but she could tell he was excited at the prospect of seeing one another again as she was. "Tonight. Are you busy? We could go for a meal, maybe over in St Mara, away from prying eyes." Said looking in the direction of the abrupt waitress who had been desperately trying to eavesdrop without making it look obvious. Jenifer smiled shyly again, happy for the first time, since her business had hit the rocks.

"Sounds lovely."

"I'll pick you up at seven, outside of Henderson's."

"Thank you." With that, the girl was gone; Nick settled back in his chair and drained the last of his beverage. Catching the waitress's eye, he smiled.

"Another coffee please. And a bacon sandwich too."

Jenifer cursed her tardiness, hoping that the real estate agent was still waiting. It wasn't far from the lunchbox café, so she left her car in the car park, believing it faster on foot. His office was in a neighbouring street to the funeral parlour, and she cringed, still remembering the day her beloved mother had been taken. When news broke of her father and brother's demise, she'd shed tears, not for their loss but because of a lost opportunity. Even as a child, she knew that the household divide was males and females and no-matter how she tried to break through those invisible walls, her efforts would have been futile. Thank God for Martha, without her love, she too may have been laying in St Helens churchyard. The lights in the office were switched off and as she tried the door handle, it was obviously locked. She tried knocking but there was no answer. Cupping her eyes with both hands, she tried to peer inside between the advertising hoardings of the window. It seemed deserted. There was a doorway to an office at the right-hand side of the room and she tapped lightly on the glass, hoping to get the agent's attention, but the entire place seemed empty.

"I can't believe I missed him, I'm only five minutes late."

"Can I help you at all Miss?" The request wasn't friendly, and his guttural tone made Jenifer apprehensive. Fred Gibson had appeared out of nowhere, and his sudden appearance made the girl jump.

"I'm sorry, I didn't see you there. I'm…"

"I know who you are miss. I'm Mr Gibson, a friend of Walter. He asked me to tell you, he's under the weather and needs to reschedule. It may need to be Monday now, after the weekend. Can't be too careful with these sickness bugs, pass them on to anyone."

"I see." The girl was unsure whether to believe him but had little choice. His demeanour reminded her of the waitress in the café, wary of strangers and untrusting of their motives. "I was planning to stay for a few days, we were supposed to go over potential buyers today but, if he's ill, we'll just have to wait." She paused, waiting for a response, none came. Gibson gave something of a grunt and walked away, back to his property. "Nice to meet you Mr Gibson." Jenifer shook her head and started back to the bed and breakfast. "Small town bigots."

Inside the estate agent's office, Walter Wilson cowered behind an advertising patrician, not daring to speak to the girl until the town meeting. "Get through today, Wally, by tonight, it's not my fault. Let fucking Brackett decide what to do, it's not my job."

Johnny Brackett only wore his police uniform for formal occasions, usually he was plain clothed, today was no exception, blue jeans, plain black t-shirt, hair slicked back with too much gel. He felt cool. And he had too, it was obvious that sometime, there would be a meeting with his former friend, the village was too small to miss each other. He hadn't slept the previous night, couldn't. Shit, he had memories too. They all did, why make a big deal of it now. The parodical son returns, bullshit. Me, Johnny fucking Brackett is the law now. No one tell me what to do now. When I see him, I'll…calm now John, just chill. Things have changed, he's the follower now, you have everything you wanted, control. He used to be the top boy, fuck that, not anymore.

The policeman's inferiority complex had returned as soon as word spread of Nick's return. As a child, he always wanted to be the Alpha male, but Castle was always in the way, better looking, stronger, better with his fists, better with the girls, better everything. But time changes people, as for Johnny, he'd taken Castle's mantle, became the leader he'd always wanted to be, whether others liked it or not. Some said he was a bully, others said nothing because they were scared too. All the way through school, people avoided him because he'd strike out for no other reason than to prove his toughness. He worked out constantly, building muscle mass, wearing tight clothes so others saw his physique. He was finally the alpha male. Getting the role of constable didn't come by accident. His father, Harry Brackett was friendly with the chief constable, played golf, even let him win once or twice. A private word with an important man confirmed the saying, "It's not what you know it's who you know." There were many more qualified people, but Johnny sailed to the top. Once more, daddy to the rescue. The real ALPHA MALE.

His police car was a Ford Granada mark II, 2.8 litre with an engine that knew how to growl. Brought in from the Hereford constabulary, former motorway chaser, Johnny's pride, and joy. When Bill Castle was constable, he barely used a car but today, they were equipped for anything. Things change. Long, white, with a red stripe through the middle, hard, powerful, the new police force, Johnny's police force.

He'd started paroling early, just quiet drives around the village, nothing in particular happening. Melrose drive was a regular visit, just in case anyone was passing by, nice and casual. Johnny didn't have the authority to question Nick officially about his visit through it was on the minds of every Hallowell resident. Everyone who knew their secrets. If Brackett junior turned up at the town meeting tonight with nothing, there'd be Hell to pay. He had to find out something. His car moved steadily into the centre of town, taking care while passing Castle's store, curious as to whether Nick could be inside. "Christ, he still could be laying in his bed, if the rumours are correct, he's probably sleeping off a hangover." Passed Gregory's butchers shop, good old Malcolm threw him a wave as the car sauntered by. The florist was quite new, Brackett didn't know the owner but there were customers going about their business. Tony Jayne was a good guy, good family. He was outside his off-licence, the sign broken with the heavy winds.

"Need a hand tony?" The car stopped, window down, community policing.

"Bloody wind through the night, came down here earlier and the bastard was hanging over the front door. I've phoned Peter Pentland over in St Mara, he'd supposed to be coming now. He put the twat up in the first place, only a fucking month ago, the fucker better not charge me, or I'll give him a slap."

Johnny smiled and shook his head as he pulled away, he counted five curse words in one sentence from Tony Jayne, hard to believe he was a volunteer at St Helens church. Father Henderson relied on the Jayne family greatly, his own family perishing in an accident a year earlier. He wondered if the priest had been informed of the town meeting, later that night. He should be involved, this one could change everything, the whole congregation would be altered if this sale happens.

"As the policeman, I would protect people as best I can but if that monster is loose…"

The car steadily turned into the communal green area. Looking toward Terry Hutchinson's pub, Brackett wondered if Nick was already propping up the bar? No, the doors would still be locked, it's only 10:15am, the sound of rolling beer barrels said that preparation was well underway. Over the street was Henderson's, where the girl was staying.

"Wonder if she's as good looking like the grapevine claims?" Across the road was the lunchbox café. There's someone inside, at the table in the window. Long dark hair can't see his dam face, turnaround, you bastard. The cup hits the table, the guy stands up, still back to Brackett, he's at the till, paying the bill, another brief glimpse, large build, broad shoulders, he turns, coming for the door, a better view, the realisation hits, Nick Castle is here.

The police car stopped at the lunchbox door just as Nick hit the street. The window down, Johnny called over,

"Do I need to arrest you to get you in my car?" Castle looked towards the voice, allowing himself a wry smile.

"No officer, I'll come quietly." The front passenger door swung open, and Nick climbed in, his 6 feet 4 inch filling the space. "So, what's it like driving a big Jam Sandwich?"

"Funny as ever I see Nick." His expression said he didn't appreciate his attempt at humour.

"Just trying to break the ice." Nick scanned the officer for weakness, wondering how much had changed, it seemed a lot.

"I like ice, leave it the fuck alone." Brackett started the car, heading in a familiar direction, this one was going to be strange.

Brackett gunned the engine, doing 45 down colliery lane, anyone else and the policeman would be producing tickets, but he was a law unto himself. Passing by the cottages to his left, he scanned Tom Daley's home for vandalism; the night after his arrest, a house-brick had been hurled through the kitchen window. The handyman, Ian Gaskins had boarded up the broken entrance, not that he any longer held an affinity with the poor chump, their friendship had ended after the paedophilia accusations had broken; not that he believed for one moment that his former best friend had murdered the Roberts boy, just didn't have it in him. Gaskins didn't even believe that Tom had been guilty of kiddie fiddling but in a village like Hallowell, you needed to choose the right side, especially when your livelihood depended on it. He'd boarded the window free of charge. There appeared no more vandalism, a lot of other people felt the same way as Gaskins even though they remained silent too. Hell, Brackett had his doubts, but the evidence said Daley, and who was he to argue.

The Granada left the tarmac road onto the gravel of the station car park. He purposely stopped the car with the windshield facing the building. Turning the ignition, the engine died, and the car was filled with silence. Nick broke it sharply.

"What we are doing here Johnny, or is it officer Brackett now?" The policeman smiled and considered his reply carefully, not wishing their conversation to be confrontational…yet.

"That's why you're back, isn't it? Dredge up the past?" Castle gave a quick retort, desperate to maintain the edge in the exchange.

"Absolutely not. I'm here for my granddad's funeral, nothing more." It was now Brackett's turn for a fast reply.

"Come off its Nick, you've been back two days, and this is the third time you've been here. You forget my friend, Hallowell has spies everywhere, nothing happens without being seen, and when things happen…I find out." Nick paused and when he tried to reply, Brackett shut him down. "Listen Nick, I understand, I really do. What happened fucked you up royally, it affected all of us, just some of us managed to deal with it better than others." Again, Nick tried to interrupt but Brackett, obviously had his speech rehearsed well and was in full flow.

"Let me finish. I'm not trying to insult you. And I'm not trying to insult your family when I say that the way they handled you and the whole situation was wrong too. That's why I came through this better than you. My dad made sure we stuck around. He sat me down and explained the whole dam thing. And as fucked up as it was…I understood. It took time, don't get me wrong but Christ, what option did they have. They tried to nail that fucker and look how that turned out. Should they do it again and see more of Hallowell's men killed? What about try and blow the fucking place up, what if he wasn't there? At least with the station intact, we knew where he was." Brackett paused for a Castle retort, but Nick was willing to let Johnny finish. "Knowing that he wasn't going to leave that place and knowing that folks realised it was off limits, well, it was the best we could hope for. Crazy as it sounds, it was like some fucked up truce. Was it perfect, hell no. was there a better option, well, if there was, you name it?"

"Bring in outside help. This isn't an island, you know."

"Small towns solve their own problems." Nick laughed.

"That is the sort of thinking from the 1800s, shit, that's the sort of thinking that got us into this mess in the first place."

"Jesus Nick, listen to yourself. It was too late for outside intervention; the village had already formed a fucking vigilante squad. Martin Graham was dead, and the village men could have saved him, did you want to see your granddad in prison? And the main fucker, Frank Graham, there was no hard evidence to say he'd done anything. The colliery disaster report said it was a natural accident, true, the investigator was probably paid off or had connections to Martin, who gives a fuck? At the end of the day, there would be no justice for the men who died, the men who were murdered, by that overgrown piece of shit, nothing, except private justice. Were they wrong? Who knows? The way it turned out, probably yes but by then, it was too damned late. You didn't have a daddy, or a brother, or a son, buried in a hole half a mile down. The relatives wanted justice, and your granddad lead the way. And I'm not blaming him, if I were a constable to this village then, I'd have done the exact same thing. That's village life."

"That's such bullshit. How many times has village life been used as an excuse for unprofessionalism? What guarantees did the residents ever have that that monster wouldn't just get bored one day and start pureeing the population? Christ, even the fence around it is fucked. Not exactly a secure location, is it? And what do you think that son of a bitch has been eating for the last decade? Don't think he's going to be too welcome nipping over to the corner shop for a snack, do you?" They were all relevant questions and Brackett's dumbfounded look told its own answer. "I'm not pointing fingers at you, shit, you are the last one I'd blame. But I just don't get how you can pretend to be able to keep this village safe when we have a psychopath on the loose in the centre of the community."

"Not in the centre."

"What?"

"You said the centre. Well, this place is on the edge of town."

"Is that really what you want to make this about; geographical location?"

"No. It's just, well…" Johnny's stammer proved he was struggling. "It is on the edge of town. And when you live here, sometimes it's easy to forget the significance."

"How the hell do you forget there's a serial killer in town?" Nick shook his head incredulously, barely able to register what his former friend had just said. Brackett paused before replying, aware that Castle's irritation level was rising rapidly. Knowing he needed a retort; his response was immediately regretted.

"You've no idea. I can go months without even passing this place, most people know the truth now, you can't keep shit like this quiet forever, so its personal responsibility to keep their kids safe. The crime rate in this village is almost non-existent, maybe a fight at the Wheatsheaf or a football breaking a window. The worst thing in two years I had to deal with was when Tommy Doyle beat up his wife after getting pissed up and putting her in hospital and even then, she dropped the charges after a week (pause) and then suddenly we have a missing kid. A missing kid and a paedophile, the last person to see him. Now you might think that Daley was some set up but here's the thing. When you are being trained for a job in the force, you are told, don't overthink things. If you

357

got a dead body with stab wounds and a mother fucker standing over the corpse with a knife and the victim's blood all over them, chances are, they are the murderer. Now Daley has history of messing with kids, a witness saw the victim running from Daley's cottage and he has the boy's blood on his clothes. Just because Frank Fucking Graham was never caught doesn't mean he committed ever crime that ever happened in Hallowell. Everything pointed at Daley. So, I arrested him, okay. I take him into custody and begin to interview him. Next thing I know, your granddad storms to the police-station and is braying on the door."

"My granddad. What's he got to do with anything?" Brackett's face flushed, the realisation that he'd said too much immediately dawning on him.

"What?" He was stumbling now, desperate to rewind thirty seconds.

"Johnny. What does my grandfather have to do with any of this?" The colour of his face suddenly changed, draining of all colours, scarcely believing he could be so stupid. This was going to cause a lot more trouble.

"Sorry Nick. I've said too much. I think you need to speak to your dad, maybe your grandma too." Brackett reached for the car's ignition but before he could start the engine, Castle stretched out a hand and grabbed the officer by the throat.

"I'm asking you." Brackett turned his head slowly to face his former friend and for a second, they were ten years old again. Johnny wanted to use his authority but understood Nick had a short temper. Plus, he couldn't believe that Castle's family was still lying to him, surely, they could see that their dishonesty had caused enough problems.

"I'm sorry Nick, I thought you knew."

"Knew what?" Brackett began his retort, slowly and deliberately, not wishing to make another mistake.

"Like I said, I'd arrested Tom Daley. We were back at the station house when there was banging on the front door. It was your granddad. He was raging, calling me a coward and a liar. Claiming that I only arrested Daley to cover my ass. Nick, no matter what you think of me, I need you to realise, I'd never do that. All the evidence pointed at Daley, Hell, nothing had happened at the railway station since we were kids, for all we knew, Graham could have been dead. Anyway, we got into an argument, Nick, I never wanted to disrespect Bill, but he just gave me both barrels."

"What happened?"

"He said he knew who the real culprit was, and he was going to the station, in case the boy was still alive. He wanted me to go too. I told him he was crazy, that Daley was responsible and if he went near that place, I'd arrest him."

"You threatened to arrest my granddad?" Castle was amused at the insanity of the statement, but suddenly became aware of where the conversation was headed.

"I know it sounds mad Nick but, well, you know how stubborn he could be."

"So, what happened?"

"Nick, this is a conversation you should be having with your family, not me." At that moment, Brackett wanted to be anywhere but where he was sitting.

"Johnny. If you're about to tell me that you let my granddad, go to that place, alone, even though you are the fucking policeman, just get it over with." Brackett grimaced.

Ten minutes later, Nick Castle was once more walking the streets of Hallowell, his thoughts clouded with frustration and rage. The punch he'd landed on the chin of his former friend had been struck in torment and the angle it was delivered from ensured that it did little damage. Brackett had expected it and refused to retaliate, deciding that arresting the enraged man for assaulting an officer would only antagonise the situation. As Castle had taken his leave, Johnny wanted to reach out once more and beg for forgiveness, Hell, he'd spent countless hours regretting the way he handled the situation with Bill and wished with all his might that he could relive the incident. Feeling a failure, he'd considered resigning his post as constable to the village, only a pep-talk from his father making him reconsider. When news broke of Nick's return, Brackett knew that this confrontation was inevitable, but he expected Castle to be more informed about the proceedings, the family continuing their lies was wrong.

The tea had gone cold; not that it mattered, it was her fourth of the morning. There had also been nine cigarettes inhaled, the residue leaving a grey cloud across the kitchen ceiling, Alice Castle's own personal addiction. Today, the circles under her eyes were a little darker than usual. The bags below them a little heavier, every wrinkle on her tired old face more pronounced. After her grandson's shocking early hours nightmare, returning to her own slumber was impossible so after trying in vain for what seemed like hours, she'd wearily returned to her favourite seat by the kitchen table, kettle boiling, china-cup and saucer beside the old faithful teapot, and a packet of embassy cigarettes and box of matches beside an ashtray. She had some thinking to do.

Seeing the anguish on Nick's face as she and Mick had awakened him from the subconscious torture, the fear, the confusion, bought back memories she'd rather not think about. Those expressions were the exact same looks that she'd seen plastered across her dearly departed husband's face, so many times, they'd always said the boy was a 'chip off the old block'. Alice was terrified they'd been only too right. Staring at the silver framed photograph for Bill, she shook her head.

"Oh, my darling, how can I make a decision like this alone? Why didn't we just move away from this evil place while we had the chance?" Opening the white cigarette packet, she reached inside and took out the last one, quickly sliding the filter between her lips. Striking a match against the box's sandpaper strip, the flaky tobacco glowed red, and she breathed in deeply. Holding the nicotine in her lungs for a second too long, she coughed as the smoke escaped into the air. "These things are going to kill me; just wish they'd hurry up." Tapping the waste into the ashtray, she gave Bill's picture a final look and suddenly, her subconscious slipped away.

Alice could still remember the first time she'd seen him. It was 1936, the cinema in St Mara had a matinee showing of Anything Goes staring Bing Crosby and Ethel Merman and she'd gone with her cousin Edna. They were just leaving the exit when that great clod had bumped into her (never did watch where he was going). Her remaining popcorn had taken flight, but he'd managed to catch her before she fell to the ground. Bill had been apologetic to the degree of grovelling, but Alice didn't mind, from the first look, she'd been smitten. The smooth Lothario took the vanquished popcorn as a doorway to asking for a date, promising to buy her the largest container they had if she accompanies him to see The Bohemian Girl staring Stan Laurel and Oliver Hardy. She didn't have the heart to tell him she couldn't stand the two British comedians and agreed and had been pleasantly surprised when the Saturday evening came, and the picture was sold out. Thankfully, on a second screen there was a showing of The Amazing Quest of Ernest Bliss staring Cary Grant. It was the English star that always reminded her of Bill, tall stature, square jawline, and the most handsome face. Though she was only sixteen and he twenty-one, they knew immediately that this was a relationship for keeps. Marriage soon followed, and they spent the next forty-four years together. If only it hadn't ended so abruptly.

Before leaving her bed, she'd heard what sounded like movement from the floor below. Seeing Nick's bedroom door still closed and after noticing his car-keys still on the fire surround, she assumed she'd been mistaken. As the time had reached 10:30 and remembering her grandson to be an early riser, she started to wonder if her first suspicions may be true. After realising that her tea had gone cold, she gently shook her head and headed for the kettle.

Nick's pace quickened as he entered Melrose drive, the family home in sight. This was the final straw; the young man had taken all the deception he could stand. The earlier mist had dissipated, blown clear by a stiff breeze and Nick walked head down, focus fixed on his trainers as they shuffled along the cracked pavement.

"Easy their young fella, you going to knock me clean off my feet." Castle looked up with a start, barely registering the stooped old man heading in the opposite direction. Harold Gregory, the former proprietor of the butchery shook his head as the young man muttered an apology under his breath, manners the last thing on Nick's mind today. Arriving at the front-door, Castle paused, knowing that this conversation wasn't going to be pleasant.

The lounge was empty, but the young man could hear water boiling in the kitchen. Purposefully, he strode through the room, aware that an argument would ensue. Entering the kitchen, Alice looked frail, the dim light seeming to shrink her diminutive frame. Nick had second thoughts, his respectful feelings for his aged sibling telling him to stay calm. Suddenly, the memories of his conversation with Brackett brought back his anger to the surface.

"Are you people for real?" The question was asked with controlled aggression, his voice low but firm, the words delivered slowly with perfect diction.

"You know, don't you?" Her tone was wavering, fighting back tears. Alice was old-school, a strong maternal leader who rarely showed weakness, but the recent events had broken the old lady down.

"Who told you?" Lifting the kettle, she poured the contents into the old teapot before stirring, the lid replaced as the liquid brewed.

"Does it matter? Did you really think I wouldn't find out? Did you really think that lying to me, again, was the right thing to do?" Striding across the room, he pulled out a chair from beneath the table and sat down. Alice lifted the teapot and joined him, before realising her cup was still across on the kitchen cabinet. Sighing with exertion, she began to rise once more. "Stay there, I'll get it." Standing by the sink's draining board, Nick whispered, "I really hoped that things had changed but it's like being a kid, all over again."

"Do you think I wanted to lie to you? I was carrying out the last wish of your grandfather."

"What are you talking about now?" Returning to the table, Nick placed the cup before his grandmother. The old woman was wearing a pale pink dressing gown with two pockets below the waistline and as her grandson approached, she reached a bony hand deep inside the right-hand side one. She retrieved a manila envelope with the words, "My dearest Alice," handwritten across the front. Returning to his seat he asked, "What's that?" The old woman slid the paper container across the table.

"Answers." Lifting the teapot, she poured herself a measure into the china-cup and left the room.

Chapter 28

My Darling Alice,

I'm writing you this letter as I know, if we discuss this, you'll just try to talk me out of doing what I'm about to do and since I've never been able to win an argument with you in forty-four years, I can't take the risk. At least this way, I'll get the final word, even if I have to mail it in.

No one knows me the way you do so I don't need to tell you what these last few years have done to me. I used to be proud of the man I was, knowing that I had Hallowell's best interests at heart and feeling respected by my peers. It's been a long time since I felt that way. That night at the railway station should have finished me off, it didn't. But a lot of good men died because of what happened and even though you say I shouldn't blame myself, I do, every-day. I can't look at myself in the mirror, knowing what happened and believing it was my fault.

I'm an old man now and I suppose quite foolish, but I can't meet my maker until I put this right. I don't care what Brackett says, Daley did not take that boy, he doesn't have it in him. So, I was thinking, perhaps the kiddie is still alive, even a monster like Graham must have some decency. I need to find out, one way or another, if for no other reason than my own sanity.

So, my darling, I'm going to search. I've asked our new constable to come with me and he pretty much told me to get lost. To be honest, I don't care, I've no wish to have anyone else's life under my responsibility anymore. Hopefully, I'll find the boy alive, but I also know that there's a chance it won't go so well.

I wish there was some other way, but I can't go on living with this cloud hanging above my head. If it ends badly, well, please forgive me. I have loved you from the first moment we met, and you and our family are the crowning achievements of my life. But without facing this demon, I may as well be gone already.

I know I'm not in a position to ask anything of you as you are probably mad as Hell with me at this moment but, I'm begging you, if this ends badly, don't tell Nick. Don't even tell him I've gone until after the funeral as he'll use it as an excuse to come home. If he thinks for one moment that that monster is responsible for my passing, he'll go for vengeance, and he has no clue as to what that thing is capable of. I'm sorry to sound so morbid but this is maybe the last chance I have to protect the people of this village and especially my family. Nick has too many of my ways inside and he won't be able to stop himself.

Tell Mick, I love him. We haven't always seen eye to eye, but I've always been proud to call him my son. And protect Nicky, I love him more than all the world.

As for you, my darling wife, just know that you've made my life more wonderful than I could have ever dreamed. With you by my side, I knew I could take on the world and you're without a doubt, the best thing that ever happened to me.

My love always,

Bill

In all his recollections, Nick Castle could remember crying only once, and that was after Julia's passing. Now, he was sitting at the kitchen table, where his grandparents had eaten breakfast at for the last forty years, openly weeping, tears flooding down his cheeks, eyes raw. After finishing the note, he'd started again, and then again, and then again. The words were hard to comprehend; was it intense bravery, or plain stupidity. He was one man, seriously outgunned. He was taking on something that had a size, age, and intensity advantage. The creature was on home ground and could hide anywhere, until having an advantageous striking position. He had no chance, and yet, he was willing to lay down his life for what he believed was right. Were there any lingering doubts about whether William Castle was his hero…they were gone now.

Bill's selflessness and gallantry were beyond reproach, but for the young man, the words took on a far more poignant meaning. He understood now, why his family had plotted the course for the direction to which his young life had taken. Hallowell as a residence for his adolescence would have been suicide, of that there could be no doubt. His natural instinct would have been to seek vengeance for Billy Scholes's murder, even though he was only a child himself. Throughout his teens, his feeling of guilt for his young friend's death had been all-encompassing, the same guilt that Bill had endured after the botched invasion of the station. Even now, all he could envision was justice for his grandfather. Taking on the beast and slaying it, one last time.

Over a decade ago, Bill Castle had seen that glint in his grandson's eye, that undeniable urge to correct a wrong, to recompense and make amends against an evil act. That was why the former policeman had worried so greatly, Nick had way too many of his own ways.

There was now recognition that his view of the world had been wrong, what his family had seen, that he was too immature to identify the seriousness, that he needed shielding from himself at all costs. That realisation was now in his grasp, and made his weeping stronger, more intense, the built-up frustrations of a decade long battle, erupting to the surface with violent connotation. The price paid was immeasurable, his relationship with both his mother and father had been fractured, possibly to irreparable extremes. His parent's marriage had splintered under the strain until they had given in and divorced. Even his kinship with Bill had been strained, and visits by his grandparents had become fewer as time went on, the old man not able to bare Nick's constant pleading for a return to his spiritual home.

So much made sense now.

Once his composure was regained, exiting the kitchen, he discovered that Mick Castle had joined Alice in the lounge. The two older generations turned to face the young man, wary of what his reaction would be. Mick had a rolled-up cigarette smouldering between his lips and after he tapped the residue ash onto the coal-fire hearth, he rose from his seat.

"You, okay?" The words were spoken with as much compassion as Mick could muster. Nick raised a hand to his face and rubbed the stubble across his cheeks, his skin still moist from the tears.

"You know what, I think I am." With the letter still in hand, he walked over to Alice's seat and passed her the note. "Thank you for letting me see this, I know it couldn't have been an easy decision to make." Her wrinkled fingers grasped the paper, and she gave her grandson a weak smile, tears welling in her own eyes once more. Nick had never seen his grandmother cry and the thought was disconcerting. Looking toward Mick, he had one question.

"You didn't know what he was about to do, did you?" The answer would ensure whether the father and son could ever have a real relationship again.

"You must really think nothing of me to be able to ask that question. There is no chance in Hell I'd have allowed him to walk into that place alone. I was over in St Mara at the cash and carry suppliers, picking up goods for shop. I came home, found the letter, and took it across to your grandmother. It was sealed. When she read it…"

Mick paused in his explanation, the latest member of the family to fight back tears. When his poise was strengthened, he continued, "When she read it, she gave it to me. I scanned the words but for some reason, I already suspected what it would say. A few days earlier, dad and I had talked, I mean, really talked. It was before the Daley debacle but even then, I could see there was something eating away at him. This was a wound that just wouldn't heal. He said there and then, he'd give his life if it meant he'd take Graham's too. I knew he was telling the truth but also, he seemed helpless; he knew he had no chance against a monster like that alone. Now, you may think I'm some kind of coward but, if I'd known what he was going to do, and I'd known there was no way to stop him, I'd have been by his side, shoulder to shoulder, no matter what. But by the time I found out, it was too late."

"So, what happened?" Nick was nervous to ask but had had no choice.

"I read the note quickly. I could see the horror on mum's face and knew it was serious. I threw down the note and jumped in the van." Another pause came but this time, he was unable to hold back the tears. "It was obvious where he'd headed, but I was too late. It was dusk, streetlights were coming on everywhere. Everywhere except at that place, I don't know if you remember but, even when the railway station was in use, the damned streetlights never worked in that road. I tore round and pulled up in the car park, I jumped out of the van and…there he was. Slumped besides the fence, same place as we found all the other victims. At first, it just, looked like a pile of rags, the lighting was terrible. I ran over and there was your granddad."

Mick's voice was crackling under the strain, but he fought on.

"This is going to sound crazy but…he looked so peaceful. There was no blood, no outward injuries, for a moment, I thought there might be a chance. I shook him, called out his name, there was no response. So, I touched his neck, to feel for a pulse. His head, lolled lifelessly to the side, his throat had been crushed." Alice had given up fighting against her tears too by now and the three were openly weeping, aware there was no shame. "I pulled your granddad into the light, but it was obvious he was dead. I was so angry, I started across the station car park. I'd got maybe, halfway, and there was a hand on my shoulder. I'd been so focused, I didn't hear anyone approaching, so I swung around and fired off a punch. Thankfully it missed because it was Johnny Brackett. Your grandma had gone to get him and the two followed me to the station. I know you have a problem with our new constable but, were it not for him, I'd probably be dead too. He and mum dragged me away and we called Fred Gibson to get dad's body." Mick cried out in shock as the cigarette he was smoking had burned to the tip and singed his fingers.

"Christ, I had no idea. I didn't mean to make you sound like a chicken, I just needed to know. I'm sorry"

"I know you don't hold me in very high esteem but, I loved my father. Sometimes we didn't always get along, what families do? But he meant the world to me, you all do. And yes, I *was* pissed, he didn't wait so I could go with him… I would have… But all the way to the end, he was protecting his family. Stupid old fool."

"So, what about Brackett? Is this just another victim we are supposed to accept?"

"Christ Nick, listen to yourself, what do you want? Is this whole set-up insane? Probably, yes. Hallowell lives at the whim of a madman. Is that what you want to hear? Your granddad was constable while this was going on, there was nothing he could do. Brackett is now our policeman and guess what, there's nothing he can do either. The people who live in this village, live in fear. Brackett could go rabble-rousing, trying to get another lynch-mob together and guess what, no one would volunteer, because the whole village lost someone last time. Be it a brother, a father, uncle, friend, employee, someone. No one wants to know. So, what's next, bring in outside help? Would you like to explain why the town waited all these years? Why so many people are dead, and no one reported it. Anyone that knew anything would be charged with withholding evidence, for perverting the course of justice. And there's still no certainty that they'd get him, he still knows that place a Hell of a lot better than any outsider. So, that's out. What else? What other bright idea is there? Blow the place up, right? Wrong. What if he's not there? Without his lair, then he turns his attention to those responsible, while they lay in their beds. Hasn't there been enough victims, enough bloodshed? I understand, this is the craziest, seriously fucked up, (Mick suddenly looked embarrassed at his use of profanity in front of his mother, though the old lady never reacted) the stupidest position any village has ever been in. Shit, if I had the chance, I'd set the mother-f…sorry, the piece of crap,

I'd set it on fire and put it out with bricks. But I haven't. I know where he is, we all know where he is, the horrible thing is, there's nothing any of us can do about it." Mick immediately apologised to his mother, it was the first time she'd ever heard him curse, though it was understandable.

"What do we do now?" Nick was legitimately stumped; he knew what he wanted to do but that would be playing to type. Everyone expected him to storm to the station and become just another victim. But though he hated to admit it, Nick knew the monster had all the advantages. He was bigger, stronger, knew every inch of that place, and was vicious and demented enough to tear Castle apart. Retreat wasn't in the young man's lexicon, but this was an unwinnable battle. Alice answered the question.

"Nothing, for now. You have your date tonight, try to put all of this to the back of your mind and have a normal evening. Then tomorrow, go see your granddad. Go see him while you have the chance. He's in Fred Gibson's funeral parlour. I saw him three days ago and he looks wonderful, just like he's asleep. All the wrinkles have fallen from his face, he looks so at peace."

"What about his neck?" The idea of seeing Bill wounded made Nick feel sick to his stomach.

"There really wasn't much to see. He had some bruising at the sides and across his throat but…anyway, he's in a silk lined casket. The only part you can see is his face. He looks like the heart-throb I fell in love with." Alice allowed herself a smile, the air of depression was lifting.

"I don't know." Nick interjected though was quite surprised at his father's response.

"It's your choice but, if you don't, I've a feeling you may regret it. It's the last chance you'll have to say goodbye." Again, Nick could feel tears, beginning to well in the corner of his eyes though this time, he managed to hold them back. "Just try to get your mind on normal things, everyday things, it's good medicine. We'll get through the funeral, together, as a family. And then, afterwards, perhaps we'll just see what happens." Both Alice and Nick gave Mick a surprised look, though for different reasons, the young man out of hope, and the old lady out of concern.

Chapter 29

Frank listened intently to his sister's childish squeals in the neighbouring room. It was the day of her 7th birthday and she'd received a 'pretty Polly' doll as a gift. Earlier in the afternoon, there'd been twelve screaming brats in the living room playing party games and gobbling down jelly and ice-cream like it was going out of fashion. He'd stayed well out of the way as his parents had pandered to the party guests every need, Martin even wore a silly paper hat and tried desperately to perform rudimentary magic tricks after the clown that had been booked cancelled at the last moment. The noise had been deafening, balloons bursting every thirty seconds and shrill screams whenever one of the snot-nosed shits won a crappy prize; it made Frank want to vomit.

Finally, around six, the last of the mob had gone home and there was a semblance of normality. He'd spent most of the afternoon, laying on his bed, getting more and more pissed, visualising crushing their irritating little heads beneath the heel of his boot. Even Martin's voice had grated on him today, playing happy families with his bitch wife and precious little Jenny, how he loathed her.

Through the wall, he could still hear her squeaky tone as she innocently played with Polly. It wasn't only the doll she'd received, no, there was the cot and pushchair too. Pink and girly and sickeningly sweet. Changes of clothing and plastic nappies…for a fucking rubber doll, how stupid, it was hardly going to shit itself. Whilst the party was ongoing, he'd crept into his sister's bedroom in the hope of finding Polly unguarded, Frank enjoyed vandalising Jenny's possessions. Unfortunately, the doll had an invite too and was being force-fed birthday cake, so its destruction would have to wait. Now, he was pacing his bedroom, her twisty tones the only thing he could hear. Even with the door shut, it wasn't drowned out and his anger was gradually growing. His footsteps stomped across the floorboards, backwards, forwards, from the window to the back wall, heart rate quickening. Lifting his hands to his head, he clasped around his ears and pressed hard. Muttering, he ground his teeth, jaws clenched in a lock; eyes closed tightly, sweat pouring from his brow, he could still hear her.

"Don't you look beautiful in your pretty, new dress. You're such a lucky girl, aren't you Polly?" Frank's fingers were now entwined in his hair, and he began pulling, the pain stabbing into his skull.

"Shut up, shut up, shut up." His face red with rage, he released the hair and began punching himself forcibly in the jaw, left, right, left right, a mistimed shot bursting his lower lip, blood immediately pouring from the open wound.

"Don't cry Polly, I know you're tired, you've had a busy day."

A shot to the gut droves the wind out him but he couldn't stop. A left to the temple momentarily dazed him and made him reach for balance. Drawing forward his right-boot, he ferociously kicked himself in the centre of the left shin, the skin immediately splitting behind his black denims, a trickle of blood clagging to the heavy material.

"I think you might need a bottle. It's not like you to be this upset. Are you hungry?"

Suddenly, his assault stopped. Breathing deeply, the wounds to his leg and lip were still oozing blood and huge clumps of hair lay scattered across the bedroom carpet. His scalp stung, and his stomach felt bruised but, there was silence. Wonderful, glorious, peaceful silence.

"There, there, Polly. That's a good girl."

Frank let out a guttural growl and headed out of the bedroom.

Jenny's door was just ten feet away and slightly ajar. There was a plaque hanging loosely on the wooden barrier saying, "princess sleeps here" and the lettering was surrounded by red roses. As he gently pushed the door, he held the plaque to avoid it banging and alerting his sister of his presence. Remembering that the hinges squeaked, he only pushed the barrier enough for him to be able to squeeze through the gap and once inside, he was surprised to notice the room was mainly in darkness, the only light coming from beneath the door of the room's on-suite bathroom.

Still that constant squeaky voice filled his head, childish giggles between water splashes and fake baby noises.

"Don't cry Polly, you know you need to have your hair washed. You want to look pretty for Froggy's tea-party, don't you?" The child was just fifteen feet away, but the bathroom door was only slightly ajar, all Frank could see was Jenny's left arm, cradling the doll across the white porcelain tub. "There, I told you the soap wouldn't get in your eyes. I'll always protect you, my little baby. Especially from my nasty big brother." The next words were whispered in the dollies rubber ear, "We hate him." Afterwards the child giggled, as if she'd revealed something that no one else knew.

Gently, the little girl poured water from a plastic tumbler over the dolls head and when she was certain that the fake hair was drenched enough, a layer of conditioner was rubbed into the rubber scalp. As Frank approached the door, his footsteps were ghost-like, almost gliding over the uneven floorboards. His breathing became laboured, his left hand clenched so tightly into a fist that calluses were forming across the palm, fingernails cutting deeply into the flesh. And in the right hand…the light from the bathroom caught the blades edge, long cold steel sharpened expertly into a lethal weapon, the wooden handle felt loose due to his hand's perspiration, its point darting in the direction of his sister.

Talking in a lungful of scented air, he reached for the wooden door, fingers curling around its edge. Slowly, it glided stealthily open, the girl now in full view. Her childish games had ensured she still had no idea of his presence, he held up the knife adjacent to his face as to strike down with greater force.

"Jack and Jill went up the hill to fetch a pale of water," his muscles tensed, "Jack fell down and bumped his crown," a final breath before the deed was done. "And Jill came tumbling after."

Click. Frank had been so focused on his target, he wasn't aware that Iris Graham was seated on the lid of the toilet, out of site to the right of the room. His head immediately shot in her direction though it was the Hechler and Kock p9 handgun pointed in his direction that took his attention, the same gun that Martin used for home security.

A maniacal grin was spread across her face, eyes of a mad person, staring full of hate. The weapon cocked and ready, his mother began to laugh, loud, insane cackling, filling the air and breaking a new-found silence. The girl turned, sporting the exact same expression and soon, she was laughing too. His body was frozen, he still had the knife on target, but it refused to strike. Limbs relinquished control, the blade slipped from his grasp and clunked to the floor with a clatter. He began to back away, slowly moving into the bedroom, flanked by his insanity ravaged mother, her laugh replaced by song.

"This is the way I kill my son, kill my son, kill my son, this is the way I kill my son, just because I want to." The pistol was being waved like an orchestral conductor's baton. The pupils in her eyes were now demonic white, as was his sisters. The child's voice had lost its innocence and between satanic laughs, she was muttering, "Frankie's going to die." All his former anger had been replaced by…fear. For the first time, the teen was terrified. His backwards steps began to quicken but the progress came to a shuddering halt, someone was blocking his path. Frank spun around to be confronted by his father, Martin Graham.

"Dad, help me."

Jenifer's laughs gained in volume as Iris slid an arm around her daughter's shoulder. She too began to roar, more gruffly than before, as if she were choking though she didn't care. Frank fell to his knees before his father and begged.

"Dad, please help me."

Martin stared down at his stricken son, then joined in the laughter. Harder and louder than both Iris and Jenifer combined, starting with a snigger, turning to a guffaw, before shrieking into a fit of howling, like the Devil's own personal amusement. The teens legs crumbled, and he scrunched into the foetal position at the feet of his family. Jenifer was now holding the blade and was feverously poking her brother with the tip. The whites of their eyes glowed in the darkness and Frank took one final attempt to gain his father's assistance. Curling an arm around Martin's left leg, he looked up a yelled, "PLEASE."

The laughter immediately stopped; silence filled the air. Slowly, Martin raised his hands to his face. Driving his fingernails deep into his own skin below his eyes, he began to shred the flesh. Blood oozed from the wounds and as he felt the sticky fluid squelch between his digits, the self-mutilation increased in ferocity. Huge handfuls of membrane tore free, ripped from the surface, and flung sickeningly to the floor; in no time, the white skeletal bones were visible. Forcing his thumbs deep into the ocular cavities, the eyes fell free with a popping sound, slickly sliding down the devastated face with the entrails still intact. The lips tore free with ease and the fatty flesh dripped across his son's face. Frank was now screaming uncontrollably but the more his wails escaped, the more his family's demonic laughs regained in volume. The jawbone of his father was hanging loosely but the tongue still helped the sounds emanation. Long strands of saliva hung between the upper and lower teeth and blood ran continually, drenching his meagre clothing. The teens head swooned dizzily and were the horrific visage not so vivid, he'd have certainly lost consciousness. Tears cascading, and his vision blurred, he could just make out that his father's hair was untouched. No, it was more than that, it was different. The colour, jet black. And its mass, almost shoulder length. Then he noticed the bones, the skeletal features of his face, no long white. They had taken on a green shade. Dark green. And the texture no longer appeared bone-like at all, it was loose and flexible, almost like rubber. Throwing arms around his head, he curled into a ball, unwilling to see the Hell before him anymore.

"Frankie? Frankie, are you okay?" Fred Gibson knew Graham refused to be seen without his mask but as the monster had his huge arms wrapped tightly around his head, forced into the filthy mattress on which the killer was sleeping, he was unsure whether the mask was in place, making proceeding a tough option to call. This visit was unscheduled and unexpected and even though the undertaker was Frank's only access to the outside world, Gibson knew better than to take their rendezvous for granted. Placing a hand on Graham's shoulder, he forcibly patted, swiftly moving clear before the angry giant awoke.

With a final cry, Frank's eyes snapped open, the mortician happy that the disguise was still in place. Inside the heavy rubber shield, his skin moist with perspiration, clinging uncomfortably to his cheeks and with the memory of his nightmare still fresh, the image of his late father masquerading as the picture of horror the rubber camouflage projected, his confused state made him more dangerous than ever.

Springing to his feet with the agility of an athlete, the monster lunged for his uninvited guest and the frightened man cowered in terror.

"Frank. Frank stop, it's me, Fred." Falling backwards, the undertaker was suddenly in the same position as Graham had been in seconds earlier during his imaginary nightmare. Seeing Gibson a blubbering wreck before him, brought the behemoth back to reality. With control restored, he turned and walked twenty feet across the room to a smouldering oil drum, which hours earlier had been a roaring fire. The ashes were still glowing red, and the killer took a handful of prepared wood from a metal container and threw them into the embers and watched as the slowly started to crackle.

"I'm sorry to come unannounced Frank, you know I wouldn't normally. But there's something you need to know."

Nick Castle had always used gentle exercise as a way of clearing his mind, and the latest revelations about the death of his grandfather had given him the headache from Hell. Seeing his father and grandmother in tears had quelled whatever anger he may be feeling and reading those words on the page humanised this horror. What did he think he was, some kind of superhero? The people of Hallowell had lived with this chaos for over a decade, wondering if that creature was still alive. Then, a body would appear, and the question would be answered. He wondered what it must be like to be a parent in this environment, like the Roberts's family who'd recently lost a child to that demonic miscreation. You'd want to warn your children, of that there'd be no doubt, but how would you do it, without emotionally scarring them. How old was old enough? How would you even start to explain things?

"Oh darling, time for bed. Have sweet dreams and, by the way, don't go in that building on the railway ground because there's a fucking homicidal maniac living there."

He'd reached the woodland behind the Graham ruins but was determined that the station was out of bounds, especially for today. The trees weren't particularly well spaced out and their height gave Nick an unwelcome feeling of claustrophobia. The ground was uneven too, risen roots mixed with fallen foliage made the young man wish he'd chosen a differing route. With the small gaps between the trees, the old mansion could still be seen. With the gentle breeze, the fresh air was ruined by the odour of charred wood, no matter how much time passed, that scent would invariably overpower nature's fragrance.

The dilemma he was fighting currently wasn't whether to take on Hallowell's bogeyman, it was whether that having a date, with his sister, was a good idea. He tried telling himself that she was her mother's daughter and only a Graham in name, but it was hard, especially after the latest unearthed news. Would his family feel he was pissing on Bill memory by dating a girl related to his killer? Nick had purposely omitted the young lady's name when he'd announced his night-time plans. So many times, he decided to cancel their assignation, surely it was the right thing to do? But then, there was a voice inside his head that argued, said that this girl was different to anyone he'd ever met, even Julia. That spark had been instant, that first moment their eyes met was electric. How could one just walk away from that? Eventually, he decided that progressing with his heart rather than his head was the way to go. Perhaps, his groin may have had a say too. The decision made, he headed home.

Nick took time to ensure, that the white shirt was intended to where for the date was pressed carefully. Alice had offered to fulfil the task, but the earlier argument was still fresh in his mind and his stubborn streak refused to accept the olive branch. After twenty minutes of trying, he began to regret that decision, household chores were not his forte. Wearing the black trousers from the suit he'd purchased from Bill's funeral, without the jacket, ensured a smart appearance without looking forced. The shirt was worn open-necked without a tie, showing just enough chest-hair to attract interest without looking sleazy. Bill had given his grandson a family heirloom for his fourteenth birthday, a pair of gold-plated cufflinks in the shape of tiny boxing-gloves. Bill's father, Arthur Castle had been British heavyweight champion for five years and had been scheduled to fight for the world title when he was called up to the forces to fight in the first world war. Tragically, it was a fight Arthur would not win, losing his life at the Battle of the Somme. They had been one of Bill Castle's most prized possessions and had caused friction between him and his son Mick, who expected to inherit the golden trinkets. For the first time, Nick intended to where them, wishing to honour his poor brave grandfather.

The words from Bill's letter had cut deeply and though it enforced his hated for that thing inside the station, it raised his opinion even higher, of his late granddad. To Nick, he was the epitome of what a man should be, bravery beyond belief, strong minded and strong willed, who would fight for what was right and what he believed in. To Nick, Bill was Superman. And as for the creature that took him, there was time.

His black dress shoes had taken time but had shined up nicely and the Brylcreem he used to slick back his long black hair gave the illusion of a 1950s movie star. He'd nicked the skin below his right ear while shaving, his hands struggling to fight the slight tremor caused by the withdrawal symptoms from the medication and he'd decided that taking two Prozac an hour before their date was sensible. They took an immediate effect and though the woozy feeling had him nervous, they did help lift his foul mood.

Nick was courteous to his grandmother, when she wished him a lovely evening, replying simply with a smile as he left the front door. They'd built bridges soon; the house was too small for hostility. Deep inside, he understood that Alice had been in an impossible position, fighting for loyalty to her dead husband's wishes against revealing the awful truth to her grandson. He'd taken it better than Alice could have ever expected. She'd had visions of needing to barricade the doors and handcuffing Nick to the furniture to prevent him heading directly to the station to try and seek vengeance. Instead, he'd accepted the horrific details calmly and maturely, though Alice was concerned that his composure may have been a mask.

The Ford's engine growled as Nick turned the ignition key, the headlights streaking a luminous beam across the dimly lit street. Using the car would maintain his sobriety for the night, the idea of being breathalysed by a smirking Johnny Brackett would keep alcohol off tonight's menu. Plus, controlling his craving after one bottle of wine would be tough, one was never enough. Normally, Nick wouldn't care but there was something about this girl, something special; that's the reason he'd tried so hard, every detail of his outfit had been carefully selected. He'd never been this excited about a date since Julia. He just had no idea why. Pressing the accelerator, the car pulled away from the kerb and moved gently to the end of Melrose drive. Turning the corner up to Main Street, he threw on some extra revs and the engine growled even harder, Henderson's bed and breakfast, his destination.

The wood had been lit from the dying embers and now the oil-drum was burning brightly once more. The natural oils from the bracken crackled and threw up some ferrous flames which lit up the whole section of the top floor of the station. The creature was standing ten feet from the burning oil drum, with the flickering reds and oranges, the mask became visible. In horrific shadow, that creation always made Gibson shudder.

Fred had been connected to Graham for some ten years and never once had he seen him unmasked. With the reflected light from the fire, that disguise seemed all the more menacing. The dark holes which concealed the monster's eyes were as dark as nightfall, and the carved rubber which made up the cheek bones threw down the murkiest shadow. Its green colour was barely visible, the fiery tones reflected back towards the flames and the straggly fake hair hung loose across the brow. From the mortician's vantage point, seated close to the fire, he could see that at the neck of the disguise, Frank's own facial hair was pushing down the rubber and protruding from its edge. Fred could only wonder just how far from human; Graham's appearance had become.

"I'm sorry Frank, I needed to wait until dusk, so no one would see me coming. If just one person knew that I visited you, those sons of bitches would tear me apart." Gibson usually spoke slowly and precisely so Graham would understand, knowing that the years of isolation would almost certainly of damaged his brain, a mind's psyche that had been fractured even before his self-imposed exile. Frank was now more animal than man, using a natural instinct to protect was he perceived as his, content to use extreme violence where necessary. Like a predator, he stalked potential targets, striking when certain his prey was at its weakest. Surviving on their dismembered remains, something Fred Gibson had taught him to do. The mortician had his uses.

"I know it's normally the weekend when I visit, but this couldn't wait. You see, there's two new arrivals in the village. Two new people, and they're dangerous."

Jenifer Graham had panicked when she remembered the clothing options she'd brought from home. The items chosen were more conservative with business meetings in mind, rather than a romantic rendezvous. After trying on her tweed jacket and skirt, the mirror reflected the item of a school mistress, hardly a sexy appearance for a first date. Not that she wished to appear flirtatious, it wasn't in her nature; she just had no wish to emerge as cold or distant, it was so confusing.

It didn't take long to realise that nothing in her wardrobe was suitable. A swift journey to St Mara solved the issue. Finding a pale pink, off the shoulder blouse and a figure-hugging black pencil skirt in a quaint little shop, half way down Craven Street, just off the centre of town. The outfit was a little more expense than she'd planned to spend but for some reason, this man seemed worth the effort.

She tried not to build up the date in her mind, knowing it couldn't possibly go anywhere, she'd only be in Hallowell a view day, but the disappointment of not seeing the real-estate agent earlier in the day was outweighed by the fact that spending a little more time in the village meant more opportunities to see her talk dark handsome stranger. This was finally an adventure for the girl who'd been coddled all her teenage life by a wonderful but over-protective adoptive mother. A mother that saw boys as the lowest form of life, who had steered her though the bad times and wanted nothing but good things for her angel. Well, this was a chance to be a little crazy with someone who, for some reason seemed as tainted by life as she was. Oh, he hid it well but, Jenifer couldn't wait for the chance to dig a little deeper.

Aware she had a fine black dress-jacket back at the bed and breakfast, she was satisfied that her outfit worked. That hadn't stopped her fretting for most of the afternoon about how to wear her hair. When just washed and left to air-dry, her long blond locked would curl naturally and with her busy lifestyle, it was her normal usage, it reflected her personality, controlled with a hidden streak of wildness. But she worried that it would appear that she hadn't made much effort for the date, just a wash and go presentation, that wouldn't do. Being a hair stylist by trade, she began experimenting, tying her locks in a beehive made her look like she'd travelled back to the sixties. Two thick pigtails and she was transformed into an eight-year-old, pulling the hair into a tight ponytail and once more, she was that school mistress. Nothing seemed to work. Remembering she'd brought along her newly purchased hair-straighteners, she began to layer her hair with the red-hot steel clasps, gently pulling through the locks until all the curls were gone, the hair perfectly straight hanging stylishly down the contours of her beautifully shaped face, with a lightly parted fringe. Even with the lack of self-confidence that plagued Jenifer, even she had to admit that she looked nice. Others may say stunning, beautiful; Jenny was content with nice. She looked at her watch and noticed it was time. Running to the room's window, she was just in time to see the black Ford pull into the car park. With a girlish giggle, she ran from the window and headed towards the door.

"You must listen Frank, this is the worst thing that could have happened. All the main players in town are going crazy, there's a town meeting tomorrow, no one knows what to do. Everyone's losing the plot." Fred's normal slow diction had escaped him, but he soon realised, and his words began to slow. The fire crackled before him and the oils from the branches made an intense heat. Sweat beads formed across his brow and a trickle soon became a river of perspiration, teeming down the sides of his pudgy cheeks. He looked across to the monster, desperate to see some kind of acceptance of the coming threat; his posture remained structured, mask unwavering, black eyeholes staring into the flames.

"This is the biggest threat you've ever faced." No change. "Firstly, after you disposed of the former policeman, Bill Castle. Well, his hot-head grandson is in town for the funeral. I spoke to him last night. Looked him straight in the eye and said he needed to leave Hallowell straight away, once is grandfather is buried. Piece of shit just smiled at me. I swear I wanted to do him, there and then. Frank, that bastard really wound me up." Gibson paused, aware that his diction had speeded up once more. Taking a long deep breath, he continued. "Anyway, he's a threat. He's a hot head, a loose cannon, fucked up mental problems as a kid. He could land here with a barrel of petrol and try to burn the place down so watch out. I can only do so much at my end to keep him away. Anyway, that's not the worst thing." Once more the mortician paused to regain his composure, knowing that this was the news that could change all their lives.

"Your sister's here." This time, there was recognition from the monster, slowly turning his head in Gibson's direction. Though the undertaker couldn't see Graham's eyes, being stared at through that disguise made him shudder. Normally, his visits comprised of Gibson bringing supplies, fruit, vegetables, human thigh meat. There would be no voice contact, no facial recognition, no thank you. Then items would be the left in a specific place, the old canteen on the lower floor; followed by any news items, either local or national that Fred thought that Graham may find interesting. The visits would be short ended with a compassionless goodbye. The mortician had considered severing ties, sometimes it felt tedious, but something always kept him coming back. Perhaps it was the unknowing as to whether he'd return home alive that kept him that made him continue. Whatever it was, he continued his weekly sojourn, knowing that he'd be ignored throughout the duration of his stay. So, for the monster to turn his head, this was progress.

"She arrived late last night. She claims as the only living heir to the Graham estate, she intends to sell off this place and the derelict mansion to developers, to flatten the whole place and built houses. From what I understand, she needs a quick sale, needs money fast. Now, I have enough stashed away to make her an offer, but people would wonder why I'd done it. Hero of the village? Protector of the village? No one would believe it. Most those bastards can't stand me, there's no way they'd believe I'd give my life savings to save Hallowell." Frank was now standing, his chest heaving up and down at the thought of the person he hated the most coming back to take his home. Gibson could see just from his stance that there was danger afoot. His hope was that he wouldn't be the first victim.

"Anyway, this meeting. Everyone who's anyone will be there. Brackett is playing lead man, the big cheese. Finally, people look to him for advice, for guidance, for leadership. What a crock of bollocks, I'd make a far better meeting chairman, I know a dam site more about this than he fucking does." Looking at the monster, he could see it was time to stop rambling and get to the point. "So, what I'm going to suggest when they ask for rebuttal, I'm going to say that all the main families put up a percentage and between us, we make an offer. I'll start it by offering five grand, that's a lot of money. I think between us, if we can reach sixty grand, she'll take the money and run. I phoned my brief over in St Mara and there's no legal objection that can stop her doing what she's doing so we have no other choice. Let's hope the greedy bastards put their hands in their pockets, and we make this problem vanish."

Frank Graham turned his body and began to step forward toward the undertaker. Gibson knew when to shut up, if the monster had decided that Fred deserved to die, he'd have no chance of escape. Silently he prayed that today wasn't the day he went to Hell. If this was the end, God would be the last one to help after the atrocities he'd performed. Graham stepped slowly, his filthy coverall boilersuit rubbing between his thick calf muscles. His steel toe-capped boots, dragging across the dust-filled floor. He was six feet away, then five, four, three. Fred looked up; the creature was inches away. The mortician could hear Frank's breathing, smell his stinking odour. As he lifted his arms, Gibson flinched backwards. Frank's massive hands, cold as ice, reached to his own neck, two thumbs slid between the thick rubber of the mask and his skin. The rustle of facial hair fighting the disguise as the killer pushed his chin free of the rubber veil. Gibson watched, frozen to the spot as the camouflage revealed his mouth. Mattered hair from a dishevelled moustache and a beard which hung down beyond the Adam's apple, the only skin visible was two withered lips. Suddenly, they opened, a thick crust pulling at the flesh.

"Bring...her...to...me."

The ground slithered under Dan Challis's feet, fallen leaves mixing with the sodden earth to form a lubricious pathway. His arms pushed away low-hanging branches, but a solitary twig swung back, a thorn embedding itself in the drunken man's skin, just below the right eye. His forward motion caused the thorn to tear a rent into the flesh and Challis cried out in pain, carefully removing the prickly spur before throwing it in anger. Lifting his fingers to his cheek, blood was escaping from the tear, a flap of skin hanging loosely. After applying pressure, he continued his fight through the woodland.

The cottage he'd shared with his late father backed onto an area of trees, the only thing that separated them from the station grounds. His home was two doors away from Tom Daley's residence and five away from the Roberts family, who had tragically lost their boy days earlier. Dan had heard the commotion, but it was normal, old Tom was a target for most of the irritating little bastards, Dan, he was a close second. With his disability, chasing them was pointless, just got a mouthful of cheek, especially off the McKenzie kids because they knew their father was a mean son of a bitch who would happily punch anyone stupid enough to have a pop at his kids, viscous circle.

Still, things could be worse, he could be Tom. Everyone knew the old boy was innocent, he was just an easy target, an easy way to mop up this mess. In time, this would all go away. The Roberts boy would sadly be forgotten about, and Tom would be released. Oh, he'd then have the reputation of being a murderer as well as a paedophile, but the evidence would be lost, and the case classed as being cold. Sad really, when everyone knew who was responsible and as usual, nothing changes.

Most of Dan Challis's Day had been in a drunken haze. Not that this was anything unusual, but todays had had a reason. Having heard rumours that Nick Castle had suffered many of the same adolescent problems as he had, it had made his own alcoholism seem more acceptable, more justified. Then, when he'd seen his old friend looking sleek and handsome, his own deterioration no longer appeared so excusable. True, Challis had always swum at the shallow end of the gene pool, with his facial features hardly attractive and his athletic endeavours zero, but that was hardly his fault, he couldn't help being ugly, he couldn't help it when he wanted to scream every time, he looked in the mirror. Obviously, he'd been responsible for the deterioration, the constant alcohol abuse had made him gain a paunch around the midriff and had helped the growth of another chin. And yes, maybe he could have visited the barber's shop once in a while instead of sporting the whispery mullet, but he needed the money for booze, again vicious cycle. One day, when the stars aligned, and the Gods smiled down, he'd kick the habit and…okay, that was probably bullshit, but he did hope that one day, he could have a normal life. And then he saw what he'd be up against. If Castle could look like that after years of hard-core drinking, what chance would Dan ever have. So, instead of stopping after arriving home the previous night, he'd drank until he passed out. Then the nightmares came.

When he'd woken, Dan had found himself on the bathroom tiles, dried vomit around his mouth, stale urine in a puddle around his crotch. It took over ten minutes to get upright, the pain from his mangled leg so severe. Grabbing a handful of Co-Proxamol pain killers from the bathroom cabinet, slowly his agony began to wear off, they helped speed up the eradication of his hangover too. Within half an hour, the pain pills had given him a warm buzz and he was ready to start all over again. His routine was drearily familiar. Strong cans of lager were consumed first, this was because his stomach was empty, and they'd slide down without a fight. After around six had been consumed, he'd move on to white cider, something that was cheap and highly addictive. So addictive, drug workers claimed that more people were enslaved by an obsession for that than all other drugs combined, mainly due to its accessibility and inexpensive cost. If he was still conscious by the time two bottles had been consumed, he'd go to the workingmen's club for a nightcap.

Tonight, the club held no interest for him. After seeing Nick Castle, the previous evening, he had no wish to be reminded of what he'd never be. Still, his home seemed claustrophobic tonight. He needed air.

Finding the lock on his front door with his key was harder than expected. The night-time freshness seemed to hit him all at once, his coal fire inside had been throwing out a torrent of heat and the cool breeze was refreshing. Dan had no idea where he was heading and started to stagger along the cobbled street. Passing Tom Daley's little home, he shook his head in disgust at the fact that someone had put a brick through the poor chump's window. It was just another excuse to target him. Was he eradicated from the village, someone else would have to take his place? Dan frowned when the realisation that it would probably be him became apparent. He'd always been a victim; he would probably *always be* a victim. Challis snarled, victim, victim, VICTIM. The speed of his stride increased, the word reverberating inside his brain, victim, victim. The cobbles were damp and uneven along the street, every so often, he'd place a hand on the cottage walls for balance, victim, victim, his eyes closed, almost at the end of the road, a door opens and a man shout. Suddenly, he's face to face John McKenzie.

"Hey there freak, drunk as usual I see. You should be fucking ashamed." The man spoke with a strong Irish accent and was close enough for Dan to know he was a hypercritic, the stench of whiskey on his breath revealing the truth. Strangely for once, Challis didn't feel intimidated even though he barely came up to his adversaries' shoulders. Still the word bounced around his brain, victim, victim. Dan stared up, man to smaller man, puffed out his chest and with all his bravery managed to say,

"Sorry." He stepped to the left to go around McKenzie, but the Irishman followed suite. Dan tried again and once more his path was blocked. Challis paused, breathed out, then looked up at the obstacle before him. "May I be passed?" The Irishman sniggered.

"You haven't said the magic word." His breath was now an unpleasant mix of whiskey and tobacco and as he spoke, spittle discharges seemed to be well aimed at Dan's eyes.

"What's the magic word?" Challis was pretty certain it would be please, and if saying please would get this shit-heal out of his face, it was a small price to pay.

"Abrar-fucking-cad bra." The bully found this highly amusing and burst into fits of laughter. He wasn't so amused when Dan arched back his neck and fired a vicious head-butt, directly across the bridge of his nose.

The Irishman fell backwards and grabbed his own front door for support. When the door swung open, he fell further, landing flat on his back, muttering obscenities as blood squelched between his fingers. When Dan realised the enormity of his actions, he fled as quickly as his withered left leg would carry him. He soon regretted that he was fleeing in the opposite direction to his home and decided that taking the long route behind the street was preferable to running by the angry Irishman. As he turned the corner at the top of the street, he heard the back door to the McKenzie's opening, a gaggle of outraged voices heading out into the night. Knowing both routes to sanctuary were blocked, the only escape available was through the fence, into the woodland, bordering the station. As he struggled to force his frame through the fractured cavity, he remembered the Roberts boy, the last soul to use this entryway.

One leg was through when the gate to his adversary's house began to unlock. His bad leg was almost there, just a last tug, but Challis couldn't take his eyes the wooden barrier. As the latch clicked open, Dan fell to the ground, inside the sanctuary the woodland provided. Scampering to his feet, he darted between the thick foliage, just as McKenzie, a blood-stained rag covering most of his face, appeared in the darkened backroad.

"When I find you, you're dead, you one-legged freak." The Irishman stepped out onto the cobbles though had no interest in giving chase. They lived in the same street; his time would come. Slowly, the aggrieved man retreated to the confines of his house, back to another double whiskey.

This was the first brave thing that Challis could remember doing in some time. Bravery was probably the wrong description of what had just happened, immense stupidity was a better characterization, a momentary act of insanity. It felt good at the time, retribution for years of bullying at the hands of this prick of a neighbour. Unfortunately, reality was now dawning, return home tonight and there was a good chance he'd be hospitalised. It wasn't just McKenzie; the Irishman's wife was also as vicious as an agitated Rottweiler. When provoked, the couple had psychotic tendencies and would happily smash a route into Challis's cottage if they believed him to be present. A hide-out was essential, if only for the night. By morning, there was a chance the nightmare neighbours may have forgotten the altercation (dependant on the amount of alcohol they'd consumed that evening). If they were still baying for blood, then Challis could always seek assistance from Constable Brackett, after all, it was his job to protect the citizens of Hallowell. Dan wanted to avoid this, if possible, but it was a preferential alternative to a painful death.

Challis's safe-haven options were limited. He wasn't about to waste money, renting a room at Henderson's guest house and friendly faces were very rare. He'd considered Nick, though felt it would appear presumptive, one conversation in a decade hardly insinuated a close bond. Thankfully, there was one option. About a half mile away was Braselton Forest, another large area of woodland at the foot of Hallowell bank. About two-hundred yards off the roadside lay a solid concrete building, buried deep inside the treeline. It was created as a small wild-life shelter, mainly for the protection of roaming deer, a refuge against the vicious wintertime weather. After falling into disrepair, it had laid dormant for generations until, as children, Challis, Brackett, and Castle had discovered it and gleefully used it as a camp, re-christening it their clubhouse.

Built from red bricks, with a solid concrete roof, it was capable of sheltering from wet conditions. Unfortunately, the frontage contained no barrier against the cold, and winds could be especially brutal. Gratefully, the Autumnal temperature was still mild and the hazy glow from another day's drinking had left Challis with an inner warmth. The £4 in his jeans pocket had been more than enough to buy a bottle of cheap vodka and as the evening grew dark and the stars appeared, Dan gently felt the earth slip away into a welcome drunken haze.

He woke with a start, his surroundings, momentarily alien. The contents of the vodka had vanished all too quickly, were he at home, some may have been saved for another day. Instead, all but a last mouthful had been drained before being rendered unconscious by its harsh effects. The inside of his mouth felt like sandpaper and a pulsing throb emanated from the centre of his brow. His body shivered against the early morning air and the collar of his denim overcoat was pulled high around his neck. Rain glistened on the outside leaves though wind had replaced the damp conditions as the primary weather. The breeze sporadically blew his damp hair down across his eyes and it was only when he removed his hands from the coat pockets to replace it did, he notice the severe chill. A crick in his neck was painful to move, the consequences of falling asleep on cold hard concrete, and he longed for home and the aid of pain-pills, his withered leg causing immense agony.

Using the brick surface for support, he pushed through the discomfort, onto his feet. His head swooned, and sickness rose from his stomach. Closing his eyes, he rested the back of his head against the wall and tried to control his breathing. Shifting his feet across the dirt covered floor, his left boot caught the vodka's glass container and it started to tilt. With surprising reflexes, he retrieved the bottle before it crashed onto its side, the last swallow of the fiery liquid like an antidote to poison. The taste was bitter and made him grimace, but the effect was soon evident. Once empty, Challis threw the bottle across the room, the material smashing into a million shards as it struck the wall.

It seemed the perfect time to head home. The cheap watch on his right wrist said a little after five, the woods were still in darkness though the sun was slowly rising to the east. Manoeuvring a path through the Autumnal overgrowth wasn't easy but Dan knew these lands with his eyes closed. The injured leg was hurting more and more, and he was relieved to find the Forest borderline, a three-feet high wooden fence leading to church lane. The wind levels were slowly decreasing, a heavy layer of mist taking its place. The steeple of the church of St Helen was barely visible and there was something distinctly unnerving about passing a graveyard under the cover of darkness. A light shone brightly from an upstairs window of the Neighbouring vicarage, Father John Henderson, the head of the clergy for Hallowell for over a quarter of a century was an early riser and it made Challis feel a little better, knowing that he wasn't the only resident stupid enough to be up at this ungodly hour. By the time he turned onto colliery lane, Dan's limp had become much more pronounced, pain shooting up his thigh and into the lower back with every movement. Thankfully, there was one last corner and he'd be home.

The street was deathly quiet, every house still in total darkness, except for one. Dan knew he'd have to pass the McKenzie house to reach his own, but he was content that the early hour would keep him safe. The scum-bag neighbours had claimed unemployment benefit for years and the only work they did was cash off the books. Challis knew there was something missing when he'd taken the corner onto colliery lane, but it hadn't registered what it was. Now he knew.

He heard McKenzie's Vauxhall Astra before he saw it. That engine was unmistakable and had been the brunt of several noise complaints in recent years, the grinding of metal on metal without the aid of lubricant. Challis's back gate was twenty yards away, he knew he'd never make it before the Astra bombed down Colliery Lane, and if McKenzie saw him and there was no witness's, God knows what he was capable of doing. A pathway between the cottages broke up the street and Dan dragged his withered leg out of site, just before the Vauxhall came to screeching halt. Challis wasn't taking any chances; being unsure whether he'd made his retreat in time, he hurried along past all the homes and into the nearby woodland. Hearing a door slam in the distance, he was relieved when he noticed the light inside McKenzie's living room, breaking the streets darkness. Still, Dan wasn't in the mood to take chances and decided to hang back for a few moments, just to ensure the situation wasn't a trap.

The earth beneath his boots squelched, the earlier shower drenching the floor, and the long grass dampened the lower legs of his jeans. His breathing was becoming less laboured though, his mind still raced; it was aggravating to know that he'd probably need Constable Brackett's help if he were to avoid a beating from his infamous near neighbour. All he wanted was his pain-pills and his bed, was that too much to ask? Suddenly, the front door to his enemy's home opened, the hulking Irishman filling the entrance. Dan stumbled backwards and prayed that he hadn't been noticed. It didn't appear so, McKenzie choosing outdoors as a more suitable location for a cigarette. Cowering in the overgrowth, Challis retreated into the camouflage provided by the trees.

Standing on the spot was more painful than walking and Dan began to slowly pace the woodland. Every few hundred yards, he'd turn to ensure he wasn't being followed but it appeared safe. Inside his denims was a crumpled box of cigarettes and he reached into the pack to retrieve one. Taking the filter less smoke between his lips, he flicked his Zippo lighter and breathed in hard, sucking up as much nicotine as possible. Holding it for as long as possible, he exhaled a long plume through his nose, harmlessly watching the cloud dissipate into the air.

The mesh fence was just away to his right. Challis had spent a lifetime avoiding this place and suddenly, there it was. Nothing ever changed. That ladder from the roof, missing the final thirty feet, the reason he'd had such intolerable pain for more than a decade. The two darkened tunnels like unblinking eyes. The enormous platform, all the same. Dan spat on the floor, more out of defiance than the need to expel phlegm. He was about to leave when; something caught his eye.

It started with a shadow. The darkness was encompassing, and the mist hardly helped, but his eyes had now become accustomed to his surroundings. Across on the platform, originally, Dan took it to be the movement of a tree in the wind, but it was more than that. A penumbra, just a partial reveal of what was to come. Though it was slow, there was definitely a developing form. The shadow was increasing in mass, blocking out the faint light coming from the right-hand-side tunnel between the main and outer buildings. Then, something lighter appeared around the edge of the corner on the main building, six feet from the platform floor, taking care to conceal its identity. It was the head of a man, peering tentatively after emerging from the tunnel. Facial detail was still too difficult to make out, dissimulation of its form essential, crouching with an arm covering the head. It was too small to be the buildings evil inhabitant and Dan immediately grew concerned as to whether it was another victim. But there was something about the way it moved. Rather than fearing attack, it seemed more concerned with being identified. It was manoeuvring its way along the platform now, in Dan's direction. The way the feet shuffled seemed familiar but still the face was obscured. Whilst passing the left side tunnel, it never peered down in a fearful fashion, insinuating that Frank Graham held little concern for him. A bunch of stones had been placed as a makeshift stairway off the platform and as the figure approached, it finally lowered its concealing limbs.

And then the truth was revealed. What was the undertaker, Fred Gibson doing leaving the station, alone at this time of day, and why didn't he appear to have any fear of the resident evil inside?

"It's a cool evening Miss Graham and rain's forecast later. You take care not to catch a cold now." Robert Henderson was standing by the front door to the bed and breakfast having just returned from walking his pet Yorkshire terrier, Scraps. His face was flushed with the Autumnal breeze and the dog was beginning to whine, expecting its dinner, immediately on conclusion to the trek. Henderson stared for a second too long at the young woman, who had prepared herself into a vision of loveliness. The town meeting was the proceeding night, to which he'd have no choice but attend, his inquisitiveness would allow nothing less. Of course, there would be a hundred questions bombarded in his direction as he was one whom had the most interaction with the young woman. He would try to fend off the intrusion, looking irritated by the interrogation when inside, he'd secretly be loving it; it was nice to be the centre of attention for a change.

"Since there's rain in the air, I've an umbrella inside if you'd like to borrow it." Before the young woman could answer, the shrill tones of Henderson's wife, Irene, carried through from a back room.

"Bobby. You let that young lady about her business and close that front door. You're letting out all the heat." His wife was the only one who called him Bobby, and he was certain she did it because she knew it got on his nerves. With a sigh, he smiled at Jennifer before closing the door behind her. Nick's ford was parked in the B n B driveway and when he saw her approach, he leapt from the driver-side door and hurried around the car, determined to appear the gentleman.

"Your carriage awaits m'lady." Immediately, Nick was content that he'd made the correct decision. Even on the drive over, there had been a nagging doubt that this was a bad idea. Seeing her clip-clop her way along the driveway, wearing heels that looked an inch above safety and a hairstyle, fit for a catwalk in Paris, all his lingering ambiguity vanished in an instant.

"Well, thank you, kind sir." She flashed him a smile that made his heart flutter and he chuckled as her tight skirt made a dignified climb into the passenger seat impossible. Eventually, she lowered her shapely rear into the Ford first, then gradually swung her legs into the vehicle. Closing the door behind her, he returned to the driver's side by the rear of the car, hoping to hide his excitement that the evening had started so auspiciously. Inside, Jenny hoped that Nick wouldn't notice that she couldn't help blushing whenever he looked in her direction.

Determined to make a good first impression, Castle had booked a table at Dante's, an exorbitantly prised restaurant on the outskirts of Carpenter. After the young couple were shown to their seats, a waiter in a dinner-jacket and dicky-bow tie brought menus across. In his precipitation to book a table at short notice, Nick hadn't been aware that the cuisine was French. Reading the options, Castle hoped that the confused look upon his face wasn't obvious.

"Nick, I'm sorry but…I can't speak French, I'm afraid you'll need to order for the two of us." Jenny's tone was whispered and apprehensive. The young man could feel his face flush but having no idea how to get out of this embarrassing situation, he decided that honesty was probably the best policy.

"I've a confession to make. Neither can I." The two giggled like naughty schoolchildren, it seemed the perfect icebreaker. "I was so positive that I wanted everything to be perfect, I forgot to ask what type of food they served." There was more laughter, though the watchful eyes of the pretentious waiter hung a cloud over proceedings.

"Is this the sort of food you'd normally eat?" Jennifer's question was asked with raised eyebrows.

"Of course not. It's just…well, I knew you came from a wealthy family, so I thought you'd be used to the finer things in life." The girl had just taken a sip of water and, after hearing the last statement, started to splutter at the thought.

"Nick, I live in a two-bedroomed terraced house in Scotland with my adoptive mother. I stopped being a Graham, the day I left Hallowell. In truth, I don't know if I was ever a real Graham, that was my father's side of the family, I was more like mum." Jennifer paused and took another sip of water. "I don't want to sound common but, I'm more a fish and chips girl. It's just the way I was brought up." Nick let out a sigh of relief.

"Thank God for that, I couldn't really afford this French muck anyway. Do you want to make a run for it?" The girl shyly nodded, and the pair ran for the exit. Castle couldn't help having a little fun at the waiter's expense and paused by him before leaving. In his best upper-class voice, Castle exclaimed,

"I've a tip for you, old chap. Loosen that bow-tie, it's cutting off the blood-flow to your brain."

The remainder of the evening progressed like a flawless dream. The couple had called into Harvey's wine bar two streets from Dante's where Nick had felt no temptation to take an alcoholic drink, instead happy to remain on lemonade, while the two glasses of sweet cider consumed by Jenifer ensured that the shy and hesitant girl allowed her guard to lower more than she'd expected. He bought her popcorn and held her hand as they watched 'The Blue Lagoon', a love story starring American teenager, Brooke Shields, in the same cinema has grandparents had shared their own first date, over forty years previously. Secretly, Nick would have preferred the Clint Eastwood comedy, 'Any which way you can', but reasoned that the 'chick-flick' was more conductive to the occasion. Afterwards, they walked hand in hand by Carpenter cannel, eating chips from newspaper, Jenifer barefoot as she'd finally had to admit defeat in her battle with the heels.

The air was cool but clear, the continuous breeze of Hallowell seemingly not having followed to the larger town. He gazed secretly at her profile as she watched the water ripple against the bankside, the clear liquid appearing black with just the moonlight as coverage. This was so confusing; he'd returned home to exorcise old demons, not to fall in love. Surely that wasn't what was happening, he barely knew this girl. Even more perplexing was, what looking at her made him want to do. Seeing her silhouette, that slim, slender frame, he knew what most guys would be thinking. Woo-her, bed-her, leave-her. This could only be a weekend fling, she'd be gone in a few days, have some fun and move on. None of this had crossed his mind. Yes, she was very beautiful, and he was certain that making love to her would be wonderful but, he couldn't remove the hope that this could be something so much more. Not since Julia had he looked at a girl in this way. No, all he wanted to do, was hold her in his arms, and tell her everything. But how could he? Surely, she'd believe him insane. Not about his own past, people have problems that could be dealt with. But he could only be completely honest if he were to tell her everything. And everything meant the station, and the station meant the existence of her dead brother. It was crazy, this was a first date, she'd run for the hills if he started talking about what she'd no doubt perceive as non-sense. But if he didn't, how could he hope to build something more, very, very, confusing.

His biggest fear was scaring Jenifer away, so he decided to remain evasive with the truth rather than tell full-blown lies, plausible deniability. If this continued going as well as to had gone so far, there would be time. Revealing that friction between his family members had caused his exile from Hallowell wasn't far from the truth and even though he'd missed some important aspects, they could be added later. All the deception he'd endured as a child made being conservative with the details difficult, but it was better than nothing.

Stroking a finger below her chin, she returned the most adorably charming smile. The cool evening air made her cheeks flush, and a sudden chill made her bundle her arms around her torso.

"What you are thinking?" Nick's question was delivered softly with an inquisitive tone. Without losing her smile, she gently shook her head as though her mind was completely clear.

"Are you cold?" Her head gesture changed direction to a nod, and he immediately wished he'd worn the jacket, so he could appear gentlemanly. He'd have offered his shirt if he thought she have accepted. "Let's head back to the car." Taking her hand, they returned to Dante's car park, hoping the wheels hadn't been clamped.

The drive back to Hallowell was taken as slowly as possible, Nick desperate to squeeze every available second from their date. He had no inclination to try to pressurize for a sexual encounter, this was worth more than that. Not that he believed Jennifer would be willing, she didn't seem that type of girl, but he knew that if he were to turn on the old Castle charm, she'd find it hard to resist. But that would cheapen what they had, whatever it was.

There were prangs of guilt, this was the first time since Julia, he'd allowed himself to see another woman in this way. Though considerable time had passed, her death was still a raw emotion, but he knew, were he ever to move on with his life, this would be a necessary step. Their relationship originally had been a means to an end which had flowered organically and though he still felt a sense of responsibility, he knew Julia wouldn't want him pining forever. Strangely, he anticipated that this was a liaison with a far greater opportunity for success, Jenifer and he had Hallowell as a common bond, even if it was the birthplace of their life's problems.

For Jenifer, things weren't so complicated. All she saw was this beautiful stranger with a mind as deep as the ocean. A man living with a world of hurt who was mysterious and as layered as another human being could be, though seeing through those complexities was something she saw as a wonderful challenge. It was scary and stimulating, passionate and inspiring all rolled into one giant thunderbolt. It was obvious, there was more to be seen, more to know, than he'd dared reveal, but in time…

Walking her to the doorstep of the bed and breakfast, they savoured every second. Just entwining his fingers around hers, the palms of their hands fusing as one, was more sensually exciting than most of his past conquests. A translucent layer of perspiration covered his back and made the white shirt he was wearing cling to his skin. Their hearts raced as one, was he strong enough to fight his natural urges? For Jenifer, she held her breath in wild anticipation, would he try to kiss her, did he find her as irresistible as she found him? She longed for the evening to continue, to feel his warm body close to hers, to share her innermost wishes and fantasies, my God, what was happening? Her track record of dating made her appear nun-like in comparison to many other girls, but here she was, desperate, it made no sense. Tonight, was too soon, but she knew she had to see him again.

"Nick, can I ask you to do something for me?" His racing heart begun to pound, please don't ask me to stay, I'm not strong enough to say no.

"Of course, name it." God, I'm weak, I know I'm weak, don't let her say it.

"Tomorrow, I think I need to see the old house." Sweet, sweet relief. "I heard what you said about the railway station, about it being dangerous and derelict but I never liked the place anyway, so I don't care about that, it was always my horrible brother's passion, not mine. To be honest, it gave me the creeps. It's just, well, the mansion, I lived there for a lot of years and it's the only place I have memories of mum. I just think I need to see it once more before it's sold, just to say goodbye. I'd appreciate some company." Castle stroked the hair away from Jenifer's face and with a smile exclaimed,

"You try and stop me."

Castle's head tilted slightly to the left, neck arched, shoulders lowered. Jenifer's eyes gently closed, her body trembling, contemplating what was about to happen. Their throats dry, excitement palpable, the few inches travelled seemed to take an age. But finally…

Their lips touched, just barely at first, the taste of her lipstick, the smell of his aftershave, the careful brush of skin on skin. When Castle was certain his wishes were reciprocated, the pressure intensified, still apprehensive of becoming too rigorous, maintaining an air of discretion when his body screamed for more, his self-discipline surprising evens him. Suddenly, Jenifer reached up, threading her fingers through his long black hair, and pulling him in closer, his will tested to the full, holding her in a lasting embrace, their tongues probing and exploring each other's mouths, bodies locked tightly together, their passion threatening to overflow them both as the rest of world fell away. At that moment, it felt as though they were the only two people left on earth. They weren't.

Across the street in a darkened alleyway by Hallowell workingmen's club, a portly figure lurked in the shadows. The only focal point was the orange glow from the tip of his lit cigarette, an open pint-bottle of vodka in the opposite hand. Slowly, the man twisted off bottle's metal cap and drained the last shallow of the fiery liquid. Carefully placing the glass container at his feet, he sucked hard on the cigarette, the residue ash tumbling across the front of his coat. Slowly breathing out a long plume of smoke, Fred Gibson emerged from the darkness, snarling a circumspect sneer in the courting couple's direction.

"Your time's coming bitch, your time's coming."

Chapter 30

Saturday October 13th, 1980.

Deep inside the bowels of Hallowell, inside a hidden bunker between the railway station and the Graham mansion, the monster stared before a dirty mirror. Fingers sliding below the rubber disguise, tearing away from diseased skin, becoming free with the sound of broken suction, tepid air rushing inside feeling colder than the temperature suggests, this freedom was rare.

Both hands inside, peeling away the confines of the flexible helmet, the stench overpowering, the mask ill-fitting now, things had changed in fourteen years. Lifting beyond the chin, and ragged facial hair falls free. The beard is mattered and thick, the residue of forgotten food with a red streak from uncooked meat down the centre. Youthful colour vanished, the edgings now grey, the volume pushing against the shield, but not soon enough.

The transformation had taken time, the life change coming as a shock. The Graham name had always carried weight, but after Martin's death, Frank's safety net was gone, he'd never envisioned what was coming. Suddenly he was alone with a village baying for his blood, it was too soon, he wasn't ready. The colliery incident had been caused due to intense provocation and losing his father had been the ultimate price. Without self-defence he'd have certainly been slaughtered. As the invaders had searched the halls of the station, the fear had been paralysing, scurrying from one hideout to another, hoping desperately not to be seen.

But suddenly, there was that boy, alone. The teenager, Dean Cundy, had let out a pitiful cry as Frank had clasped a hand around his throat, squeezing tightly, crushing the child's larynx with one swift movement. Knowing his young rival was disabled, he'd taken his time, ensuring that the point of his blade had pierced the boy's heart with the first shot. The hot jet of sticky blood sprayed forward, forming a slippery reservoir at the killer's feet. As the life drained from Dean's body, Frank grasped the hair of the Halloween mask the youth was wearing and as the child crashed to the floor, Graham gazed incredulously at his prize.

From the moment the heavy rubber disguise slid comfortably across his face, Graham immediately felt empowered. Certain that he needed to find his inner monster to survive this intrusion, the latex camouflage fired his mind into action, slicing through victim after victim with ruthless aggression without leaving a trace. The relationship had been formed, like Bruce Wayne and his bat-suit, Clark Kent with a red cape, Frank Graham had the key to a demonic switch. Being paranoid of a return invasion, Graham began wearing the horrific prop constantly, fearful that when the hoards came, he wouldn't be ready, psychologically only feeling monster-like when in character, unaware that it was his actions that made him so fearsome. The only time his face become visible was during sleep. The mouth was altered to allow food to pass freely and eventually, even night-time gave no respite.

In time, Graham's facial skin broke down and became infected. The flesh below the eyes on both cheeks became discoloured and flaky and with the constant rubbing from the mask's rubber surface, deep sores were soon created. Infection would attack, and the skin would crack in two. Each time the affected area would begin to scab over, the mask would tear away the healing flesh and the process would begin once more. Fresh air was needed to rectify the situation but Graham's stubborn reliance on the heavy hood meant things continued to worsen. Soon, the area across the bridge of the nose followed suite, and suddenly, Graham's horrific appearance had begun to resemble his actions. Scaring had ravaged his face, puss-filled scabs growing and healing improperly. The rubber began to fuse to the affected areas and during the slightest movement, the flesh would tear open once more. The stench of decayed muscle was grotesque, as were the results. Patches of facial hair grew around the slashes, mirroring a strange roadmap with lines of boundaries.

Due to a lack of scissors, Frank would hack through his thick hair with a butcher's knife to ensure that the mask still fit. Differing lengths remained, some long and straggly while other patches were torn from the root. The long scar across the crown which had occurred during the assault from the Scholes brothers while he was just a teen was no longer hidden, adding to the overall hideous vision. Frank Graham had truly become a monster in every conceivable way.

Now, he was standing before a mirror, barely recognising the creature that stared back. Knowing he'd need to summon that inner demon once more if he was going to remove the threat of his sister, this was an issue he'd never envisioned happening. As a child, the girl was more an inconvenience but now she was a mortal enemy that had to be destroyed at all costs.

The mask gripped in both hands, the rubber squeezed across the crown and over his face. The eyes barely visible, just black lifeless holes, a double gateway to the madness that was Frank Graham. A deep breath escapes and the behemoth is gone, out into the darkness of the tunnel once more.

Fred Gibson's mind was a vortex of possibilities. This was going to be it, finally, seeing another human-being extinguished from this world. God knows what torturous symphony, Frank would compose for this victim, what weapon would be used. Would it be bare hands crushing her throat? The sharpness of his blade, slicing through skin, piercing major organs? Would he tear out the bitch's heart while it was still beating? The excitement was unbearable, unpalpable, the mere thought brought tears to his eyes.

Plus... WHAT THE FUCK...he'd spoken. For the first time in God knows how long, he'd actually opened that fucking mouth and uttered words. One simple command, "Bring her to me." BRING HER TO ME. This was amazing, astounding, perhaps the beginning of a new era. We could converse, like real people do, instead of just delivering his food, telling him the news, and praying, this time wouldn't be his turn to be slaughtered. There were no guarantees. But real conversation, what would that be like? Fred could find out him his likes, his dislikes, does he know that he'd been serving him human remains for fuck knows how long. They could team up, like an evil Batman and Robin. Gibson serves them up and Graham finishes them off, they'd be a psycho dream team. Oh, thank you God, (okay, maybe not God). It's happening, it's happening, it's finally fucking happening.

The first mistake. Gibson always used the tunnel as an entrance and exit, never the platform. The platform was too dangerous, no matter what time of day, someone could always see. But in his giddy, confused, blood-lust state, normality was forgotten. He'd staggered as a drunk man, his obese, bovine-like flesh, pushing tightly against his black sweatpants, a role of blubber fighting the waistband. To ensure he blended into the night-sky, Fred always ensured his total clothing choices were a black ensemble, a thin cotton sweater squeezed of his gargantuan chest and belly, two husky arms forced through the holes provided and a rotund head and neck the final piece in the unpleasant visage. A black XXX-large overcoat worn to block out the cold early morning air.

The second mistake. Overwhelmed with the thought of bloodletting, he'd stayed longer than usual. These visits were normally, well organised, and well timed, once a week, Tuesday night/Wednesday morning. Dependant on the time of year, visitation times could vary. Summertime and the hours of darkness were considerably shortened, therefore a visit of 3 am to 4 am was all that could be allocated. The winter months, things were less rushed, so a less exact time of arrival and departure were unnecessary. This was autumn, so they were caught in between. Fred had maintained the 3 am arrival time but his departure had become less formal. Coupled with the fact that tonight had been an unscheduled meeting under extreme circumstances and Gibson had lost track of time. It had been after six before he'd left the premises and with using the wrong exit, he was certainly more prone to detection.

Stumbling clumsily through the tunnel between the main station structure and the outer buildings, the connecting roof had hidden the morning sunlight before he'd had the chance to notice it. His thoughts still elsewhere, Gibson almost feel clean off the edge of the platform, luckily, regaining his awareness at the last split-second before stepping off into a three feet fall. Fred's face, already covered with a heavy layer of perspiration, became even more deeply flushed, as he exhaled a deep sigh of relief at avoiding, what could have been a potentially painful fall. Plus, had it been debilitating, and he needed outside assistance, the tale of why he was here in the first place may have been an awkward one. It was then that the huge mistake he'd stupidly manufactured, emerged in his mind.

"What the fuck am I doing?" His head darted from side to side. Christ, there was a row of houses, across in the distance, any one of those could have someone peering from a window. Looking at his wristwatch, the timepiece showed 6.30

am, it was early, but not so much that he was safe. Scurrying backward, he retraced his steps, still scouring the scene before him for early risers; a dog walker passing the woodland, or a night-shift worker returning home and he'd be done for. It looked deserted, God willing (again, it was doubtful, the Almighty would be willing to do Fred Gibson any favours) everyone would still be tucked up in their beds. Reaching the confines of the enclosed pathway, he bounded head-long, back towards the safety of the underground tunnel, the same pathway his murderous accomplice had used moments earlier. With a final look, he sniggered to himself, "That was a narrow escape."

Dan Challis was barely conscious, the woodland by the station giving slight respite from the cool morning air. Slumped at the foot of a withered elm, a snapped branch pointed uncomfortably into his side, the pain negated by the flow of super-strength cider, the remnants laying stalely in the bottom his last remaining can.

"What…the…fuck?" Had he really, just seen, that? Was it possible? What the hell was the fat mortician doing, stumbling out of that place. Looking at the almost-empty container in his hand, he drained the dregs and crawled clumsily to his feet. "What…the…Fuck?"

Nick Castle woke with a smile, this was going to be the first day of the rest of his life. Last night had proved that his existence could still carry meaning, that the feelings of affection and, dare he admit, love, that he'd tried so hard to bury deep inside for so long, could maybe, just maybe, be resurrected from their comatose state and shared with another. Love? Surely that was stupid to contemplate at such an early stage, he barely knew her. But that spark was undeniable and the butterflies down deep in his loins that had refused to flutter since Julia had flown like the Red Arrows throughout the entirety of their date. This was something he wanted, all he needed was guts.

Leaving Jenifer at the guest house had been tough but there was time. Plus, Castle had one more thing he needed to do, something that required privacy.

Arriving back to the family home on Melrose drive, the downstairs was in darkness. Turning the key to the front entrance quietly as to not wake any sleeping residents, he noticed a crack of light around the outside of his grandmother's bedroom door, situated directly at the top of the stairs. The old woman always had a dog-eared paperback on the nightstand beside the bed and, had she heard her grandson returning home, he knew she'd feel obliged to welcome him. Pleasant conversation wasn't on Nick's mind, and he took extra care to not draw attention to his presence. Silently latching the solid oak barrier, Castle stealthily slid into the living room and headed directly for the kitchen.

The strip light crackled as it burst to life, the room now illuminated. The house remained silent as the grave, in his eye-line, the refrigerator handle inches away. The white barrier accepted defeat and swung outwards on its hinges, the fridge now open wide.

Two cans of 'Carling black label'.

Two cans of Stones bitter.

Lying flat on the top shelf, a half full bottle of vodka.

Nick reached for his choice, the glass bottle screeched across the shelfing and was suddenly in his grasp. The glass container was freezing to the touch and had not been moved in some time, residue of spilled milk had formed between itself and the shelfing and produced a momentarily sticky resistance. Gradually, there was separation and Nick grasped his prize.

He carried the bottle as a new mother would carry a baby, laying across both arms, right hand having the tension. On the draining board, there were two glasses, one a large pint glass, stolen from Hallowell workingmen's club by his granddad years earlier, and the other, a perfect four-inch shot glass.

The smaller container was turned on its end, ready to accept the vodka. It was thick and heavy, expensive with a bevelled base and crafted lines, delicately moulded to specification, Bill Castle had an eye for the finer things, even if the family rarely purchased them. The cap on the bottle was stiff and took force open it. Nick counted as the red metal spun, round and round. Finally, it was free. Holding the glass, he poured a two-finger measure.

Raising it high, toward the window, out in the dark night.

"For Billy, and for Granddad." The clear liquid glistening in the artificial light and a grimace stretched across Nick's Face as he prayed for strength to do what needed to be done.

"Good night and God bless you!"

The vodka splashed perfectly into the waste pipe of the sink. Flowing it slowly, gently watching the stream until the glass was completely empty. Nick rubbed his index finger around the inside then wiped it on a tea-towel. It was at that moment he knew…he was winning.

For once his slumber was nightmare free. Eight solid hours of restful, comatose sleep without the bogyman's invasion. Was his mind finally focusing on the happier aspect's life contained? Awaking with dry sheets was pleasurable but the smile across his face was still surprising. Had he dreamed of her but forgotten when consciousness was resumed? If so, he'd rather be in slumber-land all day. But that wouldn't do. He was about to take his comatose images into reality, today was date number two.

Unfortunately, the location was less than welcoming. Exploring the battered remains of the Graham mansion wasn't exactly romantic. But Jenifer had ghosts to exorcise too and if he could help, he would.

Descending the stairs from bedroom to lounge, he found the house empty as usual. His grandmother, Alice Castle, had returned to working at her news agency but his father, Mick, was nowhere to be seen. Nick had passed by his dad's bedroom door; it was wide open revealing a made bed and open curtains. Strange, Mick would normally still be sleeping off the previous night's drinking. Yesterday had been the same too, very peculiar. Still, most of their conversations ended in blazing rows so perhaps it was for the best.

Whilst heading toward the kitchen, Nick noticed the silver-framed photograph of Bill, laying by the central settee and momentarily frowned, the revelations of yesterday still raw in his memory. Standing proud and honest in his smart policeman's uniform, Castle could only imagine the torment his elder had suffered, feeling an obligation to protect the village of Hallowell from that monster but being only one man. Perhaps had he taken on the creature at a younger age, he may have stood a chance but…

A small, black, and white clock with Roman numerals in place of numbers seated on top of the mantle-piece read 8:40 am, just over an hour before his meeting with Jenifer. The frown was replaced once more with a disguised childish grin. It had been so long since he'd last felt excited about anything, it was almost a lost emotion. A yawn escaped and as he stretched his arms above his head, he caught a reflection in an adjacent wall mounted mirror. The Brylcreem used the previous evening to hold his hairstyle in place had forced a giant hedgehog style during sleep and that wouldn't do. Swiftly, Nick bounded back up the stairs, and headed for the shower, haste was a necessity.

Jenifer Graham had no such time concerns. Barely sleeping after their date, she'd tried to idle away the small hours by reading a ratty, paperback novel but even then, her focus was elsewhere. Was this really happening? Did this enigmatic stranger feel as intoxicated by her as she did him? If it was so wrong, why did it feel so right? Her experiences of the opposite sex were limited to a few tedious sticky fumbling's in the back seats of cars, weekend Romeos who'd say anything for a quick leg-over. Nick was different, she was certain. Certain because if he'd attempted to seduce her, the previous night, she'd never have been able to resist. Those eyes of the deepest blue, features of a Hollywood demi-god, physique of an Olympian, what woman could resist? But instead, he'd been a perfect gentleman, not willing to take advantage of her obvious weakness. Did he want something more than just a one-night stand? God, she hoped so. But how could this be anything more than a fleeting romance. Her life was in Glasgow, and he'd just returned home. Long distance relationships never worked, one of them would be forced to make a huge sacrifice. This was crazy, they'd been on one date, it was so confusing, no wonder she couldn't sleep.

By 6am, she was seated alone inside the Lunchbox Café, nursing a weak cup of tea. Twirling a teaspoon inside the white mug, she pressed a floating teabag against the pot, trying to illicit some flavour. The container scraped against its saucer and the obnoxious waitress who had served the couple, the previous day stared across the room from a wooden counter with a 'Can't you just fuck off back where you came from', look, on her face. A voice from the kitchen broke the silence.

"Ingrid, come in here NOW, there's sandwich orders to bag up, the factory lads will be in soon." The server sighed and flashed Jenifer the same fake smile as the previous day, something she was obviously well practiced at.

Suddenly, she was alone. Hallowell was gently waking, and an occasional car would pass by as she stared sluggishly from her window seat. Two men stood in the distance by the roadside dressed in coveralls, both smoking cigarettes and awaiting their lift to work. Another man with dark sunken eyes, leathery skin, and a bald head, strolled carelessly on the other side of the village green, his pace matched by the large German shepherd that was tethered by a thick silver-linked chain to the man's wrist. Occasionally, the dog would pull at the leash and the man would yank the animal to heal. Jenifer smiled, 'small town life'. Sipping on the tea, its tastelessness made her cringe. Replacing the cup to its saucer, Jenifer headed towards the exit.

At 9:45, Nick Castle's borrowed Ford pulled into the Bed and Breakfast car park. The shower had refreshed his skin but the feeling of waking without residual alcohol in his system was a pleasant victory. The occasional tremor of withdrawal still made him shudder, but things were improving quickly. The Autumnal sun was coming into view above the terraced buildings to the left and Nick pulled down the car's visor to avoid squinting. It was then that he noticed Jenifer, seated on the small brick wall around the guest house, waiting patiently for her beau. Hair tied back in a high ponytail; the white whispery blouse she wore seemed little protection against the sharp Hallowell winds. Castle pulled the car to a sharp halt and quickly shut off the engine. Leaping from the Ford, there seemed little point in closing the driver's side door until Jenifer was safely inside.

"I thought we said ten. Hope you haven't been waiting long."

"All my life." Her impish thought remained unsaid though the cheeky grin across her face told a thousand tales. "No, just a few minutes. My room just seemed so claustrophobic this morning, I thought I'd get some air."

"Yeh, some cold air, you're going to freeze without a coat. It's been known to snow in autumn here you know, don't let October fool you." Jenifer appreciated the concerned boyfriend tone, even if it was just their second date.

"Oh, don't worry, I come from tough stock." She immediately regretted the insinuation to her lineage and tried to backtrack fast. "And anyway, if it gets too cold, I'll just steal yours." Nick arrived at the passenger door and gentlemanly opened it. Before allowing her entry, Castle stretched down to kiss her cheek. Before making contact, the girl tilted her head and their lips met soothingly. It wasn't overtly passionate, just a loving touch that lingered longer than it might. As their lips separated, Nick smiled as it took Jenifer's eyes longer than usual to re-open.

"That will give the gossips something to talk about." A shrill honk from a delivery van waiting for entry broke the moment. Nick's head darted in the direction of a battered white van with Gregory's butchers scrawled across the side with black gloss paint. A kid who looked no older than sixteen with greasy hair and skin that would have been a dermatologist's wet dream was making impatient faces through the windshield. Nick returned an angry glare and the driver seemed to sink back into his chair. The passenger window of the van was open, and Castle took the few steps across to confront the irritable youngster.

"Problem?" Nick was no troublemaker, he just had no tolerance for rude people.

"Nor mate, is just I's got to get van back sharpish, me dar is off to cattle mart this savvy n if I's late, he'll tan me arse. Got an order f'd guest hoose." The young man's earlier bravado now a distant memory and Castle could see the butcher posed no threat.

"Okay, no bother. Just pull back and we'll be out of your way." Nick began toward his driver's side door when the spotty teen called out.

"You's Mrs Castle's young an ant y. And that's that Graham girl. I heard me dar saying. Is that youa lass then?" The delivery driver had this docile grin plastered across his face as though he knew something he wasn't entitled to. The smile faded when Castle's expression returned to an angry glare. Nick walked back to the open window.

"I thought you were running late?" With a final snarl, Nick rebounded to the Ford and started the engine. As the couple left the guest house car park and the butcher was certain his words wouldn't be heard, he exclaimed in a brave and bold voice,

"Bloody outsiders. Next time a sees y, al kick y heed in."

Inside the basement of the Graham mansion, the steel trim across the base of the hidden tunnel doorway screeched slowly across the concrete floor. A muffling sound of exertion buried behind thick latex followed and suddenly, Frank Graham was inside his ancestral home. Dust mites filled the disturbed air as the monster slid the barrier back into place. Across to the right-hand side far corner lay a discarded mattress which Graham had used on occasion in the winter when the temperatures were at their harshest. That was back when he was learning to tolerate life without creature comforts. Now, he'd become hardened to whatever nature had in store. Most of the work-tools that had been stored here had either been taken to the station or thieved by rogue villagers. Even now, the smell of charred material was pungent though Graham barely noticed it. Clearing a path, he manoeuvred across to the basement door and with an almighty tug, heaved the heavy wooden portal open. Twelve stone steps lay between the monster and the ground floor.

Usually, small talk was a monotonous chore for Nick Castle, but Jenifer seemed to make everything relevant. No topic was uninteresting, no conversation tiresome. Whenever they were together, Nick struggled to hide his enthusiastic beam which may have been embarrassing had he not noticed that she was having that self-same problem. It made no difference that they were heading to explore derelict ruins, it may have been a day, playing at the beach, so long as they were together, it didn't matter.

The journey by car took less than two minutes. They decided it best to park the car in the quiet, Colliery Lane, as to not draw attention to their presence. Nick felt a strange obligation to check the coast clear before exiting the car as he had no wish to add further fuel to the gossips fire. The side-road between the colliery cottages and Graham Road had just a high stone wall that bordered the Graham property with opposing, unutilised wasteland, developers being put off by the imposing, fire ravaged neighbour. Had they parked two hundred yards further down the road, every curtain of every window would be twitching with delight.

This was going to be one of those days. Johnny Brackett had been up since six, having a prisoner banged up meant long hours. He had no idea where this would lead, truthfully, he was almost certain that Daley wasn't responsible for the child's disappearance but like his father said, someone needed to be held accountable and old Tom was the obvious choice. It didn't make him feel any better though, keeping an innocent man locked up. Oh, in time, the poor chump would be released without charge but for now, Daley was his responsibility and that meant 24 hrs a day. From the flat above, Johnny had heard the big dummy crying all night, using a baby intercom was better than sleeping on that bloody uncomfortable camp bed in the next cell. By the time he'd fed him the obligatory cornflakes and coffee for breakfast, the prisoner's eyes were puffy and red. Sympathy was a dangerous emotion for a copper.

After the meal, Johnny had done the rounds. Nick Castle returning to Hallowell gave the officer a consistent bad feeling. Tonight, was the town meeting and he was ill prepared. There would be a lot of frightened faces in that crowd and his former friend was a distraction, Brackett could do without. Thankfully, the good doctor would take the brunt of the questioning, but Johnny could hardly allow his father to be hung out to dry. There needed to be a plan in place for the future of Hallowell, lives depended upon it, but angry residents eager to be heard would help little. These were the kinds of headaches he could do without.

Brackett slipped off his reading glasses and rubbed the bridge of his nose. He had a migraine coming on, stress always did it. Plus, this bastard paperwork didn't help. Johnny didn't have the budget for a secretary and had no education with computers, so everything had to be done by hand, in duplicate. Plus, listening to that maggot in the next room whine all morning had him at breaking point.

"Mr Brackett. Please Mr Brackett, I need you. Mr Brackett, can you hear me?"

"For fuck's sake, it's impossible not to hear you." Johnny pushed his chair back across the tiled floor and rose from his desk. His neck was stiff and the meagre breakfast he'd forced down was laying heavy on his stomach.

"Mr Brackett, Please Mr…"

"Can you just wait one minute, I've more to do than play nurse-maid to you." Brackett threw the eyeglasses down onto the desk, but the force was too great, sliding over the edge and crashing to the floor. The police officer snarled.

"I swear, if they're broken, you're next."

"Mr Brackett, please, I…" The words were cut off mid-sentence as the officer stormed into the holding area with an angry glare for company.

"Right, I'm here, what the fuck do you want?" The prisoner suddenly fell silent, afraid that his next words could make his captor angrier. "Nothing? Fine. Shut the fuck up then, I've work to do." Brackett turned to walk away when desperation made Daley respond.

"I've a headache. After my accident, I've had tablets from the doctor to make my headaches go away but since I've been here, I didn't dare ask for them. When I don't take them, it makes me poorly. I feel sick and my legs get restless, I can't lie still. Can I have my tablets, please?"

Johnny hadn't considered that the guy needed medication.

"Your dad gives me a per Crip, no, pre-scrip-tion. I've taken them for years. They take my bad heads away. Oh, please sir, won't you ask the doctor for my pills?" Brackett had fought the urge to sympathise with old Tom, but this was going too far. He was probably going through withdrawal on top of being locked away for a jumped-up crime, this was paramount to torture.

"I need to go out but if I get you your pills, will you please be quiet?" The policeman's tone had softened though he knew he could only allow so much.

"I promise. I'll be a good boy. I just want my pills, is all."

Johnny returned to the front office and lifted the receiver of his telephone before dialling the number of his father. It was Saturday and Brackett knew his dad didn't have a surgery at the weekend. The only time he saw patients then were emergencies. Surprisingly, there was no answer on his home number and the line to his office had been faulty for weeks. After replacing the receiver, he explained the situation to his prisoner.

"Tom, listen. There's no answer at my dad's house," Daley released at childish whine, "So I'm going to drive round and see if I can find him. If he comes back here while I'm away, tell him you need your pills and I've gone to find him. Is that clear?"

"But I have pills at home. I keep them in my little white cupboard, above the sink, in my bathroom. You could get them from there, if you like?" Brackett shook his head as he was beginning to feel more like an errand boy than an officer of the law. Fetch his breakfast, fetch his pills, this was getting ridiculous.

"In the bathroom, above the sink, right?" Daley nodded. "What are they called?" Tom pulled a puzzled expression.

"Tablets." Brackett was quickly losing his patience.

"I know they're tablets, you are fucking clown. What type of pills are they?"

"I think they called Tramadol. They green and yellow and easy to swallow." That sympathetic feeling was growing once more in the officer's mind. Two years earlier, Brackett needed an operation to repair a torn tri-cep and he'd taken that same medication for a month to ease the pain. The woozy feeling was a little too pleasant and stopping, even after such a short period had been tough. If Tom had been taking them for years and suddenly the supply was cut off, chances where he was going through Hell.

"Okay, I have your house keys in my desk draw. I'll go now but if my dad comes, tell him I need to speak to him, okay. Tell him to wait for me, is that clear?" Daley nodded dutifully, the way a child in a classroom might. With a resigned shake of the head, Johnny Brackett headed for the door.

The earlier morning sun had vanished as quickly as it had risen, weather had a habit of changing dramatically in Hallowell. Grey clouds coming in from the west threatened to spoil a potentially pleasant day and with the huge oaks towering ominously above the stone retainer, the lane took on a decidedly prophetic, sinister presence. Nick hurried around the car and opened the young lady's door. A shudder slithered across them both. Jenifer cuddled her arms around her torso, attempting to fight the sudden chill.

"Did you feel that too?" Castle's question barely required a response.

"Yes, who stole the sun?" The girl was almost trembling. "Think you were right; I should have brought a coat." Nick immediately began to remove his black leather jacket and though Jenifer playfully protested, she was glad of his gentlemanly streak.

"Nonsense take it. I'll just get pneumonia, it's no problem." Again, she protested, but not too much. Standing before her, he said, "Don't worry, if I get cold, I'll just share it with you." Her smile insinuated that he'd be more than welcome. Taking the girl by the hand, they begun a brisk pace to the properties wrought-iron gates by the front driveway. A steady smattering of leaves rained down from above and those already shed crunched underfoot. The whispery branches from the trees created malevolent shadows on the footpath before them and ghostly howls as the breeze whistled through made Jenifer even more apprehensive. Had it not been for Nick's companionship, she questioned whether she'd have the courage to explore alone. Even with his assistance, she had begun to wonder if this was a good idea at all.

Turning off Colliery Lane onto Graham Road, the driveway started a few hundred yards up on the right. For the first time in each other's presence, their conversation had become laboured, mostly because both were lost in their own thoughts.

For Jenifer, this was the first time she'd returned to her ancestral home since the death of her mother. Whatever psychological issues she felt were born from this place and the sooner she could sever all ties with it, the better it would be. Her mother lived on now, only in photographs and memories and even those were all too fleetingly rare. Today was simply about saying goodbye to the past, nothing more. Still, the shadows were long and the ghosts many, she thanked the lord that Nick had come into her life when he had.

As for Castle, he couldn't help but feel he was intruding on enemy territory. Whatever lurked in the mansions dark hallways had all the advantages. This was for Jenifer's sake, not his.

Johnny Brackett was glad to be out of the office, even if it was only briefly. He needed to check Tom's cottage today, for fear of vandalism reprisals. In years gone by, the Graham situation was limited to a select few but now it seemed most of the village knew every detail. Still, it was easier to blame old Tom for this awful incident than accept the harsh reality. A reality that was barely comprehendible, in their midst was a killer who would destroy anyone and anything that was stupid enough to enter his domain. Folks had become almost ambivert to its presence, that was until something like this happened. Johnny could only imagine what the town meeting had in store. There'd be calls for his resignation, as usual, by the same people who would crap themselves at the mere mention of another invasion. All talk and no balls. They'd rather put a brick through Tom's window than accept the truth. Johnny had considered leaving, walking away from all the bullshit, and starting over somewhere else. But when it came down to it, he still had that yearning to be a hero. To be the man who slayed the beast and freed Hallowell from the curse of Frank fucking Graham. To play a secondary role to anyone no longer, and that included Nick Castle.

Brackett's Ford Granada's engine growled as he turned onto Colliery Lane. These houses used to be nice, a reward, for the miners and their families. The maintenance subsidised by the Grahams. Now, most of them were shitholes, the roughest part of the village, except for the obvious. Johnny still enjoyed the power he felt pressing the accelerator to the floor and letting her go, who was going to complain, it was a benefit of the job. The motor was just reaching full power when he noticed a car parked out of place. Pumping the brakes hard, Brackett slid the Granada across both lanes and parked directly behind Nick Castle's vehicle.

"What the fuck is he up too now?"

Glass crunched under the monster's heavy work-boot. Windowpanes shattered under the fire's intense heat and littered the kitchen's hardwood floor. Charred debris impregnated the air and walls blackened by soot, the remnants of a kitchen table laying crumpled in a heap in the centre, camouflaged by colour and material. Graham's unwillingness to manoeuvre around the fallen obstacle forced a swift kick-out and the brittle timber is sent flying across the room, the noise reverberating throughout the entire property.

"Did you hear that?" By now the young couple were more than halfway along the driveway, the house looming large before them. Nick smiled in response.

"Don't let yourself get spooked. This place has been collapsing for years, little by little. Don't worry, I'll protect you." Throwing an arm around her shoulders, she cuddled in close, appreciating more than ever the company that Nick provided. Continuing on, the front-door in clear sight.

A door, which formed a barrier between the kitchen and hallway hung by one rusted hinge and would normally cause a hindrance, difficult to traverse. Instead, Graham lashed out, striking hard into the splintering timber, crashing the blockage to the ground with a thundering boom. As the monster forced a path through to the hallway, an eruption of ash choked the air.

"Now you had to have heard that?" Jenifer was becoming more agitated, determined that it wasn't her imagination playing tricks. The couple paused, the front entrance now just 50 yards away.

"As a matter of fact, I did." Even Castle was beginning to grow concerned. "I want you to wait here, just for a moment, just while I check this out."

"Nick, no. I want to stay with you." The young woman's protests were irrelevant.

"Just for a moment or two. I won't go inside, I just want to look through those windows at the front, just to see if there's anyone there."

"So, if you're not going inside, there's no reason I can't come with you." Jenifer seemed adamant, but Castle was quickly as intransigent.

"Jen, for me please, just wait here, two minutes, that's all I ask?" She could see he was resolute in his determination and couldn't help but feel complimented and his unrelenting stance to keep her safe.

"Okay, two minutes, that's it. And no going inside without me. Promise?" Castle nodded.

Dr Harry Brackett was in a bad mood. He'd barely gotten to sleep when, at 2.37 am precisely, the telephone beside his bed had startled him from his slumber. Sarah Thompson's baby wasn't due for another three weeks but since she already had five, she knew the early signs of labour. Her husband Peter had waited until they were certain the baby was coming before calling the town doctor. They only needed Brackett in case of complications. Peter had delivered two of their three boys but the last one, Elsa, their only girl, had been breach and required urgent medical attention. The baby had almost been choked by the umbilical cord so now, they weren't taking any chances. Sarah's age was a concern too, at 43, she was a little old to be having babies. This one certainly hadn't been planned. The contraceptive pill is only 96% safe, they'd beaten the odds.

Brackett arrived just in time to see the miracle of birth once more. When he was a younger man, he'd always taken pride at being involved at the beginning of so many young lives. Now, it was a chore. Thankfully, he hadn't been needed, mother and baby were doing fine, and the doting dad got to cut another cord. Oh, what fun.

It was almost 4:30 by the time he'd returned to his bed and even then, it seemed pointless. He had an early morning round booked at Carpenter golf club, and since his friend, Dr Harvey Samuels had given him a 'sound thrashing' the previous week, revenge was high on his list of priorities.

After another five-shot defeat, the doctor's mood was foul. Oh, he blamed the Thompson's baby, the lack of sleep, the early morning mist, anything to excuse another morale crushing loss to his rival. That was five defeats in six games and oh how Samuels was crowing. Bragging about playing a round at St Andrews and Meeting Nick Faldo. How he'd paid almost £1000 for his new clubs and his intention to retire early and play all the courses across America. What a load of caca. The final straw had come when Brackett had hurled his clubs into the boot of his Range Rover and the head snapped off his new putter.

"Bloody golf, stupid game."

The door to the police-station was locked. Harry Brackett was one of only two people to own a key to the property, a reward for having the officer as a son.

"Johnny? You are hiding back there?" The voice that returned fire made the doctor cringe.

"Mr Brackett, sorry, I mean, Dr Brackett, is that you?" The aggravated physician almost turned on his heels and left but realised that Daley was the best lead to finding his son.

"Yes, Tom. Where's John, I mean, Constable Brackett?"

"Oh Doctor, thank goodness you're here. Officer Brackett went to fetch my pills but that was ages and ages and ages ago and he hasn't come back. Can you get them for me, my head hurts really bad?" Brackett frowned, bemused as to why Hallowell's only policeman was running around playing nurse-maid to this big dummy. Passing through to the holding area, the sight was pitiful, a 58-year-old man, whining like an infant. His knuckles were gripped tightly around the bars of the cell, and the four-day grey stubble across his face made him appear dishevelled and untidy. The green sweater Tom was wearing had food stains across the front and his cream slacks were in desperate need of a belt, hanging baggily around his behind. From the redness around his eyes, it was obvious that tears had been flowing freely and the deep dark circles that entrenched his upper cheeks insinuated that sleep had been tough to come by.

"You mean to say; you haven't had you're pills today?" Daley shook his head profusely.

"I haven't had none since I been here." Brackett was amazed that the sad chump had lasted this long, Tramadol was a strong and highly addictive opiate and withdrawal symptoms could be not only severe, but dangerous. It was then a plan began to form in the physician's mind.

"Why the Hell didn't you ask Constable Brackett for your pills? Even if he hadn't had them, I would have made sure they were available."

"I was frightened to. The officer kept telling me to shut up when I tried to talk so I thought I'd make him angry if I asked." The doctor tried to show a sympathetic expression though benignancy wasn't his natural emotion. Brackett dragged over a small wooden stool from the neighbouring cell and sat face to face with the detainee.

"Listen Tom, we could help each other out here. You'd like to be a good boy and help, wouldn't you?" Daley's energetic nod returned once more. "Good. Now, you know, Johnny and I just want to help you, to keep you safe, you know that don't you?" The nod was slightly less prominent but still as obvious. "You remember last year, when those kids were throwing stones and broke your kitchen window, Johnny made their parents pay for the damage." Constable Brackett was now replaced by his Christian name so to appear warmer and less threatening. "And a couple of months back, when you lost your pills on the way home from the chemist, I gave you a replacement prescription even though I wasn't allowed too. Do you remember all that?" Tom was looking towards the cell floor, worried as to where this conversation was headed. Still, he acknowledged with an affirmative smile. "You see Tom, Johnny and I have only ever tried to do what's best for you. So, I'm thinking, maybe, you'd like to do something nice back?" This time, the prisoner refused to respond. Brackett rose from the stool and headed back to the front office, flicking the switch of a small white electric kettle. "How does a nice cup of tea sound?"

"What about my pills?" His reticent tone was barely audible.

"All in good time." Daley listened as the rustling of utensils and the boiling of water filled the air. The doctor returned with two steaming mugs and a half-full bottle of milk which seemed close to turning sour. Passing one mug through the bars, Brackett settled once more onto the stool, trying to show as little intimidation as possible. Sipping on the tea, the doctor smiled.

"That's better." Even with his slow wittedness, Tom was cautious as to his captor's motives.

"I really need my pills doctor, I feel poorly."

"I told you, all in good time." Momentarily, the scheming physician's tone returned to its sinister worst. Quickly, he corrected himself. "Let's see if you're going to help me out, then I can get your medication." The undertone sounded like blackmail but what option did the prisoner have.

"Right Tom. I want you to listen carefully here because it's important you understand. Do you know why you've been locked up?" Daley considered his response carefully and was about to answer when Brackett fired off his own retort. "It was because of the Roberts boy. Now here's the good news, I don't think you hurt Tommy and Johnny doesn't think you hurt Tommy" For once, Tom found a reason to smile, unfortunately, it wouldn't last. "The big problem is everybody else thinks you did." A low whimper emanated from inside the cell. "The people of this village are small minded and would rather blame you for their worries than seek the truth and that's why you're locked up here. Not because Johnny or I think you hurt Tommy but to stop other people hurting you."

"But I didn't do anything. Doctor Brackett, you must believe me, it was the bad man from the railway station, he got Tommy, maybe he still has him. Maybe…" Brackett raised a hand in protest and Daley immediately fell silent.

"I don't think we should be talking about that."

"But…"

"But nothing Tom. Look at it from Johnny's side. You had the boy's blood on your clothes, you were heard calling his name and you had history with him and his family. It doesn't matter what Johnny believes; the people of this village have already decided that you're guilty. Nothing will change their minds." The doctor paused, the frightened look on the prisoner's face made him feel truly guilty for the first time. "So, listen Tom, this is what I'm thinking. Do you know what a confession is?"

"I think so but…"

"Well, the thing is, Tom, a confession is like a story. You must have made up stories before. What I'm thinking is, we write us a little story. All we need to say is, what happened with Tommy was an accident."

"But it's not…"

"Let me finish. We don't say you hurt Tommy. That would be telling lies. What we say is, maybe he fell and hurt himself. That's what you told Johnny in the first place, he was climbing on your fence, and he fell and cut himself. Now that wouldn't be lying at all. But when I say we write a little story, all I mean is we add a few little bits, just for pretend. What if, when he fell, he hit his head and couldn't get up, not that you hurt him, it was just an accident. And when he wasn't moving, you panicked. You thought you'd get the blame, and no one would believe you so instead of calling the police or telling his mom and dad, you moved his body into the railway station grounds until he woke up. You weren't to know that he was badly hurt, it wasn't your fault."

"But Doctor…"

"Tom, this is your only chance. If you don't do this, people will call you a murderer. They won't believe it was someone else. You might go to jail for a long, long time. And do you know what they do to people in prison who've killed kiddies? It's not nice Tom." The captive was openly weeping now. His whole body trembled violently, and the colour had drained from his complexion. "Tom,

400

we can stop that from happening. No-one would send you to jail for an accident. All we need to do is write down a confession, just a little story, and hopefully, you'll be able to go home soon. Plus, when we finished…I'll give you your pills."

Nick tried desperately to tread lightly on the gravel underfoot, fixed on hearing any sound that emanated from the mansion. It was obvious from the blackened state of the windows that his vision would be greatly impaired but perhaps movement inside would give away a perpetrator's position. On the steps before the front-door, shattered glass from a broken security light crunched below his feet. Another pause and then he arrived at the threshold, a twisted iron handle would reveal whether the entrance was locked or open. Remembering his promise to not go inside without Jenifer, he moved slightly to the left, to a grime covered porch window and cupped his hands around his eyes to help see more clearly.

"Nick?" The girl's cry startled him, and his reflexes made him dart away from the glass. "Can you see anything?" Castle sighed and tried to slow his breathing.

"Not yet. Just give me a minute." Rubbing the pane with the cuff of his sweater's sleeve, he tried desperately to identify any interior details, but the grime was located inside. Blocking out all exterior daylight, his eyes slowly became accustomed to the gloomy surroundings. Several closed doorways leading to concealed rooms hardly helped the obscured murkiness, but a shaft of light did slightly illuminate the vestibule, emanating from a distance in what appeared to be the open doorway to the kitchen. Nick's eyes were automatically attracted to the crepuscule-like breakage, but the clearing was still slightly obscured. Nick blinked rapidly, desperate to give his sight the best possible advantage, unsure whether what he was witnessing was real. It was possible that the dimness was causing optical illusions but at the base of the staircase, there appeared to be a familiar shape, the darkened silhouette of a human being.

Jenifer's concentration was fixed completely on Castle's actions. She wanted desperately to join him, but an unnatural unease forced her to stay away. The breeze was gaining in strength and the chill was becoming more acute. Unconsciously dancing from one foot to the next, the sound of crunching gravel below her shoes drowned out all other noise. So much so, that the figure emerging to her rear had reached out a hand and grasped her shoulder before she even acknowledged his presence.

It took less than ten minutes. Ten minutes to write a draught of pure fiction, blaming Tom Daley for the Death of Tommy Roberts. This bullshit had more holes than a fisherman's net. The version gave no explanation as to why, if the death was an accident, did the poor idiot not come forward with the truth. Why if, were he not certain whether the boy was alive or dead, did he hide the body in the one location that extinguishing of life was a forgone conclusion. And most baffling, had he been responsible for hiding the child's corpse, where was the body now? It was such rubbish that, firstly, it was difficult to believe that a man of Harry Brackett's intelligence could ever imagine that the residents of

Hallowell could buy this crock, and secondly, even someone like Tom Daley, with the recognised intelligence of a primary school child, could see that acknowledging this worthless document was a huge mistake.

The doctor came as a friend, no, a saviour, but it was obvious that this confession was seriously detrimental to Daley's future. Even if the physician was right and no charges brought (which was highly unlikely, at best, Tom was agreeing that he'd hidden the corpse of dead child) his life in the village would be over. His existence in Hallowell had barely been tolerable before this tragedy, what with the false accusations of paedophilia, now, after admitting to being solely responsible for the demise of a child barely out of nursery, he'd be lynched as soon as his feet hit freedom. And if charges were brought, even lesser charges due to diminished responsibility, one thing Brackett had said was true, kiddie murderers don't last long behind bars.

Brackett had written every word without consultation and was virtually blackmailing his prisoner by withholding essential medication until he got his way. The poor chump had sobbed constantly, begging for the pills he so desperately needed. His mind was in such a state of flux, he barely knew what was happening. The skin on his forearms was scratched raw as his flesh felt alive with bugs. Blood ran hot through his taxed veins, creating an intensely unpleasant restlessness in his arms and legs, the temples on the edges of his brow pulsed and a thick coat of perspiration covered his entire body. He subconsciously yawned over and over, and his eyes watered uncontrollably. It was like the worst flu imaginable and all the time, his doctor, the one person who was able to eradicate the symptoms, kept the tablets locked down until Tom had effectively signed his life away.

The biggest mistake Brackett had made was allowing Daley out of his cell before the document was signed. Written in shorthand on a yellow legal pad, he smugly read aloud, every word he'd created, keenly aware that Tom had little option but to agree. He even held the bottle of pain killers in plain sight, the medication had been inside of the policeman's desk drawer since the incarceration began and Brackett junior had forgotten their existence, Now holding them welcomingly as to ensure his captive wouldn't have second thoughts as to what he'd acquiesced too. The medication had been hidden away for 4 days, with only the doctor aware of the prisoner's requirements. Had the officer known of the treatment, or had he even been told of their existence, the drugs would have been administered as and when required. Johnny Brackett may not have been perfect but torturing his prisoners was not on his list of sins. As for the physician, he had plausible deniability, ensuring that the medication was present, even if directives for the execution of said medication had not been forthcoming.

Such was Brackett's egotistic distain for his captive that he never considered the man a threat. Positioning himself with his back to Tom whilst writing the confession, he wasn't aware of the changing expressions on Daley's face. Had he slipped the patient his essential medication before starting his work of fiction, Tom may have been more controllable and less volatile. Perhaps, had Brackett not continued the torture, Daley wouldn't have been pushed to his breaking point. And maybe, had the doctor continued in the guise of protector rather than persecutor, the plot may have ended just as the physician had envisioned. Perhaps…

It only took one, well aimed blow. In his entire fifty-eight years on the planet, Tom Daley had never struck out in anger towards anyone. Oh, he'd been a target, too many times. But to actually deliver a blow to another human being, it just wasn't in his nature. The main reason for this was he was a self-confessed coward, violence terrified him. Strangely, that was the main reason that finally made him snap, fear. Fear of incarceration, of being mobbed together with the dregs of society, all of whom believed that he was responsible for child murder. Even with his limited intelligence, he knew that neither Brackett nor his son would allow him to walk free and even if he did, the residents of Hallowell would be baying for his blood. He had only one chance, prove his innocence.

The dramatic withdrawal to Tramadol was also a contributing factor. Though a strong opiate, they contained an anti-depressant element which controlled mood swings and without the fix could dramatically alter a person's personality. The incredible craving for the drug could drive the most mild-mannered person to extreme measures, especially towards someone who is threatening one's very freedom.

Silent tears cascaded down Tom Daley's cheeks as the first of his right hand clenched tightly into a ball. With nerves shot and self-doubt crushing whatever courage he could muster, it had to be done quickly. Scouring the room, there were no weapons to use, all he had was his bare hands. Pulling back his right arm, Tom hurled a punch with as much force as he could mobilise. Flowing from the shoulders and chest, the motion propelled so that he almost lost his footing before impact. The blow buffeted perfectly at the base of the doctor's skull, sending Brackett crashing forward, his head smashing vigorously into the wooden desk before him, and rendering him instantly unconscious. For an entire minute, Daley stood frozen at the scene, amazed at what he'd achieved and even more shocked that it had worked. Suddenly, the realisation of the situation washed over him, and his legs rebelliously, almost lost their ability to maintain an upright position. He'd committed assault, and not only that, but it was also against the parent of a police-officer. An escaping wail from deep down in the pit of his stomach seemed to gain volume, second by second. His head felt faint, and he needed the desk's sturdy rigidity to prevent him crashing to the ground.

"This is bad, this is very, very, bad." A screech of tyres from a passing motorcar on the outside street startled Tom back into life. If this wasn't going to be for nothing, he had to act now. The bottle of pills was still clenched in Brackett's sweaty palm and Daley found himself needing to pry the doctor's fingers open. Medication retrieved; he slid the container into the pocket of his wrinkled slacks. The sight of blood, seeping into the oak desk from Brackett's nose, which had shattered on impact with the cumbersome furniture, shocked the frightened man. "Please don't be dead." The doctor's chest still appeared to be heaving as oxygen escaped from his open mouth rather than the impaired nose, so Tom took that as a positive sign. Below the comatose physician's head was the fraudulent confession and the fleeing prisoner struggled to free it. Blood had quickly permeated the notepad, making it stick to the doctor's skin. Dampness made the paper tear and Tom was afraid that Brackett would regain consciousness before his task was completed. A bubble formed at the quack's left nostril and Daley turned away in disgust. Finally, the pad broke free from its captor's face and Tom breathed a sigh of relief. Loosening the grip, he'd used on the back of Brackett's hair, the head fell back to the saturated wood with a sickening thud.

"Sorry, Doctor Brackett."

Peering gingerly around the outside empty street, Tom pulled the door open wide and made a dash for freedom. He'd need to use the backroads, outside in the daylight was more dangerous than remaining in the cells. For once, Tom Daley had a focus, there was only one way he could prove his innocence, find Tommy Roberts, alive.

"NICK." The tone in Jenifer Graham's voice was a mix of anger, shock, and full-blown terror. Her eyes had been totally transfixed on Castle as he squinted into the darkened halls of the derelict mansion, the stranger who appeared at her rear had materialized without any warning. Her response was completely out of reflex.

Crack. Johnny Brackett's reaction unfortunately wasn't as spontaneous. The swat was more surprising than painful, the open-handed slap delivered had shunted his macho pride and he made a grab for Jenifer, clenching tightly into her shoulders. His body had spun to face away from Castle and as per-normal, Brackett was wearing regular clothing rather his policeman's uniform. When Nick heard the girl's startled scream, he reacted the only way he knew. The sprint from the mansion's locked doorway to the scene took less than five seconds and he didn't care who was accosting his girlfriend, just that someone was accosting his girlfriend and protecting her was that natural reaction. Planting a hand upon the officer's shoulder, he spun his shocked rival around and landed a right cross to his exposed jaw. Johnny was prostrate on the ground at Castle's feet before the realisation of who he'd punched began to reveal itself.

Had he known it was Johnny, would it have made a difference? Probably not, at this moment, he knew where his priorities laid, and they certainly weren't a former friend with an inferiority complex. Unfortunately, this was exactly what Brackett had hoped for.

Jenifer leapt into Nick's arms and huddled her head into his chest. He kissed her hair and when she tried to speak, he gave her a gentle shush. He knew what she'd ask, "Who was this crazy person who'd creeped up on her when she least expected it?" Castle sighed, without words, he knew what trouble he was in.

Brackett could feel the grass between his fingers, the dew dampening his blue-jeans, his left hand lifted to the bruised jaw. That was the second shot Castle had landed on the policeman in two days, the first could be forgiven, but this one... The five o'clock shadow felt rough beside his palm but, the injury was superficial, no teeth dislodged, no witnesses to be embarrassed before. The shot was worth it.

"Big mistake Nicky, very big mistake." The officer slowly rose from the ground but immediately felt a little dizzy when upright. "By the way, you hit like a bitch."

"Well, we can go at it right now if you like?" Castle began to believe that offence would be the best defence.

"Oh, I don't think you want to do that, surely one charge of assaulting an officer of the law is enough for one day." That smug expression that Castles had always despised was emblazoned across the cop's face. When Jenifer heard that, her eyes sprang open, aware that she was guilty of the same offence. Brackett emerged, nose to nose with his rival, a self-important glow around his aura. "So, Nicky, I'm afraid I must place you under arrest, if I didn't it might seem like preferential treatment. Now, Miss Graham, I'll accept that you weren't aware that I represent the badge and therefore, provided you leave now and be a good girl in the future, I'll let you off with a warning."

"Nick?" The girl turned to her beau, looking for direction.

"You don't question him; you listen to me. Now, this isn't optional, leave now or share the next cell, you decide." His tone was rising to the point of full-blown war-cry and the girl immediately began to feel intimidated. Nick stepped between the two.

"It's fine, just calm down. Jenifer, please, go back to the guest-house and I'll be in touch." Brackett smiled.

"Oh, that may take a little time, but it never hurts to hope." Inside his denim's back pocket, a pair of silver handcuffs with a small key lay waiting, ready to be a prop in this silly game.

"Are those really necessary?" Jenifer couldn't believe what she was seeing.

"Oh, I think so, Miss Graham. I really do. We have a dangerous man here."

For once, this felt right, constable Johnny Brackett was in charge, the alpha male. He'd altered the Police-car's rear-view mirror, so it was focused squarely upon Nick Castle, handcuffed and helpless on his backseat. His former friend sat gazing out of the side window, he looked so…mortal. This was a pissing contest and Brackett was finally in position to show he had the biggest dick. Or at least bigger balls, yes, that sounded better, Johnny had all the balls in the world. His intellect had prevailed, setting up Castle and eliminating him as a potential problem for tonight's town meeting. It took guts to take Nick's right cross and in reality, it barely made a dent. He could have kicked this Johnny-come-lately's arse if he wanted to, but this was better. If only he could convince himself that all this bullshit was true. Oh, he'd fallen lucky. It was an accident that he'd stumbled across Nick's parked Ford, and it was certainly handy that Castle's actions gave him a reason to lock him up for the meeting's duration. But none of it was planned. Still, that's the way it would play out when the residents heard the story. Even if he couldn't convince himself that he was the hero of the day, he'd ensure others thought he was. Pressing down hard on the accelerator of the

Granada, he listened to the engine growl; he smiles, what the Hell, this was still a good day.

This journey hardly required transportation, but it was nice excuse to demonstrate strength. Locking up Jenifer too would have been an option but keeping those two lovebirds separate was useful. Perhaps, she'd get bored and leave, in an ideal world…

The door to the police station was off the latch, strange. Maybe his dad was inside waiting? Still strange, they always kept the entrance locked, visitors needed the bell. The car pulled up to the kerb with a jolt. Johnny's pulse began to race, this just didn't seem right. A Vauxhall was approaching to the police-car's rear and as the officer opened the driver's door, the oncoming vehicle almost smashed it to Hell.

"Jesus, learn to fucking drive." The rant was aimed at the other car's driver though there was no chance of the fellow road user hearing the scolding. After checking the coast was clear, he darted from the Granada and rove open the back door. "Come on Nick, there's something wrong here."

"What do you mean?" Castle's response was measured, another argument wouldn't help anyone, he had to admit that his actions had been ill-timed, no matter how good it felt. Brackett's response was sharp and to the point.

"What I mean is the door to my station is open and it's never left open. It's called security." Brackett reached into the car and placed an arm behind Castle's head, the handcuffs an awkward hindrance. Pulling at his prisoner, Nick's temper began to fray.

"I can manage myself." Swivelling his legs to the outside road, he stood upright, nose to nose with the policeman. Brackett's eyes dropped first.

"Hurry the fuck up then." It was said, more a childish retort rather than a firm response and Nick could see, the balance of power was shifting back in his favour. "Come on." Brackett walked side by side with Castle, more interested about what he'd find inside the office than playing one ups-man-ship with his rival.

"Wait." Brackett paused. "I really don't want to do this but," The officer swivelled behind his prisoner. "I'm going to take the cuffs off; I might need you in there." Nick rubbed his sore wrists, strangely impressed by Johnny's coolness.

Pulling open the white, hardened plastic front door open, a chill ran through Johnny's body. This apprehension didn't make sense, but it was there, non-the less. The hinges creaked, and Brackett peered through into the gloomy room. Before he could speak, the sight of his father, lying unconscious across the desk, rattled the cop into action.

"Oh fuck, dad, are you okay?" kneeling by the chair, Johnny tried desperately to remain calm. A dark, sticky puddle of blood had formed around the stricken man's nose and mouth and for one horrible moment, the officer thought his father was not breathing. Taking the doctor's hand, the skin was cold and clammy. He tried carefully to raise the head away from the desk and the flesh across the cheek clung oppressively to the wooden surface, finally peeling free and revealing the beginning of a bruise down one side of the face. The area was ringed with dried blood though the damage appeared minimal.

Nick Castle looked on, feeling like an expendable guest at the mad hatter's tea-party. Obviously, his innocence towards involvement in this attack could be proved, he'd been with Jenifer all morning, but still, this could make things complicated. The worst Johnny could throw at him was assaulting an officer but, Nick knew that 'Mr Big-Balls Johnny Brackett', when never let something like that reach court, that would show weakness. No, this arrest was to make life awkward, lock him up till the town meeting was over then quietly let him leave. Unfortunately, this could slow things down considerably, if the doctor was seriously hurt, the gathering would be cancelled, Harry Brackett would throw a fit if decisions about Hallowell's future was made without his permission. And even if he was just banged up, the Brackett's wouldn't rest until the perpetrator was captured. Nick sighed a little louder than he meant to though the officer was preoccupied with his father.

"Come on dad. Please, are you okay?" Johnny tried gently slapping the Physician's cheeks, frantically desperate for a response.

"Do you want me to go bring a doctor?" Nick looked on impatiently.

"He is the doctor, you are fucking moron, you just stay where I say." With his attention fixed firmly on the patient, Brackett wasn't aware of the silent sniggering emanation from his former friend. "You're going to keep old Tom company."

Nick peered through to the back room and shook his head in disbelief at what he saw.

"Johnny, I know you have bigger fish to fry at the moment but, Tom's not there." The policeman's head shot around 90 degrees, his jaw dropping open, the first holding cell was empty. Leaping to his feet, he momentarily released his hold on his father and the doctor's head fell once more to the desk. Running through to the backroom, he checked the only possible hiding place which was behind the door before angrily swinging the open cell door with full power, smashing it against its latch. Reappearing in the doorway he exclaimed to no-one in particular,

"His gone. Tom Fucking Daley's escaped."

The loud clashing of metal on metal, finally revived the fallen doctor. Slowly, the muscles tensed in the back of his neck and the head raised gradually from the desk. The eyes were still closed, and a saliva bubble had formed at the corner of his mouth. Johnny walked gingerly across the room and stood erect and angry before his older sibling. Suddenly the eyes flickered and opened. And then, the room was filled with the officer's cry.

"DAD, WHAT THE FUCK HAVE YOU DONE…AND WHERE'S MY PRISONER?"

Had it actually been true? Hell, there'd been times in forgotten days when Dan Challis truly couldn't believe his own eyes. One drink too many, vision and psyche heading in opposing directions. A bad bottle of hooch and after waking, he'd had a reasonable level of certainty that his nightmares had been reality.

Pools of piss and dried vomit, unwelcome props in the game, only an alcoholic could know the rules too. But today, was different.

When Challis had returned from his night-time excursion, he refused to allow himself the luxury of sleep-in case he began to question the validity of what he'd seen, this was too important. Was he able to un-see what he'd witnessed, he'd take it in a heartbeat, not wishing the responsibility? Seeing the undertaker leaving the railway station made no sense and if slumber would allow his mind to eradicate the image… But Challis knew, were he to wake in a state of confusion, he'd never piece the puzzle back together. Therefore, remaining in a conscious state, even be it a semi-drunken one, until he could find at least some answers to these nagging questions was the only option, he owed himself that much.

If there was one thing that Dan knew about, it was loss. Loss of friends, family, loss of memories, of self-respect, of a future. If outing that fat-fuck could give him just a fraction of that back, just maybe… All he needed to do was discover what Gibson was actually guilty of.

He'd spent as little time at home as his actions would allow, keenly aware that his neighbour, John McKenzie would still be baying for blood, another of his actions he regretted when the booze had worn off. There was just time to change his weathered clothes, damp from the early morning dew, and to hunt out a hidden half-pint bottle of Gin (remembering locations wasn't always easy after drunken purchases). A double dose of pain-meds kept his battered body moving and warded off the lingering effects of the previous day's drinking. Peering down the backstreet to ensure a clear coast, he quietly locked the back door to the cottage and began his mission.

Working out a plan of action wasn't easy. Confronting Gibson alone was concerning. Not that the mortician had a reputation for being 'a hard case', it was more that Dan feared confrontation. His alcohol ravaged brain had been irrevocably altered negatively and handling verbal retorts took quick wits, something Challis struggled to rely upon. Gibson may not have been physically daunting, but his bluster and confidence meant that it was a battle the young man couldn't hope to win. Retaining allies was a better option but his choices were limited. One alternative was the town constable, Johnny Brackett but their relationship had turned foul many years earlier. The police officer siding with Challis over the undertaker was doubtful. Nick Castle was the only alternative, but they barely knew one-another anymore. Would he be willing to help out due to a long-forgotten loyalty?

Unfortunately, Challis always seemed to miss his former friend by fractions. Having called at the Castle home, the doors were locked, and the curtains drawn. Knocking three times, and finding no answer, he decided to visit the news-agency where, Castle's grandmother was busy talking to a soda company representative, keen to house his products upon her shelves. She'd been pleasant, if brief with Challis's quick question of her grandson's whereabouts.

"Sorry son, I've not seen him today. I believe he was seeing that young girl again this morning." With that her attention turned back to the salesperson, a woman who was probably in her forties who tried her hardest to appear back to her thirties. Wearing skin-tight black jeans, high-heels and way too much make-up, the appearance seemed forced.

Beyond that, the options were limited. Dan Challis appeared to the world, someone who'd try desperately to fade into the crowd, to be as anonymous as possible. But when irked, he still had spirit, gumption, acumen, sagacity, an astuteness to solve mysteries. If he had to do this alone, so be it. Booze helped too.

Challis returned to the cottage one final time before heading to the mortuary, deciding that it may be best to have some form of weapon, just to be safe. It took a few moments searching through cluttered drawers before finding his prize, a six-inch folding blade with a black rubber handle and a sharp edge. Knowing it was illegal to carry such a tool, he buried it deep into the pocket of his long grey overcoat, only willing to brandish it under serious duress, it was better to have it and not need it than to need it and not have it. Leaving the cottage, the weapon was almost required immediately.

The front door to the McKenzie home swung open, Dan, in his haste had momentarily forgotten the previous altercation and neglected to check for a clear path. Unwilling to take an unnecessary beating, Challis quickly hobbled across the street to the safety net of the nearby woodland, the same thick foliage that he'd spent much of the previous night. As the giant Irishman exited his backyard, his frightened neighbour was relieved to see McKenzie head off in the opposing direction. Still, he was taking no chances and descended further into the enveloping arms the woodland provided. Manoeuvring his way through the tightly packed trees wasn't easy and the first clearing revealed the God-Forsaken railway station, looming large in the distance. He'd seen that place a thousand times on a thousand days but today seemed different. The visual was as grim as ever, from the cracked and faded marble platform to the weathered red brick exterior. The only physical change in a decade had been the arrival of a metal supermarket shopping trolley, six feet from the platform's right-hand side corner. Challis had always wondered who would be crazy enough to get that close, then shuddered as he recalled he and his friend's own excursion into Hell.

No, the change wasn't visual, but purely psychological. Hallowell's dirty little secret was well known now, far wider than during his childhood. But Graham had become more the rat in the cellar, knowing it's there but incapable to eradicate it. Like a fucked-up truce, leave us alone and we'll leave you alone. Gibson's actions could screw that treaty up forever, venturing onto Graham lands was paramount to suicide, that was that fat bastard doing?

This was the closest Challis had allowed himself to venture towards that place in years. It had become a symbol of resentment, mirror images reflecting the man he'd allowed himself to become. While celebrating his 18th birthday, alone in the hovel he called home, his drunken experience reaching its zenith. In a fit of despair, he decided that suicide was preferential to continuing to live this waking nightmare. Unfortunately, his cowardice wouldn't allow himself to launch the conclusive blow, that was until realising that using Graham as his final act would be an ironic ending.

Just after midnight, he'd navigated the woodland to the hole in the chain-link fence. Desperate for one day's redemption, a release from the never-ending turmoil that was his life, he clambered onto the Graham lands and started across the wasteland to the station. Amazed at the ease his actions took, expecting his body to freeze with fear and finding no such restrictions, an inane grin plastered his face, an expression of glee engulfing him. Screaming Frank's name and determined his plan would work, he became surprisingly excited about the journey he was about to take. No more suffering, no more self-hatred, just the release of darkness that death would allow.

Bill Castle ensured his plan was thwarted. A chance sleepless night had brought about a late-night stroll and a fateful decision to pass by the woodland at the exact time Dan Challis had chosen to extinguish his life. The former police officer had dragged the eighteen-year-old from harm's way and remained by his side until the next morning to ensure that the insane scheme wasn't repeated once the coast was clear. By morning, Dan's drunken bravado had vanished and a stern warning from the old man made certain that a re-run was never attempted.

William Castle saved Challis's life that night, and Dan never forgave him for it.

Fred Gibson's actions had made no sense. It wasn't a childish dare or midlife crisis, he didn't look ill or suicidal, the prick had been smiling from ear to ear, hell, he looked positively giddy. There'd been no rush, no concern, the fucker had strolled, care-free, a walk in the park, a splash in the surf. He wasn't worried about the psychotic host, seeming certain that the monster wasn't lurking in the shadows. He appeared safe, content. Why? Then a thought entered the young man's mind, an image that made his blood run cold.

Chapter 31

Saturday October 23rd 11am, stage 1.

A Tractor trundled its way down the narrow road, earth embedded in the grooves of its massive wheels. Vast, spun, hay bales packed tightly into its oversized trailer cast a shower of loose wheat, down onto the concrete street below, swirling into a vortex as the mighty engine spewed out its toxic waste. The farmer, an old man with a worn, chequered shirt, flat cap and weathered skin that revealed untold signs of the harsh Hallowell seasons, sat high up in the cabin, trying to manoeuvre a path through the row of parked cars, completely oblivious to be being watched by the young man at the street's end.

Station View was usually quiet. The furthest point west of the village, where residential properties had once been a premium, the row of seven Victorian buildings with their rears facing onto the Graham lands were once considered the height of society, in terms of Hallowell residency. At one time, each property had been in the Graham family ownership, being leased to their most trusted employees but one by one, they'd been sold off whenever the family needed cash flow. Now, they were all in private ownership and because of this, their once great lustre and majesty had diminished hugely. Three had been bought by private landlords who had leased the homes to outsiders for profit. The furthest to the left was the residency of Dr and Mrs Harry Brackett, who had modernised the frontage to help their home stand out. The neighbouring house had been in the Gaskins family for three generations (the first family to purchase from the Graham's directly) but since the last lineage of the family was fifty-three-year-old mechanic Ian, who had never married or had offspring, it seemed certain that another historical property would eventually fall into the hands of outsiders. The next was empty and due for auction. The doctor had badgered his son to bid for ownership though Johnny had no wish to be tied to a long-term investment. The windows and doors had been boarded shut to evade squatters and because of this, the whole area's appearance was affected. The character of the street thankfully hadn't been completely lost, the stone-built walls and grey slate roofing gave an air of heritage that new builds couldn't hope to achieve. Each habitat had generous bay fronted windows and extended porches which cut into the outside pavement but added an old-world feel that was impossible to replicate. That was all properties, bar one.

It had always seemed a strange location for a mortuary, but Hallowell was a strange village. The final residency, on the corner of station view and colliery lane stood out for obvious reasons. Gibson's funeral parlour had altered the bay-window, squaring it off to arrange more space inside and a glass vestibule came out slightly onto the outside footpath. Three stone steps lead up the solid oak doorway and above the entrance, a gothic stone gargoyle stared out onto the street below. Above the downstairs window, a wooden sign coloured in red with Gibson's funeral parlour written in black lettering was attached to the stone wall. The sign creators had used the Engravers mint design to constitute a rather gothic feel, though one may feel a more soothing and comforting composition would have been best placed. Typical Fred Gibson. Most of the neighbours had switched to double glazing with bright u.p.v.c plastic doors and windows, and as the parlour had resisted the urge to follow the trend, the building seemed old fashioned and more out of place.

Dan Challis's right leg was beginning to throb, the pain meds struggling to contain the stress of the additional exercise. He still wasn't certain how this would play out, confronting the undertaker alone wasn't ideal, in fact it was terrifying. There was no evidence that the fat slug had done anything more wrong than be in a stupid place in a stupid time. It wasn't illegal to enter the station, it was just very, very stupid. Still, the nagging doubt, that there was something more sinister about what he'd witnessed wouldn't go away, "Why did I have to use today to start being a hero?"

He'd been here for fifteen minutes now; Gibson's was twenty yards away and still he couldn't force his legs to carry him that final lap. It would be easier if the undertaker came out, a confrontation in the street would have witnesses. What if he asked him inside? There were dead bodies in there, coffins, fuck that. No, to be patient was better, this was a nice spot, and he had a park bench, a bottle of gin to keep out the cold, there was plenty of day.

Challis couldn't help but feel depressed as he took in his surroundings. The small children's play area had been here for as long as he could remember. There'd been plenty of play-wars back in the day, himself and Brackett versus Nick and Billy (since Billy Scholes had been brought into their group by Castle, he was his responsibility). Throwing mud bombs and making obstacle courses, it had seemed like the best place in the world. Now, it just seemed to parallel the rest of this shit-hole village, old and tired. Originally there'd been four rope swings, and a large solo tyre-ride with steel cables and mesh seating. All had been vandalised. The see-saw had rusted to extinction and the metal climbing frame looked a decent breeze away from collapse. Back in his day, it was a magnet for kids, having to queue just to grab a turn. Today, hardly surprisingly, it was deserted.

A small litter bin, beside the playground's open gate rattled in the growing breeze. Uncut grass swayed, and an empty chocolate bar wrapper flew gracefully into the air with an updraft. The young man watched hypnotically as the plastic danced in the invisible air. After a final check to ensure he wasn't being watched, Challis dipped into his overly large overcoats inside pocket and produced the Gin. The cap had already been snapped and a decent-sized swallow consumed. Lifting the glass container to his lips, he was about to devour another measure when two people emerged from one of the rented houses. They were two teenagers, one boy, maybe sixteen, seventeen, wearing a black leather jacket with the lapels pointing high, toward his fashionably styled long black hair. The jacket was open at the front to reveal a plain white T-Shirt and blue jeans, this kid was an obvious fan of Fonzie from 'Happy Days' though the coolness was harder to imitate. The girl looked younger, fourteen, wearing a white dress with blue flower petals emblazoned in the material, flowing at the back but unnaturally short at the front for a girl her age. Her hair was tied back tightly in a bun to reveal a face containing way too much make up. Impressing Fonzie was a drag, man.

They walked in Dan's direction, but barely registered his presence, they were hand-in-hand, giggling at some joke or memory. Challis grimaced, he'd never experienced that, the joy of being with someone of the opposite sex, just because they wanted to be with him. Oh, he wasn't a virgin. When he had spare cash, the hookers in Carpenter were an enjoyable pass-time. As for a girl, being with him, just for him, maybe one day.

As the couple passed by, one of the girl's high heels slipped into a crack in the pavement and she almost sprawled, but for her knight in shining leather jacket, catching her before the fall. Again, they laughed, just another fun memory they can share forever. In twenty years' time, when she had four kids to four different men, she'd always remember the time when Fonzie was cool under pressure. Dan returned his stare toward the morticians, then remembering the Gin, his hand darted back into the coat and retrieved the bottle.

As his fingers clasped the glass casing, Dan sighed at hearing an unwanted voice. The gin stayed hidden.

"Danny Challis is that you?" The irritating raspy cackle of old Mrs Clarey was a once heard, never forgotten, situation. Hallowell's only octogenarian, the withered old hag was still spry for ninety-five. Secretary at Hallowell primary school for over sixty years, most expected her to die after retirement but somehow, she thrived. Charity work, meals on wheels, volunteering in St Mara library, she had her fingerprints all over the village and knew everything about everyone.

"Hello there, Mrs Clarey." Dan didn't need this distraction and the earlier double pain meds had left him with a decidedly queasy feeling. Plus, the longer she stayed, the longer he'd need to go without the GIN.

"You look as rough as ever. Still drinking, are we? Such a shame, young man like you, wasting your life." She'd never been the most tactful of people.

"I'm fine, honestly. How are you?" As the words left his lips, he knew he'd made a big mistake.

"It's funny you should ask. I was at Dr Brackett's office yesterday, do you know Dr Brackett, lovely man. Anyway, he checked my blood pressure and cholesterol levels, and he was amazed, said there was women forty years younger than me who wasn't half as healthy. I bet your blood pressure levels are high, all that redness around your cheeks is a tell-tale sign you know, you need to be careful, it's a killer. Anyway, I'm getting about, better now, I had my hip replaced last year but I won't let it keep me down. Got to use my cane but that's expected, I'm ninety-five you know. When I saw Dr Brackett, do you know him, lovely man, anyway he said that if I keep improving, soon I won't need the stick, I'll be glad too, makes me feel old. But…" The words seemed to decrease in volume as she spoke, either that or maybe, Challis had found the eternal answer to blocking out AGRAVATING BASTARDS. He was looking at her desperate not to appear rude and visualising ramming the cane down her wrinkled old throat. Just then, something caught his eye.

Challis had heard the girl was back in town and the rumours were, she was beautiful. The gossips were correct. Still, she looked bothered, exasperated, her pace quick, expression stern. It had to be her, the Graham girl, about his age, elegant, classy. When Mrs Clarey saw Dan's diverted attention, she turned to see where his focus laid.

"E, Danny, you know who that is, don't you? That's that Graham girl. Yesterday, when I was waiting to see Dr Brackett, lovely man, I was talking to old Billy Jenkins, do you remember him, he was a taxi driver before he got his cataracts and couldn't see properly anymore, such a shame. Anyway, he'd been talking to that handyman, Gaskins, I think his name is, just lives over in one of those houses. He'd been sat with Mr Henderson from the guest house in that Wheatsheaf pub on Thursday night and said she'd booked a room there for the weekend. Between you and me, I heard she's here to sell the big house and the railway station, needs money, probably drugs." At the last statement, Challis turned once more from the girl and gave the old woman a mournful glare. "Well, what else could a young woman like that need money for? Anyway, if the railway station gets sold, I don't know what will happen I mean…" The former secretary stopped abruptly, realising that she was about to say too much.

"I heard see needed the money to help her business. It is her property, after all said and done." The young man's words were said with force and vigour, hoping the tone of needle would shut the old witch up.

"Oh well, it's not for me to say. You know, I'm not one for gossip." Dan smiled and shook his head.

"Of course not, Mrs Clarey." Returning his stare towards Jenifer's direction, his eyes grew wide, mouth falling slightly open. Station View's Street of properties was long and terraced with no detachment, he'd just seen her ten seconds earlier. Squinting to check for movement, all seemed quiet. It was impossible, Jenifer Graham had vanished.

Saturday October 23rd 11am, stage 2.

"That motherfucker." Had this been a children's cartoon, there'd be steam-lines radiating for Jenifer Graham's head. Because it was reality, she had to make do with a flushed complexion and tightly clenched teeth. Even the cursing, which she rarely did, was allowed at a reasonable volume, even if there was no-one around to hear it. Around her shoulders, Nick Castle's jacket still hung loosely, there'd been no time to return it before the arrest. Not that she needed it anymore, her temper was making her blood boil and the growing migraine she was suffering forced a full body layer of perspiration.

"That God-damn piece of shit." The statement was thought rather than said though it carried no less weight. Was it a set up or just plain bad luck? The

414

previous evening, Nick had been careful not to reveal too many details of his past but had mentioned things about life, pre-leaving Hallowell. Family ties mostly, but also stories about his network of old friends (without mentioning Billy Scholes) There was a smile when mentioning Dan Challis even though there'd been sadness too when he'd talked of the young man's struggles with alcohol (there seemed little point revealing his own battles with addiction) There was warmth when talking about the good old days and Challis's casual laid-back nature being one of the things, he'd missed most about his exile away from the village. It was a friendship; Nick hoped his return could re-kindle. The opposite could be said of Johnny Brackett. Castle hadn't gone into detail, but it was obvious that there'd been an underlying rivalry and even jealousy between the two. When pushed, he'd changed the subject but had conceded a bitterness that Brackett had taken on the role of constable, this was a kinship that seemed irrevocably broken.

It had been indisputable that the officer had enjoyed the morning's confrontation, the conspicuous grin as the handcuffs had snapped into place, overt joy at pushing Nick into the backseat of the police-car. True, he'd had to endure a firm punch to the jaw, and Jenifer was certain that, in the moment, her would-be boyfriend probably relished the chance to exert some superiority. But the second the blow was dealt; the balance of power had shifted. She knew it, Castle knew it, and Brackett definitely knew it. So again, she asked herself the question, was it a set-up or an unneeded co-incidence? Whatever the answer, that son of a bitch had destroyed their day and stolen an opportunity for the young couple's feeling to grow. It wasn't right.

As they'd taken Nick's Ford for the morning excursion, Jenifer headed back to the guest house on foot. Not that it mattered, the distance was short, and she needed the air. Exploring the ruins was postponed. Jenifer had promised Nick she wouldn't enter without his presence; he'd been insistent enough to make her wary. The building was uninviting enough, and were it not for Nick, she'd have left the matter with the elusive real estate agent and headed home. Memories of her mother lived inside her heart only now, whatever ghosts roamed the detritus remains were a past she had no desire to face.

Castle had given the girl a half-hearted smile as the police-car moved off down the long gravel driveway. A surprising depression emerged fast, like a thick uncomfortable blanket and had she not been so angry, a torrent of tears would almost certainly have erupted. Momentarily, her limbs felt cumbersome, unmanageable, weighed down. This wasn't how today was supposed to go. As the car passed through the open gateway, Jenifer allowed herself a final look back towards the property. A parturient crow with a copious wingspan forced itself free from a nest inside the shattered roof. A grey slate tile worked loose and slid away from its neighbours. Torpedoing to the ground with frightening speed and fragmentizing into a hundred shards, echoing around the open space, causing more birds, hidden in the trees, to flee for cover.

Across to the far right of the lands, the outside edge of the Graham garages was just in view. This was one area not destroyed by the inferno, though part of the roofing had collapsed as the harsh Hallowell winters had taken hold. A side-entrance was open, the door hanging on one hinge. From Jenifer's eye-line, everything inside appeared black; except for one brief moment. There *was* movement, just faint, but the change in density seemed much larger than anything wildlife could achieve. The girl squinted, Autumnal sunshine hindering the line-of sight, and as nothing emerged from the doorway, Jenifer admitted defeat. Still, the uncertainty left her anxiously concerned. Letting out a protracted sigh, Jenifer began the hike back to the residence.

Apprehensively, a portly figure emerged from the cover of darkness, careful not to be seen. Running head-long into the land's wooded area, he raced to get ahead. This was his only chance.

Once free of the Graham lands, her energy seemed to return. Depression turned to aggression, and she decided to alter her destination, she'd be damned if she was going to let Nick rot in a cell without doing all she could. If imploring to the constable's better nature was futile, perhaps Nick's grandmother would have more influence. She was a Hallowell original, and her husband had been the previous law and order. It was worth a shot.

Walking by colliery lane, Jenifer remembered the area differently. The cottages were run-down and shabby; on the driveway of the first was stripped-down Vauxhall, without doors or windows, piles of bricks where once were wheels, a highly amused little boy of no more than six, playing alone inside. The child, who was eagerly about to win the British grand prix noticed the girl and rudely stuck out his tongue before shouting, "Fuck off, nosey bitch." This was not a good area. The neighbouring cottage had a pony tethered in the front garden, happily chewing what little grass remained on the lawn. Its grey coat hung loose around its belly, signs malnutrition obvious, the nourishment from the wasted garden would have been minimal. The house by the streets end had loud music blaring from its open windows. A furious argument between a man and woman could faintly be heard of the deafening noise and the front door suddenly crashed open followed by the emergence of a wild haired giant, shouting obscenities with an Irish accent. Jenifer looked to the ground, desperate not to make eye contact; Hallowell was turning to shit.

Leaving Colliery Lane, she noticed a vandalised playground on the corner of station view. Inside, there was two people who looked purposely out of place, like the punch line to a bad joke. As they feverously gossiped, the old woman made no effort to hide the fact that Jenifer was the topic of their conversation. The words were impossible to decipher but the stare held burning venom. The old bitch added hand gestures, a withered finger in the girl's direction and a nodding head, it couldn't have been more obvious if she carried a billboard. As for the young man, he appeared embarrassed at the hag's actions, but was no less interested in the subject. Still, he looked sad, desperate for pity. Dishevelled with a bad complexion, he looked a parody of what a man should be. He wasn't even confident enough to tell the old woman to shut the fuck up though he appeared dis-interested by her opinions. Stuck in position but unwilling to leave. His location seemed on purpose and not by accident, the girl couldn't help but wonder why.

That shy, innocent young woman, who'd arrived in the village just days earlier, would have blushed, perhaps turned, and headed in another direction. For now, that girl had taken a sabbatical. Recent events had altered her sensibilities. The snotty waitress, the cop with the Hitler impression, the whole village hiding behind twitching curtains and muffled voices. It was too much. Perhaps, it was genetic, that inner Graham finally coming to the surface. Or maybe it was the added strength she felt whenever Nick Castle entered her mind. Whatever the answer, the young woman had reached breaking point. There was still apprehension mixed with a measure of trepidation, but the frustration was getting the best of her.

Stopping across the road, adjacent and angry, she volleyed back a stare that meant, "I mean business." The incessant chatter paused, the man dropping his eyes to his worn-out shoes, while the old woman tried to look complacent, while finding it impossible not to be slightly impressed. An uncomfortable stand-off lasted mere seconds before the hag broke eye-line, like John Wayne's rivals in a western duel.

"So, Danny, what's your plans for the weekend?" The statement was said, more for the girl's ears than for Challis, a weak effort to disguise their previous conversation. Jenifer didn't wait for his reply, knowing that any response would once more be for her benefit only. Turning on a heel, with a shake of the head and a wry smile, she began to walk, no, strut away, striding down Station view, content with the small victory.

"Danny? Wasn't that the same name, Nick had mentioned last night?" Co-incidence? Perhaps.

The sun was just high enough to peak over the rooftops and make Jenifer squint. The breeze was growing to uncomfortable levels, and she found herself looking to the pavement rather than straight ahead. It wouldn't matter, the coast was clear. The whisper of voices was no longer relevant, the quiet click of a door opening ahead echoed though she paid no attention. The street was shrinking, the homes let by private landlords looked cold and unloved, a sad reflection of a once fine street. The spectre of the neighbouring mortuary added to the eerie outlook. An open window from the final rented accommodation revealed a television with unnecessarily high levels of volume. A Range-rover parked by the kerb, slightly onto the pavement made the girl crabwalk for space. The faint shrill screams of a new-born baby could just be heard over the Saturday morning talk-show, the same infant that Harry Brackett had seen into the world just hours earlier. Jenifer slowed, and then paused, there was something about the child's tears that made her heart ache. She wondered if motherhood would really be a good fit for her future.

Continuing, she re-focused, Nick needed her. The pace quickening, the street was reaching its end. A glass vestibule protruded before her, another unwelcome obstacle, and the morbid signage, hammered tightly into the stone wall couldn't help but attract her attention. A shudder ran down her spine.

The final time Jenifer had witnessed her mother's remains had been inside that place. Lying lifeless and wasted, 'suicide', stealing a soul to beautiful to be a Graham. Subconsciously, her head darted away, momentarily, the thought too much to bear. A queasy unease rumbled in the pit of her stomach and tears welled. For a fleeting second, she was a child again, recalling the crushing news. A bolt of electricity pulsed her body, like a lightning strike, she needed to get away. Staggering forward, her eyes barely open, the exit strategy required speed, co-ordination irrelevant, escape the only goal.

Out of nowhere, an arm shot around her neck and her legs lost all strength. Vocal cords temporarily paralysed, the scream for help refused to come. With eyes wide shut, seeing nothing, the earth spun then fell away. When her voice returned, a sweaty hand with flashy sovereign rings, clawed at her face then clamped her mouth. By the time she could make noise, the front door was closed, it was already too late.

Saturday October 23rd 11am, stage 3.

This was really happening; he'd never get a better chance. His palms sweaty, body trembling with anticipation, he'd waited for this his whole life. There was no time for self-doubt, no time at all, he could hear her footsteps growing louder with every passing stride. This was it.

Fred Gibson had lived a lifetime in one morning, peaks and troughs, incredible highs and devastating lows, his drab existence bursting with excitement. Ten hours ago, and a sixth sense told him that this would be a special day. And special occasions deserved the best. Angela Loomis was the best.

It had been the biggest risk, Fred Gibson had ever taken, but she was worth it. The girl came from a good family, the mother, a secretary for a pharmaceutical company based in Carpenter and the father, a wealthy businessman who'd made a fortune in moulded plastics before retiring. They'd had Angela late in life and because of that, their daughter had wanted for nothing. The most stylish clothing, the best education, the most influential of friends. A little spoiled but with a kind heart, her passion was animals, especially horses.

The Loomis family-owned land at the far side of town in the hills towards St Mara where they built stables, housing three; a wonderful grey stallion that had been bought as a yearling then used at stud, a fawn mare that the family had tried to race only to discover she neither had the aptitude nor the speed to be a champion and a gelding named Striker, Angela's favourite. The horse had been rescued from a nearby farm after their stables had been destroyed by fire. The black beauty previously had potential to be a champion racehorse but fractured a leg whilst trying to kick an escape from the burning holding. The D.M.V. had recommended the horse be euthanized but the Loomis family made an offer to the owner and the horse was saved. It had been Angela's pet ever since. Had the family known the ramifications of that decision, the deal would never have taken place.

Angela was used to commanding the stock alone, she'd been a well-versed rider since the age of eight and had ridden her first pony as a toddler. By eighteen, the stock and stables were her responsibility, one that she welcomed. The morning had begun like so many others. By 5:30 she was dressed and ready, only content when around the breed. Early July, the warm morning sun was giving way to clouds from the east. The forecast was storms, thundery showers so the girl knew that were she to take in a ride that day, now was probably going to be her only chance.

The mare was exercised first. Fitting the saddle and bridle took time but it was worth it to feel her react, all the horses had their own eccentricities. Alli (Allison's Flyer had been her race name) liked to canter to the top of the hill, then race into a gallop down the rails. Next was Tanker, the grey stallion, who would bolt ahead for as long as the jockey would allow. There were the first droplets of rain in the air as the girl led Striker out from the number three stable. Holding on firmly to the saddle rack, she led the animal out into the open air. After the horse had suffered the leg injury, he was no longer ridable, but Angela has happy just to exercise her around the paddock, quickening the pace when the animal wished to trot, content that this beautiful creature could still have a happy life under her ownership.

The clouds began to gather overhead, and the first rumble of thunder could have been mistaken for a passing vehicle. The second was far stronger and the gelding reared up on its hind legs, visions of the storm which started the stable fire still fresh in the horse's memory. Angela tried to calm the animal, stroking its head, and using soothing tones but a vicious crash launched a booming roar that echoed back off the Hallowell hills. The terrified horse broke loose from the reigns and ran, kicking with all its might at the invisible air around it.

Dressed in an Aurbion ladies Arlington jacket, charcoal with long white sleeves and cream high waisted jodhpurs, with her long black hair packed tightly inside a Champion X-air plus riding hat, black moulded plastic with a grey metal strip down the centre. The strap below the chin felt tight and uncomfortable as she fought to regain control of the creature, now rearing wildly with fear. It headed towards an open gate, were it to get loose, it would run blindly into the busy road outside. Another roar, this time louder still, it reached the gate, but Angela was there first, crashing it in its hinges. The gelding kicked out with its front legs ferociously, unrelenting in its desire to be free. Tears were now visible on the girl's face, these horses were her responsibility, she couldn't let this horse destroy itself. She looked around for help though none appeared nearby.

"Where was Abbey, the useless hand who was employed to help with the workload, probably sleeping off another hangover."

Angela grabbed for the bridle strap, desperate to gain some control but the horse refused to be tethered. Rain was now coming down in sheets and the thunder was almost a constant roll. The other horses inside the stables were becoming unnerved, their crestfallen cries for condolement echoing around the yard. Still, Striker was the priority. The eighteen-year-old fought valiantly, her breathlessness ignored. The horse swung to the left, the bridle strap flying and lashing the girl's face. The sudden sting made her cry out with pain, but she refused to relent. Once more, the leather lashed through the air though this time, Angela saw a chance. Throwing an arm fast, it slid perfectly through the loop.

Her grip now was key, corralling the leather with both hands. The horse kicked out violently and missed the girl by inches. Still, she refused to release the grip. Rainwater made the surface slippery, but her determination was strong. Pulling with all her might, Striker slowly began to calm. The thunder still crashed around them, but Angela now had her eyes locked firmly onto the horse's, an invisible bond between human and animal that only those involved could understand. With four hooves on the ground, she stroked the horses head lovingly, ecstatic that she'd regained control. Steadily, she began to lead the animal back toward the stable. The rumbles of thunder seemed to be passing and the rain began to ease.

Her body was discovered a little over an hour later by the stable-girl Abbey. All the horses were corralled inside, and the storm had passed. A single bolt of lightning had struck the metal stripe across the top of the helmet, immediately destroying the circular system, the lungs, and the central nervous system. The catastrophic energy pulsing through her body would have killed her instantly.

Fred Gibson immediately fell in love. The family had pleaded with the undertaker to ensure she had the best funeral, no matter what the cost. Preparing the body, he took his time.

On the metal slab in his workshop, lay the remains of the most beautiful girl he'd ever worked upon. The only sign of damage was a scorching across the crown, but her amazing black hair hid the covered corruptive affliction. The face was make-up free, pure, and natural. The hint of a smile, a slight turning of the lips, as though she was content. The eyes had been closed before the corpse was delivered but Fred liked them open, believing it was the only way to see into their soul. And what eyes, deepest blue, reflecting peace and happiness. Gibson drooled as he imaged what was next. Moving down the naked prize, the neck was long, shoulders slender, breasts beautifully formed, legs long, she even had perfect toes, he liked to nibble on toes.

This wasn't just about sex, even though he'd performed unspeakable acts upon the remains as many times as he could manage. She could be his imaginary partner, someone to play with whenever he wanted, burning something so beautiful seemed such a waste.

The parents had come to say goodbye. The mortician watched through a crack in the door as the mother sobbed and the father held a hand. She was dressed in a long white night-gown which slenderly extenuated her curves. He felt his manhood hardening, the excitement of the plan too much. As the parents wept their final tears, the coffin lid was slid over the base and the daddy kissed the name on the golden plaque.

The church blessed of St Helen, was standing room only for the service, the overload listening outside on speakers to the vicar's words. He decreed that Angela Loomis was with God now, and if they had memories, she would never truly be gone. As the congregation moved to the crematorium, Fred Gibson watched from the back of the room as he curtains opened, calming music played as the casket moved on. Out of slight, rolling into ovens fierce flames, the curtains closed, the ceremony ended peacefully.

The undertaker had won, no one had checked the coffin. His employees, working as pallbearers remarked that the casket was lighter than usual, but no-one questioned Fred Gibson. When the ashes were collected, the parents believed it was their daughter, in reality it was just wood and whatever trash the undertaker had disposed of.

With a two-inch hook forced through tightly into the skin, scraping the spinal column, the corpse hung limply in a walk in freezer in the basement of the mortuary. The head slumped forward; she still retained that cheeky smile. The temperature such that the body was persevered without being frozen solid. That way, with preparation, he could still play. Fred Gibson could make a giant tick in his bucket list, an entire corpse stolen without any questions. She was his now.

He used her infrequently, terrified to damage the prize. He'd panicked a couple of years back when a power-cut struck the entire village. Being without electricity for thirty-six hours, Gibson began to consider his options. All his prizes (stolen body parts) had begun to thaw, and Angela was almost completely defrosted. Under pressure, employees of Northern Electric worked frantically. The mortician knew that the souvenirs and keepsakes he'd taken from clients would soon begin to stink, then questions would be asked. When power returned to a village in darkness, there was a collective cheer, and the undertaker breathed a huge sigh of relief, his secret remaining intact.

Today was going to be special, he could feel it in his bones. So, before he left for the station, Gibson had removed the body, positioning the remains seductively on a black leather couch by the back wall of the basement.

Unfortunately, he neglected to turn down the central heating. The undertaker was a fan of warmth, he'd been carrying a sniffle for a few days so blasting out heat from the radiators was natural. Immediately behind the leather sofa, was a six feet long metal radiator, throwing out invisible strikes. This continued for five hours.

The undertaker was giddy when he returned from the railway station visit, skittishly mouthing the words,

"Bring her to me. Bring her to me." By the time he reached the basement, he was naked, feverously working his manhood, sweat soaking his hideous frame. When he saw he prize, he wanted to scream?

The corpse was flaccid, hanging loosely, the left arm and leg dragging the floor. Water dripped from the leather, the remains sailing past deforestation. The bottom lip of that cheeky smile had flopped miserably, one eye slid closed, the expression of contentment gone. The left breast was squashed under the body's weight and the right hung painfully. This wasn't his Angie.

"I'm sorry baby. I promise, I won't take you out again. We'll get the smile back, we won't have that smell, you'll be fresh all over again. Please, stay will me?"

The corpse was moved onto its front. The legs sliding, bent, knees on the cold tiles underfoot, two tempting love entrances pointed accessibly before his eyes.

"No, not today, no time." Fred slid his left under one armpit, the right eventually followed suit and sliding under the opposing armpit, even if it did detour to other areas on route. His torso against the dead girl's back, the skin slimy making the undertaker feel nauseous, this certainly wasn't supposed to happen. Thoughts invaded his mind. "What if this is the only way I'll see her, imagine her, my beautiful little girl." The glutinous slime that had replaced her soft skin felt like mucus, debilitated, like holding a slaughtered pig. He lifted with all his might, the flesh peeling from the leather sofa like a suction cup. The head fell back, the long black hair almost reaching the floor. It was no longer the velveteen sweep, just an annoying obstacle. With a forceable hoist, he was upright, just her feet dragging across the floor. Striding with audios laboured movements, the remains clinging to his naked skin.

"Fuck…no"

It was getting hard.

"Not now"

It was definitely getting hard.

Eventually, Angela Loomis's remains was rehung in the freezer. The mortician stepped back, staring deeply at the damage that had been done. Her skin had taken on a different colour, an unpleasant grey. The hands had been repositioned, the fingers wrapped in a semi-fist so to, well be able to slide things in and out of. The spacing needed to be perfect, to make certain he'd…checked. The corners of the mouth were re-arranged but no matter how hard he tried; the smile was impossible to replicate. That vision had gotten the guy though thick and thin. Fred Gibson closed the freezer door and wept for an hour.

It was after 9 am before he regained his focus. He had work to do.

The morning was spent tailing that Castle boy. The rumour mill had been proven correct, Nick had left the family home and headed directly to the Henderson's guest house where the Graham girl had been duly waiting. Keeping a safe distance, the couple had driven to the mansion ruins, where Fred had managed to use his knowledge of the property to remain undetected. Things had become more interesting when Dr Brackett's son Johnny arrived and arrested Castle. His distance was too great to hear details but since there'd been a violent altercation, it looked obvious that the young hot head would be spending time locked away, very useful. Gibson had considered launching his assault there and then but realised that the open spaces would give the girl the advantage. Instead, the local geography gave the undertaker a much safer option. The direct route from the mansion to the guest house passed directly past his front door.

The fading sun made the street seem unnaturally dull, second by second, light was lost, as though the weather was on his side. Gibson slid out a six-inch mirror, just past the frame of his front door, tilting it a few degrees either way to see the whole scene. There was two people at the bottom of the street, that gossiping old hag who used to work at the schoolhouse who knew everything about everybody and a young man who seemed strangely out of place. What was his business? Too old for playgrounds and all the attractions were broken anyway. Was he a spy? Stupid, paranoia was such a fucking torment. Still, Gibson knew when to be wary.

A tractor trundled into the street, leaving a trail of loosened earth from its massive back tyres. Ensuring that the door was closed to a crack so that the farmer in the cab didn't notice him, when the sound of the vehicle passed, he squeezed the door open once more, just enough to pass out the mirror to it former vantage point. And that was when he saw her.

His heart played a rhythm faster than he could count. It was too much, the mortician felt faint and nauseous, it was time to abort, this was taking things too far. People would know, or at least wonder; it was too close to home, his home, Fred Gibson, prime suspect. What if they searched his house, they'd find all his trophies, his keepsakes, his secrets? He'd be ruined, go to jail, abort, abort, ABORT.

The front door was almost closed when a rush of power surged through his body, words screaming in his brain, "Bring her to me." This was his life's work, his addiction, his fucking crack-cocaine. There would never be a better chance. Gritting his teeth till his jawline throbbed, a single tear escaped the corner of his left eye and struggled to climb the incline of his bloated cheek. Those same blood-shot eyes, wide and alert, knowing to the right was retreat and the left was attack. The time was now, choose God damn it.

The front door tilted a little wider. The mirror peaked deftly around the edge. Christ, she was twenty yards away and gaining fast. Fumes from his chloroform-soaked rag gave off a dizzying aroma that added to his nauseous feeling. Gripping the white flannel in his left hand, he swapped it to the right, no longer needing the mirrors guidance, the echo of her footsteps enough to signal her arrival. Were the odd couple at the bottom of the street still watching? Perhaps the neighbour's stationary Range Rover, parked just feet from his doorstep, would give ample cover. Their horrible loud television would help cover any scream the young woman could make. Scream, he was about to make a woman scream, the excitement was too much to bear. Five yards away, the final choice, the last opportunity to retreat. It was now or never. His left hand gripped the door handle tightly, the right squeezing the chloroform rage a little too gingerly, the fluid sliding through his fingers and dripping toward his trouser leg.

For a moment, the sound of her footsteps ceased. Had she noticed his door ajar, was his cover blown? His racing heart almost stopped, breath held; perhaps it was for the best, he'd done nothing wrong, yet. The front door edged closer to closing, the day a waste. Disappointment and anger grew, "Bring her to me. How the fuck do I..."

The footsteps restart.

"Oh Christ, this is it."

"Do it, DO IT NOW."

Suddenly, she comes into view. This was perfect, she's looking away, walking slowly. It took micro-seconds and he's on the street, holding his foul breath, his hulking frame throwing a huge shadow, altering the girl of his presence. Her head angled slightly, mouth covered by the chloroform-soaked rag, her scream immediately muffled. Her legs weaken, and Gibson drags with all his might, the two struggling over the threshold into the mortuary. Her arms fling into the air, just once, holding no risk to her captor, all strength was gone, the toxic fumes taking effect dramatically quickly. Her eyes roll back and turn to white, shoulders shrinking into Gibson's bulky chest. The tight hold across Jenifer's nose and mouth remains overly forcible and unnecessary, the battle was won. A hot trickle of blood seeps from her left nostril causing her assailant to release the grip. The young woman's legs lose their battle with gravity, bending and crashing to the ground it one swift movement, a weakened hand makes a last reflex grab for the waistband of his tracksuit trousers though the feeble digits have no chance of success. As her head slid by his left kneecap, he resisted the urge to kick out, aware that Frank wanted her healthy. As her journey ended, and her unconscious carcass crashes at his feet, Fred Gibson fights valiantly to disguise his excitement. The mission is accomplished, perfectly executed, a masterful performance. Instead of wallowing in a job well done, he simply allows himself the faintest of smiles, for there was still work to do.

Chapter 32

"Where the fuck has, she gone?" Dan Challis's face scrunched with confusion, eyes squinting towards the street's apex.

"Dan Challis, wash your mouth out with soap and water." The old woman looked legitimately shocked and when the young man realised his statement had been said out loud rather than confined to his brain, his expression turned to embarrassment, his hand clasping his lips, face reddening.

"Sorry Mrs Clarey, I didn't mean to swear." Her expression didn't seem forgiving, years of scolding naughty schoolchildren giving her a steely glare. Still, Challis had bigger fish to fry. "I'm sorry, I have to go." He didn't wait for a reply, turning quickly and starting up Station view, his withered leg screaming against the sudden exertion, dragging slightly behind.

"How rude." The old gossip's lips were pursed, an angry scowl covering her face as she shuffled away in the opposite direction. In the distance, she noticed another figure she knew. "Mr Gaskins, hello. Can I have a word?" The handyman frowned, suddenly aware that his own plans were on hold, the woman was like quicksand.

Challis began to stride away, ignoring the pain from his injured limb. "I did see her, I know I did, she didn't have time to just vanish." Listening to the unpleasant volume of the television, an open window, and a screaming baby. The couple inside seemed one step away from a major row, raised voices ready to turn into an argument, the birth of the new child not eradicating their natural instincts. Challis crab-walked past the house, the Range-Rover parked up on the pavement, the young man couldn't help but curse their thoughtlessness. Facing the window, he could see a new crib, white lace and a baby mobile, a German-shepherd laid sleeping at the foot. It was suddenly startled and saw the stranger passing the window, its bark loud and terrifying, the sleeping baby startled enough to scream. Challis upped his pace.

Moving forward, he slowed to catch a breath. Suddenly, he was aware that he was face to face with Gibson's funeral services, his original destination. Should I knock? Dan hadn't forgotten what he'd seen earlier, but the girl now had become his main concern.

Perhaps the two are mixed? Surely not? What could that fat bastard have to do with Jenifer Graham? But…what was the fat bastard doing in the station? He didn't seem afraid, Hell, he seemed, happy. Oh God, this is too much for just me. Challis began to shuffle away, this was a job for Johnny Brackett, that's what the bastard gets paid for. But still, something screamed in his brain, Jenifer Graham was inside. He had no idea how he knew that; he just did. Once more he slowed, he wanted to leave, get reinforcements, but visions of the girl in abhorrent danger forced his forward motion to cease.

Breathing an audible sigh, he turned and strode back to the mortuary doorway. Two high steps and a fucking stone gargoyle staring down. In the window, wooden caskets stood on their end, making Danny shudder. Reaching high, a large iron door-knocker huge ominously. Challis's cowardice was showing, his heart pounding violently, a sickly feeling deep in his stomach. His brain was sending signals to right arm to stretch up and knock but the limb refused to obey, self-preservation throughout his body taking command.

His teeth clenched, a layer of perspiration chilling his body in the cool Autumnal day, finally, heroically, his shoulder moved, bicep extended, fingers stretching, the cold iron doorknocker inside his grasp, he lifts it back, exhales the breath from his lungs, and decisively, inescapably…

BANG, BANG, BANG. Challis held his breath. BANG, BANG, BANG. Challis exhaled his breath. He listened intently, was there footsteps? No. How about any other movement? Not really. He tried one last time, BANG, BANG, BANG. This time he placed an ear to the cold wood. Everything seemed quiet…

"Help." The call was muffled, barely audible. Dan pushed his ear harder to the wooden surface, his heart rate gaining intensity. Had it been a misdirected scream from the noisy neighbour's television. The set was certainly blaring loud enough for the cacophony to carry to the adjoining property. Without a follow-up yell, it was impossible to be certain. Deciding to fire one last series of turbulent crashes with the doorknockers, he pulled the iron back as far as possible and detonated an explosive boom, drumming out five deafening thuds that would be impossible not to hear from any occupant inside. Returning his ear to its former position, he heard…nothing. Still, he couldn't help but imagine the girl, trapped inside, his mind was believing it without the need for evidence. The next-door TV was showing a children's programme, when was there ever screams for help on Saturday morning television? He found himself pounding with a balled-up fist against the front door, no longer afraid of a confrontation with the undertaker, but still there was no reply. Turning the handle, it became obvious that the door was locked.

"Should I try the back-door? What if I'm wrong? I could get arrested for breaking and entering. Arrested? That was the answer, do as I'd first decided, alert Brackett, get him off his arse and make him do his job." A final crash upon the wooden surface yielded no new results, so Challis stumbled back down the three front-door steps and started towards the end of Station view, the police house his desired destination.

Fred Gibson listened attentively; a pudgy, sweat-covered palm pressed tightly across Jenifer Graham's mouth. Only when absolutely certain that the young man had left did he release his tight grip, four red welts forming across the girl's right cheek where the force had stopped her blood flow. Due to the chloroform's lasting effect, her words were slurred and barely understandable, another reason why she hadn't been able to scream loud enough for Dan Challis to be certain of her presence.

"What's happening? I don't understand, where am I, who are you?" Each word seemed to trail off, as though she didn't have the energy to complete the confabulation, though she tried with every fibre of her being. The mortician was busy trying to knot a tie across the young woman's mouth, and though Jenifer continually shook her head in resistance, it was a battle she was destined to lose. Her hands were already bound behind her back, as were her ankles, and the rope which held everything together was threaded through the slats of an old wooden chair, its uncomfortableness not lost on the base of her spine. Even though she still tried to communicate, the words were now completely indecipherable, and after knotting the rope to painful levels of security, Gibson allowed himself a wry smile, content that the first part of his mission was complete. Aware that time wasn't on his side, he was determined to only allow himself a few seconds of breathing space, but, as he knew he had the girl's full attention, he couldn't resist the temptation to gloat on a job well done.

"I, you little bitch, am Fred Gibson, the funeral director to Hallowell. We met yesterday and, even though you may not remember me from our brief conversation, I've a feeling you'll remember me this time." Fred allowed himself a chuckle before continuing. "Now, what was your next question, where are you? I'd have thought that was reasonably self-explanatory, you are in my mortuary, the basement of my mortuary to be exact. And as for what's happening, that's the fun part. I'm going to ensure that you can't cause any more damage to my village by ending your stay here in the most horrific of ways. All you had to do was stay away, just live your pathetic little life, away from Hallowell and things wouldn't have needed to get messy. But you had to be greedy, when you didn't deserve a penny from the Graham estate. Frank is the rightful owner and you're trying to steal away his birth-right, and that won't do. Therefore, you need dealing with, once and for all. Oh, I could kill you myself, that would be easy, but there's someone else who'll enjoy it so much more and will cause you far more punishment in the bargain. You see, I'm finally going to prove myself to your brother, that I'm a friend and an equal, and when I deliver you to him, when I take you to the railway station and he despatches you with beautiful destructive savagery, the threat which is Jenifer fucking Graham will cease to exist." Once more, a laugh emanated from Gibson's disgusting mouth though this time, it carried more vigour, like a Bond-villain, overacted and humourless, like a joke without a punch line.

A muffled reaction came from the seated girl and though her words were still indecipherable, the change in her eyes told the undertaker all he needed to know.

"Of course, you didn't know Frank was still alive, did you? Oh the tales I could tell you if only I had the time." He rolled up his right sleeve to check his cheap, leather-strapped watch which was cutting into the skin around his wrist. His eyes grew large as he continued his retort. "But I haven't, not at all in fact. Maybe we might have time to regale some former stories once we are safely inside the station. Or perhaps, Frank will be happier just cutting off your head the moment he sees you. Either way, we're going to have a lot of fun."

The chloroform caused Jenifer's head to pound but the woozy feeling inside her brain was less to do with the invasive narcotic, and more the revelation Fred Gibson had just announced. The mere mention of her brother's name was enough to send a shiver through her body, but the knowledge of his passing had offset the horrors he'd created during their childhood. But now, if the undertaker's claim was true, if Frank had truly survived the inferno of the Graham mansion, if the teenage monster had preserved to become an adult psychopath, if Frank Graham was truly alive, the idea was almost too horrible to conceive and, the mere thought chilled her to the bone. And with the addition of the mortician, Fred Gibson, some weird superfan who seems to idolise whatever her brother had become, the pairing was terrifying, making her situation seem all the more hopeless.

Jenifer could feel her stomach churning, bowels clenching, an attack of nausea an unbearable inevitability. Her temperature began to rise uncontrollably, her skin burned, sweat emerging in waves. Suddenly, her throat began to squeeze, her windpipe tightening, her body gasping for oxygen which seemed harder and harder to replenish. Inside her skull, the white of her eyes turned bloodshot and then rolled back, the pupils vanishing giving a demonic impression. Her entire body began to shake, then violent spasms emerged, her head lashing from side to side, convulsions taking control without warning. A torrent of vomit erupted from the depth of her stomach, the side-effects from the chloroform now violently launching to the surface. An explosion, emptying the guts, squeezing painfully past her clamped throat, only to find an impenetrable obstacle, which began to suffocate the young woman slowly. The tie, which Fred Gibson had trussed around Jenifer's mouth refused to yield its position, the knot at the base of her skull holding fast. Due to her immense temperature change, hives appeared across the skin of her cheeks, everything indicated the death was emerging rapidly.

"What's wrong bitch?" it was now Gibson's turn to panic, Frank had given express instructions, the only command the psychopath had ever asseverated toward his strange friend. If the girl died, there was a good chance that the mortician may be next. Working the knot to the ligature, Fred cursed his fat, nail-bitten fingers, wishing that his tying hadn't been so rigorously veracious. Luckily, he remembered the small penknife inside the pocket of his black slacks, the one piece of equipment that he rarely left the house without. Forcing his hand inside the tight trouser leg, retrieving the weapon wasn't easy but finally, he pulled the shiny knife free and cracked the blade from its casing. Pushing the cold steel between the back of Jenifer's neck and the thick material, he began cutting, hoping her head wouldn't thrash at the most inopportune of moments. A thin layer of mucus which had escaped from the corner of the girl's mouth made gaining purchase upon the silky fabric more difficult, but slowly the tie began to fray. A pale blue colouring had formed under Jenifer's eyes and the undertaker imagined the same had happened around her lips too, the lack of oxygen shutting down her body, one organ at a time.

Suddenly, the tie broke in two and a torrent of vomit lunged forward, a projectile thrust of her stomach contents, undigested food from her meagre breakfast mixed with stale tea served from the lunchbox café. When the cascading shower finally ceased, all that remained was a translucent slime, sliding from the corners of her mouth. The lack of a choking gurgle told the undertaker that the girl had resumed breathing, her life for now was saved. Looking down, Fred noticed a fair amount of the eruption had splashed across his left trouser leg. His reaction was more out of natural reflex than planned retaliation.

Crack.

"You dirty bitch."

Smack.

"Look what you've done to my clothes."

Gibson stared at his captive who was barely conscious and suddenly realised, that was fun. The two open-handed slaps had been across the back of Jenifer's head and though the force was minimal, the feeling of power was vaguely overwhelming. Until now, he'd felt more of a prison warder than law enforcement, but the violent shots, even with the nominal velocity changed that. She really was his detainee, and he could do whatever he pleased to her without the fear of retribution. Taking a long deep breath, he realised that his life's ambition was presented before him, tied to a chair, completely at his mercy. Was it worth it? Did he still need Frank? Maybe this was the start he needed, the first victim in a series that would bypass anything his demented partner could dream of.

"Bring her to me." That was all well and good but, what did he actually owe Frank Graham? The undertaker had supported the unhinged lunatic when all others had wished him dead. He'd supplied food and information, defended him carefully with the residents whenever the topic arose, he was even willing to offer financial aid where the purchase of the Graham lands was concerned, should he be assisted by others. He'd done everything possible during their collaboration, was the killing of the girl too much to ask? But…

That cripple banging at the mortuary front-door. What was his name? Fuck it, I can't remember, his father owned the greengrocers on Main Street, that's all I can recall. Anyway, what the fuck did he want? The street was clear when I grabbed the bitch, I'm certain of that, he couldn't have seen. Oh, he was down the far side, talking to that old windbag from the primary school but, I'm certain he couldn't have seen. So what the fuck did he want? Bang, bang, bang, bang, bang, nosey bastard, nosey piss-head bastard. WHAT DID HE WANT? Could he have seen? He must have, why else would he be banging on my door? Cos I'm a fucking idiot, that's why. It was too big a risk, standing on my own front-doorstep. It was stupid, so fucking stupid. The question is, would anyone believe him, would anyone want to believe him? No one gives a fuck about Jenifer Graham; we all want her gone. I'm committing a hearty service; I deserve a medal. Plus, he's a pisshead, I'm a respected pillar of the community, and he's an alcoholic. Who would give a shit if she vanished? Challis, that's his name,

Dan Challis. He's always been a fuck-up, ever since… Oh shit, maybe no one would believe him, but he was friends with Constable Brackett, and more so, the Castle boy. I knew he'd be trouble as soon as I heard he was heading back to Hallowell. And, oh fuck, he's been seeing this bitch. The grapevine reckons they were out together last night. And the certainly looked cosy over at the Graham mansion ruins, earlier this morning. Oh, this is bad, this is very, very bad. If Challis tells either Brackett or Castle what he thinks he's seen, they'll be round here like a shot. Okay, fuck offing her myself, that's Frank's job. If they get here before I can get rid of the bitch, maybe I can talk my way clear, I mean, I was only trying to frighten her, make her leave before anything else happens, everyone could relate to that. Still, the best way to avoid that is, move this worthless cunt, soon.

Johnny Brackett's concern for his stricken father was vanishing quickly, the empty holding cell making his blood boil.

"Okay dads explain please. Could you divulge the information I need, WHERE THE FUCK IS MY PRISONER?" Senior frowned, the pain from the bruise at the base of his skull where Tom Daley had landed the perfect blow, and the uncomfortable fracture across his nose where his head had collided with the flat wooden desk, both secondary; his senses were beginning to return, the memory of the recent altercation still fresh in his mind, the acknowledgement that he'd seriously fucked-up. But Doctor Harry Brackett rarely admitted defeat and he felt that attack was the best form of defence.

"Actually, BOY," Johnny's temper was reaching boiling point, he'd been punched in the face, lost a prisoner, and it was barely past lunchtime…and to add to the worries, tonight was the town meeting.

"DON'T DARE START WITH THAT BOY SHIT. I'm fucking constable to this piss-ant village and…"

"And don't forget who got you this job." Nick was feeling uncomfortable, watching two generations of Brackett tearing each other apart was entertaining, but there was no popcorn and no trailers, just straight into the main event, Castle felt robbed.

Johnny was ready to quit. "You want to do it? If you want to be constable on top of being town doctor, feel free, here's my badge, good luck."

"GENTLEMEN, PLEASE." Nick's tone was quieter than the two combatants though somehow, he managed to gain their attention. "I think it might be best if the two of you just take a breath, swallow a chill pill, and calm down. This is Hallowell, with a giant exception of the obvious, nothing ever happens here, so whatever the problem, it can't be that hard to fix." Junior shot an evil stare at his former friend, his quick retort was direct, immediately to the point.

"Well genius, here's our predicament. Tom Daley was being held in cell number one, whether you believe he killed the Roberts boy or not, he was here for his own protection. The Hallowell lynch mob hadn't needed a trial, he was guilty by association and sentenced to…whatever they could think of. They looked at the evidence and cognized his guilt immediately. They couldn't differentiate that the Hallowell bogeyman could just as culpable."

I'm being locked up by the inventor of the dictionary.

"So that's why Tom was here. My only job was to keep him safe, out there, they would tear the poor bastard apart. The day we brought him in, I reached out to the main instigators, in their hearts they knew Tom hadn't in him to kill anyone, especially a kiddie. But in Daley, they knew there was a chance for vengeance. Whether he'd done it or not was irrelevant. And before you start with the arrest them instead bullshit, remember, your granddad had the same problems I'm having now. Back when Tom was accused of kiddie-fiddling, there was no evidence, he was never charged, but the Hallowell bad boys decided he was guilty. There was fuck all your granddad could do, and I'm in the same position now. The railway station and its occupant are carrying a dark shadow.

"So, what I was planning to do was, at the town meeting tonight, everyone will be knowledgeable about our history, I was planning to announce that Tom Daley had been released as we had evidence to prove his innocence. I was also going to give a legal warning, anyone with thoughts about paying the poor son-of-a-bitch a visit, would be in a cell faster than you could say vigilante. That way, I wouldn't need to warn everyone individually. It was a plan; the best one I could come up with.

"But here's the pisser. Every minute the poor guy was locked up in here, he was being tortured, and I knew nothing about it. With his condition, after the colliery accident, he's been on strong pain-killing medication, he's taken it for years, prescribed by our wonderful town doctor, Mr Harry Brackett. Nick knew where this was going but decided not to intervene yet, knowledge is power. Instead, it was Senior who tried to interrupt."

"Excuse me constable, but I had a reason for my actions." Johnny laughed out loud at the unbelievable retort, genuinely interested where his father was taking this.

"Torture dad. That's what you're guilty of. Remember the hypocritic oath, rule number one, first do no harm. You knew what symptoms Tom was going through, cold turkey from strong pain medication, the withdrawal could have killed the poor guy."

"Poor. Don't make me laugh. Do you remember the evidence? The kids' blood on his clothes, the argument between them loud enough for the whole street to here, Daley even chased the kid down the street. What more do you want? This comes with a bow on. A history of paedophilia, and yes I know, he was never charged, but everyone knew, the fucking guy was just weird."

"Come off its dad. You know the same evidence that I do. Tom had a reason for what happened, he was drenched and went in the house to change his clothes. The kids were told never to go inside, that was off limits. The little girl ignored that, went look for Tom and found him naked, changing his clothes. And that one instance made him a supposed kiddie-fiddler. Well sorry but that's bullshit. And as for the latest ball of shite, Daley would never have been thought of as a suspect if it hadn't been for that one event, all those years ago. The blood

431

evidence, a decent solicitor would tear that to shreds, the kid cut himself on Tom's fence getting out of his garden, a garden that he had no right to be in in the first place. Tom touched the blood and panicked, that's why it was on his clothing. As for the argument, like I've just said, the kid had no right to be in the garden, vandalising shit as usual. So, Tom shouted at him, and the kid ran. When Daley followed, the idiot climbed through into the station grounds, the rest is history."

"Who are you, president of the Tom Daley fan club?"

"No. But I've just realised, you haven't explained how the guy escaped, or how your face got all fucked up, oh, and why you withdrew the guy's medication?"

"Fine. You want the truth, let's hope you can handle the truth. I had this planned right from when he was first arrested. I knew I couldn't tell you because you're too inside the box, in this game sometimes you have to think outside the box. Now, I agree, there are two versions of what could have happened, either Daley did it, and I still think that's most probable, or the monster from the railway station got him, either way, Hallowell needed a culprit."

"What's this got to do with his medication?" It was Nick who asked the question, he'd been so quiet, the Brackett's had barely acknowledged his presence.

"This is between me and my son, thank you very much, and I was coming to the medication. I knew how it would be for Tom, going through withdrawal inside a prison cell. My plan was to leave it overnight but when I saw him then, he didn't look too bad. Little pale, little shaky, but I thought I'd give him another couple of days."

"Another couple of days for what." Johnny's tone was changing, and his father knew it, the angry Johnny Brackett was a man to be avoided. The doctor continued with caution.

"Now remember, I did this for you. This was your first real test, and the village was watching, not everyone believes in the bogeyman. If you didn't get a culprit, your position would be under threat immediately, confidence is a hard emotion to create. When I first saw Tom, I knew that he wouldn't confess, not unless I broke him. So that's why I withdrew his medication. By this morning, he was going out of his mind. So I offered him a deal, a way out. Just sign a modified confession, say you didn't mean to hurt the kid, it was all an accident and you just panicked. Do that, and I'll get your pills, hell I'd have doubled them if he wanted. Anyway, he took the deal. I wrote the confession, all he had to do was sign it."

"I don't believe I'm hearing this; you basically blackmailed a prisoner into signing a bullshit confession, which any barrister would have thrown out in a heart-beat, they'd claim it was written under duress, which of course it was. We'd still look like arseholes, and you'd have tortured the poor guy for nothing. Good plan. Anyway, obviously something went wrong. What happened?" The doctor closed his eyes for a second, he didn't like playing the fool but that's exactly what had happened.

"I fucked up. He was in the cell, whining and crying, waiting for his pills. I had them on the desk in front of me, but I wanted the confession done first. So, to shut him up, I opened the cell door. I'd finished writing and I was reading it back to him before he signed. The mistake I made; I had my back to him. It was only for a few seconds but...he hit me right in the base of my skull. I was unconscious before my head hit the desk, and I think my nose may be broken too."

"Good." Junior enjoyed that slight retort. "So what happened to the fabled confession?"

"He took it, probably burned it now. Fucker took the pills too, box with 200 inside so he's good for the next few weeks. That's all I remember, and yes Johnny, my plan was flawed, I fucked up, is that what you want to hear?"

"It's a start." The officer paused, his anger slowed waning, no matter how dumb his father's plan was, he'd done it for the right reasons. His tone changed though his words were still firm and concise. "You do know, I should arrest you. You were willing to destroy another man's life, just to keep me in a job. I job I couldn't give a shit about. This town is unpoliceable, I'm in a no-win situation here, we have a murderer living in our community and I can't take him on alone, but there's no back-up, this town is chickenshit, they'd rather blame patsies like Daley than face the truth. Even the Robert's boy's own father, he'd lost his kid and knew the culprit...and did, fuck all. No one is willing to back me up."

"I would." Castle had been so silent and irrelevant, the Brackett's were shocked at his reply, but for different reasons. It was the doctor who took the lead.

"No you fucking won't, Mr Castle. Your assistance is not welcomed." His tone was a mixture of anger...and fear; if he started rabble rousing, it could lead to trouble, this whole situation was a house of cards, disturb the incorrect one and the entire thing could crumble, and the good doctor had his fingerprints on the whole of Hallowell's recent history...dangerous. Strangely, Johnny agreed with his father.

"I'm sorry, Nick but this isn't your battle, it's none of your business so I'm telling you, as a friend to possible friend, keep out of it." Johnny wasn't certain how Nick would react to that retort and prepared himself for anything. Instead of jeering and demanding, Castle just smiled, aware of his position of power. The Brackett's had just aired the dirty laundry in public, once more, knowledge is power.

"None of my business, are you having a laugh? I've lost more than most because of that motherfucker, and I just keep on losing. Less than a week ago that cunt murdered my grandfather, so I ask you, how much more to I have to lose to make it my business?"

Brackett junior was about to reply when the police station front door burst open, a sweating Dan Challis fell inside, fighting for breath.

"Jesus' kid, you should be in show-business, you make one Hell of an entrance, you nearly gave me a heart attack." The doctor was trying to insert a slice of humour into a serious situation, though the blank expressions on the three younger men's faces told him his efforts were in vain. Instead, Johnny tried another take on the situation, this was the first time the three former friends had been together in over a decade. Playing it cool on the exterior, inside he hadn't finished scathing his father, but the less people who knew what happened, the less chance there was of the problem spreading, Nick could be a bastard, but he was no rat.

"Okay Danny, what can we do for you? Oh, and I was just curious, on your travels, you haven't seen Tom Daley, have you?" Playing it cool.

Challis's response told the room that his problem was far larger than a missing prisoner.

"No, I haven't seen Tom, I thought he was locked up?" The dried blood on the doctor's face made Challis curious but his own revelation carried far more weight. "Listen, what I'm about to say is going to sound crazy, but if you ignore me, there could be another victim on the horizon."

"Victim? Who?" It was Castle who responded first, he suddenly had a dark feeling, he just hoped that he was wrong. Unfortunately, that immediate fear soon became a reality. Challis responded, but he already knew how his old friend would react.

"I'm sorry Nick, but it's the girl you're dating, the Graham girl."

"Jenifer, what are you talking about, I only left her, what, twenty-five minutes ago, how the hell is she in trouble, I mean…" It was obvious that Castle was beginning to panic, denial was the first stage, Challis interrupted.

Over the next few minutes, the three men were told a story so unbelievable, they had no choice but to affirm it as the truth, no-one could right this shit. He revealed how he'd witnessed Fred Gibson, strolling care-free upon the railway station platform, without a trace of fear. His expression wasn't one you'd expect for one being in that area, plus it was early, around 6 am, it appeared he was leaving after a visit, anyone else walking on that platform would be looking over their shoulders, expecting the unexpected, for Gibson, there was no anxiety, no suspicion, no faintheartedness, and strangely for a man like the mortician, there was no cowardice.

Moving forward, he divulged how he'd headed to the funeral directors' home, and waited at the end of the street, daring himself to knock on the door. He'd been cornered by that old hag who just retired from the school and while she gossiped about nothing in particular, Jenifer Graham had stormed by, she looked in a bad mood. She was walking fast, with a purpose and Challis had watched for as long as possible, she really was beautiful, after all. She'd made in up to the end of the street and Dan's view was slightly obstructed by a parked vehicle but, Dan was certain she hadn't made it passed the mortuary. From his point of view, he would have seen her once more for a couple of seconds before she turned the corner, she never made it. Challis had fought his own cowardice and charged up to Gibson's front door. He'd brayed hard with the doorknocker but there was no response from inside. What he did hear was possibly a cry for help, but the next-door neighbours had their television on loud, had the windows open and the doubt was the cry had come from the next house along. Still, something inside told him the girl had been abducted. Challis had decided that this was too much just for his abilities, he needed back-up.

As Challis concluded his tale, Nick Castle began to head for the exit.

"Where the fuck do you think you're going?" Brackett junior hoped his position of authority would give him the edge in this confrontation but doubted it.

"Where do you think I'm going? To Gibson's of course. If Jenifer is there, I'll find her." The expression on Castle's face told the policeman that trying to prevent his exit may by seriously bad for his health. Still, he had to try.

"I think you may have forgotten; you are under arrest for assaulting a police-office?"

"You punched Johnny?" Challis was smiling, living vicariously through someone else was his speciality.

"I was provoked."

"Provoked or not, the only place you're going to is in my cells, and this time, no muppet is going to set you free." All eyes looked to Brackett senior who had suddenly become unusually quiet. Nick though, had an ace to play, and now seemed the perfect time, *knowledge is power*.

"Is that so constable? I take it your father will be my neighbour. That will be cool, we can have a catch up. You see, I've just listened to your father admit to a very serious crime. I won't go into details because I don't suppose you want Danny to know what he's done. I admit, I gave you a little love-tap, there was no serious injury, but the courts will find it fun that I knocked you down with one punch. I'll plead guilty, and if I get a reasonable judge, I'll get a £50 fine and a slap on the wrists. Your dad however, he can forget about his medical licence, that's gone immediately. Then there's the charge of perverting the course of justice, that won't be a fine, that's a custodial sentence. There'll be scandal, he'll be shunned by the residents, his life, as he knows it, will be over. Plus, the whole village will think you need your daddy to get the job done. In fact, you may be fired too, I mean, you claim not to have known your father's shady tactics but, well this happening right under your nose, that doesn't say much for the detective standards. Maybe…the whole Brackett family will be fucked." Castle paused just long enough for the magnitude of his threats to sink in, before continuing. Or, we cut a deal, if this shit with Tom goes to court, I'll say nothing, but I doubt Tom is bright enough to know a crime's been committed. Other than that, I walk free, I keep my mouth shut, no one is any the wiser…what do you think, do we have a deal? The Brackett's looked at one another and nodded solemnly, suddenly aware that they'd been beaten. Castle didn't wait for a verbal reply and started to the door.

"Wait Nick, I'm coming with you." The room was collectively shocked at Dan Challis's exclamation. "If I'd acted sooner, this might never have happened, I can't leave it like this." Castle held the door, happily impressed at his back-up. Looking towards Brackett, it seemed they were on their own. Challis dragged his withered leg, ignoring the pain, happy to be part of something. Before leaving, Castle had one more condition for the policeman-doctor combo.

"By the way Johnny. All charges against Tom Daley are dropped, immediately. That includes the love-tap he gave the good doctor, the silly bastard deserved it. We all know that the poor guy had no inclination to hurt anyone, especially a kid; if you want to act like a real policeman, then protection for Tom is better than torture."

"I won't agree to that, the stupid son-of-a-bitch could have killed me with that punch." Harry was soon cut off by his son.

"Yes, you will. You drove Tom to desperate measures. I agree with Nick, you deserved what you got. As for the other charges, consider them dropped, it's time to do what's right. But Nick, that's the last time you use this, we're even, okay?" Nick smiled and nodded in response.

"I'm not a blackmail guy Johnny. Consider us even. Lots of luck mate." Before Brackett could reply, the door was closed, the dynamic duo heading for the mortuary, the two generations of Brackett left with an uneasy silence. The only plus point for Johnny, Castle calling him mate, it had been a long time since anyone had used that word in his presence, it felt good.

Castle and Challis hurried off Main Street, along Myer's terrace and onto Station View. By the time they turned into their destination, they were shocked to notice Johnny Brackett's police-car parked outside the mortuary. As they approached, the vehicles door opened.

"How the fuck did you get here so fast?" Castle was strangely unsurprised by the officer's appearance, there was no way that Brackett was about to allow the other boys to take all the credit, were there something really untoward on Station View. Nick was surprised though, at how pleased he was to see his old friend waiting.

"I came in the car, dummy." Johnny was smiling, Challis wasn't.

"Could have fucking told us you were coming, the speed he's dragged me around here, I'm fucked now." Both his partners in crime laughed at the response and even Dan allowed himself a grin, though his leg was screaming.

"Now boys, can we have a little less bad language in public please, it's fucking terrible." All three smiled, for a moment, this felt like old times. Still, there was more important things than this frivolity.

The street was deserted, three parked cars, no passers-by, no dog-walkers. With greyish light, a faint layer of fog dropping gently, the wind had gone, there was a stifling lack of sweet air, the atmosphere acutely similar to an old hammer-horror movie, bereft of a gothic castle or fang-wielding vampire. A shiver seemed to slide effortlessly through all three participants, only Challis acknowledging the sudden chill, the others still determined to prove their alpha male status. The old wooden door up three steps before them, Nick looked to Brackett, aware his position as lawman gave him precedence over the other two.

Without needing an invitation, Brackett climbed the steps, this was why he wanted the role in the first place. Exhaling a deep breath, he scaled the first stone step, two more to ascend.

He couldn't use the Hearst, people would talk. If he'd pushed the stricken girl into a casket and she woke, it could turn to disaster. Still, she had to be moved, if those nosey bastards returned, God forbid, with reinforcements, then perhaps they might not find his treasures, they'd have to really look for those, but Jenifer Graham, she'd be harder to hide. He could tie her and gag her and stick her in the freezer, but there was always that fear, find the girl at the mortuary and he was screwed. Find her and they investigate, and he had a lot to lose, without his treasures, he may as well be dead. If they found his treasures, it would be life in prison. He had to move this bitch.

Malcolm Gregory was a Godsend. His best friend, (only friend) since school days, all he had to do was ask and there would be no questions, just direct conveyance. His delivery van was old, rickety, and stunk of meat, but it was road-worthy, on offer, and most importantly had no windows across the back.

Malcom's son had finished taking out his daily orders and had left the vehicle by the back door of the mortuary. Gibson had hurried out to greet the lad, not wanting any visitors inside. The keys were handed over, Fred even gave the lad £2 as a tip and then he pulled the van into his yard, as close to the backdoor as possible.

The undertaker had assaulted the young woman once more with chloroform, a danger after she'd vomited so violently earlier under the narcotics effects. Wrapping masking tape around her mouth, the entire roll was used, this time she wasn't going to scream. Another two rolls had been required to secure her hands and feet, and even then, he'd used two lengths of rope, tying tightly around her knees and torso (including her arms), unless she was rescued, Gibson was adamant she wouldn't escape.

Throwing her over his beefy shoulders, the mortician struggled through the buildings ground floor before peering around the exit. Seeing everything quiet and having the van's backdoors already open, he bounced the young woman onto the vehicle's filthy floor, a low murre escaping from behind her taped mouth, only her unconsciousness stopping her acknowledging the painful landing, her head crashing dangerously against the firm metal. Gibson hurried back inside the property, returning swiftly with an armful of heavy blankets.

Throwing them into the van, he clambered inside, pushing the coarse material around and under the girl. Once finished, it was impossible to tell if anything was being carried inside the van other than old blankets, a perfect disguise.

Peering out into the back street and still finding it empty, Gibson realised a guttural laugh, *this was working*. Entering the mortuary for a final time, he pulled a large thick black overcoat over his bulk, one that he hadn't used in years. Across his bald head, a black beanie-hat hid his obvious appearance and a thick rimmed pair of eyeglasses completed the ensemble. If he could have worn fake facial hair, he would have, but this had to do. Locking up his property, he took a last look at his prisoner, seeing no movement and slamming the back doors closed. To his horror, he realised that the barrier had no lock, he had to go and go now.

Scurrying across, he opened the back-gates wide, a final look, the street was empty. Hurrying back, he climbed into the driver's seat and inserted the ignition key. Turning over, the engine grumbled, and died. Once more the key was turned, again nothing more than a growl before spluttering to a pitiful end. The undertaker was beginning to panic, sweat covering his reddening brow.

"No, this isn't happening, please." A third effort, this time Gibson's hopes raised, the engine fought valiantly, grow, grow, grow, grow, gone.

"COME ON, PLEASE." An echo wafted across from the front of the property, someone was crashing hard on a door, on his door, he recognised the sound of his knocker.

"Oh God, please." The ignition turned once more...

Brackett thundered a booming crash once more on Gibson's front door, still no answer. Challis cupped his hands around his eyes as he squinted through the large bay window, there was no movement, just wooden coffins, one was laid in a central position, Dan wondered if it held a corpse, another shiver tickled his spine. At the base of the three stone steps, Nick Castle bobbed for foot to foot, the inactivity driving him crazy.

"If she's in there Johnny, the fucker is hardly likely to answer the door." Patience wasn't one of Castle's virtues. Brackett could see that something more extreme was required, but he was trying to leave breaking into the mortuary as the final option. Still, he could see the Nick needed something now.

"We're missing a chance hear. This has a rear exit, why don't you go check that out, if you can get over the gates, the back door might be unlocked." Castle's face suddenly glowed, like a dog that's just found a juicy bone. Without reply, he began sprinting down the street, finally this mission was moving forward.

"COME ON YOU MOTHER FUCKER." Effort seven, the ignition had been turned for so long, its engine was almost flooded. Pausing, he rested his head against the steering wheel, his face now wet, tears mingling with perspiration, the fat-man openly weeping.

"Fucking Malcolm Gregory, he told me this bastard was road worthy." One final effort was coming, if this didn't work, he'd need to take the girl back into the mortuary.

His fingers dripped with sweat as he grasped the key. He'd taken it out of the ignition monetarily, hoping the break would help. Sliding it slowly back into the ignition, he grimaced before turning, please let this work. A quick turn, the engine fired, could this be the time... Castle was slightly winded as he took the corner, running too hard, hard fast. Skidding into the back street, he hurtled towards the mortuary gates. Seeing the size of the neighbouring barriers, he was pleased to see that Gibson's gates were open. Finding the yard empty, Castle was momentarily shocked though he didn't know why.

In the distance, a delivery van trundled up the uneven backstreet, Nick had seen it earlier, the butcher's van, the kid who'd looked for trouble. Watching it pull away into the distance, the young man felt troubled, perhaps it was the current situation, maybe he was just seeing issues where there was none. This nagging doubt was one to many. He had been sure and began to sprint up the gravel track, hoping to catch up before he reached the main road. Even while he was running, Nick had no idea why, something just didn't seem right. As the vehicle gingerly travelled, avoiding potholes on the surface, Castle was gaining fast. The corner onto colliery lane was coming, the flat surface where the van could pick up speed, Castle was breathing hard, time was running out.

Gibson was being bounced around, inside the driver's seat of the delivery van. Still exhaling breaths of relief, the engine didn't sound too healthy, but it was moving. The road-surface was terrible, the local council had mostly washed their hands against work in Hallowell, and when they were willing to execute repairs, it was only if they were absolutely necessary. Potholes in back-streets were deemed unworthy of their time. Gibson had made enquires as to whether the residents of Station view would like to pool resources and pay privately to have the work done, but most were short term occupants, and the rest were too greedy to pay. Now he wished he'd bit the bullet and undertook the work himself; he could afford it and he'd have been able to brag to the occupants to tight to put their hands in their pockets.

Still, the street's end was coming, and it was only a short journey to the Graham mansion. Beside the girl in the back of the van, Fred had brought along an old wheelchair, an essential tool to get Jenifer along the tunnel and to the station, carrying her was out of the question and, even if she woke, she'd be too drowsy to walk. Forward thinking, the greatest weapon, a clear mind.

A mere glance into the rear-view mirror and the mortician once more began to panic. Was it true? The glass was filthy, he could barely see anything but, it was, the Castle kid was tearing up the backstreet, heading in his direction. His pace was amazing, even on foot he was gaining fast. The undertaker pressed harder on the accelerator, the speed extenuating the horrible road surface.

"What the fuck does he want? He can't know, surely?"

There were three houses left to pass, three more and then open road. But the bastard was still gaining, what if he dives in front of the van? Yes, I could run the shithead over but, I'd have to wait, or it would be hit and run. She wouldn't be unconscious for that long, Christ Almighty, I need to get away or...

The corner arrived but Castle was only two houses behind. With no time to wait, the mortician pulled directly out onto the open road, a kid on a bicycle jumped for cover but there were no other vehicles passing. The fat-man whooped for joy as he pressed down hard onto the accelerator, reached fourth gear in mere seconds. Castle had taken the corner too but as the van sped away, he acknowledged defeat and slowed to a halt. A murmur from the back of the van told Gibson that the Girl waking, not that it mattered, in minutes they'd be parked inside the Graham mansion compound, his only fear being someone seeing him enter. Knowing he had time, he was willing to wait until the coast was clear, finally, things were going his way, by the night-time, he was really going to see a murder, up close and personal.

Chapter 33

Nick Castle was breathless as he returned to Brackett and Challis. The concerned look on their faces told their own story, if Nick was back, something had happened. Playing it cool, Johnny was the first to ask for an update.

"What's occurring? I thought you were going to check out the back entrance, see if it's an entry point?" Castle's exhausted response insinuated that the speed of their actions needed to increase.

"I did. The door is locked, but if we're breaking in, it will be easier to smash than this one. But there's something else. It might be nothing, perhaps I'm just being paranoid but, (Heavy Breath pause) there was a delivery van, moving up the backstreet when I got there. For some reason it just seemed, out of place. It was from that butcher on Main Street." Challis broke in.

"Gregory's. That's owned by old Malcolm." Castle spoke sharply, pissed at losing his train of thought.

"Yes, we all know the name." Dan was equally distinct with his response.

"Yes, but do you know that Malcolm and Fred Gibson are drinking buddies? They've been best friends since their school days, they are together almost every time I go into the workingmen's club."

"Ah no, I didn't know that. Sorry Dan, I didn't mean to be sharp, it's just," Challis was smiling at his small victory.

"Fuck it, we're not six, I won't go crying to mummy, oops, just realised, I don't have a mummy, god I'm depressed." The sarcastic tone lightened the mood momentarily, but the seriousness soon returned.

"So, what was it about the van Nick? What made you think there was something unnatural about it?" Brackett maintained an air of normality to the situation, there was still a possibility that this whole thing had been a mistake, that Challis had misinterpreted the disappearance of the girl, Christ, she could be sitting back in her room at the bed and breakfast at this very moment. They had no evidence that a crime had been committed at all. The strange thing was, Johnny really, really wanted to believe that something outlandish, something inscrutable and ghastly and uncanny was occurring. Instead of giving out speeding tickets and breaking up fights on a Saturday night in the Wheatsheaf pub, this would be real police work, the reason he got into the force in the first place. Plus, there was one more reason.

Johnny Brackett's life was boring, a strange description for an officer of the law. His dream had been to police a big city, London, Manchester, anywhere away from petty small-town politics. That dream had turned to a nightmare. His father, the person who should naturally have wanted his offspring to follow that rainbow, to live the life Johnny truly wanted, had used every underhand tactic in the book, to ensure that the only dream Junior followed was the one senior had envisioned. Knowing that, as doctor and constable, the Brackett family would have a base of power, insurmountable by any other Hallowell resident. The physician had been patient while William Castle had been the law to the village, a man of his respect and stature was above even Harry's paygrade. But once the old legend had retired and knowing his son was training in the force, the doctor wasn't about to allow this opportunity to pass his family by.

It had taken longer than expected for his son to succumb to the pressure but when he finally did, senior had used every contact he had, to ensure that the new constable to Hallowell was his son. Some residents quietly questioned the move though only in private and most were surprisingly impressed at the young man's established use of his new-found authority. The job was hardly taxing but whatever problems arose, Johnny dealt with swiftly and with the minimum of fuss. And there began the complications.

Johnny wanted action, to make a difference, not sit on his arse all day waiting for someone to get drunk and take a swing at their wife. Hallowell was claustrophobic and the only crime that needed solving, that would make that difference, was out of bounds. So many times, he would sit in his police-car, just staring over at the railway station, wishing for just one chance, knowing it would never come. And that's why Johnny Brackett's life was boring. Until the last few day…

Involuntarily smiling, it made no sense but, he couldn't stop this fucking grin from invading his face. Perhaps, it was being around his old sparring partners, maybe it was just returning memories of days gone by but, he'd found himself in a good mood, even if his father had seriously messed up earlier. Just thirty-six hours earlier, the mere idea of his former friend returning to the village made him cringe. The doctor had spent a decade programming his son to feel a certain way about his former running-buddies, how they were nothing but trouble, headaches they could do without. Hell, the officer even allowed Nick to punch him in the face earlier that morning, just to remove his threat from the coming town meeting. It would have worked too, had the good doctor not gone into business for himself, stupid, so stupid. But in a strange way, senior had done his son a favour, and screwed himself in the bargain.

Inside Hallowell, the officer had only acquaintances, no real friends. The last time he had any real friends had been the time they all walked into an old, abandoned railway station together, Challis, Castle, and Scholes weren't the only losers that night. As a teen, he'd pined for closeness, which made his Halloween aftermath actions all the more compunctious. Daddy's plan for self-preservation, that same plan which helped the boy become cold and desensitised to the world, nice one Harry. Recently, he'd been thinking more and more about that night and just what he'd lost, what they'd all lost. Seeing Dan Challis now filled Brackett with regret. As kids, they'd been close as brothers, what justification could there be for turning his back on his best friend like that, just abandoning Dan when he needed him the most? Worse, it wasn't just abandonment, he'd treated the guy like shit. Watching as the disabled teen, who was crying out for attention, turned into an alcoholic man, aware that he had the power to help and instead being a huge hindrance.

Looking back now through a man's eyes, he wished he'd rebelled, turning to his father, and just saying no. Not that it would have mattered, the doctor had a way of manipulating those around him to get what he wanted, and Johnny was no exception. Sometimes, the young man wondered just how long his father had been planning for this eventual outcome. Pushing for his son to take a job he hadn't wanted, in a village he resented. Just how long had this life been planned out, without his knowledge?

Well fuck it, today he was going to police the way he wanted and screw the consequences, today, he was the law.

Castle paused thoughtfully before answering Johnny's question about the van's abnormality. Studying Brackett's face, somehow Nick could see that something in his former friend had changed. That anger, that cockiness, which had been prevalent during the arrest, had now vanished. He no longer seemed confrontational, he was receptive to other ideas, and most of all, he was treating his two partners with respect. Perhaps Castle was wrong but, he was certain he could detect a hint of excitement in there too, getting the officer away from his dark-cloud father seemed to have improved the policeman's mood. It was early days but maybe, the former could soon be taken out of his title.

Both Brackett and Challis listened intently as Nick gave a far-fetched though believable retort.

"At first, it was just another van on the road; I was probably just grasping at straws. But it dawned on me, why make deliveries to the rear when that road is so piss-poor. Plus, the lane's so tight, there's barely any room to move, no other vehicles seem to use it, it just didn't make sense, looked out of place, y know? I decided I was going to ask the driver some questions, had they noticed anything strange, had they seen Gibson that morning. It wasn't going fast, so I wouldn't have had much problem catching up. But the quicker I ran, the faster the van went. I think the driver must have seen me in his rear-view mirror, because he floored it. It's amazing the fucking thing didn't fall to bits on that surface, but it managed to reach the top corner first. I nearly caught up but, once it was on the open road, I had no chance. This might sound weird but, it was like whoever was driving was running away from me, I just don't understand why? Anyway, I caught a glimpse of the driver's side mirror. Now I know I was running flat out, and I could have been mistaken but, I'm certain it was Gibson driving." Challis and Brackett looked to one another, this whole thing was becoming more and more mysterious.

Brackett took a breath, aware that what he was about to say could change his life.

"Look, we need to be sure a crime's been committed, so here's what I'm going to do. I'll go round the boarding house, just to make sure that Jenifer's not there. Sorry Dan, I'm not dissing what you saw but, you said it happened fast and I'm about to put my career on the line here."

442

"What do you mean?" Challis asked the question both friends were thinking.

"What I mean is, if Miss Graham isn't in the b-n-b, I'm going to break into this fucking place and see if she's inside. I can't get a warrant in time, and I don't have enough evidence anyway. But after everything you two have said, I believe enough to think something iffy is going on here, and until that young woman is found, I'm classing her as a missing person. Now, this place is our best lead and since Mr Gibson isn't answering the door…well, fuck it. We just might have to open that son-bitch up. Just let me check the guest house first, okay?"

Pouncing excitedly into the police-car, Brackett sped away. With Challis maintaining a stance by the front door while Castle patrolled the backstreet, they were determined that, should the mortician return, they would know.

"Come on bitch." Fred Gibson grabbed a fistful of Jenifer's hair; he had no concerns as to what pain the young woman absorbed so long as she survived long enough to reach the railway station. Frank had given him one request, no, demand,

"Bring her to me."

The words had reverberated throughout his mind since they'd escaped the monster's lips. There'd been a slight waver in the mortician's mind, after enjoying the feeling of slapping the girl twice in the aftermath of her projectile vomiting, the urge to take his own violence further had been overwhelming. Causing another pain and suffering while they had been completely at his mercy had been comparable to orgasm, the feeling of power far greater than the degradation of the dead bodies in his care. But that urge hadn't lasted long, the undertaker more fearful of the creature's wrath than his own distorted enjoyment. Still, there was a short window of time available to enjoy what damage he could inflict before delivering his prize to her brother. Plus, there was still the opportunity to witness Frank dispatch the bitch, Fred's ultimate lifetime ambition, to watch the life force drain from another human being, rather than just deal with her flaccid remains. And that was coming soon, of that there was no doubt, there'd be no rescue, no escape, no chance. The hard work was done and now, there was only the reward, this was going to be fun.

The undertaker pulled the vehicle to the rear of the burned-out mansion to ensure no passers-by from the outer roadside could pose irritating questions. The backdoor to the van opened, through closed eyelids, the sudden brightness brought Jenifer back to her senses. The narcotic-forced unconsciousness, to which she'd now suffered twice, had lasting effects, the incredible feeling of nausea, which had caused an eruption of vomit earlier that morning, was back, though this time, she was aware her stomach contents were depleted, and her gag reflexes were now controlling a repeat reaction. There was numbness in her limbs, pins and needles made her fingertips uncomfortable and her head pounded.

This horrible man, who seemed angry enough to kill her in a heartbeat, was firing profanity fuelled commands, to which she barely understood, heaving her from the van, tearing on her hair, pushing her towards the Graham mansion remains.

With legs barely capable of taking her weight, Gibson had severed the ties across her knees, allowing her to walk but had given her a graphic warning about the ramifications of trying to escape. It was inconsequential, liberating her freedom with her current state was impossible, weakness entrenched inside every muscle. The undertaker's threat of serious violence should she not adhere to his commands were pointless, though it gave the bully yet more feelings of power.

The outer entrance to the kitchen was already open. Before being forced inside, Jenifer began to hyperventilate, her mouth still covered, her nose grasping whatever oxygen was available, inflating her lungs with fresh air, exhaling the last lingering stench of the chloroform, aware that in seconds, the clean air would be replaced by the funk of burned material.

The mere idea of re-entering the Graham mansion terrified the young woman almost as much as what this monster had in store for her. Secretly, Jenifer had required five years of counselling to combat the tragic events of her childhood, and all the troubles centred around this house. Every memory of Hallowell, both good and bad, started here. The news of her Father and brother's untimely passing had started her dark thoughts, unnatural feelings of guilt. Even though she was just a child, her psyche programmed her belief that, had she remained inside the family home instead of retreating to a new life with Martha, Martin's psychological problems may not have reached such desperate extremes, had she not left, not taken the coward's way out. That choice had ultimately been hers to make, she hadn't been forced, and in reality, it had been proven correct, the connection between herself and her adoptive parent had grown to almost as strong as the one she'd experience with her late mother. Her childhood had become safe and secure, happy, and healthy, at the same time as her birth father had lost his mind and destroyed everything the Graham family stood for. Even the revelation of her brother's passing had been difficult to take, though she'd never been able to figure out why? Their relationship was brittle at best, and frighteningly dangerous at worst, but her pure mind was of the belief that humans had the ability to change, to repent for their sins and become better for it. It seemed that Frank wouldn't be capable of putting that theory to the test and because of that, she'd mourned his passing. Had she been aware of what was to come, that sadness would have been replaced with celebration. The news of both men's demise was similar to an exclamation point at the end of a sentence, hard and abrupt.

This horrible man who had been responsible for her abduction and torture had seemed to take delight at seeing her distress at his news of Frank's survival. The fact her brother had taken refuge inside the abandoned railway station for well over a decade, that he'd been responsible for the death of so many good men and had remained phantasm-like, causing terror for the rest of Hallowell's residents; the entire scenario seemed too fanciful to believe, though that's exactly what she'd done. Why else would the mortician make up such a tale were it not true?

"Come on bitch, I told you to hurry up." Gibson snarled, pushing the young woman with both hands across her shoulders, delivered with such force, she almost sprawled onto the kitchen floor. Her collapse was only prevented by the dining table, central to the room, and incredibly, for a few seconds, she was no longer in this horrific, life-threatening situation. Instead, she was a child once more, eating breakfast across from her mother Iris, laughing and happy, one of the few memories that she'd been able to cling too. Those recollections were precious, and though she'd struggled to maintain those images in her minds-eye, being inside the mansion again made them vivid once more, a brief interlude in an otherwise nightmarish situation.

"Move your pathetic cunt, or I'll move you." The disgusting insult meant nothing to the young woman, though she felt it prudent not to test his patience. Once more grabbing a handful of Jenifer's hair, he yanked her in the direction of the doorway, deeper into the mansion, the image of Iris fading fast.

With the weakness remaining in her limbs, she once more over-balanced. This time without protection, she crumpled to the hallway floor. The mortician growled and again, tore at Jenifer's hair, hurling the girl back to her feet. Soot clung to her clothing, and made her cough, though the unpleasant substance had no means to pass the tight gag, more a reflex to what her mind believed should be happening. Along the passageway, another door was already open, one she could scarcely remember being there and as they headed in its direction, her growing feeling of despair deepened with every passing second.

There was still no sign of the mortician, and the three men had a growing concern that the missing girl was being held captive inside the parlour. The guest house owner had confirmed that Jenifer wasn't inside her room and the options were becoming less viable. Knowing there was only one way to be certain, they formulated a plan to gain entry.

It was decided that attempting to gain access from the front of the property would raise too many questions. So far, the neighbours had allowed them to go about their business undisturbed but that wouldn't last should they create a scene. Plus, the door was old and solid and, were they wrong, it would be expensive to replace. The rear of the property was a far safer option.

From the backyard, there was two entry-points. A flight of stone steps leads downwards directly to the mortuary, plus, there was a fire-escape style iron structure which climbed to an entrance to the residency. The former gave more cover from interested neighbours but again, the barrier was similar to that at the front of the property, thick and heavy and expensive to repair should they be incorrect. The raised entry-point was a combination of wood and glass and, should there be a key on the inside of the door's lock, the damage would be minimal. This became the obvious choice.

For one final time, Nick requested Brackett remain outside, his participation in the search without a warrant being grounds for dismissal from the police-force. Again, Johnny gratefully declined the offer, this was a chance at real investigation work, even if it required breaking the law to do it. Plus, the officer was unwilling to allow his friends to take the maximum risk whilst he watched from afar, he'd broken their trust once, he wasn't about to repeat the action, this was going to be a three-men job. For Challis, his relief was palpable, the chances of imprisonment lessened greatly if they were caught, and an officer of the law was present. The alcoholic's confidence in his former best-friend had still to grow, his unwillingness to accept blind faith was one of the side-effects that the last decade had taken on his personality, words came easy, actions were harder. For Castle, his only motivation was finding the girl alive, the ramifications of his actions could be dealt with later. He'd lost one woman through his naivety and ignorance and the memories of Julia Martin still burned deeply, if he could rescue Jenifer, perhaps he'd wake during the night no more, seeing the doctor's wife's face, hearing her cries…

Waiting by the street's end, Dan Challis signalled to his friends that the coast was clear. From their high vantage point at the top of the iron staircase, they checked the opposite direction too, realising the road was deserted, it was time to proceed.

Brackett had taken a hand-sized rock and with it wrapped around his coat-sleeve to muffle any sound, he cracked the door's glass window, creating a generous hole. Slipping a hand inside, he was elated to find a key, hanging loosely from the lock. Without hesitation, the key was turned, and, with a firm push, the barrier swung open. Broken glass crunched underfoot as they entered, the sound magnified by the wooden flooring. Challis hobbled up the steps as quickly as possible and once all three were safely inside, the door was closed behind them, there was no turning back now.

Jennifer Graham didn't even know this existed. The darkness was all encompassing, even Fred Gibson was unnerved, and he'd walked this tunnel countless times. The echo of scurrying vermin startled the mortician into reaching for his small pocket-torch, tucked inside the lining of his jacket, and when the bulb fired into life, both captor and prisoner breathed an audible sigh of relief. The wooden boards which adorned the passageway walls had warped overtime, adding to the undeniable claustrophobic feel, and the musty smell of mould soon invaded their senses. The icy temperature in the deep underground tunnel made Jenifer's skin crawl, if it were possible, the situation seemed to be deteriorating with every passing second.

"Move it bitch, we don't have all day." The undertaker walked two steps to the terrified girl's rear; she wished with all she was that the gag was removed, that way she could ask questions, or try to reason with this horrible man. There was so much she was desperate to learn, why was he doing this? What had she ever done to deserve such savagery? How had her brother survived in the wilderness for so long, and what was the relationship between Frank and the funeral director.

The frustration was overwhelming and to re-boot her mind, she tried to solve some of the questions she did know the answers too. His name was Fred something, she could recall that. He claimed they'd met before and she could remember that too, outside the reality office. Another question popped into her mind, had the real estate agent been in on this plot? She could have sworn she'd seen movement from inside. If that were true, how deep did this conspiracy run, how many other people wanted her out of Hallowell? The thought was too frightening to bare, and she pushed the images from her mind. A mind now filled with confusing facts and queries, the biggest being the survival of her brother. Another terrible question entered her head; did Martha know the truth? Her adoptive mother had tried desperately to convince the girl to abandon the idea and had Jenifer not been so adamant, the plan would never have come to fruition.

All of this speculation made concentration on the problems at hand so much harder, everything seemed to be conspiring against her.

"Go on move, or I'll move you." His threats were becoming less prevalent, had he wished to kill her, he'd have done it already. Self-preservation slowly began to kick-in.

Is there any way I can run?

With these restrictions and the lingering effects of the chloroform could I still out-run the fat bastard?

Did he lock the tunnel door behind us?

Confusion still reigned supreme. Along the tunnel, another artificial light glowed dimly in the distance. Not huge, just a strip along the floor, off to the right. Gibson hadn't seemed to have noticed it, but Jenifer's curious eyes soon became transfixed. Was it an exit? Had they reached the tunnel's end and the railway station now loomed large? It hadn't seemed to be that long of a walk but her rational of time and space was hard to compute.

"I told you to…" The realisation of the broken darkness ahead finally dawned upon the mortician. "He's come to meet us. It's going to happen right now; praise be to God. Maybe not God but…" Jenifer was temporarily paralysed with fear, the prospect of seeing her dead brother too horrible to comprehend. If what the funeral director had said was true, this was about to be the end of her existence, a lone tear rolled down her left cheek. "Come you slow bitch; we can't keep Frank waiting." Another push between the shoulder blades snapped the young woman from her funk and they moved forwards, everything now seemed hopeless.

"Jesus, boys, we better find something, I'm not paying for that glass." Challis's use of sporadic humour was welcome, their moods needed it.

"Okay Johnny, this is your show. How do you suggest we proceed?" It was tough for Castle to hand the reigns to Brackett, but he'd realised that you catch more bees with honey than with vinegar. Plus, should the shit hit the fan, it was policeman whose future was on the line, he was taking all the risks, he deserved respect. Content in his newfound leadership role, the officer began to formulate a plan.

"Thanks Nick. I think we should do this floor by floor; it will be obvious quickly if the girl's up here in the residency, but we still need a search. Dan, you keep watch by the door just in case Gibson comes back, Nick and I will do the first sweep."

"I'm not fucking useless, you know. I can do more than just standing guard." Challis looked legitimately pissed at what he perceived as a lack of faith. Brackett returned with a tentative reply.

"I know you're not useless Dan. But here's the problem. I've just made enough noise to wake up the dead, if you'll pardon the pun. We have no idea if that fucker is in here, perhaps he's downstairs. If he is and makes a run for it, we need to know straight away. That's why I need your eyes here, the flat will take care of itself, is that okay?" His words were delivered with just enough authority to avoid argument but with enough compassion to not sound condescending.

"So basically, you're saying that my job is more important than yours, maybe both of you two put together?" All three men smiled, the sarcastic tone in Challis's voice said that disaster had been averted. Castle slid an arm around the disabled man's shoulder.

"Dan, you're the man."

"Okay, enough of this mushy shit." Brackett had enjoyed the brief frivolity but wanted to refocus. "Nick, you take the two bedrooms and the bathroom, I'm sorry to have to say this but, check for blood droplets, especially around the sink or tub. I'll do the living room and kitchen; we meet back here in five."

The men headed to their designated areas without extra conversation, the mere idea of blood-splatter making Nick cringe. Trying to fight negative thoughts, he ploughed on. The bedrooms took little searching, everything neat and precise, beds made, clothes hung away, laundry dispensed in the hamper. Dark coloured carpets made sifting for blood-stains impossible, but still he rubbed a hand across the heavy traffic areas, finding all dry. Taking more care inside the bathroom, he inspected with forensic detail, the white porcelain of the tub and washbasin, discovering nothing. In fact, it appeared too clean, either the guy was a neat freak, or the room had recently been scrubbed from top to bottom. Even the black and white floor-tiles were spotless, no dirt, no dust, nothing. There was slight discolouration of the pale-blue shower-curtain, but it appeared more mildew than murder. Castle returned to where Challis was waiting, empty handed.

Brackett finished his search at a similar time, with similar results. Like the bathroom, the kitchen was immaculate, even the oven-hob was grime free. Red and white striped linoleum across the floor surface had been cleaned and the officer began to suspect a similar theory to the one which had invaded Nick's thought, this place was too clean. A majority of people, (especially single men) had something out of place, washing up in the sink, a dirty plate or cup upon the kitchen table? For Gibson, there was nothing, nothing at all.

The lounge continued the same traits, settee with fluffy up cushions, carpets vacuumed, furniture polished. Strangely though, this time there was one imperfection. The window central to the room, the right curtain was drawn further than the left, the net besides the glass slightly crumpled, and condensation had formed a smudge on one specific area, insinuating that someone had been watching out, breathing heavily, excited, or frightened, or both. To the untrained eye, it could easily have been missed but Brackett was a professional, he returned to his partners with a glint in his eye.

Moving on, they discovered the door at the far side of the kitchen which led to the mortuary below. The undertaker had made an uncharacteristic mistake, the barrier had been left unlocked. Descending the staircase, the atmosphere seemed to change, whatever small talk that had existed between the three men had now momentarily ceased. The shafts of light from outside were now dull and grey, the early morning brightness replaced with rain clouds and whistling winds. None of the investigators had bothered to check for a light-switch at the top of the stairwell, a mistake all regretted now. In sight was the main entrance to the mortuary with three other internal doorways completing the passageway. Of the three entrances, only one door was found to be unlocked and Challis was assigned that room to search. He cringed when discovering the main office, and a plethora of wooden caskets, all of which required examination. Coffins were a phobia, and a one which the alcoholic didn't wish to face while sober. When he was certain the other two were out of sight, Dan slyly produced his bottle of Gin from the inside coat pocket and consumed a generous swallow. Immediately, he felt braver.

Brackett and Castle moved on to the sealed entrances, hoping that the locks wouldn't be too difficult to break.

Nick's mood had taken a decidedly darker tone. This was taking too long, every moment that passed, was a moment more danger for Jenifer Graham. Perhaps it was just his usual pessimism or maybe just boyfriend intuition, but his sense of foreboding told him their pace needed to quicken.

BANG. One kick and the wood splintered. Challis rushed back into the passageway to enquire what had happened. Castle was no longer in view, Brackett just shook his head in Dan's direction, so much for the element of surprise. Nick found himself inside another small office, old-fashioned with an oak desk in the centre and not much else. A brief scout for evidence found nothing, discouraged, he re-joined the policeman. Johnny was trying to carefully shoulder-barge his entrance, attempting to break the lock without too much noise. Seeing Castle, he breathed a sigh of defeat, gesturing to his old friend to try it, his way.

BANG. Kick number two fired, door number two opened. Challis re-emerged, his own search completes without success.

"Do you two minds, there's the corpse of an old man in there, trying to get some sleep, you just woke him up." This time, Dan's humour didn't make a dent, Nick was too focused for joking. Challis looked for reassurance from Johnny, though he too was less than impressed. This was beginning to look like a waste of time, the officer had put his career on the line and for what? Still, it was too late to turn back now, the damage was done.

The room was larger than the others and, once a light-switch was found, its use soon became apparent. The smell of chemicals was unmistakable, and an aroma of spilled blood made an unpleasant combination. The area was quite sparse, bar for a long metal table in the centre of the floor and a set of shelving and cupboards across the back wall. Frustration seemed to be taking hold of Castle, a small steel stand beside the main table, which housed several cutting instruments became the object of his irritation, a kick sending it crashing to the floor.

"We're too late. We're too fucking late." The words weren't said to anyone in particular, though Brackett couldn't help feeling partially responsible.

"It's not over yet Nick, there's still the basement to search, don't give up." As Johnny slid an arm around his friend's shoulders, Dan noticed something of interest.

"Boys, what's in there?" On the adjacent wall to the doorway, three large rectangular spaced boxes stood side by side, each covered with white sheets. By the time his partners realised what he meant, Challis had removed a large bottle of chemicals from the first, the tarpaulin falling to the fall.

"Wait a minute, they are freezers. What the fuck is Gibson doing with deep freezes in a mortuary?" Brackett's interest had now peaked too and soon all three cold-storage units were in view. Heavy padlocks clasped the lids closed, the question was, why?

"That must be some expensive meat, to keep it under lock and key. Any of you guys see anything like that before?" Castle and Brackett declined to answer, just firing back concerned looks. Finally, Johnny broke the uncomfortable silence.

"Okay lads, let's find something to break these locks, we've smashed so much already today, a little more won't matter."

Fred Gibson pushed the door gently with his right boot.

"Frank? Frank, are you in there? It's me, Freddy." There was no returning voice, no sound at all, just the continued squeaking vermin from the outer tunnel, a stridency which always made the mortician wince. "Frank, if you're there, I have something for you, something special. I've done as you asked, remember? Bring her to me, that's what you said, well, I've done it, I have her here. I have your sister, just as you asked." The undertaker paused, awaiting a reply. "Go on bitch, get in there."

The odious bully, who was seemingly ecstatic at being able to force his punishing wishes upon the stricken girl, now appeared fearful himself, his unwavering respect for the monster's lack of mercy or empathy, always elicited a consistent buzz until he was safely back home. Today, it was multiplied ten-fold, after the peaks and valleys of the day's occurrences, how he'd risked his own future to fulfil Graham's command, how he couldn't be certain when dealing with the monster how the remaining predicaments of the day would play out, the undertaker found himself psychologically spent; and still, the day's main event was to come. Today would be the pinacol of Fred's debauchery, the height of his perverse ambition. But one thing had to happen to ensure that ambition came to fruition, just one thing, and he'd be able to see the soul of another leave their human body, to witness life's final seconds, the heart's last beat. To achieve that, he must survive to the day's end. And when dealing with Frank Graham, that was never certain.

For Jenifer, finding this hovel below ground was just one more jolt in a day of horrible shocks. It could only be described as an underground bunker, a hideaway, far from the outside world, though she had no idea why a place like this would ever be needed. It was obvious that Martin had been the architect, he was the only one with the finance and opportunity to create such a place, though why was a mystery. Even as a child, she knew that her father suffered with paranoid delusions, his actions and mannerisms were enough to prove that. Perhaps that was the reason for the bunker's inception, either way, she had more important matters to deal with.

Pushing the entrance wider, Gibson struck out once more at his prisoner, the ferocious blow landing at the base of the girl's skull. This time, the force was enough for the young woman to lose her balance, sending her crashing to the filthy floor. Unwilling to show weakness, Jenifer fought back tears, though the pain was considerable and the trauma unpleasant. Seeing her fall, the mortician had the temerity to laugh, as the young beauty sprawled at his feet. Was he certain of Frank's absence, the urge to kick out at her open body may well have been overwhelming, but for now, Gibson needed to be sure? Barging past the girl towards the kitchen off-shot, the mortician was momentarily out of sight. Once more she considered running, was this her chance? Thoughts exploded in her mind, could she actually do this with her wrists bound, was it worth trying when, if caught, she'd almost certainly receive a beating. Was there a better chance waiting for her at the end of the tunnel, had she not been gagged, maybe she could talk her brother out of doing whatever heinous act he had in mind, perhaps even convince the undertaker to change his plans. None of that was possible because of THIS FUCKING GAG. It was stick or twist, do or die. This was the biggest decision of her life; she couldn't afford to be wrong.

Less than five seconds and Gibson was back in the living quarters. His eyes grew wide, lower jaw dropped; this couldn't be happening; the girl was gone.

"NO, NO, NO." The funeral director scurried faster than his legs had ever carried him before. Instantly turning back towards the mansion remains, the blackness was overpowering. Could the dark be Jenifer's alley? Gibson was momentarily blind, before remembering the torch, tucked tightly into his back pocket of his trousers. Fumbling with the switch, the bulb crackled and went dead. The girl was nowhere in sight, panic began to rise inside him. "No, this is impossible, no one's that fucking fast."

Running whilst holding her breath as to make no noise, the young woman soon felt dizzy, though there was no way she'd allow herself to fall again. Looking back, she could neither see nor hear her pursuer giving chase, surely, he hadn't given up? He was a fat piece of shit but, this obviously meant a lot to him, he couldn't have thrown in the towel so easily.

This was so confusing, where was the bitch? It was a straight tunnel, noise carried, she could have only had a few seconds head-start, how could she simply vanish? He began to whimper like a naughty schoolboy, invisible tears escaping from his blood-shot eyes, it was impossible, just impossible, it just couldn't fucking happen.

He really wasn't chasing, she was certain. There were no sounds, no visuals, nothing. Still, she had no intention to slow down, this was her chance. She wondered, had that bastard locked the entrance to the tunnel behind them? She couldn't recall. She couldn't remember anything now, not that she cared. For the first time since leaving Nick that morning, something had gone her way. Did Nick even know she was missing? If that prick policeman had not arrested her would-be boyfriend, none of this would have happened. She wished with every fibre of her being that her mysterious stranger was here with her now.

The darkness was overwhelming, like a living breathing entity. It terrified her but, it was also her friend. Looking back over her shoulder, her pursuer could have been ten yards behind and she wouldn't know, she was invisible. She found herself running with her head facing in the wrong direction, her urge to watch for her captor more irresistible than seeing her way forward. Running faster and faster, almost out of control, it felt wonderful to be back in charge of her own destiny. She wouldn't just accept being a victim, she wouldn't just wilt like a summer rose in autumn, this was her chance, her escape, her...

The doorway she struck appeared from nowhere. Her head had twisted in the correct direction just a second too late, the force of the blow striking like a bolt of lightning. From believing there was a chance just a fraction earlier, it now returned to despair, she had no control over whether consciousness was lost or not, no control of anything anymore.

"Please God (he's hardly going to help). Where has she gone? Please tell me." Gibson was breathless, pains across the chest made him fearful of a heart attack. It was all going wrong, how could he allow this to happen, how could he be so stupid? Suddenly, from his rear, there was a crashing bang, followed by a barely conscious moan. Finally, the answer exploded in the undertaker's brain. His smile returned, and then a giggle escaped. The giggle grew to a laugh, a long, loud hysterical guffaw. It echoed across the tunnel's vast length, into the ears of Jenifer Graham, and just before she lost consciousness, two things became apparent. One, the increased volume told her that her pursuer was gaining ground, fast. And two, when she'd sprinted from the bunker, in a confused state, she'd taken a right turn instead of a left. The door she'd just smashed into, was the entrance to the railway station.

Chapter 34

Exiting the police station, the outside road was traffic-free. Crouching low, his head darted from left to right, the face of perspiration had nothing to do with heat, it was fear, confusion, concern, everything rolled into one terrible, gut-wrenching emotion, there was no turning back now.

Bounding quickly to the rear of Musgrave Street, on the corner of Graham Road, he scurried across the driveway to the newly built terrace of apartments, most of which were still uninhabited, passing swiftly to the cover of the treeline on the border of the village, momentarily able to take a breath, so far, so good.

Avoiding the internal roads of Hallowell was essential, should anyone see him in the open, his freedom could be short-lived. Inside the woodland, there was an element of cover, though that could be lost at any time. Scampering through the long grass, bypassing the tightly packed trees, the fresh air on his face felt wonderful, days of being imprisoned inside the police cell had not only taken a toll on him physically, mentally his psyche had been on the brink of shutting down. Now, with his freedom restored, he needed a plan to ensure that he remained on the outside, going back into that tiny room wasn't an option.

Launching forwards, he temporarily forgot his safety-first approach; two children who appeared around ten-years-of age each, were playing happily with a rope swing, a car tyre connected, hanging down in place of a seat, the first boy giggling with glee while his friend pushed with all his might. The fleeing man slid on a patch of damp earth, landing hard on his backside, the mild moan which escaped his lips had heads turning in his direction. Throwing himself flat on the ground, the children soon lost interest and continued their game, blissfully unaware of his presence. When certain to not be seen, he scrambled back to his feet, circumventing the obstacles, continuing along his path.

This area scared him. So much so that he'd always evaded it whenever possible. Back in the days when he still had his Yorkshire-terrier, Bobby, the mutt was never exercised around this space, and the one time it had escaped its leash, his former friend, Ian Gaskins had been the one to search the woodland, finding the dog chasing a rabbit. It always felt like night-time here, the trees were tall, and tightly packed, the branches looked like spikey arms of slender monsters, and the sections which weren't over-planted were covered with shadows, ominously shaped, reaching out, making his spine shiver. Unfortunately, today would need to be the exception, he had no other choice.

It was growing darker now, the sinister looking rainclouds merging to form a grey mass. The afternoon was becoming late, and he knew he had to hurry, soon it would be night-time.

It was time for a choice. It really was essential he stay hidden but, ever since the colliery disaster, he'd never been able to face returning to the scene. As a child, he'd been brave, he was a normal boy, doing what children do. After the accident, everything had changed, the courage he'd once felt, was lost, he was now a child forever, trapped in an adult's body. And with the regression came fear, fear of living, fear of dying, taking a risk only when absolutely necessary, today was one such occasion.

This was the main area of Hallowell for dog-walkers. The old building, which had stood of over 150 years was now in a terrible state, the colliery offices, the epicentre of the Graham Empire, was now another section of the village which had become derelict. The windows smashed, some by vandals with nothing better to do with their time, others by thrill seeking children, but mainly by irate families of the disaster victims, the structure, along with the mansion and the railway station, had become symbols of evil, the beginning of the end of Hallowell's innocence. He looked across the courtyard at the broken-down doorway, the main entrance which he'd used every day at the beginning of his shift, the same portal to which he'd been carried from, rescued but barely alive, the sole survivor of a horrendous tragedy. How many times had he wished that that liberation had been unsuccessful, a yearning to have passed with his workmates? Returning to a world he didn't understand, with a body which refused the most obey the most rudimentary of tasks, a brain irrevocably damaged. Tears began to steadily flow, remembering friends lost, his life stolen. To avoid the village streets, he'd need to cross this courtyard, bypass to the rear of the colliery buildings, but his body refused to obey, a mental block, an invisible barrier, to achieve his aims, there would need to be another way, taking one step closer to that place was simply impossible.

Instead, he tentatively left the cover of the woodland, peering across onto station view. The roads were quiet, no cars motoring, no pedestrians, an old woman sat on a park bench in the distance, waiting for passers-by to accost was the only person in sight. With his head still crouched, he ran headlong, aiming for the streets rear. A sudden bolt of terror, there were three men, outside the funeral director's property. Diving into a gate-free backyard, he pressed his back against the wall, eyes closed tightly, breath held, his body trembling uncontrollably. There was a sudden crash, glass smashing from above. He refused to move, body frozen, there weren't voices, no footsteps coming in his direction, had they not seen him? There were two people he didn't recognise but, one he certainly did. The same man who'd had him locked in the cells, the same man who'd refused to believe anything he'd said, and the same man whose father had been guilty of torture with the withholding of medication.

Poor Dr Brackett. Tom winced when he remembered how the physician had looked, slumped across the desk, blood oozing across the wooden surface. Was he dead? Oh God, maybe he was? Daley had listened sorrowfully at the untrue accusations levelled at him about the disappearance of the child, knowing he was innocent when all around was believing of his culpability. Now, perhaps he was guilty, the only difference being the victim's name.

"Oh God, what have I done?"

Tom detested violence, having been a victim himself on numerous occasions. Since the untrue paedophilia allegations, so many residents had looked to him as some kiddie-fiddling pervert, and as such had taken unnecessary pot-shots in his direction whenever they wished. Broken noses, black eyes, cuts, abrasions, too many to remember. Sometimes it didn't take physicality, a wad of phlegm spat in his direction, or a well aimed house brick fired through his cottage windows, mental violence could be just as destructive. Therefore, Tom abstained from confrontation at all costs, some called it cowardice, he preferred to classify himself as a pacifist, a trait he'd always been proud of. Now, he didn't even have that to cling too. Launching with beastly intentions, he'd struck out at the doctor with all his might. Seeing his reflection in the immediate aftermath, the scowl of fury and indignation plastered across his face, he hadn't recognised the person staring back. Yes, there'd been provocation, mental persecution coupled with devastating medication withdrawal symptoms had transformed him from a child-like mild-mannered objector to a raging, violent escapee. Had he not had a plan for redemption, fleeing Hallowell would have been the only option. Instead, Daley was about to gamble his life on a real long-shot.

The men attempting to find a way into the funeral parlour were suddenly successful and as Tom peered above the neighbouring boundary wall, he discovered the street was once more deserted. Breathing a sigh of relief, he ran, the terrible road surface causing the need for careful footing. With his increased heart rate, he was soon breathless, though his unwillingness to be discovered wouldn't allow him to slow. Reaching the end of station view, he crouched once more, peering tentatively around the corner onto the main highway. Henderson's guesthouse was across in the distance, a man Tom didn't recognise pulled into its small car park, climbing from the vehicle without paying any attention in Daley's direction. When the stranger was out of sight, Tom continued his wary journey.

Across a grassed area, the first of the colliery cottages were in view. A grimace grew across the agitated man's face, the brown board covering his back kitchen window stood out like a missing tooth in a clean mouth. He'd considered heading home for supplies before putting his plan in place, but it seemed an unnecessary risk now. He'd considered a searching for torch, an essential component, his constant fear of the dark more terrifying than whatever lurked in the shadows, but instead, he'd decided to head to his desired location immediately, hoping that the daylight may hold long enough to complete his search.

There was only one main obstacle now which could prevent his plan now. Cowering on the corner of Station view and Church Street, there was a wide thoroughfare road which continued around the entire perimeter of the village. It was well known for speedy drivers and, even running flat-out, it would be tough to avoid oncoming traffic. Still, there was little choice, it was passing this barrier or move through the residential streets. That would be suicide, so instead, Tom checked the farthest away points, seeing no emerging vehicles or pedestrians, he took a large intake on breath and ran.

Reaching the broken white lines of the road's centre, a dirty white Bedford van careered around the corner passing the church of St Helen and Hallowell cemetery at break-neck speed. Immediately, Daley knew the driver, Neil Roberts's father had bought the second-hand carrier to perform furniture removals while still claiming unemployment benefits. He was well known for driving while under the influence of alcohol and the way the van was weaving across both lanes, it looked obvious that this was one of those occasions. Tom had no time to think, of the two options, continuing on seemed the safer choice, back-track and he couldn't be certain the coast was clear. Plus, if he returned to the cover of Station view and Roberts had witnessed him, there would be no hiding place. Rushing forward, his momentum almost caused him to over-balance, and he stumbled while leaping upon the kerb. Somehow, regardless of the slip, he managed to keep on his feet, and in seconds, he was once more under the cover of woodland, the exertion forcing him to wretch when he was allowed the opportunity to stop. This was a nightmare, everything made him panic, his anxiety draining him of much needed energy. This was too hard.

Staggering a weave amongst the large oaks, Tom's head swam. Snatching the medication from the stricken doctor was the only choice he'd made today that made sense and even that was fighting against him. Four days without the pills had almost caused his body to seizure, the vile withdrawal symptoms almost as devastating as the accusations. When he'd snatched the bottle, it was as important to get the drugs into his system as it was to find an escape. Without a drink, he formed a wad of saliva inside his mouth to help the medication flow down his throat, but in his desperate state, he counted out double the dosage. Now, with the pain-killing narcotic spreading through his bloodstream, its effect attacked with ruthless aggression, his body numbing, motor skills impaired, brain overwhelmed. The anti-depressant element did help, the endorphins released after four days without left him with a euphoric high but coupled with the exertion, he had to fight the need to purge his system. For a man with limited mental capacity, the confusion was distressing but, regardless of the way he felt, he was aware that action was still required, no one was going to help him this time.

It was now or never. What option did he have? Walk away and it was a return to the prison cells, enter the railway station and…he didn't want to even think about what could happen inside. Another confusing element was why the hypothesis of entering the station frightened him less than seeing the colliery ruins. There was no resident bogeyman inside the mine, just a hole in the ground, bad memories, bad times, the ghosts of yesterday. This miscreation which towered before him, a dark, lifeless entity which swallowed souls with reckless abandon, a doorway to purgatory with the gatekeeper wearing a green-skull mask and carrying an eighteen-inch sharpened blade with psychotic intentions rather than a horned, red-faced demon carrying a pitchfork and going by the name Satan. To most, entering that place would be paramount to suicide but, that wasn't Tom Daley's view. Perhaps it was his child-like optimism, not having knowledge of what power true evil could do, or maybe, he was just at the end of his rope with nothing left to lose. Either way, the choice was made. Those clouds which had turned to dark grey just moments earlier were beginning to shed their contents. The meagre drizzle felt refreshing as it slid down his brow and across his flushed cheeks, only the afternoon chill spoiling the experience. The faint rumble of thunder away to the east was less appreciated. Tom had always been more fearful of the harmless crashes than the bolts of lightning, perhaps it was because when the streaks appeared, they would break up the night-time darkness, he hated the darkness.

He'd seen this quasi-entrance, the vandalised hole in the fencing, countless times, though had never felt the compulsion to pass further. Today, things had changed, there was a need now. The stories of the bad man who lived inside the railway station and killed people for fun were common tales, children would whisper and pretend to have seen him, others had lied and claimed to have entered and lived to tell the tale. Tom knew most stories word for word, another reason his fearful heart had ensured the derelict building was way out of his bounds. But now, he'd convinced himself that they were just that, elaborate stories, Chinese whispers added too each time they were re-told. There was a resident bad man, he'd seen as much the night Neil Roberts had been taken but, surely, he wasn't all bad, surely hurting a defenceless child was a step even the legendary Frank Graham wouldn't take? And if that were true, perhaps it would see Tom in a similar fashion? Not as a threat, for Daley was no threat. Just a childlike innocent who was there simply to rescue the boy, to save a life, was that so bad?

The plan he'd formulated; find a safe place to enter the railway station without being seen by any of Hallowell's residents. Swiftly search the inside, avoiding the bad man, being ready to run if he had too. Find the child alive, rescue him from the clutches of the bad-man, escape, and return Neil Roberts to his family. Simple.

Afterwards, all the people of Hallowell would see Tom differently, for what he really was. There would be no more accusations and lies, he'd be able to walk the streets safely without the horrid abuse, no more name calling, no more beatings, spitting in his direction, no more fear. His home would be free of vandalism, there would be no more people taking his things, smashing his windows, and breaking into his garden shed.

They'd see he was a good-boy, mam and dad always said he was a good boy. Maybe he'd be able to watch the kiddies play again, this could be brilliant.

Tom's heart was racing but whatever fear may have accumulated in his psyche was suddenly gone. A cheeky grin scrawled across his face, his plan was going to work, a fresh start, child-like excitement filled him. The whole of his body was twitching, the hysteria of the occasion becoming too much to hold inside.

"WOOO." The outburst was irrepressible, the buoyant feeling inside made him want to scream louder and louder, "WOOOO… Oh no, I must calm down, I have a job to do, afterwards, we'll celebrate."

The aperture in the fencing served no problem, Daley slid the right leg though onto the station ground, pulling the head and body inside before slipping the trailing leg in too. He felt fit, he felt strong, the double medication had now lost its woozy feeling, replenishing his soul to its regular high, the pills weren't really for pain anymore, they were his own little, private addiction. Not a lot, just enjoying the buzz they gave a little too much.

"Dr Brackett didn't know, he thought it was just for my aches and pains, the aftermath injuries of the colliery disaster. What he didn't know, I have very little pain anymore, the pills made me feel good, that's why it was so bad in prison, no pills no anything, Today, I feel good, and I have a plan."

Staggering slightly, Daley launched past the final trees, onto the railway station grounds. The cautious nature in him made watching out for other residents still vital. Leaning across a final oak tree, his scanned the area, seeing no one, the coast was clear.

Tom hated the clothes he was wearing. When he was arrested, he had on a blue boilersuit, old and raggedy, of the two pockets around the crotch, one was torn and hung loosely, the left knee was ripped too, it was only for gardening. When Constable Brackett had arrived, he wasn't waiting for a change of clothes, it was in the car, in the cells, no questions.

Now, after the adventure, when he'd found little Neil and took him home, it would have been nice to be dressed properly. Maybe people would take pictures, he would be a hero, after-all. That grin was getting wider, I'm a good-boy, no I'm the best boy. Pushing away from the final oak, he strode forward, confident, bold, courageous, a winner…

Gravel kicked under his shoes; the walkway was taken quickly. The darkening sky was a worry but, this was going to be easy. The platform was there, the next step…

Over, inside the woodland, rested, hidden, on the stump of a tree, a rolled-up cigarette half smoked between his lips, a can of Stones-bitter in his right hand, Mick Castle sat waiting. His son had been missing since early that morning and this was a possible location. Staring across at the railway station, he saw the figure of a man, middle aged, badly dressed in a scruffy boiler suit, four-day stubble and an inane grin on his face. Staring closer, he recognised the figure, Tom Daley. Poor Tom, been a victim all his life, will be a victim till the grave. Mick rose, took a breath, ready to call out, to stop this insane expedition but…

"That's not my war." Shaking his head solemnly, Castle drained the remainder of the bitter before crunching the empty can angrily between his fingers. Throwing it down, amongst several overs, he reached into a white plastic bag, magically appearing was another full one. Snapping back the ring-pull, froth foamed as he lifted it to his lips, a generous measure sliding smoothly down his throat.

458

"Anyone else, fuck you. I've had a bet with myself, sometime today, my lad will be here. I am fucking no it. If he does, I'll be ready. Until then, I have eight little friends to keep me company." The bier was flowing well, Mick Castle was determined, his son would never walk alone.

Chapter 35

The Unthinkable was happening, what was before them was so unexpected, so unbelievable, so indefinably horrific, that words could barely describe such debauchery, it had taken time for the magnitude of the situation to be revealed, but when it was…

Bracket was the first to step away, the events momentarily fracturing his thinking, a stagger backwards, the white wall saving him from crashing to the floor.

"You okay, Johnny?" He heard the phrase leaving Dan Challis's lips but only returned an incomprehensible stare, the notion that things would ever be okay again seemed overly distant, this was the worst thing to happen since…this village really was cursed.

All colours had drained from his face, shoulders drooping, air escaping from his lungs, he felt small. Johnny Brackett felt small, tiny, nominal, expendable, facing the biggest test of his life. He'd wanted this, prayed for this, he deserved more than Saturday night punch-ups, giving parking tickets when some numpty on double-yellow lines, playing mediator to warring neighbours, it was boring, stifling, monotonous. Sitting in that bastard office, doing paperwork that meant fuck all.

Since taking the job, he'd been to court once, 14-year-old Bob Dagger had been caught house-breaking but instead of just raiding the valuables and seeking cash, he'd caused damage, lots of damage. Spray paint across every wall in the house, profanity that would a docker blush, a black marking-pen had been used to draw pictures of penis's, boobs, even a crude attempt at a woman's genitalia, a large expensive-looking mirror in the living room, his sketchpad, it had taken time, the entire thing was full. A Stanley knife with a brand-new blade was used to slice through the leather of the settee, both matching chairs suffering the same fate. No ornaments had been broken, though the temptation must have been crushing, he was clever enough to know that damage of that kind would be loud, draw unwanted attention and as the visit had been during the night, the neighbours would surely have been on the telephone to Brackett and that wouldn't do, he wanted to enjoy this, take his time. Drinking a large bottle of wine from the fridge had given the boy a buzz, upping his excitement, pushing him on with his mission. The shower curtain was torn down, the bathroom eviscerated with toothpaste, shower gel, shampoo, squirted in every direction. He'd giggled like a five-year-old while pissing upon the master bed, the excrement in the wardrobe was hidden, diarrhoea splashed across dresses and into the shoes on the base, the stink ensuring the young thug closed the doors rather than suffering the rancid stench. After the alcohol really took hold, the boy rested upon the slashed couch. He got so comfortable; sleep came naturally.

He was only woken when the homeowners returned, the screams from the lady of the house at seeing the devastation, her husband ran from room to room, hoping to find the culprit, shocked at seeing the 14-year-old curled up in their lounge. With a natural reaction of disgust, Thomas Wallace beat the living shit (whatever shit was left in him) out of the lad. Strangely, the kid hadn't even tried to defend himself, just happy to take a beating. When his wife had pulled her husband off, the lad was unconscious. Her screams had alerted the neighbours, their weekend sleep-in disturbed by the horrified yells and Brackett arrived post haste. At first, he worried boy lad was dead, a broken nose had disrupted his breathing and the blood that covered Bob's face made finding details difficult. An ambulance arrived quickly, taking the pressure off Johnny's first-aid skills. The state of the house was disgusting, and he felt for the owners. He felt even worse at having to arrest Thomas Wallace. Even though the little bastard deserved what he got, the law said that this was an assault. Even worse, an assault on a child, this could be serious.

The law is an ass.

The court date came, it took twenty minutes for the judge to give the kid a 12-month suspended sentence and a £20 fine. TWENTY FUCKING POUNDS. The damage to the house ran into the thousands, the owners were considering moving, the memories too devastating. A kid they didn't know had torn through their home for no reason other than to amuse himself. It was a despicable situation, but that wasn't the end of the nightmare. Thomas Wallace was facing real prison time. No one would ask questions; he was a grown man who'd assaulted a child. His court date was a month away, Johnny had offered to speak on his behalf to which had been accepted readily. Should anyone deserve a good kicking, it was Bob Dagger.

Johnny's biggest case so far...until today.

The three men had begun their own individual searches, the padlocks snapped, freezing air rising from the enclosed iceboxes. Initially, they'd decided to check each as a group, one at a time, but Nick was growing impatient, keenly aware that every second could count in the rescue of Jenifer. Therefore, they each took an assigned freezer, not expecting to find much. They were wrong.

Freezer number 1. Dan Challis.

He opened the lid tentatively, his usual caution seemed prevalent today. Originally staring without touch, there seemed little out of place. The six feet, by four feet, by four feet dimensions appeared to be packed with joints of meat, individually wrapped in white plastic supermarket carrier bags. Inside, there was expertly prepared pieces, well severed, rolled with the skin still on, tied with butcher's string. Dan was no meat expert, the closest he came was sausage and bacon sandwiches at the lunch-box café, so acknowledging the origins of the joints was tough. Though the meat was frozen and had taken on a blue tinge, it seemed originally that outer-skin was a creamy-white. Surely, it must be pork. Recalling in his deepest memories, he envisioned the flesh on chops and roasts, just like mummy used to make. Yes, that must be it, lots and lots of pork, the only other flesh that had a colour like that was…

Dan was growing nervous, he was right, wasn't he? The other option was too horrible to believe. "Surely it couldn't be…that? Human skin was darker, wasn't it? Yes, of course it was, the fat fucker just likes pork, pig meat for a pig. That makes him a cannibal. Oh fuck…looking at this, that maybe the case, maybe this is…food."

Staring tentatively, he knew it was time to believe? Nobody eats that much pork. The joints were hard to move, the frost clinging them together, plus many were heavy, heavy as bodies? Peaking across at his colleagues, it was obvious that just looking wasn't going to get the job done. With force, Challis pulled the meat apart, his curiosity to witness what lay deeper pushing him on. When he completed his task, he suddenly wished he hadn't.

Below the prepared meat, there were clear plastic bags. Dan's body began to quiver as, even from the first glance, it became obvious of their contents. Eyeballs, lots and lots of eyeballs, human eyeballs, lots, and lots of human eyeballs. They weren't frozen in the form of sludge, meaning they had been taken at different times from different victims, as the new ones were added, the others were already frozen solid. This made the vision worse, lifting the bag from the deep-freeze, they moved, rattled, many appeared to the rear of the eye, and looked dark red with severed veins hanging stiffly, but others, the pupils, staring, it immediately felt like they were watching, directly into Challis's face, into his soul. He pushed the bag away, almost spilling the contents on the floor. The image was overwhelming, a mixture of shock, disgust, and strangely, fear. He knew he shouldn't be afraid, there was three of them against one fat bastard, but he couldn't help it. Still, he tried to control the gentle quiver, the bigger chore, hiding it from the boys.

Digging deeper into the freezer, the next discovery was ears, lots, and lots of human ears. They ranged in colour, size, age, some had residual skin where the amputation had been a little messy, others had thick entrails from the rear, again the culprit finding a simple theft quite difficult. For whatever reason, these weren't as horrific for Dan to take, strangely, he showed a keen interest in the variation. One had eardrum hair, grey and whispery, with withered skin across the globe insinuating that its owner had been an elderly gentleman. He remembered the image of Bill Castle before his death, and wondered…

The final three plastic bags contained other facial features, noses sliced off at the septum, lips sheared away crudely from chin to nasal passage. The seven tongues, which were almost enough to fill an entire carrier, barely seemed human at all, resembling a series of deceased eels. Cut with surprising precision, they stretched from the tongue's tip to the rear of the throat, far longer than one may expect and a severely repulsive vision. Challis pondered, animal tongue is seen by some as a delicacy, had Gibson seen these as merely souvenirs or were they part of his diet?

When finished, Dan waited silently, aware that his partners were probably discovering enough horrors to rival his own, this whole situation stimulated a varying range of emotions. This entire thing should have repulsed him and to a point, it did, but there was more than just repulsion. They could now authenticate that Fred Gibson was a sick motherfucker and that created a weird feeling of happiness, plus, Dan was still a man terrified of confrontation so there was still fear added too…but most of all, for the first time in years, he had excitement. He knew it was wrong but, for so long his life had seemed meaningless, but now, he was a part of something, something big. Strangely, an instantaneous grin spread across his face, his inquisitive nature started him wondering just where this could lead.

Freezer number 2, Nick Castle.

As Castle ended his investigation, he felt the strangest emotion, one that didn't fit his recent discoveries, Nick felt relief. An appeasement that overpowered all other sentiments, because the remains before him were not those of Jenifer Graham. As for the disgust he felt, that could wait.

On opening the lid to the ice-box, he'd cringed before witnessing anything, his mind was automatically programmed to see what he expected, the perfect looks of the girl he was quickly falling for, her pale skin turned to an unpleasant shade of blue, glistening with frost, lifeless eyes staring back, her full soft hair turning brittle and hard, her slender limbs crunched and distorted Instead…he found feet, lots of feet, assorted, male and female. The lady's paired, given special treatment, some had painted nails, carefully brushed with multi-coloured varnish. Others were left pure, posed naturally before freezing. All were placed inside protective clear packaging. The men were thrown inside haphazardly, allowed to receive freezer burner, no care, no attention. Most were from old men, the first steps of a sick mind, stealing body parts from those who wouldn't miss them, rough-cut souvenirs.

Below the feet, they were more layers of human artefacts. Similarly to the feet, most male hands (not all) were scattered as singles and not packaged in any way. Ranging from teens to old men, it didn't seem to matter, these were easily stolen appendages which Gibson had seen as a work in progress. The women were once more given attention, all paired, decorated with nail varnish, some with the rings they had died wearing. Nick winced when he saw one specifically, which had been posed in a troubling position. The fingers had been curled, wrapped around just tight enough to squeeze a pathetic little penis into, in a sick masturbatory aid. Castle couldn't be certain but…

Across the base of the freezer there were legs. The feet severed, some amputated at the knee, others (women's) at full length, bent so they fit. There were eight. None were wrapped in protective packaging so the skin was ice-burned, much of the flesh clasped tightly to the sides of the freezer, should any require removal, a total de-frost would be essential.

After closing the freezer, Castle certainly felt disgust, but thankful, there was still no sign of Jenifer Graham. It was impossible for her to be the victim of any of the amputated artefacts, the undertaker hadn't had time and everything inside was frozen solid. A shudder spread across his body as a hideous thought invaded his thinking. If they didn't get to her soon, then one day the girls' remains would surely suffer the same fate.

"Johnny, are you okay?" Challis asked the question a second time, though he had no idea what answer he'd receive. The policeman felt weighed down, like his life had been directed to this one exam and he hadn't revised. All eyes would turn to him now, he was the law and as such, things would need to be done properly. Unfortunately, after what he'd just witnessed, he had no idea what properly really meant.

Freezer number 3, Johnny Brackett.

Of the three, this icebox carried the most personal of human remains and as such, was the hardest to investigate. Inside were full black dustbin-liners, tied with knots, making viewing tough, but instead of fighting with the ties, Johnny tore into the plastic with his thumb, ripping an extended hole in the material. Swiftly pulling his head away in repugnance, he hadn't seen what was before him yet, but his exploring hands told him all he needed to know. For inside was a wide array of male penises, once more varying in size and colour. Some had the testicles removed, others remained. A quick glance inside added to his disgust, the numbers were scores and probably dated back several years. Brackett didn't feel the need to investigate the bag's interior further and, to ensure the plastic didn't split further, Johnny carefully lifted it from the freezer and placed it at his feet on the floor.

Another bag, similar in size but carrying additional, weight was investigated next. The officer paused before creating another hole, not yet ready to witness the continued horror. Aware he had no choice, Johnny tore a small rent in the material with his thumb, before sliding fingers from both hands into the split, pulling until there was a gap large enough to see inside. Once more he winced, as the hidden artefacts were quickly revealed to be yet more personal body-parts. On this occasion, it was a sack full of female breasts, sliced off surgically with neatness and precision, again ranging in age and size. This time, he decided to explore more in-depth, tearing the plastic so to see further detail, Brackett noticed that many were from old women, the skin wrinkled, the masses more pronounced. It was now he discovered something even more troubling, a few hidden deeper were without nipples, bite marks indented into the affected area. On one such affliction, blood had run from the wound, meaning that there was a chance that the victims may have been still alive whilst the atrocity took place. Johnny could feel anger growing deep inside, there now seemed a good chance that Gibson was not only a sick grave robber, but he may also be a murderer too.

Again, the second bag was placed on the floor, freeing up his vision towards insides of the freezer. It now appeared far was less organisation, just a series of differing body parts, most of which appeared as mere trophies, thrown inside without any thought or care. A pair of large breasts which had been too big to accompany their neighbours were part of the mix, heavily tanned which insinuated their origins being a lady of colour, once more, a single nipple missing, heavy indented teeth marks accompanying the disappearance, though this time, there seemed very little blood seepage from the wound. Brackett was thankful for small mercies. There were hands, feet, another selection of male genitalia, and a leg, the foot still connected, which had been severed at the knee. A white supermarket carrier-bag, twisted at the handle made the policeman pause once more, and when the knot was untied, Johnny reeled in abhorrence at the remains before him; the complete head of a young man, a teenager, skin carefully preserved, handsome features, with golden-brown hair and blue eyes. The amputation had taken place directly below the chin as to not waste space and the wound cauterised with a hot blade. Tying the bag once more, it seemed impossible to believe anything could top the revulsion Johnny Brackett felt at that moment, but one final manifestation that exploded before the officer's eyes destroyed everything which had come before.

In the base of the icebox, buried under various other remains, a tiny right foot came into view. So small, the policeman barely noticed its miniature toes, wrinkled skin across the sole, diminutive ankle bones, and the start of a leg, which was buried deeply. Something screamed in Johnny's brain to look no further, his troubled psyche struggling to cope with anymore unearthly visions, but the investigator inside wouldn't allow him hide. Pushing away the human debris, the full horror began to reveal itself. The right leg grew longer and soon, the left was in sight too, as it had been hidden due to its acute angle. Now, the entire lower portion of the child could be seen, a little boy. Moving away more coverage, suddenly the whole body was visible, just the head left unseen. Sliding his hands around the infant's lower legs, Brackett tugged at the remains, but frost held them firm. Terrified the body may sever, he withdrew and begun once more removing debris from above. The adult leg which had been severed at the knee was also stuck fast on the freezer base, making rescuing the infant remains more difficult, leaving the officer with a difficult decision to make. Damaging the leg could accentuate the loss of vital evidence but, content that there was more than enough evidence to procure a conviction, Brackett decided that freeing the child's frozen remains was more pressing. Therefore, with both hands gripping tightly around the calf muscle, he heaved with all his might, tearing the icy flesh from the frozen base. The adult leg ruptured, a laceration forming across the muscle, but thankfully the limb was torn away from the ice-encrusted bottom, skin being left behind. Only now, could the true horror of the situation finally be revealed.

It wasn't a child, just a mere baby. From the size, Brackett estimated its age no more than twelve months. There seemed no outward injuries, the infant appeared well fed, and the cause of death implied a mystery. The officer's eyes were transfixed on the tiny corpse, finding it impossible to accept how someone could be so callous as to leave an innocence infant's remains to freeze in the bottom of an icebox. For God's sake, the poor little mite just looked like it was just sleeping. Its eyes were closed but not in a pained expression, the arms crossed over the chest, it looked so…peaceful. The colouring had obviously changed, the regular pinkish tone replaced with a bluish complexion, frost glistening in speckles across its naked body. But, regardless of its colouring, the tiny child just looked in a comatose dreamland.

And that was what made Johnny want to scream. To yell and cry and tell the world, "FRED GIBSON IS A FUCKING MONSTER, HE'S A PERVERT AND A MISCREANT WHO DESERVES TO BE SHOT. NO, DEATH IS TOO GOOD FOR THAT BASTARD. I HOPE HE LIVES A LONG AND PAINFUL LIFE, ROTTING IN A PRISON CELL, WITH EVERY CONVICT INSIDE KNOWING EXACTLY WHAT HE'S DONE. HE WARRANTS BUTT-FUCKING IN THE SHOWER, DAY AFTER DAY, AND TORTURE NIGHT AFTER NIGHT. FUCK YOU FRED GIBSON."

This situation, it was mind blowing. Obviously, the undertaker had been keeping trophies from those in his care, though Christ knows how long this had been going on for. Then there was another thought; are any of these people murder victims? And if so, was Gibson responsible? That image of the tiny baby, its entire body frozen, the grieving parents, whoever they were, had probably cremated a log, or maybe house bricks, the ashes of the child they had lost, replaced by timber. It was difficult to believe, but it had happened. Johnny's eyes dropped to the floor, he needed time to process this.

The other two men joined Brackett, their own thoughts battling common sense against this situation. Suddenly, their self-imposed silence was broken.

CRASH.

"What the fuck was that?" It was Dan who asked the question, though again, an answer wasn't expected. Nick responded, his disheartened feeling at finding no sign of Jenifer suddenly lifting, perhaps this was her way of calling for help.

"I haven't a clue, but it came from the basement." Without the need for more words, the trio bolted for the exit, aware that the only entrance to the lower floor came from the back yard. Stumbling down the iron staircase, Castle lead the way, no longer waiting for permission to assault the outer door first. It needed three stiff kicks, but the lock finally gave way, the heavy wooden frame fracturing, the door smashing loudly into an interior wall.

The atmosphere was gloomy, disturbed dust-mites swirling in the air before them. A strong smell of must insinuated that this was a room, not regularly used. An aluminium stepladder was spread across the floor, the origin of the earlier crash becoming obvious, though how it had lost its position was harder to figure out. The area was sparse, bar for a walk-in refrigerator unit looming large of the furthest away corner. The whirring of its motor told the men it was still in working order, though why was a mystery, surely the storage of bodies awaiting funeral couldn't be used in such a depressing and uninviting location.

"Jennifer?" Castle called out though knew not to expect a reply. The room would need little in the way of searching, except for the fridge; all three were apprehensive to progress forward, but knew it was a necessary task. Nick breathed out a worried sigh but still took the lead, his partners happy to abdicate the role, neither wishing to find further horrific discoveries.

The unit's doorway was closed with a heavy, iron, locking rod, the mechanism needing force to allow entry. Castle tugged harshly, expecting more resistance, the door flying open with the first thrust. An interior lightbulb automatically fired into life, making the three men squint. When they discovered its hidden monstrosity, their heads instantly turned away in disgust.

The distorted body of Angela Loomis, the undertaker's prized souvenir, the only adult figure that he'd had the courage to keep intact, hung from a butcher's meat-hook, the spike piercing the young woman's spine at the rear of her neck. The once angelic skin now anamorphic, perverted with the heat of the earlier blasting radiator, her long dark locks hiding a face, gnarled, beauty lost forever. For a brief few seconds, Nick panicked, the terror that came from uncertainty, the hair was different to Jennifer's but in that moment, he saw only the female form. Rushing to see the face, he was unashamedly relieved to find a stranger's lifeless eyes staring back. Dan Challis feared receiving an answer to his next question but asked anyway.

"Christ boys, just how fucked up is this guy?" Terrifyingly, neither Brackett nor Castle felt confident to venture a response.

Chapter 36

"Oh, Miss Graham?" This was going to be fun, real pleasure without danger, without interruptions, there was no escape now. "Miss Graham, are you hurt?" The words just oozed from Fred Gibson's sleazy lips. "Don't you worry, Miss Graham, I'll be with you shortly."

The undertaker had laughed, roared uncontrollably, when he realised the young woman's mistake. Taking one simple wrong turn, that's all, turn right and speed away to freedom, Fred wouldn't have had the energy or the fitness to give chase, the exit wasn't locked, the damn thing didn't lock, it was just one long tunnel and at the end, daylight, fresh air, immunity from the mortician's devious plan, exemption from her brother's anger, liberty just a right turn away…and the bitch turned left.

Fred had stumbled forward, out of the room, certain his prisoner had escaped, whimpering with self-pity, wondering how he'd fucked up so badly? Running until his breathing would allow no more, he grasped his chest, he'd had pains in the heart before, but he put it down to indigestion, this was worse. It brayed a hard rhythm against his ribcage, leaning again the tunnel wall, he tried to control his breathing, but every time it seemed to slow, a vision of that bitch running away would start it pumping again. It hurts, it really hurts, this is how I'm going to go, a cardiac arrest in a fucking tunnel, no one will find my body for years, I've so much more I want to do, so much more I want to see, so much… BANG.

The crash was followed by a low whimper, and then silence. Immediately, the undertaker's breathing became controlled, his pulse slowed, his frightened, pained expression across his face turned to relief, she wasn't lost, she was fucked.

It had been that final shot at freedom, a chance she hadn't expected, a chance she was going to take. It had been mere seconds; Gibson had gone out of sight just long enough to run for it. Jenifer never classed herself as athletic, but today, she would run like the wind. Her hands were bound, but her legs were free, speeding for the door, that horrible man didn't even see her go; she'd dived out into the darkness and ran, freedom felt wonderful, the wooden slates across the floor were unsteady so watching her feet was essential. She glimpsed out before her, it was total darkness, but that darkness was good, it would keep her safe, safe from him. The echo of that man scurrying out into the tunnel rebounded off the wooden walls, she knew he was coming. Her legs wouldn't quit though, every stride felt a stride further away, his voice, all those horrid insults and threats, they were fading too, was she really running so fast? Who cares? Who cares about him, this wasn't about him, this was her, rescuing herself, finding her own freedom, it was head down, run forward, fuck the world? A swift looks over her shoulder, only darkness, he was long gone, she smiled, her head returning to a forward position, her speed still strong. The smile widened, her eyes closing monetarily, and then... BANG.

The doorway was rock solid, locked with only Gibson possessing a key. She'd struck the heavy wooden surface with such force, her head taking much of the impact, that falling into unconsciousness for a third time in one day seemed probable. It came from nowhere, she'd been running with such speed, taking more interest in her tormentor than direction, that realising she'd taken the wrong turn from the underground bunker still hadn't registered. Beginning the gradual fall to the ground, she gazed at her surroundings, barely conscious, had this been animation, there would be stars floating around the girl's head. Instead, a large gash across her forehead was beginning to swell, a trickle of blood sliding down her nose, dripping to the floor. Not that she felt much, the shock of the impact working as a natural antistatic, the pain would come later. She could hear laughing but it seemed far away. Sliding down gently against the wooden door, she felt no fear, she felt no pain, just the beautiful enveloping arms of dreamland, the world was drifting away.

"I'm sorry Nick, I'm really, really, sorry." Castle may have been sceptical at the policeman's sincerity and well-rehearsed words alone could have added further doubt, but his genuine expression would have been harder to execute. For now, he was willing to listen though, Nick still looked upon this as a setback only, he wasn't about to give up yet.

"It's not your fault Johnny, we've plenty left to do, we're not beaten yet, are we?" When the current expression was replaced with one of confusion across the officer's face, Nick began to grow increasingly concerned. "What's that look for? We do have plenty of options left, don't we?"

"Nick...listen. I wanted this to work out, I really did, honestly, it sounds strange, but I've enjoyed working with you guys, it was like I had my friends back. Unfortunately, we're looking at a bigger problem."

"What the fuck are you talking about Johnny? What can be bigger than saving a girl's life?" This was the first time Nick had forced the issue, feeling he needed back-up to achieve his aim of rescuing the girl. He wasn't here to catch the bad guys, that was Brackett's job. He was here to save Jenifer, anything else was a bonus.

"Listen Nick, I know how much this means to you but, you ask what's bigger than saving a girl's life? How about saving lots of girl's lives?" Brackett hadn't wanted this confrontation but deep down, he knew it would come, alpha male against alpha male. "This is the problem." He paused, giving the next statement the due respect it deserved. "Horrible as it may sound, the chances are, Jenifer is dead, you may not wish to admit that, and I hate admitting that but, it probably is the truth. Being held in here was the best chance she had, that's why I okayed the break in." Another pause ensued, though Castle decided to let his friend finish before delivering a retort. "And there lies the second problem. When I took part of this break-in, it was an unlawful search. Therefore, in the eyes of the law, Gibson is innocent."

"How can that be?" It was the first interruption, Dan Challis had allowed himself, aware of his role as the third wheel, and accepting it without argument. Castle shared the same question but was happy Challis seemed to be falling on his side.

"Because, without a warrant, anything found cannot be used, it's classed as inadmissible in a court of law, Understand? The only evidence against him, and I don't mean any disrespect to you here, is the word of a known alcoholic, against a well-respected businessman."

"Well respected businessman? You have got to be kidding? The guy is a creepy pervert and that's not just because of what we've found tonight. Everyone in the village knows it, most people hate his guts, he's a pompous, self-righteous mother fucker who, by the way, drinks almost as much as I do, the bastard is in the club, propping up the bar, nearly every night."

"That might be so, but it doesn't change the facts, hearsay isn't going to cut it, courts need evidence, and we don't have any." Brackett was desperately trying to keep his cool, but it was becoming increasingly difficult.

"No evidence, are you fucking kidding, there's three fucking freezers full upstairs." It had been a long time since Challis had felt this passionate about anything, he wasn't about to let this lie without a fight.

"Are you listening to anything I'm saying? We can't use it; we were supposed to be in here in the first place."

"Okay, I get that we can't take this evidence into court. But I don't see why we can't take photos, a jury couldn't argue with pictures, could they?" Challis was growing angry at his seeming irrelevance to this situation, being talked down to like a cowering child with a stern father, it was starting to piss him off. "We photograph everything we've seen here, there's not a jury in the world that wouldn't convict that piece of shit." Castle stood by and waited, his mind already preparing a retort for what he knew was coming.

"Dan, listen, to, the, words, coming, out, of, my, mouth. We can't use photos, we can't use video, rumours, or carrier pigeon. It's all inadmissible. Without the legal forms, it does not exist. Now please listen to what I'm about to say and don't interrupt until I'm finished and I'm talking to you here as well here Nick. Just let me finish before busting my balls. This might sound strange but, I'm not afraid of dying. Honestly, you can believe that or not but when I took this job, I knew it was dangerous, and when I got the role of constable for Hallowell, I knew something like this could happen at any time, that fucking railway station casts a dark shadow over the whole village. Now, if there was still a way to save Jenifer, I would risk everything to do it, that comes with the job. But miracles rarely happen and that's what it would take to rescue her now, a fucking miracle. We gave it our best shot, we were just too late, she's not here anymore. If we are right, and there's a connection between Gibson and Graham, and he's took her to the station, she's dead, plain and simple."

"But…"

"Nick please, just let me finish. Now I'm sure you would have no problem hunting the station, chasing any possible sight or sound, just in the million to one shot that you could get her out alive but Nick, Frank Graham is no kidnapper, he won't want to talk out their issues, share out the assets, if Gibson has taken her there, she is dead. But I still understand your point of view and sympathise, I honestly do. And I also know that you are so pig-headed that, whether I'm with you or not, if there's a doubt in your mind that you can save her, you'll do it anyway, even if it means risking your life alone. So, here is my offer, if you're set on heading over there, I'm with you, but you have to give me one hour first. I'll stand by your side brother, shoulder to shoulder, there's weapons at the police station we can use, but I need one hour." Castle was understandably shocked and a little relived, but had to ask,

"What good does an hour give you?"

"Here's the thing. I have one fear and it's not going in that place. I'm terrified that Fred Gibson gets away with what he's done. As I've said, at the moment, we can't use anything we've seen in here as evidence, but I might have a way of getting around that." Nick was becoming interested.

"How?"

"My father might be a dick sometimes but, he does have connections. One of his best friends is a guy called Raymond Spade. Actually, his proper title is the right-honourable Raymond Spade, he's a crown court judge, lives in St Mara, works out of Carpenter. He and dad are close as brothers, dad delivered his two daughters, so he owes him. One call from Dr Harry Brackett should be enough to get a back dated warrant, and then we're in business. It's Saturday today, so hopefully, he's at home, he shouldn't need to actually be in court to issue the warrant, and if I know Raymond, he won't even ask too many questions, he's loyal as an old Labrador. So here's what I suggest, give me one hour, if dad can get hold of the judge, I'll blue-light it over to his home, bring it back, then there can be no questions asked about whether we broke in before the warrant was issued, that bastard isn't getting off on a technicality."

"You said you need an hour but surely you'll have to do the search again, once the warrant is in place, if you're just trying to stall me?"

"Listen, Nick, I don't need to stall you, if I wanted too, I could just arrest you again, you did assault an officer of the law this morning remembers? The truth is, I don't need another fight, you're more use to me on the outside, if we are going to make these charges stick. Just remember, I'm not the bad guy here, I'm doing everything I can to make this work, I could really use some co-operation." The officer waited for a response, though strangely, it was Challis who broke the deadlock.

"What about me, I might see inconsequential but, I'm not useless."

"I know that you're nowhere near useless, and I was coming to that next. When I get back with the warrant, we are going to need an impartial witness to testify. God willing it won't come to this but, if the worst happens and Nick and I don't make it back, you are the only person who can make sure that bastard gets what he deserves. My dad would appear like an avenging father, but you could be seen as unbiased, especially with our history. Plus, you are the only other one who knows the details about what we've seen and where. Please

471

believe me Danny, I'm not underestimating you, on the contrary, there's no-one I trust more, whatever happens, you are needed."

"But surely my testimony wouldn't count for shit, I'm no officer of the law, I'm just Joe-Blow, legally, I shouldn't have been there in the first place, should I?" It was a legitimate question; one Brackett was ready to answer.

"Technically, no but here's the thing. I'm the only policeman in Hallowell. Legally, I can't ask a member of the public to put themselves in harm's way, and if anyone discovered we'd been in here without a warrant, I could be fired and you two could go to prison. But this is small town life, normal policing rules don't always apply. In the case of emergencies and when back up from other forces isn't available, I can use my digression to get the job done. Meaning, I can deputise the public in matters relating to the law, you just don't have the powers that real officers do. Plus, if you get hurt and it was your own choice to help, you're not able to sue the force for damages." Challis wasn't certain whether to feel impressed or used.

"But wouldn't I be better served with you guys looking for Jenifer? Don't get me wrong, I don't want to go near that fucking place but, if you two are, shouldn't I be there too? People are going to think I'm a pussy."

"Dan, everyone knows you're a pussy already." Castle and Brackett shared the joke with a smile, Challis just returned a famous one-finger salute. "I'm just kidding. No mate, if you do what I'm asking, we succeed with the bigger picture, no matter what happens in there. Between us, we make certain that that piece of shit can't do this to anyone else, ever again. Whether any of these poor fuckers were his victims or even if he just stole their body parts, he has desecrated their memories, he's robbed the families of the closure they thought they had and that needs to stop, now. Plus, there is one other major factor; if we are right about all of this, if there really is some sick connection between this fucking undertaker and Frank Graham, then stopping Gibson might stop Graham too. If his supply line is cut off, if he has no more means of information about the village, if he has no more supplies to food during the cold-weather months, then maybe, we put an end to this whole situation. For the life of me, I could never understand how that bastard survived without help, now, I think we have our answer. If we cut him off, perhaps Graham doesn't survive another winter, or if he's desperate enough, he comes out of that place out of necessity, giving up all his advantages and then we nail the fucker, the two of them finally pay for the crimes they committed. None of that can happen if we don't bring down Gibson, understand?" A simple nod was all the answer the officer needed, a faint smile and an air of resignation, this was one battle, Challis didn't mind conceding. With that hurdle vaulted, Brackett moved on to the next.

"So, Nick, Dan's on board, will you give me that hour?"

"Go get your warrant Johnny, I'll be waiting."

Chapter 37

The undertaker was happy to take his time, aware that the girl was going nowhere. His pulse was finally beginning to slow, the concern of potential heart failure fading. This scare had been the worst yet, the vice-like grip which had strangled his arteries and made him feel as though a truck was parked on his chest, had remained longer than usual and the tightness in his left arm, along with his incapability to take in oxygen, genuinely had him believing that his time on earth was coming to a premature ending. His mind had almost shutdown with the bombardment of emotions, differing levels of differing elements, clouding his thought process, battling his ability for rational thought.

The primary concern, obviously had been his demise, would it be instantaneous, would he linger, how much pain would need to be endured before the inevitable final breath and after that breath, where was his next destination? (It was amazing how quickly he had turned to the almighty in his moment of need) Beyond the fear of his own mortality was the chances of imprisonment. Should the girl escape, and he survive the cardiac arrest, charges of kidnapping would be waiting in the outer daylight. Unlawful imprisonment charges would lead to further investigation, and should the police search his home and discover of all his special treasures, a life sentence would be the inevitable outcome. A lifetime of incarceration, perhaps death was better? An additional concern was Frank. In a strange way, he'd grown to love the behemoth, the mortician's life revolving around their weekly rendezvous', the night-time visits becoming a bizarre addiction, which Gibson couldn't break. Without those unexplainable highs he felt on entering that place, of never knowing whether he'd walk out alive, Fred wondered if life would be worth living at all?

Now, none of that mattered, the panic was over, Jenifer Graham was trapped, like a fly caught in a spider's web, the plan was back on course.

Gibson began to whistle a non-descript tune, desperate to block out the scurrying sounds emanating from the rodent population. He shuddered at their thought, their twitching noses, and razor-sharp teeth, disgusting coarse fur and dagger-like claws. The noise from their presence had increased dramatically over recent years, the hoard multiplying constantly. The mortician's phobia had grown to such extremes that he'd considered abandoning the tunnel as a means of entry to the railway station grounds. Still, that sort of decision took thought, Gibson wasn't a spontaneous man. Today, he was content he'd made the correct choice of using this entry-way, the resourceful young woman could well have been able to make an escape had she not been cornered inside its narrow hallway, his rodent phobia off-set with knowledge of certainty to deliver the bitch to

Frank, as planned Though surrounded by total darkness, the undertaker knew there wasn't far to go, he'd travelled this walkway so often, he could do it blindfolded. As his footsteps echoed off the wooden-clad walls, an alien sound suddenly made him stop, the tune coming from his own pursed lips replaced by a low, gurgling moan. A widening grin grew across his smug face, the groan was just yards away, the distressed, semi-conscious murmuring of Jenifer Graham making the mortician giddy with anticipation. His footsteps resumed though in a creeping motion, the opportunity to startle the young woman too good to miss. Just ten feet away now, her form, a grey mass at his feet. As he approached, Gibson winced at the sight before him, the reason for Jenifer's growing distress, a large black rat was greedily gnawing at her exposed head wound.

Johnny Brackett's powerful police-car tore away from the kerbside, dust exploding into the air as the wheels spun wildly. Black tyre-marks became embedded in the tarmac, speed was of the essence. It had been decided upon that Challis and Castle would remain at the funeral parlour, hiding intently inside the back yard on the chance that Gibson returned early. Nick left the coverage of the perimeter wall, walking to the street's end just in time to see the squad-car vanish from sight, it was time to put his own plan into action.

"Nick, will you get in here, Johnny said we needed to keep out of sight?" Challis could instantly tell from Castle's expression that something had changed. "Nick, are you okay? What's wrong?"

"Listen Dan, I'm sorry but I have to go."

"Go? Go where? What the Hell are you talking about?" Castle looked towards his confused friend but paused before making a response. "Nick, I'm serious, you can't go anywhere, we have to wait for Johnny, we need to…oh…wait just a minute." The realisation was beginning to dawn on Challis. "Tell me you're not thinking about heading to that place alone, please, tell me you're not that dumb?" Castle still remained silent though his eyes told Challis all he needed to know. Nick began to quickly stride away, Dan following swiftly in his own unique way. Challis reached out and, with a forceful grip tightening across his shoulder, Castle took a deep intake of breath, aware his friend wouldn't quit without a good explanation. "Please Nick, I'm asking you, don't do this." When Castle spun around to face his pal, one final time, it was obvious that he was having one Hell of a battle at holding back tears. The disabled young man had never seen Castle this emotional and found it disconcerting. Placing both hands on Challis's shoulders in an arms-length embrace, he began a heart-felt retort.

"Dan, please listen, you might think I'm crazy, hell, you probably right, but this is something I have to do, and I have to do it, alone, and this is why. Johnny believes Jenny is dead, I don't blame him, if I wasn't so involved and was thinking normally, maybe I'd agree. He thinks she's dead yet still he's willing to risk his life, just to stand by my side. You probably think she's dead too but, were it not for making sure Gibson sees justice, then you'd insist on coming with me too. That's because you two are my friends, hell, you're probably the only real friends I've ever had, and I do appreciate that, more than you'll ever know.

But here's the thing, I asked you guys to go in that place once and it ruined all our lives. Actually, that's not true, I didn't ask, I forced, I guilted you guys into coming with me, and I've regretted the decision every day of my life since. It may not seem like Johnny's life got wrecked but, for a decade, he had to live a life without friends, that couldn't have been easy. Then, I look at you and… I feel ashamed of myself, your life became a car-crash and that was all my fault too, whether you want to admit it or not. Worst of all, there's Dilly, his life wasn't ruined, it was extinguished. He was just a baby and because of me, he's dead, I live with that knowledge every day and it makes me sick. Christ, even people like my parents, like Billy's parents, everyone got fucked over because of a decision I made. Now I'm not crying here or looking for sympathy, but I can't look at myself in the mirror without wanting to put my head through it, I have no self-respect whatsoever and it all comes down to one…stupid…choice. So make no mistake about this, I'm not about to let anything like that happen again. The circumstances may have changed but the results are the still the same, I'm the one insisting on heading back in that place and you guys are willing to back me up. Well, I'm sorry Dan but, no this time. I'm doing this alone and there's no one going to stop me. It's not fucking happening again."

"But Nick, I've just got you back. It's true, my life has been the shits, some of it coming from that night, some of my own doing. But I feel like I have a chance again now and you coming back into my life did that. I'm asking you, no, I'm begging you, don't do this. I can't lose you again." There were tears openly cascading from Challis's eyes now, the emotion becoming too much to bear. In response, Castle smiled.

"Whatever happens, you'll never lose me again, whether this works out or not, I'll always be here, in spirit if not in body. And you have Johnny back too. if nothing else, at least something good had come from all this shit."

"But…"

"Dan please, you won't change my mind. Just do one thing for me. Make me a promise. You could be so much more, have so much more, you've seen nothing of life yet. I know more than most that, it's not easy to change but, if you try, at least you'll look back with no regrets, no fear. These demons we share, they will take some beating, but just imagine if you did, stopping the booze and the bullshit, maybe you'll find the self-respect that I never could. Hell, by tomorrow, we both might. I love you brother."

With that Nick Castle was gone.

For Dr Harry Brackett, this had been a bad day. The early hour's telephone call to deliver the Thompson baby, which had already arrived before he had chance too, had set the wheels in motion. Losing another round of golf to that smug bastard Dr Harvey Samuels had made his mood ten times worse. And then there was the Tom Daley fiasco. Bad day, very bad day.

The good doctor stood in the backroom of the police station, holding a small compact mirror, his nose had finally stopped bleeding, but the bone was definitely broken, the deepening swelling around both eyes confirmed as much. Dabbing with a clean handkerchief, a dampened corner had managed to wipe away much of the dried blood, but he certainly had two shiners to look forward too.

"Fucking Daley. No more pills for that bastard, he's cut off, the big dummy will have to go over to St Mara, next time he needs a fix." Brackett's entire head ached, especially at the base of his skull, where Tom had delivered the knockout blow. "I probably have a concussion. I could be dead by tomorrow, no one cares." Still, the physical pain was tolerable, what hurt the most was Johnny's words before storming off in a bad mood.

"Sadistic torturer. How could he say such a thing, to me of all people? Ungrateful brat. I'm a doctor for goodness's sake, the hypocritic oath, I heal people, that's what I do. I didn't do anything to that big idiot, if he wasn't so dumb, he'd have asked Johnny for his pills. It wasn't my fault, am I supposed to think of everything?"

Suddenly, across the room, the front-door handle snapped up and down, rotation, back, forth, back, forth being. A bang from the same area, someone outside was shoulder barging the entrance, determined to get inside. Brackett moved away, sliding behind a wall of the rear room, pressing tightly against the painted brick surface, even though the barrier was enough to disguise his presence. Again, the handle was twisted, and then came a kick to the lower part of the wooden blockade, someone really wanted inside. The doctor found himself holding his breath though had no idea why. He was thankful his son had locked the door after leaving, the public couldn't be allowed to see him in his current state. The adjacent window became shaded, the invader peering nosily through the glass, whoever was outside was trying desperately to discover whether anyone was home. When they saw an empty interior, the loud banging began, first on the entrance and then to the window.

"Christ, can't this guy get the message, no one's here."

A thought entered the physician's head; what if it was Daley, coming back to surrender? Harry pushed away from the hide-out, and was about to reveal his presence, when the clatter abruptly stopped. Listening intently, he heard a car door open and an engine firing into life.

"Well, it wasn't Daley, the thick fucker doesn't know how to drive." Afterwards, his curiosity began to run rampant. Was it someone who'd seen Tom and needed to report it? Was it Johnny and he'd lost his key? Was Johnny hurt?

Even mentally, the words felt too loud inside his brain, this was going to be a daisy of a headache, that much was certain. "It wasn't my place to see to Daley, and it's not my place to answer the public's policing needs, that was Johnny's job, let him answer his own fucking door. Back to Daley, did he ask about medication? Did he ask for medical advice? No. No, no, fucking no, it wasn't my fault."

Deep inside, the doctor didn't actually believe any of that bullshit, but he was a great politician, if he could convince Hallowell's public that he had their best interests at heart, he was determined to try his hardest to convince himself that he was the innocent party, his narcissistic side hated to admit his failures.

"If Daley had just done as I said, all of this crap would have gone away. Tell a few white lies, make the report seem good. The residents knew the truth, they knew that moron wasn't man enough to hurt anyone. It would have been a cover story, that's all, a coat of whitewash, he wouldn't have gone near a fucking prison, slap on the wrists and Hallowell would move on. Now, with that bastard on the streets, God knows what would happen. And if he tells anyone about my, miscalculation, then my reputation could be crushed. God, I hope Johnny finds Daley before the simpleton has chance to shoot his mouth off. Maybe I should be out looking too?"

Placing a hand to the back of his skull, a large welt had grown. "Mother-fucker." Adding insult to injury, he'd been forced to make a round of telephone calls, informing the residents that the evening's town meeting had been cancelled. Keeping details to a minimum, they were told the postponement was just for twenty-four-hours, claiming that the extra day was necessary to give the gathering the updates required. That much was true, the real-estate agent hadn't had the meeting with the Graham girl yet so it was impossible to tell what her asking price would be. It also gave him time to hide his injuries and come up with a plausible explanation, if the audience saw his bruises in their current form, there would be more conversation about his personal predicament than the topic at hand. Brackett had no intention of looking weak before his public.

Lowering the mirror, Harry looked to the empty cell, vacated by Tom Daley, and gave a lasting snarl. With his attention altered, he never heard the click in the lock of the front door. Just at that moment, the entrance burst open, giving the physician another jolt. Johnny Brackett ran inside.

"Christ lad, you know how to make an entrance. Have you found Daley yet?"

"No I haven't, just be quiet and listen." The officer wasn't used to being forceful with his over-bearing father, but this wasn't a regular day. "Right, you screwed up this morning, agreed?" The doctor paused, but decided against argument, a simple nod was all the response needed. "Fine, that was very stupid, you know it and I know it. You've put me in a shitty position that I could do without, but, if you want repay that debt, here's how?"

Nick's heart was beating wildly, the prospect of what was coming filled him with apprehension and excitement in equal amounts. Of course, he was afraid, no sane person wouldn't be. He was planning on returning to the place which had destroyed his life, filled his nightmares, and potentially robbed him of a future. The prospect of facing, not only a psychotic adversary on enemy turf, but also, it's obedient minion with a fetish for deceased body-parts should have been enough to determine a wide berth, but Nick was no ordinary opponent and the opportunity to, not only rescue a beautiful young woman, but to right so many wrongs, to avenge his late grandfather and free a village from its unholy darkness, was enough to make the young man giddy with excitement.

The wind-shield wipers on his borrowed Ford were switched from intermediate to constant, the rain outside falling with increased strength, lashing with force due to the intensifying wind. The headlights were switched to full beam, lighting up colliery lane, his speed increasing to dangerous levels on the wet tarmac. Passing by that place, he'd had to fight the urge to stop, believing the need for help, more vital than catching the last of the afternoon daylight. That help wasn't human assistance, there was an item inside his grandmother's home which he hoped would sway the advantage back in his favour.

The wet conditions had made his hair damp, lank strands falling across his brow and into his eyes. A hand swept the locks back, clearing his vision and as he passed Main Street, onto Melrose drive, he wondered if this was the final time, he'd see the family home. Leaping from the Ford, leaving the keys in the ignition, ready for a hasty retreat, he ran to the house's front door, relieved to find it unlocked. Stealthily entering, he heard footsteps from the floor above, though the down-stairs rooms remained vacant. Passing through the lounge, into the kitchen, he carefully opened the door to a shelved space below the stairs, preying the item in question was still there.

It had been a Saturday afternoon when he'd first seen it. The boy was only seven-years of age, doing the thing he loved the most, spending time with his granddad, Bill Castle. Nick recalled, it was close to Christmas time, both his parents were on a shopping excursion, as was his grandmother, leaving the house deserted, bar for the two male siblings. Because there was no chance of being caught, and the old officer trusting the child's promise of discretion, he'd shared for the first and only time, his prized possession.

Passed down from his late father, Bill took a metal case from its hideout, snapped open a small padlock and produced an old service revolver. A browning, model 1900, .32 calibre, manufactured in Belgium, it was the last line of defence for squaddies in world-war 1. Semi-automatic with a 102 mm barrel, capable of firing seven rounds a minute, the policeman had cherished the black handled firearm ever since the day he'd inherited it. As Nick held the unloaded pistol in his tiny hands, he could almost feel the history pulsing through his veins. There was a bag filled with ammunition accompanying the weapon, though the officer promised his grandson that he'd never fired the gun in anger. The child noticed a faint air of regret as he heard those words and now, as a man, Nick understood why, with hindsight, a single gunshot to Frank Graham would have meant Hallowell missing out on years of destruction. The old man-made Nick promise that this revelation was their secret, that he'd never tell a soul about what he'd seen and, as the boy respected his grandfather above all others, he never did. Now, fourteen years later, he hoped that one revelation would be the difference between his success or failure, life, or death. Knowing that his grandparents were creatures of habit, he hoped the weapon would still be in the same place he'd previously been shown. The small area under the stairs was filled with clutter, old shoes and coats, tools, and bric-a-brac. A low wattage bulb fired into life, making the search easier, but for a moment, it seemed the gun had been moved. Pushing by a pile of jigsaw puzzles and old National-geographic magazines, Nick finally breathed out a sigh of relief, a black box with a small padlock keeping the lid closed appeared at the cupboard's furthest away corner. The youngest had looked at that container many times after the original introduction but, as the clasp was always secured, seeing the weapon was out of reach; until today.

The rain lashed forcibly against the kitchen window, the arriving storm making the late afternoon sky prematurely black. Just above the noise of the torrential weather was the sound of padded feet passing across the upstairs floorboards. Castle knew immediately it was his grandmother, the carpet slippers worn dulled the thuds to a minimum. Aware that time was short, Nick grabbed a thin-handled fork from the cutlery draw and began trying to snap off the padlock.

"Nick, is that you?" He paused before replying, knowing that every second counted, and the old lady would naturally come to see him, the moment she was certain of his presence.

"Yes, it's just me. I'm sorry gran, but I'm heading straight back out, so you don't need to come down, I'll see you later." Knowing his previous statement was doomed to failure, he wasn't surprised to hear footsteps descending the staircase. The lock was proving a stern adversary, but the young man refused to accept defeat, twisting hard with the stainless-steel handle until the bolt snapped, falling noisily to the floor. By now, his grandmother was almost at the foot of the stairs, time was vanishing fast, and he had no wish to ask permission to take the weapon. Not that it mattered; as the box snapped open, Nick's eyes grew wide with horror, the metal container was empty, the gun was gone.

"Have you seen your father? He was here, not fifteen minutes ago looking for you." The old lady was calling out while walking, zeroing in fast, causing Castle to grab the box from the kitchen table and find any hiding place possible a small cupboard down at his feet the easiest destination. Mere seconds later, the old woman entered the kitchen.

"Looking for me? What did he want?" Asking the questions drew attention away from the flustered expression upon his face.

"He didn't say. Just asked if I'd seen you and then took off. What *you* up too?" The grandmother's suspicious nature, coupled with Nick's troubling history, meant that his response needed to be quick and believable.

"Oh, not much. I just came back to borrow a flash-light, do you have one?" The query ensured that Alice Castle would return with another inquiry of her own.

"Flash-light? What do you need that for?" This was one reply Nick had considered before even returning home.

"I bumped into Dan Challis; do you remember him?" He continued without waiting for a comeback. "He has a little Yorkshire-terrier, and it slipped its leash over by the churchyard. He asked me if I'd give him a hand finding it, with him having a bum leg, so I figured it would be easier to spot with a flash-light, do you have one I can borrow?" The returning volley had been just good enough to allay her suspicions.

"In this weather, you must be mad."

"Probably, but I promised, do you have one?"

"Yes, it's in that cupboard by your feet, if you move over, I'll find it for you." Pointing towards the same storage area he'd stashed the gun container, Nick reacted quickly.

"No. Sorry, I mean…don't worry, I can find it." Bending swiftly, blocking the woman's line-of-sight with his body, he began to rummage for his prize.

"Can you manage? I'll find it for you if you like?" As panic grew, Castle pushed the bric-a-brac inside around until he discovered a high-powered, yellow-handled torch, hiding at the rear of the cupboard.

"Here it is, I have it." Closing the door immediately behind him, he fired off a nervous smile, hoping his reaction had been enough to allow a sharp exit.

"Are you sure you're alright Nick? Would you like me to make you some food, there's some Ham in the fridge, it'll only take a minute?" Castle was trying desperately to remain calm when all his instincts told him to get away, fast.

"Don't worry gran, I'm fine, and I've already eaten. I'm just in a bit of a hurry, Dan's waiting for me." Alice paused to consider the situation before passing judgement, she'd always been an expert at reading people's faces.

"Well, if you're sure, then you better get yourself away. Don't forget that your dad is looking for you. And take a coat if you're roaming around, the weather is bloody awful." Nick nodded, smiled, and kissed the old woman on the cheek.

"Don't worry, I'll catch up with him later, and thanks for the torch." Castle bolted towards the kitchen exit but spent a second to look back at his watching grandmother. "I'll see you later too, love your gran."

With that, the young man was gone and though the old lady appreciated the sentiment, it left her with a troubling concern, as though her grandson was walking out of her house for the final time.

The sky was almost black now, another of Hallowell's famous fierce storms driving away the last of the daylight. Head down, the young man ran to the driver's side door, pulling the grey waterproof jacket he'd grabbed from the hallway around his shoulders before leaping into the seat. The keys were still hanging from the ignition and as he started the engine, the interior light flickered into life. Catching a glimpse into the rear-view mirror, Nick let out a cry of shock, the face staring out from the back seats sending a shudder through his entire body.

"Boo." Mick Castle had always had a mischievous sense of humour.

"Jesus Christ dad, what the Hell are you doing hiding back there like the ghost of Christmas past?" Senior replied with a self-satisfied grin.

"Waiting for you. What you up to?" Nick had neither the time nor the inclination to begin the same tale he'd just told his grandmother, plus his patience was beginning to wear thin.

"Not much, I'm just going out so, if you wouldn't mind buggering off, I'm running late."

"Are you seeing that Graham girl again?" Nick smiled; the irony of the question not lost on the young man.

"Maybe, I don't know yet." The statement was true, though the circumstances were greatly different from Mick's meaning.

"Have you seen Johnny Brackett today?" The question caught Nick cold and momentarily, he paused, did his father already know the answer, fishing for details, or was it a lucky guess?

"Johnny, why you ask that, we're not exactly friends, now are we?" This time, it was senior's turn to pause, though his was done for dramatic effect.

"I was wondering… It's just…"

"Just what." This was beginning to feel like an interrogation.

"Don't get touchy. I heard he still had Tom Daley locked up for the Roberts abduction."

"So?"

"So, I was curious, that's all. You see, I was over in the woodland, same place as where we talked the other night…"

"And?" Nick's fortitude had vanished now, though he was certain there was more to his father's tale then what had been revealed so far.

"And I was there to keep an eye out, just in case you were dumb enough to try something stupid; something like, oh, I don't know, going back in that place, alone, even though you promised you wouldn't. But, instead of seeing you do something stupid, I saw old Tom doing it. Heading straight over to the platform, not a hesitation in sight. Before I could call out to the big dummy, he was gone." Junior's blood ran cold, this was a complication he didn't need.

"Okay, well, what's the problem, what's that got to do with me?" The defensive tone in the young man's voice began to put Mick on alert.

"I never said it had anything to do with you, you snappy little twat. I was just curious as to whether you'd seen Brackett on your travels. You see, when I knew I wouldn't reach Tom in time, I flew around to the police-house, but the door was locked. I looked through the window and thought I saw movement in the back but, no one answered. So, I came back here for a few reinforcements before heading back over there. I'm not going in the fucking place but, I couldn't just do nothing, the dopey fucker wouldn't stand a chance on his own." Nick was shocked, he'd never considered his father a brave man and certainly didn't look at him as community minded.

"So what are you saying? You've preached to me for years not to go near the railway station, but Tom Bloody Daley goes for a wander inside, and you come to get me?" Junior's confused tone deserved a response.

"I didn't say that. I still don't want you near that place and I didn't come home to get you." The young man was even more perplexed now.

"Listen, dad, you're not making any sense. You said you came for reinforcements, if not me then who, Grandma?"

"Don't be a dick. When I said reinforcements, I didn't mean people, I meant this." Opening the inside of his camouflage army jacket, a bulge pushed out from the lining of an interior pocket. Though most of the body was obscured, the handle was unmistakable. "It was dad's service revolver, he had it for years, but it still works."

"How do you know?"

"Because dad took it with him, the day he died. That's how the alarm was raised, people realised where he was when they heard shots. When we got his body back, the gun was still in his jacket." Junior sighed, now things made sense. The male siblings didn't agree on much, but they did acquiesce to the notion that, it would be suicide going near the railway station without a weapon. Starting the engine, Nick glanced once more into the rear-view mirror.

"I think I have something to tell you." With a screech of tyres, the Ford pulled quickly away from Melrose drive.

Strangely, Fred Gibson was aggravated when he discovered Jenifer Graham unconscious on the dirty floor, keenly aware that, if the young woman was incapable of walking, he'd need to carry her, the undertaker was a lazy fat bastard.

"Get away, you filthy creature." The mortician kicked out at the bristling vermin which had been greedily enjoying the salty treat oozing from the Jenifer's forehead. For once, the creature fought against its natural instinct to flee, desperate to take advantage of the food on offer. Momentarily, Gibson backed away, the understandable phobia making his body freeze. Finally, the rat returned to its impulsive aptitude and scurried away, hissing with a defiant audacious stare. Fred considered kicking out at the retreating beast, but thought better of it, fearful that its allies may be lurking in the shadows.

"Come on bitch, get up." Gibson hovered his left foot off the ground and using the wall for balance, began tapping the girl around the side of the head. Not hard, just enough to get her attention, though there was still no movement. "I said move, get the fuck up, you worthless bitch." His volume was increasing, as were the ferocity of the kicks, the left side of her face quickly reddening, but still, there was no sign of life. A thought suddenly crossed the undertaker's mind which made him shudder, what if the blow she'd taken to the head has killed her? If she was dead, how would Frank react? Her demise may result in his too. The smile which just moments before had settled upon his lips had now dissipated, replaced with a grimace, this was becoming a real possibility. "Oh Christ, come on, please. WAKE UP, WAKE UP NOW OR I'LL KICK YOUR FACE IN PIECES. WAKE UP, WAKE UP, WAKE UP."

Bending to one knee, Gibson began slapping the girl across both cheeks, lightly at first, increasing in force, becoming heavy-handed swots. Next, he grabbed both of Jenifer's shoulders and began to shake her, shouting in her face, insults and spittle bouncing of her skin. Tears were forming in the corners of his eyes, face dripping with perspiration, those chest-pains returning with a vengeance.

"NO, NO, NO. This isn't right." It seemed certain now, she wasn't breathing, reflexes stationary, the bitch was dead, and he hadn't even had the pleasure of committing the crime. He felt robbed, he felt insulted, he felt...

The second her eyes opened, Gibson stumbled away, falling hard onto his backside. How was this happening, was she a ghost, was she the living dead? Her hands were still bound but that didn't matter, her out-stretched fingers aiming for his eyes, falling just short but making contact with both cheeks, tearing the skin deeply. The mortician yelled out in pain but suddenly realised, "She's not dead, she's not dead, I'm saved."

Jenifer had other ideas, the quiet reserved girl with an innocent smile and a caring nature was suddenly a woman possessed. She didn't want to be rescued, she wanted to fight. Her sir-name was Graham, and it was time to prove it. Her face took on a demonic scowl, the whites of her eyes bloodshot, body darting forward, again and again, fingernails clawing at anything within reach. Stumbling backwards, body crouched low, Gibson cradled his head with his arms, the expression of fear plastered across his face manufactured by the shift in power. Seeing the opening, aware it was now or never, she launched forward, the several losses of consciousness making her brain swim, double vision, a blurring world, causing her to swing and miss, falling but fighting, not needing to defend herself because her opponent was a cowering disgrace. The mortician was flat now, the girl kneeling between his legs, face inches from his. Allowing himself a squint between a hand-clasped guard, he squealed in terror as Jenifer's jaws began to snap together, over, and over, her teeth, white and sharp, aiming for Gibson's facial extremities. Forcing a hand away from his face, he pushed at the girl's jaw, only for his index finger to find a way into her mouth, the lock-down between upper and lower rows, sinking deeply into his skin, blood immediately bursting forward, the salty taste of the sticky jet, suddenly making the events frighteningly real in the young woman's mind. All of this was completely against her natural instincts, and as such, she pulled away, shocked at these alien, animalistic tendencies. Gibson though, hadn't noticed the change, the injured hand once more part of the fleshy forcefield, protecting his face and eyes, the blood trickling across his brow, the unbelievable change in fortune astounding his confused brain.

With the sudden realisation, Jenifer reverted to her more natural inclination and began the desperate scrabble for escape, crawling her body above the undertaker's chest, a knee catching Gibson across the bridge of the nose, the bone cracking instantly and momentarily knocking him senseless. Her fingernails scratched at the wooden flooring, fighting to gain purchase, her feet pushing away from the mortician's shoulders.

The tic upon her wrists made climbing upright, all the more difficult, and now the exertion was taking a toll too. Even grabbing a breath seemed tasking but still she continued. Clambering a path to the side walls seeming her best shot of taking the lead she so desperately needed. Passing away from the undertaker's prone body, she stumbled once more, instead, crawling on all fours, determined to battle on to the end.

With the musty fog-like air making her cough, suddenly Gibson began to realise what was occurring. Second by second, her lead was growing, if she rose to her feet first, he'd stand no chance. Rolling to his knees, he stretched out an arm, his fingernails scratching the left leg on her black denim jeans. Twisting her neck towards the evil pursuer, her eyes widened, Gibson's fat slobbering face was a crimson mask, blood erupting from the broken nose, eyes squinting in fear of further retaliating strikes. Speed intensifying, she pulled her trailing leg away, once more trying to find her feet but tumbling forward again. That impetus spurred the mortician on, grabbing out, this time taking a strong hand on her right trainer-shoe. As Jenifer Struggled to find an escape, Gibson seized a second hold, his time with her opposite leg and now, the advantage had shifted.

With strength seeming to desert her at the worst possible time, Gibson used his massive bulk to heave the girl towards him. One fierce haul and the young woman was in the undertaker's blubbery grasp, his weight collapsing down upon her tiny frame, the air forced out of her lungs, spittle dropping from his quivering lips onto her expose face. Making a final lunge towards him, her teeth gnashed in the direction of his nose, though it was more instinctual than hopeful. Pulling his legs forward, knees moving high across her flattened chest, her arms were now pinned to the floor, the struggle was almost over.

The continuing tightness across his ribcage was now more concerning for Gibson than the chance of another Jenifer fight-back and pausing, he began taking in huge lungsful of foisted air, desperate for his heart rate to slow down. Showing one final act of defiance, the young woman twisted her neck, biting into the inside of his thigh.

"You are stupid, horrible, twat." Gibson snarled, the disgusting language, a penultimate, if not ignored, assault.

The final strike came after grabbing two handfuls of the girl's hair, yanking her head forward and smashing it violently to the wooden floor below. The sudden burst of excruciating pain caused her vision to cloud, the world suddenly fell to grey, before finally fading to black for one last time.

Two generations of Castle sat inside the darkened Ford, the outside sky black as pitch, the weather monsoon-like in its ferocity. The white lines of the road's centre zipped by with alarming speed, time was running out.

The older man was aware his son was hiding something, the question was, what? Nick had always had an uncanny ability to hide his emotions, the isolation during his adolescence had taught him to rely on no one. Plus, as Mick had been absent from the later part of the young man's teens, he'd missed that character development, that dexterity of looking into his son's eyes and seeing truth.

The facts were, they barely knew one another now, there was love between them, basically because it was expected, even if not always warranted. But a relationship? Whether that could be rebuilt remained to be seen. Still, there were obvious signs that the boy wasn't right. The tone in his voice took on an agitated edge, and his body seemed to twitch uncontrollably, as though tensing itself for events still to come. Mick had climbed through to the front-passenger seat and watched as Nick's hand trembled, knowing he'd have to tread carefully if he was going to make progress.

For Nick, his mission was simple; find a way to get the damned gun away from his father and lose him anyway possible. That weapon was essential and as such, he knew he'd need to lower his aggressive tendencies if he had any chance to succeed in those aims, but time was running out fast, they were almost at the railway station, passing the church, heading onto Colliery Lane. Though his mind was racing, the thoughts were muddled and confusing, he was desperate for a cover-story, but nothing was revealing itself. He grimaced at the prospect but suddenly realised, there was no other option, the truth was his only choice.

The Ford pulled up just outside the railway station carpark, neither wishing to draw public attention to their destination. Turning off the ignition-key, the engine died, the interior light automatically firing into life. The young man took a deep breath before letting out a sigh, every fibre in his being screamed not to say what he was about to say, but the options were over, every second that passed was another second closer to Jenifer's demise. He decided to just dive in, blaze out the specifics with as much detail as the time constraints would allow and hope his father didn't think he was full of shit.

Over the next few minutes, Nick threw out a tale so bizarre, it had to be true. Were they anywhere but Hallowell, perhaps the older man wouldn't have believed what he was being told, but this village was the birthplace of bizarre and as such, Mick had learned to accept what others may see as lunacy? He'd remained silent while the young man told of stolen body-parts and forbidden love, of abduction, kidnapping, and an unholy alliance. When the statement was finished, he pondered for a moment, unsure where to begin a retort. Finally, he spoke.

"You done?" This wasn't the reaction Nick was expecting.

"What more do you want?" Senior smiled, he could see the young man's point.

"I just didn't want to interrupt while you were in full flow." Now it was Nick's turn to smile.

"You're not an easy guy to surprise, are you?"

"Are you serious? Living in Hallowell, this is barely the most interesting thing I've heard today." The shared grin seemed to break the ice, now it was time for answers. "So, you're saying that our wonderful, warm-hearted funeral director, who no one would ever think of as weird, is actually a body-parts stealing, corpse snatching, son-of-a-bitch."

"Yes."

"And that same funeral director is butt-buddies with this village's resident bogeyman Frank Graham?"

"Yes."

"Okay, so next, that resident bogeyman, who incidentally killed one of your best-friends, murdered your grandfather and pretty much ruined all our lives, his sister moves back to town, you and her fall madly in love after one date, but she then gets abducted by said weirdo funeral director, for the purpose of delivering her to that evil, resident bogeyman brother, to stop her from selling off the Graham lands and making the resident bogeyman homeless. Does that just about sum up everything?"

"It's a little simplistic but, yes."

"And what you want is for me to hand over my dad's gun and all the bullets, then piss-off, while you try some half-arsed rescue mission which has got virtually no chance of success."

"I suppose so."

"I have to ask you something first?" Nick was intrigued but wary of where this was heading.

"Okay, what?"

"Are you either drunk, high, or just fucking stupid?" The young man frowned but didn't react. "You actually think that I'm going to watch while my only son walks to certain death and give you, my blessing?"

"I need that gun." Any tone of humour had gone now, this game of cat and mouse was deadly serious.

"No boy, you don't need a gun, you need a fucking lobotomy, lots and lots of brain surgery, because whatever is wrong in that tiny mind of yours is no small thing." Nick reached for the doorhandle.

"I can see this is useless." Mick stretched and grabbed his son by the lapel of his raincoat.

"Where do you think you're going?" Junior's face snapped back towards his father, in his mind, this conversation was over.

"I'm only going to ask you this once, move away from me…or I'll move you. You may not want to help, but I'm sure not going to let you hinder, I'm going in there, whether you give me the gun or not." Mick wasn't backing down.

"You really think you're some kind of hard-case, don't you? And you really must think I'm a piece of shit, if you thought for one minute that I'd let you do this. Christ, I knew there was no respect, but this is just fucking stupid, no, more than that, its fucking suicide, that's why I've been sitting in those fucking woods, night after night, in the Pissy rain, just waiting for you to do something dumb. That's the reason why dad wanted you out of Hallowell in the first place, and that's the reason why he didn't ever want you to come back, because you're predictable, and predictable people do predictable things."

The older man was red-faced and sweaty, knowing this was the last chance to save his son. "Believe it or not, I know what you're going through, I felt exactly the same when dad died, we all think about vengeance."

"This isn't vengeance."

"Bullshit."

"No. Not bullshits. Last night, I spent the evening with someone who, made me feel special, normal, like maybe, just maybe, I could have a regular life doing regular things, do you think I want to keep living in the past?"

"You're thinking with your dick, not your brain."

"That's bullshit. Yes, I could have pushed things and slept with her last night. If all I'd wanted was a quick leg-over, I'd have done it, nailed it, and fucked off home. But I didn't, I didn't. You don't seem to understand, maybe it's being back here, maybe it's being around my family and old friends, but I feel amazing, Christ, I feel born-again, and that's been bled back into me. And yes, I admit, I do think Jenifer is beautiful, sexy as Hell, and I have wondered what it would be like to be with her, but it's more than that. There was a spark, no, a fucking flame, that got lit between me and her last night, I can't explain it, but that shit doesn't happen to me all the time. Normally, whenever I feel something for someone, I run. I sprint, as fast as my legs will carry me, but this time, I'm not going anywhere. Christ, I don't know if we'd have a future, I've known her for thirty-odd hours, but I tell you one thing for sure, I'd like to find out. Can't you see, if I can do this, if I can beat those demons, face them head on, get past all the bullshit, and get some sort of life back, maybe I can find some of that happiness that everyone else just seems to take for granted. Believe it or not but, I don't want to die, Hell, I feel like I've just started living. And I know the chances of me finding Jenny alive are slim, but if I don't try, if I walk away and leave her to the whim of those bastards, then all the progress I've made just goes away, blown out, like a candle in the wind."

"You're not going to break into song are you, Elton?" Nick never reacted, just a faint smile whilst he got his breath back. "Okay then, come on."

"What are you talking about?" Junior had an inclination of where this was headed but still…

"Let's go find your girl." The statement was said with a such matter-of-fact tone, that the young was taken aback.

"You're not coming with me."

"Want a bet?"

"Dad, I mean it, this isn't happening." Nick's words weren't said with much conviction, he knew he'd made progress with the speech he'd just given, but this wasn't supposed to be the result.

"Listen boy, you're not the only one with a score to settle, he killed my father, remember? Here's the thing; if you want to go find Jenifer, we go together, that's the only way it's happening. Make no mistake about this, if you try to go in there alone, I'll shoot you. Nothing fatal, just a leg, maybe even a foot, just enough to keep you from getting away. I can't run to fast these days and, even if we went home now, I'd be awake all night waiting for you to sneak out of the house. I do accept, that you have demons, we all do in some ways, and if this is the only way you can get rid of them, then I'm in. We watch each other's backs…and fronts…and every other God-damn thing, we go in, we find the girl, and we get the fuck out. No heroics, no vigilante bullshit, you're not Dirty Harry, let's do this quick and to the point."

"Dad…please." The appeal was doomed to failure, Nick knew it, but he had to try.

"I know there's times you probably thought I was a pretty shitty father, maybe your right, parenthood doesn't come with a handbook, you just pick shit up as you go along, sometimes you make some mistakes. But I've always loved you and I always tried to do what was right, even if it didn't work out that way. Well, I'm through making mistakes, tonight, I'm fucking father of the year, now let's go."

With that, both men exited their respective car doors and silently started towards the platform. Unbeknownst to them, they weren't alone.

Chapter 38

Six stone steps at the end of a darkened hallway; that's what stood between Jenifer Graham and her pernicious destiny, the final passage to an inevitable conclusion.

Fred Gibson bent crooked, the day's events having taken a tremendous physical and psychological toll, planning to hoist the captive across his shoulders, the only option to move her unconscious weight. Propping her comatose body by the slatted wooden walls, he stooped further, placing his forearms under her armpits, her head flopping lifelessly to the left. Taking in a large gulp of unclean oxygen, he began the final preparations. With one monumental effort, her frame was lifted, feet pressed against his, toe to toe, their knees parallel, touching so Jenifer's legs couldn't bend.

His entire body was drenched in perspiration, two heart scares in less than thirty minutes had caused untold consternation, another and perhaps, his clogged arteries may refuse to continue their battle. Remaining calm was essential, even though this situation didn't promote halcyon thoughts, and the physical exertion which was still needed for this final stage was hardly the most tranquil of passtimes. Still, it had to be done, whatever the risk.

The grunt which emanated from his lips, echoed across the vast walkway, his knees had bent and almost buckled, his back screamed out in discomfort, and the sweat from his hairless crown became an additional hurdle, her legs glissading at the mere touch. But the endeavour eventually proved fruitful, the hoist a success, and though he had yet to take a stride with the girl's weight across his upper torso, the sense of achievement filling him with an idiosyncratic pride.

With his head tilted permanently forward due to the young woman's position, his eyes could see only the floor below. The six-stone steps before him were covered with residual grime, pockmarked only by his own footprints, years of making the weekly pilgrimage creating a well-worn trail. In days gone by, Frank would occasionally use this passage when taking supplies from the old, burned-out mansion, but as the undertaker now provided everything necessary, the visits had become infrequent to the point of ceasing.

Tensing himself for the climb, Gibson took the first step, only lifting his legs a single stair at a time, there was no point in rushing. Jenifer's arms hung sluggishly to the base of his back, while his own hands gripped tightly to her calves. The urge to busy himself on more private areas of her anatomy had passed fleetingly though his warped mind, she was very attractive, but his sexually compulsive requirements were locked away for now, there'd be time for that sort of thing later.

Aware of the need to make this short journey as accessible as possible, he'd taken precautions before hoisting the girl to his shoulders. At the height of the steps, there were two heavy doors, fashioned from wooden slats and containing three cross-braces each, a previous coating of creosote had long since lost its finish, though the scent still impregnated the oak material. The strength of the barrier had waned over the years, tiny indentations about the outer rim insinuating an attack of woodworm, but what the aperture had lost in durability, it gained in weight, the cumbersome hatch absorbing moisture from Hallowell's changeable weather conditions. Two strong locks, fastened to the door's inner sides, had maintained a closed position and to avoid fighting with the tight-fitting obstacles while carrying the girl, he'd taken time to force the bolts open, before pushing the barriers free, allowing a certain level of daylight into the oppressive alleyway. The cool evening air felt refreshing about his dampened skin, and he was pleasantly surprised to see the overcast moonless sky in almost total darkness. The distance from tunnel exit to the railway station main building entrance was mere yards but in daylight, there was always the possibility of being spotted, under the cover of darkness the chances decreased massively.

Staggering to the mid-way point of the flight, he paused, that tightness across the chest and discomfort down his left arm still prevalent. Pushing out a deep breath, he continued, just wanting the task to be over now. He grimaced after remembering where he'd need to reach once inside, the regular meeting point with his psychotic partner was by the burning oil-drum in the far-right corner of the top floor. Six separate flights of stairs, twenty-four turns of the spiral design, two entire lengths of the vast floor space, even thinking about the prospect made him tired.

Finally, they reached the wasteland by the side of the platform, Jenifer still unconscious, Gibson struggling for breath. Content that the first element of his plan was complete, he momentarily allowed himself the luxury of cooling his over-heated body, the lashing rain instantly dropping his soaring temperature. Tilting back his aching neck, a sudden bout of dizziness threatened to send the pair crashing to the ground. Reaching out, he placed a free hand on the drenched marble of the platform, sliding the girl from his shoulder onto the high walkway, the relief of disposing her weight, even if it would only be briefly, refreshing his flagging spirit.

Seeing Jenifer Graham lying flat, comatose, and helpless, once more aroused a stir in his over-active libido, the opportunity to sexually abuse a female before death proving difficult to resist. The girl was still wearing Nick Castle's black leather jacket and sliding her arms from the heavy coat wasn't simple, without assistance, the only way was to lift her to a seated position before tugging it free of her shoulders. As the borrowed item of clothing felt free, the sleazy mortician marvelled at the young woman's ample cleavage, her plain white blouse drenched and clinging to her skin, the lacy brazier beneath easily visible, her taught midriff and instant turn-on. As he approached the top button on the blouse, his chubby fingers trembling with anticipation, a sudden noise broke into his fantasy.

Across in the distance, two men were talking loudly, striding with purpose in the direction of the station. Gibson's eyes widened, panic erupting once more in his deviant brain. Scrambling upon the platform, he grabbed the young woman by the wrists and began to drag her mercilessly across the faded white marble surface, desperate for coverage, unsure whether he'd already been witnessed.

Why else would anyone be here at this precise moment? Didn't they know how dangerous this place was, didn't they have respect for other people's property?

"What the Hell was that?" The two generations of Castle paused and gave one another a concerned look. They were thirty yards from the platform, rain lashing across the gravel encrusted wasteland, clinks emanating from the disused iron railway tracks, growing wind howling through the roofed tunnel-like space between the massive main building and its smaller neighbours. But above the horrendous weather conditions, there was one sound which seemed out of place, an echo across the desolate wilds, of a door closing, its hinges fighting against years of rusted obsoleteness, creaking, and growling until it crashed to a definite closure, a loud audible bang, leading to deafening silence.

"Maybe it was an echo, Colliery Lane isn't far, and sound carries around here?" Mick Castle, while answering his own question, was grasping at straws, and they both knew it.

"Or perhaps the wind clashed one of the doors over on the smaller building, it's definitely strong enough?" Nick's addition to the possibilities came from the same fantasy hymn-sheet to which his father was reading from, neither man ready to contend with the real liability that their adversaries were already aware of their presence…and were watching.

Darting into the darkened walkway between the main building and the former station-master's quarters, Fred Gibson allowed himself a swift look back, only to see, to his horror, another vehicle pulling into the railway carpark. The two invader's progress across the wasteland ceased as they too noticed the incoming car. The undertaker gulped, fighting with a silent scream, deep inside his throat, as he suddenly became aware to the identity of the proprietor of that vehicle, the gravelly roar of Johnny Brackett's police-car, an unmistakable barrage of testosterone infused power. Petrified that these intruders already had knowledge of his recent actions, the mortician doubled his efforts, finding cover inside the station his only hope now.

The emerging headlights of Johnny Brackett's police-car were on full beam and as the Castles peered in its direction, the brightness caused the men to squint.

"Now what?" Mick was growing tired of the interruptions. Yes, he was apprehensive of entering that place, but standing out in the pouring rain was hardly a fun pass-time. The younger man sighed with disappointment, he'd expected the intrusion, but that didn't make it any more welcome.

"It's Johnny." Nick's voice was low, almost whispered, discouragement filling his thoughts, this was almost worst-case scenario time.

"Johnny Brackett? How'd he knows we were here?" Mick was slightly confused, though the sight of reinforcements lifted his spirits. The sound of two car doors opening and closing added to Nick's dismay, for his father, he believed there was strength in numbers.

The inclement weather, raw with coldness, the wind slicing through the men like a hot knife through butter, made a swift conclusion to this inevitable confrontation essential, but Nick was willing to argue his case if it meant getting his way. As the officer, along with Dan Challis, emerged from the darkness, an argument was imminent. Mick had time for one last question.

"Nick, I asked how he knew we were here?" As rain continued to cascade rapidly though his hair, down in a steady stream falling from the tip of the young man's nose, he wasn't in the mood for interrogation.

"It's a long story, I'll tell you later." The late-comers were in ear-shot now, the expression upon the policeman's face was one of anger, mixed with disappointment.

"One hour? That's all I asked for, one lousy hour, and you couldn't even give me that. You promised me Castle; I should arrest you now, just for the hell of it." Nick knew an explanation would probably be needed, though the worsening conditions were hardly conducive to pleasant conversation.

"You were quick? There's no chance you had time to get to St Mara and back, what happened to the search warrant, to your daddy's buddy, the judge?"

"The fuckers on holiday, won't be back till Thursday, and don't change the subject Nick, I thought we were past the biggest bollocks bullshit, why did you lie to me?" Castle returned his retort with fury, the pent-up aggression inside bubbling to the surface.

"Why do you think, dumb-ass. Because I didn't want you here. I didn't want you, I didn't want dad, and I didn't want Dan, oh, and by the way Challis, thanks for doing what I asked. Even if you couldn't stop him, you could have given me a head start. Christ, five minutes earlier and you two would have been in there before us." The disabled man was first to react.

"Listen pal, this is what you can't seem to get through your thick head. This isn't only your fight. You've been gone for over ten years; we've lived with this shit every-day. And all this guilt you carry around, like some fucking comfort blanket you can use to push people away with, you don't get it. Yes, you influenced us to go in there, all those years ago, it was your idea, it was your plan, and it was fucking stupid, but we all had a choice. You weren't holding a gun to anyone's head; you wouldn't have dumped us for new friends if we'd said no. We choose to follow you, free will, remember. And yes, it all got fucked up, Billy died, and he shouldn't have been there, but he could have said no. My leg got screwed up because I fell off a damned ladder, but I could have said no. And you have no right to keep all this guilt to yourself, because sooner or later, whatever happens inside this place tonight, it will destroy you, but guess what? That's a choice too, you can let it…or not. So yes, I told Johnny where to find you, but I only did that after he said I could come along. That was his choice, this is my choice, and there's fuck all you can do about it."

491

"But I explained to you. I can't be responsible again. Anything happens to any of you, and I'm back to feeling the way I do about Billy."

"Shut the fuck up." It was Brackett's turn to try and make his pig-headed friend see sense. "Dan's just told you, this is not your choice to make. Christ, I'm the fucking police around here, not you. If there's a chance that Jenifer Graham is in there and still alive, I am duty bound to try and rescue her, no matter how stupid that may seem. So, here's the thing. This is now my mission, Dan has asked for permission to help, I've said yes. And now, I'M ASKING YOU, will you come into Hallowell railway station with me, will you help me search for the girl, and will you watch my back?" Nick paused, Johnny's attempt at reverse psychology suddenly made sense. Or was it he just wanted it to make sense? Either way, this was happening, with or without Castle's consent.

"Shit, I used to be good at manipulating people, now, no fucker listens to a word I say." Nick smiled, as did the rest of the team. Challis couldn't resist his usual attempt at ill-timed humour. Throwing an arm around Nick's wide shoulders he said,

"I still listen to you buddy. Especially earlier when you said you loved me. I only got worried when you looked to by hiding a stiffy, but none of those matters now, if we are going in here, we're all fucked anyway."

Except Nick, the whole group chuckled.

"Clever fucker. I've just realised, you were supposed to be our safety net. If we all get chopped into little pieces in here, who's going to make sure Gibson gets what's coming to him?" Once more, Brackett interjected.

"That's where my dad comes in. He's offered to be our secret weapon. Jumped at the chance actually. I think he was worried I was going to ask him to come along, so doing this gave him an out. We explained everything we saw, and where, we told him about the plan of action and, if we don't make it back, to make sure to pull the trigger on Gibson straight away, so there's no chance of the evidence being lost. That's about as much as we could do, really." Challis continued, "No one would have taken any notice of me anyway, I'm just a piss-head with a limp. The good doctor will carry more weight." The other three weren't sure if they should laugh?

"Feel free to argue anytime boys, pack of bastards." Now they laughed.

For a few seconds, a weird silence fell over the group, the realisation that this was really happening suddenly leaving an air of impending doom behind. They all seemed to look to one another, tongue-tied, hoping someone, anyone, would have a clever continuation, but words suddenly failed them all. Because for each man, this was an upcoming nightmare, from which there was a real possibility, they may not wake from.

The rain didn't bother Johnny Brackett even though it was bouncing across his tightly shaven crown like a Las Vegas fountain, his green three-quarter length wax jacket was buttoned all the way to his throat, collar peaked, with a back woollen scarf, worn like a snood, covering his chin, riding up to his lips and protecting his ears. A pair of heavy-duty work boots completed the ensemble, giving the officer as much protection from the elements as a fucking forcefield, not that he cared, the rain didn't bother Johnny Brackett.

He'd have done this naked if the situation called for it. Because this was like some strange dream come true. Of course, it had the potential to become a nightmare rather than dream, but the optimist inside Johnny told him everything was going to be fine. Was he fearful? Obviously, he'd be insane not to be, they were going up against a legitimate monster in every sense of the word. A monster with back-up, a man so deviant that there seemed no limit to his aberrant capabilities, how long he'd managed to hide his heretical activities were anyone's guess. And to make the trifactor complete, they were about to battle on enemy territory, the place where mortal men fear to dread, the place where *he* had a 100% success rate, emerging without a blemish on his grotesque body. Taking all that into account, why the fuck was Johnny feeling optimistic?

But still, this was a dream come true. Why? Because this was his shot, his one and only opportunity to get out from that dark, icy, oppressive shadow cast by his manipulative father. Johnny couldn't give a fuck about political agendas or village popularity, why the doctor put so much credence in what the people of Hallowell thought was baffling, maybe small-man instinct. What the officer wanted, no, what he needed, was to stand alone. Instead of being seen as Brackett's boy, as Harry Brackett mark 2, he wanted to be Johnny Brackett, mark 1. A man of principal, a man of honour, courage, integrity, if that meant risking everything to make it happen, so be it.

A closing thought crossed his focused mind as he stared over at their target. He was here with people who had previously meant so much to him. It was ironic as, his only real childhood friends had re-formed, had come back together at such a pivotal moment in the village's history. Now, as men, they were ready to banish the past, to rehabilitate that pact that had once seen them all as close as brothers. Castle and he had always had an unspoken rivalry, but it had been a positive in many ways as it had pushed both boys to fulfil their true potential. When he'd lost Nick, Brackett had become lazy, more aggressive than competitive, you don't run that fast when no one is chasing you. Obviously, losing Castle had been beyond Johnny's control, but Challis, that was the officer's biggest regret. A one he desperately wanted the chance to rectify. But the past was gone now, whatever errors had come before could no longer be changed, forgiven but not forgotten. Tonight was an opportunity for redemption. Johnny knew that success was a long shot…but he was a sucker for a good underdog story, and this underdog was ready to show its teeth and bite someone in the arse.

Had this been a regular twenty-four hours, Dan Challis would probably be stinking drunk by now. His alcohol intake, which was quickly destroying his liver, kidneys, and God-knows what else, had become central to his daily existence and the sharp decrease had left him with a nervous quiver, an uncontrollable fluctuation of the hands and outer extremities which he tried desperately to hide from his compatriots. While waiting for Brackett to return from his failed search warrant expedition, Dan had finished off the vodka from his inside pocket, which had helped to kerb the need, even if the craving for more was ever-present. The handful of pain-pills washed down with the booze had also helped to take the edge off and had managed to control the agony from his damaged limb, but he knew that wouldn't last, he just prayed that adrenaline would see him though. Of course, the fear would help maintain his focus, Terror, the ultimate encouragement for a coward's mind.

Dan didn't like the cold, or the rain, or the dark, he was an indoor man. In fact, there was honestly nowhere in the world he'd rather be at less than here. This was the epitome of Challis's nightmare, the site of destruction, both physically and psychologically, and returning to the scene of the crime...the mere thought filled him with unequivocal terror. But, for Dan Challis, there was one thing that horrified him even more, something that repulsed him to his very core. What Nick had said earlier was correct, Dan's existence had become like a car-crash, an obliteration of what life should be. Living from pint to pint, bottle to bottle, pill to pill. Waking up drunk, staying that way, and then re-collapsing into an excess-induced comatose state, until the next day...then doing it all again. He'd been hospitalised with alcohol poisoning three times in the last eighteen months, and twice with accidental medication overdoses. The last time, the effects had been so extreme, he hadn't been expected to survive, and when he did wake, he found himself angry at the medical staff who'd brought him back from the brink, and at God for making him remain in this never-ending war with addiction.

So tonight, what was the worst that could happen? He'd be killed. At least he'd be dying for a reason instead of taking the coward's way out, he'd been slowly killing himself for the last decade anyway. But...if he could make it through this coming nightmare, face the demons of that night and come out the other side, then maybe, just maybe, with the right help and encouragement, there could be hope for the future. The next sixty minutes could shape the rest of his life, for now, that was all that mattered.

Mick Castle stared down at the gun in his hand, and grimaced. He'd already lied to his son tonight; senior had never fired the weapon in his life. It had taken all his time just to load the fucking bullets. The cold steel felt heavy and cumbersome, should anyone volunteer to be marksman, they were welcome to it. Anyone but Nick, he'd probably take the gun and shoot his father in the leg to prevent his participation. Stubborn twat, an unwelcome Castle inheritance.

At least Mick had come prepared. A grey chequered flat cap, fashioned in cloth with leather trim, was taking on water fast, but it still kept the rain out his glassy eyes and off his weathered face. He was wearing two overcoats, one, a thick woollen bomber-jacket with high lapels and fur lining, and the second, a thinner water-proof Macintosh with a light hood and a pull-string around the neck. The pair of camouflage trousers were army surplus and therefore heavy and fit for purpose. The only negative to his outfit was a pair of white Adidas trainer-shoes which had splits across the soles and leather uppers, the continuing horrendous conditions ensuring that his feet would be wet all evening.

Mick saw this night as an opportunity. His son had been slowly destroying himself for over ten years, no number of apologies were going to alter the role

494

senior had played in that. In the guise of doing what was best for his son, he'd managed to make the situation many times worse and though he suspected it was something Nick would always hold against him, rehabilitating their fractured relationship was the older man's number one priority. With Bill gone, Mick was now the patriarch of the Castle family and as such, his responsibilities, not only to junior, but to whatever offspring his son may produce, had increased dramatically. For he knew, if Nick couldn't proceed past this nightmare, eradicate the guilt and torment, and move forward to a happy existence, then the Castle family name would die forever. Senior didn't want this shit dragging the boy down, weighing heavily on his shoulders and commanding his future, creating another victim of the Graham curse, be it one still breathing. So tonight, the aims were two-fold; continue the repairs of their unconventional father-son relationship, and second, gain vengeance for William Castle, the man who tried and failed to eradicate the Graham curse, the man who had more courage and integrity that Mick could ever dream of, and hope, his dad looking down from Heaven, could finally be proud of him. To achieve those aims, the risk was worth taking.

Nick Castle screwed a hand-rolled cigarette between his chapped lips and quickly fired his last match from the pack, guarding the flame with cupped hands until he was sure the smoke was alight. An orange tip emerged, the only colour in this God-forsaken place, rapidly turning to grey, as whispery vapour dissipated in the night-air. Breathing in deeply until his lungs were filled, burning, and fighting to escape, he gently flowed a nicotine stream through his nostrils, like a fire-breathing dragon, preparing for battle.

Like Johnny, the elements meant nothing to the young man, his focus was razor-sharp on the task in hand. The rain had forced his long black hair back to his scalp, rouge strands falling across his brow; the grey waterproof jacket he'd borrowed proved useless, absorbing rather than repelling the constant downpour and had been discarded swiftly, now with only a white cotton shirt between him and the deluge, it quickly became almost see-through, his firm sculpted chest and powerful shoulders unshielded from the coming battle.

Nick knew that physically, he was ready to face whatever lay before him, this was death before dishonour time, all, or nothing, live or die? For that, he was a qualified made-up Member of the FUCK FRANK team. But this wasn't only a physical fight.

This is what he'd craved…this is what he feared. He wanted to face the monster, man to creature, a battle to the death…and he wanted to run like fuck away from the monster, the thing that invaded his dreams nightly, made pissing the bed a regular occurrence, leave the station, leave Hallowell, and never ever look back. Externally, he oozed confidence bordering on arrogance. Inside he was screaming. Howling at the failure.

This was supposed to be ONE on ONE. For fuck's sake, how did this happen? A straight up battle, slide inside, coolly explore everywhere, floor after floor, every nook, every corner, no hiding place ignored. And when the monster appeared, then the best man would win. Nick was hard. Not a troublemaker but, when the situation arises, Castle never took second place. He'd fought bullies who suddenly retired their imperious ways after receiving a humiliating beating. They could be older, bigger, stronger, it didn't matter, because Nick took on anything as if it was do or die. If they had a stick, he'd find a log, if they pulled a blade, he'd pull a machete. Absolutely nothing would get the better of Nick Castle for one simple reason, he didn't care. He literally would fight until he was unconscious, which never happened by the way. He didn't care if someone produced a blade and slit him from groin to sternum. That sort of fearlessness was intoxicating, because he didn't care if he lived or died. If this fight was the last fight, a bad punch to the head, brain damage, or worse, then he'd be released from the nightmare which was his life. Suicide was for losers, but death in combat? Therefore, Nick Castle never took a step backwards when a challenge arose, win? Lose? Who cares?

But now things had changed. He had his family back, his friends back, his home back. That was a lot to lose. He was desperately trying to summon that who gives a fuck spirit, and it was still there, but now…things had changed.

His final gripe…this was his fight. Not Mick's not Johnny's and definitely not Dan's. Inside that place, Challis would need protection more than he'd be a benefit, without it, he'd be a sitting duck. Brackett…Nick could understand that one better. For the constable, it was more than just being a copper, Johnny had something to prove, not just to his father, or even the population of Hallowell, he wanted to proof to himself, that he was his own man instead of daddy's shadow. If doing this helped, so be it. But then there was MICK. Yes, the guy had reached out an olive-branch, trying to stick a plaster on a broken leg. Would they ever be close, live as regular father and son? Only time would tell. But this? Tailing Nick on this mission, carrying a gun for fuck's sake, who did he think he was, Dirty Harry?

Castle was out of options, it was accepting this team or abort the mission. That was impossible, every minute that passed was another minute Jenifer needed to wait. Because that's how Castle saw her in his mind's eye, awake but strapped to a chair. Perhaps a little bruising, wrists raw from rope burns. But other than that, she was fine, and she was waiting to be rescued. Imagining her any other way and his mind would get foggy, his thoughts muddled, speech impaired. So instead of accepting the inevitable, the tiny optimist inside gave him hope. Jenifer was why he was here, Jenifer was why he was here, Jenifer was why he was here. He played the phrase over and over, forget vengeance, that could come another day, Forget Gibson, he was fucked no matter what happens tonight. This was all about rescue…this was all about rescue?

So the time had come. Four individuals, united in one goal. Nick looked across at three faces, all trying to be brave, none really managing. Taking one final drag on his dying hand-rolled cigarette, he threw the stump to the ground, crushing the remains below his boot before releasing the residual smoke once more through his nostrils.

"Are we ready?" Nick waited patiently for an answer.

"Ready as I'll ever be?" Dan Challis's retort seemed weak and immediately all eyes turned in his direction.

"Remember Dan, you don't have to do this, you don't…"

"Nick. Save your breath. I appreciate the concern, but I have demons to fight too. Let me fight them, my way?" Castle sighed, this was going to be the team, no matter what he said. Mick, who had been surprisingly silent for several moments broke his reticence with a line which would define their mission.

"Let's finish this?" Silently, they headed for the platform.

High on the top floor, the smouldering ambers inside the empty oil-drum told of a fire dying. Every week, Fred Gibson would use this as a meeting place with the monster, the heat and increase light taking away some of his fear. This was not their usual day, due to Hallowell's upheaval, nothing was usual anymore. And for that reason, Frank Graham had kept the fire burning virtually all the time. HE could appear with that bitch at any moment and though the monster's attitude to murder had changed, performing it as a necessity rather than for pleasure, the opportunity to carve up his sister was too great to miss. He still had memories, Christ, he still had nightmares, and she was always in them. Perhaps slicing that cunt in two, chopping off her head, arms, legs, Gibson could play with the rest. It would remove her threat of selling the property and feed him through the winter.

Feet away from the dying embers was the only window inside the main building of Hallowell railway station, and, deep in its shadows, staring down to the wasteland below, the monstrous figure of a man, its face masked with green latex, wearing filthy, blood-stained coveralls, with piercing eyes which saw no mercy, no compassion, no humanity. An overly large meat-clever, something which may be used in an animal slaughterhouse, hung tightly by his right leg, the grip on its handle firm and controlled. Its body did not tremble for he knew what was expected, tonight, blood would be shed, once more, an example made.

As the four intruders climbed onto the platform and out of sight, Frank Graham drifted back into the shadows, ready to do whatever was needed, like a spectral phantasm, he was gone.

Chapter 39

As quickly as it had come, the rain began easing, its earlier ferocity seeming to serve as a warning, an obstacle, go home and get yourselves dry, leave the hero-act for another day. When the cautionary downpour had failed in its task, the elements called for reinforcements. Challis was the first to hear the distant rumble of thunder emanating from the west. Most of Hallowell's fierce storms would blow in from the coast, the village was only twenty-or-so miles from the Irish Sea.

"That's all we need." Dan had never liked these types of conditions, the harmless thunder always unnerving him more than the potentially deadly lightning.

"What now?" Nick was trying desperately to focus on the matter in hand, interruptions weren't welcome.

"Didn't you hear it? Over in the distance, bloody thunder. Like this wasn't creepy enough already, now we have to have bastard sound effects. It's like living in the Adam's family house." The Castle men smiled to one another while Brackett was less dismissive.

"Let's hope it doesn't get too strong, sudden lightning could give our position away." The officer had a point, one Challis was all too ready to nod in agreement with. Not that room brightness had entered the disabled man's mind, he just didn't like the bangs.

"Shut up you tarts." Castle junior was enjoying the brief interlude of concern by his perturbed partners. "There's more chance of the torches giving away our position than the bloody weather. Plus, if we are lucky, the only flash there'll be is us, as in, quick as a… Hopefully, we go in there, find Jenny, and get back out again. Simple. By the time the storm hits, you could be tucked up in bed. Now stop rabbiting and let's get a move on, okay?" Nick took the lead, if the others wanted to dawdle, that was their prerogative, had there been a choice, it would still be preferential to do this alone, even though it seemed that ship had now sailed.

Mick was matching his son stride for stride. Out of the four, he somehow seemed least anxious. Perhaps it was just older man's experience, or maybe it was just his passion for the opportunity to avenge his late father. Whatever the reason, he was adamant that, for the next hour-or-so, he was junior's shadow, there was no way he was about to allow Nick to become another Graham statistic.

Challis and Brackett gave one-another a dubious, uncertain stare. Simple? Had Nick really said that this would be…simple? Either their friend was greatly underestimating the situation (doubtful), or he was playing down the risk for their benefit? Whatever the reason, both men knew that this mission was going to be anything but…simple.

Nick took a final opportunity to soak in the magnitude of the task presented before them. Craning his neck to an acute angle, he stared up towards the massive central building and notably, the sinister single window high on the top floor, peering out like an unblinking eye. Its interior blackness appeared slightly lessened by something. Perhaps it was just an optical illusion, a trick of reflection or an over-active imagination, but there definitely seemed to be a differing beam of energy around its perimeter, an orangey glow breaking out of the aphotic gloom. Or maybe…it was just bullshit. At this moment, he barely knew what was real and what wasn't. Standing at an impressive sixty-feet-plus, Castle felt oppressed by the building's mere presence, it's now invisible shadow still managing to add another layer of control, almost autocratic in its dominance of the skyline. Could a building actually coerce an air of brutality, simply with its appearance? Or was it just more of his imagination still playing tricks, it was currently impossible to tell?

Deep inside, there was a well of panic growing in the pit of his stomach. Not as vicious as the attacks he'd suffered in the aftermath of the nightmares, just enough to add concerns. With heart rate steadily rising, a layer of perspiration covered his back, a rouge trickle streaming from the centre of his shoulder-blades, creating a small reservoir at the base of the spine. The most vital thing though was, don't show the chaps your weakness. It was obvious that even Brackett looked towards Nick for leadership, confidence would erode quickly if their fearless authority figure happened to piss his pants.

The platform was just feet away now, cracked and broken, the white marble having lost all of its former majesty, a sad indictment of the deterioration. Taking a breath, Nick placed his hands upon the cold surface. Immediately, a sudden shock rocketed though him like a bolt of electricity, causing his legs to stiffen straight, body tighten rigidly, and his head to throw back like an army recruit before the Sergeant Major. Trying to pry his fingers away, his body seemed frozen, rooted in one position. That panic which he'd fought so valiantly to quell was back with a vengeance, turning his face ashen-white, the perspiration which had started across his torso now swelling to his brow and cheeks, and the knot in his stomach reaching football-size proportions. An uncontrollable tremor began to shudder throughout his entire body and was becoming harder to disguise. As his father approached, Mick gently placed a hand upon his son's shoulder, instinctively realising something was wrong.

"You okay buddy?" Even though Nick was far from okay, the words were delivered tenderly and with a whispery tone, maintaining a measure of secrecy as the remaining two members of their party were still several feet behind. Without waiting for a reply, the older man continued. "It's not too late, you know. No one would think any less of you if you called this thing off, the history you have with this fucking place would freak anyone out." It took several seconds before Nick could respond, the lump in his throat causing restriction on his vocal cords.

"Thanks dad, but I'll be fine. Just give me a second, okay?" His hands had now escaped the platform's grasp, the cold residue wiped upon his drenched jeans. With Brackett and Challis emerging, junior took the final opportunity at a private retort. "Just a bit of a flashback, that's all."

"It's only natural. I just want to say one thing, I'm going in there for you, no one else. I understand this is something you have to do, and I hope coming with you can start to make up for all the shitty things I've done in the past. I love you boy." Nick desperately wanted to respond in kind, but with the team now reunited, a loving smile would have to do for now. Aware of his unofficial role as group leader, Nick decided he needed a statement of intent. Blowing all the air from his lungs, he placed his hands once more on the cold marble trim, and with one single leap, bounced up onto the platform. He almost expected another bolt of electricity to surge through him and when none came, he breathed an audible sigh of relief. Offering a hand down to his team, Mick was the first to accept the assistance. For a man in his forties, senior was still in reasonable shape, even if the alcohol and cigarettes had taken a toll on his fitness. With a strenuous hoist, senior was back up, shoulder to shoulder with his son. They shared a questioning glance and Nick winked, insinuating that the recent panic had dissipated. When Castle volunteered a hand to Brackett, the officer's head shook swiftly, the alpha male in his psyche unwilling to accept facilitation. Not wishing to appear inferior to Nick's athletic prowess, he turned backwards, placing the palms of his hands onto the platform edge before thrusting up to a seated position. His three-quarter length coat made climbing to his feet a chore, but it was a small price to pay to save face. Challis had no such illusions of grandeur, welcoming cooperation from both generations of Castle, flying gracefully into the air and landing upright without the need for exertion. Step two was now complete.

The group decided against using the roofed passageway between the main building and the former station-masters quarters as a route to the entrance, instead taking the slightly longer circuit around the platform's outer perimeter, unnecessary risks being deemed pointless. Passing to the rear of the property, the sudden change in visibility levels became quickly apparent. Just moments earlier, the dark surroundings were occasionally broken by outside influences. Brightness from homes on Station view and Colliery Lane, across in the distance, at least gave reminders that there was still life away from their situation. Streetlights from neighbouring roads and the occasional passing vehicle headlights also gave a break in the opaqueness of the night-time atmosphere. But now there was nothing, all that was adjacent were desolate fields and woodland. Both Nick and Johnny had had the foresight to bring along torches, though neither had come equipped with additional batteries. Aware that inside, light would be a priority and not knowing what lifespan remained in the power-source, using the flashlights were on a need-only basis. For the moment, they'd be working blind.

They'd momentarily paused at the opening of the roofed passageway, a tiny hope that Jenifer may call out from inside the smaller building. With no noise emanating from the station-master quarters, they progressed without investigation. Continuing on the main entryway into the main building was just feet away, this was quickly becoming real.

The four team members stopped dead, as though they'd walked into an invisible wall. Initially, the sudden darkness to the rear of the property had been unnerving, but it hadn't taken long for their eyes to become accustomed to the crepuscule bleakness, distant trees and fence boundaries, hedgerows swaying at the strengthening wind and long grass battling the elements, all creating a divergence of shade and movement. But now, ahead was a total contrast to what had come before. Beyond that door was a tenebrous blockade of obscurity, the more their eyes searched for a guidance spot, the more everything merged into one.

Challis took a step backwards, self-preservation screaming in his mind, RUN... RUN, JOG, HOP, CALL A TAXI, DO ANYTHING, JUST GET THE HELL AWAY. He looked to his left and to his right, hoping to see the same concern on his comrades' faces. The interpretation of the older man's expression was hard to read, either he was a superior poker player with bluffing his specialised subject, or he knew something Dan didn't. Mick had been part of the miscarried invasion party, years earlier, so he had experience of what lay ahead. But as it had failed so dramatically, it was hard to envision how that could instil confidence going forward. Brackett was equally hard to decipher, his idiosyncratic nature and unwillingness to show weakness was illustrated in his deadpan expression and wide unblinking eyes. Was Johnny feeling as terrified as Challis as they stood on the threshold to Hell? Who knows, but as Dan studied his friend's face, a tiny tear emerged from the officer's right eye. The disabled man smirked, feeling less cowardly as the thought of the policeman's heart beating wildly registered in Challis's troubled mind. As for Nick, his recent panic attack was now just a memory. Eliminating the first hurdle, which had been climbing onto the platform, had helped his confidence grow. Though it was small in comparison to what lay ahead, he believed that this mission would be won and lost inside the mind, physical attributes taking care of themselves. They would need focus, clear and concise planning, nothing rash, audacious, or foolhardy, and to ensure victory, considered rational choices would be essential. Considered...? Rational...? Nick knew these things were completely against his personality, and in reality, the chances of him sticking to it was doubtful. Still, it never hurt to hope.

"Excuse me boys, I know this is a little late but, I have a small problem." Mick Castle's tone seemed serious. "It's about the gun. Does anyone know how they work?" Systematically, all three of the younger men raised their eyebrows, the timing of the quandary less than perfect.

"Well Mr C, what happens is, long round things called bullets, go inside. If you see something that you want to make dead, point the barrel, that's the thing the bullets come out of, in the direction of the thing you want to make dead. You put your finger on the trigger, that's the thin bit of metal hanging down under the barrel, and when you hear a bang, hopefully the thing you want to make dead, falls over. If the thing that falls over, is you, that means you pointed the gun in the wrong direction." Nick and Johnny burst into a fit of laughter, even if the volume was controlled. Dan Challis, being one of the most sarcastic people ever to walk the earth, awaited a punch from the team's oldest member, and when none arrived, he began to continue, happy to have an audience. When Mick flared an unamused glare in his direction, Challis decided to quit while he was ahead.

"Wait just a minute dad. You told me you were familiar with the gun?" Junior realised the revelation could have serious implications for their plans.

"Yep, I lied, I haven't got a clue. Never held one, never fired one, never even loaded one." Nick looked on, exasperated at his father's blasé attitude.

"You did remember to bring bullets, didn't you?" It was Brackett who asked the question.

"Oh yes, they're here in my pocket." Mick reached into his jacket, proffering several long silver lengths of ammunition. His son shook his head in dismay.

"Well, they aren't much use in there, are they? What you are planning on doing, throwing them at the bad guys?" Challis's sarcastic tone was beginning to aggravate the older man.

"Listen dickhead, at least I brought a weapon. I've never had any need to be around guns, that's why I hoped one of you might have more luck. So, does *any* of you know how these fucking things work because if you don't, we might as well chuck it in the bin?"

Both Castle men looked to Johnny, his background in law enforcement making him the obvious choice.

"Sorry, fellas, don't look at me. Armed response is a specialised unit, it's not often you need a weapon giving out parking tickets and breaking up drunken brawls." Nick's patience was wearing super-thin, aggravated massively that, had his father acknowledged his lack of prowess with a firearm back at the car, at least they'd have had a light source to help load the fucking thing.

"Well, that's just great. It's a good thing it isn't loaded, or maybe I'd have considered using it on you." Junior was staring directly into senior's eyes.

"I'll take it." Dan Challis had been reluctant to volunteer but it seemed there was now no other choice. Brackett scoffed.

"No offence mate but, what do you know about guns? With the way your hands shake, you'd probably shoot me."

"Johnny, if I shot you, it wouldn't be by accident. Anyway, clever fucker, what you don't know is this. My dad was part of a gun club over in Carpenter, since he was such a pussy, it was the only way he could get his aggression out. A few years ago, I started going with him, he was trying to play daddy, too little, too late. Strange thing is, I started getting pretty good at it, I had no experience, just a natural thing. When I got better than him, the fucker stopped me going. I haven't been in a while but, it looks like I'm the only one here who knows one end of a gun from the other. It was the only thing I was ever good at." The last part was said with a solemn tone, a faint battle with regret clouding his thoughts.

"Christ, it's Mr Mystery over here." Mick took one final look at the weapon before handing it over. Nick raised his eyes in surprise, finally pleased at his troubled friend's participation.

"Okay, Billy the kid, do you think you can handle that?" Taking the weapon in his right hand, Challis enjoyed the empowerment the cold steel delivered.

"There's only one way to find out." Flicking a lever on the Gun's left side, the magazine ejected. Finding the chamber empty, the others watched on in begrudging fascination as, one by one, the bullets were loaded. When the magazine was full, Dan snapped it back into place, cracking the firing safety switch until it was needed. "Locked and loaded boys, are we ready to rumble?" As they looked at one another in mild bewilderment, Challis stepped forward, the first man to pass the threshold to the station.

Tom Daley's heart was pounding out a rare rhythm, vibrating off his chest wall like a jackhammer. Climbing on to the platform had been the easy part, his child-like innocence making him believe that somehow, everything would work out fine. When he'd made it to the rear of the property, that miss-placed confidence had begun to erode and by the time he'd reached the main building entrance, his brain screamed out retreat. Had it not been for his overwhelming fear of being re-incarcerated, he would almost certainly have withdrawn and ran for his life. But that was no longer an option, without finding Neil Roberts, his future was bleaker than the outside conditions.

It had taken all his courage to step inside, the ungodly darkness making him feel claustrophobic, even though the room before him was vast. He cursed himself for not having the fortitude to seek out a flashlight from his little cottage kitchen. He could visualise it, hidden inside a draw by the refrigerator, complete with batteries and a little stand. How he wished it was here, things would be so much easier if only he could see. With his vision negligible, he began to rely on other senses more, mainly hearing. Taking a few strides, he'd pause, and listen. Walk, pause, listen, walk pause, listen. It would take more time, but it was safer than rushing.

It had taken more than five minutes to just pass around the perimeter of the ground floor, using the outer wall as a guild, his ears pricked, concentrating on every sound, attentive to microscopic rustles, holding his breath as to miss nothing. His eyes were still battling their surroundings, just shapes and shadows emerging from the gloom, and as he completed his circuit of the room, he was already drenched in perspiration, the convergence of the situation exhausting. The stress-headache which had begun even before entering was gaining in force and he reached into his pocket, grabbing a strip of his pain medication, and pushing two more pills from the blister-pack, throwing them to the back of his throat before swallowing. He'd already taken too many today, the woozy feeling making his body numb, but at least the pain would soon subside.

Across in the corner, Tom grimaced as his next worrying task became clear. The door-less entranceway leading to the stone spiral staircase looked grim and uninviting. Daley had heard stories about it, the kiddies who had previously played in his back-garden used to scare each-other and say there were ghosts around every corner. Now…he'd have to see if that was true. A faint whimper escaped from his tightly closed lips, he wanted to cry, he wanted to run, he wanted to be anywhere but here. His lips began to tremble, as did the rest of his body. There was a stirring in his bladder, and he squeezed tightly, determined to not allow its contents to burst free. His vision began to blur, this was crazy, he wasn't brave enough for this, he wasn't strong enough for this, he was no hero. Tom was about to turn and head for the exit when a sound from above made him freeze. It had sounded like a voice. No, perhaps not a voice, just a cry, a whimper like the one that had just escaped from his own lips. He listened intently; there it was again. It sounded child-like, someone afraid, someone in trouble. The image of Neal Roberts fired into his brain. How could he allow himself to leave? How could he run away if that little boy needed his help? His fists were balled so tightly, the fingernails were piercing the skin of his palms. With teeth clenched, a new look of determination spread across his face, with a herculean effort, he raised his right leg and began the ascension to the next level.

Step, step, pause. Step, step, pause. The darkness was all consuming, there could have been anything standing before him, and he'd have no warning until they were nose to nose. Step, step, pause. His hearing became incredibly acute, though there was little of interest to heed. The outside wind was growing and, in the distance, a rumble of thunder made Tom flinch. Other than his own heartbeat, which was still beating a quickening pace, the building was silent. Had the cry from above been his imagination? Christ, what if it was a ghost? He blocked the image from his brain as quickly as it had entered, there was enough to worry about without ghoulies and goblins.

Slowly, he arrived at the first floor. He'd decided that, instead of inspecting each floor individually, he'd climb each flight of stairs, and then wait, and listen. If Neal was here, and alive, surely, he'd hear something, some movement or whimper, anything which could give away his position. Daley had considered calling out across the expanse of each floor but decided against it, the bad man might hear. If Neal was here and not okay, Tom had decided he'd rather not find him, taking out a lifeless body might make the villagers think he was guilty even more. This was rescue only, anything else and…

Floor one, two, and three, all silent as the grave. He'd waited as long as his waning courage would allow, standing still, holding his breath, trying so very hard to see any movement, the slightest flicker of change across the dark beyond, but there was nothing. The temperature inside had plunged, his damp clothing clinging to his skin, making him tremble. His teeth chattered uncontrollably, but he wasn't certain whether it was the conditions or his undeniable fear. He'd expected things be become easier by now, perhaps growing slightly more comfortable in the surroundings, maybe his eyes becoming more accustomed to the blackness, but nothing seemed to help. Every dark shadow appeared to increase his terror, every shape taking on the form of the bad man. He scolded himself silently for having the temerity of believing he was capable of this crazy mission. Maybe he should just have stayed in the police-house, the cells were warm and safe, constable Brackett had promised to get his pills, anything would be better than this. Deciding it was madness to continue, he was about to begin a race back down the stone staircase, back to the doorway and out into the open-air. Maybe head back to the police-house and apologise to Doctor Brackett, he'd understand that good old Tom hadn't meant to hurt him, he was just desperate, that's all. Yes, that was the way to go, just run, run, and run and run until he couldn't run anymore. By then he'd be safe, by then he'd be…

It came from above. The same noise as he'd heard not ten minutes ago, only louder this time. It was a struggled cry, not clear and concise but enough to realise he was getting closer. Moving forward was so hard, everything told him that it was wrong, that it was the biggest mistake of his life. But if he didn't investigate, what kind of life would he have to go back too? More insults, more vandalism, more assaults? Leaving Hallowell wasn't an option, where would he go? His whole life was here, he'd never known anything else. If he could just find the will, the courage, to continue a little longer, then maybe he'd have his life back, all those horrible memories would be forgotten, and he could have a future instead of living in the past. What did he have to lose, living like this was no life at all?

Wiping away an escaping tear, he pushed on. One flight to go, I think. Have I climbed four flights or five? It was hard to remember. Please let it be one, it sounded like one. Every step was torture, dust mites filled the air, grey speckles dancing before his eyes in no discernible pattern, his breath visible, white, like odourless smoke. He sniffed, wondering if it really was smoke, but nothing came to his senses. Everything was confusing now, the noise from above had ceased once more, and again, he began to question whether it had been his imagination. It didn't matter now, there was three steps to go, three more steps and he was at the top floor.

He stepped out of the staircase, strangely relieved to be away from the spiral vortex. The room was slightly more visual than the previous five, across on the far wall, a long window broke up the blackness, and though the outside atmosphere had turned to night-time, the variation of shade made a slight difference and a focal point to aim for. Curiously, there was something more; to the left of the window, there was an object standing upright from the floor and though its form was nothing more than a rectangle, there was a mild brightness from the upper width. A moderate, almost benign fluctuation in the lighting, an orangey glow, hidden inside its host, revealed only by reflection, Tom studied closely, finally understanding that the source must be the dying embers of a fire. Perhaps an oil drum capable of harnessing the flames without allowing the ability to spread. Was this an opportunity, or a trap? If Neal was alive after all these days, he'd have needed warmth. Even though it was only autumn, the temperatures of night-time in Hallowell could be bitterly brutal. Perhaps the bad man wasn't so bad after all? Perhaps, he'd started the fire just for Neal, keeping him warm until deciding upon the boy's release.

Daley strode forward, step, step, pause, step, step, pause, his eyes finally becoming more accustomed to the gloomy surroundings. The remainder of the room held little interest, the dissimilarity by the window peaking the naive man's enthusiasm. Still walking slowly but deliberately, more shapes began to reveal themselves. False boundary walls, cordoning off parts of the room, a desk midway across the floor, its position a divergence from the bareness. Broken glass on the concrete flooring, announced only by the cracking under his feet. And it was this sound which created the most telling contrast.

As the crunching commotion echoed out, there was movement across the way. Two shapes; Tom stared intently as the first appeared to be a person, seated upon a low-to-the-ground chair, remaining still and silent. It was hard to be certain, the obvious solution the mind would create was a human form, and he was still too far away to say with any conviction. Daley was confident that the second form was definitely a person, the silhouette, the outline, it was unmistakable. Not only was it a human being, but it was a human being who was coming his way.

Panic suddenly filled Daley's mind once more. What should I do? If it was the bad man, he'd be helpless, if it wasn't why hadn't he spoken yet. Instinctively, he began to back away, ready to run at a second's notice. The closer the figure became; the more Tom was certain that his life was drawing to a close. Just twenty feet away now, the person's silhouette was taking on greater detail. Tom's retreat was quickening pace, though his backwards steps still allowed him to watch the emerging person keenly. The advancer wasn't tall but what he lacked in height was made up for with girth, the midsection bulbous, the neck barely visible, rolls of access fat making the shoulders and head appear as one. There didn't appear a curvature of hair across the person's scalp, and the frame of his face appeared bloated and misshapen. Suddenly, it spoke.

"Tom Daley?" The voice was one the frightened man recognised, though its identity remained suspect due to his panic. "That is you, Tom, isn't it?" The tone was familiar, not as loud or booming but still constant, and finally, something triggered inside Daley's confused psyche.

"Mr Gibson?" The undertaker was only feet away now, his unpleasant visage as repugnant as ever, even if Tom was relieved to acknowledge a familiar face. The expression upon Gibson's red sweaty face was one of bewilderment, the simpleton before him being the last thing he expected.

"Tom, what are you doing here, this place is dangerous?" The words were fired with a gruff emphasis, the conversation appearing chore-like.

"Oh Mr Gibson, I'm so pleased to see you, so much has happened, I don't know where to start. I ran away from the police-house, I know it was bad, but I had no choice. You see, I needed my pills, and no one would get them for me. So I punched Dr Brackett, I know it was very bad, but I had to, I thought I'd die if I didn't. And when I got away, I realised I'd done wrong and was going to go back, but I didn't dare in case Dr Brackett was dead. I'm in so much trouble, I thought I'd go to jail for real, so I didn't go back. I couldn't go home because they'd catch me and take me back to jail and I couldn't stand that, so instead, I came here. You see, I know the bad man lives here, but I thought, maybe little Neal might still be alive and if he was and I saved him, people would leave me alone. Maybe I'd be a hero and I wouldn't have to go back to jail, not unless Dr

Brackett is dead, then I'd probably have to go back for a little while, but maybe not for too long cos I'd say it was an accident. I don't know, I didn't want to hurt anyone, I'm so confused." He paused before continuing. "But Mr Gibson, why are you here?"

The mortician was dumbfounded, all the details which the poor innocent had bombarded him with was hard to grasp. Raising his eyebrows in strained amusement, Fred replied.

"Wow, you hit Harry Brackett. You probably are in trouble." Daley's face creased, as though he was about to cry but before tears began, the undertaker continued. "But I might be able to help you." Tom's lower jaw dropped with a mixture of puzzlement and hope. "You see, that's why I'm here too, to find little Neal Roberts. And guess what, I have found him. I knew you hadn't hurt the boy, so I thought I'd prove it by finding him. And guess what else, he's fine, just a little sleepy. In fact, he's right over there, just resting in that chair. Now, this is up to you but, if you like, we can tell everyone you found him, then you will be a hero." Daley suddenly lost the urge to fight his emotions, tears of relief cascading down his cheeks in unequivocal joy. Lunging forward, he wrapped his arms around the mortician's neck, the outpouring of alleviation overwhelming.

"Really Mr Gibson? You're not kidding. You promise you're not kidding? I can't believe how kind you are, I really can't. I don't know why people say nasty things about you. I never did, honest. I just listened but never ever joined in." The undertaker frowned, the ill-thought-out complement revealing more details than Gibson wished to know, even if he'd suspected as much. "Oh, Mr Gibson, it's hard to believe this has come true, I hoped, and I said a little prayer to God too, but I didn't think I'd find him. But now, everything can be better, I'm sorry to go on but I'm really excited, you really, really, promise that really, really, is Neal over in that chair? There's definitely no mistake?" The expression on Tom's face was so hopeful, so innocent.

"Yes Tom, he's right over there by the oil-drum, there's been a little fire burning for days, so he's been nice and warm too. But he's been through a lot and is still sleeping, so all you have to do, is go wake him. Do you think you can do that?" The mortician's words were delivered slowly with an unaggressive tone, like a parent speaking to a concerned child. Daley paused, his naivety willing him to believe everything he was being told, though their surroundings meant that doubts remained.

"But why is he sleeping Mr Gibson? It's too scary for a nap. He is okay, isn't he?" Tom didn't wish to appear cynical or mistrustful, but there had been all those rumours about how devious and selfish the undertaker was, why was he being so nice now?

"I just said he was okay, didn't I?" The mortician's natural instinct was threatening to bubble to the surface, momentarily causing the simple man to back away. Realising his mistake, Fred returned to the charm offensive. "I'm sorry, I mean, yes, of course he's fine. I was just checking on him and he was beginning to regain consciousness when I saw you. I don't think he's slept much recently, that's why he's so tired. Now, if you prefer, we can forget about telling people that you found Neal, I'll take the credit if you'd rather do it that way, but if you really want people to forget your past, and look to you as a hero, then that's probably the only way it's going to happen. But it's up to you?" Reverse psychology, a devious mind's best friend.

"No, no, please, I'm sorry, I didn't mean to sound ungrateful, and of course I believe you Mr Gibson, you've been so kind to me, it's amazing really. Nobody's been this nice to me for a long time, everybody just calls me nasty names and throws things at my home. I never did the horrid things the kiddies said I did, honest. I would never do anything to hurt those kiddies, they were my friends, and that's all I want now, I just want people to be my friend again, I've been so lonely for so long, sometimes, at night, I cry myself to sleep. I have a cuddly-toy doggy on my bed called spot, he's the only one I have to talk to. Do you think you might want to be my friend, Mr Gibson?" Tom's pleading sickened the mortician, his whining and begging reminded him of a mangy mongrel, sniffing for scraps on the street. But at least Gibson now knew, he had Daley under his devious influence.

"Okay Tommy (the Y was added in the pretence of affection) Of course, we can be friends (lies) and I never believed any of those stories they said about you (more lies), so let's start the healing. We'll pretend I wasn't even here; you can have all the credit for finding Neal, and then saving him too, it will be our little secret." The undertaker smiled at the excited man, the way a paedophile might grin while gaining the confidence of a potential victim.

Finally, things were going Tom Daley's way, his life could be rectified by this strange source, and all he needed now was a little trust and some extra courage; he smiled, I can do that.

Gibson could see his plan was working, all that remained was a final push. Placing a hand on the innocent's shoulder, he squeezed gently before motioning with his eyes in the seated member's direction. Tom nodded dutifully and began the quest across the dirty concrete walkway. The darkness ensured an air of caution was still required and as such, he trod ponderously, still aware that this was the bad-man's lair, the shadows were long and the space vast, prudence and discretion was essential.

Step, step, pause, step, step, pause. He'd involuntarily been holding his breath and when he realised, he released a sigh-like exhale. Halfway, he stopped and looked back in the mortician's direction, with his unlikely partner, this task felt even harder. He wanted to call out, ask for help, for guidance, but Mr Gibson had been so nice already, surely, he couldn't expect more? He needed to be brave, to prove he deserved to be a hero, so with a second, quieter sigh, he turned once more towards his destination and continued his journey.

Gibson's fat pudgy fingers wiped a sweaty residue across the rear of his trousers before sliding into his back pocket. Retrieving the prize from the ill-fitting clothing was difficult and required patience, and he was relieved when it emerged, momentarily concerned that it may have been lost in the earlier struggle with Jenifer His eyes had never left his retreating partner, though visual aid was not needed to transform the piece of benign steel into a lethal weapon. Using both hands, the snap as the blade from the folding knife clicked into place echoed out across the deathly quiet room. Due to his concentration, the sound didn't register with Daley, and the undertaker's pulse quickened as he began to follow along the same route.

Tom squinted, the seated member was just feet away now, their head bowed forward, resting upon the breastbone, and from the rear, all that could be seen was a slim pair of shoulders and a black leather jacket. Concern grew once more in his fearful mind as he noticed a thin pair of wrists bound with clear twine, locked between the base of the spine and the wooden slats of the hard-backed chair. He pauses once more, looking back in the mortician's direction, desperate for fatherly encouragement, but the room's extreme darkness had almost swallowed the devious miscreant. Returning his attention towards the seated person, dread was increasing by the second, that didn't look like Neal Roberts?

"Mr Gibson. I'm sorry but, I think there's been some mistake, I don't think this is Neal." His voice was shaky and on the verge of tears and as such, his volume was louder than intended, a mild echo vibrating across the floor's bare walls. Throwing a hand across his lips, he scanned the room, hoping that the bad *man* hadn't heard his cry. The undertaker was barely visible, and all Tom wanted to do was run, only decency and worry for the stricken seated person forcing him to remain. Suddenly, there was a murmur. The poor soul before him was waking, the neck twitching, slowly gaining strength allowing the head to rise. Tom looked on anxiously; he'd been right, it wasn't Neal, it wasn't even male. It was a woman, no, a girl, long dark hair hanging loosely down to her shoulders, a wound on her forehead which appeared serious, and dried blood all across the face, making her skin appear dark, broken only by streaks below the eyes and down both cheeks where tears had escaped.

"Oh dear, Miss, are you okay?" Obviously, a stupid question, it was delivered softly but urgently, with a caring tone. Her face was upright now, with her neck fighting painful stiffness at the top of her spine, she slowly swivelled her head to face her potential saviour. Though there were no restrictions across her lips, her vocal cords refused to reply, the confusion of the previous horrific events making trust a hard commodity to purchase. But the man did seem genuinely concerned for her well-being and had a kind face and innocent puppy-dog eyes, slowly she began to allow herself to believe that he could be the key to her survival. As Jenifer studied the strange person, with her head pounding and vision blurred, her body wracked in pain and her spirits depressed, she decided that he was her only hope. Delivering a wry smile, Daley grinned back, happy that, if he couldn't rescue Neal Roberts, this girl was the next best thing. Suddenly, Jenifer's smile rapidly turned to an expression of fear, her eyes widening with hopelessness, realising almost psychically what was about to happen.

The undertaker appeared out of the shadows like a nightmarish phantasm, a mask of hatred mixed with excitement plastered across his devilish face. Daley still wasn't aware of his presence, concern for the girl taking importance over self-preservation. So to appear less threatening, Tom began to Kneel at Jenifer's feet, an action which almost certainly sealed his fate.

The mortician's forearm slid menacingly around Daley's throat, the grip tightening second upon second. Shock fired inside the frightened man's mind and momentarily, his body became paralysed, with his airways blocked, panic immediately attacked. The girl looked on but still, her vocal cords remained useless, the scream she longed for refusing to break free. Gibson's bulk became his alley, from his position of strength, simply leaning forward meant his opponent was trapped, Daley's lower back silently screaming in pain, his breathing halted, and his brain fractured with confusion. Could this be an error? Had Mr Gibson mistaken him for the bad man? The innocent tried to twist his neck, hoping to make eye contact, but his body was captured in a vice-like grip, like an anaconda squeezing its prey. When he couldn't reach the undertaker's line-of-sight, he stared back towards the young woman, his eyes sorrowful and lost, his mind slowly beginning to understand his fate.

Jenifer Graham recoiled in terror as she saw the weapon inside Gibson's right hand, its usage inevitable, the form of attack less predictable. Her need to scream a warning was still hugely prevalent but still, the words refused to arrive, her fear for the man before her suddenly a greater concern than her own fate. Gibson clenched the dull steel handle, its blade reflecting an off-white sheen, raising it high above the right shoulder, the tip aimed with marksman-like accuracy, pointing in Tom's direction. His flabby left arm still pinned tightly around his opponents' neck, the crush making a breath almost impossible. Aware that the stricken man was helpless, a demonic expression of glee grew across the mortician's evil face, the realisation that his repugnant lifelong ambition was easily within reach. A sour, yellow-toothed grin emerged; he was going to enjoy this.

Instead of slashing down with the horrific weapon, Gibson changed tact, adamant that this would not be rushed. Manoeuvring the knife to the right-hand side of Daley's neck, he positioned the tip just north of the corotated artery, pressing with just enough force to make an indentation upon the flesh.

"No, please." Tom whispered the words.

"No, please." Jenifer's tone was equally as soft, never expecting the pleading request to be granted. With a sick smile, Gibson pushed added pressure, the elasticity of the skin giving way, the piercing allowing a small trickle of blood to escape. The girl could no longer watch, closing her eyes tightly and spinning her head away. The mortician noticed her reaction but now craved an audience for the abhorrent act.

"Open your eyes, bitch." Gibson snarled the words with venom, though the young woman refused to react. Growing increasingly impatient, he continued. "I'm warning you, watch, you worthless cunt, or I'll slice your eyelids off." Knowing she had little option, she blinked away tears before firing the undertaker a disgusted glare. Content that he was in complete control, Fred returned his attention to the blubbering wreck before him, blood from the wound now flowing freely. Tensing the muscles in his forearm and tightening his grip upon the handle, he increased the pressure, finding little resistance as the blade sliced cleanly into Daley's neck. Knowing enough about human anatomy to be confident that the wound's placement wouldn't be immediately fatal, he pushed harder, stopping only when the blunt edge of the handle touched flesh.

By now, Tom was barely conscious, he bodies seemingly closing down to avoid the onset of more pain. Still the mortician refused to increase his speed of attack, keenly aware that Daley's life could be extinguished whenever he wished but enjoying the torture too much to end the stricken man's suffering. The tip of the blade touched something hard, Gibson guessed it was the top of Tom's spine, so in curiosity, he began to wriggle the hard steel, scratching the internal bone, the pain returning his victim from the self-imposed psychological exile, the agony suddenly causing a huge crescendo inside Daley's fractured brain. Gently, the undertaker withdrew the knife, a forceful jet of sticky blood spurting horrifically into the air, Gibson marvelling at the spectacle. As a revolting reservoir formed at their feet, Tom's eyes rolled back, appearing lifeless, while the grin upon the psychopath's face grew ever wider, a sick sense of accomplishment taking over his thoughts. The blood-loss was growing to massive proportions, the deep-red fountain cascading sickeningly in Jenifer's direction, spray drenching her clothing, sliding stickily across Nick Castle's loaned leather jacket. As the undertaker loosened his grip around Daley's throat, the victim fell forward, his left shoulder crashing hard onto the cold concrete, followed closely by his head and torso. Though his life had yet to expire, all innocent exuberance was now deceased, the pupils of his eyes beginning to dilate, becoming unresponsive. His lips silently mouthed the word, "Why?" but the only sound released was a congestive stifled strangulate as Daley began to choke upon his own blood.

Wanting an exclamation point upon the nefarious act, Gibson pounced, his knees pressing onto his victim's stomach, and taking the knife into both hands, the mortician began to strike. There was no effort for procrastination now, the lock-knife pounded down, again and again with irresistible force, no longer aiming for definitive areas, instead just marvelling at the power surging through his body. The blade slashed between Daley's ribcage, piercing the heart, the explosion of plasma massive, even if the blood pressure had fallen dramatically. A low moan escaped Tom's mouth, his teeth jammed together, lips turning blue, his jaw locked. As the attack continued, the blade gnashed deeply into Daley's skull, crashing violently into the right cheekbone, sliding off the bone, dislodging four teeth and causing a huge flap of skin to fall away. When little blood pumped clear, Gibson knew the task was complete, the heart had ceased beating, Tom was dead.

Sickeningly, still the assault continued. A return to the chest, deep wounds upon both shoulders and stomach; the left eye exploded with a popping sound as the blade pierced the pupil, emerging from the socket as the weapon retreated. The heinous assault ended only when Gibson collapsed with exhaustion, an ungodly smile plastered across his bloody face.

Looking on, the girl wanted to vomit, the sight too much to bear. Instead, she finally recovered her voice, one scream erupting, followed more, and more…and more.

Chapter 40

"Jesus Christ, what the hell was that?" The four rescuers had reached floor three and found nothing, heard nothing. It hadn't been easy, they'd searched each level forensically, or as forensically as their nerves would allow. Taking whatever care was available, they'd stayed locked together as a group, a set of eyes focused on every direction, listening for any change in atmosphere, with only the storm outside breaking the silence. Only one torch was used at a time, the bulbs and batteries being priorities over extra short-term vision. Heart rates would rise in areas of darkened corners or obscure doorways. Pressure increasing when hideaway objects required inspection, cupboards and desks, false walls and workstations, all demanding attention, all raising their pulse-rates…none baring fruit.

Strangely, their apprehension seemed to be increasing at the perceived lack of activity, the anticipation feeling worse than whatever battle lay ahead.

From above, a series of blood-curdling screams permeated the air, shattering the deathly silence, freezing the four men in their tracks. Challis had been the first to ask the question, though the answer seemed self-explanatory. While waiting for a reply, Dan felt the gun in the palm of his right hand, finger holding firmly upon the trigger, and considered whether the safety switch was still in position. More so, you wondered if he really did have the guts to shoot another human being, should the situation dictate it? Finally, Nick Castle fired an excited reply.

"It's Jenifer, it has to be. She is here and more importantly, she's still alive." Mick gave his son a bemused frown, this was suddenly becoming very real.

"How do you know it was her? It was a scream, not a voice?" It was now junior's turn to repel a look of bewilderment.

"Are you taking the piss? It was a woman's scream, how many other fucking females do you think could be in here tonight?" He'd already begun a sprint across the room to the staircase doorway without awaiting a reply, the plan to remain together as a tightly cohesive group suddenly dissolved.

"Hey dopey, where the Hell do you think you're going?" Mick began to panic, aware that his son was too quick to keep up with, too headstrong to see sense, and about to roam the hallways of this God-forsaken place alone.

"To do what I came here to do." The reply was retorted between heavy breathes, his head twisting back across his right shoulder without effecting his speed, the burst of a sprinter rather than the endurance of a distance runner, his feet struggling for purchase on the dusty floor. Johnny Brackett looked to his two remaining team members, waiting intently for encouragement to follow his fleeing friend. Challis caught the expression and knew instantly the officer's intentions.

"Go on then, for fuck's sake, we'll be bloody fine...alone." As ever, the sarcasm was laid on thickly, his usual use of humour as a defence mechanism ever present. "But you're not getting the gun...and if any of you silly bastards hide out in the shadows, expect to get shot." Taking a breath, Challis and Castle senior gave one another a mystified glance. "Well Mr C, alone at last."

The screams had unnerved Gibson. Jenifer had been through Hell in the last few hours; abduction, assault, both physically and psychologically, loss of consciousness more times than a narcoleptic pensioner, and tolerating the repugnant stench of her heinous captor, the creature which had seemed to have made it his mission to destroy her.

But witnessing the murder of Tom Daley, the savagery and disregard for human life, had suddenly made this situation so much worse. No matter what she'd suffered previously, there was nothing that couldn't be repaired. Pain could end, wounds stitched or bandaged, emotions healed, growing as a Graham, she knew that more than most. But after witnessing that butchery, the desecration of that man's broken body, his blood spreading thickly across that filthy floor, the fountain spurting high at first, losing its ferocity as the heart ceased to beat, transforming into the totality of death, and as Jenifer watched Tom Daley die, she'd looked on in morbid fascination, hoping to see his soul drift away into the heavens. Instead, there's been nothing, just the malaise funk of execution, the metaphorical excrement of human nature, the evil that men do.

It was then that the screaming had begun. At first, she hadn't even realised, her horrified yells vibrating around everywhere except inside her own mind. And when the young woman finally did realise, she was piercing the air with her high-pitched cries, it was too late, her hysteria making it impossible to control. Her throat was hoarse, lips cracked, eyes streaming with tears; her pounding headache made it painful to even think, but still she had no authority to curb her deafening delirium.

There was a sudden realisation that her own fate was destined to mirror the bloody remains by her feet. There was so much she hadn't done yet, things she was desperate to experience, her sheltered upbringing being guarded and protected. Buying her own home, starting a family, falling in love. Christ, just hours earlier, she'd been in the company of a man who'd had the potential to share in all of those things. The enigmatic stranger with piercing eyes, who'd looked at her as more than just a sexual conquest. Just that very morning, Jenifer had felt so happy, so excited, at whatever the future may hold, how could things turn to shit so quickly. Now, she was tied to a chair in this Hellhole, head pounding, body aching, flanked by this disgusting man and with no fucking explanation. So that's why she was screaming, why she would scream, and scream, and scream, longer, louder, harder, because it was the only weapon left in her arsenal. It didn't matter that her throat was raw, her voice deserting her, her only chance was for someone to hear her plight, to launch a rescue, to...

Thwack. Gibson's back-handed slap was more shocking than painful, a red welt immediately forming across her left cheek, one nostril allowing a tiny flow of blood to trickle down to her lips. It was only the acidic taste that forced her screams to cease, it was strange that, after everything she'd suffered, a mere unpleasant sourness could bring her back from the brink of hysteria.

As for Gibson, the girl's cries had initially turned him on, he terrified yells serving as a sexual aphrodisiac to his sickening sensibilities. He'd grinned that deviant smile while watching her mental deterioration, enjoying her distress, her pain. But soon he began to realise that inside the empty shell of a building, sound carried. They were close to the open window and, even though most residents were too chicken-shit to enter this place, especially at night, there was always the chance of a good Samaritan being unable to suppress the urge to assist a woman in need. It wasn't worth the risk.

He lowered the blade to her exposed throat while yanking hard at the back of her long hair, exposing the strong line of the corotated artery, stroking the cold steel against her flesh, threatening to slice a path to her insides. Jenifer's eyes locked onto the weapon rather than stare back at her repulsive captor, the blade almost hypnotic, sorrowfully aware that her fate rested in his blubbery hands.

"Scream again, and I'll gut you like a fish." His previous threats hadn't bothered her much, believing him more an act of bravado rather than a life-or-death ultimatum. But now, she knew exactly what the undertaker was capable of, she'd watched helplessly as he'd slaughtered that poor man and realised instantly that a similar fate could easily be bestowed upon her. In fact, the bigger question was, why hadn't he done it already? There was no way he could allow her to exit alive, what was he waiting for? The mortician had insinuated that her brother was alive and waiting but it was still possible that he'd only used Frank's name as a fear-inducing tool, building his own sick gratification. She was desperate for answers, but the questions wouldn't leave her lips.

The girl had lost all hope now, just praying that it would be over quickly. That was another reason she'd forced her screams to fall silent, what was the point in antagonising the fat bastard? What was the point of anything anymore?

"Jenifer?" The voice had come from floors below, but it was a tone she recognised. Her enigmatic stranger was here, attempting a rescue, her hopes instantly soared. Gibson heard the voice too, his eyes widening, colour draining from his face. With his pulse quickening, he threw a hand across the girl's mouth, squeezing tightly, allowing no room for a scream to escape. Twisting her neck from left to right, she tried to bite at the man's flesh, but his hold was too strong. Her frustration growing by the milli-second, one more call, one more ear-piercing yell and Nick would have a location to home-in upon. She knew that Nick must have heard her previous cries, one more was all that was needed, just one more.

"Make one sound and you die, simple as that." The grip around her face was painful now, five digits crushing into her flesh, his thumb blocking her clear nostril. She breathed in hard and for a second, no oxygen reached her lungs. Her chest began to heave, the panic of a drowning person trapped under water. "Stay quiet and I let your breath, blink twice if you agree?" Her lids began to flutter frantically, self-preservation overtaking the need for rescue. A slight movement of his thumb and sweet unbridled relief washed over her, long gasping intakes making her head feel dizzy. The mortician seemed preoccupied, the voice from below creating massive alarm, who would be idiotic enough to follow them in here? Another call broke through the air, appearing closer now.

"Jenifer. Jenifer, are you there? Shout if you're there." Gibson held his breath, someone was coming, he needed help, he needed Frank, where the fuck was Frank? The undertaker suddenly had an idea. Across in the far-right corner, the old canteen area was the only available hideout. A disused walk-in freezer was still in place, the heavy door could be locked from the inside, the question was, did he have time to get the girl there before the intruder arrived? Without taking his hand from around the young woman's mouth, he began to drag her, while still tied to the wooden chair, across the room, hoping that the noise as the furniture moved would not be too great, this was his only chance.

Nick Castle paused at the top of the stairwell, at the door-less entryway to floor six. Just seconds earlier, he was certain he'd heard a door close, perhaps it was just his overactive imagination. After sprinting up three flights, his breathing was heavy, chest heaving, a chill causing his body to shiver where a layer of perspiration was now fighting against the icy temperature. His eyes scoured the expanse of the room, the dark shadows appearing as ominous as anything the young man could ever imagine. Every shape seemed massive, every silhouette giving the impression of human-like features. Squinting, he tried to find a focal point, anything to aim for rather than walking blind. Everything seemed so dark, the other floors hadn't appeared so pitch, maybe it was because previously, he hadn't been alone. Suddenly feeling foolish, he remembered their plan, sticking together no matter what, that way they could remain in an advantageous position, safety in numbers. Now, nick felt exposed, all around was potential hideouts for the monster. Castle hadn't brought a weapon, the group had retained possession of the gun, he hadn't even had enough patience to insist on use of one of the torches, stupid, so fucking stupid. He considered retreating back to his team but remembered the girl's voice, her tone, so hopeless, so afraid, what choice did he have?

A hand came out of the darkness, gripping onto Castle's shoulder with more force than was necessary. Nick span around, his complexion drained white, his right hand ready to strike out in retaliation.

"You simple bastard. What did you think you were doing?" Johnny Brackett had a face full of rage, his leadership aspirations dented with Castle's swift exit.

"Christ, Johnny, don't fucking creep up on me like that, especially not in here" His heart was pounding a speedy rhythm, even though he was elated to have a partner in tow.

"What did you expect? Was I supposed to run up the stairs shouting, don't get scared mate, it's only me?"

"Point taken." All their words were delivered with hushed urgency and for a few seconds, they fell silent, the officer discovering what his friend already knew, this place was bloody dark.

"Okay hero, have you seen anything out of place?" Castle couldn't believe the question.

"Out of place, are you taking the piss? This is Hallowell railway station; everything is out of place."

"I didn't mean that, clever twat. Have you seen anything of the girl?" Castle never replied, just a solemn shake of the head answer enough. Both men continued to scan the room, listening intently for the smallest sound, hearing nothing. Nick's eyes were growing accustomed to the surroundings, certain points of interest increasing his curiosity.

"Don't know if you can see it but, there's something over there, over by the window." As to accentuate the discovery, he pointed in the direction with his right hand, the police-man's eyes straining to fight through the gloominess, but still not visualising the object.

"I'll take your word for it." Nick sighed, the time for conversation was ending, it was time for action. Gradually, they began across the room, afraid at what they may find.

Gibson held his breath, had they made it in time? He'd dragged the girl forty feet to the canteen area, exerting more strength than he knew he possessed, the chair Jenifer was tied too scratching across the cold concrete. The lip on the broken walk-in freezer was mere inches high but it remained a tough obstacle, using all his remaining power to hoist the girl inside before quietly closing the door behind them. Inside was an entirely new level of darkness, not a crack of light breaking though, the door tight to the floor. He struggled to control his breathing after the strenuous activity, the pains in his chest and right arm once more adding to his concern.

The intruder's voice was familiar, though he couldn't place it. The accent wasn't local and from the tone, it was obviously a younger man, not carrying the emphasis of a person who'd experienced the traumas of a long life, someone beaten down by the trials and tribulations that came with maturity, an urgency without forbearance that came with wisdom, someone like the undertaker himself. Originally, he'd believed the intruder to be Johnny Brackett, the lawman of Hallowell, but again the dialect wasn't right, the regional twang more north-east than north-west. As he racked his brain, the answer suddenly flashed in his mind.

"Castle. That nosey bastard, rabble-rousing piece of shit. I knew that kid would be trouble, the first time I clapped eyes on him." The realisation came with a pronounced level of worry, if the rumours were true, he was a chip off the old block, police-man Bill's favourite off-spring. If he was anything like his grandfather, the kid wouldn't give up easily. The undertaker heard Jenifer's name called once more. It was definitely Castle and he was getting closer, in fact, he was right there on that very floor, just the heavy door between the two battle-hardened men.

"Christ, where the Hell is Frank? He's the monster, he's the killer, this is his home, and that nosey bastard is trespassing, he has to be stopped." Then another preoccupation entered the mortician's mind. What if Castle wasn't alone? Gibson hadn't heard a second voice, but surely no-one would be dumb enough to search here, *alone, at night*. The funeral director's bladder felt fit to burst and his bowels were fighting a similar battle. "What if I get caught? What would happen then? Life without parole, that's what he'd have to look forward to, a life behind bars. I couldn't survive prison, I'm not the type. Oh, why did I choose today to claim my first victim. Until Daley's demise, the worst thing I'd be convicted of is my collection of special trophies, and that's only if they searched my home. They couldn't get me for anything else, and if I plead insanity, I'd get off with a slap on the wrists and a few months in the nuthouse. I could cope with that. But there's one major problem. This bitch is the only witness to what I did. Without her testimony, old Tom's death would be blamed on Frank, just another victim of the railway station killer. But if she survives, I'm fucked."

He looked to the girl, her face barely visible in the dense blackness of the closed in freezer, and immediately knew what he had to do.

Castle and Brackett walked in tandem, their strides long and steady, both apprehensive of what lay before them. The long window on the back wall was at least a small source of light. Johnny had brought along the second of the torches but was still wary of using it, the sudden light could bring unwanted attention. Still, this seemed the correct circumstances, so he reached into the inside pocket of his jacket and produced a thin, silver-handled flashlight, its power minimal but better than nothing.

Brackett was the first to recognise the lingering scent of smoke, hanging in the air, growing stronger as the approached the open-topped oil-drum. As the largest item on show, both men's attention had been drawn towards it, and as the torch flashed across its metal exterior, both felt relieved that it was nothing but an inanimate object. Nick peered across the rim, still wary that human remains could be hidden inside and when he noticed the smouldering embers, he breathed an audible sigh of relief.

"Oh sweet Jesus." The officer had been a few yards behind and had continued his search off to the left of the former fire.

"What's wrong?" Nick's head shot in his friend's direction, Johnny's tone revealing something was seriously off. The light-beam was pointing towards the ground and from his vantage point, Castle could only see a dark mound, crumpled upon the concrete. Suddenly, a horrific thought crossed his mind...Jenifer.

Nick hurried to the officer who was now knelt by the remains.

"Be careful, there's a lot of blood and it's slippery, I don't want to have to carry you out of here." Castle heeded the warning and slowed his pace, squinting to try and make out details, hoping and praying...

"Is it?"

"No. It's not the girl." Brackett reached out towards the victim's neck, just to confirm what was already obvious, the pulse had ceased.

"So who is…" The officer paused, guilt by association beginning to grow in his disconcerted mind.

"It's my prisoner. The guy who escaped earlier, Tom Daley, it's his body." Nick was stunned, lost for words, overjoyed that the remains weren't Jenifer Graham, but dismayed at the sight before them. "This is my fault. I arrested him when he'd done nothing wrong. Hallowell needed a suspect, and he was the perfect patsy. You see, the way this town works is, if someone, *anyone*, gets arrested, then the rest doesn't need to face the truth. And the truth…is that this fucking town is cursed and everyone who lives here is partially to blame. I knew Tom was innocent, Christ, we all knew Tom was innocent, but, while he was in the cells…"

"But why's he here. He escaped earlier today, right? Of all places, why come here?"

"To clear his name, I assume. A kid went missing last week, the Roberts kid. The little bastard had been trying to break into Tom's Garden shed, and the poor chump had heard. When Daley went out to confront him, Neal jumped over the fence and cut himself. Tom went after him, just to help, I guess, but the kid ran away. When Tom followed, the little idiot climbed into the station grounds and…well, the rest is history."

"So, why's it your fault?"

"Because if I hadn't arrested Tom, maybe gave him some protection from the few locals who actually did think he was responsible, then he'd never have felt the need to come here in the first place. There's no denying it Nick, the guy is dead because of me." As Brackett rose to his feet, Castle walked to his friend's side and placed both hands upon the officer's shoulders.

"Now listen to me. You were doing your job, that's it. Could things have been handled differently, sure, hindsight is a wonderful thing. But you did what you thought you had to do, probably what anyone in your position would have done. If your arsehole dad hadn't tortured the guy with his medication, he'd have never escaped in the first place. But there's one other thing you need to consider. Whatever the reason for Tom turning up here tonight, you didn't kill anyone. That fucking piece of shit who lives here did. Now, obviously you can't bring the poor guy back. But you can make sure he didn't die for nothing. You said Hallowell is cursed, well let's break that curse. Let's find the bastard who did this and make him pay, even if it's just for Tom Daley's memory, for my granddad's memory. No matter what it's taken to get us here tonight, I believe everything happens for a reason and this village has suffered at this fucker's hands for far too long. So, tonight, we end this, once and for all."

The policeman looked back in his friend's eyes and saw the one thing he needed, truth. Yes, he could blame himself for Tom, tie himself up in knots and second guess his decisions, but Nick was right, whatever had come before couldn't be changed, tonight was their chance to re-write history, to make history of their own.

Brackett nodded solemnly and Castle smiled that quirky grin that the officer had missed so much. Unsure how it would be taken, Nick pulled his friend in closer and embraced him, just for a few seconds, but the contact made all the difference. All that alpha male bullshit seemed to dissipate into the air, maturity taking precedence over childish one-upmanship. As the separated, they shared a look, a moment that didn't require words, and then with an intake of breath, they refocused upon the task at hand.

Castle looked across the expanse of the room and noticed a large, seated area.

"What's that over there?" He was pointing towards the canteen.

"Not sure. I think it was the old food area, lunch breaks and shit." Both men were squinting through the room's gloominess and as Brackett shone the flashlight in that direction, the beam wasn't strong enough to reach the area. "What do you think, shall we check it, or go back to the others and check it when we all together?" Castle shrugged his shoulders.

"Well, we here now, we may as well take a look." Brackett nodded in agreement and the two men began across the floor, Brackett taking one final look towards Tom Daley's remains, mouthing a silent prayer as the left.

Challis and Castle senior had reached the stairwell entrance, still on floor three. Both were apprehensive about taking the steps as a pair but did take a little comfort at the fact that they were still in possession of the gun. Looking high up the spiral staircase, the ominous darkness was gratefully broken by the beam from the one remaining flashlight. More powerful than the one in use by Brackett and Castle junior, its highly forced jet of light reflected back off the brick wall-face and grey concrete steps. The men paused, listening for movement from above, hoping that their partners had found the girl, alive, and were about to bring her to safety, without the need for their involvement. Nothing could be heard.

"What do you say old man? Do we head up?" Challis was looking for guidance and hoping that senior was as terrified as he was.

"You call me old man again, and I'll take that gun and stick it up your arse." Senior was growing tired of jokes at his expense.

"No offence chief, I was just bowing to your seniority, that's all. What *do* you want to do, I'm easy?" Mick was just as concerned, even if his facial expressions refused to admit it, but knew that if he didn't suggest climbing the stairs to the other team members, he'd be insinuating cowardice.

"I suppose we better follow them. I can't hear anything and if we stay here, we are sitting ducks. And another thing, remind me to kick my son's arse when I see him, we were supposed to be sticking together."

"Will do chief."

"And don't call me chief."

"No problem chief." Castle snarled but Challis raised his hands in mock surrender, still ready to use humour as a way of hiding his true emotions.

Castle senior took the lead, taking one step at a time, aware that Challis would need extra effort due to his disabilities. The younger man continued to point the weapon ahead and Castle kept a beady eye on the gun's direction, determined not to be shot by accident. It seemed to take an age, but they arrived on floor four. Peering out into the empty space, Senior felt an icy chill shiver down his spine.

"Do we investigate ourselves or carry on and find the others?" Challis really hoped the answer would be the latter.

"I think we better off doing this as a team, like we were supposed to do from the beginning, let's keep climbing." Challis smiled.

"Whatever you say chi, sorry, Mr Castle." Senior knew that this wasn't the time or place to have an argument, so he let the last one slide. Carefully, the continued.

The shooting pains throughout the young man's left leg was growing worse with every step climbed. Stretching the hamstring, then putting weight through the muscle as his body was hoisted forward, was becoming seriously uncomfortable, and he paused, just allowing the older man to take an extra step lead. Looking downwards, he rubbed vigorously upon the pained limb with his free hand, trying to get some ease from the debilitating strain. And then it happened.

Senior was a few steps ahead when he realised that Challis wasn't directly behind him. He stopped instantly, staring down towards his struggling partner, a mixture of concern and agitation etched upon his face.

"Are you alright lad?" His shoulders were swivelled, neck tilted, eyes peering down in the darkened stairwell. The older man was carrying the torch and when he shined it in Challis's direction, the younger man squinted at the sudden burst of brightness.

"Yeh, I'm coming. Leg's killing me but I'm okay. It's just that... OH FUCK, MICK, LOOK OUT."

The monster appeared out of nowhere, just a dark shadow and an evil silhouette, a shaded rubber mask in the form of a rotting skull and black dishevelled hair hanging across the crown. Challis's hands were shaking as he grasped the weapon, pointing it upwards, desperate not to miss. The creature had Mick Castle by the throat, the frightened man pinned up against the red-brick wall, his body frozen, his eyes locked on the monstrosity before him. His limbs were paralysed, fear shutting down his motor skills. And then he saw the knife.

Challis pointed the weapon high and to the left, wary of hitting the wrong target. His hands shook uncontrollably now, the torch having fallen from Mick's grasp had dropped to the floor, shining in Dan's direction, the strong beam making his vision impaired. He took a step forward, hoping for a clearer image but still everything seemed blurred. His terror increased dramatically when he noticed the large butcher knife inside the psychopath's right hand, raised at shoulder height, pointed towards his stricken teammate. Dan knew it was now or never and squeezed the trigger firmly. Nothing happened.

Frank Graham's fingers crushed deeper into his rival's throat, not to strangle him, but to ensure there would be no fight back. Senior's hands had now found some life and were grabbing towards the monster's body, desperate for some leverage and spacing between the two, knowing that Challis needed a clean shot to take the creature down. Time stood still as the razor-sharp edge of the butcher's knife hung in the air before him. Senior made a final effort, aiming for the mask, trying for the eyes, anything that would slow the assault down. But it was too late.

The blade shot through the air with ungodly speed. Its direction was altered as Mick's left hand rose it intercept it mid-flight, causing the knife to deflect from its original target of his heart, upwards, piercing deeply into left shoulder. The weapon ploughed into the thick muscle, causing the older man to scream out in pain, a sudden spurt of blood firing out into the air. Three steps below, Dan Challis fought with the safety switch on his weapon, finally discovering its location before taking aim once more. The torch began to steadily tumble down the concrete steps in Dan's direction but there was no time to waste, he needed to fire on instinct now. The beam flickered as the torch picked up speed, its metal casing creating a clunking sound as it fell. Closing his left eye, he stared down the barrel, the staircase was in almost total darkness, the flash-light's bulb crackling to its death as it reached Challis's feet. He whimpered a low prayer as his finger squeezed hard upon the trigger. There was a sudden flash of light, and then came the darkness.

Chapter 41

There were broken chairs strewn across the flooring, as though something in a rage had taken out their frustrations at whatever came to hand. A table too was tilted onto its side, one wooden leg missing, another hanging loosely by a bent screw. Across the back wall and besides a dividing patrician, long workbenches with draws and cupboards below encircled the perimeter, the rest of the inner floor-space taken by the remaining seated area. Thick dust and cobwebs covered every surface and above, a light-fitting had been torn from its holding, a long wire with a bulb still attached suspended lifelessly in the air. To the far left-hand corner of the canteen stood a large self-contained storage unit, its door closed.

"What do you think that is?" Nick pointed across the space, pausing while waiting for a response.

"Looks like a walk-in freezer, maybe a pantry, something like that. I suppose we better take a look." Pushing the residual furniture from their path, they cut a route to the hideout.

Both Gibson and Jenifer could hear the men's voices clearly. The girl wanted to cry out, scream Nick's name and beg for rescue. At the very least, warn the would-be heroes of the threat they faced on the other side of the barrier. But she knew that creating the faintest of sounds would result in her demise, the cold steel of the mortician's folding knife was pressed hard to her throat, the slightest increase of pressure and her veins would open. As for the undertaker, he found himself holding his breath, petrified that his discovery was imminent. Inches from the girl's face, he dared himself to whisper a message, his putrid breath and tobacco-stained teeth making the young woman gag.

"One sound. Just one sound, and I'll slice your throat. Mind me now, and you might make it out of here alive." She so desperately wanted to believe the monster, but in reality, knew that her chances were slim. Still, she chose to remain silent, at least it could keep Nick safe. The mortician's bladder finally conceded defeat and a trickle of yellow urine flowed down in trouser leg; Jenifer noticed and though it made her captor seem even more repugnant, she was cautiously elated that Gibson was showing signs of apprehension too.

Castle was the first to reach the freezer entrance. Brackett was searching inside the larger cupboards, warily opening doors at arm's length, relieved when finding nothing. The men began to wonder, had they been mistaken? The scream had seemed to emanate from this floor, it had seemed distant, but perhaps the perpetrator had cried out from floor five, maybe even floor four, it was difficult to tell now. Nick placed his fingers around the iron handle housed upon the door's left-hand side. Unsure whether to wait for Brackett, he paused, looking over towards the officer. It was then they heard a gunshot.

Dan Challis picked up the fallen flash-light and shook it violently, relieved when the bulb crackled into life. Mick Castle had slid down the wall, blood drenching his clothing, thick red jets emerging quickly from the open wound. The younger man stepped forward cautiously, the gun pointed ahead, the torch quivering in his left hand extracting a shaky beam. The monster was nowhere in sight.

"Mick. Are you okay? How badly hurt are you?" Dan knew they were stupid questions, but his mind had more important quandaries to deal with.

"Of course, I'm not okay, you are fucking idiot, I've been stabbed." Castle senior looked helpless as the light flashed incandescently in the direction of his face. While Mick Turned his head away at the sudden brightness, Challis saw the wound for the first time. Even though the victim was pressing down hard at the opening, blood still flowed freely between his fingers and his young partner realised immediately that they needed to act fast if the man was going to be saved.

"Where did he go? Did I hit him; did I kill him?" Dan asked more out of hope than expectation, unsure if Castle had seen the monster's retreat.

"I don't know. I was too busy bleeding to worry about him. Why didn't you fire sooner?" Challis looked down embarrassedly, having hoped the question wouldn't be asked. He considered lying but felt he owed Mick the truth.

"Yeh, I'm sorry about that, the safety was on. I was sure I'd checked it but…" Mick simply shook his head, this was no time for admonishment, maybe there'd be time for that later.

"What the fuck was that?" Brackett's words stopped his friend dead, his grip upon the freezer door slackening. They both looked to the staircase entranceway and realised the others were in trouble. Listening for a second bang and hearing none, they had no idea of the seriousness of the situation.

"It was the gun; Dan's just fired the gun." Without the need for additional words, the pair sprinted towards the staircase, praying to make it in time.

Challis slid off his jacket, the gun still pointed in the direction of the upper steps, ready to fire again if called upon. Balling the coat tightly, he handed it to the stricken man.

"Press this hard against the wound, it should slow the bleeding down." The seated man did as suggest without argument, the sudden blood-loss making his head swim, dizziness making the walls shake in his eyeline. Castle's breathing was beginning to labour, his complexion turning ashen white, his time running out. "Listen Mick, I know you don't want to leave the others, but if I don't get you out of here soon, you might not make it, you're losing too much blood."

"I'm not leaving without my boy." His answer was stern and uncompromising, even though he knew himself the ramifications of his choice.

"I know but…" There was movement from above, the sound of emerging footsteps on the stone stairs. Challis braced himself, taking a firm stance and aiming the weapon with both hands. The safety was checked, the bullets were loaded, the gun was cocked and ready. Both men weren't sure, the footsteps were emerging quickly, increasing in volume the closer they came. Were they single or plural, was it Graham or their team-mates? They collectively held their breath. Who was about to emerge from the darkness?

Gibson breathed an audible sigh of relief. He'd heard the gunshot too and became worried for his psychotic partner, but for now, the undertaker himself was safe from detection. He looked to the girl as he gently opened the freezer door, the hinges squeaking quietly as it swung to the maximum. There was a choice to be made, kill her, or wait? With Jenifer gone, a major threat would be neutralised, there'd be no fear of his position being compromised due to an errant scream, the only witness to the murder of Tom Daley would no longer be capable of testifying and obviously, there's be no more concern of her escaping. But the mirror image had compelling arguments too. Without the girl, he'd have no leverage, no hostage should he need one in a battle to escape. Knowing now that the intruders were armed, and also being aware that there was more than just a solo rescuer, there was a strong possibility that Frank may not overcome their challenge. And with Graham gone, he'd need all the advantages he could get. And the final point of debate, Frank had wanted the girl for himself. If the mortician did eliminate her, would the monster turn its aggression towards Gibson himself? Fred pondered the situation and decided to give the girl a stay of execution, keenly aware that making the wrong decision could prove fatal.

The footsteps were just around the corner now. Challis was ready, the weapon was ready, it was now or never.

"Don't shoot." Mick Castle saw the two men first, his positioning low to the ground ensuring the perfect view. Challis breathed out and lowered the weapon, strangely disappointed that his opportunity to be a hero had been thwarted.

"Christ dad, what happened?" Nick was kneeling by his stricken father, his left hand touching the escaped blood. The young man was close to tears, the fractured relationship with Mick had just begun to show signs of repair, now there was a chance Nick would once more be robbed of a father.

"He came out of nowhere, there wasn't time to act. Dan saved my life, if he hadn't shot when he did, I'd have been done for sure." Mick winked in Challis's direction and the disabled man suddenly felt a cheat, a phony. He was about to reveal the truth when Nick rose, throwing an arm around his narrow shoulders and squeezing him tight. Whispering in Dan's ear he said,

"I'll never forget this, and I'll always owe you, no matter what." That made Dan feels even more maligned and he still wanted to reveal the truth, but the words wouldn't come.

Junior rested a hand to his father's brow, the skin felt clammy and cold, the pale complexion ghost-like, a constant tremor adding to the unholy image. Mick's eyes were glazed, his stare unfocused, his consciousness no longer certain.

"Right dad, your evening's work is done, time to get you the Hell out of here." The young man tried to hide his anxiety while inside, his mind was screaming. Their relationship had finally started to grow organically after years of mistrust and misinterpretation, Nick was adamant he wasn't about to lose his dad without a fight. Because, until this very moment, junior had never realised just how much he'd craved a father-son relationship. Having spent the last few years playing the role of lone wolf, deflecting human interaction so he could continue to wallow in his self-pitying stupor, Nick had finally realised what he'd been missing, a family, a home, a life.

"I'm going…nowhere…without you." There was little eye contact, but the older man's voice remained steadfast, intransient toning without the aid of strength. Nick passed a glance towards Brackett and Challis, hoping for support, finding none.

"Do you think I'm nuts? Don't you worry dad, we're all leaving, we tried, we failed, but this shit is too serious now. I don't mind risking my own life, but I'm not about to lose any of you." The remaining two team members gave a perplexed stare to one another but weren't about to argue, if their mission was over, it was over, at least they'd tried.

"Really?" Mick's eyes rose to meet his son's, unsure whether junior was being truthful, hoping that catching his line-of-sight would answer his query. Looking away meant the kid was talking bullshit; Nick's stare remained true. Apprehensively, the older man admitted defeat, it was time to leave.

It seemed to take an age but, eventually the group descended to the ground floor. Nick and Johnny had given Mick support, almost carrying the wounded man down the flights of stairs, while Challis remained vigilant, gun aimed, ready to shoot on sight. They were content with the theory that Graham had to be on a higher floor, in the aftermath of his attack, Challis had been positioned lower and with the belief that the staircase was the only escape, the monster had to be above, ensuring that maintaining a safety-net only required watchfulness to the rear. Even though, every corner was taken with due care, each floor entrance passed tentatively, haste could still facilitate mistakes.

Reaching the ground floor, the injured man was barely conscious, the blood loss increasing due to the exertion of movement. It was obvious that, without urgent medical attention, there was a serious possibility that Mick Castle wouldn't survive. Exiting the tight walkway of the spiral staircase, they returned to the vastness of the open room, the group collectively praying that their journey would be completed without incident. The massive doorway was in sight, the outside storm seemed to be calming, the sweet smell of uncorrupted air a refreshing change. As they closed in on the exit, Mick looked to his son and smiled.

"We tried son…we tried." The words were delivered without force and the statement seemed to appear as a conclusive proclamation, as though the older man was slipping away.

"We gave it our best shot, but don't you give up on me now. We nearly there, just keep going."

"Don't you worry boy, I'm going nowhere." Mick propelled that crooked smile, with a devious glint in his eye, causing Nick to chuckle. "I love you son, never forget that."

The effort of carrying the injured man's limp body down three flights of stairs had taken a toll on both Nick and Johnny, their relief palpable as they reached the exterior platform, the claustrophobic darkness of the building's rooms replaced with the cool autumnal air, the temperature barely changing from the icy conditions inside. Across the wasteland, a wild rabbit twitched his nose as it scurried through the bushes, jumping nervously as an unexpected breeze swayed the twigs, the last of the year's leaves losing their battle of life. Junior changed his position, moving to his father's rear and sliding his arms beneath the older man's armpits and as Brackett leapt from the platform to the gravel below, they began the task of lowering Mick to a seated position. When the patient was firm, Nick stretched out an ache in his back, his dad's blood covering much of his raincoat. The makeshift bandage that Challis had presented was now drenched too and Nick slid off his jacket, balling it firmly and replacing the heavily soiled one. As Nick noticed just how much blood had been lost, he realised that urgent action was needed.

"Johnny, can you get your car all the way around here? It would be better than carrying dad out?" The wasteland was poke-marked with potholes and discarded rubbish, broken tree-stumps, and overgrown foliage.

"If I'm careful. There's a section further up where the railway tracks are missing, I'll pull round there but it will take a few minutes. I'll radio to my dad too, get him ready for when we come in, it'll be safer than trying to get to the hospital in Carpenter." Without waiting for a response, the officer began the sprint towards his patrol car in the railway car park. Nick watched as Brackett sped away, thankful that after a decade apart, his friends could still be relied upon when most needed.

"Can I have the gun for a second mate?" Nick delivered the request with a casual manner, ensuring that neither his friend nor his father suspected his motive. Dan passed the weapon over and Castle clicked open the chamber, finding five bullets still inside. Realising it was now or never, he looked towards the open entrance.

Challis had steadily climbed to the floor adjacent to the platform and was standing directly before the injured man, watching for the smallest change in his consciousness. The two had formed a strange bond over the last thirty minutes, Castle senior hadn't had to defend Dan over the late gunshot, he owed him nothing, and the fact that he had, proved the type of man he was. Challis had considered revealing the true sequence of events but, partially out of respect for the older man, held his tongue. Mick had said what he said, for team morale, taking a bad situation and putting a positive spin on it, turning Challis's actions from a delayed mistake to a life-saving intervention. It was a brave selfless act, and now, Dan was determined to do everything he could to ensure the injured man's survival. It was due to this preoccupation that he hadn't noticed his friend moving back towards the main building entrance.

A sudden loud clap of thunder, directly overhead, made the disabled man cry out with fright, tiny speckles of raindrops falling across his face insinuating that another downpour was imminent. Glancing upwards, Dan momentarily had lost sight of his friend.

"Hey nick, what you doing?" The young man appeared out of the gloomy doorway, pushing heavily on the left of the two massive iron-edged doors, the movement causing the swelled obstacle to scream out a high-pitched crunch as the metal fought against the concrete platform. Forcing with his shoulder, he grimaced as the barrier moved into place, years of immobility causing rusted hinges and weakened joints. "Good idea locks the bastard inside. Try quieten it down though, we don't need more attention." Nick's lack of response made Challis concerned, he'd seen that look in his friend's eyes before, it was never good. When Castle began to close the second door, his position seemed to signal his motive, remaining on the inside of the barrier. Dan had finally realised what was about to happen and though he knew it was too late to intervene, he felt obliged to try. Rolling back onto the platform, he battled to his feet just as his friend's image vanished from sight. The doors were closed tightly but the disabled man knew Nick would still be able to hear his voice.

"Nick, Christ, Nick please, don't do this." Pounding with the flat of his palm, across the massive door, the sound reverberated around the entire area. Suddenly, a voice from inside replied to Challis's plea.

"Danny listens, I'm going after Jenifer, I heard her voice, I know she's alive. You shot the bastard so we know he can he hurt; I'm just going to finish the job." Dan Challis had tears in his eyes as he knew there would be no reasoning with his head-strong pal. "Please mate, don't try to follow me, I'm blocking the door, just take care of dad, that's your job now." With that, he was gone, Challis wondered if he'd just spoken to his friend for the final time.

Chapter 42

Nick decided to roll the dice with regards to using the torch, trusting that the batteries were good and the bulb strong enough to maintain the lighting he so desperately required. He could still hear Challis's protests from the opposing side of the door (the good side) his voice raised to a higher octave and an occasional kick against the barrier in retaliation to his friend's STUPID DECISION. Hell, even Nick knew this was stupid, aware that the chances of success were minimal, that he may never walk back out of this place alive...but he was still doing it anyway. The question was, why? For Jenifer? He barely knew her; yes, they'd shared an unmistakable connection, an instant bond which Nick had only experienced once before, but was she worth dying for? Hard to say. Was it for the good of Hallowell? Bullshit, he didn't owe those people a God-damned thing and had it not been for their series of idiotic choices, then this situation would probably have never existed. Frank Graham and his piece-of-shit father should have been dealt with swiftly and decisively before they ever had the opportunity to fuck up the village. Hindsight? So why? Was it a test of his masculinity, a chance to slay the beast and prove his alpha male status? Not a chance, there were easier ways to show the size of his balls without risking his life.

The reality was, he didn't want to do it, he needed to do it, he had no option. Was he to cower away and run, his life would never change? He'd be trapped in that shit-hole flat in Bishopsgate forever, drinking and drugging and pissing the bed after his nightly dream-fest, living scared and hiding, running, and hiding, running, and running and running until he could run no more. Then what? Curl up in a ball and die, if that was his destiny, why wait? Why not just roll the dice and see where it lands, could be good, could be bad, but at least he'd be making a difference, becoming the captain of his own ship, he could live with that.

Was it worth investigating every floor again? Her was certain that Jenifer's voice had emanated from level six. It had definitely come from above and as they'd been positioned on the third floor at the time, the options were limited. The location of Tom Daley's demise appeared to have been on that upper level, his corrupted remains serving as a reminder as to what evil Nick was facing. And also positioned on the top floor was that walk-in freezer. Ever since the moment Castle had noticed it, something triggered in his mind, a cautionary curiosity that deserved investigation. It was one of the few free-standing areas inside the building, large enough to be used as a hideout, and though he had no wish to witness Jenifer's body if the worst had happened, at least he'd know the nature of his mission, be it rescue, or revenge. He cursed himself for not taking the few seconds needed to open that door and as such, it remained a massive area of interest. Knowing this, Castle began his tentative walk to the staircase.

The more Nick tried to keep his body loose, the stiffer he felt, his actions almost robotic, left arm stretched out straight, pointing the flashlight forwards, his right arm bent touching his upper chest, the gun held tightly in his grasp, first finger touching the trigger, desperate not to add undue pressure, the ammunition was scarce.

None of this felt natural, for years, he'd travelled through life either over-medicated or in a drunken haze, but now, his system was clean and alert, his senses overly heightened to the point of hyper-activity. His legs remained bent slightly at the knee, ready to pounce or fly, run or fight, whatever the situation required, his feet pacing lightly and without sound, careful not to allow his shoes to squeak on the concrete below. His eyes had adapted surprisingly quickly to the gloominess, finding shapes and shadows in the darkest of corners, and his hearing was suddenly incredibly acute, though the quietness inside was disconcerting. A stale mould-like stench, the result of years of dampness and a lack of warmth, was unpleasant without being overpowering, for there was something else too, a smell he couldn't place no matter how hard he tried.

The cold night-time air hung around him like a bad memory, and then, something did dawn on him, the reason why much inside felt so familiar. When he'd explored earlier with his other team members, he hadn't taken in the eccentricities of the building, instead guarding against potential attack rather than taking in his surroundings. But now he remembered. Every detail from his horrific recurring nightmares were right there, exactly where he'd expect them to be. Scanning across the ground, he noticed the metal shaft protruding from the concrete floor, crudely hacked to about a foot from ground level, the same obstacle he'd fallen over, again and again in his nightmares. The way the room felt larger to the left than away to the right even though the huge entranceway appeared central to the building. And then there was the staircase; a door-less entry point leading to pitch blackness, concrete steps, five lifts then a turn, repeated four times until the staircase would be broken for an entrance to the next floor. Stoic, daunting and constant, solid red-brick walls bordering a floor of dark grey, no handrail, no windows, simple, fit for purpose, uninviting.

Pausing at the foot of the first flight, he breathed out, the air visible due to the decreasing temperature, smoke-like, ghost-like. There was a choice to be made. The options, remain silent as the grave, check his footing, watch for potential obstacles, even maintain the weapon in a cocked position as to not allow a sound reverberating click to echo off the emptiness, or, let the station inhabitant know of his presence. Take the fight to the monster, draw him out and as such, force Graham into a mistake (wishful thinking). Certainly, should Jenifer hear his voice, her spirits would be heightened, realising that rescue was possible. Nick had considered both options carefully before deciding upon the former, believing that it was the best opportunity for success. Inside this Hell, the monster held all the advantages, therefore there was no need to concede the only element which could remain in Castle's favour, the element of surprise. True,

Graham knew of their presence, but hopefully, it would expect the intruders to flee after the attack on the older man. By the group decreasing to a single member, it was possible that that element of surprise could still return to the young man's advantage. Really, who would be stupid enough to enter this place alone?

The monster was hurt. Attacking Mick Castle, Frank hadn't expected the interloper's partner to be armed.

Graham had seen it all before; intruders idiotic or ignorant enough to enter his home. Some with the intention of thieving whatever they could, believing that certain valuables may remain inside, even down to something as small as scrap-metal was deemed important enough to risk their lives for. Others were just idiots, youngsters wanting to prove their courage to their sheep-like friends with a need to exult a blustering boast of 'conquering the station'. Maybe they hadn't been warned, perhaps they had and were just too moronic to heed that caution. Then there was the final category, the homeless and desperate. Some needed shelter, like the two teens just a few days earlier, hiding from either the elements or the authorities, whichever caught them first. Believing that entering his home was preferential to freezing on the streets. They were no danger, no challenge, but still, the monster had dispatched them with his usual ruthless effectiveness. Others were the crazed fool's incapable of rational thought, alcoholics, drug-addicts, glue-sniffers, anyone who wanted privacy to partake in their sordid mind-altering pass-times, his station appeared the perfect location. Many had entered, few had walked away. Some had even used Frank as a form of suicide. Too pathetic to end their own lives, they had used Graham's unique abilities to help them pass over. The monster was always happy to oblige. Some remains would be returned, serving as a warning to others, while some was used as sustenance for the lean winter months. But today was different.

He'd began as ever, using his definitive knowledge and the element of surprise to launch his attack from the shadows, disabling his opponent with his effortless strength advantage before dispatching the interloper with the help of his razor-sharp steel weapon. And as ever, it was working, his grip around the intruder's throat had been enough to freeze the terrified man, his aim with the blade had been slightly array, piercing the upper shoulder rather than the intended chest cavity, but when the knife was retracted for a second effort, he was content that the inevitable was nearby. But, when the sudden gunshot had echoed out into the stale night-time air, targeting Graham's upper body, the monster had been stunned. The bullet had intercepted the right-hand side of his chest, just wide enough for the projectile to deflect from one of the higher ribs, instead slicing through his skin and smashing into the red-brick wall. Though the wound wasn't serious, it did force the creature to retreat back into the covering darkness, regrouping, re-evaluating his next strike, unnerved that an intruder had managed to cause him injury.

Graham checked the severity of the wound before a broken mirror in a partitioned off section of floor four, a hidden flickering candle the only break in the darkened off-shot. An area of spilled blood made it appear worse than it really was, the skin opened to a five-inch gash, straight across the side of the upper ribcage, its position awkward, restricting his right-arm's mobility, tearing further with any movement. The pain was minimal, years of contending with the elements, had made him battle-hardened, immune from things which others may find debilitating.

As ever, the mask retained its place. Frank had lived with the latex shield across his skin for so long, it had become as natural an element as any other part of his body, facial features becoming a forgotten memory of a by-gone era. Even on the rare occasions he was forced to hack away facial hair, the mask would only be lifted enough to access the areas required. He'd come to rely upon its horrific appearance as a reminder of what he truly was, an undeniable monster and harbinger of death. Glancing into the cracked mirror, he briefly caught a reflection, the green colouring barely definable in the dim flickering light, but the moulded rubber features, pronounced jawline and ghoulish cheekbones, a dull tip-less nose and repulsive foul teeth scattered around an enlarged mouth-hole, two large pits hiding his black merciless eyes, it truly was an image to send shudders through the bravest of men, to create inescapable nightmares.

Rejuvenated and ready for battle, the creature took hold of his blade once more and stared towards the entry-point of the staircase, keenly aware that tonight, more blood would need to be spilled.

Arriving at the entrance to the first floor, Nick breathed out a silent sigh, content that the first climb was over, but knowing the mission had only just begun. He stared out across the room's vastness which contained few hideouts, the area mostly empty bar for certain broken items of furniture and overturned machinery, nothing large enough to hide Graham's colossal frame. The torch beam was strong enough to illuminate most of the darkened corners and though Castle couldn't be certain, he was convinced that the monster wasn't lurking on this floor. Before beginning his climb, he'd decided that re-investigating each level once more, space for space, shadow for shadow, wasn't the best option. Leaving the sanctuary of the staircase would result in him having no clue to the monster's location, Graham would have the opportunity to pass to the lower levels whilst Nick's inspection took place. Retaining his position until he reached the highest level, Nick could investigate floor six and work his way downwards, having the positional advantage from above, provided nothing occurred on the staircase beforehand. The lower levels had been checked as a team and Nick still had that nagging feeling about the walk-in freezer on the top floor, knowing that until he witnessed its interior, he'd always be curious.

Having a final scan with the flashlight across the first floor, he returned to the staircase. Hoping his instinct was correct, he pointed the torch above, aiming the weapon forward, and continued the climb.

Graham had now reached the entrance to the staircase too, passing over the empty space of the fourth level with silent footsteps, ghost-like strides from a creature that knew every inch of his home. As he was about to begin his descent, something alerted him to a coming danger. Like a sixth sense, as though he could feel the vibrations in the air, he knew the interloper was close. Though there was heavy coverage of rubber from the mask across his ears, he picked up the faintest of noise emanating from the steps below. The deft layering of rubber sole on concrete, the mildest shuffle of clothing, the briefest exhale of breath, Graham sensed it all. He paused, contemplation of his next move vital. Squeezing hard on the knife's rubber handle, his decision was made.

Nick tried to control the speed of his footsteps, his natural instinct to hurry forwards boldly being opposed with an understandable caution, an obvious wariness that came with the territory. In his left hand, the torch leads the way, its forceful beam reflecting back against the rough red-brick wall, the light arriving around corners for his body to follow. And held tightly in his right hand, the gun, loaded with just five bullets, five projectiles between himself and helplessness. His first finger hovered across the trigger, ready to fire at any sign of danger, but also aware that the ammunition must not be wasted on speculative shots. His cheeks felt hot and flushed despite the freezing temperature, his body stiff, muscles tight, the tension making him feel physically exhausted, though his mind was sharp and alert.

One more turn, five more steps and he would be in the doorway to floor number three. It was time for another choice, maintain his plan or investigate the level? Knowing the monster had to be aware of his presence and feeling certain the creature would have a plan to deal with the intrusion, Castle thought hard.

"If I was in the bastard's position, what would I do? Would I use the claustrophobic surroundings of the staircase, aware that my adversary had a gun? Or would I use the open spaces of the larger rooms, lurking in potential hideouts for a chance to strike? In the open, the gun would prove more dangerous, to launch an attack, Graham would need to be up close, whereas in the open, the monster would be defenceless should I get a clear shot from distance. He would want that closeness; he would want that element of surprise. Therefore, he would want to remain mobile, he would want to use the staircase."

Nick knew it was a 50/50 choice, there were no guarantees, but his instinct had worked so far, and his instinct said, stay on the steps. With the decision made, he passed by the opening to the room and continued the climb, floor four his next destination.

Every step felt torturous; Castle's apprehension was growing with every passing second. He knew that Graham was almost certainly lurking inside one of the station's upper floors, but those upper floors were vanishing quickly. Every step was a step closer to a potentially deadly encounter, the opposition, evil incarnate, a demon who would eliminate human life without blinking and who already had a history of murder, devastation in close quarters, slicing through invader after invader without so much as a scratch. Castle tried to block out such thoughts, look upon Graham as a man rather than monster, but it wasn't working, the memories of their only previous encounter returning with a vengeance. Images of that beast, that mask, the invader of his nightmares, the murderer of his grandfather, the…

That was different. Nick had got used to the way the torchlight beam would react as he approached each corner, the brightness dimming as it became obscured on its journey, losing a percentage to the area he could not see yet. But this time, it was being reflected back, at the foot of the coming corner, something was blocking the path. He stopped dead, waiting for movement, the gun cocked and ready, his finger over the trigger. Gently, he moved the beam up and down the wall, the blockage vanishing the higher the torch was raised. Was it the monster, crouching low, ready to thrust forwards, bursting from the darkness with speed and power?

He waited, and waited, and waited, still there was no movement. Was he wrong? Was it an optical illusion, a fault in the building design? Or was it a trap? A blockage set to attract Nick's attention while the monster appeared from behind. The very idea made his head dart backwards nervously over his shoulder. He suddenly felt trapped, incapable of going neither forward nor backwards. He found himself subconsciously retreating, his back pressed tightly against the red-brick wall, his face contorted, his bladder fit to burst. Legs cramping, stomach cramping, fear replacing rational thought. Then suddenly…he remembered.

The pain of the past, the eradication of the life he'd once known, all perpetrated by this thing. And then there was Jenifer, he owed it to himself and to her to push on, no matter what the cost.

His clothes still scraping against the red-brick surface, he crab-walked up the first step, determined to maintain as much of his panoramic view as possible, both above and below. Craning his neck to the right, Nick tried desperately to see the blockage around the upper corner, but it still remained hidden. Tentatively, he took the next step, the torch positioned oddly, still in his left hand but raised high above his head, stretching to a position to maintain the irregular beam without turning his body. Such was the movement, the torch almost slipped from his grasp, the beam suddenly pointing towards the floor, his eyes automatically following, and it was only now that he noticed the discolouration of the grey concrete. Originally, it appeared only as a wet patch, perhaps a collection of water from a leaking roof, but on closer inspection, Castle realised that the substance was red, blood red. It wasn't a flood, just enough to create a small puddle, but it was still growing, a steady trickle drifting from the edge of the top step, whatever was around the corner seeming to be the obvious source. Nick suddenly remembered; Challis had shot at the creature. There was immediate hope, had the wound been fatal, was the blockage hidden around the next bend the remains of Frank Graham?

With a sudden burst of expectation, Nick took the remaining stairs swiftly, his apprehension momentarily gone. Taking the corner, the torch beam swelled at the revelation, causing Castle to grimace in repulsion, the devastated remains of Tom Daley had been moved, dumped as a reminder of what the resident evil was capable of.

This made no sense, why use deceased remains as a sick prop? Nick's heart was pounding, the anticipation of a deathly encounter suddenly replaced with this vision of destruction. It had been posed, propped up like a store-front mannequin, its back pressed tightly besides the red-brick wall, the legs crossed, child-like, with the arms tucked in neatly by its side, helping with the balance. Had Nick not known differently, the corpse could have been mistaken for a living soul, the eyes were open and staring out into the darkness. The white skin across the complexion was pale, drained of all colours, the remnants of a final terrified thought engrained in his features. Nick found it impossible to remove his stare from the corpse before him and as his pulse began to slow, he allowed himself a moment of contemplation. Kneeling before the poor man, he placed the torch on the ground, if only for a second, so to perform a tiny gesture, the closing of Tom Daley's eyes. He mouthed a short silent prayer (it was strange how his lost faith had suddenly been re-ignited as the events inside the station unfolded, it was safer to edge his bets) before saying out loud the words,

"Sleep well old boy, your pain is over now." Resting a hand upon the dead-man's brow, the skin felt cold and clammy, and he had to fight the urge to withdraw. Instead, gently stroking downwards, the eyelids were closed, making the young man feel surprisingly worse, the totality of death rearing its ugly head once more.

Castle had no idea why, but he knew he was being watched. There was no change in sound, no movements, no smell, taste, nothing, he just knew it. Grabbing for the flashlight, a single word exploded in his brain.

DECOY.

A sudden kick rocketed out of the darkness, a steel toe-capped work-boot cracking the young man just below the right temple, the force so great, it sent Nick hurtling down the first flight of five steps. His head took a second blow during the downward plummet, crashing across the central stair slicing a four-inch rent just above his hairline, a prompt showering of thick squelching blood erupting from the wound. During the descent, he also suffered a painful impact to the right elbow, his entire arm suddenly going numb causing his grip upon the gun to slacken, the weapon falling to the concrete floor below. Without interruption, Graham followed swiftly, ready to press home the advantage. Castle's natural instinct was to shine the flashlight in the behemoth's direction, horrified by the cat-like speed of its descent. The work-boots pounded the concrete surface, silence no longer a consideration. Nick fumbled across the ground for his grandfather's Browning service revolver, panic creating its own problems, but finally he found the gun teetering precariously on the top step of the next flight. He grabbed the handle, the feeling in his right arm was still impaired, the grip unnatural. He swung to aim the pistol in the savage's direction, but Graham was already too close. Towering above his stricken opponent, a firm swat sent the Browning tumbling from Nick's clutches once more, the gun crashing into the darkness to the foot of the next flight of stairs. The beast was unrelenting, grabbing a fistful of Castle's long black blood-filled hair and dragging the young man to his feet, the two major head concussions making the world spin, turning his rational thoughts into paralysing fear.

A sudden burst of realism brought Castle to his senses, aware that fast action was needed were he to stand any chance of survival. As his body scrapped its way upright, he brought his left fist forward in a lightning strike, the monster's groin his designated location of choice. Graham crouched slightly at the sudden blast, loosening his clinch on Nick's hair. The shot was just enough to buy the young man a precious second or two and without hesitation, he leapt from the platform, down the next flight of stairs. As he took flight, he heard the clunk of steel meeting brick, the beast had fired a lunge in Castle's direction with the huge butcher knife, the penetration missing by inches, lashing into the wall instead. Nick heard a low moan emanating from the hellion's mouth, the attack had been delivered with such force that, when the knife struck the red-brick surface, his fingers had slipped from the handle, sliding down the edge of the razor-sharp blade, slicing deeply into the flesh of all his fingers. A second clunk of steel on concrete echoed out as the deadly weapon fell from the creatures' clutches, crashing to the floor. Castle knew this was his chance.

This second leapt had been less destructive than the first, clearing four of the five steps before tumbling off the edge of the final one. On landing, the torch had cracked against the lower wall, the round glass coverage in front of the bulb smashing, causing the flashlight to be extinguished. He cursed the mistake, the sudden blackness coming as blindness, realising his other senses would have to be heightened because of the loss. There was a warning coming from the concrete above as the demon retrieved his weapon, the blade scratching against the floor as it was raised up. Immediately, it was followed by the sound of footsteps quickly descending in his direction and once more, panic began to well in Castle's brain. He began to scramble across the floor with both hands, desperate to find the Browning, praying for one clean shot to end this nightmare. The space was small, only a surface of five feet square and it quickly became apparent that the gun was missing. Had it fallen further? Perhaps it had landed on a higher step, and he'd missed it during his leap for freedom? There was no time for guessing, the beast was approaching fast, and Nick knew that in this close proximity, he'd stand no chance.

Taking one stride, he began to leap for the next flight of stairs, but Graham was too quick. The monstrous psychopath stretched out a leg, just as Castle took to the air, the displacement causing him to lose balance and height, ensuring that he'd clatter to the stone steps, thundering into each one as his body rolled and rolled. The young man's left kneecap became twisted and blasted into the central step; he let out a scream of agony as he began to realise the extent of the injury. He came to a shuddering halt at the bottom of the flight, landing across his shoulders, the base of his skull coming down hard on the unforgiven concrete. Once more, the world began to swim, though this time, the feeling was more severe, his focus had become blurred, double vision adding to the already gloomy surroundings. Pain was wracking every part of his body and he had to fight the urge to drift into unconsciousness.

Graham seemed to sense victory was in sight and took his time descending the steps, a steady torrent of blood flowing from the beast's injured right hand. The strides were slow and deliberate, the creature seeming to enjoy the sudden change in fortune. Nick was laid flat on the floor, unable to move, his hopes dissipating along with his strength. He tried to bend his legs in a futile effort to push away from the advancing demon, but he knew his race was run. The series of horrific events seemed to mirror uncannily to the images of one of his recurring nightmares, the detail of his collision with the crudely hacked away fencepost in the space of the ground floor replaced with a fall down the stone steps, both concluding with a similar finale, a debilitating injury which prevented him from fleeing the killer. The only difference being, in his dream-state, he'd wake before the final deadly blow.

More out of instinct, than a belief that there still remained an opportunity of survival, he still tried pushing away as Frank drew closer, his feet failing to gain purchase on the dusty floor. With his eyes locked firmly on the demon, he tried a final futile grasp across the concrete, praying that the gun may still be found. The battle had moved out inside floor number three now, the flight of stairs ending at the level's entrance. Still, the weapon was lost and though his spirit wanted to fight on, his broken body was no longer capable.

Frank Graham was just a yard away, staring down at his fallen opponent, strangely respectful for the young man's gutsy performance, but still remaining unwilling to deliver any mercy. Castle was angry, finding it difficult to believe that he'd come so far, just to fail now, perhaps it had been his destiny all along?

The beast grasped the butcher's knife in both hands, holding it tightly and raising it high above his head for maximum force.

"Fuck you." It was Nick's final rebellion, his body broken but his spirit finally free. The monster took in a deep inhale of breath, the battle was over now, Castle closed his eyes…and waited.

The gunshot which rung out into the stale night-time air was as much a surprise to Nick as it was to its intended victim. The young man had accepted his fate, his shattered body unable to continue his valiant effort and by sealing his eyelids closed, he'd anticipated the Beast's final strike. Contemplating his demise had been surprisingly cathartic, the mistakes of his short life seeming to dissipate, aware that his effort to slay the beast had been courageous if not successful, and the fact that his death would come about in the aftermath of a heroic failure made him magnanimous in defeat.

Awaiting the kill-shot, he'd instinctively tensed his muscles, as though the flexing would guard as a wall against the knife's penetration. He began wondering what lay ahead, was it Heaven, was it Hell? He was aware that he'd spent much of his life squandering his God-given talents, more interested in punishing his parents than progressing a future. Would that be enough to deserve an eternity of damnation? Nick knew he'd never purposely set out to hurt another human being even though his stupid actions had been responsible for the passing of his one true-love, Julia Martin. True, it had been her jealous psychotic husband who had landed the killer blow, but it had been Castle's hot-headed stupidity and lack of trust which had alerted Dr Allen Martin of his wife's infidelity. If only he'd trusted her intentions, if only he'd kept his mouth shut, if only…

So perhaps he did deserve this fate, perhaps he did deserve an eternity of pain and torment, perhaps…

The bullet struck Frank Graham in the left shoulder, the knife immediately falling from his clutches, hitting the concrete floor with an echoing thud. The deafening blast from the pistol automatically made Nick's eyes spring open, the shocking destruction of silence taking his breath away. Incredibly, the beast remained standing, shocked at the sudden searing pain, confused at the location of the shooter. He looked to Castle, just to be certain that the young man wasn't armed, then returned his attention to his own fallen weapon, aware there still had a job to finish. He began to bend his legs to retrieve the blade, but Castle was faster, his injured body obeying his orders in one last stand of defiance. Managing to angle his left foot to the correct level, the knife was thrust across the floor into a darkened corner, rendering it inconsequential. Though no expression could be seen through the maniac's rubber shield, his body told its own tale, its chest heaving, exhaling the lungs-contained air in harsh bursts, shoulders raised and square, head pointed down angrily at his fallen opponent, irate that the young man would have the temerity to thwart his attack.

Instead of tracing the knife, Graham began to loom over Castle, realising that the old ways would need a swift return, instead of weaponry, his massive bulk and willingness to crush with his bare hands becoming his only option. Nick's confused mind tried to fire his body into action, twisting to his knees in an attempt to regain his footing. A shuddering pain exploded as his injured limb hit the concrete causing him to scream out in agony but still his battling attitude refused to allow him to accept defeat. Pushing with his right leg, he stumbled forwards, though the beast was waiting, once more a handful of Castle's long blood-stained hair swung into Graham's reach. Pulling back furiously causing the young man to fall back to the ground, Nick could only stare back, that final retaliation draining his last resources of energy, that sudden hope that had momentarily grown diminishing to a forgotten memory. A guttural grown escaped the rubber mask as the colossal savage reached for Castle's exposed throat, its own injured shoulder decreasing its mobility. Nick's eyes drooped once more, the end near...

The second gunshot struck the creature with far more ferocity, exploding into the chest cavity just left of its throat, launching it backwards and sending it crashing to the floor, the tight grip upon Castle's scalp ensuring that a huge clump of hair flew backwards with it. Blood began to jet forwards from the wound and immediately, it looked certain to be fatal. The young man, breathing in deep lungsful of corrupted air, searched the shadows, unable to comprehend where the unbelievability welcome assistance had originated from, his vision was still blurred, head pounding, psyche barely able to absorb what had just happened. Slowly, a figure began to emerge.

Though it was just a silhouette, Castle knew immediately who his savour was, the pronounced limp, the left foot dragging slightly behind, the stooped, odd-shaped physique. Dan Challis came into view, a mixture of revulsion and self-satisfaction plastered across his expression. The smell of gunpowder was thick in the air, the barrel of the browning still smouldering and hot to the touch.

"I thought I told you to stay outside." Nick's words were delivered softly and with an air of resignation, something inside had told him that his friends would be there right to the end.

"Good job I ignored you, isn't it?" Challis's entire body was trembling, the realisation that he'd just shot another human being (even a monster like Graham) lying heavily on his soul. "Is it dead?" Dan had no wish to get too close to the dying monster, his bravery strongest from twenty yards away.

"If he isn't, he soon will be." Challis approached his friend and now could see the extent of Nick's injuries. "How? I mean, how did you get…"

"The gun?"

"Yes, the gun, how did you get the gun?"

"When I saw Johnny's car pulling across the wasteland, I knew your pops wouldn't be alone for long. I also knew that, if Johnny saw you'd gone inside, he'd have followed you first, but since someone needed to see to Mick, and I knew Johnny couldn't leave him alone, I took my chance. I guess I thought I had less to lose than he did. So I followed you, the door wasn't too hard to open, and I stayed a floor below you, I knew if you knew I was in here too, you'd be pissed, so I stayed quiet."

"Devious fucker."

"Yeh, anyway, when I heard you in trouble, I set off up to help, and when you dropped the Gun, thankfully, I found it." He offered Castle a hand. "Can you walk?"

"With a little help. Fuck, what about Jenifer?" Challis shook his head, amazed at his friend's selflessness, the fact that his own body was broken but still he was worrying about others.

"Let's deal with one problem at a time, okay. Your hunting is over for tonight my friend, let's get you outside, then we'll decide what's next to be done."

A final, gurgled choking sound came from the creature, a huge reservoir of blood had pooled around its shattered body. And then…there was silence. Move movement, no twitching, no life.

"Should I put one in its brain, just to be sure?" Dan hoped for a negative response; his actions already had taken a toll on his troubled mind.

"You could, but we not outside yet, you might still need the bullets." Challis nodded dutifully, happy that his involvement seemed to be drawing to an end. Taking the pressure through his good leg, he helped hoist Castle to his feet, the pain on his friend's face etched in stone. Sliding an arm around his shoulder, Nick paused for one last statement.

"I don't think there's any way I can repay you for what you've done tonight, but whatever you ever need, no matter what it takes, I'll be there, I promise, this will never, ever be forgotten." The tears in his eyes told their own story and had they not still had a task to complete, he would almost certainly have broken down and wept.

"Don't you worry pal; I won't let you forget. Now, can we get the fuck out of here please?" Nick nodded and as the two limped towards the staircase, their eternal bond was recreated forever. As they passed by the fallen beast, Castle spat out a blood-filled wad of phlegm, landing on Graham's latex shield.

"I hope you never, ever rest in peace, you over-grown piece of shit." Challis smiled at his Friend's rebellious statement, but suddenly, a voice from the shadows would stop them in their tracks.

"Nick." The name was called out barely above a whisper, her battered body barely able to remain standing. The fat slug that crushed in tightly to her back held a blade to Jenifer's throat, the edge shuddering as his sweaty hand struggled to control its aggressive shake.

"Jenifer? Oh Christ, Jen, are you okay?" Castle suddenly lost his concentration upon his own injuries, his preoccupation for the young woman's wellbeing taking precedence.

"Yes, she's okay but for how long is up to you." Gibson's voice was as dithery as his body, threatening to break at any time. The men were close enough to see the pained expression on his face, the beetroot red complexion across his perspiration-drenched skin told of a man on the edge. "I won't hurt her, provided…" He paused as though catching a breath was a burden, "Provided you give us a path to…" Again, a tightening across his voice-box made the words jam in his throat. "A path to esc…" The sudden tightness in his chest made the deviant fall backwards against the entrance to the staircase, the girl suddenly able to seize her opportunity to escape his grasp. His left hand dropped his weapon and clutched for his chest, the vice-like grip around his arteries told of a man suffering a heart attack. He stumbled forwards, the fear of death causing his condition to worsen by the second. "Help…me…you have to…help…me." A sudden burst of self-preservation made him turn towards the steps, but the chance of escape had gone. Tightening, the squeeze across his chest was unbearable, his breath trapped inside lungs which refused to exhale, the pressure, the weight, the…

Gibson fell to his knees with a heavy thud. He turned his head back to the watching group, desperate for assistance, praying for mercy from the same person he'd tortured for hours. Jenifer cringed as the mortician stretched out an arm, his fingers grasping for help which ultimately, he didn't deserve. Her natural instinct was to assist anyone in need, but this miscreant had put her through Hell, he deserved his fate. A sudden fleeting glance of humanity swept his face, a lifetime of debauchery and wickedness finally filled him with regret, his actions ensuring which direction he'd take in the afterlife.

Epilogue

It seemed to take forever, but eventually Nick Castle, Dan Challis, and Jenifer Graham found their way to the railway station exit. Each had been scarred in different ways, physically yes, but more so…psychologically.

Dan would never have believed that he'd have the gumption to take another's life and though his gunshot had eliminated a monstrosity of nature, the image of that creature, blood oozing from the wound's that Challis had created, didn't make him feel warm inside, there was no heroic celebration, just apathy, a removal of emotion, for jubilation at the death of another human being just felt, wrong. In time, perhaps he'd change his view, when word would spread around Hallowell that he, Dan Challis, had been the village's unlikely saviour, and the triumphant slaying of the beast would result in his honouring from people who before, would cross the street to avoid his presence, maybe he'd be able to accept the magnitude of the achievement. Until then, he had his friends, for now, that was enough.

Jenifer hadn't spoken much yet. Naturally, it would take time, so much had happened in a few short hours, processing things in her current state would be too much to ask. In time, there'd be questions that would need answers; how had her brother survived for so long without her knowledge, why had Hallowell not done more to eradicate his reign of terror, why had that horrible mortician treated her in such a despicable way? Obviously, there'd be more too, but for now, she was just glad to be alive. How long it would take to emerge from this trauma was anyone's guess? Would she every truly recover from such a deplorable series of events? Would anyone? As for her handsome stranger, the man who'd risked everything just to rescue her. Would they see a future together? That was for tomorrow, as for today, Jenifer hadn't spoken much yet.

Was this retribution? Nick Castle didn't know, couldn't know, everything was too raw. In time, he'd no doubt be proud of what they'd achieved today. The fructuous relationship with his father showed real promise, the man had been willing to lay his life on the line, just to protect his son, that had to count for something, didn't it? Would it eliminate all the mistakes of the past, who knows? Maybe they both needed to leave prior events in the rear-view mirror, set a new precedent and set afresh. Could they? Only time would tell. Nick's relationship with his two old friends was easier to predict. Years before, they'd felt deserted, betrayed by Castle's absence, but still, when they were needed, they broke from the pack and stood shoulder to shoulder with him, no matter what the odds. Nick had no idea where his future laid, but if it was in Hallowell or not, Johnny

Brackett and Dan Challis had proved, they were friends for life, he'd never leave them behind again.

As they'd emerged from the giant doorway of the ground floor, Nick had seen straight away, his father being treated by the town doctor, Harry Brackett. Even he had taken up the call to arms; when Johnny had radioed to the police-station that there was a casualty, the physician had arrived swiftly, and had refused to leave with the patient until he knew everyone else was safe. A makeshift first-aid kit had stemmed the blood-flow from Mick Castle's wound and a shot of pain medication had taken off the edge. He'd survive, senior was tough.

As for Johnny, he'd met the survivors on the staircase of floor number two, unwilling to wait for safety even though he had no idea whether the mission had ended in success or failure. Taking his role of constable seriously, he was willing to risk his own life to help rescue the others, a heroic feat in itself. There was still a lingering feeling of disappointment, it would have been nice to land the killer blow upon the beast himself, but the creature had been vanquished, that was reward enough, and eventually, all the residents would know of Johnny's involvement, his position of a leader in the small village would be set forever. That had suddenly become important to him, maybe he was his father's son after all?

Inside, the remains of Fred Gibson lay prostrate on the cold concrete floor, an ironic ending for such a miscreant. He'd passed almost instantly, the heart failure a fortunate ending for one who lived for the suffering of others. The fact that his life-long ambition, to murder another human-being, had been completed just moments before his own demise seemed a salubrious, if not pugnacious achievement, and if there was an afterlife, a points system to dictate the next destination, the heinous murder of innocent Tom Daley would certainly ensure that the undertaker was not Heaven-bound.

Due to the lateness of the hour, the injuries sustained from the horrific encounter, and the lack of any lighting or lifting equipment, the group decided that the bodies could remain inside the station until the following day, only then could they all accept that this nightmare was truly over, there was no rush.

Fifteen feet from Fred Gibson's remains, a reservoir of blood had pooled on the railway station floor, its donator, the beast, the monster of Hallowell, the Graham curse, the taker of souls, Franklyn James Graham. There'd been no movement since the second gunshot had struck his chest, the immediate blast enough to kill almost any human being. The blood-loss had been massive, the tissue damage immense, the devastation complete…almost.

For when the building had emptied, when the interlopers had retreated to the safety of the outside world, when the battle appeared over, there was a twitch. A single straightening of the right hand. Was it a final reflex of a decreased body, the last expel of air from the lungs, the onset of rigor-mortis?

The green latex image of a rotting skull hung tightly to Frank Graham's skin, his face a long since forgotten memory. A trickle of blood escaped from his dehydrated lips, a sign of organ failure and internal bleeding. There'd appeared no intake of oxygen, no rise and fall of inflating lungs. Inside the mask, two black pits hid demonic eyes, cold, merciless eyes, clamped shut.

Until a flicker, a single twitch, steadily, gradually…